A Time for Healing

Michelle Denison

First Edition

NEWMAN SPRINGS PUBLISHING
320 Broad Street
Red Bank, NJ 07701

First originally published by Newman Springs Publishing 2024

ISBN 979-8-89308-321-7 (Paperback)
ISBN 979-8-89308-322-4 (Digital)

Printed in the United States of America

To John, for all the never-ending support you've given me…even when I don't deserve it!

1

A PERFECTLY FORMED TEARDROP, as sparkling as early-morning dew, formulated in the corner of Brye Grayson's right eye. Midafternoon sunlight spilled into the spacious photo studio, traipsed upon the solitary teardrop, and burst into a kaleidoscope of colors. The dazzling spectacle gradually trickled down flawless skin.

Picture perfect!

So intent on warding off the nebulous thoughts fogging her present modeling assignment, the supermodel took no heed to the trickle of moisture clinging to her eyelid.

Through the lens of her Nikon D850 camera, high-fashion photographer Tenisha Davidson cast a photogenic yet contemplative eye. A lovely sight. It was also one of the saddest. Quickly and efficiently, she danced around the supermodel as she captured the profoundly melancholy scene at various angles.

Soft, sensuous, sadness: Brye Grayson's trademarks.

Brye had been a second-year college student the first time Tenisha had laid eyes upon her. Witnessing the halo of pain encircling the strikingly beautiful woman, an extremely photogenic young woman, Tenisha could not walk away from the enigmatic sight nor could she allow it to go undiscovered. The twenty-three-year-old photographer had cautiously broached the guarded woman. Amid debilitating meekness, Brye declined the photo opportunity awarded her.

Determined to set the modeling industry on fire, Tenisha's dogged persistence chipped away at the young woman's resistance. Ultimately, Brye allowed her image to be replicated on film.

The initial shots, and the subsequent others, skyrocketed the two women toward the glamorous world of beauty and fashion. Now, six years later, fame, fortune, mutual respect, and a perpetual attachment linked the two women together as lifelong friends. Through it all, a shroud of deep-seated sorrow stained a permanent source of turmoil within Brye's troubled soul. And Tenisha remained oblivious to the origin of that pain.

One final shot, the session concluded, Tenisha dropped her camera to her side. "You can come back to reality, Brye. We're done."

Brye blinked. Once. Twice. An unconscious sweep of her hand shoved the single tear into oblivion. Disoriented with time and place, she gradually acclimated herself to her present surroundings.

An old abandoned warehouse had given birth to Tenisha's midtown Manhattan photo studio. The empty shell of a building had been stripped to the bare minimum, then undergone a miraculous facelift. The one-story brick building now accommodated a reception area, kitchen, dark room, prop room, dressing room, and lofty thirty-by-thirty workspace. Transom windows and skylights were strategically situated to gather every morsel of natural lighting. A solid oak flat-top desk and chair, a spruce green love seat with kick-pleat skirt, a cheval mirror, and a ten-hook oak coatrack spanned one half of the ample room. The second half of the studio—the half utilized for all in-house photo shoots—was now adorned with an industrial-sized fan, an antique slipper chair with crush red velvet upholstery, and a photographer's backdrop which, at the flick of a wrist, displayed a multitude of picturesque backgrounds.

Shocked at observing Tenisha command her post with diet Coke in hand instead of a camera, Brye blurted, "Are we done? How did we finish so quickly?"

"It wasn't all that quick." Tenisha frowned. "You just happened to be visiting another dimension during the last thirty minutes." Her frown surrendered to eagerness. "Your last shots were remarkable. I'm anxious to develop them." The lack of response confronting her candid praise, coupled with the inability to throw off the mound of concern riding shotgun amid her wearisome brain, urged Tenisha to acknowledge, "Something's troubling you." She scowled and hustled to rectify, "Something more than usual, I mean."

Off-kilter all morning, since waking up, foreboding images diligently sought an audience within Brye's debilitated thoughts. Somehow she had managed to detain the apocalyptic shadows at a stifling distance, but she would lose her strong hold if she allowed Tenisha to continue probing into her innermost thoughts. And she could not allow that to happen. Not today. Maybe not ever.

To gain a tighter grip onto her faltering mental stability, Brye shoved her lackadaisical mood into a not-so-far-removed corner of her brain. "Nothing's troubling me," she unconvincingly established. Movements calculated, she relaxed her pose and stood. Dispensing with the dressing room, Brye gingerly strayed toward a fabric-inserted dressing screen planted in a corner of the studio. In search of impenetrable safety, she hastily ducked behind it.

"Yeah…right," Tenisha retorted to Brye's retreating backside. Brye's blatant refusal to discuss her momentary memory loss reinforced Tenisha's determination to uncover the truth. She stationed her tall, slim frame in front of the five-paneled screen. Holding vigilance, she prepared to assault Brye with a frontal attack.

Behind the screen, Brye replaced her shimmering fabric of elegance with baggy jeans and sleeveless V-neck T-shirt. Her mind wanted to retreat to safer grounds. Therefore, it took every atom of strength to concentrate on Tenisha's pronounced allegations.

"You are a wonderful person, a sensational model, and my closest friend. But when I look at you, I realize that I've only scratched the surface." Tenisha paced in front of the screen. "I know very little about you, Brye."

The words traversed the circumference of the room, veered around the dressing screen, and slammed Brye in the center of her quivering chest. The direct blow lowered her defenses a notch. She fought the compelling urge dictating her to shrivel up inside herself. "You know all there is to know?"

Tenisha halted in midstream. She turned and confronted the screen. "But you haven't told me anything about yourself."

"There's nothing to tell." Forgoing the nervous rumble agitating her churning gut, she bent forward and tied her Reebok shoestrings.

"I know nothing of your personal life," Tenisha persisted.

Please don't do this to me, Tenisha! her mind screamed out in anguish, but her voice upheld its modeled composure. "That's because I don't have a personal life." Her defense shield lowered several more notches. If her internal barricade continued to disintegrate, she would be ineffective in protecting her mind from the faded memories clambering for release. At all costs, it was imperative she step out of this unwanted spotlight.

On unsteady legs, Brye stepped from behind the screen. She stuffed her fingers inside her pockets to draw attention away from her trembling hands. Tenisha's concentrated stare heated her cheeks. Body tensed, Brye studied the statuesque woman standing before her. And momentarily, the photographer's unconstrained beauty jarred Brye.

Tenisha retained sole ownership of exquisite attributes; with a mere wink and a nod, the wisest of men would willfully jump though fiery hoops if the action alone complied with her very wishes. Shoulder-length chestnut hair accentuated flawless hazel skin. Sublime caramel-colored eyes could melt the most frigid of smiles. Well-formed, perfectly sized breasts—breasts most women would spend a fortune to own and most men would give a fortune to fondle—also endorsed her praiseworthy assets. From the moment the two women had met, Brye remained curious as to why Tenisha flung a camera around her neck instead of posed in front of one.

The two women had been raised within the realms of two entirely different worlds. Tenisha had been cultured inside a supportive, two-parent, middle-class, African American household. She advocated a solid sense of self-worth and had never struggled with her own identity; at all times, she recognized herself as her own person and diligently labored to obtain the strenuous objectives she'd set for herself in life. Whereas Brye's parents, with their unconventional lifestyle and irrefutable lack of parental skills, left their daughter burdened with irrecoverable uncertainties—within herself as well as with mankind in general. Over the years, Brye had learned to maintain a tight rein on her cryptic emotions.

"I know nothing of your past," Tenisha was saying. She benched her untouched Coke can on top of a narrow windowsill. Hands on hips, she continued with this impromptu inquisition.

Brye sighed...heavily. How strange. Up until now, she'd always presumed she and Tenisha were the same height. Today, her imperious friend loomed over her by several feet, like judge and juror anxious to condemn. She steadied herself against Tenisha's accusatory glare. "My past is in the past, Tee. There's nothing to tell."

The air thickened. Tenisha sensed the supermodel's withdrawal. All too often she collided into a brick wall whenever Brye's past became the target of their undivided attention. To prevent a full retreat, Tenisha opted to back away from her original strategy. "I know nothing of how you conducted yourself prior to six years ago. For all I know, you could be a reformed terrorist."

Brye laughed. The mellow sound carried with it a lightness infiltrating her troubled heart. "Yeah...right," she responded, grateful for the slight reprieve. "So explain to me why I allowed you to plaster my face on this side of planet earth these past several years?"

"That's easy," Tenisha promptly answered. "Reconstructive surgery."

"Good answer. But not a realistic one." With the shift of conversation, Brye felt more at ease. "When you met me, I barely had enough money for college expenses. Where would I have found the funds for reconstructive surgery?"

Tenisha ignored the question, casting more frivolity into the light of day. "You changed your looks to throw the police off your trail."

Brye's shoulder's shook as she battled the upsurge of laughter. In less than thirty seconds, her wary guise had undergone a 180-degree transformation, her defense shield clanged securely into place, her veiled secrets surviving yet another day. "The police are no more interested in me than I am with continuing this idiotic conversation. But since you brought up reconstructive surgery"—Brye squinted at

Tenisha's heavily painted features—"why are you wearing so much makeup?"

As a rule, Tenisha rarely applied makeup during shoots. Today, foundation glazed her face like a thick layer of chocolate frosting. Brye found herself wondering if they'd need a putty knife to scrape the glutinous layers away.

A dark speck peeked from underneath the mulberry rouge riding Tenisha's left cheek. "You have a smudge," Brye took note of. She gently swiped at the out-of-place spot. But a startled heartbeat later, her brain disturbingly registered what her eyes and fingers gingerly poked at: the minuscule dot grew larger.

A bruise the color of an overripe plumb gawked menacingly at Brye. "Oh my god, Tee!" Her concern gushed forth like a severed artery. "What happened to your face?"

The tables turned, Tenisha now stood in center stage. She welcomed the attention with as little, or less enthusiasm as Brye had manifested just moments earlier.

Spine rigid with agitation, Tenisha reeled from Brye's prying fingers. "Nothing happened." Flying around her cluttered work desk, she plopped into a rattan-back swivel chair. Makeup kit and mirror instantly materialized. The damage was hastily repaired.

Panic inched along Brye's backside at a slow crawl. But her alarm was not born from the possibility that Tenisha would gain access to her own buried secrets. Brye's dread had given rise to the horrors Tenisha, herself, sought to conceal.

Brye spoke in a non-accusatory tone. "You have a bruise on your face the size of my fist, Tee. A person would have to be legally blind to miss it. Please don't tell me nothing's wrong!"

The makeup brush poised over Tenisha's right eye began to shake involuntarily. Grief swallowed her soft features. How was she supposed to admit to Brye of the indignation she'd suffered at the hands of her own husband? What did she have to gain in confessing that she'd changed into someone other than the same strong-willed, independent, self-assured individual her parents had nurtured with a firm yet gentle hand? How could she explain that every day she electively remained with her husband—a man who'd taken up fighting his wife as a pastime sport—meant surrendering a generous portion of her inner self? Invariably, why would she admit to anyone that she was a mere shell of the woman she used to be?

She wouldn't. She couldn't. Therefore, she remained silent. Her hand dropped listlessly to the desktop.

The silence between the two troubled women elevated to an unascertainable altitude. Breathing in the thin, frigid air, Brye crouched beside Tenisha's chair. Tenacious fingers gripped the wood armrest. Inhaling deeply, Brye blindly stabbed in the dark. "Did TyJuan do this to you?" Greeted with more silence, she urgently appealed, "Please, Tee. I'm not prying. I just want to help."

Tenisha's lower lip trembled. Her shoulders drooped in abysmal resignation. A sigh, drawn-out and oppressive, invaded the mummed ambiance. She wanted to entrust her fears and concerns with someone—God knows she couldn't go to her parents—but the embarrassment, the loyalty to her husband, influenced her speechless tongue. In the end, a profound sense of sisterhood won out; a tragic event—not from the distant past but inside the near future—would solidify the two women's friendship for life. Premonition alone propelled Tenisha forward.

Wearily, she began, "TyJuan's been searching for a job since the layoff at Panasonic. He's been looking for six months but hasn't found anything suitable. He's frustrated and unable to hide it any longer." Tormented eyes fell on Brye. "He started drinking. "Yesterday, he spent the entire day with a bottle of Jack Daniel's attached to his lips. He was drunk by the time I returned home." She broke her concentration and carefully weighed her next set of words. To Brye's astonishment, instead of questioning her own feeble motives for tolerating the abuse, Tenisha proceeded to defend her husband's barbaric behavior. "It's been hard on him. His pride—" Her voice trailed off before continuing, "He thinks he should be taking care of me." Her voice cracked. "I don't think he's ever really gotten used to the fact that I make more money than him. He even threw it back in my face last night." Tenisha cringed as she recanted the painful memory. "We argued. He stormed out. But not before he attempted to punch a hole in my face."

"My god, Tenisha!" Brye exclaimed in horror. "Has he hit you before?"

Tenisha's silence carried with it a startling revelation.

"He has, hasn't he?"

"Once," Tenisha reluctantly admitted. "But he'd been drinking that time as well."

"You can't use his inebriated state as an excuse, Tee. Drunk or sober, he has no business striking you."

"I know that." Her voice hardened, as if steeling herself against the sincerity of her husband's remorse. "Both times it's happened, he's been extremely apologetic."

"And both times, I bet he's promised never to do it again," Brye stated, the sarcasm oozing through her clinched teeth. "Can't you see, Tenisha? The morning after, even the *second* afterward, once they sober up, if they retain one ounce of remorse within their pathetic bodies, the guilt takes over. And at *that* particular moment, they're willing to do anything, say whatever's necessary to gain forgiveness."

Brye pushed herself up from the floor and propped her perfectly rounded bottom against the edge of Tenisha's work desk. A disheartened sigh whistled past her lips. This was hard. Much too hard. Confronting Tenisha's pain meant confronting her own. And she could not do that. She was not prepared for that. Steeling her sanity against the wrath of her own shameful history, she searched for the suitable words that would not betray her past. "You have to realize that it doesn't matter how many times he apologizes. It doesn't really matter how nice he is afterward or what he does to make up for his behavior. What does matter is that if he's struck you twice before, the chances are high that he'll do it again."

Tenisha deduced that there was more to Brye's impassioned statement—more than she had actually verbalized or admitted to; the supermodel was using Tenisha's unfortunate circumstance as a smoke screen to shelter her own obscure weaknesses.

How can Brye help me when she can't even help herself? The realization bowled over Tenisha with a two-ton steamroller. Infuriated at Brye's impertinent boldness, Tenisha barked, "Is this the voice of experience speaking?"

A crippling chill immobilized Brye's arms and legs. Frozen to the spot, she could not break away from Tenisha's icy glare. She could, however, avert her eyes.

The bridge of her nose pointed toward the floor. Brye answered with intended vagueness, "I've studied the subject extensively. I've gathered enough information to draw my own conclusions." She then gathered enough courage to challenge Tenisha front and center. As she continued, however, her frontal visage thrived with unspeakable apprehension. "He needs to get a handle on his emotions *now*, Tee! And if he can't do it on his own, he needs to seek help." She laid a gentle yet strongly supportive hand upon Tenisha's forearm. "If he doesn't seek early intervention, his problems can escalate into something more threatening."

"There's no need to worry." *Who exactly am I reassuring?* Tenisha wearily asked herself. *Brye, or myself?* "TyJuan is having a difficult time dealing with his long-term unemployment, but he'll find a job. She sighed. I know he's been drinking more and more lately, but he's not an alcoholic. He does not drink every day."

Afraid Tenisha flounced in crippling self-denial, Brye mechanically recited well-documented facts. "A social drinker can have a drink every day and not be classified as an alcoholic. And whether you believe it or not, an alcoholic doesn't necessarily drink every day. Many tend to drink in spurts—sometimes going days or even weeks without lifting a bottle to their lips."

"College classes begin in, what?" Tenisha scanned her desktop calendar. "Several months? But your first assignment is giving me a psychoanalytic interpretation of TyJuan's behavior. Is this piece of information free of charge? Or do you plan on sticking me up with a consultation fee?"

"That's not fair—"

"What's not fair is you labeling TyJuan an alcoholic," Tenisha angrily interrupted.

"I did not label him an alcoholic," Brye cautiously disputed. "I merely pointed out that he could get outside help if there is a problem."

"You mean therapy?"

"If it'll help him focus his frustrations down a more constructive path, yes, maybe he should look into therapy."

Incredulously, Tenisha gaped at Brye. "You're kidding me, right? You're the national poster child of misery! You make your living by selling a woebegone expression! *You*, who refuse to talk about your past, your pain, your fears *and* your future! I can't believe you're suggesting TyJuan get therapy!" Slapping open palms against solid desktop, she propelled out of her chair. "I'm sorry, Brye, but you aren't qualified to suggest how TyJuan should fix his morning eggs."

The hurt generated by Tenisha's caustic pronunciation did not meekly tiptoe around Brye's motionless body. Instead, it daringly stomped on her tightly reined emotions. She bowed in somber surrender. Of course Tenisha was right. Brye had no business butting into someone else's life when she couldn't get a handle on her own crippled emotions. Able to accept the disturbing truth that Tenisha did not want her help, her advice, or her company, she pushed away from the desk. Brye drifted toward the coat rack and gathered her backpack. Voice flat and unemotional, she apologized, "I'm sorry. You're right. It's not my place to interfere."

Detesting the twang of remorse storming Tenisha's acrid taste buds, she choked back displaced anger. The ill-tempered attack had been misdirected. Her insolent husband should be the beneficiary of her foiled tongue. Not Brye.

Unable to allow the supermodel to flee without soliciting some form of reconciliation, Tenisha quickly closed the gap between them. Playing tug of war with the strap of Brye's bag, Tenisha gained possession, then hung the long strap over the coat hook Brye had just removed it from. Hurriedly, she rushed to justify her anger. "The reason I'm acting like such a bitch is because I'm on edge." She dragged Brye over to the love seat and pushed her into the soft cushions. "It's getting harder to go home after work." Tenisha folded her body next to Brye. "When I do go home, I never know what to expect. TyJuan's moods are so erratic he stuffs everything I say back down my throat."

Tenisha shrugged in defeat. Her lower lip dropped in fatigued exasperation. "Frankly, I'm growing tired of reaching out to him when all he does is bite my fingers off. Once, I suggested he come to work for me. Needless to say, the idea didn't sit well with him. I've suggested he forget job hunting and go back to school. He says he refuses to live on my charity. Whatever I propose, he shoots down." Tenisha sat up straighter. She stuffed her hands between her thighs. Her voice turned stiff and unrelenting, as if she'd finally put the blame where it belonged. "TyJuan sits at home and grows bitter by the minute. He's groveling in self-pity and he's drinking himself into oblivion."

More than anything, Tenisha sought Brye's understanding. She wanted the supermodel to acknowledge that she wasn't an abused wife. Not really. A pet owner does not put a dog to sleep just because he wets the carpet. Nor does a wife give up on a marriage at the first sign of trouble. Tenisha and TyJuan were battling rough waters. She could not jump ship without attempting to save the boat first.

"I can't write TyJuan off." Tenisha caught and captured Brye's undivided attention. "We've been married three out of the six years we've known each other. When he apologizes for striking me and promises to cut back on the drinking, I *should* give him the benefit of the doubt."

Brye's fingers brushed against Tenisha's leg. She reassured with a light squeeze. "Of course you should remain supportive of TyJuan, just as I will remain supportive of you and any decisions you make concerning your marriage. But Tee, when you and I first met, your inner strength is what impressed me the most. You're independent, assertive, beautiful, and you hold yourself and your life in such high regards—which is the way it should be."

Brye puckered her lips. "First and foremost, you have to remain loyal to yourself, Tee. Don't give TyJuan the authority to turn you into something you're not."

Tenisha smiled fondly at her dearest friend. As long as they'd befriended one another, Brye had never been anything less than supportive. A twinge of guilt trampled across her mental awareness. Tenisha rushed to beg forgiveness. "You didn't deserve me going off the way I did. And when I said you had no business interfering... well...I was way off base there as well. The fact that you care gives you every reason to interfere. So forgive me, please, and let's move on to more pleasant thoughts."

"There's nothing to forgive," Brye assured. And although she couldn't easily set aside the damaging disclosure Tenisha had thrust upon her, she would let it go for now. "Did you have a pleasant thought you wanted to share with me?" she asked, willing to play along.

Gloomy clouds dispersed. The sun burst forth in the form of a dazzling smile. Like a panting man gulping down that much needed breathe of fresh air, the photo studio greedily inhaled the polished brilliance. "I have good news." Tenisha's grin broadened. "Well…it's good news to me." Knowing full well what Brye's reaction would be, she added, "You, on the other hand, might not think so."

Brye grimaced. Certain of where this conversation was going, invisible shackles clamped around her ankles and wrist. Cold steel bit into tender flesh. "Well?" she prompted, casting a suspicious eye.

"You have an interview with Romanique Cosmetics. Ten o'clock. Monday morning." Tenisha's face squinted in transparent anticipation. An attack was forthcoming. Whether it came in the form of a hurricane, a tornado, or a blast of hot air, Tenisha did not know.

Fear pricked at Brye's skin like a hot, blustery, sand storm. She clamped her eyelids shut, as if the action alone could squeeze the mounting dread out from under her aggrieved premonition. Dragging in several deep breaths to quell her racing heart, she mumbled, "You mean this Monday? This coming up Monday? Three days from today…Monday?"

Tenisha slammed the brakes on her mounting smile, but was unable to clamp a lid on her volcanic elation. "The one and the same."

Reopening her eyes, Brye fixed Tenisha with a hard stare. "But why are you just now telling me? I'm not ready for this. I need time to prepare."

"Because I knew you would react this way and I wanted to put it off for as long as I could. And what the hell do you mean you aren't ready?" Gulping down the laughter tickling her persistent patience, she continued, "Damn, girlfriend! We're talking about a simple interview! You're not preparing for a psych test, for god's sake!"

"Then why does it feel like I'm suffering pretest jitters?"

Tenisha grinned. She refused to cater to Brye's groundless insecurities, nor would she allow the supermodel to succumb to them. Brye would never have achieved the monumental success she had acquired to date had Tenisha allowed her to wallow in her own self-induced fears. "You'll make a great spokesperson for Romanique Cosmetics."

Brye shook her head in uncertainty. "I don't know, Tee. I've never padlocked myself to a long-term assignment before." She pulled her lower lip between her teeth and benevolently sucked. Arms folded in her lap, she rocked back and forth.

Whenever Brye contracted her services, purposely, she accepted short obligations lasting no more than a week or two. Professionally, she remained accommodating and prided herself in achieving a reputation for completing jobs in record time without creating major hassles or inciting power struggles amongst her colleagues. But once she fulfilled her assignment, she moved on.

A loner, Brye could not chance endangering the defense shield she resurrected around herself. And repetitious contact with others could actualize what she would consider to be her worst nightmare.

Brye echoed her trepidation. "I don't know if I can handle the pressures or responsibilities expected of a national cosmetic's spokesperson."

"You'll do fine." Tenisha peeked at her watch. She had been hired to fashion a modeling portfolio for an adorable seven-year-old. The doting mother retained great aspirations for her precocious daughter. The shoot was scheduled to begin in Central Park in one hour.

Oblivious to Tenisha's time constraints, Brye dropped her gaze to the ceramic floor tile. Her voice followed suit. "I don't know about this."

"Yes, you do." Tenisha stood. She strolled toward her desk. Turning to confront Brye, she repeated, "You'll do fine. You work well with others. You're wonderful in front of a camera. You're erotically appealing—to all age groups and sexes." She paused. "They sent me a copy of the contract, Brye. I looked it over. My lawyer looked it over. By mutual consensus, we think you should sign."

"Thank you," she dryly stated. "I'll take it under advisement."

"This is a wonderful business arrangement, Brye. It's a multimillion-dollar deal. Do you realize how many years you can keep Brylinn going with this kind of money? Not to mention what I could do with my 10 percent?

"They're allowing you a lot of concessions," Tenisha continued. "Plus, they're willing to work around your college schedule once fall classes reconvene."

"And what are they asking in return?" Brye asked, unable to disguise her normally suspicious nature.

"Exclusivity. But it's a good business decision for everyone involved. And trust me, Brye, it'll be worth it.

"I'll interview with them," Brye promised. "Afterward, well… we'll see."

Tenisha generously accepted her terms. "It's all I ask."

The doubt raking across Brye's mournful expression enticed Tenisha to repeat, "Trust me…okay?"

Dismissed, Brye floundered out the room as trepidation crashed over her head like an incoming tsunami. A sense of foreboding flooded her. Swimming down uncharted channels would conceivably upset the scale of her perilously balanced world.

Brow furrowed in profound concentration, Chad Collier—acting CEO of Romanique Cosmetics—examined Brye Grayson's modeling portfolio. Emotions entangled, a surge of desire slammed against his agitated loins. Anger, frustration, it took an immeasurable amount of effort to cast his inflamed reflections elsewhere. Restless eyes torpedoed the span of the office he had occupied for the past six months. Massive by anyone's standards, the room spread before Chad like an overdressed peacock strutting its prized feathers.

Glass, brass, and gold. Blinded by the overabundance of the three sparkling elements, on days when the sun seized the room within the realm of its blazing clutches, Chad considered donning sunglasses.

His desk was one thick sheet of glass. He sat in a black leather high-back chair with brass base and casters. Contemporary oil paintings wrapped in antique gilded frames, ornamented marigold-painted walls. A built in elaborate glass and brass entertainment system featuring a fifty-inch LED television, with blue-ray and a universal remote, adorned one wall. A well-stocked wet-bar flanked the opposite wall. An inner door led to a private washroom; with its gold sunburst mirror and gold and glass shower and sink fixtures, the bathroom was a mere continuation of the office. The massive office also contained a sitting area with a European-style leather sofa, matching rocker-recliner, and beveled glass cocktail and end table with gold-inlaid bases.

Home away from home, Chad distastefully mussed. The cultured marble fireplace with solid brass three-panel fire screen proved to be the only redeeming quality within the entire room, yet Chad had never harbored any desire to light a fire and relax inside the antiseptically designed room.

Two French Empire chairs, with intricately designed hand-painted silk upholstery and solid gold detailing, fronted Chad's glass desk. Brian Paxton filled one of the two matching chairs. Chad's wandering eye finally rested upon the sandy-blond-haired man. "What do you know about Brye Grayson?" His voice sounded gruffer than intended.

When the Collier Corporation appropriated controlling interest of Romanique Cosmetics, Brian Paxton had been a twenty-year veteran of the company. Hired at the age of eighteen, he was now highly skilled and well-versed in every sector of the nationwide company. For that reason alone, Chad had taken him on as his right-hand man.

Expecting to encounter some degree of resentment once he stepped into the driver's seat, Chad had been pleasantly surprised, and pleased, at Brian's honest nature, his willingness to assist, and the never-ending mound of facts and figures he could yank off the tip of his tongue at any given moment. And now, as usual, Brian did not disappoint. He answered in his usual proficient manner.

"Brye Grayson was working as a waitress before Tenisha Davidson stepped in and recognized her potential. The photographer convinced her to pose for Marsetta's Fashions. Her inaugural shots were sold for an outrageous sum of money. And the rest, as they say, is history."

Leather squealed in protest as Chad pulled his six-foot-three frame straighter inside his chair. His mind shifted into overdrive. Chad's silent meandering drowned out Brian's incessant medley of facts. A waitress? But how could that be? She had banked enough money to have hired a staff of attendants to fulfill her every beck and call. So why the sudden drop in lifestyles?

"Why was she waiting tables?" Chad demanded, cutting into the admiral praise Brian flourished upon the rising supermodel.

Brian paused. Mentally collecting his facts, he confirmed, "She was struggling to put herself through college. She obtained her bachelor's in sociology—graduated summa cum laude. Afterward, she received her master's in psychology and is now completing her final studies for her PhD in social psychology. She's—"

"Does she have a family?" Chad struggled to keep his voice on an even keel. "A husband? Kids?"

"No," he promptly answered. "She's never been married and there are no children. She lives a low-key life, doesn't frequent any of the local digs, and her name hasn't been linked to anyone on the dating scene.

"Today, not only is she the most sought after supermodel around, but she's the most intriguing as well. She's strictly freelance. She's selective in her choice of assignments. She can, and usually does, write her own ticket."

Chad had heard enough. "I want her as our spokesperson. I don't care what it takes or how much it costs. If we have to revise the initial contract to accommodate her needs, then do it!"

Brian's roving eye dropped to the fashion photographs scattered across the glass tabletop. He lifted an eight-by-eight-inch glossy by its edge and stared at the stilled magnificence. Her beauty equated with a blinding ray of light; the more he gazed upon her inspiring loveliness, the more difficult it was to see. And although the brilliance is what initially drew him toward her, going beyond the light remained his primary goal. Because beyond the light lay a potpourri of lofty secrets as well as hidden treasures. And Brian earnestly recognized that almost every sighted man alive—including himself—would give anything to be given the chance to break through her glowing yet enigmatic exterior.

As if he handled the actual being, Brian delicately lowered the glossy back to the table. "Sounds to me like you may be a tad bit smitten with our Ms. Grayson," Brian reflectively observed.

"This has nothing to do with a rise in my libido!" Chad impatiently snapped, lips taut, unable to subdue his growing irritation. "This is strictly a business decision. Without a doubt, her devoted contributions to this company will make a substantial difference to our financials."

Eyebrows raised in curious skepticism, Brian replied, "It was an innocent remark, Chad. You don't have to bite my head off for it. After all, I'm sure many red-blooded males fantasize about her at one time or another." He reached across the table and picked up another of Brye's photographs; a full-bodied shot of her standing barefoot in a field of white lilies. Her skirt fluttered in billowy swirls around well-defined legs. The aesthetic sight depicted the inner essence of the supermodel.

Brian had never worked with Brye, although he had followed her steady rise to fame. More times than not his fantasies harbored on meeting the supermodel—and he considered himself damn lucky to know he hadn't gotten so old he'd forgotten how to daydream over beautiful women.

He retained no inhibitions in sharing his innermost thoughts and desires. "Do you know what my fantasies are when I look at this?"

Startled by the question, Chad stared in cryptic silence as he waited for Brian to relay his migratory whims.

Brian needed no prompting. His voice lowered, gradually dipping to a hypnotic phase. "When I look at this, I want to enfold her in my arms. I want to hold on tightly...secure her trust...urge her to confide her worst fears...protect her from those fears. Then I'd ease her aching heart and make damn sure she remains happy." He picked up another fascinating photograph. "A woman like this deserves to be happy."

The environment surrounding Chad grew turbulent. The air swirled and whirled, scattering his embroiled thoughts. Unable to collect himself, Chad remained quiet and turned toward a large picturesque window. He stared out over the magnificent skyline overlooking Manhattan. A hodgepodge of architectural delight sprinkled the eastern horizon. The sky glistened a sapphire blue. Several pigeons strutted contentedly along Chad's window ledge. But none of this went observed to his wandering eye. He pooled his concentration into quelling the unjustifiable surge of jealousy heating his fiery blood. *This is ridiculous*, Chad grumbled in agitation. *Why should I care if Brian fosters deep feelings for that woman?*

Because you have deep-seated feelings for her as well.

Before the unconscionable thought attached and sunk its piercing claws into Chad's spiked awareness, he sprang from his chair and stationed himself in front of the fireplace. He stuffed his hands deep within his pockets. A slight throbbing in his right temple confirmed his inner turmoil. In the hope of getting his haphazard emotions under control, he trained his attention on the gold anniversary clock perched on top of the marble mantel. Several intense moments later, he finally found his voice.

"Since you're so enamored with her, I'll allow you the honor of interviewing her."

"It's an honor I would eagerly fight to the death for." Brian's amber-colored eyes twinkled in absorbed merriment. Chad encountered a second spasm of uncontrolled jealousy.

Ignoring his squandering emotions, Chad trudged back to his desk and gathered Brye's stirring portfolio. "It's settled then."

Meeting adjourned, Brian reached over the glass tabletop and relieved Chad of the photos. He sauntered across the massive room.

"Oh...one more thing." Chad halted Brian in his tracks. Waiting, Brian leaned his large body frame against the wide doorjamb. "Can you explain to me how Ms. Grayson advanced to the top so quickly?" Chad continued.

Brian stared with guarded features. "I don't think I understand the question."

Chad looked over at the assembled photographs, then back at Brian. Facial lines solid as granite, he asked, "Has she been linked to any scandals?"

An unwavering light of comprehension burned a steady pathway toward the forefront of Brian's mind. "You mean," he pointedly interpreted, "has she gone to bed with a potential employer solely to further her career?"

"One way or another"—Chad maintained a hard, fixed, stare—"I want you to find out if she's willing to go to any lengths to obtain this job." Chad settled into his chair. Stoic eyes remained trained on Brian. "I owe it to this company to hire the best spokesperson attainable. And if there's a chance her past is tainted or if she can pollute this company in any way because of deviant behaviors—sexual or otherwise—I'd like to discover it before it's a done deal." It was a flimsy excuse invented on the spur of the moment. "We need to familiarize ourselves with her morals as well as her code of conduct."

Lips pressed together, Brian listened without comment. Since the commencement of this meeting, he'd noticed the not-so-subtle changes within Chad's temperament; his mood swings vacillated between confusion, anger, and drunken agitation. For the first time since knowing Chad, his boss appeared unreadable, out of control—as if he'd lost all objectivity. And although Brian could not pinpoint the exact cause of Chad's uncharacteristic behavior, he believed Brye Grayson, unwittingly, had punctured a hole in the center of his usually composed exterior.

"I think you're way off base here, Chad." Brian's fingers closed around the brass doorknob. "But I'll see what info I can stir up." Rotating on his heels, he walked out.

Alone, Chad leaned heavily into the back of his cushioned chair. Slowly, he blew out a puff of insipid air. A number of collective thoughts traipsed along his firing synapses. Behind closed eyelids, he reflected over the last six years of his life.

The first three had been flagrantly unproductive. At the age of twenty-four, acquiring a master's in business administration, Chad Collier held a sense of what he expected out of life. His father, a multimillion-dollar real-estate mogul, waited with open arms for his son to join him in the family business. It was a task Chad had looked forward to with confident expectations. Then a dramatic incident in which he held no control or understanding of curtailed his meticulously designed plans; his personal life shattered into thousands of unserviceable pieces. Inner turmoil wreaked havoc on his mental stability. Needing to detach himself from the world at large, he staggered out of his prevailing existence and tumbled, headfirst, into a nonexistence.

In total disregard to his own life, his parentage, or his father's lifelong dream to join forces with his industrious son, Chad bottomed out of the societal and business world.

Dodging his own volatile emotions, along with normal day-to-day responsibilities, he hitched a one-way ticket onto the fast lane. His embroiled travels led him down a collision course on the brink of disaster. Drinking, womanizing, gambling, it all came to an abrupt halt two murky years later when Chad awakened in an unfamiliar house. He found himself lying in a strange bed, sleeping next to an unknown woman, unable to remember how he'd gotten there. His life had spiraled dangerously out of control. It was only then did he realize he had to pull himself together.

In his decision to rejoin the ranks of the living, he was met with relieved gratitude from his estranged parents.

On his return to the workforce, his misbegotten adventures proved to have held no lingering effects. What emerged, however, was a man who had become cynical in nature with life and love. Working hard, playing little, Chad buried himself deep within his work.

Quick to discover he possessed a natural flair for business practices, under his father's prudent tutelage, and his never-ending quest for higher supremacy, the Collier Corporation flourished to monumental heights. In his own right, Chad Collier had carved a niche for himself in the corporate industry.

When the opportunity to purchase controlling interest of Romanique Cosmetics arose, the enticing proposal could not be dismissed.

Although Daniel Collier employed a proficient staff fully capable of entering and running Romanique, the real-estate mogul wanted a firsthand, sweeping, no-holds-barred report attained from his son.

Once the shares had been appropriated, strictly as a personal favor to his father, Chad stood at the helm of Romanique Cosmetics. It was a position he had looked upon with minimal ardor—a number of other projects battled for Chad's immediate attention.

From top to bottom, Chad scrutinized the company with a keen eye and a firm hand. Six months later, he imparted his seal of approval; Romanique Cosmetics proved to be of sound body structurally as well as financially. And in the months of working with and developing trust and respect toward Brian Paxton, Chad was confident he was the right man to run the newly acquired company. Chad was prepared to entrust permanent position of CEO to Brian.

And then, unexpectedly, minutes before finalizing his official report, Brye Grayson's portfolio trampled across his desk; the sudden intrusion hacked a jagged path along a nerve which had been festering for more years than he cared to admit. The commanding photographs motivated Chad to set his findings aside. Indefinitely.

Chad's empty stare guided toward the photograph he absentmindedly held in his unstable grip.

Long, luxurious hair feathering exquisite features proved to be a master of colorful illusions. Chiefly jet black, yet natural shades of mahogany-red and chestnut brown, infiltrated the thick velvety strands. Prominent cheekbones. A nose that could not have been more perfected had a plastic surgeon chiseled the delicate flesh. Full, sensuous lips slightly turned upward. Luscious, long eyelashes highlighted eyes the color of predawn blue. A blue so deep they actually appeared violet. Mesmerizing violet-colored eyes which sent his heart fluttering over the edge. Violet-colored eyes urging him to—

Chad's head snapped forward. This would not happen. Not again. He would not let her deceptive magnificence suck him into a deadly cesspool a second time.

Beauty, pensiveness, vulnerability, innocence, trepidation; Tenisha Davidson managed to capture a multitude of Brye's inner essence. *She wears sadness like a lovestruck man wearing his heart on his sleeve,* Chad ironically scoffed. *But this woman is an elaborate delusion: an embellished trick of the camera.* Not for one second did he believe the femme fatale to be vulnerable *or* innocent.

Disapprovingly, Brian's blundering statement hit Chad like a boxer striking his opponent with a sucker punch: *Sounds to me like you may be a tad bit smitten with our Ms. Grayson?*

Smitten wouldn't even begin to describe the tumultuous antagonism Chad harbored for this woman. In a word, he hated Brye Grayson.

But as he tenderly ran his index finger along her delicate, stilled features, he could not stop himself from acknowledging the fact that there was truly a fine line between love and hate.

2

FRIDAY AFTERNOON RUSH HOUR traffic had not yet exploded into exalted chaos. Given plenty of space to maneuver, thirty-year-old Marcus Lindell, a chemical engineer, whizzed his black Lincoln Navigator southward bound on I-95. He'd shortened his work day to begin preparations for the evening's party he was hosting for coworkers and friends. And although he believed his attempt would be futile, he also petitioned for time to convince Brye into making an honored appearance.

His next door neighbor of three years, he had never known her to date, party, nor go out on the town for an evening. She did not have a significant other, nor did she have any desires to begin an intimate relationship.

With Brye, trust did not come easily. Hell, Marcus swore to himself, 98 percent of the time, trust didn't come at all.

When he'd moved next door, vividly, he recalled how difficult it had been to stir up an ordinary conversation with the ambiguous supermodel. From a distance, if their eyes met, she waved, then hurriedly moved on—as if attempting to dodge a near-death experience. At a much closer range, she would exchange obligatory pleasantries, then politely excuse herself. After a while, Marcus wondered if she retained misgivings living next door to a Black man.

Fortunately, nothing could have ever been further from the truth.

Eventually, their rickety acquaintance soared into an everlasting friendship. But Marcus credited his Scarlet Macaw for procuring Brye's affection.

Ahead, Interstate 287 accelerated toward him. As Marcus grabbed the westbound exit, his mind trekked back into time…

Tensed, Marcus stood on the arched fieldstone porch. Stabbing at the orange-lit button, he nervously waited for a response. Before he could mentally prepare himself to ask a favor, the door graciously swung open.

Astounded to see his six-foot-four frame hovering at her doorstep, Brye studied him for a quick second. "Marcus…to what do I owe the honor?"

"I was wondering"—his mouth suddenly went dry—"I mean…I needed to ask—"

"Would you care to come in?" Brye interrupted, clearly witnessing his visible apprehension. Stepping aside, she allowed him entrance.

Brye led him through the vaulted ceiling foyer, past the angular staircase, and into the spacious living room. As he followed, Marcus completed a visual inspection of his present surroundings. Not at all what he expected, the home did not give off the appearance of being too showy or ostentatious; it exemplified class and comfort. A blend of contemporary and classical furnishings in soothing shades of peaches and cream attracted his attention. Damask balloon shades beautified the expansive living room window overlooking the front yard. Solid pearl Regency chairs and tea table gave rise to the scenic view peeking into the polished room.

"Would you care to take a seat?" Brye's sonorous voice channeled into his deviating course of action.

Grabbing the closest chair reaching out to him, Marcus dropped his hefty body into a peach cotton-and-silk blend upholstered, camelback sofa.

"Can I get you something to drink?" Brye offered, standing over him.

"No…yes…no," he stuttered, indecisively.

"Water? Diet or regular Coke?"

"Water will be fine." Marcus stretched his long legs outward. His eyes took inventory of the seven-foot grandfather clock. The elegant craftsmanship, the massive swinging pendulum and ornate chimes, the beveled glass shelves, the engraved brass nameplate. However, all this combined was not what captured his fascination. His focus had immediately homed into the treasured collectibles—porcelain birds of all sizes, color and variety—displayed under the enhancement of halogen lighting.

His observant eye landed on a yellow and red parrot. His nervousness abated somewhat but mounted again upon Brye's expeditious return. She carried two tall, frosted glasses. Marcus swigged down half his beverage in one enormous gulp. Surprisingly, his nervousness seemed to put Brye at ease. Parking beside him, she patiently waited.

His facial muscles twitched. Nerves bunched, he rushed through his impromptu visit. "My company is sending me away on business in a few days." He stalled and rested the half-empty glass on top of his knee. "This trip caught me off guard, and I was wondering… well…I have a favor to ask of you."

Emotionless, Brye blinked at him.

"I have a parrot…a macaw, actually," he rushed to amend. His eyes fluttered toward the porcelain parrot. "With my recent move to New York, I have no friends or family who could take on the care of Rainbow."

"Rainbow?" The tip of Brye's unadorned mouth raised in quizzical wonder.

"I named him Rainbow because of his coloring," Marcus explained. Having gained momentum, he pushed forward. "You shouldn't feel obligated in any way, and I can understand if you wouldn't want to, but the only reason I'm asking is because I don't have anywhere else to turn."

A bewildered brow unfolded into confirmed understanding. Brye questioned, "Are you asking me to babysit your bird while you're away?"

He nodded. "I'll only be gone for five days. And Rainbow really isn't any trouble."

Instantly warming to the idea, Brye shrugged her shoulders in capitulation. "Why not? How difficult can it be to take care of a bird?"

Tension visibly ebbed from Marcus's anxiety-filled features. Shortly afterward, it returned in full force. "Would you care to meet him?" he asked, springing off the sofa like a kid on a pogo stick.

Again, Brye shrugged in agreement. "I'd love to."

Marcus drifted toward the door. Tensed fingers gripped the brass doorknob. He paused for one uneasy second. "I'll be right back."

Fifteen minutes later, he stood at Brye's door with Rainbow perched on his shoulder. "Okay, Rainbow," he uttered to the macaw, "I want you on your best behavior."

Rainbow released a high-pitched squawk.

Forgoing the doorbell, Marcus lightly tapped on the redwood door. Brye yelled out for him to enter.

"I'll be out in a sec," she acknowledged from deep within the interior of the home. When she entered, abruptly, feet came to a dead standstill, her bottom lip stretched out in bewilderment, her eyeballs popped out of her head as she gawked at Marcus's bird.

"Oh my god!" she wailed. "That's not a bird! He's big enough to be a living...breathing...person!" Inching closer, she inhaled the size of the macaw. From the top of his head to the tip of his tail, she calculated him to be three feet in length. "There are children running around smaller than him." Her groping eyes settled on Marcus. "By any chance, is he potty-trained?"

In high-pitched resonance, Rainbow chose to address Brye. "Hello... Pretty lady...hello."

Perplexed, Brye's eyeballs bounced from Marcus to Rainbow. She slid closer. "He talks?" It was more a statement than question. "In the hopes of winning me over, you made him say that, didn't you?"

"He mimics words," Marcus clarified. "And contrary to popular belief, birds talk at random. Although at times it may seem as if Rainbow knows what he's saying, there's no rhythm or rhyme to his pattern of speech."

Brye switched her gaze back to Rainbow.

Head cocked to one side, the macaw studied Brye intently. In turn, she inhaled his colorful personage.

His name deemed apropos. Eye and cheek area gleamed white against a multicolored background. Crown, nape, forehead, breast, and tail illuminated a brilliant red. His greater wings and shoulders radiated a lustrous yellow, shades of green poked from underneath, as well as bordered along the ends of his features. Primary and secondary wings blazed a brilliant blue. Lower back, rump, upper and lower tail prevailed a light blue.

"He's beautiful," she finally admitted.

A small plastic bag filled with fresh orange slices materialized inside Marcus's stalwart clutches. "Would you like to feed him?

"It's okay," he urged, deciphering her hesitancy.

Casting a tentative smile, she removed an orange slice and offered it to Rainbow. Without hesitation, he picked it from her fingers and gobbled it down. Next, he gracefully glided from Marcus's shoulder down to Brye's. She, in turn, smiled up at Marcus. It had been the beginning of a beautiful friendship.

In an affluent suburban subdivision of White Plains—the birthplace of New York and Marcus's place of residency—Marcus steered down a superbly manicured, tree-lined street. Rolling toward a cul-de-sac, he pulled into his drive, fronting one of the two-car garage, shut down the engine, and piled out of the Navigator.

He ambled through the front courtyard. A low brick wall directed him toward the covered porch and front entrance to his sprawling brick home. Mid-June, and stifling pre-summer air clutched at his three-piece suit like condensation on a Coke can. He loosened his tie and shrugged out of his jacket. Picking his daily newspaper off the lawn, he ambled toward the front door. As he stood poised, keys in hand, a blistering breeze carrying a boisterous shrill whipped past his ears. Abruptly changing his route, Marcus retraced his footsteps.

Detouring past his bay window, the thriving Rhododendron plants, and the multicolored rock bed, he skirted around the side of his house. In the back, he spotted Brye perched on her knees, planting lavender delphiniums and purple lobelia inside her commodious flower garden. Rainbow flittered contentedly around the thriving yard. Unobserved, he watched as his macaw pushed at a spray bottle with his massive beak.

"It's a little late in the afternoon for a spritz bath, Rainbow," Brye spoke as if the macaw understood every word. "If I spray you down now and your feathers don't dry by the time dusk settles, Marcus will kill me."

Rainbow continued to push the bottle at her. When the container bumped against her leg, he pointed, pleading yellow irises up at her.

Brye moaned. "Don't look at me like that."

Rainbow released her name in a high-pitched screech. He then whistled.

Brye laughed. "You're a bird after my own heart, aren't you, Rainbow? Well"—she picked up the bottle and spritzed him down—"I guess I can always throw you into the clothes dryer."

Rainbow let lose a bloodcurdling scream.

"Jeez, Rainbow, calm down." Brye giggled. "I was only kidding." Smiling, she turned and caught Marcus wandering toward her.

"Hi," she greeted, sheltering her surprise. "I hope you don't mind my removing Rainbow from his cage." Doleful eyes lowered to her soiled gardening gloves. "I needed the company."

Sadness palpated Marcus's racing heart. He found it hard to accept that Brye would rather spend time with macaws and children rather than with her own peers. Towering above her, he visibly washed over her bent head with a gentle caress. "If it's company you need, why won't you agree to come to my party?"

"Because I can do without *that* kind of company." Brye bit back her irritation, but the strain she'd been under all day darkened her soft features as she glared up into Marcus's concerned expression. "I don't need you setting me up on dates, Marcus."

"I'm not talking about setting you up on a date. I'm talking about a party...a small gathering of friends...a change of pace...a chance to mingle with a variety of personalities."

The thought of subjecting herself to a room filled with leering men and patronizing women frightened more than irritated Brye. Exhaustively, she tossed her garden tools into a small canvas bag. Finger by finger, she accentuated each word as she peeled off her thick gloves. "Can we talk about something else, please?"

Although dark glasses shadowed a big portion of her features, Marcus acknowledged the hint of fear playing behind dark lashes. For now, he decided to concede to her request. Offering his hand, he pulled her to her feet. "Can you at least help me take inventory of my wet bar? Maybe even help me make up several trays of hors d'oeuvres?"

"I believe I can handle that." Brye smiled in gratitude. Earlier she had found herself embroiled in an emotional battle with Tenisha. She didn't have the strength to live through a repeat performance with Marcus. She wiped dirt particles off the front of her tan shorts. "Give me a few minutes to clean up, then I'm all yours."

"You got it." Marcus hunkered close to the ground to allow Rainbow access to his shoulder. He released a low whistle, Rainbow flew to his left shoulder. Straightening to his full commanding height, he turned and trudged homeward bound.

Fifteen minutes later, showered and dressed in a pair of walking shorts and tank top, Brye entered Marcus's front door. Soft music—Kenney G's "Breathless,"—played softly on his surround sound system.

Elegance stood out in every area of his dwelling. A window wall blessed a two-story living room with vaulted, sloping ceilings. Massive brick fireplace—a Macon stone mantel displayed crystal candlesticks, Westminster chime clock, and cherished family photographs—floor-to-ceiling cherry-finished wall units, handcrafted figurines and delicate collectibles, custom-designed furniture and prized paintings—thousands of places dust specks loved to frolic. A housekeeper's nightmare.

Marcus maintained his home just as he kept himself: meticulous. Regardless of date and time, if Brye performed an on-site white glove test, he would pass with flying colors with each inspection. Brye remained stumped on how precise he maintained his home, particularly while Rainbow commandeered jurisdiction over the entire abode.

"Marcus?" she called out.

His deep voice filtered into the entryway. "In here."

Brye navigated past the twisting stairwell, the downstairs bathroom, and the grand living room. She halted inside the dining room's arched doors.

Formal elegance. Neutrally colored walls, a two-tier crystal chandelier dangled above a Queen Ann-style dining set, solid brass candlesticks and eye-catching silk flowers; Brye's vision swept past the Dutch inlaid chest. She found Marcus on his knees, polishing the wood baseboards.

"One of these days," she lightly teased, "you're going to make a wonderful wife for some lucky woman."

Marcus's polishing rag halted in midair. Dark features brightened into an elusive grin. "Is that a proposal?"

Brye moved further into the room. "You wouldn't know what to do with it if it had been."

"You're assuming I'd want to do something with it. In all actuality—not that I don't think you're one fine piece of artwork—I'll always remain true to my color."

"It's a good thing too," Brye was quick to answer, "because you wouldn't have had a chance with me anyway."

"As if any man has a chance with you." He pushed himself upward. Before giving her time to sprout her protests, he grabbed her by the arms. "Dance with me."

Startled with the tactical maneuver, Brye found herself locked within the province of his muscled arms. Movements obstinate and unyielding, she gradually relaxed and permitted the mellow music, his gentle touch, to invade her rigid body. Loosely she secured her arms around Marcus's neck. Her head rested comfortably against his broad chest.

They danced for several minutes without speaking. When Marcus sensed the withdrawal of her inhibitions, he asked, "Don't you miss this?"

The steady strumming of his heart resonating against her eardrum controlled her hypnotically. The feel of his sturdy body gliding against hers inaugurated a warm feeling inside. Much to her amazement, being enfolded within Marcus arms did not cause her to want to crawl out of her skin; she did not acquire an overwhelming sensation to throw up. She closed her eyes and tightened her grip around his neck. "Miss what?" Her tone sounded distant, serene.

"Dancing with someone you care deeply about. Close companionship… Intimacy… Waking up in the morning in someone's arms."

Brye's chin lifted. She stared into a handsome face. Pearly white teeth gleamed bright against a bronzed, smooth complexion. Thick bushy hair covered an area just above his upper lip. He unveiled warm, sensitive, brown eyes. Concern lines burrowed deep into a prominent forehead. "I don't allow myself to think about it," she finally admitted.

"And you don't believe something's wrong with that?"

The precarious change in topic slowly dissipated Brye's somnolent mood into thin air. "I believe that how I lead my life is of no concern of yours," she apprised. "And I believe you are the last person to question my sex life, particularly since you spend so much of your time babysitting *me*…worrying about *me*…trying to take care of *me*…that you don't have time to pursue any lasting relationships of your own!"

"At the moment, there isn't anyone I would like to pursue a lasting relationship with—"

Brye knew his statement was a lie, yet she chose not to draw attention to it.

"But I still spend time with women. I date them. I have fun with them. I still get—"

"Laid," Brye finished for him. Pushing away, she abruptly ended the dance. "What a wonderful accomplishment to boast of. Especially since, in this day and age, having casual sex outside a monogamous relationship could very well bring on unwanted consequences!" Swinging doors separated dining room from kitchen. She hurried from one room to another, as if the transitory response alone could distance herself from the shaky subject. Not willing to allow her to sidestep the subject entirely, Marcus followed at close heels.

"I'm not talking about you going out and having casual sex," Marcus retorted. He flung open the refrigerator door and pulled out packages of thinly sliced ham, deveined shrimp, green onions, cream cheese, milk, and a block of cheddar cheese. "I'm talking about a woman who functions normally in the public eye but privately has shut down all emotion or contact with the outside world."

Brye snatched the green onions out of his hands. She carried the long stalks to the sink and rinsed them clean. "Is it a crime to want to guard my personal life?" Shaking off excess moisture, she carted the onions to a chopping block gracing the kitchen counter.

"Are you happy?" Marcus asked. He began putting together a cream cheese filling for the ham slices.

Brye's answer was slow in coming. "I'm…satisfied."

"But is that good enough? Will it ever be good enough?"

"I don't know if it's good enough," Brye replied honestly, "but it's…safe."

"It might be safe, but it's also a hell of a lot lonelier," Marcus intentionally pointed out.

"This is who I am, Marcus." As she diced onions, the paring knife struck against the chopping board and emphasized her every word. "I don't need the glitter of nightlife. I don't need a man to define who I am. And although I'm the center of media attention at the moment, if it were all taken away from me tomorrow, I wouldn't be devastated. I certainly wouldn't feel as if my life had come to a crashing halt."

"This is not who you are, Brye. This is who you have become over the last several years. The *real* Brye Grayson is burrowed deep beneath a blanket of fear, insecurities, and hurt! The *real* Brye Grayson is afraid to peek her head out from underneath the thick covers! The *real* Brye Grayson deserves a better life than the one she's created for herself! She deserves to be happy. She deserves to be cherished by a man who knows how to take care of a precious gem."

Pain spilling from her eyes, Brye startled them both by admitting, "I don't want to open up to people, Marcus. In all my experiences I've found that whenever I open my heart, someone throws salt into the newly exposed wound. And I don't need or want the pain and aggravation."

"You've allowed Tenisha into your life. You've also allowed me… and Linn. Are you any more worse for wear than when you first met us?"

"*We* becoming friends was not anything forged out of the unordinary, Marcus." Brye tilted the chopping block and dumped the diced onions into the cream cheese mixture. And with her mind navigating on copilot, she stereotyped the formation of their close alliance. "It's a well-documented fact that people become friends with the ones they see the most…the people they work with…their neighbors."

Marcus had been vigorously blending the green onions into the cheese concoction with a wooden spoon. On the closing of Brye's psychoanalysis, he angrily shook the utensil in Brye's face. His bronzed features deepened to a darker shade of anger. "Spare me the psychobabble bullshit, Brye!" he snapped in annoyance. "The fact is, you did allow us into your scrupulously guarded world. Which means there's room for a few others if you—"

"I don't want to leave myself open to be used, abused, cheated on, or lied to!" Brye barked, spinning away from him. "Why can't you leave it alone?"

"Because you're so afraid of being hurt, you've shut yourself off from the world at large."

"I'm not afraid," Brye vehemently denied. "I just believe that if you expect more from an individual, you get hurt when those expectations fall short of what was expected. Therefore, I don't expect anything…from anyone!"

"I'm not asking you to go out and find yourself a husband, Brye." Turning back to the job at hand, he slathered a thin layer of cream cheese filling across the length of a ham slice. Carefully, he rolled the meat into a log, sliced it in half, and then stuck a toothpick in the center. Brye worked beside him, substituting chunks of cheddar cheese for cream cheese.

"I'm also not asking you to take on the entire population of New York. I just want you to get a life—"

"I *have* a life," Brye testily interjected. She slammed her rolled ham down on a silver platter.

"I want you to go out every now and then," Marcus continued as if she hadn't interrupted. "You need to seek companionship from others...mingle a little with the outside world. Nothing too drastic, Brye. I'm talking about baby steps." He stopped working and flung a caring visage at Brye. "I promise I'll be right behind you, ready to pick you up if you slip."

Brye smiled, unable to remain perturbed with his intrusive yet well-meaning meddling. Grateful he cared enough to make an issue of her stark lifestyle, reflectively, she easily recognized that he was the first man in her life who concerned himself with her needs, her wants, her happiness, without taking anything for himself.

"And I suppose you want me to begin these baby steps by way of your party tonight?" Brye asked, her irritation forgotten, merriment darting along the boundaries of each word.

Busted. He grinned sheepishly. "It would certainly be a good place to start." If asked, Marcus would contribute the deep-seated concern he fostered for Brye to his parents. His life had been cultivated on a solid foundation. His parents had shared an equitable, devoted partnership. Raised the youngest and only male amongst three highly energetic and vexatious sisters, aside from the trouble they'd steered him toward while growing up, he'd been taught to respect and safeguard the women in his life. He'd also been taught to protect children, the elderly, and those who could not fend for themselves.

Although Brye did not fit into the last three categories, to Marcus, she resembled Pavlov's dog. For reasons foreign to his understanding, she'd been condition to shrink inside herself whenever a member of the opposite sex invaded her close, personal space. And since Brye had no one—no family, no love interest, not even a devoted pet—he had self-ordained himself as her personal savior, guardian, and friend. It would take time but he pledged to recondition her conditioned mode of behavior.

Brye stood on her toes and planted a kiss on Marcus's cheek. "Thank you."

"For what?"

"For being my friend." It meant a lot to Brye. It meant more than she could ever put into words.

"Does that mean you'll come to the party?"

"No." Brye pulled away. Her efforts turned toward concocting a shrimp dip. "But I promise to think about what you said."

Frustrated, knowing it would do no good, nevertheless, he urged, "If you change your mind—"

"I won't. But thank you again." She smiled. "Now let's finish up before Rainbow gets bored with his playthings and comes looking for you."

He decided to let it drop for now. She may not be coming to his little soiree tonight, but he remained determined in adding a little spice into her mundane existence.

Tenisha entered her upper Manhattan apartment. Stillness engulfed her. She peered around the empty room. Total chaos. After the argument the night before, she had grabbed pillows and bed linen and sought refuge on the living room sofa. The rumpled sheets were now haphazardly tossed aside.

Early morning, TyJuan had entered the living room with breakfast tray in tow. He'd sought atonement for his rampant actions of the night before. Morning dishes aligned the fossil stone cocktail table. Shoes, clothing, and morning paper decorated the light-colored carpet.

Fatigued from her overextended workday, Tenisha inspected the disorderly room with an exhaustive eye. "I know you said you were going job hunting today, TyJuan," she mumbled to herself, "but you could have picked up some of this clutter before you left."

Tenisha saddled up to the custom-designed banquette sofa snuggled deep inside the corner wall. She bent forward to pick up the fallen linen. Then, unfolding at the waist, she stared at her reflection inside the sofa-length, gold-leaf accented mirror. Face streaked with a pound of makeup, troubled eyes, grim line molding stark lips—a total stranger glared back. The force in which uneasiness bashed against the side of her head sustained just as much impact as if she'd been struck by a baseball bat.

Tenisha felt sick to her stomach. She did not like the woman staring back at her. Unable to peer at the sullen face any longer, she hastily turned away. Skating around the room, she picked up the fallen disaster. As she cleaned, she strove to keep the dwindling devotion she elicited for her husband at bay.

No doubt TyJuan's recently acquired aggressive behavior accounted for some of the lack of passion she felt toward him lately. But a steadily growing concern forced her to realize that her love for him had begun to wane long before he'd taken up drinking as a hobby.

Which came first, the chicken or the egg? She grimly smiled as she mulled over the philosophical saying. Was she falling out of love with her husband because he had undergone a Dr. Jekyll–Mr. Hyde transformation? Or was she using his erratic performance as an excuse to put an end to a marriage she had become disillusioned with long before their troubles surfaced?

Tenisha understood all too well that people change…circumstances vary. But she also understood in her heart of hearts that she had not been the one who'd changed during the course of their marriage. TyJuan had.

He resented her success. He resented the circle of affluent individuals she cavorted with. Not receiving a college education himself, he'd always felt inferior to others who had clawed their way up the educational ladder. And since he'd taken on the title of joblessness, he sank heavily into despair like a man drowning in a pit of quicksand; the more he struggled, the more he was rendered immobile. Tenisha didn't know how to go about tossing him a lifeline.

An apprehensive sigh filled the boundaries of her kitchen wall. *Maybe you're struggling to hold on to this marriage because you feel like you owe him,* she thought to herself. Shoving the unreceptive notion toward the back of her mind, Tenisha piled dirty dishes in the kitchen sink.

"We need to put a little romance back into our lives, TyJuan." Opting for a long, hot bath, she strayed toward the bathroom. Afterward, she would prepare TyJuan's favorite meal: Cornish hen, corn bread stuffing, green bean casserole, and New York-style cheesecake for dessert. And then…well…she would see where the evening guided them.

TyJuan Davidson flaunted brooding eyes and inharmonious features. He wore a cocksure attitude and paraded himself to the world as if it owed him a favor. When given the opportunity, he eagerly spoke with blatant hostility on how the white man pitted himself against the Black man.

A rebel with a cause.

He wasn't an exceptionally good-looking man, but he possessed an all-empowering smile that could halt the mightiest of trains in its tracks. Women flocked to him. And if it was his devil-be-damned spirit that attracted the ladies, his charismatic smile is what influenced the most devout of Christians to sing praises to that same devil.

"This beats pounding the pavement for a job." Contented, TyJuan polished off his fourth beer.

"You got that right," Steve, his friend since high school, seconded. Midmorning, he called and invited TyJuan over for a poker game. TyJuan needed no encouragement. He readily agreed. Now they were sitting in a local bar, tossing back mug after mug of draft beer.

"Man," TyJuan validated, "you don't know how much I appreciated getting your phone call this morning." Underneath the high-pedestal pine table, his foot tapped in rhythm to the music streaming out of a corner jukebox. "I need to get out more with my dawg!"

"Yeah, bruh! You been hangin' out with the rich and famous too long. You've forgotten where you come from."

"Yeah…well…thanks for the reality check." His table was posted several feet from the bar entrance. Patrons steadily traipsed in and out. The grating mumbling passing over his head did not drown the vivid images of the fight he'd sustained with his wife the night before. She had jumped down his throat the moment she'd stepped inside their apartment. His drinking was driving her crazy, he recalled her saying. *Hell*, he thought to himself, *what did she expect?* She didn't have a clue as to what was going on inside his head. She had no idea what it felt like to fall on hard times. Her daddy—an Uncle Tom if he'd ever seen one—had pampered Tenisha her entire life; he'd given her everything she'd wanted in life.

Damn you, Tenisha! He cursed himself. Why did she always have to sweat him? On and on she went, her harping grinding on his ever-lasting nerve. It had culminated to the point of him hauling off and hitting her. But dammit, she had deserved it. And to add injury to insult, he had been duty-bound to suck up to her the entire morning to secure her forgiveness.

TyJuan's dispirited tone, the anger fueling his heavy mood, impelled Steve to deduce, "What's the matter? Is Tenisha bustin' your balls about your current job situation?"

TyJuan signaled for another beer. Sitting up straighter inside his rattan bar stool, he replied, "She don't know what I'm dealin' with every day. She can't even pretend to imagine how I feel.

"Every morning, I go out in search of a job. Every day, I get slapped in the face with: 'Sorry Mr. Davidson, but we're not seeking job applicants at this time—try back in several months' or 'Fill out the application and we'll get back to you.' Only they never do. And then there's 'I'm sorry, Mr. Davidson, but we're looking for someone more qualified… Someone with more experience…someone more *White*.'"

"Yeah, man," Steve agreed. "I hear where you comin' from. Whatever the reason 'the Man' gives you, it all translates into the same fuckin' thing: 'Get your Black ass out of my office. You're smelling up the place.'"

"It's the way it's always been."

"It's the way it'll always be."

"And we're supposed to just bend over, allow them to stick it to us, then say thank you when they're finished screwin' us over."

As the waitress returned to replace empty beers mugs with loaded ones, TyJuan floundered in his own chaotic thoughts. It had been six months since his layoff; lack of seniority, his superiors—his *White* superiors—had cited to him. He'd worked his tail off for seven years, and all he'd gotten in return was a kick to the curb. Hell, he could understand why a high percentage of disgruntled postal employees returned to the workplace, packing pistols. Work had been their livelihood. And in the few short seconds it took for "*the Man*" to say, "You're fired," his livelihood, his dignity, his honor had sunk like a man drowning in water. For far longer than TyJuan cared to admit, he felt like dog shit.

Once the beer server swaggered away, TyJuan belted down half his mug. His fifth beer went straight to his brain and erupted in the form of a tyrannical tongue. Slamming the mug down, he swiped his mouth with the back of his hand. "To top it all off, I have Tenisha breathing down my neck. She expects to walk into a clean apartment and find a hot meal simmering on the stove. But after I've been confronted with rejection all day long, I'm in no mood to play housemaid."

"So why not play the part?" Steve's shoulders lifted in inquisitive astonishment. "Tenisha doesn't care if you go back to work. With the money that woman makes, hell, you can sit on your ass for years and never feel one moment of discomfort."

The concentrated alcohol hunkering in the core of his stomach provoked his mounting outrage. "Just because your sorry ass will lie back and let a woman take care of you doesn't mean I'll go there. I'm not looking for a free ride. I believe in takin' care of my own."

"Then what do you plan on doin'?"

TyJuan picked up his mug and tipped it toward Steve. Neglectful of the authoritarian words he'd spilled seconds prior, he admitted, "Maybe I'll start spending more days like this one." He shook his head. "It sure as hell beats hangin' out at those dull parties Tenisha's always harping on me to attend." He frowned in distaste. "You should see the way the high and mighty look down on me when I tell them

I'm in-between jobs. They treat me condescendingly…as if I'm just another Black man riding on a good woman's coattails. And they look at Tenisha with pity. As if to say, 'You poor thang. Is he the best you can get?'"

"Hey, man!" Steve interjected. "It can't be that bad."

"You're right," TyJuan agreed. "What's worse is the way Tenisha looks at me, with shame in her eyes—as if I need to be pitied." His fingers tightened around his mug. "Sometimes, I feel like knockin' that smug look right off her."

"TyJuan, is that you?" a female voice—hot, throaty—ebbed over his right shoulder.

TyJuan turned toward the mellow sound. The trespasser's hair was styled in cherry-red micro braids, with loose strands trailing past her shoulders. Thin eyebrows, pointed nose, deflated lips. Her mahogany features wasn't anything to write home about, but that body…

Although TyJuan hadn't spoken to the woman in years, he would have recognized that body anywhere. Built with authentic materials, a well-formed structure, solid with curves in all the right places. A brick house personified. TyJuan was prepared to move in. He hopped to his feet. "Vanessa… Baby, it's been a long time."

She laughed. "Three years. But who's counting?" Her hands lingered longer than necessary at the back of his neck. Gradually, her fingers trailed around the front of his face and rested on his cheek. "You're as handsome as ever."

"And you"—his fingers overtly examined her hourglass figure—"feel as good as ever." Reluctantly, he pulled away from the promises her body offered. "Why don't you let me buy you a drink?"

Pulling out a barstool, he introduced Steve. Pleasantries exchanged, Vanessa settled close to TyJuan's side. The palm of her hand rested lightly on his knee. TyJuan's insides churned with an intensity he could barely control.

"So"—she smiled lasciviously—"are you still married?"

"Yeah." He grinned back at her. "But don't hold that against me."

"I won't if you don't." Her fingers climbed higher. She squeezed the solid thickness of his quivering thigh. "How about going somewhere more intimate…share a quiet dinner? We can catch up on old times."

By the lusty glaze of her eyes and the determined feel of her fingers rambling up and down his leg, TyJuan understood she offered more than a hot meal. The question not voiced, however, is would he take her up on the offer? He had no doubt that Tenisha would be home, awaiting dinner. Yet the more he played that sorry scene in his head, the more he resented returning home to nothing but indulgent sympathy and faithless charity.

One eyebrow cocked in question, he flung a look at Steve that asked: *What do you think?*

In turn, Steve shrugged his shoulders to give his endorsement. "Don't let me hold you back, man. Drop me home, then follow wherever the night leads you."

What could be wrong with wanting one night of no expectations, no demands, no worries, and no one reminding him of his failures?

TyJuan needed this. He wanted this. He desired spending time with a woman who held no preconceived notions of what he should be doing with his life.

Yes, he thought to himself, *I'm going for it.* Dropping his hand over Vanessa's, voice low and husky, he demanded, "Let's get out of here."

"I thought you'd never ask." Eagerly, Vanessa waited while TyJuan and Steve settled the check. The evening was turning out better than she had hoped for. Traipsing out the bar arm-in-arm with TyJuan, she practically devoured him with a gluttonous stare.

3

DUSK CAUTIOUSLY GATHERED THE bustling city underneath its gloomy wings. Dusk tantamount to the malaise befalling Brye. Malaise which had threatened to overpower her the entire day. Somehow, however, she had managed to keep the shadowy images outside the perimeter of her restless thoughts. Now, all alone, it was inevitable that her wandering mind would catch up to her stalled body.

Music coming from the direction of Marcus's home drifted along a lofty breeze. Laughter rose, then gradually tapered off in the midst of the steadily darkening night. For a brief moment, Brye's attention turned toward the number of cars aligning her neighbor's drive.

"Maybe I should reconsider," she softly spoke into the warm night air. "Marcus would be happy to see me make an appearance."

A motion sensor lantern planted inside Marcus courtyard winked on and off, its twinkle insistently inviting her over.

"No." Brye shut her eyes against the enticing summons. "I'm not ready for that yet." She pulled away and accepted the protection her humble abode provided. But once inside, she realized that the confining space was anything but safeguarded.

As she took in her oppressive surroundings, the walls appeared to come alive, swelling, contracting…breathing…sucking up the bulk of her strained ventilation. Tiny hairs along her arms and legs prickled. She shuddered and labored to slough off the strong sensation that she wasn't alone.

But she couldn't. Because she wasn't. His crushing presence made up the very core of her home…her soul.

Brye covered her heart with trembling fingers. And she felt the very essence of his spirit flow through her. A heartrending sob rose from the back of her throat. She needed to get out. Leave. Flee from the stranglehold he sealed around her neck. But tonight she could run to the depths of hell and back, and he would continue to ride shotgun. Tonight, there was no escaping him. In the end, she decided to endure his obscure presence.

There was no sense of direction as she gingerly drifted through her home. In short order, she opted for a relaxing shower.

Hot water sluiced down her tensed shoulders, backside, and chest. A feeling of melancholy washed over her. Face raised to the steamy downpour, she waited for the tears to flow. But the weeping did not come.

Heavy-hearted, she slid open the glass shower door and climbed out. Unlike the stream of water Brye easily turned off with a flick of her hand, she could not halt the steady flow of vexed images inundating her weary mind.

Toweling herself dry, she slid into a sleeveless, cotton nightshirt. Seconds later, she found herself standing in front of her bedside table. Slowly, painstakingly, she bent at the knee. Cautiously, as if expecting an apparition to halt her unsteady motion, her right hand nervously extended forward. Drawing open the bottom drawer, a leather-bound photo-album poised at her fingertips. She lifted it from its resting place.

Brye clutched the album to her chest as she climbed into bed. With back cushioned by a thick cloud of pillows, she raised her knees. Drawing the covers over her chilled body, she propped the large album against her upper thighs. Then, inhaling deeply, she opened the front cover. Distraught eyes swept downward and confronted what she had unfailingly attempted to run away from all day.

Brye came face-to-face with an eight by ten glossy of a young, beautiful, teenage boy. Jet black hair, violet-colored eyes, and tender features—the spitting image of Brye.

Her brother. Her twin. Born five minutes apart—Brye being the older of the two—and christened Bryson and Tyson Gray. Today was the eighth anniversary of his death. Fifteen years old at the time the photo had been taken, he had died two and a half years later at the sweet age of seventeen.

Time heals all wounds.

Whoever composed that compelling statement had never walked in Brye's shoes. For she had lost a twin brother...a piece of herself. Her pain was just as great now as it had been on the eve of his death.

The problem, of course, could be that she refused to confront the origin of her intrinsic pain. And the only time she consciously solicited memories of her twin brother originated and concluded on the anniversary of his death.

Nimble fingers turned the page of the large book. She then confronted an eight-by-ten glossy of her parents: Ashley and Lawrence Gray. Both Bryson and Tyson had inherited their strikingly good looks from their mother. But their charm, their youthful appeal, the hypnotic violet-colored eyes, had been personally handed down to them on a silver platter from their debonair father.

To the outsider looking in, the Grays were a handsome couple who had created handsome twins and lived a handsome lifestyle.

The observation, made by others, had been a calculated falsehood created by Brye's parents. Or maybe it wasn't calculated. After all, inside her parents' eyes, they *had* led a fairy-tale life.

In reality, Bryson and Tyson Gray had been abused. To her parent's credit however, the twins had not been physically mistreated. Nor had they been physically neglected. Properly fed, clothed, and groomed, they had been raised in a luxury Manhattan, four-bedroom apartment aligning Park Avenue. Nevertheless, as a teen, Bryson had been able to put a name to the mistreatment she and her twin brother had endured at the shrewd hands of her parents: they had been mentally, emotionally, and sexually abused.

Despite their lavish lifestyle, her parents did not work. At least not in the traditional sense of the word. Brye's parents spent their entire lives making money by *entertaining*. Her parents had adopted an "open" marriage policy and had lived successfully off the sexual promiscuities of others. Although they kept their eccentric lifestyle hidden from the public eye, they never kept their amoral ideology concealed from Bryson or Tyson.

It had become a fact of life for the twins, witnessing the stable of wealthy, prestigious women and men entering and exiting their lives at diverse times of the day or night. Yet due to the Grays' extremely absorbed schedule, very little time had been devoted to Bryson and Tyson—the twins were given free rein to raise themselves however they saw fit. Therefore, Bryson had devoted all her time and energy into raising Tyson. For as long as she could recall, she had been the most mature of the two.

It was she who put Tyson to bed at night. She was also the one to wake him in the morning. She dressed him, fed him, comforted him, amused him, and taught him right from wrong. More times than not, she was both mother and father. In her guardianship of her twin brother, she learned independence, whereas Tyson became codependent.

As Bryson grew older, wiser, increasingly self-reliant, she accepted her mother's and father's lack of parental nurturing. Tyson, however, forever sought maternal affection. Enamored with their mother, he obsessed over her beauty and grace. He would do anything to gain his mother's favor—and that included selling his soul to the devil.

Much to Tyson's delight, shortly after reaching puberty, their parents began showering them with more of their time and attention. And with impressionable minds and an eagerness to please, it wasn't difficult to mold—or corrupt—young, naive souls.

Distinctly, Brye recalled when the nightmare began. And as she was sucked into the deepest, darkest recesses of embroiled slumber, she dreamed of her fourteenth birthday…

4

ABSORBED IN A GAME *of chess at the ivory-finish dining room table, Bryson and Tyson called a halt to the game as their parents entered the apartment.*

"How're my sweethearts doing?" Ashley planted a kiss on Bryson's cheek. She then stood behind Tyson's chair, leaned forward, and tossed her arm around his neck. "Did my baby have a good day in school today?" she asked him.

"It was okay," Tyson responded, reveling in the warmth his mother's embrace provided.

"Well, you are going to have a better evening." She smiled at Bryson. "Because your father and I plan to spend the entire evening with the two of you."

"That's right," Lawrence confirmed. A DVD materialized from behind his back. "And while your mother fixes your favorite dinner, we're going to watch a movie."

Bryson witnessed the elation drizzle over her brother's head, immersing him in his entirety. Intimate moments spent with her parents were few and far between. Yet she had no idea how intimate the moment would get until the four of them joined ranks on the sofa.

The movie started out innocent enough. But five minutes into the scene, a man—a well-endowed man Bryson couldn't help but notice—initiated intercourse with a much eager woman.

A pornographic movie. Inwardly, Bryson tensed. This is wrong! *She told herself. But as she glanced at Tyson, she witnessed his enraptured expression, and his salivating tongue. He did not share her nagging concerns.*

But then why should he? On many occasions, he had spied on his parents and their guests as they "screwed each other's brains out"—as he so elegantly worded it.

Yes. Tyson was having the time of his life. What fourteen-year-old boy wouldn't enjoy watching an X-rated film? Particularly when he retained the endorsement of his parents.

Bryson turned her attention back to the TV screen. She felt disgusted and dirty. Nausea reached up and grabbed her by the back of her throat. If she continued to gaze at the overdramatized sex scene, she would vomit.

Mumbling something incoherent to her father—she couldn't remember what—Bryson sped to her room.

Fifteen minutes later, her mother waltzed in. "I think it's time we have a little girl talk," she informed.

Closed-mouthed, Bryson prudently surveyed her mother as she crossed the room and perched on the edge of Brye's white canopy bed. Seconds into their "talk," she realized that this would be her mother's adulterated rendition of the birds and the bees.

"Sex is a normal part of living...it's a fundamental component of life." Ashley reached out and grabbed a lock of Bryson's lustrous hair. Her touch was gentle as she wound the velvety fibers around her index finger. "It's nothing to be ashamed of. It's certainly nothing to run and hide from. You have really blossomed this past year. You've turned into a beautiful young woman." Ashley dropped her hand to the bed. She stood and walked to the window covered with an Irish lace curtain.

Unable to grasp the context of what this conversation entailed, Bryson sought to control her steely tongue. And as the words continued to flow from her mother's ruby red lips, comprehension hammered a massive crater in the center of Bryson's guarded consciousness.

"Men only want one thing from a woman—particularly a beautiful woman. And your male classmates are going to do anything—say whatever is necessary—to gain access to your virginal body. The bottom line is this: none of those boys can offer you anything except a scrambled lay in the back seat of a car. Nothing romantic. Nothing memorable. Rest assured, you'll go unfulfilled."

All too well, Bryson understood her mother's flagrant implications. She asked anyway. "What are you trying to say to me, Mother?"

Ashley's curvaceous body sashayed across the room. She sat and covered Bryson's hand with her own. "There are wonderful, experienced men who would love to spend time with you. They'll go first-class all the way and will happily pay a fortune for your innocence, youth, and beauty."

There it was. Short and sweet. Her parents wanted to pimp Tyson and herself out to the highest bidder.

No longer could Bryson stand to listen to the load of crap her mother spewed at her. Shooting Ashley a withering eye, voice strangled, Bryson pronounced, "Maybe I'm wrong to feel this way, but I'd like my first time to be with someone I love...someone who loves me...someone who respects me for who I am, not what I look like."

The corners of Ashley's lips twisted in a show of disgust. A flint of anger sparked the natural shade of skin color—from alabaster to fiery red, her irritation visibly noted. "If you insist on remaining starry-eyed and go into a relationship, expecting a storybook romance, you're setting yourself up for a huge fall. Trust me, Bryson. Given the chance, a man—all men—will use you, abuse you, and then throw you out with the garbage. It's up to you to prevent that from happening. You and you alone have the power to remain in control."

She pushed herself off the bed and sauntered toward the door. "I'm not trying to push you into anything, honey. I only want you to think about what I'm saying."

Standing at the threshold, Ashley swirled in a cloud of jasmine-scented perfume. She smiled her most enticing smile. "Men think with two brains, sweetheart. And if you do your job correctly, you can manipulate one in order to control the other. It will be a horrible waste if you give yourself away for free. Especially when there are men willing to pay well for your exquisiteness."

Alone, Bryson tore off her clothing. Hastily, she dove into the shower. For reasons utterly clear to herself, she felt unclean.

Month after month charged forward. True to her word Ashley never pressured Bryson. She would, however, subject her to inane statements such as, "We are put on this earth to satisfy a man's lust" and "Men like to be complimented by a beautiful woman at their side. They are willing to pay—be it money, clothing, cars or jewels—for that beauty." At other times, Ashley would say, "Your father and I are driven by our strong sexual drive. And you may not see it now, but it'll be the motivator of your actions as well. You are a part of us, Bryson. Genetically, we are of one. It may take you a little longer to discover your inner self, but eventually, you'll come around to our way of thinking. It's in your blood."

Deep down, barring their looks, Bryson prayed there was nothing genetically compatible between herself and her parents.

Although her mother's incessant prattle went ignored by Bryson, with growing trepidation, she watched as her brother willingly followed them into their sacrileges lair.

With their father's enthusiastic assistance, Tyson took up drinking. The more he drank, the greater his personality change.

He skipped school often, causing an immense drop in grades. Encouraged to do so, he began sleeping with older, wealthy women. And he treated Bryson with abominable contempt and disrespect.

Bryson continually confronted him with her increasing concerns. The road he'd chosen to travel was contemptuously immoral, and there was no reason for him to mimic their parents' sordid lifestyle. To no avail, the more she condemned her parents, the more Tyson idolized them and struck out at her. And it was one evening, shortly after their fifteenth birthday, he introduced Bryson to the depth in which their parents had managed to bury their poisonous claws into Tyson.

When entering the apartment, the stench of alcohol instantly assaulted her senses. She found Tyson nursing a glass of brandy.

A trail of fear skittered downward, pulling at her lower intestines. The love and devotion she fostered for him could not escape her tender tone. "Do you realize what that stuff is doing to you?" Gently, she removed the glass from his clenched fingers.

The hostility he discharged with a mere flicker of an eyebrow startled Bryson. "Spare me your holier-than-thou attitude, Bryson!"

Bryson's heart ripped in two. Disheartened with the carelessness in which he treated their relationship, she wearily plopped down beside him. "We used to be so close. We could talk to each other about anything." She ran the back of her hand along virgin skin shaping itself to grow facial hairs. "Why am I losing you?"

His eyes, the tone of his voice, softened. "I'm still here, Bry. I haven't gone anywhere."

Sadly, Bryson pointed at the bottle of liquor gracing the coffee table. "That has changed you, Ty! Our parents have changed you!"

Tyson's face darkened. He shot off the couch. "Don't even go there, Bryson! I've heard enough criticism from you to last me a lifetime."

"What am I supposed to do?" Bryson countered. "Do you expect me to just sit back and allow you to destroy your life? You should be doing things other normal *teenagers do."*

"What the hell do you know about normal teenagers? You've spent so much of your time smothering me, you've never made a life of your own. You couldn't begin to guess what the life of a normal teenager entails!"

"I know that a normal teenager wouldn't prostitute himself!" she angrily retorted.

Offense taken, Tyson paced back and forth in front of Bryson. "Dad was right." He halted long enough to throw daggers at his twin sister with piercing eyes. "He says you're a stuck-up bitch who thinks you're better than the rest of us!"

Bryson stiffened. The complete lack of morality startled her. Her voice lowered several octaves. "That's not true, and you know it."

"Dad said that you would understand our way of life if you just went out and got fucked." He sneered. "I'm beginning to think he's right."

Bryson loved him too much to hold him accountable for his harsh words. "Now you're allowing the alcohol to speak for you."

"Yeah." He raised an unabashed eyebrow. "Then let's see how much more I can get it to say."

He made a mad dash for the bottle. Bryson shot off the couch and, reaching it first, she sprinted toward the kitchen. "I can't condone your drinking!" she shouted over her shoulder.

While dumping the entire content down the sink, his powerful grip sealed around her upper arm. Jerked backward, she found herself pivoting on her heels.

With the speed of lightening, Tyson's arm whipped through the air. A dazzling string of lights danced before Bryson's eyes as the back of Tyson's hand caught her on the side of her mouth.

Once the fierce sound of skin connecting with skin trailed off, ominous silence swallowed them whole. Several attenuated seconds later, Bryson's mind and vision cleared. Horror-stricken, she could only stare into Tyson's alarm-colored eyes. Ironically, his expression reflected that of her own. The same thought rushed through both their confused minds: how could he have raised a finger to harm her?

Remorse ripped through him like a rabid dog sinking his barbed teeth into an unsuspecting victim. Frozen to the spot, yet his body shook uncontrollably. When he recaptured control of his voluntary movements, he grabbed Bryson and hauled her to his heaving chest.

"Oh god, Bry!" His wretched sobs grazed her temple and spilled into the oppressive atmosphere. "I don't know what came over me. I swear I don't. Hitting you was just like hitting myself. I didn't mean to hurt you."

Pushing her at arm's length, his fingers shook as he examined her bruised mouth. "I'm sorry," he repeated over and over. "Can you forgive me?"

The bitter taste of blood jarred Bryson's tingling tongue. Nevertheless, she chose to ignore it. The compassion her brother exhibited overrode the pain. "I'm all right," she rushed to assure. "And, yes, I forgive you. Just please...please...can you slow down on the drinking?"

Tears fogged Tyson's aggrieved eyes. He nodded, then pulled her back into his arms. And for a short while, Bryson believed her brother had come back to her.

Days later, Tyson broke his promise. And the more he drank, the more he exhibited uncharacteristic signs of aggression.

Numerous times, his anger got the best of him, and he would come to blows with his twin sister. Each time, profound remorse surged through him. Each time, Bryson forgave him.

He was her twin brother. She loved him dearly. A bond prolific of love and solidarity united them as one. No outside force could ever sever that tie. And after dedicating her entire life to his care, she knew she would never let go or give up on him. But slowly and surely, she lost sight of him. Seeing and feeling him slip away was synonymous to having a large chunk of her heart ripped out of her chest.

Day after day, week after week, month after month, Bryson's world crumbled into a rancid pile at her feet. She was the outsider...an outcast.

In the hopes of keeping her sanity intact, she buried herself in her school work and spent the entirety of her time studying, reading, learning. And as her family pursued their own soiled agenda, they diligently labored at persuading her into joining the ranks of their contaminated immorality.

Ring!

The blast of the doorbell infiltrated Brye's somnolent state. She woke with a start. Golden touches of sunlight cantered along her bedroom walls and traipsed warmth and color along her pallid cheeks. Plagued with recurrent nightmares of her teenaged years, she slept fitfully. But before she could reflect upon her disturbing night, once again, the doorbell stabbed into her hazy awakening.

Shaking her head to scatter the foggy swampland weighing her down, she vaulted out of bed, grabbed her robe, and flew down the stairs.

Much to her surprise, Tenisha stood at her doorstep.

"You look like hell!" Tenisha greeted, immediately taking note of Brye's haggard appearance.

"Thank you. So do you," Brye responded, gaping at the heavy bags underneath her friend's veiled eyes. She stepped back, allowing Tenisha entrance to her home. "I take it you had a rough night?"

"Apparently not as rough as yours." She trailed Brye into the kitchen. "So…do you want to talk about it?"

"No." Brye plugged in the coffee peculator. Her left hand leaned on the butcher-block island, her right hand rested on her hips. Facing Tenisha, she asked, "Do *you* want to talk about it?"

"No." She threw herself into a kitchen chair and visibly pouted.

The coffee on, Brye pulled up an arm chair. Staring at her over the claw-foot oak table, she asked, "Have you eaten any breakfast?"

"I can't deal with breakfast at the present moment," she curtly replied.

Indifferent to Tenisha's brusque attitude, Brye shrugged. The thought of food did not sit well on her stomach any more than it did Tenisha's. Elbow on the table, she propped her chin on her knuckle.

As the fresh aromatic blend of French Vanilla coffee permeated the room, a pair of cardinals soared past Brye's patio door. The red birds landed on the deck railing. Several sparrows pecked noisily at the bird feeder. The cardinals stared in open curiosity before joining the feeding clan.

The flurry of activity erased the memory of Brye's night terrors, yet lingering uneasiness forced her to heave a disconcerted sigh.

"TyJuan didn't come home last night?" Tenisha carved into Brye's wayward thoughts. "I fixed dinner, put out the good china, lit candles, and dressed in his favorite negligee. Only he never showed."

Apprehensive eyes lit into Tenisha. "Have you heard from him?" Brye interrogated. "Is he okay?"

"Why don't you ask the bitch he woke up with?" she sneered maliciously.

Brye was startled with the vicious nature behind Tenisha's verbal attack. "Do you know for sure he slept with a woman last night?"

"He finally called this morning and said he ran into an old friend. He claims they got together, had a few drinks, talked over past experiences, and forgot about the time."

"Are you sure that's not what happened?"

Tenisha experienced the initial stirring of a stress headache. In circular motion, she applied temperate pressure to her right temple. As she did so, she glared at Brye as if to say, "Get real, girlfriend!"

But why should I care what TyJuan does? The refractory thought shot at her from the midst of her drumming skull. *Let the bitch have him. At least then the guilt wouldn't be on my shoulders anymore.* She sighed. "When he called, I heard a woman laughing. She sounded close…as if she was lying on top of him."

Brye could easily rationalize the situation. She could have readily accused Tenisha of suffering from an overdose of an overactive imagination. Yet if she did, it would seem she had sided with TyJuan—and that meant she would be doing a terrible injustice to her friend. Therefore, she asked, "What do you want to do about it?"

"I don't know." Tenisha dropped her hands to the table. Where had she taken the wrong turn in her marriage? How had everything gone so bad? *You know where*, she told herself. *It was when you absolved TyJuan from striking you…twice. Just like you'll exonerate him from not coming home last night…just like you'll exonerate him of all future sins. The man's got you feeling guilty because you've made a huge success of your life. He's convinced you that you're to blame for his inadequacies—and you're buying into his bullshit.* Lips stretched into a tight frown, Tenisha scattered the disturbing thoughts. "I don't know what I want to do," she repeated. "I do know that I don't want to think about it any longer."

Nodding in understanding, Brye set aside her empty comments. She would not attempt to sway Tenisha one way or the other. Instead, she shoved away from the table and poured two mugs of freshly brewed coffee. Tenisha, alone, had to do what was best for Tenisha.

She carted the steaming hot liquid to the table.

Silence befell the room as each woman nursed her own tortured thoughts. Not wanting recollections of her past to dominate her temperament all day, Brye's mind reached outward for ideas to occupy her time.

But before her flaying thoughts could step past her morning cup of coffee, a key turned inside her entrance lock, and the sound of her door swinging open invaded the bleak setting within her home.

"Brye?"

"We're in here, Marcus!" she yelled out.

Marcus entered the kitchen with Rainbow on his shoulders. The macaw cackled, "Hello" several times in quick succession. The jovial greeting coerced a smile from Tenisha.

Marcus sensed the dark mood flowing between the two sedate women. It did not in any way overshadow the exhilaration motivated by Tenisha's lovely image. He moved over to the percolator and grabbed himself some morning brew. Joining the ladies at the table, he pulled up a side chair across from Tenisha. "So," he asked, tipping his mug to his lips, "are you two holding a contest to see who can draw the longest face?"

Tenisha rolled her eyes over Marcus. A slow inventory took in his freshly shaved face, meticulously trimmed mustache, smooth dark skin, lopsided smile breaking into handsome features, and bulging biceps accentuating a much worn tank top. An unexpected band of butterflies detoured across her lower abdomen. "Didn't you have a party last night?" Not waiting for a response, she added, "Shouldn't you be home, nursing a hangover?"

Marcus peered at her through vapors rising above the rim of his cup. He replied, "I don't drink. But I may be induced into taking my first if I'm forced to continue looking at sorry-ass faces the rest of the morning."

His remark roused a smile from Tenisha. Marcus's heart tugged at the dazzling sight.

"There's an obvious remedy for your dilemma." Tenisha pointed her ceramic mug toward the patio door. "And don't let it hit you on the behind on your way out."

A robust laugh rising from the depths of Marcus's massive lungs tickled Tenisha's senses. He looked down at his watch. "One minute, forty-five seconds. This is a record. I'm usually in the company of a beautiful woman for at least five minutes before she puts me out in the cold."

"It's nice to know you reap the same effect on every woman you come across."

"It's part of my innate charm."

"Charm?" Tenisha repeated with a skeptical grin. She was enjoying this playful exchange more than she cared to admit. "Is that another word for someone who's full of sh—"

"You know," Brye strategically cut in, guiding the subject to safer ground, "in two weeks, I'm giving a surprise birthday party for the kids at Brylinn."

Tenisha's uplift in spirit convinced Brye that Marcus was just what the two of them needed to divert their attention elsewhere.

"Are you trying to tell us that fifteen kids have birthdays on the same date?" Tenisha asked in stunned disbelief.

"Actually, it's the twins' sixth birthday," Brye explained, "but I thought I'd buy everyone gifts."

"You spoil those kids," Marcus proclaimed, none too harshly.

"Yes, I do," Brye blithely agreed. "And I'm enjoying every minute of it. Anyway, Tenisha, we can spend the day shopping. You can also help me order a cake and pick out the decorations. And"—Brye smiled at Marcus—"Marcus can tag along and carry our packages… can't you, Marcus?"

Since making his entrance, Marcus's interest had lingered on surreptitiously embodying himself into Brye's and Tenisha's day. Brye had just given him the opening he desperately longed for. Feigning irritation, he growled, "You wish to enlist my brute strength for the day and you can't ask me any better than that?"

"What are you complaining about?" Tenisha quipped, appreciative of the prolonged distraction Brye offered. "At least she *asked* you. She didn't give me a choice."

Brye stood and placed her empty coffee mug in the double sink. She turned and faced her friends. "You want a choice? Okay, here it is: my offer's on the table… take it or leave it."

"We'll take it!" Tenisha and Marcus shouted in unison.

"Good." Brye waltzed toward the kitchen door. "Let me jump in the shower and throw on some clothes, then we'll be on our way." Grateful to be spending the day with her friends, a notable spring dictated her step as she exited the room.

The two-toned stretch limousine idled alongside the curb of Terminal B inside Newark International Airport. In a matter of seconds, the luxury car filled with traveling passengers: Chad and his parents—Elizabeth and Daniel Collier—settled into the plush seats. The limo crawled its way past congested lanes spilling with cars, buses, taxis, and courtesy vans. Inevitably, it hooked its exit and manipulated its way onto the New Jersey Turnpike. And like a marathon runner pacing himself for the duration, the grand ride settled in for the thirty-mile jaunt to Somerset, New Jersey.

"Did you enjoy the South of France, Mother?" Chad reached into the refrigerator and found his mother a diet Coke.

Although she'd only taken a few steps from strolling out of the airport and settling into the luxury vehicle, the parched heat had drained her of all moisture. Appreciative of the offer, she seized the cold can and resisted the unladylike urge to swipe it across her forehead. "I would have enjoyed the trip more had your father spent more time with me. His business affairs kept him so bogged down, more often than not, I had to fend for myself." Adoration spilled from blue-gray eyes as she gazed at her husband of thirty-three years. Married directly out of high school, Elizabeth had devoted her first few years to marriage as well as college. Born into prestigious families with old money, a six-year difference in ages separated Elizabeth and Daniel. Childhood sweethearts, although the two families approved of their marriage, Elizabeth had gone against her parents' wishes by legally uniting before obtaining her college degree.

Two years into the marriage, she had given birth to her one and only son. A devout mother and wife, she suffered no regrets in placing her family's needs before her own.

Daniel lovingly squeezed his wife's fingers. "We'll be leaving for the South Hamptons in a few weeks. And I promise you, dear, for the next month afterward, I'll be at your complete disposal."

In Daniel's earlier days, as a young, power-driven entrepreneur, he sought his own fame and fortune—he refused a ride on his father's coattails. Ruthless in nature, he cut a number of unscrupulous deals. Never breaking any laws when pursuing business affairs, nevertheless, he usually teetered close to the edge. Not once had he lost sleep over crushing heads as he stomped his way to the top. Although he was not well-liked in the corporate world, he remained well respected.

Daniel smiled at his greatest achievement: his son. Expecting nothing less, he proudly looked on as Chad left his own imposing footprints throughout the industry.

There had been a time in Chad's life when his future was uncertain. Touch and go for several years, Chad had finally hauled himself out of the chasm of self-pity. Ambitious and highly motivated, he plunged into his work as steadfast as a lion going after its prey. Industriously proving himself Daniel's son, no man had ever made a father more proud.

"Have you wrapped up your work at Romanique Cosmetics," he asked, smiling at the pride of his life.

Averting his dad's question, Chad aimed a cryptic eye outside the limousine window. Beyond the smoked glass, cliffs, trees, houses, and businesses soared past in distorted panorama.

No, he was not ready to sign off at Romanique.

For years and from a distance, Chad stood sentry over Brye Grayson's meteoric climb to fame. With restrained impatience, he'd confronted the supermodel's magazine layouts, billboard advertisements, television commercials, and music videos she'd costarred in. As long as she'd maintained her distance, he had been able to sustain a tight cork on his flaying emotions. The day her portfolio surprisingly crossed his path was the day she'd unleashed a festering volcano. Unleashing the fire of his swelling wrath now, Brye Grayson consumed his every conscious as well as unconscious thought. She governed his every move, which was something he knew his father would never tolerate.

Evasive in his answer, he stated, "I've decided to stick around a little longer…complete a few projects…tie up loose ends."

Intolerant to the idea, his mother harshly voiced her objections. "No, Chadwick. I expect you to spend the summer in the Hamptons with your father and I."

"I can still come out on weekends, Mother."

"But I've invited Jennifer and her parents to join us for the Fourth. They'll be spending several weeks with us."

"Whenever you make plans concerning my future," Chad retorted, his voice rising in irritation, "I'd appreciate some advanced notice."

"You may be grown," Daniel mildly chastised, "but you're still expected to treat your mother with respect, young man."

Anger abated, Chad smiled. Despite his age, inside his parents' eye, he remained their little boy. "You're right." He leaned over and kissed his mother on the cheek. "I apologize, Mother. But I *am* extremely busy. It's impossible for me to get away right now."

Daniel stared at his son with a skeptical smirk. "Several months ago, you were willing to give your right arm to get away from the cosmetic business. What's changed, son?"

Unwilling to admit to his father or himself that one Brye Grayson stood behind his sudden change of heart, he merely shrugged. "Believe it or not, the ins and outs of the cosmetic industry have intrigued me."

Extremely proficient in reading between the lines, Daniel interpreted more behind his son's reluctance to leave Romanique Cosmetics.

Instinct alone had driven Daniel to the level of success he had achieved throughout his life span. Daniel never ignored gut feelings. And now he was certain his son held a hidden agenda. For reasons known only to himself, Chad was intentionally being cryptic, concealing significant information Daniel wasn't sure he would be pleased with. At all costs, he would find out what Chad was deliberately keeping from him.

"I'm hoping you and Jennifer will announce your engagement this summer." Elizabeth smiled warmly. "You know you aren't getting any younger. It's time you give your mother a granddaughter to pamper and your father a grandson to spoil."

Involved with Jennifer for the past several years, at one time, their engagement had appeared inevitable. Now he wasn't so certain. Now he had Brye to contend with.

Not allowing his mother to witness his hesitancy, he grinned. "Don't worry, Mother, when I decide to get married, you'll be the first to know." Then, burrowing himself further into the malleable cushions, Chad retired from the conversation and gave way to his own transient thoughts.

Twelve hours overflowed with shopping, roller-skating, carriage rides, and literally stuffing their faces with junk food, Brye, Tenisha, and Marcus toppled into Brye's living room, exhausted yet content.

Arms abundant with packages, Brye collapsed onto the winter-white carpet. Tenisha slouched down onto the sofa, her shopping bag spilled onto the floor. Across from Tenisha, Marcus lowered his huge frame into a Regency chair. His large parcels rested at his feet.

Sliding out of her Skechers, Tenisha heaved a huge sigh of relief. Her eyes rolled over the many presents they had spent a good portion of the day buying. Her vision then panned over Brye. She cast a knowing glimpse at Marcus.

In anticipation of the monumental job Brye expected of Marcus and herself, Tenisha slipped her feet back into her shoes. Struggling to her feet, her words ran together, "I think it's time I should be heading home."

"Oh no you don't!" Brye exclaimed in a warning tone. "You're not going anywhere until you help me wrap these gifts."

"But Bryeeee!" Tenisha moaned, falling back onto the sofa. "There's so many. And the party isn't for another several weeks. Can't we do this later?"

"No. We can't," Brye spoke softly, as if speaking to a spoiled child. "Because if I let you go now, I'll never see you again until after the party has come and gone."

"But I don't like to wrap," Tenisha whined. "And I'm soooo hungry!"

No more thrilled to be wrapping presents than Tenisha, her statement left Marcus with an opportunity of his own. He stood. "I've got a pound of ground sirloin thawing in the fridge." He smiled innocently at Brye. "Why don't I fire up your grill? I'll cook up some of my famous Marcus burgers."

"You only want to use my grill so you won't have to clean your own," Brye protested, throwing him a sour look.

A man who fully believed in paying for all his gift wrapping needs, Marcus would promise anything if it meant getting out of a job he considered mundane. He practically begged, "I promise to clean up afterward."

"In that case, you have a deal." Brye searched through bags, seeking out the various gift wrapping paper they'd purchased.

Marcus thrust a triumphant chin toward Tenisha.

"Traitor!" she yelled at his back as he slipped outside. Her gaze remained on the door long after he'd disappeared.

Unfamiliar feelings generated by Marcus's overpowering presence flooded Tenisha's overtaxed system. Feelings she did not want to think about. Feelings that frightened as well as excited her. Funny, but she had never looked at him as an obtainable man before. She'd merely treated him as Brye's good friend. Today, spending the day with Marcus, getting to know him better, her image of him had changed dramatically. Despite his brute strength, he was not afraid to reveal the gentleness. He could be earnest or he could be funny. Handsome, courteous, an avid conversationalist, and well-educated, he was exceptional at focusing in on a woman's mood swings. He also knew how to respond appropriately. Tenisha was curious as to why he hadn't been snapped up by some energetic, confident, young woman before now.

"Tenisha!" Brye's sharp tongue sent Tenisha's thoughts scrambling for cover. "Are you going to help me out here? Or are you going to stare at the door for the rest of the night?"

With great effort, Tenisha slid her body down the front of the sofa. She landed next to Brye and began separating gifts from shopping bags.

"What were you thinking about?" Palms flat on the ground, Brye shoved herself off the floor. Strolling into the kitchen, she pulled scissors and tape out of a utility drawer.

"I was thinking about Marcus…how sweet he is," Tenisha answered as soon as Brye reached hearing distance.

Brye stopped dead in her tracks. Head tilted, she appeared to be weighing a heavy decision. Should she or should she not tell Tenisha of Marcus's true feelings. Quickly resolving her dilemma, she sat cross-legged on the floor next to her friend. "He's in love with you, you know!" she blurted out.

Startled with the unexpected revelation, Tenisha gawked with wide-eyed naiveté. "But how could you— He's never done anything— He's never said anything!" she stammered uncomfortably. Outwardly, she appeared taken aback; inwardly, she was thrilled by the unexpected revelation.

"He wouldn't," Brye stated with certainty.

"Then why would you say that?" Tenisha insisted in a state of uncertainty. "After all, I *am* married."

"Which is the reason I decided to tell you. I wouldn't want you leading him on…prompting him into believing something could transpire between the two of you."

"Dammit, Brye! I would never—"

"Not intentionally," Brye interrupted. "I know you wouldn't. And the only reason I'm bringing this up is because I think you should be careful. You don't need any complications in your life right now…at least not until you straighten out your relationship with TyJuan."

Marcus and Rainbow entered the room, giving Tenisha no opportunity to respond. The girls, buried knee-deep in gifts, influenced him to shuffle as fast as his size sixteen shoes would carry him, away from the unpleasant task. Rainbow flew off his owner's shoulders and landed in the middle of an unrolled sheet of gift wrap.

Brye shooed him away. "If you can't help, don't hinder my progress."

Looking to be scratched, Rainbow rubbed his head against the back of Brye's hand. New feathers had emerged in sheaths around his neck and head region. Gently prying the tips of the feathery sheaths open, she then pushed him away. "Now go away before I wrap you in purple paper and stick a bow on you."

Rainbow released a bloodcurdling screech. He half flew, half walked to the other side of the room.

Incredulously, Tenisha stared at Brye. After that unexpected bombshell her friend dropped, how was she expected to sit here and calmly wrap presents? In all actuality, she wanted to confront Marcus and the feelings he retained for her. Or…maybe not.

Maybe she needed to confront the feelings she held for Marcus.

No, she didn't want to do that either.

Besides, Brye could have misread Marcus's good-hearted intentions. She could have mistaken an innocent remark for something more meaningful. She could have—

Tenisha halted in mid-thought. In the grand scope of things, whatever Brye believed, and whatever Marcus felt, could never be validated. Because in the end, she remained a married woman.

Tenisha dropped her gaze to the toy she held tightly within her grip. Releasing a dismissive sigh, she decided to concentrate on the task at hand.

Seconds later, she frantically searched through shopping bags. "Brye?" Lips crinkled in quizzical fashion, she said, "Call me crazy, but when you give someone a birthday party, isn't it customary to buy the honored guests a present? Bethany and Anthony?" Tenisha rushed forward, not giving Brye time to respond to her frantic inquiry. "We bought everyone else something. Did we forget the twins?"

"No, we did not," Brye reassured. "I won't pick up their gifts until the day of the party." A shimmer of light danced around an all-knowing smile. "And trust me, they're going to love it."

The only time Brye appeared genuinely happy, Tenisha observed, was when she spoke of the kids at the Brylinn Residential Home for Children. Tenisha wondered why that happiness did not spill over into other areas of her life. "The twins mean a lot to you, don't they?" she somberly asked.

"All the children hold a designated place in my heart. And although I would never show any favoritism toward any of the other kids, the twins are very special to me."

"And why is that?" Tenisha began cutting out a strip of paper large enough to wrap an iPod.

Because of the similarities I see in myself. Brye said, "When they initially arrived at the home, Bethany and Anthony were extremely introverted. They shied away from everyone, including children their own age. They trusted no one and were suspicious of everything. Bethany, the oldest only by a few minutes, was a ferocious protector of Anthony." As Brye talked, she wrapped present after present—a kite-making kit, a Barbie doll, computer software, a gift certificate to a bookstore, a pair of rollerblades. Each present had been painstakingly selected to match the personality of the child receiving the gift.

The children in the home all came from low-income, dysfunctional families. All had been used and abused in some form or another. Yet, despite their trials and tribulations, their spirits had not been broken. More than anything, Brye respected their tenacity and ability to bounce back. She would do anything to bring a smile to their faces. She would give anything to put a ray of sunshine into their dreary lives.

"Anyway," Brye continued, "Bethany and Anthony needed extra attention. They needed to learn how to trust."

"Trust?" Tenisha croaked. "Now that's funny coming from you...the woman who lives, breathes, and eats distrust and cynicism."

Brye wrinkled her nose at Tenisha. Choosing to ignore the remark, she continued, "I began spending more and more time with them. I wasn't making much headway until I took Rainbow for a visit." Brye smiled. She watched as Rainbow amused himself with a Macy's shopping bag. "He brings out the best in everyone."

"Now that," Tenisha laughed, "I can wholeheartedly agree with." She snatched the thick handle from Rainbow's beak. Lifting the bag, she dropped it over his body. The paper sack rustled loudly as Rainbow worked his way out.

"They really opened up after his visit. They questioned me endlessly about macaws, where they come from, what they eat, how one cared for them. They tossed inexhaustible questions at me. I finally presented them with detailed books exploring the many species of the macaw. They were fascinated with the subject. And in the aftermath, we've become good friends." Brye's tone had taken on a distinct quality, a manifestation of motherly devotion.

"Sounds to me as if there's more going on besides a mere friendship," Tenisha thoughtfully noted.

Circumstances had thrown the twins and Brye together. The parallelism between the three is what sealed their unity. Brye wanted to disclaim the strong attachment she felt toward Bethany and Anthony, but she could not deny those feelings any more than she could deny her own identity. "I care a lot for them...yes. I can't ignore what I feel for those two," she openly admitted.

The gifts found themselves wrapped in no time as Brye and Tenisha endlessly chatted. Just as the last package was stacked, Marcus hauled them in for dinner. Laughter brightened the kitchen as they dined on grilled chicken, corn-on-the-cob, stuffed mushrooms, and a spinach salad. Tenisha stuffed the last mushroom into her mouth.

"Marcus is a man of many hidden talents," Brye said as she popped a cherry tomato in her mouth.

"Is he now?" A glint of mischievousness brightened Tenisha's spirited features. She captured Marcus's gaze with an amused eye. "And what does a lady have to do to uncover those 'hidden talents?'"

"It depends on what the lady wants and what she's willing to do to get it," Marcus replied, lips formed in a devilish grin.

"Well, I don't know about your other lady friends, but I'm willing to do anything if you can pull dessert out of your bag of tricks."

"Now that," Brye stated as she shot out of her chair, "I can handle." She pulled open her freezer and stuck her head inside. Her voice seeped from around the door, "Fast, convenient, low in calories, and sinfully delicious." With a flourish, she pulled out several packages of Weight Watchers Sweet Celebrations desserts.

"Weight Watchers!" Tenisha shrilled with glee. "I love their desserts. But the portions are so skimpy. I generally eat more than one."

"When they advertise 'total indulgence,' somehow, I don't think they meant eating the entire package." Marcus stood and snatched a box from Brye's hands. "I got dibs on the chocolate eclairs."

"I'll trade you a Triple Chocolate Caramel Mousse for one of your eclairs," Tenisha bargained.

"Deal!"

Brye laughed and sat down with a package of Praline Toffee Crunch Parfait. Dipping her spoon into the plastic cup, she stuck a generous portion of ice cream into her mouth and savored the inviting taste. Brye knew she'd gone completely overboard in her caloric intake for the day. Generally diet conscious, in accordance to healthy eating habits, she did not maintain a strict regimen. A supermodel by trade, she had never bought into the Twiggy-thin image. She was not an emaciated waif. Nor was she obsessive in her eating habits to the point of suffering from an eating disorder. At five-foot-ten in her stocking feet, from top to bottom, her poised frame displayed a well-proportioned reflection. From sheer observation alone, she maintained the ability to halt the most sophisticated of men while they mindlessly drooled down their chins.

"Now that I've indulged myself and I'm feeling completely disgusted, I think it's time to go home." Finishing one eclair and one chocolate mousse, Tenisha hoisted herself out of her chair while heaving an agonizing groan. "It's midnight now. Do you think I can waddle out to my car before the break of dawn?"

"Why don't I walk you out?" Marcus offered, pushing himself away from the table.

"Why don't you eliminate some of my misery and carry me? No," she promptly reconsidered, "forget I said that. The faster I get these weighted-down feet to move, the faster this food'll metabolize…which means, hopefully, the faster I'll feel better." She pulled Brye into a hug. "I'll see you later, kid."

Brye pulled away. She shared a meaningful glance with Tenisha. Once her friend walked back into her home, she would be entering unfamiliar territory; there was no way she could guess the mood TyJuan would be in. "I'll be at Brylinn all day tomorrow. Call… if you need anything. If you simply need to talk. Don't hesitate to call…anytime."

Tenisha nodded, then walked out. Marcus trailed behind her.

In Brye's driveway, Tenisha halted beside her Ford Explorer. She turned and faced Marcus. In the several years they'd known each other, they had never been alone nor had they been in such close proximity of one another. Now that it was time to depart, mixed feelings overtook her: maybe it hadn't been such a good idea to be alone with him. Head tilted upward, hands captured behind her back, silently, she stared up into his eyes. Kind, gentle eyes. A kind and gentle man. For a brief moment Tenisha wondered what it would feel like to be held by this man. Heat swirled around the pit of her stomach and worked its way down to the most intimate part of her being. She grew warm at the thought of being loved by this man. Then, recalling Brye's earlier warning, she hastily thrust thoughts of falling into his arms aside.

A full moon loomed overhead. A diaphanous haze had formed around the incandescent orb, creating a mystical appearance. One mile away, lake water shimmered in the moonlit night like a thousand glimmering fireflies. Melodious night sounds added to the twilight charm.

A lazy breeze swathed Marcus within its spirited clutches. The balmy air felt good against his heated skin. It felt almost as good as the love he felt for this woman. A love he would never be able to act upon. Regrettably, he sighed.

"I had a good time today." Tenisha was the first to break the tension forging its way between the two fidgety bodies. She smiled, a brilliance competing with the glistening moon. The glorious sight sent Marcus's heart on a speedy cadence, heating his blood to a noticeably high level.

"We should do this more often," Tenisha continued.

"Yeah?" Marcus raised a questionable eyebrow. God, how he would love nothing better than to spend time with this enticing woman. "Are you serious?"

"Well… No…yes…maybe…I don't know," she stumbled.

Marcus nodded. They would be embarking upon a dangerous game if this continued; a game of chance. An accidental slip of the tongue or an unrestrained gesture might make Tenisha take a step backward. He would not jeopardize their alliance for a romance that may never come to be. If Marcus couldn't have her as a lifelong mate and lover, he could still cherish her as a friend. "I understand," he somberly stated.

Nothing else needed to be said. Tenisha climbed into her Explorer. The engine roared to life. She drove off without a backward glance.

Hands stuffed deep inside his pockets, Marcus stood sentinel over her departure. As her taillights diminished into tiny red pinpoints, mixed emotions gripped him by the balls, clung tenaciously, and refused to let go. She was married. He was sorely aware of that fact. But the more time they spent together, the less time he thought of her marriage. Married or not, he wanted her. He desired her for more than a one-night stand. And God help him if she ever encouraged their relationship. Because if she did, he would not have the strength to turn away from her. No-holds-barred, like a professional poker player, he played for the entire kitty.

Somehow he managed to break away from the disabling clench affixing him to the spot he stood in. He turned and entered Brye's home. Marcus found her scrubbing down the charred grill work. "I thought I was supposed to clean those?"

"It's okay," Brye scrubbed vigorously at the hardened stains. "It's late. I have to be up early in the morning. Go home, Marcus!" she commanded.

Collecting Rainbow, Marcus left through the back door. He crossed the yard and went home. Through her kitchen window, Brye kept a unwavering vigilance until his large frame completely disappeared from sight. Subtle as it were, Tenisha had begun to exhibit genuine feelings for Marcus. Brye wasn't sure how she felt about that. With everything TyJuan put Tenisha through, God knows her friend needed someone as wonderful as Marcus in her life. But she did not need a lover. And Marcus didn't need to get caught up in the middle of Tenisha's domestic problems.

Brye sighed. She scrubbed with the vigilance of a woman trying to eradicate the thick shadows settling around her.

5

BRYSON GRAY WAS UNDER the terrifying clutches of a nightmare; at least her tormented mind tried to convince herself that it was only an illusion. The cold, slimy snake slithered along her tender body. Slowly, steadily, sickeningly, its squalid trunk shimmied its way past her stomach, between her breasts and around her neck. She shuddered from the revolting touch and tried to awaken.

As she fought her way back to wakefulness, the snake grew larger, became heavier. It covered her entire body, pressing oppressively into her constricting chest. The snake prodded her mouth open. She could feel him slinking down her throat. His thick skin imprisoned her breathing. She cringed with fear, gasped for air, and forced her eyes open.

Now, fully awake, nothing in her wildest nightmares could have surpassed what she presently endured. A human snake—one of her mother's creations—with beady eyes and putrid alcohol breath, had crawled his way into her bedroom and inside her bed. He now lay atop her, stuffing his glutinous tongue down her throat.

Bryson's chest heaved as she struggled for air. She only succeeded in drawing in his rank breath.

"Relax," the human reptile hissed. "I promise you'll enjoy this."

Indignant more than afraid from having her privacy invaded, her body soiled, and the reprehensible assumption made by a scaly creature that she was no better than the rest of her vile family, Bryson did the first thing that came to mind: she bit down on his putrid tongue. Hard. She drew enough blood to coat the inside of her mouth.

The snake howled. A bloodcurdling scream. His tongue no longer restricted the fresh air clamoring to gain access to her lungs.

Before he had time to physically act out his outrage against Bryson, she grabbed her phone from her bedside stand. Slamming it against the side of his skull, he howled again, grabbed his head, and rolled onto the hardwood floor. Bryson leaped out of bed. Hurling her furor toward the withering creature, she spat into the darkened room, "Maybe next time you'll think twice before entering someone else's territory without an invitation!"

Racing out of her bedroom, weak-kneed and sweaty palms, she didn't stop until she was safely locked and sheltered inside her own private bathroom. And when she stood under the drenching pour of a hot shower, gargling with bottle after bottle of peroxide, extinguishing the repugnant taste overriding her shuddering system, only then did she collapse in fear.

Early Monday morning Brye's eyelids sluggishly split open. Vacant eyes remained fixed upon the bedroom ceiling. Blinking back soft tears, the reality of surviving the weekend—the anniversary weekend of her brother's death—slowly sank into her fogged brain.

Pulling herself into a sitting position, she grasped her pillow and hugged it to her chest. Cold moisture permeated the rose-colored pillow case. The wetness, soaking into her trembling body, did not prohibit her from embracing the cushiony softness. Eyes, ears, and her sixth sense welcomed the serenity encompassing her intimate environment. Sometime during the wee hours of the morning her brother had been exorcised from her home…her soul. No longer was he a part of her physical world. His spirit had receded into whatever world he'd risen from. Now she only had to contend with her night visions.

Because of Brye's refusal to confront her past inside the light of day, more times than not, her teenage years, her brother's death, her living nightmares, continued to plague her as she slept. Eight years later, still, she sought no exoneration for her sins. Nor did she ask for clemency from the apparitions convening at her bedside as she slept. In fact, she readily accepted it as a natural part of her bleak existence.

Nights, Brye usually obtained no more than three to four hours of sleep. Days—as a stalwart testament to her mental and physical stamina—she pushed herself well beyond her limits, specifically to hamper the night terrors from disrupting her every waking moment. Between college, her modeling career, and Brylinn Residential Home for Children, she inexhaustively maintained eighteen- to twenty-hour days, running on pure adrenaline alone.

While completing her dissertation, Brye tenaciously studied all modalities of human behavior. Effortlessly, she could recite scientific data shaped by the intricately functioning mind and body; how the mind worked in conjunction with the body; how an individual reasoned and learned; how and why human beings react differently when confronted with similar disasters.

As to her method of coping with her own personal tragedies, she, as well as other experts, would say: challenge your fears, embrace them, accept truths for what they are, forgive, then let go.

Maybe, deep down, Brye didn't want to let go. Maybe this was her way of punishing herself; she was alive while her immediate family members were dead.

Because of her uncertainties and her unwillingness to face her truths, she would never be able to employ a career in psychology. For how could she offer any form of therapy, for anyone, when her own emotional stability could be called into question? How could she expect others to confront their fears, embrace their terrors, when, for eight years, she ran from her own? For Brye, it was much easier to run, than to face the destruction and devastation her parents rained down on her emotional well-being, still, long after their death.

Pulling herself together, inhaling a deep cleansing breath, Brye climbed out of bed. It was time to prepare for her interview at Romanique Cosmetics.

Two hours later, she emerged in front of Romanique Cosmetics wearing a soft peach double-breasted jacket, matching tailored trousers with white tailored shirt and jacquard print tie. The pantsuit did not in any way camouflage her flattering figure. Her dark hair, pinned high off the collar, accentuated her prominent features and violet-colored eyes. Diamond stud earrings graced dainty earlobes.

Ten o'clock, and the sun's fiery rays had already taken the city hostage. Agilely, Brye stepped out of the stifling heat of Madison and East Seventy-Ninth and moved into the cool interior of the spacious atrium. The sudden drop in temperature forged goose pimples along her arms and neck. Removing her sunglasses, she waited for her eyes to adjust to the change in lighting before proceeding toward a security officer posted in the center of a large circular information desk. Courteously, he directed her toward a double set of elevators.

Brye's heels tapped rhythmically against the black marble floor as she advanced toward the closed doors. Majestically, steel jaws gracefully slid open, presenting itself to her like a carriage awaiting its royal subject. Plush red carpet, wall-to-wall mirrors applied in parquet squares, exquisitely detailed brass trimming, Brye rode to the tenth floor in polished magnificence.

The interior decorating on the L-shaped tenth floor proved just as refined. Two cabriole leg wing chairs fronted a corner fireplace. To her left, a skirted settee lined a fabric-textured wall. To her right and at a distance, she encountered an empty reception desk. Brye drifted to the right.

Halfway to her target, a young woman loaded down with stacks of files shot from around the corner. Her body jerked forward, then came to a complete halt at the sight of the much-anticipated visitor. "Ms. Grayson." Despite her frenzied entrance, she attained complete control. Sporting cheerful facial features and a welcoming smile, she immediately put Brye at ease. "We're expecting you, and I apologize for not being at my desk upon your arrival. Mr. Paxton will be here in a moment. Can I get you something to drink while you wait? Coffee? A soft drink? Iced tea? The heat is kickin' butt today."

Brye laughed, taking an instant liking to her colorful characterization. "Yes, it is at that, Ms."—she glanced down at the receptionist's name tag: Rhonda Reece—"Ms. Reece. But no, thank you. I'm fine."

Rhonda dropped her files on top of her white oak desk. "Why don't I get you settled? We—"

"Ms. Grayson?"

With the gracefulness of a ballerina, Brye pirouetted toward the sound of the eager, male voice. In one quick swoop, she took in his kindhearted smile, his easygoing disposition, intelligent eyes, trimmed sandy-blond hair, and comely features as he approached her. In two-inch heels, she stood right at six feet tall. Their eyes met on an even keel as his right hand stretched outward. Brye slid nervous fingers into a warm, secure grip.

"Ms. Grayson," he repeated, "I'm Brian Paxton. I hope you don't think ill of us for keeping you waiting."

"On the contrary," Brye challenged, knowing the wait had only been several seconds at best. "Between the limousine picking me up at my door and Ms. Reece's welcome"—she shot an indebted eye toward Rhonda—"I'm highly impressed."

Brian smiled at Brye. Her return smile rendered a heart-faltering reaction. "Well, let's see if we can keep your initial perceptions of us soaring." He placed his hand under her elbow. It was an innocent touch. Brye warded off the impulse to shy away from the light handling. "I thought we could begin with a tour of our facilities. Afterward, we'll go back to my office to chat."

As the tour commenced, Brye listened intently as Brian spoke of Romanique Cosmetics financial stability and its continued growth. He proudly acknowledged future projects as well as future expectations. Impressed with the zeal in which he lectured, simultaneously, Brye found his enthusiasm infectious as her nervousness abated.

Brian also found himself stirred by Brye's fascination with Romanique Cosmetics. She reviewed it all with more than polite interest. Her questions were in-depth and well thought out. Absorbed with the tour, she listened to his every word. Beneath intellectual eyes, she digested, then stored away information to be analyzed at a later date.

Much to Brian's chagrin, where it concerned Brye Grayson, he found it laborious to maintain his proficient objectivity. There was more to meet the eye than just a beautiful face and intelligent mind.

And as they strolled and conversed, Brian studied her. Deep from within, he sensed the loneliness, the sadness, the vulnerability. It was an integral part of her identity—sorrow interwoven within her soul.

Romanique inhabited the top twenty floors of a thirty-story steel, concrete and glass high-rise aligning the cluttered Manhattan skyline. Cornering the market on a wide range of perfume, cologne, and beauty products, Romanique was also responsible for a monthly publication featuring the latest in fun, fashion, fitness and finesse.

Brye traversed the multileveled structure fashioning Romanique Cosmetics, meeting many of the department heads, as well as a good number of staff members. Greeted warmly, as Brian escorted her about, she found herself submerged in relaxed conversation.

Their final destination brought them to the chemical laboratory. Standing outside the wide double doors, Brian looked at Brye with a cat-that-swallowed-the-canary grin. "I have a surprise for you." He pushed the swinging doors apart and entered the aseptic work area. A powerful intermixture of obliging aromas permeated the bustling atmosphere. Making his way toward the center of the massive room, Brian halted at each lab station to introduce the diligently working technicians.

"Alvin?" Brian greeted, braking in front of a short, studious young man wearing horn-rimmed glasses which magnified sea-green eyes to a greater degree. "Meet Brye Grayson."

He smiled tentatively, yet enthusiastically addressed, "Ms. Grayson!" His grip was hesitant, moist, and exposed a touch of meekness. But as she smiled into his thrilled expression and awarded him encouragement, his shake grew firmer, bolder, giddy. "I'm honored," he beamed. "I've been on pins and needles all morning waiting for your endorsement."

"Please…call me Brye," she prompted for what had to be the hundredth time that morning. Painstakingly, she removed her numb fingers from his bobbing clutches. With raised eyebrow and crooked smile, she blinked at Brian and repeated, "Endorsement?"

"Please forgive me if I'm being too presumptuous," Brian stated, "but I noticed you weren't wearing any perfume."

Flushed with embarrassment, Brye answered, "No. I didn't want to insult you by wearing a fragrance made by one of your competitors. And since my agent informed me of our meeting two days prior to today, I didn't have time to run out and buy something created by Romanique."

There was no rancor or opposition, only a rumble of unpretentious laughter expunging Brye of her expressive misdeed. "I should praise you for the conscientious manner in which you handled the situation. But the reason I ask is because I'd like you to test something for me."

Alvin presented an atomizer filled with a honey-colored fluid. Brian asked Brye to present her wrist. As she did, he graced her delicate skin with a dab of the fragrant substance.

Brye sniffed. The premium fragrance immediately embraced her senses. Not too overpowering nor too weak, a mixture of scents she could not readily identify stirred her inner senses. A touch of floral, a pinch of spices, a dab of springtime, an array of island breezes… Regardless of the composition, it was all rather soft, subtle, sensuous, and extremely mysterious.

"It's wonderful!" Brye pronounced. Again she deeply inhaled the elegant aroma. "I love it."

"May I?" Brian asked, dropping his gaze to her wrist.

With wrist floating just below Brian's nose, his nostrils flared as he inhaled the unique aroma. "On several occasions, Alvin has given me the opportunity to inspect his creation," Brian informed in a state of awe. "From the first moment of conception, I believed the exclusive scent manifested exceptional qualities. But oddly enough, the fragrance's true virtues hadn't been revealed until now…as you gave it life when you placed it upon flesh."

Somewhat confused, Brye breathlessly queried, "What does that mean, 'I gave it life?' Have I been given the honors of inaugurating this fragrance?"

"It was principally created with you in mind," Alvin informed with discernible exuberance. "There's also a line of body products."

Stunned yet feeling equally touched by the magnanimous display of faith in her abilities as the Romanique Cosmetics' spokesperson, she uttered, "You mean you..." A lump, mingling at the back of her throat, rendered her speechless.

Alvin's head bobbed up and down in uncontrollable pleasure. "We are mulling over the name Mystique...subject to your approval, of course."

Like a flying tennis ball in the midst of a tournament, Brye's gaze bounced from Brian to Alvin. Then, unexpectedly, amused laughter, mixed with the delightful fragrance, encircled Brye. "You guys don't believe in putting on the pressure, do you?"

In unabashed amusement, Brian admittedly noted, "We believe in pulling out all stops when going after something—or someone—we want."

"And enticing me with my own line of body products is pulling out all stops?"

"The fragrance, amongst other things," Brian admitted.

"I'm afraid to ask what the 'other things' entail...or what you'll do if I turn down the position."

Brian groaned and grinned, leaving Brye with the distinct impression that he would fight till his dying day if that's what it would take to convince her into accepting the position. "I've chosen not to think that far ahead."

"For a businessman, that's not being very practical, don't you think?"

Again, Brian grinned. "I also choose not to answer that particular question."

All three laughed. Several commodious minutes past as they discussed several of Alvin's other major projects.

The final stop of the tour, Brian escorted Brye into his office. Richly decorated with Italian leather, Honduras mahogany, and scenic paintings, Brye easily noted that the only items missing were the enrichment of family portraits. Curious about his personal life, the question of marriage floated along the perimeter of her composed thoughts.

Twenty minutes into discussing her college schedule, her expected duties and planned appearances as spokesperson, and going over the terms of the contract, Brye took it upon herself to call a halt to the interview. She slid the contract into its manila folder. Although Tenisha had given her the go-ahead to sign the contract, she found herself floundering in a sea of uncertainty. "If you don't mind, I'd like to take this home and examine it further before committing myself."

Her closing remarks reminded Brian of his promise to Chad: to validate Brye's worthiness of the position. After spending the biggest part of the morning with the supermodel, he sincerely believed she would never forfeit her dignity or pride, under any circumstances, to enhance her career. Nevertheless, stemming from an urgency to prove to himself that her integrity was nothing less than impeccable, he took a deep breath and proceeded.

"It's almost one o'clock. Why don't I take you to lunch? We can discuss the terms of your contract in extended detail. We can go somewhere *private*." Subtle as it appeared, the insinuation hung in the air. Tensely, he waited for her response.

It appeared in a cloud of indignant rage and distrust. In the attenuated second it took for her emotions to color her face, Brian sensed he'd lost her.

Shocked into silence, fear beat at Brye like a bat flapping frantic wings. How had she missed this? How had she been blindsided by a proposition she should have seen coming from miles away? At an early age, necessity alone had impelled Brye to learn how to detect, intercept, and deflate any and all veiled overtures thrown her way. It frightened her to think that Brian had been so smooth on his initial approach that she had somehow neglected to spot his final landing.

She sat perched on the edge of her seat, prepared to soar out the office if he approached any closer. "Is having lunch with you a prerequisite for obtaining this job, Mr. Paxton?" she stiffly spoke, acrimony laced her every word.

Afraid her fleeting retrieval was complete, there were several roads Brian could have traveled to handle this cataclysmic situation. He could have fallen over himself attempting to adequately explain the invitation away. He could have apologized profusely after insisting she'd misunderstood. He could have retracted the request and pleaded temporary insanity. But given her highly visible standing and a soaring probability that she'd heard every come-on line invented by man, he decided that honesty was the best policy.

"I'm sorry, Brye…Ms. Grayson! Please allow me a few minutes to explain." He pushed himself out of his padded leather chair and walked around his large desk. Taking a seat next to Brye, he silently cursed himself as she visibly cringed at the close proximity of the two bodies—he stood his ground and pleaded his case. "I've worked for Romanique Cosmetics my entire adult life. I've dedicated my life to upholding our high standards, cardinal standards which have played a major role in building this company to the monumental success it has become today. We can't afford scandals, Brye"—again he stammered—"Ms. Grayson. And if by chance you could prove to be an embarrassment to this company, I needed to know…now. Not after the ink has dried." His body went taut with his efforts to beg her forgiveness. "Essentially, I propositioned you merely to observe your reaction."

Rigid during his entire discriminate explanation, gradually, Brye's tense facial features loosened its knots, her eyes recovered their illustrious shine, and her back released its stalwart flexibility; Brye had begun to relax.

Much to her puzzlement, she believed him, which was a major scoop in itself. And a much relieved Brye was grateful her initial impressions of Brian had been restored.

"Did you really think I would have taken you up on your"—she hunted for an amended interpretation—"solicitation?"

"My every instinct told me you wouldn't."

Brye studied the words as well as the man. She perceived both to be honorable. "I appreciate your candidness and your vote of confidence." She no longer sat ready to bounce from her chair. Completely at ease, she said, "Thank you."

Brian breathed a prolonged sigh of appreciation. "Thank you for still speaking to me."

Brye's features shadowed. She sat with clasped fingers folded within her lap. She then lifted a contemplative eye to Brian. "Tell me something, Brian, if I had agreed to go to lunch with you, if I'd welcomed your advances, what would you have done?"

"I would have instantly retracted our offer," he stated without hesitation. Then a guilty grin refined his boyish good looks. He spoke with incertitude, "Well, maybe I wouldn't have *immediately* retracted the offer." His youthful grin widened. "After lunch." His chin bobbed up and down in feigned contemplation. "Definitely after lunch. Maybe?" Hopelessly, he shrugged. "What can I say? I'm an avid fan of yours."

It was his mock indecisiveness and impish charm that won Brye over. Refraining from laughing, she guided the contract out of its folder. Brye studied the papers intently for several seconds.

This past Friday, Marcus had suggested she begin with baby steps. About to take the biggest leap of her career, she prayed the blind jump wouldn't send her plummeting off the face of the universe.

On pins and needles, like a caged animal, Chad paced back and forth between the confines of his office wall. Unable to concentrate, he'd given up all pretense of working. Ultimately, afraid he would wear the carpet thin, he flung himself into his swivel chair.

He stared at his gold Rolex. One o'clock. Turning his attention toward a stack of documents mounted on his desk, he merely found himself tapping the tip of his gold pen against his glass desk top.

Agitation or apprehension? Within the building, the presence of Brye Grayson carried with it emotions he could neither capture nor subdue.

"Dammit!" Chad tossed his pen across the room. It bounced off the wall, then fell soundlessly to the carpeted floor.

Dangerously close to losing control, Chad squeezed his baby-blue eyes shut, groaned inwardly, and raked his fingers through stands of his thick swarthy hair.

Anticipating her arrival all weekend long, now, with bated breath, he anxiously waited for some word of her appropriation. Realistically, he understood that the chances of her signing a contract after her initial interview deemed slim at best, but it was all Chad had to cling to.

Getting up to retrieve his pen, he jumped as an excited Brian burst through his office door.

"It's time to break out the champagne," he cried in elation. "She just signed on."

Stunned, Chad flopped heavily into his chair. An abundance of unexplainable emotions flooded his overwrought senses: satisfaction, repulsion, eagerness, heartache, hatred. Aware that all of his focused emotions were enticed by one person alone, he governed to keep the tremor out of his voice. "How did you get her to sign so quickly?"

In rapid summary, Brian replayed the entire morning's events. In greater detail, he repeated the ambiguous advance thrown at Brye. He exposed the negative response drawn from her. And, finally, he relayed how he had obtained her trust.

Noncommittal, Chad surmised that Brye's portrayal of an offended woman could have been a calculated ploy on her part solely to win Brian's confidence. Chad, of all people, had witnessed her deceit firsthand. He also remembered how fast she could conjure up her mystical charms. And by the look of admiration illuminating Brian's eyes, and the animated manner in which he spoke of her, Chad guessed that she had already cracked her witchcraft over his head. He frowned. "Sounds to me as if she's got you hooked."

"She's an enigma. Attempting to fit the puzzle pieces together would be an improbable task in itself." Brian shrugged, unable to disclaim Chad's observation. "She fascinates me. I don't deny that. But this is a business deal. And I would never do anything to jeopardize Romanique Cosmetics."

Chad openly stared, uncertain if he believed Brian, even more uncertain as to why he cared. Nonchalantly, he lifted a stack of papers and tapped the edges on the desktop. "When do I get to meet our illustrious spokesperson?"

"I can take you to her now," Brian notified, standing up. "I have Rhonda arranging a press conference. Brye's in my office, making some phone calls—she wanted to notify her business manager before it was announced on the evening news."

"I can introduce myself," Chad stated, placing the documents back on his desk. "Why don't you check on Rhonda, see how she's handling the press conference?"

"All right," Brian readily agreed, anxious to announce to the world that Romanique Cosmetics had done the impossible: they had snagged the famed Brye Grayson in an exclusive contract.

"Brian?" Chad called out as Brian reached the door. "If I haven't said it before, I want you to know that you are doing an exceptional job here. It's to your credit alone that we were able to procure the acclaimed model. Congratulations!"

Pleased with the winning commendation, yet feeling it was all in a day's work, Brian answered modestly, "It's my job." Saying no more, he walked out.

A thunderous torrent of blood pounded relentlessly against Chad's temple. In a matter of seconds, he would confront the exalted lady. Instead of encountering a swill of exhilaration for having attained the unattainable, he felt nothing but scorn for the woman who had almost cost him his sanity.

Silently, Chad coasted up to Brian's office door. Glancing inside, he was immediately assaulted by her dark crown of thick hair. Sprays of sunshine sprawled through the office window, sprinkling shades of mahogany red and passion purple throughout the imprisoned strands. His torturous past scurried to gain access to the here and now. Unable to deal with the emotional entanglements, Chad shoved back the toxic memories, hunched his shoulders, and hardened his mind to the woman he was about to confront.

An ear-piercing scream erupted from the opposite end of the phone receiver. For fear her eardrums would split, Brye thrust the receiver away. When she thought it was safe to reestablish contact, she asked, "Is someone attempting to murder you? Or can I take that as a scream of elation for my impulsive exploit?"

"You know damn well what that scream meant!" Tenisha shrieked in exhilaration. "I can't believe you did it! You actually signed the contract!"

"Of course I did." Brye's knees rocked from side to side as she twirled around in Brian's chair. With each passing moment, she was beginning to believe she'd made the right decision. "You told me to sign. Don't I always do what my agent and manager orders me to do?"

"Don't make me laugh, Brye," Tenisha growled good-humoredly. "As long as I've been your manager, Brye Grayson's only done what was best for Brye Grayson."

"First of all," Brye said, "you say that as if it's a bad thing. Secondly, without your advice, your input, your guidance, *and* your support, I wouldn't be where I am today—which is the reason I'm calling."

"What is it now? Do you want me to hold your hand while you sign the contract?" Tenisha asked in mock irritation.

"Actually, I handled that part very well all by myself, thank you very much! I didn't stab myself with the ballpoint pen or smear ink all over the contract…or Brian." Brye tapped a peach-colored nail on top of Brian's desk. "But what I do need is for you to come over and hold my hand during the press conference. It's several hours away, and I'm scared to death."

"With or without me, you'll do fine. You always have, you always will. But," she rushed to add, "it's nice to be wanted. So as soon as I rearrange my schedule, I'm all yours."

Brye's apprehension eased…somewhat. "Thanks, Tee. It'll be nice looking across the room during the press conference and seeing at least one friendly face."

"I'll see you in a little bit." Tenisha severed the connection.

Toward the end of their conversation, a shadow had traipsed across the inner office floor. As Brye hung up the phone, she looked up and smiled. The exact moment of eye contact, hospitality faded into full-blown panic.

Mind exploding with confused terror, heart thumping wildly, the sudden presence of Chad Collier hovering just inside the door produced an involuntary gasp. Shooting out of her chair, she stumbled backward until solid wall slammed against her rigid back.

Speechless, Brye absorbed every inch of his stalwart six-foot-three-inch torso. Conservatively dressed in a charcoal gray business suit with burgundy silk tie, he presented himself as the epitome of power. Amazingly handsome, Brye was overwhelmed at the alteration in the baby blue eyes she had at one time come to know and love. His intense stare had drastically hardened over the past few years; his eyes were now as cold as the Arctic Ocean. A numbing chill penetrated the depths of her entire being; agitated insides solidified into rock-solid ice cubes. "You orchestrated this entire event, didn't you?" she finally managed to mutter, painfully aware that she had just locked herself into an iron-clad predicament. The first stirrings of fear enveloped her, emotionally crushed her. "Somehow you maneuvered my coming here today, didn't you?"

Terror outlined her frozen flesh. He overlooked it, misinterpreting her alarm for irritation. "Do you think I can orchestrate events by simply waving a magic wand in the air?" he sneered, moving further into the room. Firmly, with determined irrevocability, he closed the door behind him.

Immobilized, the cold frost crawled inside Brye's whirling head. She had unwittingly stumbled inside a predator's lair, with Chad being the ferocious lion, and she his much-awaited meal.

Every deliberate step drawing Chad closer was filled with menace and hatred. "What's the matter, lady, does guilt yield paranoia?"

Baffled with his odd choice of words, Brye had done nothing to plead guilty to. Instead of addressing the issue, however, she whispered, "What are you doing here?"

His laugh was harsh, threatening, bouncing off walls like the caustic screech of fingernails deliberately drawn across a classroom chalk board. She could not control the shudders vaulting through her body.

He speared her with a sharp-edged glare. "You're looking at your new boss?"

Wounded by his words, frigid blood pooled inside Brye's heart, shoving much needed oxygen out of her lungs. "Why? What do you want from me?"

"We have unfinished business to contend with," he sneered, his features crippled with thoughts of revenge.

"You're wrong," Brye informed in a soft undertone. "We have *nothing* to discuss."

Chad stepped closer, never taking his eyes off Brye's bewildered, vulnerable expression. He willed himself to ignore the despondency and anguish he detected within her violet-colored eyes. Deceptively beautiful, he established how much he hated her.

No…that wasn't true. Now, face-to-face, he knew he had been deluding himself for far too many years. He did not hate her. He hated the feelings she incited within his mind and body…still. After all these years, after all her deceitfulness, she retained the power to turn him into molten wax. He felt himself faltering but refused to act on his weakness.

"Sit down, *lady*," he gruffly commanded.

The contempt he displayed toward Brye astonished her. If anyone had a right to exhibit loathing, she deserved the honors. What he had done to her had been contemptible…unforgivable. And if she had possessed at least one cruel bone in her body, she would have attacked him with the viciousness of a scorned tigress the first moment he had entered the room. She fronted him with a defiant stare, yet her back continued to beat against the wall, as if seeking refuge. Amazed she had full control over the tremor in her voice, she again asked, "What do you want?"

Chad now stood dangerously close. A scowl transformed his cloudy features into something frightening, something unknown, something inhuman. "For starters," he demanded, "you can tell me what happened to the baby."

Taken aback, Brye stared in total disbelief. To curb her rising anger, she spoke with composed indifference. "I find your concern commendable, although long overdue. Don't you think?"

Chad ignored her play at sarcasm. "What I think is that there was never any baby. It was all a ploy to weasel money out of my family."

His indignant conjecture sent a wave of agony charging through Brye's unmoving torso. Her skin blanched. The hurt clearly visible, she diverted her attention toward the floor. How could he intentionally be so cruel? Yet, despite his taunting, she refused to give him the satisfaction of seeing her cower. Regaining control, resigning herself to seeing this through to the bitter end, she repeated the question one last time, "What do you want from me?"

"Dammit, lady!" he exploded, ripping a hole in Brye's cool exterior. "I want some answers. You owe me an explanation!"

"Brye," she spoke barely above a whisper.

"What?" Chad's lips flattened into a grim line, his anger ripped apart by inner turmoil.

"My name is *Brye*," she tolerantly repeated. "And if being on first name terms is much *too* personal for you, *Ms.* Grayson will do just fine."

"I'm well of aware of your name, *Brye*!" he spat angrily. Unable to control himself any longer, a sudden burst of energy propelled him forward. Chad found himself towering over the supermodel. His crippling grip cut into her upper arms, rendering her motionless. His wounded pride thrust inches above her, he viciously hissed into her stunned expression. "I wasted two fuckin' years of my life trying to erase your name off my tongue! I strove to wipe the memory of your angelic face from my tormented thoughts! I battled to forget the feel of your body pressing into my yearning loins! And I squandered two years of my life trying to cope without your damnable presence!"

An outstretched hand flew up and dangerously cloaked her tapered neck. "I could kill you for what you did to me!" But as he spoke, the steady beating of her heart caressed the unprotected recesses of his skin, his mind, his soul. Her life flowed through his fingers and mingled with his own. Two hearts began beating as one. And the potent memories of what they once shared strained to ignite once again. The passion burnishing within his eyes doused the fire of his condemnation.

Brye's insides threatened to implode. From fear or desire, she could not differentiate. Determined not to betray her internal mutiny, she met him with a rock-solid stare.

So close. They stood too close. Chad could not ignore the sudden rise of her body temperature. Or maybe it was his own body heat climbing. He wasn't certain. And as he looked down into vulnerable, pain-filled eyes, he was certain of only one reality: the identical force that had drawn him toward her years ago remained as intense now as the day he first walked upon her saddened spirit. At this moment, he wanted to drag her into his arms and make wild passionate love until she cried out for sweet release.

His treasonous body responded severely to the sizzling images implanted in his mind. The crux of his desire ached to be extricated from the constraining confines of his slacks. Grunting incoherently, he forcibly thrust Brye aside. Spinning on his heels, he turned his back on his embroiled emotions. More than slightly unnerved, his shaking fingers combed through his dark hair. No longer could he halt the influx of memories storming his overwrought system. Entangled in the moment, like an all-consuming vacuum, memories of the past sucked him down…

Heart flailing inside his chest, Chad stared unseeingly at the copy of a million-dollar check attached to a signed contract.

"She came to me looking for money, son. I'm sorry. I know how much you loved her, but all she wanted was a piece of your wealth: a million dollars in exchange for her silence. Otherwise, she threatened to make your life miserable."

No! This could not be happening. Brye would never betray him. Not like this. Chad's entire world had just come to a crashing halt. "But the baby?" he painfully mourned.

"She all but implied she wasn't pregnant. She said she wouldn't have married you regardless. If I give her the money, she promised to disappear. I wrote her a check and demanded she sign a contract relinquishing you of any and all rights. I made certain she wouldn't come back into your life flinging someone else's bastard child in your face." He sounded concerned, like the loving father Chad knew him to be. "I did it for you, son. I was looking out for your best interest."

"I loved her, Dad. She *loved* me. She would never do the things you're accusing her of. I know her...sometimes better than I know myself."

His father stared at him, sympathy and condolence wavering in the balance. Shaking his head as if he pitied being the one to kick his son when he was already down, he said, "Her real name is Bryson Gray, Chadwick. Not Brye Grayson as she introduced herself to you. That should tell you enough."

That was the day Chad lost one life but found another...inside a liquor bottle. It was the day the world had ceased to exist as he had known it.

Chad's control dangled by a flimsy thread. He turned to confront Brye. His confusion, the anguish coloring his eyes, was not lost in the glacial surroundings. Their close contact had also left Brye floundering on shaky ground. And despite the pain endured by his hand those many years ago, more sympathetic to his suffering than he deserved, she wanted to reach out to him. Comfort him. Reassure.

"If you feel this way, then why?" Brye's eyes begged to understand. Against her better judgment, she reached toward him. "Why did you—"

A knock on the door tore them apart. Feeling as if she'd been caught dipping her fingers in the cookie jar, Brye's arm futilely fell to her side. Pulling back, she moved as far away from him as the four walls would allow.

Stepping aside, grappling to deflect his confusion elsewhere, Chad threw open the office door. Brian and Rhonda, riding on the tail end of a warm draft, trailed inside and melted the ice crystals circulating the frostbitten air.

Apprised of a four-thirty press conference, Chad rushed to remove himself from the binding imprisonment Brye's nearness forced upon him.

"Everything seems to be under control," Chad acknowledged as he ambled toward the door. Before leaving, he turned a circumspect eye to Brye. "Welcome aboard, *Ms*. Grayson." A trace of sarcasm tinted the air. "We're glad to have you join us."

"Thank you," Brye mumbled, blanching under the final wintry scowl he thrust upon her.

Chad strolled out after promising to brief her minutes before the press conference.

6

WITH THE EMINENCE OF a man ready, willing, and able to toss his overpowering supremacy around, Daniel Collier filled the industrious corridors of Romanique Cosmetics. Meticulously dressed in an Italian three-piece suit and black wing-tipped shoes, power exuded from every miniscule pore on his body.

With each step he executed, the surrounding atmosphere turned hushed. The overwhelming presence of "the Great Man" mingling amongst the commoners induced the sudden stifling milieu.

Yet despite the subdued transformation, Daniel sensed a titillating undercurrent buzzing through the offices. Foresight alone warned him of a major feat in the workings. Instinct also enlightened him to the certainty that no answers would be coming from his son's direction. He made a direct beeline to Brian's domain.

Not deeming it necessary to be announced, Daniel heedlessly barged into Brian's office. Startled with the unexpected intrusion, the sitting man vaulted out of his chair.

"Mr. Collier," Brian honored him with a courteous smile. Extending his hand, he circled his desk and advanced to Daniel's side. "What a pleasant surprise." While pumping his hand, he apologized. "I wasn't expecting you, and therefore I must beg your forgiveness for not having a secretary here to greet you. Rhonda's filling in for the receptionist today, and—"

"Think nothing of it," Daniel impatiently waved his rushed explanation aside. "I was carrying out an impromptu visit with my son, but he wasn't in his office," he smoothly lied.

Instantly reacting, Brian stretched for the phone. "Why don't I track him down for you?"

"Nonsense." Daniel waved Brian back into his chair. "You can apprise me of current events as efficiently as Chadwick could. So"—tugging on his pants legs, he sat in an evergreen Chippendale chair fronting Brian's desk—"tell me what's got everyone humming around here."

"Brye Grayson," Brian answered with swollen pride. "We just signed her on as spokesperson."

"Brye Grayson?" His voice took on a cutting edge, face impenetrable as steel.

The sudden change in attitude smothered Brian's fresh air. Still, he did not let the sudden stuffiness in the atmosphere arrest the thrill of the moment. "We're very excited about it."

Incapable of hiding his irritation, Daniel barked, "Does my son know about this?"

"Of course he does," Brian replied, struggling to repress his own rising agitation. Electing not to mention that it was Daniel's son who had personally handpicked the supermodel, he appropriately informed, "Chad is fully supportive of this decision."

Jaw muscles twitched irritable as Daniel stood up. "I think you'd better locate my son."

Several phone calls later, Brian informed Daniel that Chad had returned to his office.

Without so much as a goodbye, Daniel stormed out with his rage encircling him within the confines of a turbulent whirlwind.

In disturbed disbelief, Brian stared at Daniel's fleeting backside. *Something has definitely crawled up the ol' man's butt*, he grimly thought to himself. But unless the problem was directly related to him or this company, Brian would not expend the energy needed to fret over the matter. He glanced at his watch. Fifteen minutes till showtime. His priority prevailed at seeing the press conference go off without a hitch.

"What the hell is the meaning of this?" Daniel angrily bellowed, storming into Chad's office.

On the phone to a major distributor, Chad motioned for his father to sit. Despite Daniel's pronounced agitation, Chad continued with his conversation. As he guided the discussion to its conclusion, he searched his father's face for some clue to his obvious outrage. Whatever the issue, by the protruding eyes, the puffy cheeks, and the flagrant scowl, Chad expected theirs would be a conversation he would not welcome.

"What's got you hot under the collar?" Chad calmly asked, uniting the receiver with its base.

Dispensing with preliminaries, Daniel summed it up in two words: "Brye Grayson."

The air went deathly still. Several strained seconds later, Chad asked, "What about her?"

"Don't play me for a fool, Chadwick!" he exploded. "Why did you hire her?"

"It was purely a business decision."

"How dare you make this decision without consulting me!"

Losing a grip on his control, Chad spat out, "I wasn't aware I needed my *daddy's* approval."

"Don't you dare get condescending with me!" Daniel leaned over Chad's desk. Baby blue eyes darkened, resembling the color of hell. "I'm here out of concern for you. And if you can't look out for your own well-being, you damn well better believe I'll do it for you."

"Look, Dad"—it took some effort, but Chad capped his rising anger—"I'm grateful for your concern, but I can take care of myself…I have been for years. I don't need you looking over my shoulders, second-guessing my every decision."

"Have you forgotten what she's done?"

"No!" Chad roared. His rage threatened to blow like a sprouting whale coming up for air. He shot out of his chair. "I'm perfectly aware of what she's done." He walked over to his window. The animated city buzzed beneath him like a mammoth hornets' nest. "And I don't need any reminders from you."

"I want you to get rid of her. Tear up her contract. Tell her that her services are no longer needed." Daniel moved around the glass desk. He stood at his son's backside.

"No, Dad," Chad quietly informed. He turned toward his father. "Today, in our procurement of Brye Grayson, Romanique Cosmetics has pulled off a major feat. We were able to do what no other company could." Sliding past his father, Chad leaned his left hip against the edge of his desk. "Despite what you think of her... despite what *I* think of her...with her distinguished recognition and her intellectual prowess, she'll be a great asset to this company."

Visibly backing down, with deliberate calculation, Daniel matched his son's tone and allowed his fatherly concern to seep through. "But are you sure you can work with her? After everything that's happened?"

No. Chad wasn't certain he could work with her. Nor did he want to. What he wanted was revenge. "It was years ago, Dad. It's over. Besides, what happened back then was personal. This is business. And believe it or not, I do know how to keep the two separated."

Acting as if he prepared to drop the matter, pretending to comply with his son's wishes, Daniel shrugged in feigned acceptance. "It's your call," he cleverly noted.

"Yes, it is," Chad verified. "And I want you to stay out of this."

"If it's what you want."

"It is." Chad glanced at his watch. "Ten minutes to press time. Would you care to join us?"

Daniel waved him on. "Be there in a moment. I need to make a few phone calls."

"I'll see you in a few minutes then."

Alone, Daniel allowed his submissive facade to slip. Frowning, he couldn't believe the bullshit his son had omnisciently dished out to him. Whatever the excuse Chad chose to use, Daniel knew better. This entire affair did not reek of business. The decision to hire Brye Grayson was strictly personal.

Truthfully, however, it didn't matter how his son had arrived at his decision. Daniel would not allow his misguided judgment to stand. Grateful, he'd had the foresight to devise an alternative plan should Brye once again cross paths with his son. Although they were traveling on the same road at the moment, Daniel would personally see to it that their journeys did not steer toward a collision course to destruction. Soon he would sever this caustic alliance permanently.

Placed in a small room furnished with board table, a host of upholstered swivel chairs, and one coffee pot, Brye roosted amidst a pile of thick-volumed procedural manuals. For the past several hours, she'd been inundated with a wealth of information. Brian had even taken it upon himself to provide her with the history of Romanique Cosmetics as they devoured turkey sandwiches on wheat bread.

Fifteen minutes to go before showtime, and her head threatened to rupture. Tediously, she lowered her face into her hands. The blood in her temple pounded obtrusively against her fingers. And, unsuccessfully, Brye attempted to restrain the influx of throbbing recollections attacking her swelling brain.

Chad Collier. Eight months after the loss of her twin brother, he had insinuated himself into her dreary existence. Despite her desires to remain detached from the world at large, apart from the lack of trust with men in general, aside from the solitary lifestyle she had created for herself, utilizing patience, sensitivity, and an overabundance of kindness, Chad had released her from her own emotional self-confinements. Slowly, surely, he worked at building up her trust. He taught her how to laugh, to feel, to enjoy life to the fullest. She learned how to receive as well as give love. Unfortunately, he had robbed her of all she had to give.

Now she knowingly accepted that Chad had used her for his own mercenary purposes. Viciously, he had ripped her heart apart, intentionally severing the very same lifeline he had thrown out to rescue her with. In the end, he had left her treading in a sea of loneliness and despair.

Most of Brye's teenaged years, her mother had spewed words of self-proclaimed wisdom: "Men only want one thing from a woman, and that same man who professes his love one minute will chew you up and spit you out the next. We, as women, have to protect our own emotional well-being. We need to empower ourselves. When it comes to being held accountable, men are willing to pay for their extracurricular activities. And they'll pay big. And as soon as you accept that fact, Bryson, you will be a much happier person."

In the short time span of loving Chad, he had merely validated what her mother had relentlessly preached. A sobering sigh rose from the depths of her soul. And as Brye massaged her temples, she reached back into time.

Quietly entering her parent's apartment, Brye quickly discovered her discretion was unnecessary; her parents waylaid her as she entered the front room. A man standing several inches shorter than herself, balding hair, bulbous nose, and eyes two sizes too small for his face stood upon her entrance.

Her father was the first to cross over to her. "We've been waiting for you, Bryson. This man represents Chad Collier. He has something for you."

Brye's stunned eyeballs darted back and forth from one individual to the other. Three people stood in the middle of the front room, ridiculously smiling at her like they'd just discovered they held the winning million-dollar lottery ticket.

Brye soon discovered her assessment was not far from the truth.

"Why does Chad need someone to represent him?" Brye asked, not liking the offensive smell suddenly taking up residency in the front room.

"I'm disappointed in you, honey." Ashley came up and grabbed Brye by the hand. "Why didn't you tell us you were pregnant with Chad's baby?"

Stunned, Brye spun out of her mother's touch. "How did you know I was pregnant?"

The balding man stepped up to bat. Handing Brye an envelope, he said, "Chad informed me of your predicament."

Predicament? Brye shrieked inside her head. *My baby is not a predicament!*

"Chad would like you to accept this as payment in full," the balding man sneered. "Afterward, he does not want to see you, hear from you, nor be notified when the baby's born. In essence, he's relinquishing his claim to you and your unborn child."

His sharp tongue jabbed at her with the cutting edge of a knife. With each downward slash, he ripped away a jagged hunk of her heart. Her hands trembled as she tore open the envelope. She stared at the personal check made out to her for one million dollars.

"Why?" Brye croaked, her legs melting in a pot of steaming anguish. If she didn't sit soon, weak knees, trembling legs, would send her crashing to the floor.

"Sign the contract and you get to keep the million bucks."

Brye scanned the agreement giving her sole custody of their child. She took note of an added provision emphasizing her options; if she aborted the unborn child, she would gain another million.

How magnanimous. He was giving her uncontestable control to do whatever she saw fit as long as the ultimate resolution didn't drag him under.

"Chad wants me to sign this?" Tears swelled. Torment and pain crippled the very trust Chad himself had indoctrinated within Brye. Would she ever be able to get beyond this point in her life? Could she ever trust again?

"He wants you out of his life for good." The balding man pulled a gold Cross pen out of his breast pocket. He shoved it at Brye.

Shutting down her mind, Brye dove in headfirst and signed her name on the designated line. She relinquished her hold on the pen, the contract, as well as the acrid check. "Tell Chad I don't need nor do I want his blood money."

She turned her back on her parents, the balding man, and the life she thought she had secured with the man of her dreams…the man she swore to love for the rest of her life, her soulmate.

As downtrodden feet made their way up the stairs and to her bedroom, a massive chunk of her heart fell away, leaving a hollowness in her chest she would carry with her throughout the duration of her life.

Brye cried long into the early dawn hours. She wept until there were no more tears to spill. Only at the cusp of daybreak, when the sun scorched a jagged pathway toward her aching soul, did she pull herself together.

For many, the birth of the new day symbolized life. For Brye, it represented death. Shoving aside her grief, she buried her tears and shrouded her heart inside an iron-clad will of determination.

Now more than ever, Brye recognized that when a person opened their heart to another, so comes the susceptibility of suffering a mortal wound. Never would she allow herself the luxury of caring for another man. Nor would she permit a member of the opposite sex to walk within miles of her shattered vital organ.

"Don't tell me you're already regretting this?"

Brye dropped her hands from her eyes. She encountered a concerned Tenisha. Her smile grim, facial cast mournful, she feebly asked, "Is it too late to back out?"

Tenisha rushed to Brye's side and sat down. "What happened between now and the time you called me?"

Chad Collier happened. Increasing her efforts to broaden a smile, Brye said, "Nothing happened." Hopelessly, she shrugged. "I guess I'm just having last-minute jitters." She reached toward Tenisha to procure a much sought-after hug. "Thanks for coming. I need you here to pick me up when I fall flat on my face."

Tenisha pulled out of Brye's needy embrace. She shook her head in snarled bewilderment. "I swear, Brye, sometimes I don't understand you at all." She squinted with mild disapproval. "Why are you sitting here preying on your self-doubts? Especially since you're going to be in top form as soon as you step in front of that lectern. In fact, the insecurities you're experiencing now will be a distant memory as soon as you shift into go mode."

Brye laughed. "Why do you always say that to me?"

Tenisha joined Brye in her short-lived moment of joviality. "Why do you always prove me right?"

Brye instantly sobered. She laid her head upon Tenisha's supportive shoulder. "Thanks for always being here when I need you. I couldn't do this without you."

"Yes...you could," Tenisha candidly contradicted. She tossed her arm around Brye. "But it's a genuine uplift to my ego to hear you say it."

"Can we interrupt?" Brian and Chad entered the modest room.

Tenisha and Brye pulled away from each other. For one excruciating second, Brye's eyes locked with Chad's. Then, diverting her gaze to Brian, she introduced, "Brian Paxton...Chad Collier...have you met Tenisha Davidson?"

"Mrs. Davidson." Chad reached for her hand. "It's a pleasure meeting you again. I'd like to personally thank you for the part you played in effectively bringing this union together."

"Call me Tenisha," she proposed. "But I can't take credit for any of this. I merely sent you a stack of photographs."

"Modesty is a virtue we rarely see in this business," Brian praised, sliding his fingers into Tenisha's extended palm. "I've had the pleasure of observing your mounting career over the past few years, and your photographs are anything but modest." Pulling away, his smile held a tinge of regret. "I would like to continue this conversation further, but we have a press conference to attend."

Brye stroked Chad with apprehensive eyes. Lids narrowed in distressed humility, she quietly appealed, "You wouldn't by chance consider rescinding my contract, would you?" Tenisha and Brian accepted her words as a joke. Chad understood otherwise.

His heart tugged in his throat. He might just allow her anything if she continued looking at him in such a fashion. He averted his stare and responded not so kindly, "Now why would I do such a thing?"

"Oh, it was just a thought."

Gaining control once again, Chad smiled, a sinister, drop-dead grin launching Brye's heart into ventricular tachycardia. Opening the door wider, he ushered Brye and Tenisha out. "After you, ladies."

Brye brushed against Chad's shoulder as she walked through the door. Sparks instantly ignited. Her limbs tingled with an identifiable sensation she hadn't experienced in years: lust. Pure unadulterated desire. Inwardly groaning, she questioned why her life had suddenly taken a turn for the worst.

Two hours into the press conference, and Brye continued to parry questions with the skill and ease of a woman used to being scrutinized by the press. Questions regarding her contract with Romanique Cosmetics, the appearances she would undertake, the original perfume she was now endorsing, her tour schedule, her personal life—particularly her love life—and her own personal views were main topics of interest.

Questions regarding the company Brye answered openly and as honestly as possible. Questions relating to her personal life she answered with charming witticism. The press had fallen in love with the sparkling supermodel.

"She handles herself well in the public eye, don't you agree?" Brian whispered to Chad as the conference continued.

"She's definitely a pro," Chad generously offered, covering his sarcasm. He stood with legs apart, hands folded over his chest.

"The entire audience is entranced," Brian countered.

Caught up in his own web of intricate emotions, Chad blocked out everyone other than the dark-headed, violet-eyed puzzle standing at ease before a room full of reporters. "This is the first time she's ever granted an interview. Every reporter here is anxious to find out as much as they can about her."

"I'm amazed she hasn't lost her composure with the inquisition they're putting her through."

She's good at putting on fronts, Chad thought to himself. He said, "Maybe you should rescue her. She's been at it long enough."

Accepting the challenge, Brian inched his way toward the lectern. He listened as Brye answered a question posed to her.

"I think a woman should give only as much of herself as she can afford to give without endangering her own identity." Smiling, she pointed to a cocky, young, attractive male reporter with long blond hair pulled back into a ponytail. "Yes?" she queried.

"Would you consider giving me a tiny piece of yourself after the press conference by going out to dinner with me?"

Undaunted by the question, highly proficient at warding off overt advances, Brye released a euphonious laugh. "I would hate to be accused of trading personal favors for a good write-up in the paper."

"I don't think there's a male reporter in this room who wants to give you a bad write-up," he answered with an artful grin.

"You see," Brye teased, innocence playing on her every word, "my virtuous charm is already working on you."

The four walls ballooned with generous laughter.

Brian joined Brye at the podium. When the chortle died to a reverberating murmur, he announced, "We'll only be taking one last question."

"Yes?" Brian indicated to an academic-looking woman with large round glasses, shoulder-length hair, wearing a blue-and-white-striped business suit.

"You mentioned the conception of Mystique perfume. When will the complete body line be on the market? And are there any samples available?"

Brye yielded to Brian, entrusting him to be more knowledgeable on the subject.

"We are expecting Mystique to be out within the next several weeks. The introduction of the new fragrance will coincide with Brye's first official appearance. A schedule—as well as the dates and cities of her promotional tour—will be announced within the next several days. And as for samples, I regret—"

Discreetly, Brye lightly nudged Brian's shoulder with her own. Gratified to have had the foresight to apply Mystique to her pulse points several minutes prior to the start of the conference, she rushed to intercede Brian's next statement. "Yes, there does happen to be a sample…and you're looking at her. I happen to be fortunate enough to be wearing Mystique." Invitingly, she smiled. "I'll be stationed at the door at the conclusion of this press conference. If anyone's interested in sampling the fragrance, feel free. I welcome any and all comments or suggestions you might have."

Turning the floor back to Brian, Brye breathed a sigh of relief as minicams and cameras were shoved aside. Anxious to talk privately with her, reporters clambered out of their seats. As promised, with Brian at her side, she seized a stance at the entrance.

"You were wonderful, Brye," Brian complimented seconds before they were waylaid by the eager assemblage.

Reporters circled Brye like vultures swooping down on their prey, leaving her with no time to respond. For forty-five enduring minutes, she lingered with the press. Brye encouraged them to converse with her, sniff her, joke with her. At one point during her one-on-one chat, she looked up to see Chad intensely scrutinizing her. For one brief moment, she witnessed designs of jealousy sprouting from his graveled expression. Instantly dismissing the thought, she hypothesized it to be the florescent lights playing along his face and deceiving her own eyes.

"Ah…Brye," Daniel greeted, taking it upon himself to address her by her given name without gaining permission first, "your beauty is only outshone by your intelligence, your witticism, and the articulate way in which you represented yourself and this company." Remarkably, he meant every word. And although she had impressed him with her staunch qualities and the indisputable ability to be a great asset to this company, he harbored no remorse for the plans he would soon initialize. He shed no qualms in destroying her, or her illuminating career.

In his pompous eye, Brye was no one; she was of little consequence to him. Not born of old money, she held no prominent social echelon. There had been no proper training in elegance, grace, or mannerism. And she had come from unsuitable breeding. In short, Brye was nothing but a lowlife. Born of low class, she would never be good enough for his son. And no amount of wealth she earned over the years would ever change that fact.

"Thank you, Mr. . . ." Brye had demanded names from everyone she had spoken with during the conference. She expected no less of the omnipotent presence standing before her.

"This is Mr. Collier, Brye," Brian formally introduced.

"Mr. Collier?" Brye repeated, brow constricting in cautioned confusion.

"Chad's father," Brian clarified in the light of her baffled state.

"Mr. Collier!" Brye extended her hand in sincere graciousness. "Please forgive me. I'm embarrassed. I didn't know—"

"There was no reason for you to know, my dear. Think nothing of it."

An ominous force enveloped this man. Every ounce of Brye's being sensed it. His smile was one Brye knew so well: a politician's smile. A carnivorous leer. And as he held her hand longer than desired, Brye detected malice in the depths of his baby blues. But just as the sinister look appeared, so did it disappear. Instinctively, she shied away from him once she removed her fingers from his unduly clutches. Now, as he exhibited nothing but praises and encouragement, Brye remained on red alert.

Chad, with one ear to Brye's conversation, the other on Jennifer—who'd arrived several minutes after the commencing of the press conference—glided up to the threesome. Tenisha, who'd also been accosted during the afternoon by many a highly motivated reporter, had also finally made her way to the eminent group. She walked up on Daniel Collier as he verbally issued an invitation to a black-tie affair he was hosting in several weeks.

Brye rushed to turn down the regal gesture. "I don't think—"

"Nonsense," Daniel terminated her refusal long before she could issue it. "Of course you could. Tenisha should be there as well," he cunningly extended the request, knowing Tenisha would be his tool in convincing Brye. "It's going to be a special night. I'm even hopeful my son will announce his engagement to Jennifer."

Brye believed *that* piece of information had been divulged for her benefit alone. She glowered at the tall, striking female acting out as Chad's overprotective arm piece. Her immediate impression: she confronted a woman absent of all natural beauty. Her magnificence had been constructed under a skilled surgeon's knife. Impeccably dressed in a Versace creation accentuating an hourglass figure, the sultry outfit particularly emphasized large, silicone-implanted breast. Brye took note of her long, fake eyelashes, sculptured nails, and spa-induced tan. Dyed platinum-blond hair intricately styled, every precious strand spritzed in precise position. Permanently tattooed makeup artfully fashioned, Jennifer stood erect, sophisticated, perfect, and totally fabricated.

Standing next to a living, breathing masterpiece, after the boisterous events of her day, Brye believed she, herself, exemplified nothing less than a cheap copy.

Entranced with the idea of announcing their engagement, yet bowing to Chad's hesitation in asking for her hand, Jennifer flashed her refined dental work. "I would love nothing better than to announce our engagement, but marriage is a subject to be discussed by the two parties involved…Chad and myself." She staked her claim by linking arms with Chad. "And as of this moment, I haven't been asked."

Brye couldn't understand why she experienced a tremendous sense of gratification hearing *that* shred of news.

"A mere oversight on my son's part," Daniel assured. "But nevertheless, Brye and Tenisha, I'd love to have you there. In fact, I'll have a messenger hand deliver the invitations."

After spending twenty more horrendous minutes of witnessing Daniel and Jennifer commandeer the conversation, Brye politely excused herself, begging the use of her phone. But several minutes later, Brian walked into his office to find Brye sunken into his sofa, eyes closed, head tossed backward and resting against the soft leather. The unwelcome intrusion strained against her much-welcomed respite. Drawing in a deep breath, she sailed off the couch. Cautiously, she reconstructed her well-disciplined façade. Within seconds, it appeared as if the taxing day had not taken a huge bite out of her weary soul.

"No," Brian signaled her to sit. "You don't have to get up on my account. I know how overtaxing this day has been."

Slowly, Brye eased down into the couch. Her back remained upright and stiff. Smiling brightly, she said, "It wasn't bad at all. In fact, this was nothing compared to my usual chaotic day."

Brian lowered himself down beside Brye. Knowing he must keep their coalition on a professional level, he resisted the temptation to reach up and run the back of his knuckles against blushed cheekbones. Disappointed she would not allow him to permeate the exterior of her solidly constructed perimeter, he softly reproached, "Don't do that."

"Do what?"

"Put on the face you show to the general public." He looked around to stress his point. "We're alone here. It's okay for you to be yourself."

Appreciative of the invitation, more drained than she cared to admit, warily she lowered her guard—somewhat. Her rigid back grew pliant under the smoothness of the sofa. Squeezing her eyes shut, confidentially, she informed, "Emotionally, this day *has* been a bit taxing. It feels as if I was skinned alive by every reporter in the state, let alone New York City. And to be honest, it's a little terrifying to be on alert every second of every minute. I was afraid I would say the wrong thing...make a wrong move."

"After your performance today, and the way the press took to you, even if you had said the wrong thing, no one would have noticed...or much cared."

Fatigued eyelids opened and produce fatigued iris-colored eyes, which were directed toward Brian. The strain she'd been under all day finally erupted in the form of laughter. It built from deep within, then intensified and fell upon Brian's ears in melodious splendor.

"Against my better judgment, I'm going to take that as a compliment," Brye stated as soon as her laughter died.

Against Brian's own prudent advice, peering down into Brye's unarmed expression, he found himself asking, "How about letting me take you to dinner? I'll be more than happy to take you home afterward." Inside the violet intensity of her eyes, a flash of fear materialized, then dissipated into the waning light. Seconds later, she confronted him with nervous ambivalence.

"I can't," Brye somberly stated, feeling it necessary to give him an explanation yet finding it difficult to conjure one.

Brian hid his disappointment well. "Then whenever you're ready, I'll summon the limousine to deliver you to wherever you want to go."

"I appreciate the offer, but that won't be necessary either." Brye lifted her head from the back of the sofa. "Tenisha will give me a ride home."

Brian smiled. "You were phenomenal today. Go home and get some rest. I'll call you tomorrow. We'll begin setting up your summer schedule."

Brye stood, anxious to seek out Tenisha. Before leaving the office, startling herself, she sought out Brian's friendship. "How about a rain check on that dinner?"

"Just say the word and you got it." Alone, Brian beat his head against the wall for his inane mistake.

Stupid! Stupid! Stupid!

Starting here and now, where Brye Grayson was concerned, he would definitely have to keep his priorities in check.

7

THE RADIANT DAY HAD given way to a dull slate gray. But at a distance along the horizon, the sun slowly settled into a bed of mauve linens. Speeding down I-95 in her Ford Explorer, Tenisha maintained a steady, unsafe distance between herself and the light tan BMW flying in front of her. The car windows were tightly rolled up to limit the noise and air pollution to its bare minimum. The air conditioner and car stereo quietly hummed in the foreground. On their last leg to Brye's home, Brye pulled out an unexpected question. "Tell me what your opinion of Jennifer is?"

Taking her eyes off the taillights of the BMW, Tenisha raised a questioning brow to Brye. "You mean the Stepford Wife wannabe?"

Brye strove to ignore Tenisha's hostility. "Every part of her body was perfectly"—she struggled for a suitable synonym—"imaged."

Tenisha grunted in agreement. "You got that right, girlfriend! Every part of her body has been chiseled under a surgeon's scalpel."

"Nevertheless," Brye persisted, "she's beautiful."

Rolling her eyes toward the roof of her Explorer, Tenisha barked, "It isn't real, Brye. Every inch of her body was conceived by one surgical procedure or another."

During the short-lived conversation Brye had held with Jennifer, Chad's superficial girlfriend had contemptuously glared down her impeccable nose at Brye. Not allowing the shallow behavior to settle into her calm frame of mind, Brye giggled. "She was certainly nice enough, in a condescending sort of way—it must be those social mores she picked up at that preppy ivy-league school she attended." Brye did not perceive the woman to be compassionate, kind, or approachable. So what did Chad see in the hollow clone of a woman?

"I'll give her that." Tenisha swung the Explorer around a crawling 1976 Chevy Impala. Once again, she kissed bumpers with the soaring BMW. "She certainly doesn't discriminate by color alone. Tonight, after the way she spoke and looked at you, it's apparently clear she looks down her snout at everyone hunkered below that impossible-to-achieve standard she's created for herself."

In the early-evening shadow filtering inside the Ford Explorer, Brye cast a thoughtful eye at Tenisha. She then switched her gaze back to the land whizzing past the utility vehicle's window.

Falling silent, Brye pondered over her own defamed childhood. Her parents had never informed her of their love for her. They had never praised her excellent standing as a student or a daughter. Instead, within Brye, they had created feelings of guilt and insecurities for not living up to the expectations imparted upon her. In effect, she had gone through life never feeling worthy.

Several strained minutes later, Brye picked the conversation up again. Much to Tenisha's surprise, Brye began with a subject she rarely spoke of.

"Before my parents met, they had two things in common: born from the wrong side of the tracks, both were incredibly knock-down, drop-dead gorgeous. Eventually they learned to use their looks to the best of their advantage.

"By the time we"—Brye instantly retracted her negligent slip of the tongue—"*I* was born, my parents were doing very well for themselves. But the mode in which they earned their living, in most states, is considered legally, ethically, and morally wrong. So it didn't matter how much they educated themselves. It didn't matter how much money they made or how established they had become. Because if you took away their clothing, the jewels, the money, *and* the education, deep down, they were the same two people born from the wrong side of the tracks."

The quality of Brye's voice changed, growing unsettled… murky. "Don't get me wrong, Tee. I'm not saying that people can't change. They can. I'm just stating that when my parents crossed to the other side of those railroad tracks, they forged a desecrated trail behind them."

Up until this point in the conversation, Brye had been staring out the window as she embraced her innermost thoughts. She now faced Tenisha and spoke with heedful conviction. "I have never deluded myself into believing my parents were anything other than amoral, defiled people. I've never pretended to be more than who I am. And as far as where I come from…I can't change that reality any more than I can change who my parents were. All my life I've struggled and am still struggling to become a better person. And more days than not, particularly during my modeling assignments, when I'm given preferential treatment or when fans swarm around me for my autograph, I can allow myself the luxury of forgetting the ties that link me to my past—even if it's for a little while." Brye sighed. She clamped her fingers together. "But then people like the Jennifer Cavanaughs of the world, with an insignificant look and an indirect word, slap me in the face with their 'I'll-always-be-better-than-you' mentality. They indicate that I don't deserve to breathe the same air they're inhaling. They say I'm not worthy of their company." Emotionally, Brye could barely contain herself. She could feel her composure slipping precariously through the cracks. "How do you deal with it, Tee? The prejudices…the put downs…the holier-than-thou attitudes? How do *you* manage?"

Tenisha lifted, then dropped her shoulders in a docile shrug. Being Black, it was a topic she related to well. It was also the focal point of TyJuan's animosity since losing his job, which meant she endured his rabid histrionics on the indignities he was forced to endure by the brutal hands of the White man. But when she spoke, there was no hint of bitterness. "It's something I don't easily accept but have learned to let float over my head. Ignorance…insecurities…jealousy…the three top reasons why certain individuals strike out at others." Once again, she steered her gaze away from the road and directed them at Brye. "Let's face it, Brye, we can't control what people say or do or think. So the only thing you and I can do is depend on our inner strengths to guide us through those rough waters."

Tenisha paused to collect her thoughts. For whatever reason, Brye had chosen to divulge a small portion of her past. There was no need to read between the lines. The signs were clear: her friend had not lived a typical childhood. And since Tenisha had been raised by two wonderful parents and had endured an idealistic home life, she could not relate to Brye's unsettled past. She could empathize, however, and she could send out her full support. "You have to learn to *not* dwell on the bad. You have to let go of the past, Brye."

"Sometimes it's just not that easy to do," Brye oppressively admitted. Somehow, Tenisha knew Brye wasn't solely speaking of the Jennifer Cavanaughs of the world.

With the exception of Mariah Carey's "Vision of Love" softly piping through the interior of the Explorer, all went quiet.

Visions of Jennifer clinging to Chad sent a jealous streak racing along Brye's backside. But how could that be? She hadn't seen Chad in over six years. What did it matter who he dated? *Because you're still in love with him. After all these years, after walking out on you and your unborn children, you continue to love him.*

Slicing through the restrained ambiance, she asked, "How long have you known the elder Colliers?"

Tenisha's gaze skimmed over the highway sign indicating the White Plains' exit. She flipped on the right turn signal and eased the Ford into the appropriate lane. "I did a photo layout on their Southampton mansion several years ago."

Abruptly switching subjects, Brye battled to keep her voice neutral. "How much do you know about Chad and Jennifer's relationship?"

"I know they've been dating exclusively for several years," Tenisha offered, highly curious of Brye's sudden inquisitiveness with the Collier family, Chad in particular. "Rumor has it they'll eventually marry. Personally, I don't believe it'll happen."

"Why not?" Brye asked, gingerly maintaining a light and airy tone.

"Because theirs is not exactly a match made in heaven."

"Why not?" Brye repeated.

"Chad is well known for being hard yet fair. He's highly competitive, and when he wants something, he pulls out all the stops to acquire it. In the end, he usually obtains what he went after, but you better believe he used honest business tactics to gain access.

"Above all else, he's fair-minded with people in general. He doesn't single out any *one* person or a group of people. He does not automatically condemn anyone for who they are. Whereas Jennifer… well…you were acquainted with *her* today, so do I need to say more?"

No, she did not need to elaborate. In one day, Brye had her fill of one Jennifer Cavanaugh. Instead, Brye mulled over Tenisha's characterized description of Chad. She also recanted how Chad had initially viewed her with nothing but contempt one moment, then innate confusion the next. The beginnings of a twisted plot began to take root. To Brye's weary soul, it all appeared to have begun and ended with Daniel Collier. Grasping for answers, she asked, "Chad and his father are complete opposites, aren't they? They don't apply the same business tactics, do they?"

Tenisha's brow arched in hushed acquiescence. Off I-287, she halted at a red light. "That's an understatement if I've ever heard one. But if you have never met Daniel Collier before, how would you know that?"

"A feeling I perceived…when we shook hands."

In distinct understanding, Tenisha's head moved up and down. "He has that aura about him. He exemplifies omnipotence." The Ford went on the move again, rolling smoothly along Westchester Ave. "And although he's extraordinarily successful and is usually victorious in the majority of the business dealings he puts together, he doesn't exactly win popularity contests when enforcing his scrupulous business tactics. In fact—"

"He's a Machiavellian," Brye softly interposed. Inwardly, she shuddered with apprehension at the vibes Daniel provoked. Something dark and foreboding frightened her about him; her survival instinct warded her to stay away.

"A what?"

Less than a mile from home, Brye stared at a male jogger sprinting down an empty sidewalk. She slowly enunciated, "A Mach-i-a-vel-li-an. The name was derived after an Italian statesman—N. Machiavelli—born in 1469. There's a book titled *The Prince* in which Machiavelli rationalizes the behavior of political leaders. In order to achieve strength and authority, there are certain considerations one has to incorporate into their intended stratagem—considerations such as disregarding all dimensions of morality." Brye turned back to catch Tenisha's attention. "It's a good book. If you like, I'll let you borrow mine."

History stood outside the boundaries of Tenisha's literary preference. Besides, the only Prince she was interested in knowing was of the "Purple Rain" persuasion. Her lips puckered in distaste. "No thanks." Her eyes flew back to the road. "I think I'll wait for the movie reviews to come out."

"It really is interesting," Brye persisted with a contrived smile.

"Why don't you tell me about this Machiavellian thing?"

"A Machiavellian will uncover your weakness, then prey on that very same deficiency with the sole intent of destroying. Machiavellians exhibit no remorse or shame in creating situations that would normally embarrass others, which means they'll always gain the upper hand, even if it means placing themselves in a compromising position. When a Machiavellian sets his sights on something, he'll use any and all methods accessible to achieve that goal. And when negotiating with a Machiavellian, someone like *you* or *I* will undoubtedly succumb to his dishonorable business tactics because someone like *you* or *I* will play by the rules—whereas the Machiavellian wouldn't."

"All this just to say he's basically a bad person willing to break the law, along with other people's dreams, to satisfy his own self-serving quest," Tenisha smoothly surmised.

"Well," Brye leniently granted, "in the usual sense of the word, Machiavellians aren't necessarily bad. They do not carjack, they do not rape, rob banks, or murder. They're merely remarkably adept in grabbing and maintaining control by any means necessary. They seize on any opportunity given them—although most will toe the line, very few topple outside the limits of the law."

"How interesting." Tenisha steered the Explorer into Brye's drive. Shifting into park, she left it to idle. "You perceived all this from a mere handshake?"

Hand perched on the door, Brye abruptly changed the subject. "Tee?" Her voice was as unsettled as the undulated sounds invading the rapidly approaching night. "I don't want to go to that party."

Brye's tone was that of a small child begging for a reprieve from nap time.

In the dim light of evening, Tenisha smiled to herself. As usual, she would furnish Brye that much-needed boost. And as expected, Brye would do what was best for Brye.

"Of course you want to go," Tenisha cheerfully informed. "It'll be a chance to go in there and show them the kind of stuff we're made of." The interior of the Explorer lit up with a mischievous gleam illuminating from Tenisha's dancing eyes. "Besides, you may be able to steal Chad right out from under the Ice Queen's nose."

Brye's heart hammered recklessly in her chest at Tenisha's blundering choice of words. "What do you mean by that?"

"During your press conference, I saw the way he looked at you, Brye. I know the signs. The man is thoroughly hooked. And the way I see it, he's tired of play-acting with a woman whose primary goal in life is to impersonate a Barbie Doll. I believe he's ready to settle down with a real woman. And *you* are that woman."

Brye forced a light, teasing laugh. "You perceived all this from a look?"

"A smoldering, consumed-with-lust, Lord-I-gotta-have-that-woman look!"

Brye pushed the door open. She then turned and met Tenisha with a sullen eye. "I don't even have a date."

With an unconcerned lift of her shoulders, Tenisha freely teased, "Tomorrow we'll announce in the *New York Times* that you're looking for a date. Five minutes after the paper hits the stands, I'll bet you'll be loaded with requests by the majority of the single men in the state, and probably half the married."

Laughing, Brye leaned over and pecked Tenisha on the cheeks. "Thanks."

"Anytime, kiddo."

Semi-revitalized from undergoing a long, hot shower, Brye slid her arms and head into a tank dress with sweeping skirt spilling freely above her ankles. Sliding her feet into a pair of leather thongs, she tediously trudged to the kitchen. Not in any mood to prepare a several course meal, she pulled out a box of Grape Nuts. Several elongated seconds of frowning at the box, unsatisfied with her choice of dinners, she eased the cereal back onto the shelf.

Grabbing her cell phone, she nervously stabbed at the numbers. "Hey, Marcus!" she cheerfully greeted. "What're you up to tonight?"

"I'm watching you…on the news. I guess congratulations are in order."

"Do you approve?"

"You know I do. Why? Are you having second thoughts already?"

Yes. "Now you sound like Tenisha." Brye ran the tip of her toes back and forth across the kitchen tile.

A deep chuckle erupted from the opposite end. "We know you so well."

"Do you know me well enough to know I'm calling because I'd like you to take pity on my weary soul?" Palms open, she reached over and slapped the kitchen cabinet door shut.

"I know you so well. I've already put an extra place setting on the table."

For the first time since awakening, a genuine, carefree laugh punctured the apathetic exterior Brye had worn most of the day. "Will you marry me, Marcus?"

"Not on a bet."

Brye grinned into the phone. "A refusal such as that would make a lesser woman question her desirability. As it is, I only want your food."

"The grub will be served in five minutes," Marcus announced with no indication of rancor.

"I'll be there in one."

Brye stepped into the brightly lit kitchen. A savory aroma permeated the air.

"We're having stir-fry chicken," Marcus declared.

Staring at Marcus's expansive backside as he transferred their dinner from the wok to a dinner platter, an idea struck Brye like a bolt of lightning searing an agitated night. "You want to get the iced tea from the fridge?"

Brye remained rooted to the spot. As nervous as she felt, she'd probably spill the pitcher over the front of her dress.

Turning away from the stove-top range, Marcus practically stumbled over Brye's stagnant frame. The fact she'd made no effort to move commandeered his attention. Keeping his voice light, he circled her rigid structure. "What's up?" He placed the steaming platter in the middle of the tile-top table.

Brye did not, or was unable to respond. Marcus prodded, "Brye?"

Unsteady on her feet, Brye visibly faltered. She felt as awkward as the class geek inviting the school jock to her senior prom. "I was just thinking… Well…I was wondering… Daniel Collier…he invited me to a party…a couple of weeks from now."

"You're going, aren't you?" Marcus asked, grasping the fact that in conjunction with the days surprising events, Brye was once again taking monumental steps in overcoming her hidden fears.

Gifting Marcus with a tentative nod, she uttered, "Tee thinks I should."

"So what's the problem?"

Shifting back and forth from one foot to another, falling mute, she crossed her arms behind her back.

Again, Marcus gently pushed, "Brye?"

"I was hoping…I mean…I thought…if you might consider escorting me?"

One bristly eyebrow lifted in unmitigated shock. "You mean *you* and *me*?"

Brye pulled her bottom lip between her teeth. Anxiously, she nodded.

"You mean go out on and date?" Incredulously, he repeated, "*Me* and *you?*"

"Well…not exactly a *date* date." She now shifted her entire body weight to her right side. "If you don't want to…or if you've already made other plans for the night… well…I'll understand."

"I'd love to go with you," Marcus nonchalantly informed, understanding how difficult it had been for Brye to accept an invitation to a party she held no desire to attend. Acting on impulse, and to put her out of her misery, his virtuous expression displayed purity of heart. "Just don't expect me to put out afterward."

The tension gradually trickled from Brye's rooted torso. She experienced a gracious swell of affection and appreciation toward this gentle giant. A huge grin broke across her troubled features. She went to retrieve the pitcher of iced tea. Pouring them both a tall glassful, she impishly retaliated. "I hate to burst the bubble in what you affectionately call your male ego, but if I were offered twenty million dollars to have a baby, and you were the only virile man available to me, no amount of money could entice me to ask you to *put out*."

"I find that kind of interesting." Marcus slid a chair out for Brye. "Particularly since, for *no* amount of money, you asked me to marry you less than ten minutes ago."

The clickety-click of Rainbow's toenail's tapping against the floor tile redirected Brye's attention. "Go answer the phone," he squawked in high-pitched voice as his slow and clumsy gait carried him closer to Brye.

"I was wondering where you were hiding." Brye tossed her napkin over her lap. "Now that you've made an appearance, say goodbye, Brye."

"Goodbye, Brye!" he mimicked.

Brye laughed. Being party to Rainbow's frivolous antics were equivalent to taking 10 milligrams of Valium; the day's strain dissipated into the jovial atmosphere. And one hour later, relaxed, her mind back on an even keel, Brye drifted homeward bound.

Trepidation, however, began to challenge her placid disposition as each step drew her closer to her back door. The thought of entering her home did nothing to help preserve her jocular mood. Once inside, she would be alone with inescapable memories of Chad—

which translated into enduring another tedious, restless, energy-depleting night.

Downtrodden feet gingerly climbed the steps leading to her patio deck. Immediately entering her dark kitchen, restrictive tentacles of solitude promptly encircled her throat. Not allowing the enclosing sensation to cloak her completely within its deadly clutches, Brye veered through the house and out into her connecting two-car garage. Folding herself into her light-blue Camry, she buckled herself in, locked the doors, slid the sun roof open, and then put the car stereo in blast mode, allowing for nothing other than upbeat music to infiltrate her unsettled thoughts.

Impatiently, she tapped her fingers on the steering wheel as she listened to the garage door smoothly hoist up on its casters. Once there was enough clearance to maneuver her car through, she roared out of her driveway while simultaneously stabbing her garage door opener. The gate silently glided to its final resting place.

Not knowing where she headed, raven black hair flapped around her face as the potent wind entered the open roof. The blaring sound of the musical group Earth, Wind, and Fire pounded in her vexatious head. As she drove, this night, she intended to outrun the apprehension, the formidable memories, and the haunting face of one Chad Collier.

Five-year-old Bethany Harrold sensed her twin brother's hovering presence long before the serene slumber she had sunken into released her from its downy clutches. Groggily, her eyes flickered open. A shaft of moonlight penetrated the room, casting an eerie glow around everything lying in its wake. Bethany stared up into a face identical to her own: serious expression, intense baby-blue eyes, hair tint so dark, numerous strands were dependent upon how the sun goddess waved her glittering wand over his diminutive head. Some days it appeared uniformly black; other times, it cast shades of burgundy and brown.

Neither twin spoke. Soundlessly Anthony crossed the room and paused at the door. Bethany followed with a steady eye, then climbed out of bed. Careful not to wake her two roommates, she silently floated past the foot of their beds.

At the door, Anthony turned and walked out with Bethany immediately behind. Stealthily, they crept down the expansive staircase. It wasn't until they were sheltered in the perimeter of the library, door shut tightly against the evils at large, when they dared speak.

Anthony's presence at her bedside only meant one thing. "You had another bad dream?" Bethany earnestly perceived.

Anthony nodded in affirmation. "I haven't had one in over three weeks, though."

Bethany inclined her head in corroborated satisfaction. She hadn't had a bad dream in several months and contributed it to the recent change in their living arrangements.

Together they crammed their diminutive bodies into a single wingback chair. "Brye says there's two things we can do when bad dreams occur. We can either talk it through, or try to understand what's really bothering us, or we can try and set it aside by focusing on all the good things that's happened to us since we've been here."

The need to guess what really bothered Anthony deemed unnecessary. Both knew it centered around their abusive relationship with their birth mother.

The room flowed with the silence of the night. Mystical shadows pranced across the twins' sullen faces as the full moon filtered in through the bay window. Images of rustling elm leaves danced like pirouetting ballerinas throughout the shaded room.

Anthony mulled over his choices. Months before they had taken up residency at Brylinn, the nightmares had begun to plague him. Many of his dreams were reoccurring. Some were original. All dealt with the abuse he and Bethany suffered at the hands of their mother.

In most of them, however, as he attempted to elude his drugged-out mother, she came at him with a hot iron. He ran away from her. Relentlessly, she gave chase. Always he found himself caught with his back against a wall. Frozen in a puddle of fear, he stood in the direct pathway of a sizzling iron, the hot appliance floating precariously over his left eye. As he quivered in fright, the iron would draw closer…closer…

And when the blistering heat radiated across his face and threatened to incinerate the surface of his tender skin, he awakened—the beginnings of a scream formed on his rounded lips, his terrified body trembling, bathed in a cold sweat.

"I hate her!" Youth and charm gave way to antipathy and bitterness as he spewed the embittered disclosure. "I hope they never find her!"

Intelligent well beyond her years, Bethany prevailed the stronger of the two. It had always been she who comforted Anthony at moments such as this. In her mother's defense, Bethany would invent excuses for why she abused her children—mentally as well as physically—while abusing her own body with the continuous consumption of drugs and alcohol. But right now, Bethany could not put together the words to mollify her twin brother because her sentiments matched his own.

As with Anthony, a similar dream haunted her. Hers, however, centered around the outright separation of Anthony and herself.

The dream had begun the same night she had overheard her mother attempting to sell the twins for crack-cocaine. Fortunately, the would-be buyer refused. Her mother then offered to sell one child. Once again the woman rebuffed the suggestion. Yet the possibility of the twins becoming permanently separated remained a toilsome burden within the confines of Bethany's tortured awareness.

Vowing to take whatever steps necessary to keep them together, much to her astonishment and relief, their mother had disappeared two days later.

For two weeks afterward, Bethany had gotten them off to school. Although their meals were meager at best, she fixed breakfast in the morning and dinner at night. During their two-week reign of freedom, Bethany *had* managed well. And not until the landlord appeared for the month's rent did their secret unravel.

Not wanting to get involved with the police, the landlord delivered the twin package to Brylinn's. It was Brye who had admitted them and, eventually gained temporary custody. And with her kind eyes, charming smile, gentle nature and inherent devotion, along with Linn Davies unrelenting manner and motherly practices, plus the camaraderie amongst the other children within the home, Anthony and Bethany found themselves casting aside their guarded demeanor.

"It doesn't matter if they find our mother or not," Bethany stated matter-of-factly, "because Brye says that whatever the future entails, she'll always be here for us. She says she'll never let anything happen to the both of us and she promised not to ever separate us."

Wrapped within the enfolds of obscure lighting, Anthony met Bethany with an earnest eye. "Do you believe her?"

Prior to coming to live in the Brylinn Residential Home for Children, the twins had been met with nothing but mistreatment and suffering. They knew nothing of love, or reassurances, or kindness. In their short time span of living, all they understood was cynicism, abuse, and distrust. But in this one instance, Bethany was quick to respond. "Yes…I believe her."

"Do you trust her?" Wide eyes spilling with apprehension gleamed brightly into the filtered light.

Although Brye's profession kept her on the road a great deal of time, she also managed to spend inexhaustible hours at the children's home. And on every occasion, when one or the other twin floundered inside destructive nightmares, miraculously, Brye appeared, out of nowhere. It was as if she had a direct pipeline to their emotions... to their innermost fears and considerations. She was always there to ease the lingering pain. And somewhere along the way, Bethany had detected a strong bond linking both Anthony and herself to Brye. She couldn't identify where the tie stemmed from nor did she understand why she felt this extraordinary attachment, but without question, she accepted Brye at face value.

"Yes...I trust her," she readily admitted.

Anthony nodded as if having sought, and found, confirmation to his own questioning thoughts.

Just then, the library doors slid apart, and Brye's head peeked inside a room bathed in midnight twilight. Her gaze swept past distorted images: a philodendron plant with animated six-foot dangling arms itching to reach out and throttle its unsuspecting victim; a closed roll-top desk resembling the Hunchback of Notre Dame; legs of a coffee table appeared identical to a bronzed lion crouched and ready to attack. Instinctively, her eyes zoomed in on two peas scrunched in a pod. Brye smiled, her relief evident. "I thought I'd find you two here." Moving over to the chair, she folded her pliable body onto the armrest. She swung her arm over the back. "What's the matter? Did one of you have a bad dream?"

"Anthony did," Bethany propelled a knowing look at her twin brother. Somehow, neither found Brye's unexpected appearance strange.

"Are you okay?" Brye drew him into a solace embrace.

"I'm fine." A warm glow settled around Anthony's tiny body. Hugs had been nonexistent while in the care of his mother, nor had he ever been the beneficiary of kind words. But with Brye, she issued them both freely and from deep within her heart.

Brye also reveled in the comfort his closeness provided. For two hours, aimlessly, she had driven around the outskirts of the city. Unaware of where her scrambled thoughts lead, she found herself in Greenwich, Connecticut, scurrying the lengthy drive leading to the children's home. Upon finding the twins' beds empty, she understood better the powerful tug pulling at her soul, propelling her forward to Brylinn; the twins had been mentally calling out to her.

Releasing Anthony, she captured his hand and asked, "Do you want to talk about it?"

"No." His nightmare now a distant memory, Anthony's eyes lit up like a bedecked Christmas tree. "I want to talk about our birthday party."

"Oh you do, do you?" Brye's words hinged on laughter.

Excitement spilled from Anthony's dilated pores. The reality of him attending his first party was thrilling enough, yet knowing this party was given on his and Bethany's behalf induced sensations of exhilaration. "I'm especially interested in *my* birthday present."

"Anthony!" The most mature of the two, Bethany recognized that it was in bad form to ask for presents. After all, it was the thought that counted. And whatever thought Brye had put into buying them a present, it had been a lot more than their mother had done their entire five (almost six) years of living. "Whatever it is, you should be grateful."

Oblivious to his sister's disapproving glare, he pushed on. "I should at least have the say in what I want…I mean, it *is* my birthday and all."

"Anthony!" Once again, Bethany took it upon herself to chastise her brother. "How can you be so…so…"

"It's all right, Bethany," Brye laughingly intervened. "He's right. He does have a say in what he would like."

Anthony grinned in triumph at his twin.

"But not this year," Brye quickly added. "Because *this* year, I've already picked out your presents."

"You have!" both exclaimed in blessed wonder.

"I have."

"What is it?" Despite herself, Bethany could not conceal her ever growing excitement. "Please tell us what it is. Please…please… please!"

"Oh no you don't, young lady." Brye clambered off the armrest. "You couldn't drag it out of me if you tore out my nail beds one by one."

"Oh, Brye!" they both moaned in unison.

"Don't 'Oh, Brye' me, you two. Subject is closed. Besides, it's extremely late. If I don't get you off to bed soon, Mama Linn is going to tear all our nail beds out." As soon as her words spilled into the serenity of their fellowship, a panicky expression altered Anthony's youthful appearance. Brye offered her hand. "It's okay. I'm going to stay the night. The both of you can sleep with me. Between the three of us, I think we can chase the nightmares away."

Contented, Anthony and Bethany grabbed an outstretched hand. Trampling down another flight of stairs, the three bypassed a recreation room. Several years earlier, Brye had added an additional room—an extra bedroom for purposes such as this. At times, she would spend over eighteen hours at the home. Too fatigued to drive the twenty-mile jaunt back to her home, or when they were short-staffed, she elected to remain and help out.

Clamoring into the bedroom, the twins jumped onto the queen-sized bed as Brye ducked into the adjoining bathroom. She hurriedly undressed while carrying on a cheerful conversation through the semi-ajar bathroom door. Pulling on a pair of cotton pajamas, she smiled at the twins as she strolled toward the bed.

"In the morning, you know Mama Linn's gonna have a cow about this." Bethany looked none-too-worried as a smile threatened to attack the seriousness of her expression.

Brye hopped between the small bodies. "Yeah, I know." She plopped a kiss on Bethany's cheek, then Anthony's. "But between the three of us, I think we can take on the world."

Anthony reached over and flipped the bedside lamp off. The room was washed in total darkness. Several hushed moments later, he broke the sheltered stillness. "Brye?"

"Yes, sweetheart?"

"I love you."

The three wondrous words washed over Brye like warm, melting butter. It had been much too long since anyone had said that to her. Nothing had ever felt so good nor sounded so wonderful. Drawing him closer into the confines of her body, she proclaimed, "I love you too, honey-bunch." Amazed at how easy the words flowed, Brye knew she meant them. And as she listened to their light breathing as they drifted off into an unruffled repose, she grew confident that three tormented souls would not endure the presence of unwanted apparitions the remainder of this night.

Lying beside Jennifer, Chad listened to the unvarying resonance of her shallow breathing. Sleep, however, eluded him. Despite having just engaged in sexual intercourse, unharnessed tension tormented his vigilant thought waves.

Behind troubled eyelids, Brye's enigmatic features lingered precariously in the balance. And the more he attempted to eradicate her from the bowels of his snarled deliberations, more vividly, her image emerged.

When isolated from Brye, he despised everything she stood for. But today, as they stood in close proximity, with his fingers dangerously close to squeezing the breath out of her lungs, when he gazed into her troubled eyes, while she confronted him with her quiet dignity—the same, refined self-respect she presented to the reporters as well as to Jennifer—Chad registered mixed feelings of the person he discerned as one Brye Grayson. He could not relate to the demoralizing portrait of the conniving, money-hungry, self-centered bitch his father had painted of her. In Chad's mind, that person didn't exist… had never existed.

Irritably, he tossed the downy comforter aside. Arms sliding into a belted shawl collar robe, he imperiously stormed out of the bedroom. Standing in the middle of his veiled living room, he found himself at odds with his emotions.

"Dammit!" Chad jammed his fingers through his hair. "What the hell have you done to me, Brye? Why can't I get you out of my head?"

Squeezing his eyes shut, he concentrated on shutting down his brain. Slowly, he counted to ten. Then twenty. Then thirty. Unable to break away from his tortured musing, he frantically reached outward for something...anything...to occupy his mind. He dropped his distracted frame onto his cream-colored sofa and began organizing his schedule for the following work day in the hopes it would drive his traitorous thoughts away from Brye. Rolling his weary head from side to side, he eased down further into the beckoning sofa. And with overcast eyelids, once again, he found himself held hostage by an influx of precious memories. Chad drifted back to a time lived long ago that he had never been able to put aside.

Downy, mammoth-sized snowflakes generously fell, covering the hardened ground with a light, luxurious mantle of frosted splendor. The February air felt more invigorating than biting to the exposed skin. Still, NYU students scampered in search of warm, dry shelter. Twenty-four-year-old graduate student Chad Collier also hurriedly trampled across the sodden campus. His thoughts teetered between holding up in his apartment the duration of his weekend and working on his thesis, or living recklessly by shoving his post graduate work to the back burner and partying for the next several days.

Leaning toward working on his thesis, an amazing sight hindered him dead in his tracks. Awestruck, he gawked at what appeared to be an ethereal snow angel. As other student bodies scurried past the still frame, oblivious to the cold—as well as the descending snow—she sat on a bench, eyes pressed into a book. Resplendent flakes settled around her unconfined hair, fashioning a crown of soft light. The powdery mist draped agilely around her frame like a weightless, protective, blanket. Wisps of snow sprightly danced at her feet. The image she depicted was genuinely virtuous. So heavenly...so pure.

Unable to turn away from her virginal profile, Chad watched as she lifted her gaze from her reading and shifted them toward his directions. An empty gaze barely skimmed over Chad, leaving him the impression that her mind had not registered his presence.

Oddly enough, as she hugged her book close to her body, Chad's heart tugged restlessly in his chest. As he studied her, the eyes, the gentle rocking of her body reflected abysmal sadness. Chad longed to cross over to her, drape a protective arm around her lamented body, and shield her from harm's way. His every instinct barred him from acting on his swelling need to comfort her. He continued to look on as she wiped a snow-laden wisp of dark locks away from her face, vented an abstruse sigh, then stood and progressively walked out of his life.

The entire weekend, his mind returned to the dark-headed, picturesque beauty. In a matter of minutes, she had managed to ingrain herself into his spirit. Somehow, unwittingly, she had captured his heart. He feared it would not continue to beat if her inspirational presence did not become a part of his stale life.

Like a man sitting on death row fearfully awaiting his final day on earth, Monday afternoon, finally, came to fruition. He needed to see her. He desired to set his yearning eyes upon her once again. And if he couldn't find her, well, the possibility of never seeing her again seemed too unbearable to envision.

At the appointed hour, Chad rushed to the very same location he first spotted his snow angel. Each step drawing him closer hauled with it a sense of hysteria. But as his feet docked upon the identical site he stood at three days earlier, he sucked in a much-needed breath of relief.

Issuing a silent prayer to his maker, he had just been granted a last-minute reprieve. For she sat directly in front of him, reading her book while foregoing the cold, crisp air. Instinctively, he wanted to confront her, but her guarded demeanor warned him away. On that day and the subsequent others, he maintained a harmless distance away.

Days fell into weeks as Chad pondered his precarious situation. Afraid to approach her, his every instinct inferred that she would bolt like a scared rabbit when he initiated their first interaction. So anywhere from thirty to forty-five minutes a day, he upheld his watchful vigilance and sought solace in her ruminating presence. And if she had ever become aware of his unrelenting appearance, she elected to ignore him.

Unbelievable as it seemed, Chad found himself falling in love. He didn't know when it happened, and God knows he wasn't aware of how it happened. He didn't know her name, had never heard her speak, and could only imagine how her heartfelt smile would transpose her melancholy yet angelic features into something softer, but he was thoroughly, irrevocably in love with the mysterious woman.

Promises of warmer days hung heavy in the air as spring rapidly approached. Although the harsh winter did not eagerly relinquish its icy clutches from around the arctic city, it yielded to a number of unseasonably tepid days.

It was on a temperate afternoon when Chad spotted his snow angel sitting on the ground with back resting against a dogwood tree. Numerous reference books stacked by her side, legs bent, she read with a college manual balanced atop her knees.

After his last class, Chad's professor had delayed him by one half hour, questioning him on the business composition he'd recently turned in. Much to his disappointment, no sooner than he settled on a bench close to his engaging enigma, she gathered her reading material and scrambled to her feet. On her way up, her body brushed against the rough bark of the tree. Losing her balance, she gracefully readjusted herself, but her books tumbled carelessly to the ground. Bending in an effort to retrieve her materials, a mere streak of lightning, Chad suddenly hunkered beside her.

"Please…let me help," he offered, staring into soft, violet shaded eyes—eyes reminding him of the feather hyacinths his mother's gardener had recently planted in her butterfly garden.

"Thank you, but it's not necessary."

Her harmonious voice, playing at his heart strings, set music to his soul. Her smile, although guarded, was more beautiful than anything he could have created in his wildest imagination.

"I don't mind." The glowing ember she incited within him the first moment he'd laid eyes on her raged into a full-fledged fire. Spontaneous combustion. A mere touch of her fingers, and his body shot up in flames. Much to his disappointment, his snow angel pulled away—but not before reclaiming her books from his smoldering clutches.

Hastily stuffing the volumes in the crook of her arm, unsteadily, she stood up. "I can manage…really." No sooner as the words slipped out, several of the smaller editions slid out from under the protection of her arms and landed at Chad's feet.

Chad rushed to gather them. "I don't question your managerial abilities," he mildly assured, the lines around his mouth aching to smile, "but don't you think you could manage more efficiently as well as expeditiously with the assistance of a helping hand?"

She hesitated, then cast her gaze over his left shoulder. Behind expressionless eyes, she gingerly weighed her decision. With bated breath, he waited.

Then, much to his relief, she laughed—an intoxicating chime assailing Chad's apprehensive stance.

"Of course…you're right," she acquiesced, capturing his stunned gaze. "I graciously accept your offer of assistance." She pushed her heavy load at him. Eagerly, he accepted her humble offerings like a starving man gone without food for much too long.

He steered the conversation to neutral territory as he walked her to the car. General topics ranged from the weather to upcoming college events. And when they finally reached her car—a late model gray Mercedes—he carefully stacked her books into the back seat.

"My mother's car," she felt the sudden urge to explain. "I normally walk, but I knew I'd be loaded down with—" She trailed off. A frown jarred her delicate features, as if perplexed with the sudden untenable desire to justify her actions or denounce her very stature in society. She turned away, prepared to drive out of his life forever. "Thank you for your assistance."

Unable to let her go, Chad laid a courtly hand upon her arm. A medley of emotions coursed through his fingers as she tensed under his clinging touch. First fear, then cold indignation, and finally passive indifference. Gradually, she relaxed, then turned a questioning eye to him.

"I'm Chad Collier." Sustaining a detached visage, he released her arm and thrust his right hand toward her.

She blessed him with a tentative smile. "Brye Grayson." Met with scrupulous silence, seconds passed before she accepted his hand in greeting.

Pleased to have a name to go along with her unforgettable face, he said, "Thank you, Brye Grayson, for allowing me to assist." Dainty fingers settled lightly against his powerful palm. Brye felt diminutive and fragile in comparison to his huge, stalwart grip. Reluctantly he released his clinging grasp. No other words were offered as she climbed into her car. With his hands thrust deep into his pockets, he silently watched her pull away. Questioning the fear flickering in her composed demeanor, determined to go slowly with the relationship, Chad stole away to the campus book store.

The following afternoon, he openly approached Brye; he towered over her dark crown as she embraced her reading materials. "Do you mind if I join you?"

She lifted her face, and his heart skipped a beat. The afternoon sun served as a backdrop for his hulking body. She squinted against the bright sunlight. "If you don't mind sitting on hard ground."

Chad collapsed beside her. His back brushed against the rough bark sheathing the tree. "What're you reading?"

Using her finger as a bookmark, she flipped the college manual around for him to see.

"Socrates?" Chad pondered over the title with an arched eyebrow. "He makes for some interesting reading." His gaze lifted. Wanting to learn as much as he could, he asked with absorbed interest, "Is this for one of your classes?"

"I'm writing a thesis on ancient civilization," she verified. "Initially, I intended to devote my paper to Plato, but as I researched his works, I discovered that many of his readings were based on Socrates. And I guess, just like Plato, I grew to admire Socrates's unwavering character. He was a wise and intelligent man—although by his own admission he was neither wise nor intelligent. And I know this is going to sound crazy because the man lived hundreds of years before Christ, but if I were given the chance to go back into time to meet the one person I most admired, it would be Socrates." She shrugged, unable to explain the abstruse feelings she held for a man who had lived centuries before her existence.

Chad, however, needed no explanation. After all, he was in love with a woman he didn't know and only had the pleasure of partaking in two conversations with—if he could add this one to his count. "It doesn't sound crazy at all," Chad assured. "In fact, I agree with you. He was a great man."

For the first time since meeting her, Brye gaped at him with new found curiosity. He desired to retain that interest. "Socrates dedicated his entire life reflecting upon philosophy. At the drop of a hat, he benevolently discussed it with anyone and everyone he came into contact with."

"He simply wanted others to understand that what they held as truths, beliefs they took for granted, were not necessarily correct. He wanted others to explore everything put before them—not just accept what was already a given. His lectures were meant to compel individuals to look within themselves for answers, and not rely on the perceptions of others' so-called realities," Brye explained with abandoned ardor.

"But it was those same sermons which influenced a group of young nonconformists to lead a revolution to overthrow the government. And it was because of his outspoken convictions, when democracy had finally been restored, that he was tried, convicted, and condemned to death for corrupting the minds of vulnerable young men," Chad proficiently stated.

"The man asked questions," Brye responded with intensified loyalty. "He built his life on questioning others. He never instructed a bunch of disgruntled men to go out and overthrow a government. He simply taught them to see what was before their very eyes. It wasn't his fault they didn't like what they saw.

"In all actuality, it was Socrates's sanctimonious accusers who refused to look beyond their own noses. It was their unswerving ignorance which unjustly indicted him for something he had no control over."

Touched by her impassioned allegiance to a man whose virtues and ideology managed to endure thousands of years after his death, Chad wondered if she embraced love with that same fiery devotion. Delicately, he stated, "But he did have a hand in the coup to overthrow the government. Granted, it was a hand never meant to intentionally push, but it was definitely there, guiding all the way."

"But how can you say that?" Brye's chin jutted forward in indignation. "He didn't—"

"I say it because it was Socrates who captured those young men's minds in the first place. It was he who helped get their analytical reasoning up and running," Chad interjected with tangible certitude. "And Socrates understood this. In the face of adversity, he held steadfast to his principles and graciously accepted the death sentence put before him because he felt as if he had been put on this earth to teach independent thinking. And the young men who acted out against their government were independently thinking. So, although he couldn't justify them bucking the system, he had to praise them for striving to institute their own ideals. And although he was put to death by drinking a cup of hemlock, he knew there would be more like him to continue with his cause."

Brye nodded, unable to find a valid reason for disputing Chad's inscribed allegations. "It's just so sad that people are ready to condemn others because of a difference in opinion or because they refuse to conform or back away from their beliefs."

"People are afraid of what they don't understand," Chad pointedly concluded.

"Yes," Brye agreed, her voice sounding far removed and constrained. "People *are* afraid of what they don't understand."

Somehow, as Chad stared into her glazed eyes, he believed she wasn't talking about Socrates any longer.

"You're very well versed on Socrates," Brye noted, snapping out of her self-hypnotic state. "Is it for your own personal gain or was it something demanded for a class study?"

With a casual shrug of his shoulders, Chad said, "I've been known to take a little interest in the men I admire." Although he spoke the truth and did respect the Greek thinker, it was only when he noted Brye's reading materials the day before that he rushed to the bookstore and bought the very same textbooks. Acknowledging to himself that the reading would be extremely burdensome, determined to familiarize himself with topics that were of great importance to this soft-spoken woman, he spent the entire night educating himself on the preacher of philosophy. Within the first few pages, however, he had read with more enthusiasm than anticipated. And the loss of sleep had been a relatively small price to pay in exchange for witnessing the entranced expression etched along Brye's cautious features as they conversed.

For several minutes, Brye remained in reflective contemplation. She tucked her college manual under her arm. The silence between them stretched out in time yet did not grow uncomfortable. When she ultimately spoke, her choice of subjects startled him. "You've been watching me for weeks now." Her tone was not accusatory. She merely stated a fact. "Why is that?"

Chad sat up straighter. The bark of the tree tugged at his leather jacket. Within his mind, he frantically rummaged for an appropriate answer. But when his prudent eye confronted Brye, he found himself flirting with the truth. "You…fascinate me."

She appeared to be taken aback by his answer. When she found her tongue, she noted, "But up until yesterday, you never attempted to approach me."

Again, he answered honestly, "I didn't think you would welcome the intrusion."

Brye dropped her eyes to her lap. "That's never been enough to stop a man before."

"It was enough to stop me."

Their eyes met and held for a surmountable amount of time. The first to break the profound contact, Brye gathered her belongings and clambered to her feet. "I have to go," she hastily announced.

Chad shot to his feet. "Brye?" He grabbed her arm in the hope of preventing her rapid retreat.

Pulling away, she repeated, "I have to go."

Afraid he frightened her off for good, Chad's question expelled in one tangled rush. "Will I see you tomorrow?"

Ignoring his question, Brye turned and walked away.

"Brye...please..." The desperation in his voice carried in the cool breeze.

Unable to disregard his exposed distress, Brye halted, turned, and replied, "You already know the answer to that." With that, she swirled on her toes and dashed off.

True to her words, the following afternoon, and the many afternoons following, she continued to frequent her favorite resting spot. And as each day passed, easily, they slipped into relaxed conversation. Chad promptly noted that although she remained on the defense at all times, she was well-versed and articulate in all subjects they deliberated over. More and more, he coached hesitant grins out of her and battled to induce genuine gales of laughter. But it was on those rare occasion, as a passionate smile touched her violet-colored eyes, that she melted his heart.

The days steadily grew warmer. And as flowers and plants blossomed, so did a budding friendship flourish between Brye and Chad. But as their camaraderie progressed, Chad could not move their relationship beyond the realm of the campus grounds. On numerous occasions, he offered to buy Brye dinner, maybe attend a movie, take in a play. With each petitioning endeavor, a fixed denial followed. Thwarted yet unprepared to give in to her rejection, he opted to bring dinner to her.

Armed with a large wicker picnic basket packed with goodies, one radiant spring afternoon, he settled down beside her. Together, oblivious to the students trampling around them, they dined on finger sandwiches stuffed with a mixture of deviled ham, shrimp, cream cheese, mayonnaise, and minced onions. A fresh mushroom salad and a variety of cheeses and vegetables also pleased their palate. A large container of freshly squeezed pineapple-citrus punch quenched their thirst. Towards the end of their Epicurean meal, Brye halted in the middle of savoring the delectable taste of a chocolate-filled croissant. She arrested Chad with a pragmatic eye. Her question shot at him from out of nowhere.

"What is it you want from me, Chad?"

Caught off guard, Chad almost choked on his strawberry-filled croissant. Gulping the flaky pastry down, he intended to tread slowly and carefully. "Everything you have to offer." *So much for treading carefully*, he quipped to himself.

"But what if this is all I have to give?" Never releasing him from her staunch gaze, Brye opened her arms to include the campus grounds, the dogwood tree, this stolen moment. She was informing him that she may never be able to go beyond this point.

"Then I will graciously accept your decision." It pained Chad to think he might trudge through life without her by his side. But he loved her enough to let go if it was what she so desired. "I don't want to." He reached toward her face. Fingers perched in midair, realizing his presumptuousness, he dropped his arm heavily to his side. "God knows I don't want to lose you. But I'll stand by whatever decision you make concerning our relationship."

His painful words drizzled around him, withering his skin like spilled acid. But strangely enough, his virtuous statement released the debilitating grip rendering her an emotional cripple; visibly, Brye assented to entrust herself to his love.

A slight smile shuffled along the confines of her lips. Long, dainty fingers lightly slathered across his sensitized chest. Smoothly trailing her open palm up and around his neck, Brye left behind a pathway of burning desire. Flexible fingers molded to his neck, pulling him downward, anxious to gain a taste of his senses.

Her initial kiss shyly graced the corners of his mouth. With a slight tug of his head, her second kiss snared him full on the lips. Hesitant at first, warm, moist with a hint of chocolate, lips trampled over his belted emotions. Motionless, finding it difficult to breathe as well as control the urgency to make love to her underneath the blooming tree, he granted her the liberty of sampling as much, or as little, as she felt necessary.

But just as her tongue snaked out and lightly grazed his lower teeth, snapping to her senses, she pulled away.

"I'm sorry," she apologized, blushing from the heat of the sun, or from the kiss, or possibly both. A tantalizing smile teased the bottom of her lip. Her cheeks colored with the warm flush of heated embarrassment.

"Don't be." Chad grinned down at her. "But if you feel you must make it up to me, how about dinner tomorrow?"

Her violet-colored eyes emitted an illustrious beacon of sunlight. Readily, she promised, "I'll eagerly follow wherever you graciously lead."

Chad woke with a start, practically lunging out of his slumped position. Laborious breathing jaggedly poured out of his lungs and cut into the stillness of the room. His overactive libido painfully stabbed into his unceasingly mounting rage. Brye's reappearance had caustically disrupted his carefully established life. With excruciating slowness, he pushed himself off the sofa. Starting toward the bedroom, he suddenly shifted directions and headed to the main bathroom. Although his body craved sexual release, he did not seek Jennifer to free himself. It was time for a much-needed, long, cold shower.

9

DRUNKEN LAUGHTER THREATENED TO crack the impenetrable armor Brye had resurrected around herself. The invisible shield would aid her in surviving the evening's gala festivities. Looking on, she appeared composed, aloof, self-assured. No one would ever be aware of the forces inciting her internal struggle; it took every ounce of willpower to not turn tail and flee.

In spite of their flagrant cultural differences, Brye and Marcus emerged as an impressive couple. In notable magnificence, the pair paused just inside the interior of a large opulent room as they were directly accosted by one of Marcus's business associates. As they lingered by the entrance, every man taken note of their late arrival tossed the newcomers a look of admiration coupled with envy.

Introductions completed, as Marcus engaged in obliging conversation, Brye's disengaged glare waft over the disseminated crowd. Standing on a marbled-floor rising, she peered over the cumulative heads sifting through the sunken room.

A pit of vipers, she regarded with disdain. At any given moment, anyone in the vast room could and would strike out at her. With no personal knowledge of the chosen invitees, from past experiences, she knew all too well how she would be accepted.

The men, in their overindulgent drunken stupor, would openly paw and disgorge suggestive remarks.

And then there were men who treated her like they were God's greatest gift to women; they believed to be providing a community service when asking her out on a date. And, finally, the married men. With a flirtatious wink and a subtle smile, they expected Brye to imbibe in a quick go round in the back seat of their chauffeur-driven limousine.

In addition, there was the severe nature in which her own gender tolerated her. With their pristine etiquette and their keen sense of smell, they sniffed out her sordid past like a hound in pursuit of a rabbit. They surreptitiously prejudged her by looks alone, automatically assuming her to be a calculated bitch who would readily and with no conscience whatsoever jump into bed with a man, *any* man—married or otherwise—to further her well-established aspirations. And although most of these women wouldn't openly shun her—it went against every grain of refinement they'd ever been taught in their aristocratic upbringing—they obligatorily endured her only as long as it deemed necessary.

Mistreatment and misjudgment had become a fact of life with Brye. It was something she had learned to deal with since the ripe old age of fifteen. But it was the game, the power play, the phony facades she abhorred being drawn into. She desired to take no part in the hypocrisy of it all. Now, standing amidst the overly rambunctious predators, she only wished she had been more adamant with her refusal to attend.

As she continued to scope the extravagantly furnished room, an indomitable presence sizzled in the air, latched on to her, and allured her toward an all-powerful vision rising from the midst of the crowd. Her eyes fell and lingered on a pageant warrior; her knight in shining armor. His virility, his sensuality, his omnipotent strength snatched at the very air she labored to draw into her lungs. Involuntarily, the adrenaline churned unsteadily through her collapsed arteries. He stood tall and handsome. Raven hair blazed brilliantly against a white tuxedo. His eyes were as intense and as esoteric as the deep blue sea. A prominent cleft enhanced a squared chin. His athletic physique was not in any way hampered by his tuxedo jacket and ruffled shirt. An aura of compassion offset his blue-blood credentials. And right now, the compassionate side of Chad homed in on Brye like a beacon light guiding the troops home.

Unable to tear her eyes away from the all-powerful man, or the woman he was engaged to be engaged to, Brye watched as both heads lifted. Her feathers remained unruffled as the three visions entangled. Boldly, Brye captured and held Chad's wary gaze. And much to her surprise, she attained a sense of perverse pleasure knowing she was the catalyst lighting the fuse to the stick of dynamite set to explode.

Jennifer ostentatiously went on the defense. "My god!" she gasped in transparent distaste. "Surely someone educated the woman on the *image* she's expected to uphold for Romanique Cosmetics? Certainly there was a stipulation in her contract on the distinction of *men* she would be allowed to associate with?"

Brye was a little under two hours late. Chad had given up on the idea of her making an appearance. Now she made her grand entrance with a tall, black, and generous-in-all-the-places-that-count, escort joined to her side. Mesmerized by her presence, he had to bite down the strong stirring of jealousy souring his mouth. "And what type of *man* do you suggest we have her associate with, Jennifer?" Listening to the agitated woman fuming at his side, he was hard-pressed at keeping his petulance from showing.

"Don't you dare patronize me, Chadwick Collier! You know damn well what I mean! She's your spokesperson, for god's sake. Therefore, she should act accordingly!"

Barely able to focus on Jennifer's erroneous protestations, as his eyes remained trained on Brye, the entire room seemed to fade away. He and Brye remained the only two people visible.

From head to toe, baby-blue eyes colored with unadulterated lust drank in every inch of her well-proportioned frame. She wore a sleeveless floor-length dress perfectly matched to her eye color. A single white gold bracelet glinted on her wrist. A hint of blush brushed her cheekbones, a light layer of soft lipstick touched her full lips. Tonight, Brye catered to the natural look. Lustrous strands of silky hair smoothly stroked exquisite features while coursing over beautifully formed shoulders and back. Simple yet elegant. The significance of her silent declaration submitted for the entire room to interpret: she didn't need to hide behind heavy makeup or adorn her body with extensive jewelry, to validate her beauty and femininity. With a straight back, a defiant uplift of chin, Brye Grayson stood tall, confidant, and all woman.

To his disappointment, his trance was dispelled when Brye broke eye contact and focused her attention on her male companion. Chad attempted to divert his attention back to the scowling female standing beside him. He stared into a face marred with arrogance and repulsion. His train of thought lost, having stepped out of their conversation minutes earlier, he wasn't certain if she waited for a response from him.

"Why don't you wipe your mouth?" Jennifer finally scoffed. "You're drooling like a sex-crazed teenager." Angrily whirling on her five-hundred-dollar designer heels, she stormed off.

Instead of responding, Chad found himself glancing back toward the entrance. Sometime during Jennifer's wrathful quip, Brye and escort had blended into the crowd. Turning in the opposite direction Jennifer had struck out in, he did not feel inclined to appease her soiled temperament.

All-in-all, Brye couldn't write the entire evening off as a total calamity. With Marcus at her side, he turned out to be the barricade deflecting zealous suitors' advances. And with Tenisha acting as her personal liaison for the *National Enquirer* and awarding her with the dirty lowdown on a large number of the invited guests, the evening proved to be informative if not stimulating.

Painfully aware of Chad's irrepressible aura, somehow, fortunately, she managed to remain out of reach from his sharp tongue and glowering accusations. Determined to keep the vast stretch of the grand room a corporeal obstacle between them, Brye dictated her movements in direct opposition to Chad's. If he turned right, she turned left; when he moved forward, she inched backward; when he crossed the room, she headed in the opposing direction. At all costs, she was prepared to take whatever steps necessary to avoid an emotional, verbal, and sexually charged confrontation.

Hours into the evening, Marcus strayed from Brye's side. This left her vulnerable to the salivating wolves. Amusing herself by closely examining the luxurious furnishings surrounding her, Brye hoped to create the illusion of someone more interested in her present environment than in indulging in polite conversation.

Brye's astute eye took in the opulent setting. Intricately detailed crystal chandeliers, antique-framed mirrors, outrageously expensive custom-designed furnishings, original artwork, priceless flower-filled vases…it was all so untouchable, all so elegantly cold and impersonal. Brye found herself wondering if Chad had enjoyed his childhood living in a home that lacked warmth or soothing qualities.

"Are you done casing the joint?" a voice absent of emotion smashed through Brye's reflective musings.

Brye turned to confront Jennifer standing well within the boundaries of her personal space. The scowling woman's stance was that of a fighter sizing up an effectual adversary. The impertinent remark did not incense Brye. Instead, she found it rather amusing that Jennifer was so bothered by her presence, she was willing to step out of her Miss Congeniality role and step into a more crude personality.

"*Case* the joint?" Brye elevated one beguiling eyebrow. "Have you been staying up at night watching midnight B flicks?"

"Do you like what you see?" Jennifer ignored Brye's taunting statement.

"Actually, I prefer homey accommodations myself." More from needing to occupy her hands rather than the sudden need to quench her thirst, Brye removed a champagne glass from a passing tray. As she did so, Jennifer's perfectly arched eyebrows caught her skilled eye. Brye wondered if the brows were Jennifer's or merely perfected artwork. *No,* she thought after a closer inspection, *they're definitely not hers.*

"Are you saying this home doesn't live up to your standards?" Jennifer asked with a cynical tightening of her jaw.

Feeling generous, Brye offered her an amiable smile. "This house is extravagant and would fair extremely well under the Queen's scrutiny. I was merely stating that everyone has different taste, and I tend to lean toward a more comfortable atmosphere, a home where I can kick my shoes off, put my feet up, and relax."

"With a beer in one hand and a cigar in the other, no doubt." Jennifer dropped all pretense of sustaining a cordial conversation. She took a step backward as if the smell in the room had gone rancid.

Brye's smile vanished into the surrounding elegance. Not wanting to turn this into open warfare, she asked forthright, "What is it you would like to say to me?"

Jennifer scowled with open hostility. In the past several weeks, she had been made aware of an unpalatable change within Chad. He'd become distracted...moody. The only recognizable factor—or thorn, she established with rancor—recently inserted into their predestined lives had been the presence of one Brye Grayson. Polite prattle dropped insidiously by the wayside. She drove straight to the point. "What is your interest in my fiancé?"

Brye ignored Jennifer's use of the word, 'fiancé'. Without taking a sip, she twirled the base of her crystal stemware. "Outside of Romanique Cosmetics? There is no other interest."

"I don't believe you."

"It doesn't matter what you believe."

"Chad seems to be...curious about you," Jennifer reluctantly understated. In reality, he acted as if this woman was leading him around by the nose. "I want you to stay away from him."

"It seems to me you should be speaking to Chad about this matter."

"I'm speaking to you." Her perfectly arched eyebrows narrowed into a pencil-thin line. "If he approaches you, I want you to deflect him."

"Why would you want to marry a man you can't trust?"

Up until this point in time, Jennifer had every reason to trust Chad. But now her every instinct told her otherwise. It also informed her that Brye was the culprit behind Chad's inexplicable behavior. Since meeting her future intended, Jennifer had staunchly set her sights on him. That hold had been strengthened with the endorsement by both sets of parents. And in the face of rivalry—substantiated or otherwise—Jennifer intended to come out the victor. "*That* isn't your concern." Jennifer closed in the space between them. With three-inch heels, Jennifer stood two inches above Brye. Fiercely, she peered down Brye's nose. "What *is* your concern, however, is that you do as you're told."

"And what if I don't?" Brye retorted with a sparse smile. "Will there be pistols at twenty paces at the break of dawn?"

Jennifer's smile turned deadly. "I wouldn't let you off that easily."

Brye's smile faded into dull disillusionment. "Why do you dislike me so?" she asked in cryptic curiosity. Although she cared little of this woman's hatred for her, she remained interested in not just Jennifer's boorish behavior but with anyone who prejudged without facts.

"Because I know of you…your type…what you stand for."

"No." Brye's violet eyes shadowed, then regained its celebrated magnificence. "You know nothing of who I am!" she sharply dismissed. Having had enough, Brye executed an about-face, then walked away with poised elegance. The evening went downhill from that moment forward.

Fifteen minutes after the scathing confrontation with Jennifer, Brye—with Marcus at her side once again—found herself ambushed by her host and hostess along with Chad and Jennifer. After discovering she had embarked upon postgraduate work for her PhD in social psychology, for reasons foreign to Brye, Daniel Collier initiated a discussion on Sigmund Freud, which soon turned heated.

"He was a cocaine-snorting, egotistical neurotic who dabbled in the study of perversity," Daniel degraded with a vengeance.

Brye cringed at the acrimonious description. "He was a great man," she calmly counterpoised, "who was greatly misunderstood. One fails to understand that despite his brilliance, despite his paving the road for others in the study of mental illness, he was an individual first. And individuals are not without fault. We are not prone to perfection. The majority of us cannot live our lives problem free.

"In spite of his problems, Freud pushed himself onward. He was an extremely productive, insightful, determined man who believed in his work despite being ostracized by others."

Chad, who'd only acknowledged Brye by a curt nod of his head, now listened with consumed interest. It had never ceased to amaze him on how avidly she defended her mentors. Impressively, he was also amazed at the candid manner in which she had taken on his father. She spoke to him with the patience of a teacher rationalizing a laborious riddle. *She's getting to me again.* Chad averted his stare. *I won't let that happen.* But on his own firm decree, and against his own volition, his eyes tugged back to Brye.

"Ah!" Daniel presented Brye with a most agreeable smile. Aware of the sizzling current flowing between his son and this woman, he was about to set the stage for the final act which would rid this social misfit from his son's life forever. "You mentioned Freud's work. He wrote a paper—one of his most notable works I believe—I had the pleasure of reading some years back." He paused, fingers stroking his stalwart jaw, as if trying to recall the title. "Three Essays on Sexual—"

"Three Essays on the Theory of Sexuality," Brye corrected with forced proficiency. An air of puzzlement centered around this entire line of conversation. All along, she'd been painstakingly aware that the discussion on Freud was merely laid groundwork for bigger revelations to come. Promptly, she understood she was about to embark on a journey she had no inclination to travel. Acting on an unconscious level alone, Brye shifted toward Marcus. As if seeking comfort and protection, she rested her fingers along his arm.

Chad took note of the intimate touch. Once again, jealousy cinched him tightly around the chest.

"That's the title," Daniel sprouted with forged enthusiasm. "I couldn't quite get the gist of his basic concepts and was wondering—for purposes of comprehension only—if you might consider explaining his ideology to me in layman's terms."

Knowing his interest was feigned, Brye guarded her words. "His conceptions are extremely complex and would take more than a few minutes to untangle."

Daniel spurned her ineffectual excuse with a wave of his hand. "Summarize as best you can."

Although Daniel displayed the most charming of smiles, his generosity did not reach his eyes. Something sinister lurked just beneath the surface. Brye didn't know when or where he would strike, but she was certain it wouldn't be pretty. "Of course." Brye resigned herself to comply with his puzzling request.

"Please forgive me, dear," Chad's mother interjected, aiming her apologies at Brye. "And please don't think me rude, but conversations such as the one you're about to embark upon do bore me."

"I understand," Brye answered with genuine kindness. When introduced to Mrs. Collier, Brye had not sensed a hidden agenda where the refined, elderly woman was concerned; she did not mean to intentionally harm Brye. In fact, Brye had found her direct manner, pleasant features, and jocular tongue quite refreshing in comparison to the miscellany of individuals composing the Collier guest list. "Then I will take my leave." She acknowledged the small group with a dignified nod of her head, then courtly slipped away.

"You may begin now," Daniel commanded in an air of authority.

Brye refused to allow him to rattle her. And when she spoke, her voice resounded with confidence she did not feel. "To understand 'Three Essays on the Theory of Sexuality,' I should at least begin with Freud's theory of the composition of the psyche. Originally, he believed the psyche was composed of three elements: the conscious, the unconscious, and the preconscious. Eventually, he decided the terms were merely simplifications. He later identified the id, the ego—or self—and the superego as small groups of mental processes in which each serves a distinct purpose. Now," holding Daniel with a firm gaze, she said, "having said that, I will briefly outline the 'Three Essays.'

"Basically, the first essay emphasized the cultivation of sexual anomalies induced by inadequate or inappropriate child-rearing development. The second essay dealt with sexuality in the infant. Freud theorized that every newborn baby is inherently sexually perverse, but in the face of a healthy, nurturing development, the growing child will subsequently subdue their perversion. The third essay pertains to sexuality on the onset of puberty—"

"I'm interested in the first two," Daniel crudely admitted, cutting her off at the pass.

Why am I not surprised? Brye concealed a scathing look. She bowed her head in acknowledgment, but her mind screamed out, *Whatever possessed me to come here tonight?*

Suppressing signs of her inner turmoil, her voice remained steady and cocksure. "According to Freud, all infants are born with sexual desires. Also, within newborns, all mental processes are unconscious functions—or id derivatives. There is no rhyme or reason to the id process. It is basically instinctual. It seeks satisfaction of rudimentary desires without regard to social rules or regulations." Brye smiled at a redheaded male joining the small group.

"In accordance with healthy child-rearing days, eventually, and for reasons that are too extensive to go into in this discussion, around the age of five, the child has repressed his or her sexual instincts."

"What do you regard as healthy child-rearing days?" a male guest with bushy brows and thick jowls questioned.

Vastly, the group continued to grow by several numbers. Addressing the man standing on one side of Chad, she answered, "Healthy child-rearing days are when a parent or other suitable facsimile nurtures, trains, and educates that child. They bestow healthy doses of love, they instill significant values, they punish their children when it deems fit. They are, in fact, the guiding force tutoring them on how to properly behave within the confines of the social system. They instruct that one does not bite, steal, curse, or masturbate—"

"At least not in public," a male guest with sly grin and leery eyes interjected. His statement was met with a chortle of laughter.

"Exactly," Brye laughingly agreed, turning a blind eye to his blatant, prurient stare. "Which brings us to the ego—or self. The ego digests these instructions. And in the normal progression of development, the child learns to identify with social morals and injunctions set upon himself by the same-sex parent. He learns to accept his parent's beliefs as his own—this is identified as the superego. The ego self-controls, but the superego oversees the ego. It's because of the superego that we behave accordingly."

"What if a child is not met with healthy needs?" Despite himself, Chad found himself drawn into the impromptu discussion.

Brye found herself mesmerized by his baby-blue eyes as she stared into his breath-stealing, alluring face. Since their forced reconciliation, this was the first he had spoken to her with no infliction of hostility insinuated into a scathing tone. Fearful she would stumble over her own tongue, she paused before answering.

"Freudian theory argues that in a child's life, psychologically, the most critical events will take place between the ages of three and five. By that age, the child's sexual urges tend to gravitate toward the one person who provides sufficient gratification. And the person with the highest probabilities of being chosen is the parent of the opposite sex.

"As I stated earlier, if the child is reared properly, those sexual urges are locked away in an inaccessible part of the id. Hopefully never to be heard from again, at least until they reach proper age and their sexual urges are geared toward a more suitable partner.

"If a child is not reared properly, if they are overly criticized, or if there is negligence in halting forbidden sexual impulses, that child might not progress to the next level of child development. And that lack of progression may appear later on in life in the form of sexual abnormalities."

Brye swallowed and continued, "In summary, in an individual who, psychologically, develops normally, the ego maintains mental harmony. But if the id is the strongest of the three, a person may take on the characteristics of a psychopath. And when the superego is the stronger element, neurosis develops." She looked around at the male faces surrounding her. Proffering a smile that belied her shaking innards, she said, "I hope I wasn't too long-winded." She then addressed her next statement to Daniel. "And I hope I was of some help in simplifying the 'Three Essays.'"

"Actually, I do have a question." Daniel's expression emerged as innocent as a newborn babe.

Brye tensed. *Here it comes*. "Yes."

"If a male child is not nurtured during the early stages of life and has not psychologically matured yet loves his mother and yearns for her affection, would he develop sexual aberrations later in life? Possible in his teen years?"

Brye's heart skipped a number of beats, then began to pump erratically. A surge of blood pounded profusely against her ear. Her mind screamed out, *Why are you doing this to me*? Calmly, she spoke, "It's possible."

"Would you even go as far as to say that he might be so obsessed with his mother he might just engage in incest for the sole purpose of gaining and retaining her affections?"

"Freudian theory would substantiate those beliefs," she vaguely replied, her heart thundering wildly in her ear.

"Freud's theories were highly castigated by many. I want *your* own personal opinion?" A sardonic edge fused with his persistent tone.

Hesitantly, she replied, "Yes." Barely able to maintain an even gaze, her tumultuous insides belied her calm exterior. "I would go as far as to say that *some* misguided children, who have been wrongfully neglected by a mother's love, would do just about anything to gain her favor. Now"—she firmly gripped Marcus's arm, determined to bring an end to this line of questioning—"if you'll excuse us, I think I'd like to dance."

"Just a minute, Brye."

His sharp tone nearly sank the smile off Brye's face. She laboriously succeeded in keeping it afloat. "Yes?"

"Actually, I have a trivia question I'm sure you can answer if no one else can."

Brye stared into eyes baring a remarkable resemblance to Chad's yet were also frighteningly opposite. There was no warmth, no compassion, no tolerance. And as Brye took in his deceptively humane expression, she knew—just as she knew the sun would rise the following morning—that this was the man who had altered her destiny many years ago. This was the man who had taken Chad away from her. And somehow, she understood, without a shadow of a doubt, he dangled her lifeline over her head. Soon—maybe not tonight but soon—he would reel her in for the kill.

Brye refused to cower. "What's the question?" she asked, unwavering.

"Based on Freud's theory, what's the one psychological emotion holding our society together?"

A number of answers were thrown out by the small assemblage, with each answer subsequently being rejected.

"Love?"

"Gratitude?"

"Sex?"

"Sex is a state of being, not an emotion," Marcus gamely acknowledged.

"Remind me of that when I'm crying 'I love you' in the throes of passion," a short Asian man remarked. Earlier, he had been introduced to Brye as a dermatologist.

Another bout of laughter ensued.

"Fear?" Someone shouted as the laughter petered out.

"Close but no cigar," Daniel rejected, clearly enjoying the game. "Brye, would you care to enlighten my guest…if you can?"

"Guilt." Her answer resounded clear and definitive over the ferocious roar of the party.

"Guilt?" Jennifer jeered in unmitigated disbelief. "You expect us to believe guilt upholds our civilization?"

"Guilt," Brye repeated with fake indifference. "Freud believed that guilt is the reason many of us would observe a pile of money lying on a table, no one around, yet walk away without taking a dime. He maintains that guilt is the reason why many of us would stop at a red light in the middle of the night, no other car in sight for miles, yet we wait for the light to turn green. He implied that our guilt is the reason we are able to maintain a civilized society. Of course, he based his theories on the assumption that we *live* in a civilized world." She confronted Daniel with an incisive stare. "But we know this world isn't always civilized, don't we, *Mr.* Collier?" She abruptly pulled away, dragging Marcus with her.

Touché. Daniel angled his glass toward Brye's retreating backside in a show of tribute. A worthy adversary, she had remained unflappable throughout his demanding interrogation. Daniel had driven many a great opponent to his knees with only a withering glance. Brye hadn't batted an eye. The game he had embarked upon would prove to be most enjoyable. The great man considered playing cat and mouse a while longer before eating Brye alive.

10

"How rude," Brye overheard Jennifer as she made her quick exit. "Some people don't know what manners are, let alone how to use them."

Out of range, Brye missed the malevolent response.

"Brye?" Concern for Brye ripped Marcus's chest open from bow to stern. The urge to shove her out of harm's way overrode everything else.

"Marcus!" Tenisha's spirited presence burst upon the scene like a display of fireworks ablaze a midnight-blue backdrop. "We haven't danced yet. Would you care to accompany me on the dance floor?"

"Where's TyJuan?" Brye blurted with lack of thought.

Tenisha shoved Brye with an extraneous look that was easily interpreted: *I don't know and I don't give a damn!* She asked, "Do you mind, Brye, if I borrowed your date?"

Marcus, torn between the two women, turned an agonizing eye toward Brye. This was an opportunity of a lifetime—dancing with the woman he cared so deeply about—but he was caught between desire and gallantry; it was time to return Brye to the safety of her own insulated world.

Behind his all-inclusive expression of uncertainty, Brye witnessed Marcus's internal struggle. Setting out to reassure, her smile irradiated encouragement as she pushed him toward Tenisha. "You two go. Dance. Have several. Don't worry about me. I think I'll step out on the terrace and take in some much-needed fresh air."

"Are you sure?" He peered down at her with troubled eyes.

Brye smiled and squeezed his arm in reassurance.

Oblivious to Marcus's internal struggle, not waiting for a response, Tenisha grabbed Marcus by the arm and excitedly pulled him out on the dance floor.

Not wanting to hang around any longer, hastily, Brye went in search of freedom.

Stepping through French doors, the warm night welcomed her. To the right, the shimmering waves of a lighted swimming pool beckoned. She strayed in the opposite direction. The lighting more obscure, she started down a flagstone pathway. A multitude of trees and flowers succulently embraced Brye. The sweet smell of honeysuckle drew Brye to a granite bench located in the midst of the glorious landscaping. She sat. From a distance and peeking through several flowering pear trees, she was offered a side view of the French doors; she would be able to spot Marcus when he came in search of her.

Above, a quarter moon decorated the starlit night. Below, the melodious sounds of crickets carried in the breeze. In short order, Brye became oblivious to everything laid out in front of her. She fought against it but couldn't thwart Daniel's imposing image from trespassing on her restless thoughts. Begrudgingly, her mind relived the peculiar conversation she had engaged in with Daniel Collier. The very reason Brye did not consort with the fast crowd, the slow crowd, or anyone else in between was because others had a way of inadvertently tapping into innermost private secrets. But Brye didn't believe Daniel Collier had accidentally trespassed upon her darkest thoughts; she believed he had purposely orchestrated the discussion in its entirety.

But how could that be? she coerced herself into rationalizing. She had met Chad months after her twin brother's death and she had never mentioned him. And above all else, she had enrolled in college under the name of Brye Grayson, not Bryson Gray.

More than anything, Brye wanted to write the unfounded vibes off to merely unsettled paranoia. But better judgment said otherwise. No, she would have to wait and see what he held in store for her.

Deep in thought, Brye nervously played with her bracelet. Absentmindedly, with trembling fingers, she slipped the shining band on and off, on and off. Unaware of her actions, with one long sigh, she removed the bracelet and placed it on the bench. Tenderly, she touched her flat stomach and remembered a pregnancy that never came to be.

Three days after the balding man had made his appearance, Brye confronted her father. She couldn't recall ever seeing him drunk before. Always having prided himself in commandeering complete control, today that control was floating somewhere in the ozone layer.

"I wanna talk to you, youn' lady," he bellowed as she trudged up the stairs to flee to her room.

Three steps from the top, Brye turned. Hand outstretched, her father stumbled up to greet her. "I wan' you t' sign this check ova' t' me," he ordered, his words uncharacteristically slurred.

Only two steps higher than her father, Brye looked down on the million dollar check he clutched tightly within his possession. "No!" Contempt was the only emotion Brye could muster. In search of job and an apartment, hopefully soon, she could leave this house of horrors and be out of her parents' life forever. "I refuse to take Chad's guilt money!"

"I said sign it!" Fangs drawn, snarl deadly, despite the intoxicating liquor, his words rang out loud and clear.

Brye had long given up hope on procuring a genuine father–daughter relationship. She no longer held any respect for her parents and could not remember when she had ceased being afraid of them. Undaunted, she tore the check out of his hand and ripped it in two.

"Go to hell!" She swung her back on him and started up the stairs.

"What that fuck did you just do?" Watching the now ragged pieces of paper flutter to the floor sobered him up quickly. Grabbing her by the elbow, he roared, "Don't you dare walk away when I'm speakin' t' you!"

"Take your filthy hands off me!" Brye pulled free. But before she could get away, he grabbed her shoulders and roughly towed her backward. Brye lost her footing. Caught between a crazy tug of war between gravity and stability, gravity won out as she fell head-over-heels down the stairs. Like a fallen sparrow with broken wings, excruciating pain ripped through every conceivable part of her body as she laid sprawled at the bottom of the steps. Seconds later, she felt the warm flow of blood spilling down her legs. Then, blessedly, darkness took her hostage.

Under the protection of the iridescent moon, Chad situated himself nearby while keeping a conjectural eye on Brye. Shortly after seeing her walk away from the party, he had slipped out behind her.

Sitting amongst the picturesque efflorescence, Brye's untouchable beauty didn't merely add to the floral garden, she enhanced it. Irrespective of the gathered twilight, the honeysuckle vines danced merrily to the mollifying chant of the evening breeze. Chad couldn't dislodge his eyes from the enchanting scene, yet his mind deliberately replayed earlier events.

For whatever reason, his father had baited Brye tonight. The purpose of his urging the psychology student to discuss a subject he cared very little for escaped Chad. Warning bells clanged loud and merciless. And for the life of him, Chad had no idea why he cared—or why he *should* care—what his father or Jennifer or anyone else, for that matter, held in store for Brye. If anything, he should luxuriate in witnessing stalking wolves closing in for the kill, with the remaining bones left for dust. But in all honestly, he felt protective of her.

Vulnerable in seeing her now as he did the first day he had run across her path, if Brye approached him begging for forgiveness, he would readily grant it.

Dammit! he swore to himself, pushing sentimentality aside. It was deadly harboring these irrational feelings toward her. Single-handedly, this woman had almost ruined him…his career…his life. He wanted revenge. And he planned on having it.

First and foremost, he longed for answers. For his own peace of mind, he needed to know why all the lies. Why ask for a million dollars when she could have married him and possessed it all? He would have given her the world had she asked.

Secondly, he wanted to possess her as she had him. Treading slowly, lightly, calling upon every morsel of charm, persuasion and patience inherited from his father, his intentions were to secure her confidence...her devotion...her love. He would have her, all of her...totally, completely. Afterward, when he was certain he owned her body, mind, and spirit, he would single-handedly split open her chest with his own hands, rip her heart out, then cast it aside for the scavengers to finish. Then, and only then, would he feel vindicated.

Vexatious eyes focused once again on the mesmerizing scene. He watched as she shook her hair freely in the opiate breeze. With a heavy rise of her chest, she stood. Turning back to the house, she spotted him and abruptly halted.

Confusion flanked Brye's troubled brow. How had he slipped out without her being aware? Chad and Chad alone, with his male prowess and intrusive sensuality, held the power to shatter the securely guarded wall, solidly constructed around her frail emotions. She could not and would not allow him to strip her to her bare essentials. Steeling herself, with a defiant thrust of her chin, she stood poised for the frontal attack. Cautiously, she waited as he advanced with the grace and beauty of a black panther stalking his unsuspecting prey. More composed than she felt, she asked, "Is there something I can do for you?"

Desire gushed from his eyes and forged a burnished pathway through the eerie glow of moonlight. "For now"—slow music drifting from the New Jersey mansion aroused an urgency to rekindle the feel of her body in motion against his—"you can dance with me."

It was not a request. Simply put, it was a demand. Too emotionally frayed to challenge him, complaisantly—or was it willingly?—Brye silently slipped into his able arms.

On contact, Chad violently reacted to her supple body molding into his. Blood pulsated erotically throughout his loins. Evidence of his wanton urges relentlessly catapulted into Brye's lower abdomen. Surprisingly, she did not edge away. Instead, her body pressed closer.

Within the confines of his arms, every fiber of Brye's being soared into the heavens. Nerve endings bloated with drunken desire, begged for immediate relief.

Much too long, Brye thought to herself. All emotions and sensations had been gathered, sequestered in a strong box, and padlocked for safekeeping for far too long. A key—the one and only—had been pilfered by Chad years ago. Tonight, he had subserviently produced that key, unlocked her restraints, and was now pillaging her soul by the mere touch of his body.

Bodies blended into one as they seductively swayed together. Legs rubbery, Brye securely wrapped her arms around his neck. Content for the first time that evening—for the first time in what felt like a lifetime—she nuzzled her nose against his neck.

Groaning, Chad pulled her closer. His face lowered into fragrant, velvety strands of hair. "You are an enchantress," he mumbled under his breath. "You're a bewitching seductress. And you've placed me under your spell."

Lifting her face to the heavens, Brye stared into an expression distorted with mixed impressions. She could only imagine what was going on in his mind, but she understood perfectly the sensations altering her own churning thoughts. If asked, she would without a doubt abandon her self-imposed prison and give herself freely to this man. The feelings he incited within her warranted nothing less.

Running her fingers through thick, raven hair, she captured his head between open palms. Dragging a steady finger down his stalwart features, she glided her index finger along his top lip.

Slowly, sensuously, Brye slid her finger into his mouth. She drew in a sharp intake of breath as his restless lips enclosed over her finger. The deliberate pressure exerted upon her sensitized digit sharpened her senses. Every inch of her body tingled with desire.

Chad witnessed the urgency in Brye's eyes and knew it was a mere reflection of his own. For days, he'd been plagued with an uncompromising libidinous strain in which Jennifer had not and could not assuage. It was time to obtain the cure.

There was no gentleness in his touch as he dropped his mouth on hers. Years of pent-up frustrations erupted in a maelstrom of greed. Eagerly, he assailed Brye's mind and body. An emaciated man embarking on a palatable feast, Chad devoured Brye. Hungrily, his lips—his tongue—claimed her flaming mouth, her swollen breast, her fluttering abdomen, and her trembling legs as he inched lower.

Between thumb and forefinger, he advanced her long skirt high above her hips. An unrelenting tongue followed, dwelling at a heated stopover along the way. He embraced the essence of her womanhood as he stroked her through the thin layer of lace panties.

Brye ransacked his hair with roving fingers. Head thrown back, eyes blurred, she pulled him deeper into her impassioned body. For years, she had walked around as one of the living dead. But under Chad's ravaging guidance, she reveled in her rebirth. She shivered in growing anticipation as Chad hooked his fingers around her panties and tugged. But before he could slide them past the well-rounded curves of undulating hips, the sudden burst of laughter erupted into the heated night.

The unexpected interruption propelled Brye backward. Cursing to himself, Chad painstakingly climbed to his feet. Brye's rejection irritated him to the point of losing all rational thought. Voice thick with venom—or was it lust?—he angrily retorted, "If I didn't know better, I would think you had missed me over the years. But then again, maybe it's your intention to charm your way back into my life, renew our relationship, regain my trust, and then appropriate even more funds from my family."

His acerbic assertion seared a scabrous pathway down to the very core of her essence. Yet his were the words that verified her earlier presumptions: Chad Collier had nothing to do with their unmerciful dissolution. Her love, given freely and completely, had not been tossed negligently aside. He had not, with malice aforethought, dissolved a relationship because of its hindrance on his career…his life. Behind veiled eyes, Brye's mind reeled as she searched for answers.

Daniel Collier! she groaned. What had she done to deserve such mistreatment? What had Chad done to deserve having his life ripped apart? What kind of picture had Daniel Collier painted for Chad to neglectfully turn his back against her and their unborn without so much as a backward glance?

Down-trodden eyes mourned their lost years as Brye somberly informed, "I've never taken a dime from you *or* your family."

"An extortionist and a liar too!" he spurned.

His bluntness, his inflexible conviction that she had wronged him, pained her more than living without him the past six years. "I don't know what I can do to convince you—"

"Don't even try," he impatiently interrupted, his words hardened by the scowl maligning his face. "I doubt if I'll ever be able to believe a word you say."

"What do you want from me, Chad?" Her eyes were big, pleading, and reflected the partial orb of the glowing moon.

All pretense of gaining her confidence long forgotten, he vengefully sneered, "I want to *fuck* you! Pure and simple."

"Sex?" His nauseating words struck a chord so deep within Brye, she had trouble crawling out to see the light of day. "It all comes down to a quick roll in the hay?" *He's just like the others*, she told herself. He's just like every other man who held no desire to look into her mind because they were too bent on attacking her body. But even as she repeated the words to herself, deep down in her soul, she knew it wasn't true. Chad was not like the others. Chad's harsh words, unlike others, stemmed from the coexistence of living with what he believed to be betrayed love.

"That's *all* it meant to you six years ago. But then again," he maliciously rectified, "maybe it wasn't the sex. For you, it all boiled down to money." Moving in closer, Chad ran a turbulent finger down her heaving chest. Roughly, he enclosed a quivering breast within the clenches of his powerful grip. "Well, sweetheart, maybe I've decided that I didn't get my money's worth and have come back for more! Or"—his grin reeked with lasciviousness as well as contempt—"maybe I'm willing to pay you another million dollars for one weekend of mindless fucking."

A prostitute? Chad wanted to treat her like a common street hooker. Any other time, at any other place, with any other man, Brye would have attempted to rip out his tongue for maligning her self-guarded morality. She and only she could defend her honor. But God help her, as Chad's caresses moved lower and embraced her womanhood, as she recklessly arched her body against his shameful touches, as she bit her bottom lip to keep from begging him to do so much more, she understood how powerless she would be if he took her right now. And that realization alone scared her more than anything else in the entire world. Because sleeping with Chad meant betraying herself and every principle she had created and lived her life by; lying down with Chad meant sleeping with another woman's man. And some promises, when made to one's self, should never, ever be broken.

Brye had to flee from here. She had to get out from under his hypnotic clutches. Now. Before she lost her self-respect; before she lost herself forever. Yanking free of his overpowering touch, she shrieked, "Keep your hands off me, Chad!"

"You didn't seem to have a problem where my hands or lips were a few minutes ago," he leered.

Two red spots suddenly enhanced Brye's heated cheekbones. She prayed the encircling nightfall shielded her undisguised embarrassment. So as not to call attention to her disgrace, she pushed past him. "Stay away from me, Chad!"

With quicksilver swiftness his hand snaked out and grabbed her by the wrist. Pulling her against his chest, he growled down into her startled expression, "That would be difficult to do since you work for me."

Brye fought to maintain an unwavering eye. "My resignation will be on your desk first thing Monday morning!"

"No!" That one word roared like a lion defending what was rightfully his. Anger—or was it fear?—rocked his entire system. He could not let her go. Not now. Maybe not ever.

Why can't you let her go, Collier? An inner voice questioned. *Is it because it would be easier to stop breathing than it would be to live without her in your life again?*

Convincing himself he would only be keeping her around long enough to destroy her, he drove his panic into blinding rage. "We have a contract!" he hissed, neck veins popping to the brink of explosion. "And if you so much as *think* about trying to get out of it, I swear, the only camera you will ever step in front of again will be the pocket kind."

Brye blinked blankly at him. Internally, she heated up with hysteria. Why was he doing this to her? What did he want? Not allowing her apprehension to seep through and be interpreted as fear, she stated with contrived calmness, "Let go of me, Chad!"

"Let her go!" Marcus ordered in a no nonsense tone. Coming up from behind Chad, he addressed Brye. "Are you okay?"

When Chad released her wrist, she sought protection at Marcus's side. "I would like to go home, please."

Nodding, he openly gawked at Chad with a harsh eye. "You go ahead, I'll be right behind you."

"Marcus?" She wrapped resolute fingers around his muscled bicep. She didn't know how much Marcus had heard or how much he thought he might have heard, but she didn't want a midnight brawl erupting on her behalf.

Marcus stared down into Brye's face with such warmth and tenderness, Chad's stomach did a double somersault. Again, he felt that same nuance of jealousy that had jostled him all evening when confronted with the two of them together.

Gently, Marcus disengaged Brye's fingers. "It's okay, sweetheart," he assured. "I promise I'll be right there." He watched her until she moved out of hearing distance. Turning hardened features to Chad, he harshly stated, "I don't know what the hell is going on here! I wouldn't even care except it concerns Brye. Whatever you may think, whatever your so-called friends and family think, Brye has more class and dignity in her one little finger than the collective batch of vultures circulating throughout this entire mausoleum." Marcus shook his head in utter disbelief. "I'm the one who urged Brye into striking out…opening up more to people. Hell," he swore, talking more to himself than to Chad, "I practically pushed her into the lion's den." Redirecting his anger, he ended, "I think you need to be reminded that Brye is a lady first and foremost. I expect you to treat her as such."

Marcus did not wait for retaliation. Doing an about-face, on an afterthought, he swung back to face Chad. Plucking a silk handkerchief from his breast pocket, he thrust it at the scowling man. "Let me give you a fashion tip, *Mr.* Collier. I'd change the color of your lipstick if I were you. Not only does it *not* coincide with your skin tone, but I don't believe it's the same color that your bitch of a girlfriend is wearing." Once again, he turned and stormed after Brye.

Marcus entered the grand reception hall in time to hear TyJuan's rapid-fire diatribe on the injustices Black men suffer under the White man's dominance. By the stench of liquor billowing from his body, and his unbalanced stance, he diagnosed TyJuan to be flying higher than a commercial jet plane. Rolling his eyes heaven bound, he had not believed that the evening could have gotten any worse.

"Let's go home, TyJuan." Tenisha's expression teetered between anger, embarrassment, and a please-help-me-get-him-the-hell-out-of-here attitude.

"I axed Brye a question." Words slurred, TyJuan's tongue hung heavy with booze. "How dozzit feel t' hav'va Black woman indebted t' you?"

Brye shot Tenisha a supportive eye. Together they flanked TyJuan. "I don't think I understand what you're asking," she placated, sliding her arm around his waist.

"Yo' fame an' fo'tunes made my wife a rich lady." TyJuan tore away from the two women. He circled the round entrance table and scowled over a Venetian crystal vase overflowing with fresh pink, white, and yellow tulips. "I think it's mighty *white* o' you t'let her ride on yo coattails."

Stunned, Brye gaped at TyJuan with wide-eyed confusion. This man was her friend, and the recently developed transformation taking place within his face...his eyes...scared the daylights out of her. TyJuan was drowning inside of bitterness and hostility. This was not the man she had come to know and respect.

Altering her tone, she spoke distinctly and patiently, seeking to throw water on smoldering embers. "If you believe what you've just said—and I don't believe that you do—you hold a distorted view of your wife's capabilities and you lack appreciation for her remarkable talents." She reached out to subdue him. "If anyone owes anything, it's I who owes Tenisha. If it wasn't for her, I wouldn't be here today."

"With o' without my wife, you'd have made it." Tossing back his head, he gulped down half the glass of whatever potent drink he clung to at the moment. Launching a sharp eye, he threw poisoned darts at Brye. "With no known skills, you've made a nice livin' steppin' 'n front of a camera. But fo' o'va two hun'nert years, yo' people have oppressed us—we can't ev'n get jobs cleanin' the fuck'n camera lens. Where's the juz'tice?"

Your people? How ironic. Brye deliberated over the genuineness of his biased declaration. A misfit her entire life, outside of abused children, she had never considered herself a spokesperson for one person, let alone an entire human race.

"TyJuan!" Tenisha warned, stepping up to her husband.

"TyJuan, what?" he bellowed, half stumbling into her. "You know damn well what I'm talk'n about! We have t' work twice as hard t' go half as far. And most of us still can't get a fuck'n shake."

Brye's temper rose, like the mercury in a glass-column thermometer. So the man wanted to discuss oppression. Well, Brye could say a lot on that subject. Her emotional stability was on hold indefinitely because of oppression. And injustice? What about the injustices she'd suffered at the hands of her own father, her brother, and the men who, with no conscience to think of, thrust themselves upon her, presuming they could snatch whatever they desired in return for a few measly bucks as payment.

"How *dare* you stand here and profess how horrible you've had it or how bad others have treated you!" Brye seethed. Her ironclad will had just skidded into nuclear meltdown. "My life has not been a bed of roses either. But at least I don't stand around wallowing in self-pity. Every day's a struggle for me. But at least I push on. I don't blame my problems on anyone else."

"'Cuze me?" TyJuan cupped his fingers over his ear. "Did I just hear you right? Did you just fix yo' mouth to say that yo' life hazn't been a bed o' roses? Well…I think it's time you had a reality check, White girl. The color of yo' skin dictates the life you've led. It dictates how far y'all go in life. Havin' a bad hair day, breakin' a nail, wakin' up with a zit plastered all over yo' face, doesn't 'xactly warrant y'all a nomination fo' the bes' sob-story-of-the-year award!"

"Please," Brye spat back at him, "spare me the I'm-a-po'-Black-chile-trying-to-make-a-livin'-in-the-White-man's-world speech!"

Red-rimmed eyes blazed with indignation. TyJuan's words tore from his throat in a strangled cry. "You can't 'magine what it feels like to be looked down on because of who you are! To be passed o'va for jobs! To be—"

"Shut up!" Brye's face raged with indignation. The strain of the entire evening's fiasco smacked her dead in the center of her brain. This was insane. Catering to TyJuan's alcohol-induced tongue was madness. With the exception of Chad, each time Brye had been waylaid by a man, liquor had been a major contributor. Brye could not listen to him any longer. She could not watch him wallow in a bottle of self-pity. She wrapped her hand around TyJuan's fingers, which remained adhered to a half empty glass of scotch. "The only problem you've created for yourself is this!" Teeth clenched, mind locked in the past, Brye braved a maddening desire to fling her repressed rage into his face. "This is turning you into an embittered man. You've methodically lost sight of rational thought and reasoning." Crushing her fingers against his, she shook the highball glass until the amber fluid washed over the sides.

"Step off, bitch!" he screamed, drawing his free hand backward.

Prepared to hit her full force across the face, in a matter of seconds, Marcus shot forward. His hand snaked out like a pit viper and locked around TyJuan's wrist. Caught off guard by the sudden outburst during the heated altercation, Marcus had stood mesmerized, permitting the reckless drama to unfold. He'd never known Brye to verbally attack anyone; she generally remained placid in the face of adversity. This had been a first, and TyJuan's drunken rambling had been the catalyst egging her forward.

"I think it's time you left," he acknowledged in a dangerously low tone.

"Why you wanna sweat me, man? The only place I'm go'n is back in there to get anotha' drink," he tipsily announced, heading straight for the main room.

"Wrong," Marcus decreed, eyes blazing. Four inches and fifty pounds heavier, Marcus was prepared to forcibly remove Tenisha's husband if necessary. Glaring down at TyJuan, he wordlessly let his intentions be known.

TyJuan took one look at Marcus's raging expression and knew he wouldn't hesitate to carry out his threat. Swaying from side to side, under his own prowess, he turned and stumbled out the door.

"I'm sorry, Brye." Tenisha pulled forward to embrace Brye. "He's having a rough time."

Brye smiled weakly. She pulled away. More than anything, she wanted to crawl in a hole somewhere and forget this night ever happened. "I'm the one who's sorry," she countered, not commenting on the cancerous growth overriding TyJuan's system or the destructive path it had taken. "I shouldn't have egged him on." Nervously, her eyes flittered around the empty reception hall. "I just thank God no attention was drawn to us."

A taut smile stretched Tenisha's comely features. Always grateful for Brye's support, she was also aware there was so much more her friend could say yet chose not to. She turned to confront Marcus. The adoration pouring in her heart for this man had shot up several notches. Honorable and chivalrous, Marcus had gallantly rode in on his white stallion to protect a maiden in distress. In this day and age, knights in shining armor where nonexistent. Her smile was hesitant yet displayed a great deal of pride. She laid an earnest hand upon his arm and thanked him.

Lord, save me! Marcus moaned. If she only knew what she did to me. Her fingers were feather-light against his jacket sleeve but weighed heavily on his heart and mind. She raised defying eyes to him, warning him to not take pity on her soul. But in contrast, her quivering chin sought understanding. Marcus would give her all he had to give. "I haven't done anything to warrant a thank you." Barely able to conceal the love he felt for this woman, he rebuffed the desire to crush her to his chest.

"Yes, you did." She stared earnestly into genteel eyes. "You didn't ask me what I was doing married to such an ass?"

"I would never say that." *I would, however, say I love you.*

"I know," Tenisha gratefully acknowledged. She found herself getting lost in those sensitive brown eyes of his. Or maybe she wasn't getting lost. Maybe she was finding herself. Being with Marcus, dancing with Marcus, being held by Marcus had helped her feel alive again; she felt more like herself. And if she looked hard enough, and deep enough, and long enough, she could forecast her future—the kind of future she longed to have.

Without exhibiting signs of jealousy, or the need to compete for her time and love, Marcus would allow her to grow unhindered. Through good times and bad, he would remain a solid bulwark at her side. He was the kind of man she could proudly display to her folks. She could marry this man. Make babies with this man. Live a healthy, happy life with this man. She could—

Tenisha broke visual contact. She strove to slow her racing heart. *See*, she mentally chastised herself. *See what looking into his eyes does to you. He makes you forget you already have a life. He makes you forget you have a husband. He makes you want to throw caution to the wind and follow him to the ends of the earth.* Stumbling backward, Tenisha squeezed the dangerous thoughts out of her mind. "I should be going. In TyJuan's state of mind, he may wander around all night in search for the car." It was a feeble attempt to lighten the air.

"I'll walk you," Marcus offered.

"It's okay." If Tenisha didn't break away from him soon, she might be tempted to go home with Marcus and leave TyJuan to his own befuddled devices. "I'll be fine."

"I'll walk you anyway," he reiterated, more firmly.

Tenisha opened her mouth to protest, but Brye interjected. She wanted to put as much distance as she could between herself and this godforsaken night. "Marcus is a gentleman through and through. He'd feel derelict in his duties if he didn't see you to safety. Don't argue with him or we'll never get out of here."

Tenisha agreed to the escort. Marcus firmly nestled his right hand at the small of her back. Sandwiched between the two women, he guided them out of the den of iniquity.

The black Lincoln Navigator whizzed north along the New Jersey Turnpike. Highway beams glaring at them from moving vehicles traveling southbound flew past like shooting stars. The night was hot and muggy, with no promises of rain in the approaching future. A half-moon played hide-and-seek behind a bank of crystalline clouds. Miles of silence stretched between Marcus and Brye. Separated by their own individual thoughts, they were not aware of the lingering stillness.

In analyzing the evening, Marcus held a better understanding of Brye's aversion to parties. He also understood why she rejected the fellowship of others: no one had ever given her reason to trust.

Men had salivated like wolves when coming in close proximity with the supermodel. But the women—the ones insecure with their own self-worth—subtly renounced her from the sisterhood. In foresight, Brye anticipated the reaction of others. In spite of it all, she had chosen to confront the battle with a distinction of nobility. Through it all, with her soft-spoken manner, her aura of vulnerability coupled with inherent strength and dignity, Brye had managed to pacify a number of egos. In the end, she was able to win respect as well as some hearts. It was no wonder she was one of the highest-paid, most-sought-after supermodels in the country. If she chose to forgo psychology when retiring from the modeling industry, Brye could effortlessly slip into the world of public relations.

His aspirations of protecting her soared higher than the bank of clouds overlooking the moving SUV.

"Why did you go tonight?" Marcus broke the hushed atmosphere, aware that Brye had not only been dissed by party guest, but by an assumed friend as well.

Brye shrugged. She linked her fingers and settled them on her lap. "I was under the impression that one does not refuse the boss."

"Does that include sleeping with him?"

Brye confronted him with a cryptic gaze. His tight expression dodged in and out of shadows as they drove past lighted lampposts. "What kind of question is that?"

"I sure as hell didn't walk out in the middle of you and Collier imbibing in afternoon tea. By his manner alone, I assume he wants more than an employer–employee relationship. Hell!" Marcus squinted as a set of high beams distorted his vision. "Every man in the place looked at you as if they would willingly give their lives if it meant having you as their last supper."

"You don't look at me that way." The statement had risen more out of gratitude than reproach.

"If I did, I wouldn't be here now." He stated with a cynical lift of his chin. "Besides, tonight has only reiterated what I've guessed all the years I've known you."

"Which is?"

"Which is: you need more friends than lovers."

Brye fell silent. Beyond the window, city lights twinkled like fireflies against the black night.

"Do you want to talk about him?" Marcus asked in gentle undertone.

Brye threw the ball back in his court. "Do you want to talk about Tenisha?"

Knuckles tightened around the steering wheel. Several strained seconds later, he gruffly responded, "There's nothing to talk about."

"My sentiments exactly." Attentions were directed back to the road. Overrun with guilt for her unnecessary curtness, Brye faced Marcus again. She spoke with conciliatory awkwardness. "Thank you."

"For what?" Marcus slowed his speed by twenty miles to advance past a construction site.

Her shoulders lifted, then dropped in a poignant shrug. "For caring. For being you. For always being here for me—even when I'm not always the easiest person to get along with. For taking me to the party and looking after me." She shrugged again. "Pick one of those reasons...or all of them. In the end, the message is the same: I'm grateful you're my friend."

Marcus reached over and covered Brye's hand. Huge bear paws affectionately squeezed long, delicate fingers. "I'm grateful you chose me as a friend."

Brye grinned, sloughing off the ill effects of the evening's madcap festivities. "You sure know how to exert your charm when winning a girl's favor."

Squinting at Brye in the dim interior, Marcus feigned annoyance. "Is this an ego thing with you? Do you think every man you meet want to bump uglies with you?"

"Bump uglies?" Brye laughingly repeated. "What a piquant way to say you'd like to take me to bed."

"I don't recall saying that I'd like to take you to bed. In fact, I can unequivocally say that I suggested no such thing. What I *do* recall, is asking if you believe every man you meet want to take you to bed."

"As a matter of fact, yes, I do believe it," she halfheartedly joked. "So get in line, bud! And rest assured, you're the elite standing amongst the elitists."

Marcus laughed. If Brye could joke on a subject she tirelessly strove to avoid, then at least for the moment, the dark cloud hanging perilously over her head had drifted beyond the range of her private grief.

Adding to the joviality, her psychology degree became the target of his light bantering. Marcus noted that after three years, if her analytical interpretation of him was that of a man lying in wait for the chance to steer her into his bed, then she needed to reconsider her job options.

The miles piled behind them. Before they knew it, Marcus was pulling into his driveway. Accompanying Brye to her door, he offered her his customary ear. If she needed to talk, he would listen without judging. Brye declined his generosity. Marcus saw her into her front door, then hightailed it back home.

First on his agenda, he entered his den to check on Rainbow. The large macaw engaged himself by gnawing on the fresh supply of branches his owner had furnished inside his enormous birdcage. In his prolonged absence, Marcus had turned on the radio to keep Rainbow company. Softening the music, he opened the cage door to allow Rainbow access to roam before bedding down for the night. Marcus did not verify if Rainbow took advantage of his newly acquired freedom. He silently slipped out the room.

Shedding his clothing, he dove into the shower. Hot, steamy water channeled down his massive shoulders and expansive back. The pulsating stream of water gradually loosened his tight muscles. But as he began to relax, visions of Tenisha threatened to send body and mind over the edge.

She had made her entrance in a royal blue, off one shoulder, ankle-length dress. The tantalizing gown seductively hugged her well-endowed bodice. The tapered skirt fell in soft gathers around symmetrical ankles. With each step she maneuvered, a side slit projected a hint of shapely thigh. Baring just enough to turn his brain cells into scrambled eggs, his tongue had been laden with lumpy oatmeal when he greeted her. Even now, commemorating on the feel of her supple body brushing against his as they danced spurred him into increasing the flow of cold water.

The torrent of frigid water pummeling over his head carried with it thoughts of TyJuan. There was definitely trouble in paradise. Tonight had been the first time he had ever met the man. His drunken demeanor and total disregard to human life said to Marcus that Tenisha and TyJuan were obviously a science project gone awry.

Earlier, Tenisha had thanked him for not asking why she had married the ass. Although honestly replying that he would never say such a thing, in reality, the thought had traversed down the intricate pathway of his thinking process.

Respecting Tenisha's privacy, as well as protecting the deep feelings he held for her, Marcus had never questioned her marriage. Having assumed the marriage was a healthy one, after one encounter, he knew now that her marriage was anything but healthy. He needed answers. And Brye was the only person who could satisfy his curiosity.

Shutting the water down, Marcus stepped out the shower. He dried himself off and dropped the thick terry cloth towel into a wicker hamper. Naked, he padded out the humid bathroom and into the master bedroom.

About to throw himself on top of his king-size bed, he paused with hand resting on top of the bookshelf headboard. He listened and heard her puttering around in his kitchen. The aromatic smell of baked cookies drifted up the stairs. Donning a robe, he secured the belt and darted out the bedroom.

Her back fronting him, he watched Brye pull a sheet of oatmeal raisin cookies from the oven. Evident by her wet hair, her Garfield nightshirt, and face scrubbed free of makeup, she had taken a quick shower then shot back to his place. The picture of youth and innocence, Marcus wondered about Tenisha's appearance when she stepped out the shower. Did she look as young and vulnerable as Brye appeared now? Or given any situation, did she always appear to be strong and in control? Tonight, she had not been in control. Which led him, once again, to question the circumstances of her marriage.

"You're out of the shower." Brye removed her kitchen mitt. She twisted at the waist to retrieve a cookie spatula from a kitchen drawer.

"I thought you were turning in for the night?" He slid into a kitchen chair.

Brye looked sheepish. One by one, she scooped up cookies from the insulated sheet. "I decided to have a nightcap." In all actuality, after entering her sedate home, in her weakened mental capacity, she did not believe she could face the personal demons lying in wait, ready to pounce. "I didn't think you'd mind."

"You know I don't." He cautiously followed her movement with his eyes.

The microwave timer sounded. Brye removed two steamy mugs: one filled with whole milk, the other brimming with low-fat hot cocoa. She placed the milk in front of Marcus. Retrieving the platter of warm cookies, she hauled them over, then sat down across from Marcus.

Marcus silently studied her. Her hair flowed freely, tumbling in pleasant disarray around sloping shoulders. Her eyes were wide and appealing, like a frightened puppy dog beaten once too often. Her skin was as pale and translucent as skim milk. Drained and distressed, the evening had taken its toll. He sensed her need to talk yet knew she wouldn't initiate the conversation until absolutely ready.

Willing to give her as much time and space as needed, he slowly sipped his milk.

As a toddler, when sleep was long in coming, his mother would bring him a cup of warm milk and two oatmeal raisin cookies. He would climb onto her lap, and she would rock him until his lids grew heavy with fatigue. As a teen, if he couldn't sleep, he would sit at the kitchen table with his mother and drink his milk, eat his cookies, and discuss whatever problem plagued him. Inevitably, the bedtime ritual turned into a proclivity he carried through to adulthood—particularly when he remained alert at the end of a winded day.

He grabbed a cookie. "Whenever I drink this stuff, I can still picture my mother telling me to drink my milk if I wanted to sleep." He bit down into the cookie. "Whenever I questioned her on why warm milk induced drowsiness, she'd tell me to shut up and eat my cookies." Laughingly, he admitted, "She never could give me a reason, but I was always able to finagle more cookies out of her."

Slightly distracted, Brye nodded. She slid two fingers beneath the curved mug handle. Guided by her subconscious alone, she absentmindedly blurted, "Serotonin."

"Excuse me?"

"Serotonin." Brye stared at the linen-textured walls. "A chemical in the brain that regulates sleep. When tryptophan—a chemical component of milk—crosses our blood-brain barrier, it converts into serotonin. Cookies are an added bonus to help clear the pathway for tryptophan." Blank eyes focused on Marcus. "I'm surprised you don't know this, you being a chemical engineer and all."

Marcus shrugged. "I must have been out sick the day we discussed the effects of milk and cookies on the brain."

Brye smiled. "You mean out playing hooky, don't you?"

Like two school chums sharing a secret, they grinned at one another. Slowly, the two grins faded, the room grew quiet. Brye was the first to look away. She stared into the light brown liquid as she swirled the cocoa in its mug.

Taking in a deep, steadying breath, afraid to begin, afraid not to, she established, "I never told you this, but I had a brother." She looked away, staring out the kitchen window and into the abysmal night. "He died when we…when he was seventeen years old." She dipped her eyes under the weight of Marcus's taciturn gaze.

Propelling forward, she continued, "I loved him…more than words could explain. My brother meant the world to me. He was a part of me. And when I lost him, I also lost a huge chunk of myself. After his death, I didn't think I could go on without him. But I *did* survive—not because I wanted to, but because *he* would have wanted me to.

"That same year, I enrolled in college and plunged heavily into my studies. I filled my days with classes, my nights with studying, reading, researching. Nothing else, no one else, mattered to me. Finally, eight months after my brother's death, I met Chad Collier. Actually"—she paused before clarifying—"I did not meet him in the normal sense of the word. He didn't openly approach me the way other men would have. He didn't directly come to me and introduce himself." A trace of a smile dramatically altered her desolate expression, much like a blazing sun exploding upon a cheerless day. "He thought he would frighten me if he openly approached me." Brye's fingernails tapped a nonsensical tune against the tiled tabletop. "Up until that time in my life, I'd had nothing but vile experiences with men." Brye clamped her eye shut against the repulsive memories. Her pain magnified amidst the quiver of her voice.

"There were men"—Brye swallowed back the clump of desperation pooling at the base of her throat—"older men who…who wanted to—" Her eyelids shot open. Her mouth laboriously worked as she struggled to release the words.

Marcus witnessed the terror in her eyes, the same terror darting along his rigid spine. *Good Lord, no! Is this the reason for her mistrust in men? Had she been forcibly violated as a child?* He reached across the table to cover her hand. "Brye?" he spoke with muffled urgency. "Did anyone ever—" He trailed off, unable to verbalize his suspicions.

Brye shook her head. She drew courage from the quiet strength he offered. "No, I was never raped. Not physically anyway. Mentally, however, I was robbed of my youth and innocence. The harsh realities of life forced me to grow up faster than I should have. And whenever someone"—she struggled for a word and wished more than anything she could cry—"whenever someone confronted me, I fought with everything I had within myself to keep them from—" Brye stared at the slew of veins blazing a crooked trail inside Marcus's forearm. The blood vessels contracted as Marcus offered her support in the form of a gentle squeeze. "I vowed I would never, *ever*, let a man violate my body…or I would die trying." Her fury raged into a blinding storm, then settled into a steady dribble.

"Chad was different. He never approached me, and only watched me from a distance. And while he studied me, I studied him. For some inexplicable reason, I didn't feel stalked, or threatened, or misused, or abused. In fact, he was the first man who had ever intrigued me. And when he finally introduced himself, in his immeasurable patience, he drew me out of my shell."

Brye lifted her eyes to Marcus's face. "Before Chad, I was merely going through the motions. I was sleepwalking. Chad awakened feelings I never knew I had inside myself. He opened my eyes and gave me reason to trust. He led me down a pathway rich with love and laughter. And I was finally able to give myself freely, and completely, to a man I learned to love more than life itself. Chad taught me the difference between having sex and making love. And whenever we made love, he helped me to forget."

The faint pitch of Brye's wavering voice dipped into a transcendental state. A smile amended her features as she allowed the memories to flow.

Deep shades of orange, yellow, red, and violet invaded the darkening sky as the sun fell behind the Catskill Mountains. The hypnotic consonance of night tunes sounded as comforting as a baby's lullaby to Brye's sharpened ears. Her acute eyes swept over the highly forested area and rested on the privately owned lake.

The cabin, the oversized pond, the ten acres of land stretched beyond Brye's vision belonged to Chad's family. Two weeks prior to the commencement of the fall term, Chad had convinced Brye to take a week-long sabbatical in isolated seclusion.

"I promise I'll be the perfect gentleman," he convincingly argued against her vacillating position.

Five months of dating Chad and still the perfect gentleman. Despite their sharing of sweltering, clinging kisses, which left Brye aching for more, Chad continually pulled away first.

With each passing day, with each intimate touch, Brye's body begged to join Chad in the way a woman united with the man she loved. She wanted to give herself to him freely, totally, completely. She wanted to lose herself within his touch, his kiss, his body. Never had Brye known such intense desire. Never had she felt a deep-seated need to be fulfilled. Chad lit an internal burn that threatened to incinerate her alive. It was also Chad who capped the lid on her mounting combustion.

Four days. Four days of living with Chad in undiluted bliss. Four days of sharing everything except a bed. True to his word, he had not attempted to make love to her. And she questioned her desirability as a woman. Maybe Chad retained lingering doubts of taking their relationship one step further; maybe he desired her as a friend, not a lover.

Whatever the reason for his maintaining a self-imposed abstinence, Brye had three more days to confront him. More importantly, she had three days in which to seduce him. And despite her inexperience, she was prepared to do anything to entice the man she loved.

The front door of the cabin opened. Brye sensed, more than heard, Chad silently slip up to her backside. Capable, assuring arms secured her waist. Warm breath fondled her cheek as he nuzzled her right ear.

"Are you glad you came?" He spoke barely above a whisper.

Brye could feel his thready heartbeat beneath his sleeveless T-shirt. She also felt the beginnings of his arousal. Turning in his arms, she trapped his face between the palms of her hands. Pulling him downward, their lips rested a hairsbreadth apart. Seductively, Brye breathed, "Let me show you how glad I am."

Lips parted, hungrily, eagerly, she ravaged him with her passion. Her fiery tongue roamed over every inch of his mouth, seeking, capturing, pleasing. Satisfied with the reaction she procured—Chad's body pressed urgently into hers as he met each of her kisses with an ardor of his own—Brye pressed her open palms between the two impassioned bodies. Errant thumbs drew scalding rings around his hardened nipples.

Intent on transferring her lips to where her fingers toyed, roughly, Brye found herself hauled against Chad's feverish body. Entrapping her within his iron grip, he securely held her against his chest; Brye found her struggles to be futile. Hot, ragged breathing pushed past her ear. The erratic pounding of his heartbeat greeted her own jagged pulse.

Minutes later, Chad's breathing settled into some sense of normalcy. Voice thick with desire, he uttered, "Maybe we should take a dip in the lake before settling in for the night?"

Disappointed, forcing the uncontrollable emotion back into concealment, Brye placated, "If that's what you'd like to do."

"It's not what I'd *like* to do," he gruffly admitted, "but it's what I *have* to do."

The candor of his words sharply pricked at Brye's heart. Uncertain as to why he faltered when they drew close to making love, she did sense that his resistance wore thin. Whatever it took, Brye would continue to chip at the indiscernible obstacle hindering them from uniting as lovers. Pulling away, she sprinted down the stairs. "Whoever reaches the lake last has to fix breakfast in the morning!" she yelled over her shoulder, pulling her T-shirt over her head.

Laughing, Chad charged after her.

Later that evening, dripping wet, Brye stepped out of her private bathroom. Instead of donning nightclothes, she snatched the hand-stitched quilt folded at the foot of the queen-size sleigh bed. Barefooted, her steps were smothered against the Persian wool carpet. Moving through the large archaic furnished cabin, she gathered the quilt around her naked body. Brye stepped into the still of the night and folded onto the porch steps.

High above, a galaxy of stars scintillated like flawless jewels. In awe, Brye blinked at the lovely sight.

Oddly enough, for the first time in her life, she felt at peace. Unlike the everyday dilemmas confronting her existence within the real world, this place was her hideaway from the insufferable afflictions weighing heavily on her mind. This place was a fairy tale come true. It was her salvation.

A contented sigh escaped her sullen lips as Chad slipped beside her.

"Are you okay?" he asked, interpreting her exaggerated exhalation as one of weariness.

As usual, whenever he drew near, Brye felt the early stirring of a craving begging to be satisfied. Soon she would be experiencing the effects of full blown hunger pangs gone unsatisfied. It was time to seek sustenance.

Leaning into him, she rested her head on his shoulder. "I'm not sure," she answered with a contemplative sigh.

Brye lost the warmth and support Chad's massive body provided as he silently slipped out from under her. Under the shadowy blanket of the fallen night, his handsome features grew cloudy with worry. "Tell me what's wrong?" he disturbingly beseeched.

"I'm experiencing sensations I've never felt before," she answered, a teasing lilt belied her contrived distress. "There's a high probability that I've fallen in love." She heard his intake of breath and felt the tension drain from his body. "But I'm not really sure because I've never been in love before. So…I was kind of hoping you'd help me sort out my feelings by detailing the major symptoms."

Astonished pleasure exploded deep from within. Intertwining their fingers, Chad lifted her hand to his mouth. Brushing his lips against the back of her hand, he spoke softly against smooth, soft skin. "Love is a feeling…an unmanageable fluttering sensation boiling in the pit of one's stomach. It augments in intensity whenever the loved one crosses the mind."

Unconvinced, Brye prudently shook her head. "That could be indigestion…or a bleeding ulcer."

"Love is when exposed skin ignite into a burst of flames from a mere touch or a light caress," Chad pressed forward, drawing a steady finger along the hollow of her neck.

"Sunburn," Brye easily repudiated, quivering under his nimble touch.

"It's the middle of the night."

"Delayed reaction."

Chad smiled. He took a different approach. "A couple strolling in a pasture find themselves confronting a charging bull. Love is when one pushes the other aside and places himself in the pathway of impending danger."

Dauntless, Brye affirmed, "That, my love, is sheer stupidity."

A cacophony of night sounds sliced through the ripened darkness. Chad's laughter dissected the congested euphony. Deliberately, his face inched toward Brye. Dropping his mouth on the tip of her nose, he replied, "You know, it really doesn't matter if you're unsure of your love for me." His tongue delicately stroked her upper lip. "Because I'm safeguarding enough love for the both of us."

"Are you really?" Brye murmured against his roving lips. Opening her mouth wider, she drew him into her private sanctum.

"I love you, Brye," he breathed into her eager mouth.

Abruptly, Brye pulled away. Eying him somberly, she asked, "If that's true, why haven't you tried to make love to me?"

"It's not because I don't want to." Grave eyes converged onto her anxious visage. "I've wanted you since the first day I met you."

"It's been five months?" She left the question hanging in the air.

Chad clasped her fingers between his powerful grip. "Brye… Baby…from the first moment I saw you, I knew you were like no other woman I have ever met before. Once I came to know you, you proved me right.

"I've loved you long before the first time we spoke. But I knew if I pushed too hard, the risks were high that I'd lose you." Tenderly, he squeezed her fingers. "I'm playing for keeps, Brye. And if it means waiting until you are ready to handle an intimate relationship, then I'll wait for as long as it takes."

Her smile was hesitant, shy. "Maybe I wasn't prepared for what's transpired between the two of us over the past few months, but since I've known you, you've taught me so much about relationships. You've taught me that there could be so much more between a man and a woman besides sex." Brye broke loose from his comforting grip and ran a steady finger under the length of his freshly shaved jaw.

"I've never been more certain or more ready of anything in my life. Please, Chad. Please make love to me."

Chad reached up and, once again, captured her fingers within his. "Brye…"

Brye took note of the inferred rejection she heard in his speech. She noted the hesitation in his eyes. Suddenly, she felt like the rejected suitor. Chad did not want her. At least not the same way she wanted him. Her pride deflated. How ironic that so many men had thrown themselves at her for years, and here was Chad, a man she would willingly give her heart and soul to, turning her down flat. She swung her back on him while choking down a sob.

"Brye, don't." He wrapped his arms securely around her. Lowering his face into aromatic strands of her thick hair, he begged, "Don't turn away from me." Soft lips traced the outline of her ear, down the side of her face. "I *do* want you…more than anything else in the world. But when I convinced you to take this trip with me, I also promised that I'd be the perfect gentleman. And the only way to ensure that pledge was to come up here without any"—he faltered—"protection."

The strain of the past few moments trickled from Brye's body and dissipated into the blackened night. She turned to face Chad. "I don't care about protection," she groaned into his neck. "I love you so much. And I trust in you. By my own free will I give myself as a token of my commitment to you." Pushing away, she captured his gaze with her own. "If something happens, if I do become pregnant, I trust you—I trust *us*—to come to a rational decision that will be in the best interest for everyone involved. And that doesn't mean I'm expecting you to cart me off somewhere and marry me. It merely means that together we'll decided on the best course of action."

Chad pulled her into his impassioned body. Clinging to her tightly, he whispered against her ear, "Are you sure about this?"

Brye pulled away from his imperial hold. She stood. Parking herself in front of him, she lowered the delicate quilt. It fell in soft gathers around her bare feet. Pleased with the sudden reaction emitted from Chad—lust tinted his eyes, an audible gasp escaped his lungs—Brye purred, "Is this proof enough for you?"

"Come here." Desire heavily gushed from the two spoken words.

Brye inched closer. She straddled his lap. The essence of her womanhood immediately tingled with heated pleasure as her inner thighs rubbed against the solid bulge straining against the thin material of his shorts. Seductively, she ground against him as he slipped a swollen nipple between moist lips. Nimble fingers lightly kneaded the opposite quivering breast.

Brye glided impatient fingers down the rock solid peaks and valleys of his rib cage. Her fingertips slid inside the elastic band cinching his channeled waist. "I don't want to wait any longer, Chad. Please, make love to me."

Climbing off his lap, she hooked her finger over his shorts. With his assistance, she hustled to remove the only opposition standing between them. With wide-eyed amazement, she stared at his well-endowed asset.

"Chad," she nervously uttered, managing to tear her gaze away. In her eyes, he appeared larger than life. Suddenly feeling eminently awkward, and very much inexperienced, she feebly smiled. "I'm not very worldly at this. I haven't…"

"It's okay," Chad reassured. He guided his fingers around her waist. Pulling her into him, his lips prowled along the slightly convex yet taut arch of her abdomen. Inching lower, his face sunk into the covert of fine, dark, velvety strands of hair sheltering her womanhood. He spoke with muffled voice, "We'll go slowly. And only when you're ready."

He used his fingers to part sensitized folds of delicate skin, but it was his tongue that infringed upon the warmth moistness of her insides. With the proficiency of a man understanding the complexities of pleasing a woman, Chad soothed, caressed, and teased her into complete submission. With each pleasurable stroke, she shamelessly lost all control of rational behavior. Pants and whimpering—sounds oblivious to her own ears—scampered from low inside her throat. Threading her fingers around strands of his raven hair, she hauled him closer. Knees slightly flexed, she rocked with unbridled movements as she generously offered herself to him.

Floundering dangerously in the midst of a turbulent wave, Brye no longer retained sole ownership of her quivering body. But despite the all-consuming force rendering her helpless, she was not ready to drown in a sea of abandoned love. Abruptly vacillating on her feet, as well as in her mind, she pulled away.

"Please...Chad." She breathed the words in short puffs. "I want...my first time to be...with you...inside me."

Raising his face to hold her impassioned stare, he asked, "Are you sure?"

She nodded. "I've never been more sure, or ready, of anything in my entire life."

On the porch steps, once again, Brye straddled his legs. And as he guided himself into her, solicitously, Brye lowered herself onto his throbbing organ. Body empowered with a deep longing to be fulfilled, she only felt a fleeting measure of discomfort as an inextricable thrust perforated the barricade covering the most intimate haven of her body.

More concerned with the sensation of his thickness overriding her every awareness, she stiffened for a brief second, then allowed him to continue filling her with his manly strength.

Once every inch of him hid inside her eager body, breathing a sigh of contentment, Brye collapsed onto his chest.

"Are you okay?" Chad raised his face to meet hers. Soft, fragrant hair spilled over enraptured features. He tenderly pushed the strands aside and stared into violet-colored eyes intoxicated with love.

"Mmm." Brye smiled down into his concerned features. "Sitting here with you warming my insides feels so-o-o-o wonderful."

"Oh yeah?" Chad's eyes twinkled with laughter. "If you think this feels good, let me show you something you'll really love."

Brye bent forward and began nibbling on his earlobe. "By all means, Mr. Collier. Class is now beginning. And being the eager student that I am, I'm ready, willing, and able to learn—with profuse enthusiasm, I might add."

Under the cover of flirtatious stars, Brye and Chad lost themselves within each other. Two fervid bodies danced in pleasurable unity to the rhythm of the night. Strangled cries of ecstasy bounced off immersed blackness. Each deliberate stroke Chad rained upon Brye met its intended purpose. Within a matter of seconds, Brye took flight. Towering high above the trees, bursting through the clouds, she found herself soaring amongst celestial bliss.

A millisecond later, Chad joined her in the conquest to grab a piece of the sparkling sky. Together, gasping for air, clutching frantically at one another, they recklessly descended to planet earth.

Bare breast beat erratically against bare breast. Labored breathing overcame the chaotic harmony whispering through the tree branches. The first to recover, Chad attempted to pull out from under Brye.

"No…don't." Brye nestled more comfortably in Chad's lap. "I love feeling you inside me."

Securing his arms around Brye's trembling body, silently, Chad reveled in the aftermath of their lovemaking. "You were wonderful," he breathlessly praised.

"You *are* wonderful," Brye announced with a sanguineous grin. "So much so I'm ready for class to begin again."

Chad chuckled. "Just give me a few minutes to recuperate."

Instinctively, Brye's pelvic muscles contracted against him. Slowly, steadily, she forged a trail of kisses from the tip of his head down to the hollow of his neck. "Is there anything I can do to speed up the process?" she whispered seductively.

"Oh god, baby!" he groaned in distinct pleasure. Still inside her, he found himself growing hard again. "You're doing it."

"Do you think you still love him?" Full of questions, Marcus listened to her tale of love in silent support.

Brye frowned. "I never allowed myself to think about him at all." It was the truth, albeit a distorted one. On a conscious level, she had pushed him back to the remotest section of her brain. But just like her parents and twin brother, he continued to plague her within the obscurity of her tormented sleep.

Confusion overrode her bellowing emotions. "It's strange, but after all these years, he still has the power to turn my life upside down. God, Marcus!" Her voice trembled at the horrific acknowledgment. "He still turns my insides into quivering Jell-O every time he touches me...whenever he looks at me."

"Maybe Chad's suffering from the same dangerous afflictions," Marcus established, forming his own opinion after analyzing the events of the night.

Astonished with his unanticipated proclamation, Brye asked with trepidation, "You met him tonight for the first time. How can you draw that conclusion so fast?"

"From what little I witnessed, by the way he looked at you, the way he responds to you," Marcus answered with certitude. "He appeared to be a man struggling with his own inner turmoil. Pain... anger...distrust...and if you dig deep enough, you would also uproot remnants of love."

An infinitesimal ray of hope glittered in the violet recesses of her troubled eyes. "Do you think there's a chance—" She put an abrupt halt to her wistful thinking.

Immediately picking up on her yearning thoughts, Marcus asked, "If the love you felt for him has remained intact, if it was potent enough to withstand years of separation, why did the two of you call it quits?"

Brye rushed to explain how their relationship had progressed, then abruptly shattered into irreparable fragments with no forewarning. She also enlightened Marcus of the sentence—she believed—that had been handed down to her, as well as Chad, by the scathing hands of Chad's father.

"Tonight, I'm finally able to accept that he remains a big part of myself. He's in my blood. He's the first man—the only man—I've ever loved. We had a wonderful relationship, Marcus." She greeted his skeptical sneer with a determined eye. "And I think I can get it back."

"I don't know about your past relationship with him, but I know how men think. And I know about holding on to grudges." Marcus's nostrils dilated, resembling a charging bull. "Chad wants revenge, Brye. He thinks you drew first blood, so he's returned to extract his pound of flesh."

His large hand continued to shelter Brye's. Speechless, she shoved away from him. She circled her mug with her fingers and took a sip. The liquid had long grown cold. Brye clucked her tongue and set the mug down.

Time trudged slowly forward. The hand-painted clock hanging on the kitchen wall ticked at a sluggish beat. Even Marcus's breathing deliberated at a leisurely pace.

Brye's cheeks puffed out like a filled pastry, then slowly deflated as the air pocketed in her mouth expelled through compressed lips. Gathering her thoughts, she finally admitted, "Chad's hurt. I realize that. But I also recognize that if he didn't still care, if he didn't harbor deep-seated feelings for me, I wouldn't be able to incite his fury." Brye dropped her hands to her laps. She leaned heavily into the back of her chair. "If he treated me with relaxed indifference, then I'd know it was really over between us. But he can't do that. Because the feelings are still there. And they're so strong, and so real, it's killing him to think I threw away the life we could have shared together."

"Why don't you tell him the truth?" Marcus stood, carrying the two partially filled mugs with him. Rinsing the cups clean, he stored them inside the dishwasher. "Why not tell him what his father has done?" he asked as he returned to the table.

With pained expression, Brye readily admitted, "Because I want him to realize that I would never betray him. I want him to learn to trust the feelings we had for one another…still. I was wrong for instantly jumping to the wrong conclusion. I should not have readily believed that he wanted to buy me off those many years ago. I realize now I should have confronted him myself. I should have trusted him. But I was mad and I was hurt, and past experiences established my frame of mind at that time." Brye leaned forward. She hugged herself just below her breast. "But *that* was in the past. If I can confront him with an insurmountable wealth of patience and understanding now, I know I can turn his pain around. I know I can get back what we used to share."

Marcus was in love with a married woman. For that reason alone, he could not crush Brye's hopes in achieving a dream that may never come to be. Hell, if anyone knew about going after the unattainable, he did. But because of the high probability of failure, because of the pain he endured every day in yearning over a woman unavailable to him, as a friend, he would be derelict in his duties if he didn't say, "You may be setting yourself up for a great fall, Brye. He may never get over his pain. And in the process, he may hurt you more so now than you've ever been hurt before."

It was Brye's turn to push away from the table. She grabbed the platter of cookies and turned her back against Marcus and her shame. And she did feel ashamed. Because she was about to break one of her own carefully guarded rules. How could she tell Marcus that it didn't matter how hard Chad struck out at her? If he sought revenge, so be it. How could she tell Marcus that she, for the first time in her life, would willingly accept whatever abuse Chad rained upon her? How could she explain that in the course of one night, Chad had turned her entire world topsy-turvy? And topsy-turvy felt a hell of a lot better than the pretense of an existence she had survived thus far.

The remainder of the cookies stored away in the Victorian-designed cookie canister, Brye swung around to face Marcus…to face herself…to seal her fate in stone. "I love him, Marcus. In the short time he's returned to my life, I've been able to breathe again."

Marcus stood, hip resting against the edge of his table. Brye strolled to his side, eyes locked and begging him to understand. "Tonight, when he touched me, when he *kissed* me"—her stomach danced wildly at the remembrance of his lips pilfering every ounce of her self-control as they inched their way down her fevered body—"when he set my soul on fire, I knew I wasn't dead. And I know that *he*, and only *he*, can remove the shroud covering my stalled heart. His love is the only thing I'll ever need to make me complete…to fulfill my needs." Brye gripped his forearm tenaciously, as if afraid he would walk away before he gained understanding.

"And if bitterness and anger is all he has to offer, I'll surrender to that pain as well. Because when I feel his rage, it means I'm feeling *something.* And anything is better than this empty hollowness I've endured the past six years without him."

Marcus grabbed her arm and swung her into his chest. His arms went around her waist, his lips nuzzled the side of her head. Marcus had grown to care deeply for this tortured young woman. Maybe because she remained so vulnerable—even when she seemed in control. Maybe it was because she didn't have anyone who cared—at least not the way she deserved to be cared for. But the love he sheltered for Brye did not go beyond the boundaries of anything other than sisterly devotion. And what he was about to say, what he would be forced to do if necessary, he knew, would be nothing less than what he would carry out to protect his own blood born sisters. "If you love him that much, if you feel you have to pursue this, I won't interfere." Pushing her at arm's length, he stared intently into her eyes. "But you have to know, up front, that I will not stand idly by and allow him to hurt you."

"Oh, Marcus." Brye planted her palms against the side of his face. Her skin paled in comparison to his dark honorable features. She insulated his evening's growth of whiskers within the warmth of her touch. This was new to her: caring for a man who cared for her, not as a sex object, but as a person and friend. She wanted to say she loved him, but the uncertainty of her feelings staid her tongue. She wanted to stretch upward, balancing on her toes, and kiss him dead on the lips, but didn't know if it would be deemed appropriate. She wanted to indicate how much she appreciated his kindness and concern, but wasn't certain if he'd misconstrue the depth of her feelings. So, instead, she satisfied herself with saying, "My guardian angel. What did I ever do to deserve you?"

11

*B*RYSON STEPPED INSIDE HER *parents' apartment and came face-to-face with the big bad wolf disguised in grandmother's clothing. She gaped at the dirty brown fuzz sprinkling the top of his head, the leering brown eyes, the massive snout, the sharpened incisors, the massive drooling tongue, the thick batch of hair covering his paws, and a scathing voice inside her head taunted…*

"My, my, my…what big hands you have."

"All the better to grope you with, my dear."

"Where're my parents?" Leery, Bryson stood with back against the entrance door.

"They stepped out for the evening." The wolf smirked, anxious for the games to begin.

Bryson's eyes grazed past his shoulder. She skimmed the elegant living room in search of Tyson.

"We're all alone," the mangy wolf purred at her with a sly grin.

He inched closer. His huge feet tapped noisily on the foyer floor. "Your mother tells me you're a virgin."

Bryson glanced to her right. She was scared but refused to show it. Stay calm, she told herself, calculating the distance between herself and the stairs. "I fail to see what that has to do with you." Her voice remained placid in the face of adversity. Bryson turned her back to the filthy animal. Her hands curled around the crystal doorknob. The door was half open before the thick paw shot past her shoulder and collided against the white oak gateway to freedom. Bryson cringed as the alarming sound of safety slammed shut in her face. She grew rigid as his front rubbed against her backside.

"I can do so many things for you if you let me," his gruff, repugnant voice bellowed in her ear. "I have money, and I'll pay well."

If his spoken intentions weren't clear, his talons, kneading her breast like a farmer milking a cow, said it all. It was too much for Bryson to handle.

Crazed, she whipped around to face him. Her elbow hooked him under his eye. He howled and doubled over in pain. Bryson darted around him. She dashed into the kitchen. A cutlery block containing eight various-sized butcher knifes topped the utility cart. Bryson grabbed the most menacing-looking blade and cautiously crept her way past the living room.

"You bitch!" the wolf growled. His good eye zoomed in on the knife—the right eye was beginning to resemble an overripe tomato. "Who the fuck do you think you are? I got half a mind to—"

Bryson closed her ears to the slew of insanities flying at her. Fronting him, knife angled to slash if necessary, she carefully backed up the stairs. At the top of the landing, she turned and fled to her room. With the bedroom door closed and locked behind her, she slumped to the floor in unbridled terror.

Four hours after leaving the safety of Marcus's kitchen, Brye woke with a start. It was not unusual for her to wake with tearstained pillows. This morning, in addition to the waterlogged cases, her bed sheets were soaked as well. Sometime during the night, she had broken into full-bodied night sweats.

Images of unborn babies flickered dangerously close to the border of her consciousness, the same images that had tormented her during her restless sleep. Her defense mechanism instantly shifted gears and slid into automatic pilot. All traces of past skeletons were pushed back into the closet.

Rolling onto the floor, Brye stripped the bed of its sheets. Steadfast, she went about her daily routine with animated movements. Loading the washing machine, remaking the bed with a fresh set of linens, preparing clothing needing to be dropped at the cleaners, none of her chosen tasks required a conscious effort on her part. She carried them through with the efficiency of a programmed computer.

Two hours after climbing out of bed, Brye dove into the shower. Hot, steamy, invigorating water pellets revitalized her fatigued soul. Closing her eyes, she lifted her face to the showerhead and marveled at the soothing efficacy induced by the cascading deluge.

For several seconds, she stood motionless. Finally, pulling away from the mainstream of water, she poured a generous amount of shampoo into the palm of her hand. As she worked up a thick lather, she began putting her day together.

Having formulated no earlier plans, she thought about driving to Brylinn. The mercurial kids would keep her mind, as well as body, thoroughly occupied.

"Brye?" Marcus's voice filtered into the shower stall. He maintained a respectable distance by standing just outside the open bathroom door.

"Marcus?" Brye yelled over the cascading water. "What are you doing up so early?"

"It's eleven o'clock, Brye."

"But I didn't leave your house until four this morning. Didn't you get any sleep?"

"I could ask you the same question," Marcus keenly remarked. "I saw you out on the patio refilling your bird feeder." In all actuality, with mind speculating over Tenisha's plight, he fitfully dozed off and on for several hours. Finally giving up all pretense of catching any sleep, he'd gotten up to make himself a strong cup of coffee. That was when he peered out the kitchen window and spotted Brye. In worrying on how the woman he secretly desired fared overnight, he elected to accost the closest source.

"So…" Brye smiled to herself. She smoothly teased, "Did you come over to wash my back?"

"If I had intended to wash your back," Marcus countered with lightness, his elbow resting atop her armoire entertainment center, "my clothing would be strewn on the bathroom floor and I'd be in the shower with you by now."

"I guess I should take that as a no."

"You damn skippy, you should!"

Brye laughed. "Then what can I do for you?"

"I was wondering if you would care to jog to the lake, do a few miles around the path?"

"I think I'd like that," Brye readily agreed. Back turned to the faucet, chin pointed to the ceiling, she rinsed the lather out of her hair.

"Good. I'll wait for you downstairs." Marcus hesitated before moving away from the door. His intentions purely selfish, he planned on spending the entire day with Brye in the hopes of hearing from Tenisha. Yet, suddenly, he wondered if Brye had already heard from her this morning.

"Brye?" he cautiously advanced. "I was wondering if Tenisha made it safely home last night. Have you spoken to her?"

"No," Brye admitted, recoiling at the thought of having pushed Tenisha out of her mind until now. "I'll call her as soon as I get dressed. If she doesn't have anything planned, I'll invite her to join us—if you're not in that much of a hurry to get going."

It took every ounce of manpower to refrain from dropping to his knees and singing praises to the Lord. "No," he kept his voice level, "I'm not in any hurry." Exiting her bedroom, his feet floated above carpet as he took the stairs down two at a time.

Halfway to the bottom, the doorbell erupted the stillness of the house. Thinking it could possibly be Tenisha, he dashed toward the door and practically tore the heavy wood off its hinges. Much to his disappointment and stupefaction, Chad hovered at the threshold.

Both men covered their surprise well. Both men eyed the other cautiously. Chad was the first to break the culpable silence. "Is Brye here?"

"Yes."

They stared at each other a bit longer.

On the realization that Marcus was not about to volunteer any more information than necessary, Chad pushed on, "May I see her, please?"

"If you don't mind waiting. She's taking a shower."

Chad was taken aback but strayed from his true emotions. "I don't mind."

Marcus looked past Chad's shoulder. In contrast to the steamy night, the day roused with a teasing sun and playful, nonvirulent clouds. The insistent roar of lawn mowers ensnared the newly developed subdivision, the smell of cut grass permeated the air as neighbors took advantage of the languid morning.

Marcus focused on the bright red Maserati, barely clearing the ground, parked in Brye's double drive. Eyes falling back on Chad, he gave him a look that said, *So you like playing with toys?* The practical side of him asked, "How does that thing fare in New York winters?"

"It doesn't."

"I didn't think so." He stepped aside.

"You don't like me very much," Chad pointedly asked as he brushed past Marcus.

"That's not true," Marcus just as pointedly answered. "I haven't known you long enough to pass that kind of judgment." He directed Chad to the living room and urged him to sit. Still standing himself, he added, "Of course, I believe I've known you long enough to say that I don't respect you. But then a man with your wealth and power can buy all the respect he'll ever need."

"Ouch. After last night, I guess I deserved that," Chad conceded.

Marcus seared him with another look that stated, *You'd know better than I.* He said, "Can I get you something to drink?" He ambled toward the kitchen. "Of course, since Brye doesn't drink, she probably has nothing stronger than bottled water."

Curious about the big man's presence, more curious with the familiarity of his moves inside Brye's home, Chad resolved himself to question Marcus's alliance with composed subtlety.

Forgoing the offer of a drink, his next question was as subtle as an alley cat in heat. "Do you live here?"

If Marcus was surprised with the question, he did not appear so. Taking his time, he ambled to the Regency chair opposite Chad. He folded his large body into the soft cushions. Leaning forward, he planted his elbows on bare, muscular, thighs. He could barely contain his amusement. "It depends. In what context are you using the word *here*?"

"In what context should I be speaking?"

"In general terms, yes, I do live *here*...in this neighborhood. Specifically, I don't live in *this* house. Brye and I are next-door neighbors."

Chad's next question was as subtle as the first. "Did you sleep here last night?"

One eyebrow raised, he asked with no hesitation, "Are you asking in the capacity of Brye's employer? Or have you taken a personal interest in her sleeping habits?"

"Does it make a difference?"

"As a matter of fact, it does. If you're asking as an employer, than I can only answer by saying: how Brye spends her personal time, and who she sleeps with, is of no concern to you or Romanique Cosmetics. But"—one eyebrow raised in amused consideration—"if your motives are strictly personal, I might be inclined to respond."

Chad held Marcus's gaze with an unwavering eye. The entire night, he had brooded over the inconsistent behavior Brye invoked within himself. It was imperative he gained her trust. In order to carry through with his plan, he needed to procure her confidence. But he could not secure a relationship with Brye if he couldn't keep a plug on his own pain and bitterness. Somehow he sensed that if he wanted to get near Brye, he needed to go through Marcus. And if it meant treating this large man with kid gloves, then so be it—Chad would do whatever necessary to achieve retribution.

"My inquiry has nothing to do with the company," Chad ultimately assured.

Marcus weighed Chad's response carefully. Studying the man intently, he was unable to decipher the wheels turning behind the cryptic gaze. Still, there was a deep emotion lingering just beneath the surface that could not be suppressed. An emotion Marcus could easily decipher as love. *Maybe Brye's right*, he told himself. *Maybe she will be able to break through the surface of his unmitigated anger.*

He decided to go with the truth. "No. I did not sleep here last night."

"What's going on between you and Brye?"

"Brye and I are close friends."

"How close?"

"Close enough to value our friendship. Close enough to have formed an instinctive need to protect her. Not so close we're sleeping together."

The room fell quiet as Chad mulled over the answer. Marcus settled more comfortably in his chair. He observed Chad with a keen eye. Twenty questions had come to an end as far as he was concerned. It was time to collect answers of his own.

"What's the purpose of this visit?" he began.

Chad's lips tightened in a gaunt smile. "I've come to apologize...to Brye. And since you're here, I'd like to apologize to you as well." He dug inside his shirt pocket. "I'd also like to return her bracelet. She left it in the garden. Things got a little...heated, last night," Chad annotated as Marcus reached across the round table to take the bangle. "My behavior was out of line. I—" He trailed off as the sound of Brye's voice filtered into the room from the entryway. The adrenaline took flight and pulsated throughout his system.

"Have you seen *Whatever Happened to Baby Jane*, Rainbow?" Chad heard her ask. He could not translate the high-pitched voice that followed.

"Well, how would you like to be served up on a silver platter for dinner?" the high-pitched voice began to laugh.

"You think that's funny," Brye responded. "Let me catch you in my body powder again and I'll show you—"

Brye entered the living room. She halted in midsentence at the sight of Chad, looking as dazzling as ever, in worn blue jeans and beige-colored polo shirt.

Both men stood upon her entrance. She focused on Marcus first. Confusion played across features untainted with makeup, as if Chad had suddenly materialized from the fine threads of her living room carpet.

As soon as the look appeared, so did it disappear. "Look, Rainbow," she said, "we have company. Say hello."

"Hello," Rainbow squawked.

Turning her attention back to Chad, Brye graced him with a smile she reserved for the general public: engaging, welcoming, yet slightly detached.

"To what do I owe the pleasure of this visit?"

Chad experienced the familiar tug in his groin as he responded to her overt sensuality. Like a man who'd thirsted much too long for water, he gluttonously drank in every inch of her succulent torso.

Hips and thighs hugged spandex shorts. Floral sports bra doubled as second skin. Soft, feminine curves, well-designed arms and legs, smooth healthy skin, Brye represented a walking Rembrandt. And added to the picturesque sight: a large, tropical bird rested contentedly upon her bare shoulders. At this moment, Chad accepted the fact that he would do anything to possess her—body, mind, and soul.

Thrusting the unconscionable thoughts from his head, he plastered a demure smile across his lips. "We need to talk."

She shot him a quizzical eye. "You could have picked up the phone…or waited until I came to the office."

Chad maintained enough grace to lower his eyelids. "I wasn't certain you wanted to come back to work."

Brye lifted a defiant chin to Chad. "Did you leave me with any other choice?"

"I want to apologize for that."

"Why don't I leave you two alone?" Marcus interrupted. He released a sharp, shrill whistle. The colorful bird gracefully flew to his shoulder. "Brye, I left a bag of Rainbow's mixed fruits in your bedroom." He shoved her bracelet into her hands. "Could you get it for me?"

Brye hurled him a questioning stare. When he innocently stared back, she elected to do his bidding without objecting.

Once she left the room, Marcus hauled his muscle-bound body over to Chad. He stood dangerously close. Eyes sunk deep into his forehead, his face took on a menacing shade. Voice low and cocksure, he snarled, "Whatever's going on between you and Brye is *your* business. But the moment you lift a finger to hurt her, you better believe I'll make it *my* business." Talking through clenched teeth, he readily assured, "I don't give a *damn* who you are, I don't care about your powerful connections. If you harm her in any way, shape, or form, I swear you'll pay."

"Marcus?" Brye stood, just inside the arched entryway, holding the bag of dried fruits.

Marcus's face cleared. A smile catered to his good looks. In long strides, he met Brye. Slipping the bag from her fingers, he bent to kiss the corner of her mouth. "I'll wait for you at home."

Brye had entered on the tail end of Marcus's brutal admonition. Where she was concerned, he sustained a protective streak a mile long. For that reason alone, she could not fault him, nor did she register any rancor toward him. She smiled appreciatively. "Thanks, Marcus."

The grin he returned endorsed genuine feelings; he offered unconditional support. "Chad?" He strolled over, smile in place, right hand out, no bad feelings clouding his congenial mood. "It's been a pleasure. I'm sure we'll be meeting again."

Neither intimidated nor frightened by the gallant threat, Chad apprehended a deep-seated respect for the man's need to safeguard Brye. His smile was equally as pleasant. "Of that I have no doubt," Chad agreed, accepting his hand in farewell.

"Can I get you something to drink?" Brye asked upon the closing of the front door.

"Marcus offered…I turned him down. But thank you."

She nodded, expecting nothing less from Marcus. "Would you like to sit down?"

Chad returned to his vacated chair. Determined to maintain her distance, Brye retreated to the farthest, most distant corner of the room. Sitting, she clasped her fingers together and rested them in her lap. Guardedly, she waited.

Chad's initial response was to leap at her, pull her into his arms, and kiss her into complete submission. He wanted to crumble that resolute demeanor she so diligently upheld.

He remained where he sat and studied his surroundings "You have a lovely home."

"Thank you."

"It's soft…refined…comfortable?"

"It's not what you expected?" she asked with a cocked eyebrow.

"Someone with your…resources…" He shrugged, allowing her to draw her own conclusions.

Brye immediately went on the defense. "Did you expect something flashier? Something more conforming to my lifestyle, something sitting in the neighborhood of several million dollars?"

Chad refused to be goaded. "Actually, this house is just what I would expect from the Brye I *thought* I knew…the Brye I fell in love with."

"The Brye you *thought* you knew is sitting in front of you."

Anger flashed. "The Brye I *thought* I knew never existed."

"Yes…she did." Brye looked imploringly into his eyes. "You have to know that she was real…and desperately in love with you."

The pleading in Brye's eyes touched Chad's heart. Her look melted the quintessence of his soul. Part of him wanted to believe her. Another part felt himself being sucked into a whirlpool of deceit yet again. This time, he would not fall for her pack of lies.

"Then you're a damned liar!" *So much for gaining her trust.* Chad loosened the rein on his repressed anger, his expression darkened. "The only thing you loved, or cared about, was my money. To you, I was a pawn. A puppet on a string. And like a fool, you had me dancing to the tune of one million dollars."

Once before, Brye had denied his caustic allegations. It was pointless to deny them again. Yet she was unable to let the claim stand. "I never used you, I never took money from you, and I never, *ever*, lied to you."

Brye studied him with a contemplative eye. She stood and moved to his side. Sliding down beside him, she laid a tentative hand across his forearm. "Tell me something, Chad, why did you really come here today? Why did you follow me out to the garden last night? Why did you hire me in the first place? And why, where I'm concerned, do you handle matters that Brian can just as efficiently handle?"

Chad could not think with her sitting so close. His thought patterns scrambled for cover as he took in her sweet scent, her vision of loveliness, her mollifying touch. Disoriented, he could not formulate a response.

Brye took the moment to answer her own earnest questions. "Is it because you're having doubts about me? Maybe beginning to believe that I'm not really the manipulative bitch you thought me to be?"

Her words seemed to discharge another wave of anger. Chad broke free of his paralysis. He smiled, a chilling sneer turning Brye's blood cold. Unerring menace accentuated his every word. "You tell me something: what purpose did you have for rearranging the letters in your name, Brye Grayson…or should I say Bryson Gray?"

The name, vehemently spewing from his tongue, hit her chest dead center and knocked her back several years. Brye's eyes enlarged with fear. Her entire body went frigid, then began to shake uncontrollably. This could not be happening. Daily she struggled against all odds to bury her past in the vaulted confines of darkness. And now she fought even harder to clear the fuzziness of pained memories long suffered. But Chad sat before her, slapping her in the face with harsh realities. "Get out of my house!" To her astonishment, her voice remained amazingly steady.

"What's the matter, *Bryson,*" he ruthlessly taunted, "have I touched a nerve?"

"Don't call me that!" She struggled to hang on to some resemblance of civility.

"Why not?" His sharpened glare cut a hole in the middle of her cool exterior. "Was that an alias you used to con someone else out of their money?"

Brye skyrocketed to her feet. Sailing to the front door, furiously she yanked it open. "I want you out of here…now, please!"

At his leisure, Chad meandered toward the open door. Halting just outside the threshold, he glared down at Brye. "What's the matter?" he gnarled. "Does the truth hurt?"

"You wouldn't know the truth if it walked up and introduced itself to you!" She diverted her eyes so he would not identify the pain she endured.

"Nevertheless, you owe me the truth."

"I owe you *nothing*!" Her self-restraint crumbled, and she slammed the door in his face.

"Dammit!" Chad scoured his fingers through his hair. *So much for maintaining my composure,* he ruminated to himself. Why was she able to push his buttons so?

Because she's right. You're having doubts about the relationship, how and why it abruptly ended. You're having problems with writing Brye off as nothing other than a second-rate con artist, a common run-of-the-mill swindler.

The pieces of the inextricable puzzle just didn't fit. Everything about Brye, the self-sustained determination, her unwavering dignity, the ability to preserve her equilibrium when pushed to the limits, indicated to Chad that something profound—something she was ashamed to admit—had compelled her to end their love affair. His every instinct screamed that there had to be extenuating circumstances.

Chad needed answers. And if he didn't receive them, he would continue to act out his frustrations on Brye. For it was her illusive refusal to provide him with the unmitigated truth that spurred his illogical behavior forward. But how the hell was he supposed to earn her trust if he continued to attack her at every corner he turned?

He had blundered his entire objective today. He turned and stepped off the front porch. It was time to start over from the beginning. Where Brye was concerned, he had to trample lightly.

Behind closed drapes, Brye watched the red sports car careen out of her drive. Too shaken to comprehend fully what had just transpired, she did, however, understand that Chad knew more than she had initially suspected. But how much more?

Falling into a chair, she lowered her face into awaiting palms. The pounding of an irregular pulse beating relentlessly against her temple negated her ability to think clearly. She thought about fixing herself a soothing cup of chamomile tea but, shaking severely, didn't think she would be able to carry out the feat without a few mishaps.

Maybe it was time to accept the inevitable. Maybe it was time to confront and accept her past head-on. Acceptance being the first step in healing—a healing process she had never exposed herself to—maybe it was time to forgive her parents for ruining her life.

No, Brye halfheartedly denounced. Technically, they had not ruined her. Reasonably sane, she had managed to trudge through life without killing herself, the people she worked with, or the neighbor's pesky dog who persistently dropped his mother lode onto her front yard. Somehow she had made it to this point in her life with minimal catastrophes. And although she didn't consider herself to be a fairly well-adjusted individual, to the public eye, she successfully presented herself as such.

But every night, her subconscious, in the form of nightmares, worked overtime at attempting to balance the scrupulously guarded scales of her mental stability; her subconscious hoped to force her conscious to evaluate and accept the situation, then take corrective measures and go on with life. Yet consciously, Brye thwarted the intrusion. She held no desires to relive the acrimonious reality of her earlier years.

Yet she had carried the open wounds of her childhood into adult life. And the open wounds continue to fester…still. She and only she retained the power to heal herself. She empowered people like the Colliers by giving them the ammunition needed to use against herself. Brye understood the necessity to make peace with her past, but she could not relinquish the overinflated terror of seeing her past come to light.

Brye groaned inside the palms of her hand. *Why do I fight it so?* she pondered, lifting her head.

"Because the memories are too painful to recall." Her voice reverberated off ivory-painted walls that taunted her.

Well…maybe it's time to get past the pain.

"Maybe I don't want to get past it."

Maybe you're afraid of what lies beyond the pain.

"Maybe I just don't care to know what lies beyond it."

The day you learn what's behind the pain will be the same day you begin to heal.

The blare of the telephone broke into the one-sided controversy.

Maybe it was a blessing in disguise. Getting up to answer, Brye buried the rebellious thoughts deep within the dark recesses of her mind.

❧❧❧

It had become a nightly ritual to bed down on the couch. Last night had been no exception. Tenisha pulled herself upright. Stretching upward, she drove the kinks out of her knotted shoulders and back muscles. The night had been long, sleepless, unnerving.

Aware that her thoughts should be focused on her husband's explosive behavior and accelerating deterioration, instead, she continued to replay the dances shared with Marcus the night before.

As they floated across the dance floor, she had experienced feelings that had become foreign to her over the past several months. With bodies brushed together, a sweltering heat nibbled at her insides. As they slowly rocked from side to side, painfully—or was it deliciously?—she was made aware of him…as all male. Rock-hard thighs, large, powerful arms, broad comforting chest, massive back and shoulders. "God, the man is big." Tenisha swooned at the memory. "But ohhh…so gentle." Tenderly, he had embraced her, handling her as one would a prized possession.

A woman could get lost wrapped inside the feel of his brawny grip. And lost she had become. He'd made her feel safe, secure, and very much desired.

Eyelids at half-staff, she sank back into the sofa. A dying ember suddenly rekindled, surged through her in the form of burning desire. Visions of entangled limbs traipsed along her overindulgent imagination. And as the illusion took flight and grew in brilliance as well as intensity, Tenisha could actually feel the heat of their bodies pressed ardently against one another. She could feel…

"Oh my god!" She jerked upright. Her eyes flew open. "What the hell am I doing? What the hell am I *thinking*?"

I'm not attracted to Marcus, she struggled to convince herself. The amorous sensations she exhibited toward him stemmed from the intimacy she lacked within her own unbalanced marriage. Hell, the sight of hummingbirds pollinating sent her nerve fibers rocketing to places unknown. In a word, Tenisha was hot…she was horny. Any man looking at her sideways could cause this heated reaction.

No. Disinclined to accept this simple explanation, Tenisha recognized it as a blatant attempt to appease her guilty conscious; she sheltered feelings she refused to open up to.

As a child, whenever falling out of sorts, her father would coddle her within his stalwart grip. His strength, his imperious assurances, left Tenisha feeling invincible. She believed her father would bear the brunt of her distress; he would do whatever necessary to keep her out of harm's way. Within herself, Marcus evoked the same sense of security. Marcus, just like her father, was a protector of women. And although both men believed women were just as capable in accomplishing their endeavors, Marcus, as well as her father, had been raised to respect and protect their more delicate counterparts.

For far too long, Tenisha had been the driving force keeping her marriage together. But having traveled too far and too long on her own, she was now ready to hand over the steering wheel. Marcus, she knew, would have no problems taking control.

Tenisha dragged herself off the sofa. She had to stop occupying her mind with Marcus and start concentrating on her own disintegrating marriage.

Stumbling into the bedroom, Tenisha looked on with distress as her gaze fell upon TyJuan's inert body. Fully clothed, he lay spread eagle on the very spot he passed out on the night before. An obnoxious snore exploded from the boundaries of his lungs; his chest heavily rose and fell. Spittle drizzled from the corner of his mouth. Sickened with the man he had become, Tenisha turned away from the nauseating site.

Brye was right. TyJuan needed serious help. The kind of help she could not provide. But whenever she broached the subject, he flew into a blind rage.

She moved around the room with caution as she dug through drawers and closets. In search of clothing, she soon discovered that her efforts to avoid disturbing him proved unnecessary; the sudden cutting blare of the phone didn't alter TyJuan's breathing pattern in the least.

Dashing back into the living room, she grabbed his cell phone and was greeted with caustic static. Knowing the lines remained open, she barked several times into the mouthpiece. Receiving no response, her mind furiously whirled as she considered the caller on the other end.

Lately, he had been receiving a number of hang-ups when she answered his phone. And then there were nights when TyJuan didn't come home. The line "wives are the last to know" had to have been invented by a man. Tenisha didn't believe for one moment that a woman could not sense when her man was being unfaithful. She could, however, come up with three good reasons why women chose to ignore the intelligible signs: she was legally blind, she was deathly afraid of losing him, or she just didn't give a damn.

Sharp-edged eyes glared at the phone before she threw it on the bed next to her husband. "To hell with this!" she exclaimed.

Retreating back to the living room, she picked up her phone. She angrily stabbed at numbers.

"Hello?"

"Brye?" Tenisha responded, surprised someone sounded more depressed than she. "What's wrong? You sound…distracted?"

"No…no…nothing's wrong." Her voice grew stronger with each word. "You just caught me in the middle of something."

"If I'm interrupting—"

"Of course not. I was about to call you anyway." Brye paused. "Are you doing okay?"

"I'm fine," Tenisha answered in a tone meant to deter Brye from asking too many personal questions. "Actually, I'm calling to see if I could take you out to dinner tonight. You've been on board with Romanique for three weeks now and we haven't had time to celebrate."

Brye smiled, grateful for the distraction. "Sounds good. We'll make a girl's night out of it."

"Actually," Tenisha intervened, none too cautiously, "we had such a good time with Marcus the last time we were together I thought we could invite him as well."

Silence.

"Of course, if you'd rather not—"

"I'd love to have Marcus join us," Brye finally announced, "but what about TyJuan?"

"He's made other plans." Tenisha rolled her eyes with her blatant lie—or maybe it wasn't a lie. *Maybe he does have plans with either a bottle, or another woman, or maybe both.* To Tenisha, it no longer mattered.

Brye understood her friend's state of mind, even if Tenisha, herself, didn't. As a friend, she felt obligated to remind Tenisha that the troubling situation she found herself in would not repair itself.

"TyJuan is sick, Tenisha."

"Don't even go there, Brye!" her voice raised in uncultivated irritation. "I'm not in the mood to discuss my husband. And neither should you be. Particularly after what he almost did to you last night."

"I don't fault him for his behavior, I fault the alcohol—"

"How magnanimous of you." Tenisha eased her body into a high back chair with channeled arms and pleated front.

"You're only going to perpetuate the problem by acting on emotions alone," Brye calmly continued."

"Damn you, Brye! You can't possible know what my emotions are!" Unable to control her rising irritation, the mounting energy propelled her out of her seat.

"I know you're feeling unjustly mistreated and your frustrations are telling you to turn your back on TyJuan. I know you're looking at Marcus as some kind of diversion for the emptiness you're experiencing. I know Marcus is a kind, decent man who deserves a woman who can come to him without the excess baggage of an alcoholic husband. And I know"—Brye paused, her tone softening—"I know that I care for you...and you don't have to go through this alone."

Brye was unaware she had lit a stick of dynamite underneath Tenisha heels. She was also unaware that her last revelation had diffused the raging fury burning within her friend. Tenisha understood Brye spoke only out of concern; she spoke as a close, caring friend. Tenisha's tightly gathered composure shattered into a million tiny pieces. "I…I don't know what to do." Her voice shook uncontrollably.

"After dinner tonight, why don't you come back to my place, spend the night even? After we send Marcus home, maybe, if we put our heads together, we can come up with something."

As if the world had been lifted off her shoulders, knowing she didn't have to face this alone, Tenisha breathed a sigh of relief. "It's a date."

"Good. When can I expect you?"

"I have to work several hours at the studio." Mentally Tenisha began packing her overnight bag. "So I'll see you around three."

"See you then," Brye finalized.

"Hey, sister girlfriend!" Tenisha sounded more confident.

"Yes?"

"Thank you."

12

Late Monday morning, after three hours of heedlessly peddling papers around his desk, Chad remained unsuccessful in keeping his mind on work. Hell, he'd been unable to function as a sane human being since the Saturday confrontation with Brye.

Confusion. Chad floundered in a sea of disorder. No matter which way he turned or how hard he fought, he could not connect with solid ground.

On one hand, he wanted to impose a form of punishment on Brye. On the other hand, he wanted to declare his eternal love; a person who had loved as deeply as he had could not just wave a magic wand and make the feelings disappear.

One way or another, Chad needed to resolve his and Brye's precarious situation. His gut feeling told him to dig deeper into their reckless breakup. The answers, he knew, would be found there. For some inexplicable reason, he also understood that he could not confront his father—doing so, he believed, would only escalate the problem further.

"No," he mumbled to himself, "Brye holds the key." It was imperative he extract—employing any means necessary—the answers needed to mollify his own peace of mind.

He peered at his gold Rolex. Almost noon. Brye had been in a photo shoot since early morning. Maybe he should invite her to lunch. After their latest fiasco, however, he didn't doubt she would refuse.

Giving in by default, needing to start somewhere, he lumbered toward his office door.

Once in the studio, Chad not only discovered Brye wasn't sitting for a shoot, but she hadn't been in all morning. Informed that a change in schedule had been approved by Brian, amidst the fury of a summer hurricane, Chad stormed into his right-hand man's office.

"Why the hell didn't you inform me of a change in schedule?"

Brian's gaze lifted from the contract he was preparing to fax overseas. "It was a simple schedule change. I didn't find it necessary to call your attention to it."

"Soon," Chad needlessly pointed out as he glowered down at Brian, "Brye will undertake a six-week tour. She has a demanding schedule, yet she was given final approval. I shouldn't have to remind you that it's vital she sticks to her arranged commitment. Otherwise, it will cost us greatly."

Brian resisted the urge to mention that he knew all too well of Brye's absorbed schedule, particularly since he was the one who had arranged it to her specifications. Instead, he elaborated, "Late Saturday afternoon, Brye called to ask if she could take several hours off today—she cited personal reasons. Since she dove relentlessly into her work last week, she's moved way ahead of schedule. She's already completed several layout shoots, she's done several personal appearances, and tomorrow she'll shoot her first Mystique commercial." Brian grinned. "This morning, Zach said he's used to pushing the models to the limits, but he's not used to being pushed by the models. He said he's the one begging for mercy at the end of a day's shoot with Brye."

By the scowl on Chad's face, Brian could tell the man was not amused. Undaunted, he continued, "Under the circumstances, we could afford to allow her the day off."

Late Saturday evening, Brye had called Brian, Chad repeated to himself. *I was at her home and she couldn't ask me?* Blinded with the knowledge that Brye had deliberately forsaken him for Brian, rational thoughts turned into irrational ones. He pictured Brye toying with him, deliberately mocking him, provoking him.

Sadly enough, if he asked himself to evaluate his behavior at this very moment, he would find his actions intolerable. Still, he was unable to suppress the anger. He found himself acting like a total idiot. He barked, "I want her back on the shoot today."

"That's not necessary." Brian rebuffed with an unflinching stance. "As I said before, she's way ahead of schedule."

"Are you questioning my judgment?"

"I'm questioning the motives behind your judgment." The behavior Chad exhibited was highly uncharacteristic—just as Daniel Collier's behavior had been the day he'd been informed of Brye's acquisition. Some underlying cause—with Brye being the center of their discord—had arisen from…where? Brian didn't know and couldn't begin to understand. Chad appeared to be exhibiting signs of… what? Something Brian also couldn't readily identify. Somewhere, Chad had lost all objectivity.

Brian tossed his pen on top of his desk. Propelling himself out of his chair, he informed, "I don't know what the hell's going on here! And any other time, I would agree that it's none of my business, but when it affects this company as well as the welfare of one of our valued employees, I think I have every right to ask for an explanation."

Jaw muscles twitched as Chad's brain worked furiously. Every instinct told him to shut down, plead temporary insanity, get out while he could still extract a scant amount of respect from Brian. His tongue, however, functioned independently of his brain. "We hired Brye to do a job, and I expect her to do it. I looked at the layouts you placed on my desk, and many of them are not up to our standards. I want her here for a reshoot."

Brian had inspected each one of Brye's photos prior to passing them on. Not one of her shampoo layouts could be classified as anything less than perfect. Stuffing clinched fists deep inside his pants pocket, Brian sidled up to the window. He turned a stiff back to Chad.

"I believe, for reasons unknown, you're having problems keeping your personal and professional life separated. And if that's the case, then maybe it's time *you* take some time off." He pivoted on his heels and confronted Chad.

Brian had struck a raw nerve. The embittered man angled his profile to keep the gnawing truth away from Brian's probing eye.

Chad's voice remained low yet commanding. "Let's keep my personal life out of this."

"I will if you will," Brian sourly agreed. "And only if you can honestly explain to me why you really hired Brye Grayson?"

"You already know the reason—because she would be a great asset to this company."

"Then why aren't you treating her as such?"

Chad could not come up with an answer—at least none born out of rational thought. He wandered toward the door. "This discussion is over." His uncompromising body filled the empty space between the doorjambs. "I want her back in here…after lunch."

Brian's expression remained stoic. He fell back into his office chair. From the very first day Chad had walked into this business, he'd never thrown his weight around. Nor had he treated the employees as underlings. But today, Brian had no trouble segregating boss from subordinate, a defiant streak running a mile-long, raced impishly across Brian's consciousness. "I mean no disrespect, *Mr. Collier*." If the boss wanted to treat him as an inferior, he sure as hell could act the part. "But it's my belief that Brye's doing an outstanding job and it was *I* who gave her the day off. Therefore, since *you're* the one who's having the problem with her layouts and *you're* the one who's demanding she return, I think it's only proper that *you* be the one to track her down and explain your reasoning, *Mr. Collier, sir!*"

If the provoked dig meant to shame Chad into rethinking his outlandish conduct, the ploy worked. At a loss for words, Chad spun around and left the room.

Not stopping until he was well hidden inside the perimeter of his office, Chad dropped his weary body into his chair and his fallen face into his open palms.

This is not going to work, he thought to himself. *I cannot continue to run around here acting like a crazed lunatic*.

He couldn't even begin to imagine what Brian thought of him.

Actually, Chad *could* imagine what he thought, and it wasn't flattering. Soon he'd have to apologize to Brian for his outlandish behavior today. But now, Chad's first concern was Brye. What should he do about her? How could he calm the stirring waters she managed to agitate every time he thought of her, spoke to her, talked with her.

He reached for the phone. Punching in a number he'd committed to memory long before Brye had come to work for the company, he waited anxiously for her to answer.

She didn't.

But a young, strong baritone did. "Brylinn Residential Home."

"Excuse me?" Thrown off-kilter, Chad wondered if he'd memorized the wrong number. He hadn't.

In a matter of minutes, Chad discovered that with the wonders of modern technology, Brye was not only forwarding her calls, but her cell phone was being forwarded to a children's home she owned, operated, and financed.

His blazing surroundings dimmed with each passing second as he found himself sinking into a black abyss. This was just another shocker added to the knowledge that she'd changed her name many years ago. Despite how intimate he and Brye had become, he knew very little of her. More and more, he wondered if he had known her at all. Instead of finding answers, he continually banked questions.

He pulled himself out of his numbed stupor. It was time to go after answers, and the Brylinn Residential Home for Children was as good a place as any to start. Obtaining directions, as well as the name of the young male he was speaking to—Kirk—Chad informed Rhonda he'd be out of the office the remainder of the day.

A congested, lung-burning heat swallowed the residents of Harlem. Bloated water particles floated above Harlem River, then dissipated into the oppressive wind—the added moisture sent the heat index soaring to an all-time high. Tiny dust specks clogged window units and exhaust pipes, leaving individuals with no place to chill their baked bodies and no transportation to seek more conducive surroundings. Heat, dirt, sweat, Harlem bathed in it.

TyJuan, smoldering on a vinyl-covered bar stool in a dark and gloomy tavern on West 138th, felt just as hot, just as dirty, and just as sweaty. The back and armpits of his wrinkle-free oxford shirt was doused in sweat. His sleeves were rolled high to the elbows; his suit jacket was wound carelessly in a tight ball and parked on the stool beside him. Sweat droplets dotted his forehead and trickled down the side of his face. The fatigued air conditioner and creaky ceiling fans ran sluggishly and offered minimal relief from the external heat. But the beers were cold and fast in coming and more than made up for the inconvenience he may have suffered when first entering the bar.

TyJuan Davidson's day had started like shit and had rapidly slid downhill afterward. Guzzling down the cold brew, he slammed the empty mug on the bar top. Thirty seconds later, a fourth beer had taken its place on the scarred pine. The frothy liquid immediately wet his lips, cooled his parched throat and stomach, yet fueled his anger against the morning's luckless events.

First, Tenisha had taken it upon herself to set him up on a job interview, a plant factory manufacturing plastic containers. He kept the prearranged appointment only because he never would have heard the end of it from his wife. Once there, after completing the initial preliminaries, he'd met with a pencil-packing, fake-grinning, butt-kissing, prune-faced White woman who'd probably never been laid in her entire life. She'd pompously informed him that the only positions available were of the custodial nature. Of course, in this new age of being politically correct, the official job title was Environmental Engineer.

She met him with a granite-eye stare as if genuinely expecting him to consider the position, as if she expected him to do nothing better with his life other than scrub floors and wash toilets.

Subsequently, he verbally ripped into her. She urged him to stay calm. "Calm?" he'd screamed back at her. She should consider herself damn lucky he'd displayed enough restraint to not lunge across her desk and snatch that condescending grin off her pale face. Seconds later, he'd found himself thrown out on his butt by a pack of security officers.

He'd then made the mistake of visiting his mother. She had asked to borrow $400 to help out with the month's expenses. He said he didn't have the cash. And as if she'd already expected as much, without blinking an eye, she demanded he get it from Tenisha.

She had actually demanded. *What the fuck?* Who did she think she was?

TyJuan blew a heavy sigh into his beer mug. He watched as the beefy bartender swatted a fly with a rolled newspaper. The crushed remains were brushed to the hardwood floor.

TyJuan went back to his raging reflections.

When it came to the expectation department, he'd always fallen short. With Tenisha, when they'd first met, she had looked at him with nothing less than hero-worship illuminating her eyes. Now he was just another man who could not hold down a job nor lay off the heavy alcohol. With his mother, he'd always been the black sheep of the family, the troublemaker, the selfish son. His father, who only made appearances whenever he couldn't get laid elsewhere, expected TyJuan to be nothing other than the pain-in-the-ass son he proved himself to be. Even his grandmother used to say, "Boy, you ain't worth two nickels rubbed together. When you grow older, you ain't never gonna amount to nuttin'."

TyJuan stared at his reflection in the wall-length mirror behind the bar. He tipped his glass in a salute to his dead grandmother. *Here's to you, Gran. It should make you proud to know your prophecy's come true.*

The youngest of three boys, TyJuan could never live up to his older brothers' standards. In comparison, he'd always been smaller, weaker, inferior. His older brother had worked his way through medical school and was currently practicing in Los Angeles. The next to the oldest was a computer programmer who had set up his living in Texas.

All his life, TyJuan had been criticized as well as ostracized. Repeatedly, he'd listened to, "What the hell's the matter with you? Why can't you be more like your brothers? Why can't you do better in school? Why don't you want to go to college and make something of your life? Why do you have to stay in trouble?" On and on it went. Over and over. The repetitious assertions deposited on his brain cells like infested body tissue. As the years swept past, so did the decaying sores cultivate, trampling on his compassion and sensitivity.

TyJuan heaved another downhearted sigh. His eyes were empty and unseeing, his brow was disfigured with despondency, his mouth was rumpled in sadness. Not once had anyone said they were proud of him…of his accomplishments. Although he'd been a rebel, he'd never been arrested. Although he hadn't made As and Bs in school, he hadn't flunked out. Although he hadn't gone to college, he'd graduated from high school. And although he hadn't become a rocket scientist or nuclear physicist, he'd maintained a steady job until he'd been canned—through no fault of his own.

Once…just once…he wished someone would praise him for not being a bad person.

His entire life, he'd been put down, laughed at, stomped on, cast out, and no one in his immediate family had ever cared about, nor even considered, the depth of his pain.

TyJuan gulped down the remainder of his beer. He belched and felt a hand glide over his tensed shoulders,

"You look like you need a friend."

TyJuan turned toward the soft, feminine voice. His vision was slightly off kilter but clear enough to recognize a fine woman when he saw one. Her skin was as brown as chocolate milk. her eyes and hair looked as smooth as honey. Her tank dress was short, riding high above firm thighs. Her legs were short and muscular; her toes were stuffed inside a pair of leather thongs and painted with glittery decals displayed against a red background. She looked good. She looked damn good. And TyJuan wouldn't mind gaining access to a little piece of her.

"Do you want to be my friend?" TyJuan's eyes, once again, inventoried her valuable assets.

The woman slid into the barstool beside him. The entire time they spoke, as if she understood his every need, her fingers gently kneaded his neck muscles. Fifteen minutes later, together, they left the bar. In the raging Harlem heat, they trudged north on Lenox Avenue and turned right on W. 142nd Street. When they were tucked away in a well-kept brownstone, TyJuan was introduced to another friend. Crack-cocaine. And as he succumbed to her soothing touch and gentle nature, he knew he had found a friend for life. For his newfound friend did not belittle him, nor did she condemn him as a bad boy. Instead, she whispered words of endearments in his ear. She encouraged him to reach out and take whatever his heart desired. And under her supportive supervision, he found himself accomplishing dreams he'd never thought possible. He found himself soaring, and excelling, far beyond belief.

It was a euphoric sensation. It was a sensation no one had ever allowed him to experience before. It was love at first sight.

Instant replay. Like a woman watching her favorite taped program with remote control in hand, memories of Tenisha's weekend slowly reeled behind closed eyelids. Specific scenes would be repeatedly rewound, then replayed over and over. At times, she slowed down the speed to leisurely relive cherished moments spent with Brye and Marcus. Other times, she would fast forward, then pause, entrusting individual frames to memory for the entirety of her life.

To celebrate Brye's recent procurement of spokesperson for Romanique Cosmetics, Tenisha had invited Brye, along with Marcus, out to a congratulatory celebration dinner. Instead, when she'd arrived at Brye's home Saturday afternoon, she'd walked into a home saturated with an appetizing aroma. She had walked in on a team effort: Brye and Marcus creating a five-course dinner from scratch. The menu consisted of all her favorites. Mushrooms stuffed with a spicy cream cheese and sausage filling. French onion soup. Baked from scratch sourdough bread. Caesar salad. Chicken marsala, twice baked potato, green bean casserole. And the highlight of the meal included her all-time favorite dessert: sweet potato pie topped with whipped cream.

Tenisha had been flabbergasted as well as pleasantly pleased. And when Brye proclaimed the elaborate meal to be eaten guilt-free—dues to be paid on a later date—Tenisha delved into her dinner with animated ebullience. The food had been wonderful, conversation enlightening, and the company couldn't have been any better had she dined at the dinner table with the president of the United States.

After dinner, they had stumbled—with bloated bellies—into Brye's living room. Beginning a game of Pictionary, they only discontinued the game when the sheet-rock threatened to crumble into medium-sized chunks from the blast of riotous laughter rebounding from one wall to another.

Ready for a little relaxation, with a bowl of popcorn and pretzels in hand, the three gathered in front of the television to watch a ten-hour mini-series which had premiered on prime time television months earlier. Brye had DVR'd the entire episode. Fast-forwarding through the commercials, sometimes stopping to critique a certain scene or particular actor, they finished the movie in its entirety in a little under six hours.

Afterward, a one-hour discussion ensued, and then Brye kicked Marcus out of her home.

Close to two in the morning, Tenisha did not want TyJuan to infringe upon the wonderful evening she'd just shared with Marcus. So when Brye extended the invitation to discuss Tenisha's current predicament, Tenisha turned the offer down—she wanted to go to bed with pleasant thoughts circulating throughout her system.

After only three hours of sleep, at five in the morning, Tenisha found herself rolling out of bed with Brye pushing her the entire way. It was payback time for their incredible dinner they'd eaten the night before. For three prolonged, painful, piteous hours, under Brye's harsh dictatorship, she found herself jumping, running, squatting, and moving to the beat of every fat-burning exercise imaginable. Amazingly, Tenisha forced her aching body into distorted contortions no human body should ever have to subject itself to.

At the end of her torture session, she was allowed to take a quick shower. Next, Brye whisked her out of the house. Thirty minutes later, she found herself at Brylinn's, lining the bright walls and ceilings with birthday decorations. With breakfast out of the way, for several more hours, she was bombarded with what seemed like millions of mind-boggling, pistol-packing, doll-toting, crayon-carrying youngsters.

Under normal circumstances, Tenisha wouldn't have minded the attention the kids rained over her, but after three short hours of sleep, followed by three long hours of vigorous exercise, her mind and body was not equipped to tackle overzealous youngsters, nor overly fresh teens.

Fortunately for her, Marcus had stopped in for several minutes to drop off presents for the twins. Wishing them an early happy birthday, he apologized for his short stay. Before giving him the chance to walk out, Tenisha caught him with a mournful eye. She begged him to take her out of this madhouse.

Minutes later, after issuing goodbyes, she nestled into the soft leather seats of Marcus's Navigator. Eyes closed, head fell backward and settled on the headrest. Blowing out an exaggerated breath, she quoted Dr. Martin Luther King, "Free at last. Free at last. Thank God Almighty, I'm free at last!"

Sliding his key into the ignition, Marcus's laughter sent shivers of pleasure rolling down her inner thigh. Had she not been so bone weary, the sonorous sound would have been enough to revitalize her.

"Don't tell me you're having problems hanging with Brye," he asked.

"Okay," she mumbled, her eyes remained shut, "I won't tell you."

Again, Marcus laughed. "I'll let you in on a little secret: I have problems keeping up with her as well."

"God, Marcus!" Her head flew upright. She turned a questioning smirk at Marcus. "We had just barely gone to bed when she pushed me out of it. We were up with the early birds. Hell…we *woke* the early birds." Shaking her head incredulously, she asked, "How does she do it? Where does she get the energy? She's just like the Energizer Bunny. She keeps going and going and going."

Marcus had thrown her a sideways glance. His well-trimmed mustache nervously twitched above his upper lip. As if weighing a decision, after several somber moments, he finally said, "She's running from something. When she sits, she's afraid whatever she's running from will catch up to her—so she doesn't sit."

Tenisha twisted her body around to better observe him. Studying his handsomely chiseled profile, she brushed aside the urge to run her index finger along the shapely bridge of his nose and down full, enticing lips. "You've noticed," she said, forcing her mind back on the subject. "It's so sad, but what do we do about it?"

"Nothing." Marcus took his eyes off the road and rested them on Tenisha. "We wait until she's ready to confide in us."

Nodding in agreement, Tenisha fell back into her seat. Neither spoke the duration of the ride back.

Pulling into Marcus's drive at twelve-thirty, he offered to fix them a light lunch. Accepting the invitation, she crumbled onto his sofa. When Marcus retreated to the kitchen, she promptly fell asleep.

The weekend had been loaded with games, giggles, and deeply felt camaraderie. Negating her own personal conflicts, Brye had gone out of her way to ease Tenisha's aching heart. And Marcus...excessively tall, disarmingly handsome, eminently self-reliant, and daringly delightful, he was all that plus a double dip of chocolate chip ice cream. Tenisha chuckled to herself at the thought of him being served up with a mound of whip cream and a maraschino cherry on top.

God would surely strike her down for comparing Marcus to TyJuan, but Marcus was everything her husband was not. He was everything she wanted and needed in a man.

The impetuous thought promptly slammed Tenisha back down to planet earth. Her eyes darted around her photo studio. A variety of photos—different shapes, different sizes, different subjects—ornamented the wall adjacent to the entrance of her office. Her roving eye searched the span of the pictures. Despite the number of years she'd been married, in spite of the large number of photographs she'd taken of her husband, there was not one picture of him hanging in sight.

An omen.

Perchance, subconsciously, she had known her marriage had been doomed from the start. Possibly, her father had been right to disapprove of her marriage with TyJuan. Conceivably, as she looked back, she could have been in love with the idea of being in love; or maybe she liked the idea of loving someone so far removed from her own lifestyle, and who was so amazingly different from her father. Ripe for the taking, TyJuan had entered her world, with his sharp edges, charismatic demeanor, his hardened good looks. Easily she found herself drawn to his reprobate appeal. The fact that her father disliked him enticed her even more. The harder he had worked in hoping to establish TyJuan's unsuitability, the more adamant she had become in proving him wrong.

She loved her father with all her heart and soul. Having spent his entire life protecting her, why had the only time she had chosen to revolt, been when she had gone against him and married TyJuan?

Hindsight was definitely twenty-twenty. Looking back now, she accepted the fact that marrying TyJuan had been the biggest mistake of her life.

Sighing heavily, she dropped her chin into her cupped palm. It was time to make some major decisions in her life. Brye was right. She couldn't get involved with Marcus. She had made a commitment to her marriage. Even though she knew she could not spend the rest of her life with TyJuan, she cared for him deeply. She could not just turn her back on his suffering. She could not walk away from his drinking problem. She had to convince him to seek help, get his life back together, cut loose the pent-up bitterness. Afterward…well… she just had to wait and see. But until then, she needed to steer clear of Marcus.

"Your two o'clock photo shoot is here," Tenisha's assistant announced, popping her head inside the room.

"Give me a few minutes to set up."

Her assistant nodded, then ducked back inside the inner office. Dragging herself out of her chair, Tenisha began rearranging her cameras. Like the 200 mm autofocus telephoto lens she utilized on many outdoor stills, her mind automatically zoomed in on her current assignment. At least for the next several hours, she would be able to block out the mesmerizing way Marcus had looked at her when she had awakened, stretched out on his sofa, after four hours of blessed sleep. Until she finished for the day, she expunged the blazing trail of desire burning a pathway all the way down to the depths of her soul. For now, she would halt her fantasizing of awakening encased within the protection of Marcus's hard-muscled arms.

Stopping to change into a pair of jeans and sleeveless T-shirt, Chad jumped into his black Jeep Cherokee and, forty minutes later, found himself pulling in front of a grand, unique-shaped, three-story home. Three painted steps led him to a wraparound verandah. He noticed another verandah overhanging the front door. Before announcing his arrival, he walked partially around the huge estate. Exquisitely manicured hibiscus, hydrangea, and rhododendron shrubs, aged oak and maple trees, and a melody of flowers and plants added to the mystic charm. Chad could not believe this place flourished as a children's home.

He turned back toward the front and rang the doorbell. Minutes later, a tall, young—no older than seventeen or eighteen—teenaged boy opened the heavy door. Long, reddish-blond hair pulled back into a ponytail, greenish eyes, a welcoming smile, he held his hand out in greeting.

"Mr. Collier?" the teen hesitantly asked. "I'm Kirk," he addressed on the end of Chad's nod.

"Nice to meet you, Kirk." Chad was met with a strong, assured grip.

"Please, come in."

Chad stepped into a huge two-story foyer. A large, arched window inundated the open space with bright sunny rays.

"I'm sorry Brye isn't here to greet you. She's passing out presents." He chuckled in amused glee. "Every birthday we have around here, she buys presents for the entire lot, and Moms Linn threatens to strangle her for the unnecessary spending of money."

"Moms Linn?"

"She's a combination foster mom, den mother, dorm director. She runs this place—"

"I run this place with an iron grip."

Chad turned toward the husky voice. African American in descent, silvery-gray hair pulled back in a tight bun accentuated strong, inflexible features. Tall, she stood six feet in flat shoes, a large yet not cumbersome frame. Middle-aged, Chad's trained eye guessed her to be between the ages of fifty to fifty-five, although she didn't appear a day over forty. Definitely not the demure grandmotherly type. Chad had no doubts she ruled with an ironclad will and a firm grip. He also believed she praised when praise was due, freely embraced when hugs were needed, dished out smiles at times most vital.

"Mr. Collier," she greeted, sweeping through the room like an unexpected windstorm. "I'm Linn—the keeper of this zoo. And if you'll excuse me, the animals are getting restless."

"Linn?" Chad curiously eyed her as she continued down the foyer.

"Brye will be with you as soon as she can," her words floated over her shoulders. "In the meantime, Kirk will take very good care of you. Brye apologizes for the wait."

"Brye knows I've come?" Chad addressed Kirk. After their heated altercation Saturday, he was surprised she approved this visit.

"Of course." He flaunted an apologetic smile. "If it was any other day, she would have greeted you herself. But today is kind of special…for the twins. It's their sixth birthday, and they've never had a birthday party before. Brye really wanted to make it special for them."

"It's all right," Chad reassured, recognizing a golden opportunity; he would be able to extract more information from this young man than he could obtain from Brye. "I understand perfectly. Besides, it will give us more time to talk…you can tell me about this place."

Kirk led Chad into a spacious office adorned with two oak desks, wood file cabinets, a computer, live plants, beautifully framed oil reproductions, and plenty of natural lighting. He directed Chad toward a tailored, overstuffed, sofa.

Curious about the twins, Chad settled more comfortable into the sofa. Question and answer time had just commenced. He asked, "Tell me about the twins?"

"Bethany and Anthony," Kirk established. He pulled his tall frame atop the desk closest to the window. Bright rays of sunlight streaked across his upper body. Bending forward, his elbows rested on top of his thighs.

Vividly, in great detail and with adorned admiration, he familiarized Chad with the twins. And Chad developed a horrifying picture of a drug-abused mother who interchangeably beat and severely neglected her children. He cringed at the mental and physical abuse two five-year-old kids suffered at the hands of their own flesh and blood. And he questioned a society in which abuse was able to augment to such damaging proportions. His heart reached out to two human beings he'd never met.

Unable to hold his tongue any longer, he asked, "You said Brye had never counseled any of the other kids before. What made her change her mind with the twins?"

Kirk's eyes swooped toward the multipaneled windows. A flower garden lay beyond the paneled glass. The young man tracked the route of a bumble bee dancing from flower to flower. "I know this is gonna sound strange, but Brye doesn't believe in the system. She doesn't hold a lot of faith in state paid therapists either. Not because they aren't qualified," he quickly interjected, "but because they are extremely overworked. That's why she wouldn't allow a therapist to come close to the twins." His stoned expression suddenly cracked. A smile appeared. "I'm not saying Brye treated them any better than the rest of us because she treats us all equally as well, but there does seem to be an attachment formed between those three." He shrugged in indifference, no measure of jealousy displayed. "It probably has something to do with the amount of time she spent with them while trying to draw them out of their shell."

"How many children are under her guardianship?" Chad asked, engrossed.

"Today the census is fifteen." Pausing, he then amended, "Sixteen if you include me. But besides being my guardian, she's also my boss and mentor." Kirk pulled himself up to sit straighter, prouder. "The number can change at any moment. We can comfortably handle twenty and squeeze in twenty-five if need be."

"How did Brye get involved in this?"

"To explain that, I have to talk about myself and how I met Brye." His gaze fell to the floor, his expression turned serious. His words slowed, became shaky, as if the memories were too painful to expose. "I was raised by an abusive father. When I was ten, my mother got fed up with his bullshit"—knowing Brye would not approve of the language, apologetically, he grimaced at Chad—"she ran off and left me there to keep him company. At fourteen, my ol' man and I engaged in hand-to-hand combat. He must have knocked some sense into my head, though, 'cause after I regained consciousness, I realized that the next time he hit me, I might never wake up. I had no family, and most of my friends didn't have it any better than I, so I decided to take my chances on the street. I wasn't doing a good job of taking care of myself when Brye spotted me. She strolled over and asked if I'd had a hot meal lately."

For the first time since trespassing on his not so distant memories, a wide grin materialized and trailed across his youthful face. About to share a man-to-man secret, his voice lowered. It surged with conspiracy. "Don't tell Brye I said this, but when she approached me, I thought it was because she wanted to sleep with me. And I thought, what the hell? She's fine-looking and all. But during dinner, it took a while for me to realize that she was not interested in my body, but in me, as a person. She grilled me to no end…wanting to know why I was living off the streets, why I had quit school, why I couldn't go back to my family. In the end, not only did she convince me to come live with her until she could find better living arrangements, but she hauled my butt back to school before breakfast the following morning." Kirk tightened his lips in buried concentration.

"The first week I was with her, she spent a lot of time with me…actually talking *to* me instead of *at* me…helping me with my studies… She showed me that I wasn't as stupid as my father had led me to believe.

"The second week, she convinced me to call my father and tell him I was okay. I told her it was a big mistake, but she said she needed to gain legal guardianship of me and could not do that without his knowledge or permission."

Kirk jumped off the desk. He sank into the sofa next to Chad. Chad, mesmerized with the story, remained quiet. "When he found out I was living with a supermodel, he attempted to extort money out of her by selling me…for $50,000." Closing his eyes tightly, Kirk inhaled deeply. His voice cracked. "All my life, my father said I wasn't worth a pot to piss in, and there he was, asking Brye for $50,000."

Stunned by his revelation, Chad found this information difficult to digest. As a child, he had lived a charmed life. His parents' boundless love and support had never been called into question. So how could a man offer to sell his own son…his flesh and blood…an extension of himself?

Needing to know the final outcome, Chad asked, "Did she pay it?"

"No." Kirk opened his eyes. Unshed tears glistened…tears of admiration. "She hired a lawyer and fought for me. My father also hired a sleazebag of a lawyer. He had a shark smile and a slick tongue. And when he spoke to Brye, he said he'd give her one week to reconsider her position. If she didn't, information might leak to the press that our relationship was strictly sexual." The rage quickly emerged and spilled forth like spewing froth from an open champagne bottle. "That fuckin' law—" He cut his words, along with his anger, as he remembered where he was and who he spoke to. "I'm sorry, Mr. Collier, I didn't mean to say that."

Chad wanted to reach out and touch Kirk, comfort him in some way. But this was new to him. Out of his element, unsure as to how he should show his support, he compassionately offered, "It's okay, Kirk. I understand your anger."

Kirk smiled in gratitude. "Anyway, the same night he threatened Brye, we spotted Moms Linn on the news. We hadn't known her at the time, but prior to that night, she'd been cited on many occasions for her selfless acts in working with runaways and abused kids. She'd given a lot to the community, but on this particular night, she was asking for help. Her house had burned down, putting her and four wards out on the street.

"Brye called her up and they met that same night. Stating our case, Brye said they could form a coalition mutually beneficial for the both of them. And before I could regret the trouble I was causing Brye, she'd bought, furnished, and moved Moms Linn, her entire clan, and me in here. And with the connections Moms Linn had, not only did Brye gain custody of me, but my father's lawyer was brought up on charges of extortion and blackmail."

"Are you telling me Brye financed this entire venture?" Stunned out of his chair, Chad parked himself under the doorsill. He stared down the extended foyer. Taking in the massive size, vaulted ceilings, the curved staircase, the patterned wall paper and polished hardwood floors, he estimated the cost of the home to have set Brye back several million dollars.

"She used her own money and hired a cook and handyman. And as this place grew in reputation, more staff was added. We even do our own in-house schooling."

"Tell me something, Kirk, if you don't mind?" Chad leaned his body against the threshold.

"Not at all."

"Tell me something about Brye…what you think of her…what kind of person is she? She doesn't talk much about herself…her personal life." Hands stuffed in his pockets, he faced Kirk once again. "I knew nothing about this place."

Kirk nodded. It was as if he understood Chad's curiosity because he was just as curious about his godsent benefactor. "As for Brye's personal life, she doesn't talk much about it or of herself. But I can tell you how she's affected me over the years. I can tell you how she's changed my life."

As he spoke of Brye, he appeared to sit up straighter; the luster in his eyes radiated unadulterated admiration, his voice resounded stronger, more confident.

"Brye believed in me long before I believed in myself. She had faith in me even when I didn't. Whenever I fu"—he stumbled, then picked himself up—"uh, whenever I screwed up, Brye never spoke down to me. She never attempted to lessen or humiliate me. She spoke to me as a person…as a human being…as an equal. And she always talked straight to me.

"When she fought to gain guardianship of me, she asked me to trust her…and I did. And every child that's come through here, she's asked them to trust her as well. Not once has she ever let any of us down."

Kirk raised unsettled eyes to Chad. He suddenly sounded troubled. "Although more times than not, we've let her down. Kids come here angry…sad…troubled. Some have stolen from us, some fight for apparent reasons known only to themselves, some are filled with so many unredeemable qualities that even I want to give up on them." His words were suddenly laden with pride. "But not Brye. She never gives up. She enjoys working with the kids. She enjoys putting smiles on our faces. She enjoys spoiling us."

Chad was amazed at the young man's astuteness. He was also impressed with Kirk's maturity. Before he could comment, however, Brye sprinted down the hallway.

When she spotted Chad lingering at her office door, her steps slowed, then halted altogether. Her tenacity spilled out into the sunny foyer as she stared into his handsome face.

Every day, the walls of Brylinn pulsed and throbbed under the energetic impulses of spirited children. The moment Chad had entered the home, his galvanized presence seemed to dampen the accustomed vibrancy stirring the air. Unfortunately, knowing he was in the house had overshadowed the twins' party; it had overshadowed her awareness of all else. When Kirk first informed Brye that her former lover had called to say he would be visiting, she could do nothing but surrender to her inflating apprehension.

She forced a smile and urged her feet to move. "Chad, what are you doing standing in the doorway? Kirk was supposed to see to your comfort."

"He did." Chad smiled at Kirk as the young man slid past him and stepped out into the foyer. "He's also been very accommodating in answering my questions."

"What do you think of my pride and joy?" Brye grabbed Kirk by the arm and pulled him to her. "He's really grown up over the past few years, and I'm proud of his past as well as his future achievements."

Kirk blushed under Brye's unsolicited praise. Needing to give credit where credit was due, he said, "Who I am, what I've accomplished, I owe to you. After all, it is you who inspire *me.*"

"Please," Brye said, casually brushing his comments aside. "Don't get sappy on me now, Kirk. I had nothing to do with the person you are inside. I merely opened some doors. It was you who chose to walk through them. Now"—she smiled brightly at Chad as she skillfully switched subjects—"please forgive me for keeping you waiting. But if you can bear with me a few minutes more, I need to go check on the twins' birthday present. Afterward, I'm all yours. In fact, if you'd like to come with me, we can talk now."

Chad agreed to accompany Brye. Brye excused Kirk and piloted Chad toward the kitchen. Arms and shoulders brushed together as they walked side by side. More conscientious of Brye than the distinctive surroundings, Chad fought relentlessly to avert his eyes from the woman striding beside him. But it was the fragrant smell of her glowing skin, the haphazard way her hair roosted atop her head, the oversized cotton romper which emphasized the splendor of her shapely legs and thighs, and the soft slapping of bare, pedicured, feet against hardwood floors that promoted the realization of how perfectly Brye blended into this charming atmosphere.

"You look lovely today," he found himself saying.

A nervous laugh erupted from the boundaries of Brye's tightening throat. "I look like I've been wrestling with a bunch of hyperactive kids, which is exactly what I *have* been doing all morning long."

They stepped into a sunlit, spacious, country-decorated kitchen. Antique copper pots and utensils climbed the softly painted walls. Built-in appliances and pantry, range-top island/breakfast bar, plenty of cabinet and storage space—any cook would be honored to yield a variety of culinary creations within a room so grand.

Chad caught Brye by the wrist and swung her around to face him. "I have a desk filled with your recent glamour shots, and I wouldn't dare trade the settled look you have now for a million of the glossies you took last week."

The sincerity in his voice warmed Brye's heart. Violet eyes searched baby-blues for signs of mockery. There was none. Staring at a face portraying nothing but open honesty, she could not contain the question she'd ached to ask since learning of his planned visit. "Why did you come here?"

Chad needed answers. To obtain them, he needed to instill her trust. And to do that, he needed to bestow honesty. As if ashamed of his earlier actions, his eyelids dropped to the handmade tile. "You asked for the day off without my permission."

Brye stood as frigid as a frozen ice-cream treat. She stared up into an expression bowing to humility. What happened next surprised them both. The tension visibly melted, her face broke into an amused grin. "So…you came to drag me back to the salt mines?" Prepared to surrender to his merciless demands, as if consenting to handcuffs, she stuck her wrists out in front of her. "If you insist, I'll go peaceably."

That she could make light of the situation made Chad shrink more into himself. He wiped a stray strand of hair away from a face scrubbed free of makeup. God, she was so damned irresistible. She was also a paradox, an intricate puzzle, a perplexity of assorted emotions and intrigue. And before he permanently severed the emotional attachment enslaving the two together, Chad vowed to learn everything there was to know of one Brye Grayson.

His tone matured, grew confiding. "I'm ashamed to say my actions today were brought on by anger. And jealousy," he added as an afterthought. "It incensed me knowing you sought out Brian instead of me when requesting the day off."

"You haven't exactly been civil to me." Brye didn't intend for her words to sting. Nevertheless, Chad winced.

"I'm sorry, Brye. I know I haven't." He ran the back of his hand down a face livid with bewilderment. "And the only explanation I have is," he shrugged, then admitted, "you drive me crazy. I didn't think bringing you back into my life would turn my world completely inside out…but it has. I deceived myself into believing you couldn't affect me any longer…but you can."

Brye found it difficult to maintain a steady gaze. His fingers warmed her cheeks beneath his savory touch. Not able to fully grasp the context of Chad's words, she prayed for this to be a significant sign to a possible reconciliation. She threw a wavering glance over Chad's shoulder. Her eyes landed on a hall painting: a cocker spaniel flooding a toddler's face with an insistent tongue. "What is it you want from me, Chad?"

He shrugged, as if uncertain himself. But he knew. God help him, he knew. "For now, I'd like to call a truce. I'd like for us to start over."

Prior to this day, whenever she and Chad confronted each other, a heated conversation ensued; verbal punches were tossed left and right, urging Brye to duck before she sustained severe emotional trauma.

Now, coming out of nowhere, Chad stood before her, offering a ceasefire, asking for a new start. Brye didn't think she was mentally incapacitated. She wasn't stupid enough to believe he was willing to let bygones be bygones. Needless to say, she had every reason to be suspicious. She also had every reason to believe he hadn't generously swept the hurt he'd suffered right out the front door, his anguish whisked away in the wind, never to be seen nor heard from again.

Brye had to assume he was not being entirely truthful. But until he proved otherwise, maybe they could fashion some semblance of a friendship. Sighing to herself, she hated to admit it, but she liked it better when Chad was going for her jugular. At least then, she knew where she stood. "Is that what you really want?"

"For my own sanity, as well as my peace of mind, it's what I need."

Something other than his own power drew him closer to Brye. His head bent over hers, their lips inched closer. But just before they made contact, Brye stumbled backward. She couldn't do this. Not yet. Not now. She moved toward a glass door in the back of the kitchen.

With fingers resting on the doorknob, she said, "Let me finish here, then I'll walk you to your car."

"I've decided to spend the day with you," Chad quietly notified.

Brye's head snapped backward. She twirled like a spinning top to face him. "Are you sure you want to do that?"

"Of course. Unless there's some reason why you wouldn't want me here."

"I'd love for you to stay," Brye admitted, her eyelashes dipped with a shyness she felt. "But things can get pretty hectic around here. The kids can get unruly at times."

"I promise to let you know if it's too overwhelming for me."

Brye allowed the last few weeks to slip out of her reach. This was as good a time as any to begin anew. And she planned on wisely using the time given her. "Have you had lunch?"

"No." Chad ruefully smiled. "I was too bent on striking out after you."

"I'll fix us something as soon as I give the twins their birthday present." She opened the door to the glassed-in sunroom. "But for now, come see my two new additions to the household."

Chad stepped into a sunroom doubling as a tropical forest. Sunlight was abundant. A variety of trees, plants and flowers flourished wherever his gaze landed. Dark, wicker furniture with floral cushions gripped his attention. But the item holding his complete fascination was the large birdcage adorning one entire wall. Two large, brightly colored birds, perched on thick branches, cracked nuts between powerful beaks.

"Macaws," Brye stated, reading his mind. "Ara ararauna. Or as they're commonly known, blue and yellow macaws." She moved over to the cage and opened the wire mesh door. "George—our gardener and handyman—assembled the cage last night. I carried the macaws in this morning. It took the effort of all of us to keep the twins away from here for the past twenty-four hours."

She clucked her tongue. Offering her finger, the parrot closest to her readily climbed on. Pulling him out of the cage, she presented him to Chad. "Go ahead," she prompted as his hesitancy tinted Chad's eyes to a sapphire blue. "Take him. He's hand-tamed, and he loves being around people. Say hello," she voiced to the bird.

"Hello!"

Chad laughed as he carefully handled the macaw. "He's remarkable."

Brye handed Chad a few nuts from the bird feed. She then took possession of the other macaw.

"Tell me something about them?" Chad requested. As he listened, he studied the bird's magnificence. A band of olive green covered ear and neck area. The macaw's underside burnished a bright yellow-orange. His backside, including wings and tail, blazed a glossy blue. And Chad marveled at the macaw's powerful grip as it traipsed along his bare forearm.

"Blue and yellow macaws are widely known for their lovable dispositions. And these two are no exceptions." Proficiently, Brye explained the care, breeding, speaking, and diet habits of the Ara ararauna. She also explained how she was able to acquire two young, tame macaws.

"These two have a different coloring compared to the one I met Saturday," Chad commented.

"They're from the same class but different species. Rainbow is an Ara macao or what's commonly known as a scarlet macaw."

"You must have paid a fortune for these?"

"It'll be worth it to see the smiles on the twins' faces."

Chad studied the seriousness in Brye's visage. *Kirk is right,* he thought to himself. *The twins mean more to her than she's letting on.*

"Kirk says you've formed a distinctive attachment to the twins," he asked, hoping to gain an entry port into Brye's ambiguous past.

Dazed, Brye fell heavily into a wicker rocker. How had she become so transparent? Despite the strong attachment developing between herself and the twins, she'd been certain that no amount of impartiality had ever played in her judgment or treatment of the others. "How does Kirk know that? I don't believe I've treated the twins with any favoritism. I haven't given them special privileges while foregoing the others." As she spoke, her fingers automatically played along the macaws head and body.

"So it's true." Chad watched his macaw take flight and gracefully glide to the floor. Struggling to understand Brye, he knelt by her side. "I'm sure you've taken in many kids over the years, so what is it about the twins that's captured your attention?"

Brye fell silent. She handed the macaw an apricot slice. In going over Chad's question, the need to confide in him heightened in intensity. If he saw the twins for himself, he would have his answer. Deciding to tell the truth, she could not control her flow of words. "I look at them and see—"

Linn stuck her head in the sunroom. "What's taking you two so long?" she asked, halting Brye in midsentence.

More relieved than disappointed for the interruption, Brye wasn't certain she wanted to entrust Chad with her innermost secrets.

Yes, like opposing magnets they were drawn to each other. Yes, she remained in love with him. But no, she could not confide in him...not yet anyway.

She unfolded from the chair. Avoiding eye contact, she skimmed past Chad's kneeling body. Scooping up the second macaw, who pecked contentedly at a large, ceramic planter, she stepped through the open glass door. "We're coming now."

Chad pushed himself off the ground. Actions spoke louder than words, and Brye's body language resembled a human advertising billboard equipped with flashing neon lights that blinked on and off at him. *I do not trust you!* they brilliantly shined.

It's okay, Brye, Chad assured himself. *You may not see your way clear in giving me answers now, but you will. Believe me, I can be very patient—as well as convincing—when I have to be.*

Following her, the moment Chad encountered Bethany and Anthony, his heart spun like a rabid tornado. Incredible as it may seem, as soon as his eyes fell upon the two precarious wards, Chad easily recognized Brye's interest. Their hair color wasn't as raven black as his but more of Brye's distinguishable dark coloring. And their eyes...sparkling baby blues, as if he'd genetically passed his DNA over to the twins. He could have easily fathered Bethany and Anthony. Brye could have easily been their mother. And when he sought and captured her gaze, he knew that she understood, how quickly he had detected the remarkable resemblance.

13

"We work in conjunction with the state but aren't financially dependent upon them," Linn explained. Sitting on the porch swing, she used the tip of her toes to rock back and forth.

Now seven o'clock, Chad had spent a colorful afternoon at the Brylinn Residential Home for Children. Much to his amazement, and despite his reasoning for being here, he'd enjoyed himself immensely. Children of all ages, sizes, color, and personality traits delighted as well as intrigued him. Yet it was the twins his wayward thoughts continued to migrate toward. His heart wanted to reach out to them.

Drawing his attention back to Linn, he questioned, "Kirk tells me that Brye foots the entire bill for this place. Is that true?"

"It is. Or it was," she quickly amended. "Last year, we were featured on *20/20*. Since then, we've acquired many loyal financial supporters. And rest assured, we are totally committed to the children. Every dime donated is utilized for the sole purpose of improving the lives of battered, abused, and neglected children."

Sitting on the back porch steps, Chad examined the tranquil surroundings. The large estate sat amidst five acres of land. Many of the older kids had gone off to the movie theater, to the mall, or left to visit friends or family—very few had remained behind. Most of the younger kids were playing in a sandy section of the backyard. A playground equipped with swings, slides, jungle gym, mazes, wading pool, and other playful objects guaranteed to keep a child's mind and body occupied, covered half an acre. A vegetable garden lay to the east of the land, a flower garden to the right. Dogwood and Sycamore trees provided shelter from the sweltering sun. An inviting hammock hanging between two Cypress trees swayed in tune with the early-evening breeze. The perfect place to rear children.

"I'm in no way criticizing," Chad said, his business sense kicking in, "and I wholeheartedly approve of what you're doing, but don't you think your money could go a lot further if you cut back on the extravagance? There are lots of kids with good, stable, two-parent homes that don't live this well."

"Don't let all the perks fool you." Stepping through the sliding glass door, Brye slid out of the air-conditioned home and moved outdoors into the warm, humid air. She sat on the steps next to Chad. Their bodies so close, Chad could feel the heat exuding from her bare arms and legs. "Linn is as stingy as I am generous."

"Stingy!" Indignant with the inharmonious characterization, Linn strongly objected. "I am not stingy! What *I* am, young lady, is economically attentive."

"Anyway," Brye continued, smiling at Linn's high-minded description of herself, "we maintain two separate corporate accounts here. All money donated to Brylinn is placed in one. The other is made up from my own personal reserve.

"One of Linn's duties is to keep the two accounts separate. All necessities—food, clothing, utilities, salaries, normal wear and tear—are paid out of one account. All other items Linn considers as foolish and nonessential comes from my pocket. Every month, she sends out complete, itemized statements to all our financial supporters."

"It's a duty I take seriously," Linn solemnly admitted. "But it's also one that Brye deals me a fit with. I can send her out for hot dogs, and she comes back with lobster. She can take the kids shopping for T-shirts and underwear but come back loaded down with shopping bags from Saks or Bergdorf. In a blatant disregard to who the children are, where they came from, and where they're going once they get out from underneath our protection, Brye rains on them an unrealistic, lavish lifestyle. And time and time again, I've chastised her about her reckless spending. She's entirely too generous. She spoils them endlessly, she doesn't deny them a thing, and she's contributing to their inability to be able to distinguish between reality and fantasy."

"Excuse me!" Flecks of irritation maligned Brye's violet-colored eyes. "From the day these kids were born, they were bombarded with lethal doses of reality. Pain and suffering has been forcibly shoved down their throats. What's so wrong about wanting to insert a bit of fantasy in their severely shattered lives?"

Much too late, Chad realized he'd made a grave mistake. By the sudden heaviness swallowing the air, he had adventitiously lit a match underneath an ongoing heated subject. Not knowing what else to do, he maintained his silence and let the storm run its course.

"It's wrong when fantasy infringes on reality." Linn's rocking slowed to a turtle's pace. An irritated twitch developed underneath her left eye.

Sighing wearily, Brye asked, "And what's that supposed to mean?"

"Take the two birds you gave to the twins, for instance." Stopping long enough to chastise a towheaded boy with devilish eyes and a mischievous grin from pulling the braids of a winsome redhead with deeply indented dimples and freckles dotting her nose, she then turned back to Brye. "I don't think you realize the repercussions of your actions."

"I bought a couple of macaws." Brye flexed her bare foot. She crossed ankles. Chad attempted to tear his gaze away from her shapely legs. "I didn't go out and rob a bank. What kind of repercussions are we talking about here?"

"In the short time the twins have spent with the macaws, they're already attached. What's gonna happen if their mother—or any other member of the family—reclaims the kids but not the birds? And the rest of our kids? How're they gonna handle being reinstated in a home that's barely pulling in enough money to feed the entire family?"

"They will handle the changes with the same bravery, strength, and maturity that's carried them this far in life." Brye stretched her crossed legs out before her. Heaving a sigh of frustration, she leaned backward and rested on her elbows.

The sight of her cotton knit romper stretched tightly against full, perfectly proportioned breasts, drew long, labored breaths from

Chad. Trying not to be conspicuous, desirous eyes trailed down a body ripe for the taking. And dammit, right now, he wanted to take her.

The rambunctious giggling of a Shirley Temple look-a-like dashed past Chad, snapping him back to attention. Fixing his eyes on children rollicking close by, he tuned his ears into Brye.

"I know you don't agree with what I'm doing. But I enjoy making these kids happy. I enjoy witnessing a genuine smile and hearing the sound of real laughter. And if I can put a little laughter in their saddened hearts, then it's worth it."

"But you can't make them happy for the rest of their lives, Brye. You can't always be there for them. And you can't save every abused child you come up against."

"I'm not talking about taking these kids by the hand and walking them through life. I'm not talking about saving every abused child out there—although I have to admit that I'd like to try.

"I just want to make these kids' lives a little better now...today. And I think I've done that. So don't expect me to feel ashamed or guilty for giving them a little piece of happiness. Because all that I give, I give from the depths of my soul."

Linn sat forward. She planted her feet firmly on the wooden floor. The porch swing slowly came to a standstill. She spoke quietly, apologetically, as if knowing what she was about to say would hurt but was nevertheless necessary. "You're overlooking one significant component, Brye. You can't buy happiness. And all the gifts in the world ain't gonna solve the real problem here: it's not gonna fill the void you have in your own life."

Chad felt, rather than saw, Brye's back stiffen. Not knowing what to expect by way of her answer, he waited with bated breath.

The response never came. An ear-piercing howl shattered the tensed moment. All heads jerked upright. The Shirley Temple look-a-like had been tripped, or pushed, by the towheaded boy.

Barefooted, Brye sprinted toward the howling child. Chad and Linn followed close behind. Falling to the ground, Brye's knees buried into tiny sand particles. Gently grabbing the bawling child by the shoulders, Brye cradled her inside a comforting embrace. Bodies swaying, she asked, "What happened, sweet pea? What's wrong?"

"Billy pushed me down…and he did it on purpose!" she wailed.

Linn promptly carted Billy aside to deliver a stern sermon on why little boys shouldn't push, hit, or disrespect little girls.

"Are you hurt, Kayla?" Brye pushed her at arm's length. Eyes soft with concern critically examined diminutive arms and legs. Gently, she brushed off the sand dusting Kayla's pink top and red shorts.

"Yes." A prominent childlike pout exacerbated a quivering bottom lip. Huge crocodile teardrops moistened adorable sun-bleached eyelashes.

Despite the gravity of the situation, Chad found himself smiling. Although the Shirley Temple look-a-like bawled as if her hair was being pulled out of their shafts strand by delicate strand, the heartwarming image depicted a scene straight out of a Norman Rockwell painting.

Touched by Brye's never-ending patience, and the little girl's overt plea to gain attention, Chad found himself drawn into the quaint scene. "Where, sweetheart?" He knelt beside the two huddled bodies. "Where does it hurt?"

Large, gray eyes stared with open interest at Chad. After several seconds of contemplation, with the aid of Brye's reassuring smile, along with a slight nod of her head, Kayla decided she could trust the tall man with the pretty blue eyes and condoling smile.

Presenting her arm to him, she whined, "I hurt right here." She pointed to a spot in the middle of her forearm.

"Oh my!" Brye gasped in feigned astonishment. "You do have an *owee*!"

Blinking several times to clear his vision, Chad stared down at Kayla's tiny arm.

Nothing.

She appeared unmarred. There was no broken skin, no bruise, no swelling, not even a hint of redness to indicate she'd been hurt. Brye's response, however, implied otherwise.

"That looks as if it really hurts," Brye indulged with practiced ease.

"It does." Her bottom lip trembled.

"I think I've got something that'll help the pain."

"You do?" The trembling stopped, the tears dried. Blind faith. An unwavering trust prevailed. If Brye said she could stop the pain, the pain would cease to exist. Impressed, entangled emotions in overdrive, Chad found himself falling head over heels in love with Brye all over again.

"Yes, I do." Brye released Kayla. Her hand plunged deep into the side pocket of her romper. She pulled out a Band-Aid branded with pictures of Mickey and Minnie Mouse. Ripping open the outer wrapper, she carefully adhered the bandage to the "injured" spot.

"There. Does that feel better?"

"Much." Kayla's smile beamed several times brighter than the steadily plunging sun.

"Do you think you feel up to playing a little while longer?" Brye winked conspiratorially at Chad. "Or do you think you need to go to bed early tonight and rest up your arm?"

"I think it's healed enough to play. But if I have a overlapse—"

"Relapse," Brye gently corrected, fighting to keep the edges of her mouth from curling upward.

"If I have one of those," Kayla happily continued, "I'll let you know."

"You do that." Brye hugged Kayla, pulling her snugly into her chest. Giving her a light pat on the bottom. She then tenderly shoved her aside.

"You were wonderful with her," Chad praised as they walked back to the porch steps. "Who'd have thought a Band-Aid would do the trick?"

Brye produced a lighthearted grin that pierced Chad's heart. "Didn't anyone ever tell you that a Band-Aid is the cure-all for whatever ails you?"

Chad skimmed Brye's unclouded expression with a caressing eye. As he silently studied her, he caught a glimpse of movement behind her. Rolling his eyes in that direction, enclosed in the sunroom, he observed the twins playing with their newly acquired pets.

Recalling the question that had plagued him since first making his acquaintance with Bethany and Anthony, Chad grew somber.

"But it isn't a cure-all for whatever ails *you*. Is it, Brye?" he spoke quietly, somewhat urgently.

Brye turned her head to follow his stare. Seeing the twins, she matched his tone. "No, it isn't."

Chad faced Brye. He lightly brushed the back of her hand with his fingers. The compassion in his touch sent them both reeling. He no longer believed Brye would fabricate a story behind an unborn baby…*their unborn baby*…not after witnessing the maternal instincts she showered upon these kids. Nor did he believe she'd run off with a million dollars and abort their unborn infant. She cared for children too much. "What happened to the baby, Brye?"

For a brief moment, she held his gaze. Confusion ripped through her, tearing away a massive chunk of the steel plated armor she maintained around herself. She wanted to tell him the truth, but it meant opening herself up to a host of questions. Questions she was not prepared to deal with.

"Please, Brye," Chad appealed with repressed ardor. "I need to know. Please…"

His subdued plea touched Brye more than she cared to admit. The remnants of her steel sheath melted away. Momentarily, she allowed her past to invade her present.

"Babies," Brye whispered with downcast eyes. "I was carrying twins. One week after you and I…split up, I…tripped…fell down a flight of stairs and miscarried."

Uncertain he'd heard right, incredulously, Chad repeated, "Twins?"

Brye turned wild, panicked eyes on Chad. Her grief burst into senseless vocalizations. "I should have foreseen it coming. I made a mistake in thinking he would leave me alone. But he didn't. I should have gotten out before…before…" Suspended in midsentence, Brye covered her mouth to halt the turbulent flow. Her fuzzy vision cleared. She looked at Chad as if seeing him for the first time. Regaining control, she submitted a feeble smile.

"They were a part of you…a part of us. They were conceived out of the love we shared for each other. I wanted our babies more than anything else in the world."

Chad could have overlooked her pain, but the anguish was clearly discernible and as contagious as a childhood disease. He could have established her unexpected misfortune as poetic justice. He could have said people reap what they sow. He could have noted that she didn't deserve to be happy because, in a blink of an eye, she had snatched his happiness away…forever.

Chad could have responded with a number of antagonistic euphemisms with the sole intent of belittling her pain. Instead, he wanted to pull her into his arms and share her grief for the babies they had lost, the babies they would never know.

"Brye?" There were too many observant eyes. Chad couldn't comfort her the way she deserved. He couldn't take her in his arms and make love to her. He couldn't ease her pain…his pain…their pain. He opted to squeeze her fingers. For now, it would have to be enough.

For Brye, it was enough. The warmth his tender touch offered, the promising look in his gentle blue eyes gifted her with a ray of hope; he gifted her with assurances for their future; he issued a silent plea for her to trust him, confide in him.

"Chad?" Brye wanted to give in to his silent plea. Beneath his consoling grip, she rotated her hand. Open palm against open palm. Eyes cast downward, she examined the back of his sinewy hand. A road map constructed of fine veins diverged across tanned skin. Masculine fingernails clipped low and even, nail beds donned a clear, healthy gloss. Smooth, callous-free skin radiated warmth and strength. She couldn't recall when an innocent touch had felt so good. Guiding her fingers in between his, she sealed their intimate clutch. "Maybe later we can talk…really talk."

"Brye! Telephone!" Damien Jordan, a sixteen-year-old, medium-built, medium height, light-skinned African American male burst through the sliding door. Short, wavy hair, congenial good looks, cocky grin equating with a cocky attitude. High-spirited, eminently articulate, initially introduced as the resident lover, Chad suspected Damien spent more time trying to talk his way out of trouble than the actual time it took in committing the crime.

"Can me and Kirk borrow your car tonight?" he asked before handing over the portable phone.

"It's Kirk and I," Brye corrected, hastily pulling away from Chad. "I thought you were grounded?"

"I was paroled less than an hour ago. Kirk and *I* are hookin' up with two fly babes, and—"

Brye reached for the phone. "We'll discuss it after I take this call."

Pulling the phone out of reach, honey-colored eyes pleaded, "Pleeeez, pleeez, pretty pleeez."

Lunging toward the phone, none too harshly, Brye barked, "Don't make me hurt you, Damien!" She carried the phone to her ear. "Hello?"

"You wouldn't really hurt him, would you?" a deep bass joked over the phone lines.

Instantly recognizing the caller, Brye beamed. "How could you ask such a question, Jeff? You know that we, at Brylinn, frown on any form of corporal punishment—not to mention that child abuse is punishable by law."

Jeff, Chad repeated to himself. *Who the hell is Jeff? And how is he able to put that huge grin on Brye's face.* Wanting to eavesdrop on Brye's conversation, knowing it wouldn't be setting a good example for Damien, he turned his attention toward the zealous teen. "Was there a good reason for your grounding?"

A lazy grin materialized across Damien's cocksure features. "Me and Hector"—he fired a solicitous eye at Brye—"Hector and *I* borrowed Brye's car two weeks ago. We went to a house party and accidentally got drunk."

"Accidentally?" Chad hoisted a skeptical brow. "How does one accidentally get drunk?"

"The punch was spiked." Speared by the suspicious leer Chad jabbed at him, he begrudgingly admitted, "Okay…so maybe I knew it was spiked as soon as I took my first sip. I just wasn't expecting it to sneak up on me as fast as it did. Anyway, I knew I was wasted when Rayana, a walking advertisement for Keebles and Bits, started looking like this month's centerfold in *Playboy*." He shuddered violently, as if the nagging thought refused to lie down and die. "And I knew Hector wasn't in any better shape than me when he watered the rubber plant—without a water can in hand."

Chad's outer facade remained expressionless, yet his insides shrieked with laughter.

"Anyway," Damien continued, "I knew if I managed to make it home while driving Brye's car without killing myself, Hector, or some other innocent bystander, I'd have to worry about what Moms Linn would do to me…not to mention what Brye would do to whatever was left over after Moms Linn finished with me.

"I ended up calling Brye, and she was real cool about the whole thing. She picked us up, took us back to her place, and let us sleep it off. The next morning, after we'd sobered up, she talked to us. Really *talked* to us, like adults, about the downside of alcohol. And when I asked her about our punishment, she said I handled the situation like an adult so she would treat me like one. Then she got this funny grin on her face and said, 'Besides, Mama Linn will take care of the punishment for the both of us.'"

"So she grounded you?" Chad asked.

"Yep!" Slightly embarrassed, Damien grinned. He bent forward and plopped a kiss on top of the head of a chubby toddler waddling by. Straightening his back, he added, "But I wasn't grounded for the actual act of getting drunk. I was grounded because I lied about it."

"I'm not sure I'm following. Brye knew you were drunk before she picked you up." A large ball rolled toward Chad's feet. He picked it up and tossed it over to two prattling eight-year-olds.

"After I called Brye, I had enough presence of mind to call Moms Linn. I told her we would not be coming home but would be spending the night at Brye's. The following morning, I called Moms Linn again and said Brye was called out for a layout shoot earlier than normal, so Hector and I would just hang out at her crib until she finished for the day.

"It would have worked too. Hector and I would have been free and clear, except the parents of my partner who gave the party found out about the booze. She dropped a dime on me when she called Moms Linn to apologize first, then made sure everyone got home safely second.

"Moms Linn was waiting for us when we walked through the front door. And you can believe me when I say I wasn't—" Damien slowed down. He stared at Brye's grave expression as she hit the button on the headset, calling an end to her conversation. "Is it bad?" he asked, knowing the phone call had to be about an abused child.

"Two sisters—age five and eleven. They've been in and out of emergency rooms for 'random' mishaps occurring in the home. The doctors suspect child abuse, and on numerous occasions, the doctors, neighbors, and the extended family have hot-lined the mother and her live-in boyfriend. On each occasion, the sisters denied the abuse occurred. Up until three weeks ago, for whatever reason—the most obvious, however, being that they were tired of getting the holy crap knocked out of them—they decided to turn their mother's boyfriend in. The problem arose when child services stepped in and, for lack of room, separated the two sisters. After living apart for one week, both sisters recanted their stories. And with the mom rallying to regain custody, the judge had no choice but to reverse his earlier ruling and reinstate them back into their abusive environment."

"Jeff wants you to go and talk to the family?" Damien asked, understanding all too well the gravity of the situation.

Brye nodded. "Child Services has agreed to temporarily place them in our custody if I can convince them to admit to the abuse."

"If anyone can do it, you can," Damien stated with emphatic certitude.

Thanking him with a poignant smile, she said, "I have to meet Jeff in thirty minutes at the home. I'm sorry, Damien, but—"

"It's okay, Brye." His high-spirited pretentiousness slipped away, to be replaced with earnest simplicity. "I understand." And he did. He owed his life to Brye. If it wasn't for her humane and generous nature, he could still be mixed up with gangbanging. Or worse. He could be lying in the city morgue, his body pumped full of bullet-riddled holes.

Forever indebted to Brye and the continuous war she waged on aiding him, as well as other misguided or abused kids, after meeting Brye, the two abused sisters would promptly realize how lucky they were to have someone like her rallying to their defense.

"Listen"—he planted a kiss on her check—"I won't even waste my breath saying good luck because you'll do everything in your power to have them here before I've told Kirk our plans are off for the evening."

"Why don't I drive you where you need to go?" Chad offered, his reasons strictly self-serving.

"I couldn't let you do that," Brye halfheartedly protested. In reality, she, as well as the children, had enjoyed his company. The entire day, he'd been extremely attentive. Not once did he utter an irritant word—particularly when Deanna painted his shirt with mocha fudge ice cream, or when Jason bombarded the middle of his back with a medium-sized water ballon, or when Jessica asked for a horsey back ride, then attempted to pull out every strand of his gorgeous downy hair as she clung to his head and giggled to her heart's content. Through all the inextricable madness, he'd surprisingly taken it all in stride. And as Brye observed the industrious patience he harbored for the children, she found herself reminiscing over days long gone. She mused over times she would never be able to recapture. She commemorated over the love she and Chad had shared in the past, and the love that continued to hinder her from initiating any kind of an intimate relationship—sexual or endearing—with any other man. Yes, she wanted him to stay with her a while longer, yet she found herself protesting, "You've spent the entire afternoon with us. I'm sure you've other important matters to concern yourself with."

"None as important as this. I'll even stick around and drive you home later."

His baby-blues reached outward and caressed Brye's soul… molded her into complete acceptance, aware she would not only wholeheartedly agree to his charitable offer, but had they been alone, she would have agreed to almost anything.

Averting her gaze so he could not detect the lust spilling from her eyes, she turned to Damien. "Looks to me as if your plans can stand."

Damien discharged a thunderous whoop of joy.

"Before you get too carried away, maybe you should get Kirk out here and go through the verbal drill before taking off in my car."

"Aw, Brye. We'll be good ol' boys," he drawled in a Southern accent.

Brye caught his face between four fingers and thumb. Firmly squeezing, she declared, "No speeding, no foolish stunts, no drinking, no spilling fluids of either beverage or other bodily form—"

"Aw, Brye," Damien groaned in disgust, understanding all too well her inferred message. Chad almost strangled on his attempt to hold down the laughter.

"Wear your seat belts. And I want you and Kirk back here by midnight."

"One o'clock," Damien countered.

Brye cunningly smiled. "How about if you two stay in for the rest of the evening?"

"Midnight," Damien saluted as he righteously accepted. He turned his charismatic smile on Chad. "Thanks, Mr. Collier. And the next time you come, we're gonna have to sit down and discuss your intentions with my homegirl here."

"Damien!" Brye warned.

Once again, he pecked her on the cheek. "Be careful," he offered, before darting into the house. "Bring the sisters home safely."

"Bring yourself home safely," Brye rebutted.

Suddenly feeling uncharacteristically shy after Damien's departure, for several frantic heartbeats, Brye observed Linn playing "Simon Says" with the younger children. It took a great deal of effort for her to push Chad into the back of her mind. His compelling presence overwhelmed her senses. The masculine scent of his cologne sent her mind into a tailspin. The friction of his taut flesh lightly rubbing against her bare skin was the only catalyst needed to melt a body frozen in suspended animation for many years gone by.

Dammit! Dammit! Dammit! She unceasingly cursed herself. Right now, she wanted to concentrate fully on figuring out how to convince sisters needing her assistance, that they truly needed her assistance. She had to come up with a plan to broach two girls who probably didn't trust any more than she did.

The task deemed futile until Brye took note of Chad openly studying her. It was his eyes. Those enchanting, drop-dead gorgeous, erotically appealing, baby-blue eyes. The same impressive eyes the twins replicated. And that's when it dawned on her: Bethany could help. Bethany, the nurturer. Bethany, the more caring of the two twins. Bethany who, at the age of six, understood life better than many three times her age. There was no one better equipped to talk to an abused five-year-old other than another person who'd survived an identical ordeal.

"I'm going to slip into my shoes, then grab Bethany. I've decided to take her with us. Could you inform Linn of our plans?"

Surprised Brye could consider dragging Bethany into this convoluted affair, Chad instantly voiced his disapproval. "Why would you unnecessarily involve Bethany in this? She's just a child, for heaven's sake."

Chad's concern for Bethany astounded Brye. They'd only known each other for one afternoon. Was Chad already developing a sense of kinship toward the twins? The thought pleased her.

In normal everyday situations, his question would have been warranted. The difference here was that Bethany had never lived a normal life, and this was not a normal situation. Chad's question was implausible at best. Patiently, she explained why.

"Bethany is already involved…so's everyone else who's ever been abused, neglected, or exploited. And although chronologically these kids are young, mentally, they've aged well beyond their years. In their brief lives, they've experienced more pain and suffering than you will ever undergo in your lifetime."

Chad instantly took note of her choice of words. She used the singular *you*, not we. She had not included herself. What was the significance behind her exclusion? Had she been abused? How? When? By whom?

As he stared into saddened eyes, he realized she was right on all accounts except one: she may believe he knew nothing of the perils of suffering, but he had undergone the greatest anguish he would ever endure in his lifetime. He had lost his one true love. She had walked out of his life. His world had been radically altered.

Sliding the back of his hand along the side of her delicate features, he said, "Why don't you get Bethany? If you can tear her away from her macaw, I'll let Linn know where we're going."

Brye tilted her head into his soothing caress. Closing her eyes, relishing in the comfort and reassurances his closeness provided, she longed to lose herself within his touch, inside the sheltering confines of his arms… She longed to drown herself in a motley of passionate kisses.

What are you doing? Out of nowhere, the thought sideswiped her. For one afternoon, Chad had methodically invaded her life and appropriated the children's approval. He was now working on untangling her tangled emotions, repairing her shattered heart, and easing her violated soul. And through it all, she totally disregarded her own uncommonly good sense. Right now, she had business to contend with. For the moment, her musings had to be shoved aside for later analysis.

Backing out of his reach without uttering a sound, she turned and slipped into the house.

Mystified, Chad stared at her backside as she strolled away from him. On several occasions this afternoon, Chad had thought he'd snared her. He'd actually thought he'd secured a sense of trust, only to watch her cautiously slip out of his precarious hold.

Determined to work harder at procuring her confidence, he turned toward Linn. Much to his surprise, she stood, eyeing him, lips puckered inquisitively. From the critical stance she had taken, to the curious expression she fired at him, he knew she retained questions about his and Brye's relationship. Squaring his shoulders, he headed toward her while preparing to fend off the inquisition.

Later that evening, traveling from bedroom to bedroom, Chad issued his good nights, then trailed down Brylinn's winding staircase. The lights were dimmed to a soothing pink tint. A contented sigh breezed through the estate walls. Appreciative of the few hours reprieve the home had been granted, a revitalization cycle geared into high speed in preparation for the following day's misadventures. With each step carrying Chad to the lower landing, images of Brye, along with Bethany, sent a surge of what? Pride? Admiration? Love? Entangled emotions coursed a direct pathway straight to his heart. Woman and child were so much alike, Chad almost found it impossible to believe, that not only were the two not blood related, but they'd known each other for less than a year. At times, they appeared so much in sync with one another.

Chad hadn't realized the extent of their unity until he'd delivered Brye and Bethany to the alleged abused sisters' place of residence.

Prior to entering the home, Jeff Packard—NYPD—had cautioned Brye. He believed the attempt at convincing the sisters to turn in their mother's boyfriend would be futile at best. But much to everyone's surprise, less than two hours later, it had been a fait accompli. With Bethany sequestering Jamie, the five-year-old, and Brye pulling Jordan aside, in no time at all, the two had worked magic. Jordan and Jamie, although somewhat apprehensive, confronted the truth head-on.

How Brye and Bethany achieved success was somewhat of a mystery to Chad. They had not collaborated on their approach with the sisters. They had not worked out a specified strategy. Instead, issuing a multitude of kind words, presenting themselves as sincere, caring individuals, promising the sisters only what could be adhered to, Brye and Bethany took on a situation, knowing what needed to be done, and, together, it had been done.

Impressed, amazed, fascinated beyond believe, Chad now saw Brye as a provider, nurturer, guidance counselor, role model, and friend.

Chad silently crept down the shaded foyer. A diaphanous glow peeking around the semi-closed door of Brye's and Linn's office caught his attention. He moved on, not wanting to disturb Linn as she labored over last-minute obligations before carting herself off to bed. He continued toward the kitchen and unintentionally stumbled into a scene which would etch a permanent spot in his memory banks forever.

Bathed in intimate lighting, two bodies were huddled with heads close together at a solid oak kitchen nook. The harsh realities of the past several hours dulled—if not in their hearts, then in their faces—by the soft colors floating around them. Parked on the edge of the L-shape bench, Brye sat with Jordan's meek body standing comfortably between her thighs. As Chad looked on, Brye exhibited extreme selflessness toward the older of the two sisters they'd rescued. She remained pacifying as well as supportive. Unnoticed, Chad leaned comfortably against the kitchen's doorjamb as a somber conversation, afflicted with tear-jerking torment, consumed him alive.

"I don't understand." The lines in Jordan's childlike face contorted in anguished confusion. Tears of despondency spilled from eyes begging to understand. Her mother had always been so kind, so loving, so understanding, until she'd started living with *him*. He hadn't even had them settled into the house before he started hitting on Jordan and her sister. And whenever he beat them, he made sure their mother wasn't around. He'd also hit them in places where it wouldn't leave a mark. "Why doesn't my mother believe me when I tell her he hurts us? Why does she only listen to *him*? What did my sister and I do to make her so mad at us?" The last sentence erupted in short, sobbing bursts.

"It's okay to cry." Brye pulled her into a consoling embrace. Jordan relaxed her cheek against Brye's chest. "But it's *not* okay to blame yourself." Soothingly, she strummed her fingers through Jordan's stringy blond hair. "You know how you get confused sometimes?" Brye felt a timid nod of the head. "Well, your mother may be your mother, but first and foremost, she's a person…a human being. She, just like the rest of us, makes mistakes."

Jordan pressed closer into Brye. Her mother used to hold her like this…before *he* came along. She missed her mother's hugs, their playtimes, the bedtime stories. The happy memories seemed so far removed from her life, and the sobering thought launched another round of sobs.

Pressing the teary child securely against her, Brye gently swayed from side to side. This was the hardest for her to handle: The misplaced blame, the self-administered recriminations, the implanted wounds. In most of the child abuse cases Brye was pulled into, the victims generally harbored a deep-rooted conviction: "I should have been a better person...tried harder...done more to make my parents love me."

With Brye, their pain was her pain. She suffered along with them. And despite the many times she relived the moment, with each child she comforted, her pain never lessened; the anguish ripped at her heart.

Hoping to confine the staggering situation within perimeters Jordan could understand, Brye asked, "Do you know anything about drugs?"

Pulling out of Brye's warm embrace, Jordan lifted wide, tear-stained eyes. Stifling a sniffle, she asked, "Good drugs or bad drugs?"

"Do you know the difference between the two?"

Nodding, Jordan wiped at fallen tears with the back of her hand. Her tongue barely grazed along her bottom lip as she considered the question. "We learned in school. When a person's sick, they go to a doctor. Doctors prescribe good drugs. But illegal drugs like heroin and crack cocaine are bad drugs."

"Very good," Brye openly praised. "Sometimes people can be considered as drugs." Brye paused. Capturing Jordan's full attention, she continued, "Your mother's boyfriend is like a drug to your mother...a bad drug. For reasons you and I don't know and may never come to understand, he's gotten into her system, and she's become addicted to him...she's grown dependent upon him. She can't think of anyone else but him." *The same way I am with Chad.* "And all the while, he's turning her into something she isn't. It's because of him she's lost sight of who she is. She's lost sight of her own self-respect and objectivity. And that's not to say she doesn't love you or Jamie any longer. It only means she's misplaced her good judgment for the moment."

Brye pushed several strands of hair away from Jordan's troubled eyes. As she lowered her hand, the front of her own romper caught her attention. Jordan's tears had altered Brye's bib from teal to forest green. The piteous sight sent tears scurrying close to the surface; tears which would never be shed. And then she felt him. His consoling presence, his voiceless support, warming Brye's inside like a cup of hot cider on a brisk October day.

Brye's gaze lifted. Wrapped in faded lighting, his immense mass could not be concealed. She felt, rather than saw, his smile of encouragement. It gave her strength to carry on. "Despite what you believe, none of this is yours or Jamie's fault. Nothing you can say will make your mother believe her boyfriend's bad for her. That's something she'll have to figure out on her own. So the best thing you can do for your mother is to pray for her well-being."

Jordan threw her arms around Brye's neck. She buried her face into Brye's shoulder. Her voice muffled, she cried out in drowning despair, "If love makes you forget who you are, I'll never fall in love." It was a reckless declaration made from a desperate eleven-year-old who wanted her mother back.

Brye tightened her arms around Jordan's fragile frame. "Oh, honey." Tenderly, she stroked Jordan along the back of her head. "How do I explain so you'll understand?" Brye wasn't certain she could explain it to herself. After all, she saw herself altering her own rules to accommodate Chad. And in her eyes, it didn't make her any smarter than Jordan's mother. Sighing deeply, she maintained her eye on Chad as she pushed forward. "Love is an intricate part of life. We can't always predict who or when or where we'll fall in love. And we can't guarantee who we'll fall in love with or how we behave when we do take the plunge. So...the only thing you and I can do is hope we don't lose ourselves in the process. And if we do, let's pray we have the common sense, as well as the strength, to listen to others when they try to inform us of our weird behavior."

Chad's heart convulsed for several agonizing heartbeats before plowing into an inconsistent beat. He's knees grew rubbery. Had the arched doorway not been holding him upright, his weakened body would have slid to the floor. Brye could have easily been talking about himself. She could have been commenting on his own irrational conduct.

And today, after spending time with Brye and the kids of Brylinn, he scrambled to pull his thought patterns into some semblance of comprehension. He had to deal with his own runaway emotions, yet seek understanding in the demonstrative bond Brye procured with the children. She related well with them, as if she'd trudged heavily in their shoes. At times, she also appeared too close to the situation, as if she relived her own painful experiences while confronting theirs. But through it all, she engendered trust and respect. When conversing with the younger generation, she remained honest and aboveboard. She never promised what she could not deliver. And above all else, she handled the kids with never-ending patience and understanding.

He, on the other hand, couldn't profess to understand traumatized children. If he had sat down and held the same conversation with Jordan, he would have said all the wrong words, made all the wrong moves. He would have asked Jordan to give him reasons for why she gave a damn about a woman who apparently didn't give a damn about her own two daughters.

So what did that tell him? It told him Brye related well because she'd suffered the same afflictions. But to what extent? And by whom?

Deliberating over Brye's veiled suffering, it saddened as well as frightened him to think she may not have had someone like herself to aid in easing her aching heart as she endured the tragedies altering her life.

14

Bryson stayed away from her parents' apartment for as long as she could manage. With no friends, the museums and public library closing, and the inflexible restrictions placed on her tender age, the possibilities of remaining away from home for an immeasurable period of time was limited. Straight up midnight, she finally let herself inside. The apartment was quiet, dark, untainted. Breathing a sigh of relief, Bryson closed the distance between the entrance door and the kitchen. Halfway there, she heard a low, strangled snort. Or maybe it was an unwieldy wheeze—a coarse, torturing hiss resembling a terminal emphysema patient agonizing over his final, lingering breaths.

Heated blood rushed to her head and pounded frantically against her folded temple. Acute awareness kicked into high gear. Gingerly slipping past the sofa, she lurched for the crystal column table lamp.

Rose-colored tint splashed about her but did not flush out every corner in the shadowed room. The rhythmic rasp, however, extended to every nook and cranny. Angling her body toward the amplified pitch, Bryson was able to distinguish the large, hunkering figure spilling from a leather-bound chair.

She drew in an alarmed breath and forgot to exhale.

A pig. A massive, fleshy, grunting, smelly animal poured into a polyester suit and tie. Pin-pricked eyes were red-tinted and sank deep inside a protruding brow; a pug nose flared arduously with each strained breath; his puffed jowls dangled weightily and bared the color of steamed shrimp. His pink skin emerged tough, leathery, peeling, as if he'd spent the better part of his life lazing in the sun. A bloated belly nestled snugly inside a mammoth lap. He leered greedily, like she was pig slop, and he could gulp her down in less time than it took her to scream.

Bryson coughed, battled a forceful spasmodic episode, and then sucked in a badly needed breath as her lungs screamed for air. Backing away from the apparition, her heel caught on the edge of the Persian rug. She teetered backward, arms spiraling like a windmill. Several wavering seconds later, she righted herself.

The pink puffer instantly recognized her immediate withdrawal. "No. Don't go! We can do so much for each other." The bloated ball of blubber struggled to extricate himself from the confines of the tight fitting seat. The leather chair bunched and crunched and made loud sucking noises in its attempt to cling to its overstuffed occupant.

The nauseous sight soured Bryson's churning stomach. Fleeing the room, she didn't stop until she was safely tucked away inside her own bedroom walls. Leaning against her door, chest heaving, she realized nothing short of a train could stop the three hundred pound animal if he wanted to plow through her door. Her eyes spun wildly, resting upon her student desk. Slowly, tediously, she dragged it across the room, heedlessly scarring the hardwood floor. The raw sound scraped endlessly at her firing synapses. Once the desk was secured in place, she slid her dresser drawer over and pushed it in front of the desk. Certain he could not invade the confines of her room, she stumbled onto her bed.

"Damn them! Damn them! Damn them!" Bryson beat her fist against her pillow. Tears blinded her vision. Torment and pain reared up and violently shook her world senseless. "Why are they doing this to me?" she wailed. "Why can't I feel safe in my own home? Why can't I be safe?"

Bryson dropped her head into her hands. She released a strangled sob. "Parents are supposed to shelter their young. They're supposed to see to their welfare and happiness." She fell back onto the bed and wound her shaking body into a tight ball. "I can't keep living like this. I can't continue fighting off these animals. One day, I'm not going to be so lucky. One of these days, I'm not going to get away so easily. This has got to stop…now!"

Bryson's tears gradually tapered off. She unraveled her body and pulled herself up. She sat with rigid back, as if warding off the cruel world. Tucking her knees under her chin, she wrapped her hands around her legs. As she rocked back and forth, an inspiration penetrated the core of her fear and progressively swallowed it alive.

A gun, she thought to herself. For the first time in her life, Bryson considered seeking protection in the form of a firearm. If her parents refused to see to her safety, she damn well better learn how to safeguard herself...

The following morning, although Chad had drained several cups of strong, percolated, black coffee, his human battery continued to recharge sluggishly. Still at half power, he debated on downing another cup but didn't believe it would satisfactorily pick him up to the degree he demanded to function properly.

Sinking further into his executive chair, his head rolled on top of his shoulders. All night, his mind had reeled over yesterday's events; staggering thoughts of Brye had played havoc with his raging hormones. At length, he had fallen into a restless sleep just at the break of dawn, only to be abruptly thrown out of bed by the jolting shrill of his bedside alarm clock.

Chad yawned. His arms and upper body stretched toward the ceiling. Kneading the hard knots swelling his screaming neck muscles, he contemplated the mound of work piled atop his office desk; would it all disappear if he ignored it long enough? Too weary to do anything but close his eyes, Chad replayed events of the night before.

Early morning—1:00 a.m., to be exact—he'd dropped Brye at her doorstep. For Chad, the drive to White Plains had been a soul-searching experience. An unspoken truce had narrowed the menacing chasm assembled between the two. They had not treated each other like enemies lying in wait to cut the other's throat. Instead, they traipsed lightly, cautiously, searching for neutral territory, seeking to mend crumbled fences.

The drive to Brye's had also been informative. Brye had openly discussed the psychological characteristics of an abused child. Regardless of the pain caused by the hands of a parent, woebegone children continued to love them. Parents could commit the most heinous of crimes, but, not out of the ordinary, and, because of the familial bond forged at birth, the offspring endured the guilt and blamed themselves for the sins of their parents—all in the name of love.

Strangely enough, as Brye spoke, the cadence in her voice became distant, automated, as if her body remained with him, but her mind had traveled beyond the realm of time.

Concerned with her detached behavior, Chad had reached over and shielded her clenched, fisted, hands within his own.

When she had laid a soft, saddened eye upon him, he was apprehended by two mind-boggling facts. One, she was just as vulnerable today as she had been the day he'd first met her. And two, he no longer wanted to hurt her.

Since joining his father in business, Chad had never shied away from power struggles; he was quick to join in corporate games. He, just as his father, played well and played for keeps. He, unlike his father, refused to resort to unfair, underhanded practices. Until now.

With Brye, he'd embarked upon a torrid game of revenge. Little had he known how risky it would become, or that he had set himself up to the dangers of fighting an emotional battle. He should have known the probabilities of losing this war would be relatively high. In fact, it was safe to say that his chances of surrendering had just risen to 100 percent.

Giving in to a resolved sigh, the lid containing all his vindictive intentions, solidly slid into place. Whatever had transpired between them in the past, he remained deeply in love with Brye. And that was an undisputable fact.

Resolute in solving the mystery behind their unpredicted separation, now, however, his intentions were strictly honorable.

During his visit to Brylinn, he'd been amazed at how the kids openly discussed their troubled past with Chad. "It's part of the healing process," each child heartily acknowledged.

Chad wanted to be able to openly discuss his and Brye's tormented past. And although he didn't know what their future entailed—he did have Jennifer to think about, although she seemed to be slipping further away from his reality more and more these days—he wanted to begin the healing process as well.

The office phone rang, abruptly interrupting the quiet milieu of his surroundings, as well as halting the pensive meandering of his silent reflections.

Stretching toward the blaring instrument, he instantly changed gears. His mind shifted into business mode. "Collier."

"Hi."

If undiluted caffeine pumped intravenously into his open veins, it still would not be as potent as the efficacy caused by the delicate lilt of her voice. The adrenaline in his system revved up to speedway mode.

Sitting up straighter, he asked, "Is everything all right? I thought you were on location, shooting the first Mystique commercial."

"I am. We're on a five-minute break. But I wanted to take the time to call…to thank you…" Shyly, her voice trailed off.

"Yes?" he mildly prodded. His gaze settled on the brass umbrella stand parked to the right of his closed office door.

"Actually, there are two matters I'd like to discuss with you."

"Yes?" He repeated, leaning into his desk.

"First, I'd like to thank you for the two dozen red roses you sent Bethany this morning. Linn says her expression was priceless when she read the belated birthday card. And the radio-transmitted airplane you had delivered to Anthony… Needless to say, he was ecstatic."

Silence fell upon anxious ears. Chad couldn't imagine why it meant so much to him, but he desired to gain her approval. He also wondered how she had obtained knowledge of his gifts so soon—he'd only had them delivered a little over an hour ago.

"I just called and spoke with Linn, as well as the twins," Brye announced, translating his thoughts. "Really, Chad, I do appreciate the thought, but you didn't have to go—"

"I wanted to," he said, cutting her off. "Bethany reminds me of a little lady." *She reminds me of you.* "She deserves something as delicate and as beautiful as she is. And I was impressed with Anthony's interest in aviation. He showed me the scale-model planes you helped him put together. I thought he needed a radio-controlled Cessna to add to his collection." His eyes grew restless. They traveled the length of his richly decorated office. "If it's okay, I'd like to take him to Central Park so we can fly it."

More silence. Then she asked, "Why are you doing this, Chad? You have your own life to lead." She wanted to add that he had Jennifer, but somehow managed to hold her tongue. "You are a very busy man, and your time is valuable. I'm sure you've more important things to do besides entertaining a few kids."

Chad pushed his chair out from under his desk. His knees pivoted toward the closed vertical blinds. "Believe it or not, I enjoyed the time I spent at Brylinn. I honestly enjoyed getting to know the kids."

"They enjoyed spending time with you." *I enjoyed spending time with you.* She deliberated for a few seconds before adding, "God knows my kids do not have enough positive male role models in their lives, but I don't want you thinking you're obligated to be that role model."

"Why don't you let me worry about my time and what I want to do with it. Okay?"

"Okay."

Separated with miles between them, Chad sensed her smile. He felt a slight pull of his stomach muscles. "Was there something else?" he asked. "You said there were several matters you wanted to discuss."

"I'm taking the kids, as well as my employees and their families, to Lake George this weekend to celebrate the Fourth. We were traveling in several cars and vans, but I was wondering—" She toyed with the question and wondered if she was overstepping boundaries. "I thought I'd ask you about leasing the company bus for five days. I'll be happy to pay whatever you think is fair."

Dazed with her altruistic generosity, once again, Chad entertained plausible excuses for the genuine reasons behind their dishonorable split. Maybe she had extorted the money not for herself but for someone else. Maybe someone had forced her into it. Maybe—

"Look, Chad, I'm sorry," Brye apologized as an excruciating stretch of silence punctured her eardrums. "This isn't business. It's for recreational purposes only. I shouldn't have asked."

"It's okay, Brye." Snapping out of his reverie, he tried to make light of the strained silence. "I was thinking about my own plans for the weekend. They don't sound one-tenth as interesting as yours." He swiveled in his chair, drawing his eyes away from the window and down to his desk. "Of course I'll donate the use of the company bus...for as long as you like. After all, it's for a good cause."

"I'd be more than happy to pay—"

"It's okay, Brye," he repeated, slightly breathless. Vivid images of a passionate weekend he'd once spent with Brye held him fast to his seat. Shaking the debilitating thoughts out of his mind, he asked, "I can call over and make sure the bus is serviced and fully gassed. When we remolded it for long distance travel, I believe they put the extra rows of seats in storage. I'll make sure everything is arranged for your trip." He began to mentally check off a list of things needed to be done in preparation. "How soon do you need it?"

"George can pick the bus up Thursday—right at the close of business hours—if it's all right with you. He's an excellent driver and has a CDL license to operate it."

"Thursday will be fine," Chad assured. "Is there anything else I can do for you?"

"It's kind of you to offer, but where the kids are concerned, I think you've gone above and beyond."

"I'd like to go above and beyond where *you* are concerned—if you'd let me." The words came out low, seductive, anxious to satisfy.

Brye's voice caught in her throat. She'd like nothing more than to allow their relationship to flourish. But how did one relinquish a love/hate relationship in a matter of days? Afraid they were moving much too quickly, Brye could not arrest the compelling force urging the two of them to reunite as lovers. When she was finally able to cough out her words, she choked on them. "Chad, I... We... I..." Stopping to catch her breath, flustered, she blurted out, "They're calling me. I have to go." Another pause. "I'm going to be extremely busy the next two days with department store appearances and a final layout shoot. If I don't see you before I leave for Lake George, I hope you have a wonderful and safe holiday." The line went dead.

Slowly, Chad replaced the receiver in its cradle. Smiling to himself, he realized, by a single sentence, he'd completely discombobulated Brye's customarily imperturbable exterior. Determined to keep her off balance, he began constructing a plan to accomplish just that.

Fifteen minutes into finalizing those plans, his fingers brushed against his forgotten coffee cup. Again, he smiled. "One phone call and I'm completely recharged," he muttered to himself.

Acutely aware he was hyped up enough to tackle any situation thrown in his path, he decided this to be a good time to seek out Brian and apologize for his less-than-charming performance of the day before.

Chad opened his vertical blinds before striking out toward Brian's office. Rich sunlight spilled into his office and brightened the weary recesses of his mind. Reborn, he was more than ready to confront Brian.

"Is Brian in?" he asked as he sided up to Rhonda's desk, his gaze steered down the hall toward Brian's open office door.

The steady clickety-click of her computer keyboard ceased. A trained eye rolled over her expansive office phone. Every call coming onto the floor initially went through her phone system. Checking Brian's lines, she noticed one lit, another flashing like a warning beacon.

"He's in, but he's taking a call and has another one on hold," she answered in her usually efficient manner.

"Does he have any appointments scheduled?"

Rhonda flipped her attention toward Brian's day planner. "Nothing so far."

Chad pushed away. "If anything comes up, I'll be in his office."

A slight nod of acknowledgment, and Rhonda dove back into her work.

Finished with one call, by the time Chad reached his door, Brian was stabbing at the second line. Hearing a timid sound tapping against his doorjamb, he looked up to see Chad block the outer office's florescent light from traipsing upon the mollifying confines of his office. Waving him into the room, he stuck two fingers out in front of him to indicate he'd only be a few minutes.

Nodding, Chad entered. Gathering his pants legs, he landed in the middle of Brian's sofa.

Brian maintained a steady conversation, but from the corner of his eyes, he kept a vigilant watch on Chad. Aware the disgruntled man had been on the warpath the day before, Brian was now curious as to if his boss's incoherent tantrum had ultimately tapered off. Also aware he had stormed out of the office in search of Brye, Brian wondered if there had been a cataclysmic explosion when the two heads collided. Was she any worse for wear if a heated conversation had ignited?

Calling an end to his phone conversation, Brian met Chad with a businesslike smile. "I'm glad you came in. There's a few things we need to discuss."

Able to put off eating humble pie a few minutes longer, Chad was all ears. "We were having problems with an overseas shipment when I took off yesterday," he noted. "Was the problem rectified?"

"As of this morning," Brian assured. Leaning back into his swivel chair, he settled his elbows on top of the padded arm rest and locked his fingers in front of him. "Actually, I wanted to discuss Brye's exclusive contract with Romanique."

Chad lifted one questioning, curious brow.

"Tenisha received a phone call from Daunte Jeans. They'd like to enlist Brye's services for advertising and feature her in a magazine layout." Brian sat forward. He laid his clasped fingers on top of the desk. "Tenisha informed them of Brye's exclusive contract." He smiled. "If, however, they were willing to feature the ads in our magazine, she might be able to see her way clear in approaching us with this business proposition."

Much to Brian's amazement, Chad laughed. A rich, unassuming chortle. Once he settled down, he asked, "If Tenisha continues to secure referrals, we may have to add her to our payroll."

Brian chuckled. "She *is* quite the businesswoman."

"So…" Chad settled his right ankle across his left knee. Stretching his left arm across the back of the couch, he asked, "How do you think we should handle this?"

Brian shrugged. "Since Daunte Jeans are not in direct competition with Romanique, I say let's go for it. In the end, Brye makes money, we make money, Daunte gets its much wanted supermodel, and everyone's happy."

"It's settled then." Chad stood up. "Arrange a meeting with Brye to discuss it. If she can manage to book it into her busy schedule—and I have no doubt she can—let her know she has our full approval."

Shocked Chad had acquiesced so easily, Brian dropped his gaze to avoid eye contact. After yesterday's unexpected turn of events, he'd predicted this conversation to have gone in a completely different direction. Vying for more time to regain his composure, he grabbed a pen and scribbled on a yellow sticky note: "Brye. Mtng. Today?"

"What're your plans for lunch?" Chad asked, blocking Brian's doorway.

"I plan on working through it. Maybe have Rhonda send out for a sandwich."

"Why don't you join me? My treat." The surprise springing along Brian's sardonic expression was just as imposing as the sudden appearance of a teenage girl's first zit. "Come on, Brian," Chad appealed to Brian's wavering hesitation. "Don't make this harder for me. Can't you tell when a person's being humble? I mean, I *am* trying to apologize for yesterday's behavior."

Twirling his Cross pen between his fingers, Brian leaned back into his chair. Grinning up at Chad, he asked, "Is that what you're trying to do?"

Chad looked chagrined. "You mean you couldn't tell? Of course that's what I'm trying to do."

"In that case, how about lunch at the Four Seasons?"

A five-star establishment featuring a sweeping selection of magnificently prepared cuisine, amused laughter danced around the perimeter of Chad's eyes at Brian's impetuous suggestion. "You have expensive taste, my friend."

"Hey," Brian smartly answered, "apologies don't come cheap."

Chad laughed. "I guess they don't." Skimming the face of his watch, he said, "I'll have Rhonda make the arrangements. Let's say… hour and a half from now?"

"That's fine with me," Brian confirmed.

Chad slipped through the door. On afterthought, he faced Brian a split second later. Tapping the doorjamb lightly with his fist, he stated with abysmal sincerity, "I really am sorry about my behavior yesterday. I can only explain it away by saying I allowed personal feelings to get in the way of my business sense. It will never happen again."

"Apology duly noted and accepted." Rising from his chair, he strolled over and patted Chad on the shoulders. "We all have our off days, Chad. It's something we can't always avoid. But you know if you ever need someone to talk to…if you need an ear to vent to, I'm here for you."

"I'm aware of that, Brian. And I appreciate the offer." Turning to go, he said, "I'll see you for lunch."

Thoughtfully, Brian maneuvered around his desk. Falling into his chair, he picked up his pen and tapped it against his desk. Questions filtered in and out of his mind; what was behind Chad's dramatic mood swings? Why did he believe that Brye stood knee-deep in whatever plagued Chad?

Stretching toward his phone, he hit Rhonda's intercom line.

"Yes, Brian?"

"See if you can contact Brye. When and if she can fit me into her schedule, arrange a time for us to meet. Make sure she understands it's important, but it isn't a dire emergency. If she can't manage today, schedule for when she can."

"Will do. Anything else?"

"That'll be all."

Brian turned his mind toward his work. Working diligently, it startled him when Rhonda's voice burst through the intercom system.

"The limo's here to drive you and Chad to the Four Seasons."

"Thanks, Rhonda. I'll be right there."

"You have a four-thirty appointment with Brye," she also informed.

"I'll be back long before then."

"Have a good lunch."

An audible sigh rolled over Brian's tongue. Brye retained the key needed to unlock this mystery. She stood at the center of whatever ailed Chad. And although he and Brye were vastly establishing the boundaries of their friendship, Brian wasn't certain he felt secure enough to infringe on her personal life. However, if the chance did arise, he would not hesitate to ask.

Sometime during the late 1800s, Southampton—one of the oldest English settlements in the state of New York—gained a reputation as a stomping ground for life's most rich and famous. Within the summer resort, the past melded graciously with the present; luxurious beach-front properties hobnobbed with classical Victorian, stylish ranch, and brick colonial.

The Colliers summer "cottage," created in stucco and glass, stretched three stories skyward, embraced ten thousand square feet of pedigreed distinction and bedded in the midst of fifteen acres of prime oceanfront property. A stable, tennis court, guesthouse, and Olympic-sized pool named a few of the amenities gifted to family and friends. And at the present, Jennifer Cavanaugh indulged to her heart's content.

"Damn him to hell!" she cursed, tossing the portable phone onto the tempered glass top snack table. The maid cringed at the harsh pitch infringing upon the late morning repose. From the first moment the thin, mousy woman had confronted Jennifer, she'd been intimidated. Today was no different. Drawing up into herself, as if the simple act would aid her in disappearing into thin air, the servant continued to clear away the morning meal from the wheeled cart/server.

"You will not get away with this, Chad Collier!" Jennifer angrily vowed, taking no notice of the maid. Flying out of her cushioned chaise lounge, she slid her dark-red lacquered toes into a pair of leather slip-ons. Flinging a matching cover-up over a respectably tailored maillot swimsuit—God forbid she should present herself to the elderly Colliers as a woman with a reputation nothing short of virtuous—with as much ladylike grace as she could muster, she tore through the resplendent grounds in search of Daniel Collier.

Of course she could go to Chad's mother with this unanticipated turn of events, but she wanted immediate results. No doubt, Daniel Collier was the man to furnish her with a much better outcome.

As an invited guest, and at Chad's insistence, she'd come down one week earlier to await his arrival for the Fourth of July weekend. *He probably wants to explore time alone with that bitch of a spokeswoman*, she scornfully conceived. Her parents were arriving within the next several days. Jennifer would not be made a fool of in front of them, nor did she have any intention to remain down here, reenacting the life of the Brady Bunch clan while Chad was out somewhere screwing the hired help.

She skirted around the pool house and trudged down the stone-laid trail leading to the tennis court. Bypassing the professionally trimmed hedges and artfully laid flower garden, eyes and mind blocked out all else but the situation at hand.

Not once, in the years she'd spent with Chad, had there ever been any hint he catered to a wandering eye. And although he'd never actually stated he loved her—which Jennifer considered to be a major flaw on his part—mentally and physically, he'd remained faithful.

At least until Brye Grayson entered the picture. Hell, she wasn't blind. She hadn't been oblivious to the strained tension gripping Chad's balls whenever she materialized. Jennifer wasn't unmindful of the recent strain evolving around their lovemaking.

But none of that mattered. To be honest with herself, she could care less if Chad fucked Brye's brains out until the cows came home. As long as he was discreet, and Jennifer received the ring on her finger, what did it matter to her?

Chad belonged to her. If not in mind and spirit, at least in body. Whatever it took, she would acquire the Collier name, fame, and fortune.

Jennifer smiled mercilessly to herself. Another woman she could handle. And if she had to pack up her bags, leave Southampton, and head back to the city to get a better grip on the situation, she would not hesitate.

"Damn you, Chad!" she mumbled to herself. "I've worked too hard and much too long to create the kind of wife your parents would be proud to call their daughter-in-law." *We will get engaged,* she thought to herself. *I will become your wife!*

Spotting Daniel walking off the tennis court, she forced a smile and slowed her gait. "Did you enjoy your game?" she questioned, drawing closer.

Midmorning, a desirable breeze drifted off the ocean surface and counterbalanced the hovering sun. And although the heat had not climbed to a fatiguing level, beads of sweat adorned Daniel's heavy brow. His chest heavily rose and fell as his lungs laboriously sucked in much-needed air. "I'm getting too old for this," he good-naturedly grumbled, swiping the sweat off his face with a white towel. "I think I'm ready for a shot of Geritol and a nice long nap."

"Nonsense." Jennifer smiled judiciously. "You're in the prime of your life…and look every bit of it," she added for good measure, but meant every word. Although he wasn't as tall as his son, he was just as handsome. And in his white shorts and polo shirt, he exhibited a solid, tanned, healthy body misrepresenting his fifty-eight years of age.

As if he'd expended no energy at all, Daniel's personal trainer sprinted up to the stationary couple. Blond, beautiful, brainless, the beguiling bodybuilder asked, "Same time tomorrow, Mr. Collier?"

"I'll be here. Unless I have a heart attack first."

"No chance of that happening while under my supervision." Grinning, he dipped his head at Jennifer, turned, and sauntered away. Jennifer was hard-pressed to keep her eyes off the piquant sight of those sexy taut buns ambling away from her.

"Did you come down to see to my well-being? Maybe hold me up on the walk back?" He tossed the towel over his right shoulder, then indulged himself with a squirt bottle filled with spring water.

"Actually"—her eyes lowered to the green tennis mat, her voice grew sullen—"I wanted to talk to you about Chad."

"Chad?" Daniel lowered his bottle from his lips. His Adam's apple bobbed for several seconds before halting at midline. "What about Chad?"

"I just got off the phone with him." Eyes spilling with concern, she carried them back to Daniel. "I'm worried about him… this job…" There was a calculated pause. "He's not coming down for the holiday weekend. And with the inauguration of the promotional tour next week, he maintains that he has loose ends to tie up."

Much to Jennifer's delight, she'd appropriated the precise effect she'd hoped for. A lesser person would not have witnessed the gales of provocation-induced smoke pouring from Daniel's ears and swarming around his pulsating temple. Her face immobile, she watched with self-possessed elation as Daniel silently fumed.

"He told you this?" His mind furtively searched for an appropriate solution to challenge this unforeseen obstacle. It was not long in coming.

Jennifer wrapped her arms around her chest as if the fire of the midday sun wasn't enough to maintain her warmth or well-being. "I know this company is important to Chad…to you…but I was so looking forward to spending the Fourth with him." The quivering of her bottom lip added an extra intimate touch. Silently, she praised herself.

Throwing his arm around Jennifer's shoulders, Daniel led her back toward the massive estate. As they strolled past a bank of cedar trees, Jennifer continued to confide in him.

"Since they hired that spokeswoman, he's been exceptionally busy. He's been…distracted." She didn't want to lay it on too thick, nor did she want to out-and-out accuse Chad of cheating on her. She wanted Daniel to draw his own conclusions.

He did.

Patting her lovingly on her upper arm, he appeased, "Don't worry your pretty little head over this, my dear. I will speak to him personally."

"Would you, please?" Jennifer's face lit up like a dog being offered a bone.

"I'll drive up tomorrow and get to the bottom of this."

"Maybe I should drive up with you?" she tentatively asked as if she'd suddenly given birth to the idea.

"That's very commendable, Jennifer, dear. But it's not necessary." Daniel planned to confront Chad himself. If there were any unforeseen problems cropping up at Romanique, he wanted immediate feedback. And if there were foreseen problems—such as Chad getting involved with that Brye woman again—he was prepared to take whatever steps necessary to end it before his son's infatuation flared into epic proportions.

Issuing an affectionate squeeze to her shoulder, Daniel added, "Trust me to take care of this little problem."

Jennifer held her triumphant smile in check. Her insides tickled with glee. She had no doubts Daniel would handle Brye Grayson. And with any luck, before the weekend was out, an engagement ring would be adorning the appropriate finger.

Brye knocked before entering Brian's office. Wandering over to his desk, she beckoned him back into his chair. "Don't get up," she requested, handing him one of the two bottles of ice-cold lemon-flavored water she had carted in with her.

"Well…look at you." Brian took his offered drink, then flopped against the back of his chair.

Given her position as Romanique's spokesperson, Brye mistook his open-eyed expression as one of disapproval for her nontraditional appearance.

Lighthearted, her eyes rolled down the length of her body to inventory each piece of her attire. Sleeveless open print vest over a twist front bandeau top, loose-fitting shorts cinched at the waist by a rope belt, slouch socks, combat boots encasing size eight feet. From her left ear, a medley of gold chains jiggled with each toss of her head, her right ear sported a diamond stud earring. Hair piled haphazardly atop her head, abandoned curls streamed along the side of a face donned with light makeup.

This was her hip-hop look created by the youths at Brylinn. The male teens went as far as to say she looked "fire," which was a term, she soon discovered, meaning she looked terrific.

Twinkling eyes settled on Brian. "I've been working for the company for what? Four weeks now? Well, I hate to say it, dear heart, but the honeymoon's over. I'm letting my kids dress me now."

Brian failed miserably at maintaining his professional image, nor could he keep his eyes on her face. Instead, they migrated southward bound—following the pathway along a bare midriff, traveling down the road to long, curvaceous legs that stretched outward to eternity.

He'd seen her at her most glamorous, her most fashionable, and her most professional, but he'd never seen her like this. Not ever like this.

Wow!

Brian's brow deepened into an appreciative groove. "I don't think so, Brye. In fact, I believe the honeymoon's just beginning. And if you give me a moment to pick my tongue up off the floor, catch my breath, and control my racing heart, I'll proclaim just how good you do look."

Brye laughed. Accepting the compliment for what it was worth, she then let it go.

During the past few weeks, she and Brian had begun to forge an amicable relationship. Initially, Brian had shown mild interest in forming a close association. Soon realizing she was not prepared to advance into anything more intimate than affable banter, without exhibiting any rancor or disgruntlement, he immediately backed off. Brye liked that. And she liked Brian. This was the first male companionship she'd pursued since her friendship with Marcus had taken root.

Parking herself on the leather sofa, Brye said, "I missed you at the Collier party—it was such a *wonderful* affair."

The emphasis placed on *wonderful*, the rolling of her eyes and scrunching of facial lines, indicated to Brian that the party was anything but wonderful.

"Actually," he stated, attempting to brush it off as an insignificant concern, "I wasn't invited."

"Oh." Cocking her head to one side, Brye studied Brian. With his one simple statement, she was able to assimilate their parallelism with very little strain. Brian, just like herself, wasn't seen as anyone of importance to Daniel Collier. Brian, just as herself, was merely a servant. Someone to hang the coat up at the door. An expendable apparatus ready to be shoved aside when services were no longer rendered.

Somehow, the dreary thought did not depress her. In all actuality, it pleased her to be standing in such fine company. Aligning her face with the most innocent of expressions, she repeated, "You weren't invited?" Leaning closer, her voice lowered conspiratorially. "So tell me, Brian, how did you get so lucky?"

Brian did not readily react. Several impossible seconds later, he accepted the irony of the situation. For weeks, he'd silently brooded over not being one of the chosen assemblage invited to Daniel Collier's social gathering. Now, by way of a haphazard razzing remark, Brye had forced him to see that Daniel Collier did not recognize Brian as someone worthy of being in the presence of his greatness.

Several seconds of conjoined, unrestrained laughter filled the room, The first to wipe the mirth from his eyes, picking up his bottle of water, he held it out for Brye to tap with her own.

"Touché," he remarked, downing a generous amount.

Under control once again, Brian lightly teased, "The day you signed aboard our company was definitely a turning point for Romanique. By all indications, you're going to take us through a ride we'll never forget."

"Should I take that as a compliment?"

"You certainly should."

Completely at ease, Brye let her guard down during the entire two-hour meeting. Finalizing plans for the promotional tour, arranging a conference call with Tenisha, Brian, and Daunte Jeans, fine-tuning last-minute details, at the conclusion of the business conference, Brye prepared for her departure.

Climbing to her feet, she noted with a hint of an apology, "I've kept you long past business hours."

Fingers lightly sprayed against the small of her back, Brian gently guided her to the door. Standing in the opening, he turned to face her. Half-teasing, half-serious, he said, "I guess this is where I ask if you'd like to go out to dinner."

The corners of her lips turned upward in an apologetic grin. "I'm sorry, Brian, but with preparing for my weekend trip, as well as the promotional campaign, I have very little time for myself."

Maintaining a constant smile, Brian nodded in understanding. "One of these days," he dawdled, leaving the sentence open for suggestion.

"I'm going to hold you to that," Brye freely promised.

"Brye!"

Brye swung in the direction of his enticing voice. Her heart quickened at the sight of him standing just outside his office door. Her insides churned to liquid. Ambling toward her, he wore the most dazzling of smiles.

"Chad," she heavily exhaled, "what a nice surprise. I wasn't expecting to see you."

"I'm finishing up paperwork." His gaze captured Brian. "Working late?"

"I also have a few loose ends to tidy up, then I'm out of here."

"Good." He turned his charming smile back on Brye. "Are you leaving?"

"I am," she verified, hoping against all hope he'd offer to walk her to her car.

"Can I walk you out?"

Internally, Brye jumped up and down in sheer jubilation. Externally, she calmly accepted his offer. "I'd like that."

Issuing their good nights to Brian, side by side, Brye and Chad wandered toward the elevator.

Staring after the two retreating bodies, Brian's mouth pinched into an inquisitive scowl. Yesterday, Chad had screamed bloody murder behind Brye's absence. Today he stared at her as if they were… what? Star-crossed lovers?

"What the hell's going on here?" he mumbled to himself. Sifting his fingers through layers of trimmed hair, he stepped back into his office.

As soon as the elevator door smoothly sealed shut, Brye realized her mistake. Haphazard sparks instantly exploded within the confines of the enclosed space. Backing as far away from the influx of sizzling sensation his nearness provoked, Brye moved to the farthest side of the elevator. Pressing her back flat against the wall, she willed Chad to maintain an appropriate distance.

A shimmer of amusement—or was it desire?—stained Chad's irises into a shade richer than the imposing deep blue sea. Brye found herself plunging into the very depths of his turbulent gaze. Hoping to resist the powerful pull he exerted upon her, as if she could fuse with the wall, she squeezed her body tighter against the solid barrier.

Oblivious to her distress, Chad positioned his hulking physique directly in front of Brye's cowering body. Hands plunged deep inside his pockets, he made no effort to reach out to her. Instead, he torched her with a smoldering glance. But the heat in his eye was just as dangerous as if he stroked her trembling body with a persistent touch.

"Do you know how appealing you look?" Chad asked huskily.

Brye didn't respond. She couldn't respond. Her entire life she'd remained crucially in control of her feelings…her emotions. And as she began earning a living under the scrutinizing eye of the camera, she was proud of the strict discipline she maintained with every detailed movement she executed. Every facial muscle, every move she instigated, every pose she struck was carefully orchestrated. But here, under the power of Chad's swaying eye, she couldn't lift a finger to push him away.

"Brye?" Her name rolled off his tongue in a seductive whisper. Her nearness exerted unconscionable acts upon his mind and body. Unable to control himself, an overwhelming craving goaded him into shutting down the elevator and taking her right here…right now. He pulled his right hand out of his pocket and traced a soft line from the hollow of her neck to the exposed crevice above her breast.

Rooted to the spot, Brye watched as his head dipped closer… closer…

Ding!

Saved by the bell. The elevator doors glided open.

Wearing a roguish grin, Chad collected himself and backed away. Gingerly inching around him to prevent any further contact, Brye stepped out into the stifling air. Sweltering heat, entrapped within the confines of the underground parking garage, soaked up every ounce of moisture from her parched skin, like a vacuum sucking up minute traces of dust particles.

Car in sight, Brye slid between a Mustang and her Toyota. "Thank you for walking me to my car," she courteously acknowledged, digging deep into her purse for her car keys.

Chad removed her key from her hand. His fingers lingered on hers longer than necessary. "How about dinner?" he asked, locking eyes.

Brye actually considered accepting. But dinner would probably lead to "other things." And Brye was not prepared to face the "other things."

Shaking her head in reluctant refusal, she apologized, "I'm sorry. I can't. I'm going over the books with Kirk tonight. It's end of the month, and our accounts have to be balanced."

Although disappointed, he bowed his head in gentlemanly acceptance. There would be other times, Chad acknowledged to himself. He hit the key fob, the car dinged in acceptance, the doors unlocked. Pulling the door open, he promised, "Some other time then."

Before she was able to climb in, Chad bent forward and kissed her on the corner of her lips. Again, he lingered several seconds longer than necessary. Brye took in the heady smell of his intoxicating cologne. She experienced a wisp of his tongue as it flickered lightly against her parched skin. Closing her eyes, she imagined her lips avidly mingling with his. If she only moved her head slightly to the left. Just one fraction of an inch…

Chad straightened. He issued her that drop-dead gorgeous smile. "Don't work too hard tonight. And tell the kids I said hello."

Brye nodded. She fell into the interior of the car with fob in hand. Chad slammed the door behind her and was gone.

En route to Brylinn's, Brye mulled over her nonsensical behavior. His nearness had caused her to act like a flighty schoolgirl teen exhibiting her first crush on the drastically handsome gym teacher.

Inwardly, she groaned. She promised herself she would keep him at arm's distance. At least until she discovered his actual game plan—if there was a game plan. Maybe he really did want to call a truce. Maybe he wanted to explore the possibility of their getting back together...forever. Maybe it was impossible for him to resist her as she found it difficult to maintain her distance from him.

There was, beyond a shadow of a doubt, an electrical current veering back and forth between the two of them. The sizzling current remained constant, operating on a consistently high voltage.

Images of Chad, his magnificent body, their love-making, ran an intricate channel through Brye's weakening composure. An old familiar swell congregated at the apex of her thighs. Not wanting to think about what she'd denied herself all these years, not wanting to think at all, Brye flipped the air conditioner to full blast. Determined to maintain a tighter grip on her cataclysmic emotions while in the presence of Chad, she pushed all thoughts of her former lover out of her mind—at least for the moment—and battled the rush hour density storming the streets of Manhattan.

The following afternoon, Brye stepped out of Macy's department store and stepped foot onto the congested pathway of 34th Street and 151st.

Inexorably warm, the imposing orange-red ball hovering above Brye's head cast a fiery glow along the beaten sidewalk. The consuming heat fried everything in its wake yet barely forged a dent in Brye's cool, calm exterior. Oblivious to the appreciative stares thrust her way, and the maddening blare of the traffic-infested streets, she slid large dark shades over her squinting eyes and blocked out the enraged scowl glaring down at her from the unrelenting sun. She peered up and down the swarming street. A two-tone stretch limo gracefully pulled to the curb. The engine idled. A medium-sized driver wearing the normal chauffeur garb along with a gnarled expression—Brye wondered if he suffered heartburn—stepped out of the car.

"Ms. Grayson?" he approached.

"Yes?"

"This way, please."

Brye allowed him to pilot her—none to gently—toward the limousine. He pulled the door open, and with his cumbersome hand splattered between her shoulder blades, she was assisted—or was it thrust?—into the back seat. Once the chauffeur settled inside, the luxury car silently merged with the stifling traffic.

The posh, air-conditioned interior did not delude Brye. She had just stepped onto a battleground. Signing on with Romanique Cosmetics had been tantamount to enlisting in the armed forces. And now she was about to embark upon a major confrontation: the battle of the wills. Her steel armor clanked soundlessly into place.

Attentive to the wisdom that body language exposed all, Brye understood this man to be proficient in reading voiceless dialect. She would rather be strung up on a torture rack, limbs stretched from here to forever, before she gave him the opportunity of interpreting hers.

With a slight shift of her body, she made herself as comfortable as she could allow.

While climbing into the limo, her above-the-knee linen skirt crept higher, exposing more of her silken-clad thigh than she preferred. Not wanting to seem prudish, she made no effort to slither her skirt downward. Not wanting to appear flirtatious, she didn't cross her legs to expose more of her fleshy thigh. Not wanting to give the impression of being too confident, she did not slink back into the invitingly lush upholstered seats. Instead, she sat with spinal column straight, shoulders back, chin fearlessly tilted upward.

Remembering her sunglasses, she debated on uncovering her eyes. Of course, she had nothing to hide behind the dark shades. Or did she?

No, she did not.

Nothing?

Other than the reality of wanting to be with this man's son. She wanted to make love to this man's son. She wanted to marry him… make babies with him. She wanted to spend the rest of her life with him.

She removed the glasses. Violet-colored eyes stared innocently at the aristocratic man sitting across from her. Back stiff, smile in place, she presented herself in a dignified manner; she presented herself as the lady she knew herself to be.

As always, her composed restraint, the cryptic air she assumed, much as a police officer donned his badge, impressed the hell out of him. Contrary to popular belief, just like Jennifer, he could give a shit if Chad fucked this woman until he was blue in the face. Hell, he'd had a few affairs of his own in his day. He understood what it felt like to have a woman dig herself so far underneath the skin, not even a stick of dynamite could blast her out. But a few hours of abandoned lovemaking would not fulfill lifetime goals and accomplishments. And a woman not of the marriage persuasion would hinder, rather than enhance, a natural born leader. And Brye Grayson—holding a past that made a porno queen look like Mother Theresa—was definitely not marriage material.

"Brye," Daniel Collier acerbically grinned at her like the devil incarnate. "So nice of you to come."

Unadulterated evil waved a hand over Brye's soul. Inwardly, she winced.

"I was surprised when I received the note summoning my presence," she candidly admitted.

To break down her solid reserve, Daniel let the seconds slowly tick past. With deliberate slowness, he sipped at his Chivas Regal. Markedly, he studied her over the rim of his crystal glass. Several dragging seconds later, and no visible signs of distress forthcoming, he said, "I wanted to spend a few minutes with you…to hear firsthand how you were doing."

Brye knew better than to believe he'd called this private meeting out of concern for her own personal welfare. Yet she would follow wherever led. "I'm extremely busy," she admitted, maintaining a stoic vigilance, "but in retrospect, I've gotten quite a bit accomplished."

He crossed his legs and flicked the hand holding the drink over his knee. "There has been a steady rise in sales since you've joined our team."

Brye nodded, not batting an eye. "Brian's kept me apprised."

"There is also an unofficial count of the number of Mystique gift packages you've sold today. Preliminary numbers supports record sales. I'm impressed. Obviously your personal appearance turned out to be a huge success."

Small talk. What the hell is he up to? "I've enjoyed it," Brye admitted, "although it feels I'm suffering writer's cramp. I'm amazed at the number of individuals asking for my autograph."

"You have quite a following. It's one of the reasons Chad hired you." He paused for effect. "Did Chad tell you he was going after a much wider target range? He wanted to bring more of the male population into the fold. And he hoped you'd be the one to reel them in."

Facial expression blank, Brye answered, "All business matters are corresponded through Brian. And, yes, he mentioned some of the efforts marketing and research were incorporating into their advertisement campaign."

"I trust you will do all that is necessary to help expedite the growth of that particular target group."

There was a suggestive lilt to his tone. A quality Brye felt nothing but revulsion toward. An influx of bile rose to the back of her throat. She struggled to keep it down. "I will do what I was hired to do, to the best of my ability. Nothing more, nothing less."

Daniel had made the off-color remark, looking for some kind of reaction. Instantly, he'd witnessed a flash of what? Anger? Hate? Nevertheless, the flash was gone a millisecond after it appeared. She cloaked it well, but a quiet storm raged behind those compelling eyes of hers.

"I think I've offended you in some way," Daniel auspiciously cited. "If I have, I graciously apologize."

The car phone rang, saving Brye from answering. Daniel lifted the receiver and carried it to his ear. No words crossed his lips. Seconds later, he replaced the headset. "We have arrived at your car. Are you sure I can't interest you in having dinner with me?"

Brye smiled graciously—this one way ticket to nowhere was coming to an end. "It's kind of you to offer, but no, thank you." Again she smiled sweetly, refusing to supply him with a reasonable excuse for her refusal.

The limo door swung open.

"What are your plans for the weekend, Brye?"

It came out of the blue. He spoke calmly, but beyond lay a dangerous edge to his words. The interior of the limousine grew ominous. His eyes, the same color he'd passed down to Chad, turned a menacing shade of evil. He glared as if he could extract an honest answer from her. Fortunately for Brye, she had an honest answer to give.

"I'm taking twenty underprivileged kids to Lake George." A narrow groove appeared over her eyebrows. "Is there a problem?"

"No." The atmosphere in the limo returned to its former state. Daniel's eyes cleared, his expression brightened. Pleased with her answer, knowing his son as well as he did, never in his wildest dreams could he believe Chad would ever spend time playing big brother to a bunch of impoverished, ill-mannered, ungrateful brats. "No," he firmly stated again, "there is no problem. I merely wanted to wish you a safe Fourth of July."

"I wish the same for you, Mr. Collier." She pushed her legs out the door. "Now, if you'll please excuse me."

"One more thing, Brye."

Brye halted. And waited.

"Did Chad discuss his weekend plans with you?"

Flipping around to face Daniel, she tilted her head to one side. Surprised, she stared with open-eyed interest. "What reason would Chad have in discussing his plans with me?"

Stone-faced, satisfied he'd secured the answers he had come for, nonchalantly, he brushed the question aside with a wave of the hand. "There's no reason he should."

A *USA Today* newspaper lay by his side. Picking it up, spreading it open, he ducked his nose behind it. No longer a concern to him, nor an imminent threat, the high and mighty promptly dismissed her.

Brye stepped out of the twilight zone and walked right back into reality. Standing in the middle of the midtown parking garage, she stared after the limo. Daddy Collier had gone on a fishing expedition. But what was he fishing for? Was he merely keeping a prudent eye on her? Did he fear she and Chad were growing closer? Did he fear that a reunion was imminent? Where had his perceptions come from?

Brye should have been upset. But she wasn't. She should have been fuming. But there was an absence of smoke.

Instead, it warmed her heart to think Daniel Collier saw her as a possible threat to his son. It sat well with her knowing he'd taken time out of his busy schedule to extort some unknown piece of information from her.

Not wanting to speculate on this sudden turn of events, Brye elected to sit back, relax, and watch the drama unfold. For the time being, it was all she could do.

15

"ANYONE NOT DOWN HERE eating breakfast within the next two minutes will be staying behind with me!" Linn's thunderous bellow swept up the circular staircase, crashed onto the second-floor landing, and tumbled down the hallway, invading every nook and cranny lying in its wake. If she wondered whether her flagrant threat touched every youthful ear in the commodious estate, her doubts were extinguished as soon as the stampede erupted.

Smiling to herself, she trekked down the parquet foyer and entered the large, brightly lit kitchen. "You have a visitor waiting in the great room," she informed Brye.

To simplify meals, all dishes were presented buffet style. A set of food warmers aligned the cook-top island. Pouring scrambled eggs into one of the silver servers, Brye stalled her progress. "Who is it?"

"Hmm?" Linn hummed, feigning distraction. Her gaze flipped to the sunroom. "Why are they out there playing with those birds? Have they eaten?" Not waiting for a reply, she turned back to Brye. "You plan on keeping your guest waiting much longer?" Then, storming over to the sunroom, she flung the glass door open. "Bethany, Anthony, I want those birds back in their cages, you out of there, washed up, and eating breakfast in five minutes!"

Brye threw up a knowing eyebrow. Mary Ann—the thirty-five-year-old cook and mother of three—caught it.

Mary Ann Carlisle, a battered wife who'd walked out on her husband three years prior and found her way to Brylinn, winked at Brye. In a matter of hours, Linn would have the place all to herself. Clearly, she wanted it sooner.

"But Mama Linn"—Brye's ears fell on Anthony's protestations as she completed her task and wandered out the kitchen—"we wanted to say goodbye to Fred and Wilma."

"Mail them a letter."

At the kitchen entrance, Brye was bombarded with a brood of screeching, scurrying, excited human beings. Sidestepping the entire lot, she entered the great room with an absorbed smile. The grin fizzled at the sight of her unexpected visitor. And like a starving beggar deprived of sustenance much too long, she greedily devoured every inch of his stalwart torso.

Hungry eyes fed upon thick raven strands of hair. She gorged on his modeled profile, lapped up his strength, virility, and commanding power. Clad in a body-hugging sleeveless T-shirt and pleated cotton twill shorts, she drank up his jutting biceps, slim waist, and powerful thighs. She nourished on her warrior, her conquering hero, her knight in shining armor.

But he wasn't her hero. If he had been, he would have fought for her, for what they had shared those many years ago, for the love he claimed he sheltered for her. But he hadn't fought. He'd only walked away. The agonizing thought forced her to swallow a lethal dose of reality. And the truth ate at her like acid searing the walls of her intestinal lining.

"Chad!" Heart chugged erratically against her breast bone. "You didn't have to come see us off."

Portraits of children at various ages adorned the mantle of the two-sided fireplace. While waiting for Brye, Chad studied each intently. The sound of her harmonious voice induced a feeling of sheer euphoria. Rotating on his heels, he confronted her. His breath caught in his throat to see her dressed in a pair of stretch leggings, a white oversized V-neck tunic with sleeves pushed up to her elbows, and long dark hair pulled back and tied with a white bow. Small white roses pierced her delicate earlobes. Suddenly, the temperature in the room climbed twenty degrees. "I didn't come here to see you off."

More confusion. "Then why are you here?"

"I plan to go with you."

Brye's eyelids widened in surprise. Ingesting his words, she tore her eyes away from the all-consuming vision and lifted them toward the vaulted ceiling. Her mind reeled with disharmony.

This is what Daniel Collier's impromptu meeting was all about. Chad must have abruptly altered prearranged plans; plans involving his entire family—plus Jennifer. The thought of Chad spending the holiday with her sat as heavily on Brye's stomach as day old, extra spicy chili. But what weighed more heavily was the excuse Chad used to break away from his prior commitments. Had he lied about his whereabouts? Had he begun to lie about her?

Brye wanted Chad, but not like this. God help her, not like this. She didn't want to base a relationship on a pack of lies and a surreptitious rendezvous. She did not want to be some man's play thing; a diversion for when times grew boring; a piece of meat served up whenever the master requested.

An involuntary shudder rocked her body with thoughts of what her mother would say, if she had been alive. She'd be taunting Brye this very moment—telling her how alike the two of them really were. But, dammit, Brye was not like *her*. She was not like *them*. And if she had to spend the rest of her life proving it, then so be it.

Squeezing her long-lashed eyelids tightly shut, gradually, she inhaled a stabilizing breath. She had informed Marcus, as well as herself, that she would willingly accept Chad's abuse if that was all he had to offer. And she had meant it. At least when he fought with her, he dealt in honest emotions. But this was not honest; sneaking around as if ashamed to be seen with her in public was not virtuous. And she would not, and could not, condone being treated like a mistress.

Brye exhaled, opened her eyes, and greeted Chad with a leveling eye. Tone neutral, she asked, "You invited yourself?"

"No." Chad took one step forward, delivering himself closer to Brye. "Linn invited me."

Deep from within, Brye could feel the kindle igniting. She took a step backward, maintaining ample distance between them. "You're joking…aren't you?" she tenuously added on the off chance he might not be.

"George is loading my bags as we speak."

Beyond the great room's arched entryway, an uproarious cadence drummed in Brye's ear. Kids yelling at kids, adults bellowing at kids, parrots screeching at everyone, Linn screaming at the parrots. To top it all off, rap music played loudly in the background. This was a typical morning at Brylinn. Although she stood in another area of the mansion, Brye never remained far removed from the chaos.

"Spending a few days with these kids is in diametrical contrast to coming over here and spending a few hours, Chad," Brye quietly established, belying her inner turmoil. "I don't think you realize how energy-draining, nerve-racking, ear-splitting they can be."

Her attitude, more reserved than usual, ruffled him. The less-than-warm reception left much to be desired. He had believed… hoped…his being here would…what? Entice her to jump into his arms and swear her undying love? Since notifying him of this trip, this was all he had thought about: spending time with her without job constraints; without the pressures of their past weighing them down. Chad thought of this trip as a new beginning…for the both of them.

He forced his mounting frustration down, imprisoning it underneath the surface of his skin. "If I didn't know any better, I'd think you were trying to discourage me."

"Don't you think somebody should?" she huffed at him.

Chad stepped closer. "If you don't want me here, Brye, just say so."

The trouble was she did want him here. But the paltry five days he offered was merely a drop in the bucket compared to the never-ending well he awarded Jennifer.

Jennifer? From everything Brye learned of Jennifer's and Chad's relationship, marriage plans would soon be in the makings. So why was Chad here? Why wasn't he spending the Fourth with his own family? Why was he earnestly pushing himself at her? And, more importantly, why was he doing this behind Jennifer's back?

Brye didn't know the circumstances behind his appearance today. Maybe she shouldn't care. He wanted to spend time with her.

She loved him. It should have been all that mattered. It should have been that simple. But it wasn't.

Whoa, Brye! She slowed her thought processes down. *Your ego is running on overtime. Chad has not once mentioned getting involved in an intimate relationship with you.*

Maybe she was overreacting, she tried to convince herself. Maybe he really enjoyed spending time with the children. Maybe he wanted to form an alliance with them.

If that is the case—again she attempted to rationalize—*who am I to interfere?*

"We'll be leaving soon." She shrugged in a state of resolution. "Have you had anything to eat?"

"Just a cup of coffee." Seconds afterward, neither spoke. But the tension flowed between them. The distance she positioned between them was maddening. Chad wanted to blast the steel armor she resurrected around herself into a million tiny pieces. He wanted assurances that she'd never be able to right that wall again—at least where he was concerned.

"You better grab some breakfast before we go." Brye turned her back on him. "We'll only be stopping for one fifteen-minute stretch break."

Mindfully, Chad studied Brye. He'd gone through the trouble of rearranging his schedule to be with her, yet she did not act pleased with his decision. But then, thinking about the unexpected appearance of his father the day before and the ensuing conversation, Chad wasn't too pleased with himself.

His father had asked for Chad's motives for altering well-laid plans. And although Chad hadn't lied, he hadn't been entirely truthful either. "Important business only he could attend to," Chad had explained. He failed to mention that his business revolved around Brye.

A grown, unattached man, Chad didn't know what was behind the sudden urge to maintain secrecy. What he did know, however, was that he hadn't been himself since Brye had reentered his life.

He also knew it was time to get his life back on track. Only right now, he didn't want to think about his life. He didn't want to think about the woman his friends and family expected him to marry. The only thing he could think about, the only person he coveted, was his pure, violet-eyed, snow angel and the promises the weekend conveyed.

"Does that mean you're allowing me to go?" His attempt at concealing a fast growing smile was futile at best.

Not sharing in the momentous occasion, Brye swung around and caustically acknowledged, "Since when did anyone ever *allow* a Collier to do anything? I was under the impression that the exalted family did whatever they wanted, whenever they wanted, and to whomever they wanted to do it to!" As soon as the words rolled from her tongue, Brye felt instant remorse. Dismayed, her eyes grew distortedly larger. Her hand flew up and covered a mouth formed in a perfect circle. In utter disbelief, she shook her head back and forth.

"I'm sorry," she whispered. "I didn't mean that. I didn't..." She trailed off. Despite the buzz of excitement permeating the large estate, the atmosphere in the great room had lost its zeal.

Before she could reactivate her defense shield, Chad's overpowering presence stood at her side. Over four weeks ago, he'd bestowed her with a look so frosty, he'd exposed her to the potential dangers of frostbite. But the look he honored her with now was so full of heated passion, her force field shifted into involuntary meltdown.

Stunned by the nature of her attack, any other time, Chad would have come out swinging. Now he only sought understanding. Clipping her defiant chin between forefinger and thumb, he inched it upward and captured her full attention. His tone was gentle yet insistent. "Where's all this coming from, Brye?"

Hypnotized by his mesmerizing eyes, his caressing tone, and his soft manner, Brye's misgiving slipped away. She erased the rising dissension goading her sudden outburst.

This man—a cross between obstinate indignation and undiluted compassion—with a mere touch and a humble nod, could make her forget all else except the passion they'd once shared.

The wrinkles aligning her brow and around the edges of her eyes and mouth evened out. An apologetic grin toyed with the corners of her lips. Chad wasn't certain what had precipitated her fury, but whatever sin he had unwittingly committed, he knew all was forgiven—at least for the moment.

"Mr. Collier!" An excited Bethany skidded into Brye's and Chad's unstable world. "Are you coming with us?"

Chad reluctantly released Brye's chin, but his face lit up with the attachment he'd unsuspectingly formed for the precocious child. "That I am." He bent at the knee, lowering himself to Bethany's level. "That is, if you don't mind my tagging along. I've never been to Lake George."

"I've never been either." She stared at him with those innocent baby blues. Chad felt his heart melting. "Anthony and I have never been anywhere."

"Then the trip will be even more special for you and your brother."

The tip of her tongue slipped out of her mouth and ran across her top lip. Deep in thought, she nodded. "It would be even more special if we could bring Fred and Wilma with us."

"Fred and Wilma?" Chad raised a questioning half smile to Brye.

"Their macaws." Brye grinned. "Anthony and Bethany are *Flintstones* fans. But we've been through this already, Bethany." Brye laid an affectionate hand across the top of Bethany's pigtails. "You know they can't come with us."

Two months ago, even two weeks ago, Chad could not have handled pouting children or sneaky teens, but since his affiliation with Brylinn, his proficiency in handling troubled kids steadily cultivated. And today, he surprised himself by rushing to intervene.

"I don't think Fred and Wilma could handle the long bus ride anyway." Obviously the touchy subject had been discussed beforehand, and Chad had no intentions of escalating it further. "Besides, how would you feel if they suffered from car sickness—or in this instance, bus sickness?"

"I'd feel awful." At the mere thought of Fred and Wilma getting sick, an anguished expression contorted Bethany's tender features.

"Of course you would." He reached out and sheathed her small hands into large powerful ones. "Mama Linn will take wonderful care of Fred and Wilma while you're gone. And when you get back, although it won't hurt them to be separated for a short period of time, the parrots are going to love you that much more because they'll have missed you just as much as you missed them." He squeezed her fingers. She squeezed back. The simple touch sealed a friendship pact for life. "So…the only thing you should concern yourself with is having a good time." Tenderly, he pulled her into a loose hug. "Do you think you can do that?"

Bethany nodded. She surprised everyone by wrapping her arms around Chad's neck. Although she had made remarkable progress in opening up to others, there remained a slight reserve she could not shake when relating to the male population; she'd been hurt too many times by her mother's male friends to just easily forgive, forget, and trust the male gender. From the first moment she'd met Chad, he'd treated her with the gentleness and kindness all loving parents treasured for their children. He'd given her flowers, he'd stopped by—without Brye's knowledge—to say hello…to ask how her day had gone…to talk. He'd shown her and her twin brother undivided attention. He had made her feel good about herself. And no other male species had ever done that before.

"I'm glad you're coming, Mr. Collier."

"We're all glad he's coming." Surprising herself, Brye's words had suddenly taken on a life of their own as they forced their way out from the back of her throat.

Chad straightened upright, exchanging glances with Brye. He asked with a mere look, *Are you really?*

The upward turn of those luscious lips, the slight nod of her head, it was all the answer he needed.

Clearing her throat, Brye said, "I think we better get moving. You haven't had breakfast yet, and I still have a few things to do before we take off."

"Can we call Uncle Marcus and see if he'll bring Rainbow over to play with Fred and Wilma?"

Brye laughed. She interlaced Bethany's fingers with her own. "You, young lady, are incorrigible. And yes, we'll call Uncle Marcus and see if Rainbow can visit. And I will particularly ask him to stop by every day and see that the macaws get their daily exercise, their bath, fresh air, and whatever else they'll need while we're gone."

Bethany turned a sheepish face to Brye. "It's not that I don't trust Mama Linn, but we all know she's so much better with people than with birds."

Brye's lip muscles twitched as she fought to slam the lid on her rising laughter. Over Bethany's head, she caught Chad staring at her mouth.

Every morning, as soon as Chad rolled out of bed, he mentally prepared a list of duties needing to be completed by the end of that particular day. This morning, closely watching Brye, he placed at the top of his agenda his need to kiss her as soon as they were alone.

As if Brye could read his thoughts, two rose-colored spots rode high along her cheekbones. Needing desperately to put her mind on track, she looked down at Bethany and said, "You know, sweetheart, just because Mama Linn isn't overly fond of animals, it doesn't mean she would intentionally harm Fred or Wilma."

"I know that," Bethany answered in her uncanny adult manner. "And even though you two run neck and neck with parenting skills, her parroting skills leave a lot to be considered."

Brye grinned. Specks of glitter tickled her eyes. "I'll call Uncle Marcus."

"Good." Bethany stretched her empty hand toward Chad. Inviting him into the close, intimate fold, the three walked out of their quiet setting and into the mad rush of the household.

Less than an hour later, Linn stood at the front door, visibly inspecting each child scooting past. Most were given a hug, a kiss, and a hearty farewell, then sent out to board the bus. Some were sent back to their room to change out of provocative clothing and into more suitable attire, a few were asked to scrape off pounds of effulgent makeup, and one had to retrieve medication for his asthma.

But when every child was accounted for, when the bus was loaded and rolling down the winding drive, Linn stood with eyes closed, chin lifted, crown resting against the heavy oak door. She blew out an exaggerated gust of air and listened. Nothing.

The sweet sound of silence caressed her inner ears. Wrapping her arms around her weighty chest, a slow smile crept along a face sketched with contentment. She pushed away from the door. Light on her feet, her hefty body executed a graceful jig as she ambled toward the staircase. Seven o'clock in the morning, and she was about to do something she hadn't done since…when?

Linn couldn't remember nor did she care. What mattered was now, this moment, this very second. Momentarily, she would climb back into bed and set her alarm to go off upon the commencement of *Young and the Restless.* After she watched her favorite soap, she would…what?

It didn't matter. Linn had all weekend to make plans…or not.

At the top of the stairs, she smiled to herself. She truly loved her kids, but solitude was something she usually only dreamed of. The next four and a half days were hers…to do with whatever she damn well pleased.

Ain't life grand?

Unlike Linn, Marcus was going into his lone holiday weekend with as much enthusiasm as the Buffalo Bills stepping away from their fourth Superbowl loss.

Ordinarily, he'd spend weekend holidays back home, in Chicago, with his parents and three sisters—except three days ago, his parents had flown off to Hawaii. And since their omnipotent presence remained the magnetic force drawing their adult children back to home base, his sisters had elected to bestow their presence at novel tourist attractions in various states throughout the country.

Born in a close-knit family, each of his family members had invited him along to join in their Fourth of July festivities. In the small hope he'd see, talk to, or spend a few moments alone with Tenisha, going against his own better judgment—good judgment he was now seriously questioning—he had graciously declined.

He, Marcus Alloysius Lindell, was a fool; a sheer, unadulterated, lovesick, moron. Why in the hell was he fawning over a married woman? More importantly, why was he putting his life on hold for a married woman? By today's standards, he was considered a good catch. Reasonably intelligent, he earned a substantial living. He was not hard on the eyes by any means, and given the risk of appearing egotistical, women crawled out of the woodwork, asking him out on dates.

Hell, he could have any woman he sought. So what was the problem?

In a nutshell, he had fallen in love with Tenisha. Granted, he had fallen for a woman swimming knee deep in a troubled marriage. Nevertheless, it remained a valid marriage. And although he understood he couldn't control when or who he fell in love with, he sure as hell could control his actions surrounding that love. No way, no how, would he do anything to encourage an illicit affair. No, sir, he was not about to buy himself a one way ticket to disaster. He held too much pride and respect for himself, as well as for Tenisha, to allow such an affair to take place.

So…with that settled, he decided he was not going to spend his entire weekend lazing around the house, daydreaming of a woman he would never know on an intimate level. He would not waste his time remembering the sight of her relaxed, motionless, body sinking deeper into the thick cushions of his yielding sofa as she dozed. He refused to recall the short, sanguineous, sighs crossing moldable lips as her weariness overtook her. There would be no drooling over the recalled vision of long, curving eyelashes trailing along elegant cheekbones. Marcus refused to waste the weekend remembering sitting across from Tenisha, contentedly watching over her while she slept. He spurned the enticing sight of the gentle rise and fall of firm breasts during her peaceful slumber. He rebuffed his need to recant the iniquitous thoughts of wondering what it would feel like to stretch his yearning body out beside hers; to enfold his body over hers; to enter her…

Jesus! Is this what his life had come down to? Spending his weekend mooning over a married woman while babysitting a couple of Rainbow's distant feathered relatives?

Blinking his eyes into focus, Marcus peered around his immaculate kitchen and wondered how it had gotten so immaculate. When had he stacked his dirty dishes in the dishwasher? How long had it taken him to wipe down cabinets, counters, and tabletop?

Deeply absorbed in his downtrodden meandering, he'd inattentively plowed through the semi-disorderly kitchen, scrubbing down everything in his path. Folding the yellow-and-brown-checkered dish cloth into thirds, he carefully hung it over the sparkling, stainless steel faucet.

Five o'clock, he noted on his quartz watch. Early Friday evening, and he held no definite plans for the evening.

Yes, you do, he thought to himself. A female coworker had invited him to a small dinner gathering hosted at her Queens' apartment. Although Marcus had made no promises of attendance, he'd just made up his mind; he was going to a dinner party. And, of course, the party would take up a few hours of his time, but what was he going to do with the remaining seventy-two hours left in the holiday weekend?

Lumbering out the kitchen door, he sighed heavily. This was destined to be one hell of a long, miserable weekend.

16

IN THE NORTHEAST REGION of New York, sweeping a substantial range of over six million acres in length—nearly one-fourth the size of the state—the Adirondack Mountains lay positioned. A succession of ridges compiled some of the oldest rocks known to man. One peak amongst the many ridges, Mount Marcy—ranging 5,344 feet above sea level—remained the tallest point in New York State; an accumulative forty-five other peaks extended well beyond four thousand feet in height.

Celebrated for their lush, awestruck forests, thousands of miles of flowing streams and rivers, the Adirondack Mountains also boasted more than two thousand ponds and natural lakes. Two such well-known natural lakes, Lake George and Lake Champlin, aligned the eastern border of the majestic region.

Lake George, a 32-mile-long lake ornamented with 365 surrounding islands, succeeded as a prevalent tourist enticement, yet it was Chad's first visit.

Over the lake, Chad had just witnessed one of the most dramatic sunsets he'd ever had the pleasure of viewing. Hues of resplendent colors drizzled the unruffled lake as the sun drowsily sank beneath the lush horizon. Watching the magnificent sight, Chad held one regret: he wished Brye had shared the stunning view with him.

The day had proved to be hectic. Enduring the scenic route along Interstate 87 in a bus filled with shrieking kids, unloading and reorganizing suitcases, orientation/get acquainted meeting, exploring their home of the next four days, and finally, thank the Lord, the day had settled into uncomplicated bliss.

Accompanied by a few other straggling couples, Chad sat on the main house's two-tier deck overlooking the shimmering lake. Redwood patio furniture covered with wild rose floral pattern cushions adorned the lower deck; the upper tier occupied an octagon-shaped Jacuzzi.

Camp George—a lodge, a retreat, a mixture of old-fashion charm and present-day design—catered mainly to large groups: church retreats, weekend fraternity parties, school gatherings, women's groups, and family reunions.

Sitting amongst a lush tranquil setting, the camp offered a wide variety of supervised, and unsupervised, activities: tennis, hiking, water sports, game room, private beach parties, golf, horseback riding, fishing, and babysitting. Experienced staff available twenty-four hours a day organized fun and games for the young, and the young at heart.

The supervised activities had been the deciding factor enticing Brye to book the lodge exclusively. While each child participated in a chosen sport, every adult could spend his or her time as each saw fit.

Wanting the fifteen adults to enjoy themselves to the hilt, Brye had booted every individual over the age of twenty out, ordering them to spend the last remaining hours of the evening in the company of their peers and without interference from an overly zealous child. Brye had selflessly remained behind to oversee bedtime for the smaller youths—the long day had finally taken its toll and many were literally falling asleep on their feet.

The woman is relentless, Chad thought to himself. The infinite source of energy she possessed steadily gushed from an overflowing fountain. While everyone else—including himself—wilted in the midst of a taxing day, Brye flourished, remarkably, much the same as a rose sprouting robust petals amidst the heart of an inflamed desert.

Right now, Chad was bone-weary. A hot shower, a warm bed, he looked forward to both with withered enthusiasm. His body sank deeper into the cushions as the constant pitch of chirping crickets lulled him into a state of—

"So, Chad," Lisa, the most outspoken of the bunch, sliced into his nebulous images, "what is your take on all this? How come you decided to spend your weekend slumming with us lowly spirits instead of jet-setting with the rich and powerful?"

Chad shoved his haziness aside. The cushions in his patio chair produced a soft crinkling sound as he dragged his weary body straighter. His eyes dropped on Lisa. Pale skin, thin lips, slightly crooked nose, she made up in personality what she lacked by way of looks. Chad searched her expression for signs of maliciousness. There was none. He saw only candid curiosity, coupled with a tinge of mischievousness.

Sitting here with this benevolent group, Chad realized that in his world, he towed a different line and mingled with a different class of people. Sadly enough, he traveled in a snobbishly conceited circle who only associated with other affluent individuals. Individuals who wouldn't give this bunch the time of day. In contrast, everyone at Brylinn had generously opened their arms and invited him into their realm.

Anticipating her question, surprised it hadn't been addressed before now, Chad answered, "I've been thinking about becoming a financial supporter of Brylinn, so I wanted to see firsthand how my money would be put to use."

In the failing evening light, she hit Chad with a skeptical glare. "We get a lot of financial backers, but none have wanted to spend hours, let alone *days*, physically offering a helping hand with our kids. Usually, the offer of money is enough." She grinned, a sly I-know-something-you-ought-to-know grin. "Well…maybe it isn't enough for some, but it's all they get."

"Lisa!" Mary Ann spoke sharply—a definite warning.

"Oh come on, Mary Ann," Lisa shot at her. "You know you're just as curious as the rest of us."

"Maybe she is," George blurted out, "but at least she's got enough sense to know when to stay out of Brye's business."

"Pleeeeze!" Lisa dragged the word out. "You're itching to know just as bad as Mary Ann is. I just happen to be the only one brave enough to ask."

Chad shook his head to clear it. "I know I'm tired," he readily acknowledged, "but did I black out for a few seconds and miss something here? What did you mean when you said that for some, the offer of money is not enough? And what is it everyone's curious about?"

Lisa flashed a triumphant smile at George. To Chad, she spoke candidly. "Some of our financial backers—not all because most of them really are concerned with helping abused children—offer donations because they're looking at a much larger picture. When they donate money, they think they're buying their way into Brye's bed." She met his gaze head-on. "Of course, you probably want to see your way into her bed too."

Chad felt the heat rise underneath his skin. Hopefully, the night camouflaged the crimson red coloring his facial features.

"But you're going at it in a different way."

"Are you suggesting that I'd use the kids to—"

Lisa flapped her hand in the air, gesturing to silence him. "I'm not suggesting anything. But since you mentioned the kids, I'd like to say that you're very good with them. And that's a plus in your favor. But you do have something else going for you."

"I'm afraid to ask," Chad said, absorbed, just like the others, with Lisa's boldness.

"Brye likes you. In fact, as far as any of us can see, you're the first man she's ever shown a real interest in." She enfolded the other couples inside her perceptive gaze. "I think it's safe to say that all of us care for Brye very much. And we've seen the way she looks at you. And we've noticed the way you look at her. Something more involved is going on here.

"I know it's not asked for, but we"—again she gathered everyone together with a silent embrace—"offer our full support."

Chad found himself sitting on the edge of his chair. Unsettled, he cleared his throat. "I'm not admitting nor denying your speculations where Brye and I are concerned. But I am curious as to why you're willing to give me your support?"

For the first time since Lisa began this line of conversation, Mary Ann decided to have her say. "Brye's a good person. She's real. There's nothing pretentious about her. And out of the kindness of her heart, she's helped every one of us in one way or another. But, despite all she's done for us, she's never given us the opportunity to return the favor. It's sad," she stated contemplatively, her chest expanding as she filled her lungs with the crisp mountain air, "because she's drawn this imaginary line around herself. She won't step over it nor will she allow us to." Mary Ann stood. She walked over to the chaise lounge Jack, her current boyfriend, inhabited. Plopping herself down, she wedged her body between his thighs.

Jack wrapped his arms around her chest and finished what Mary Ann started. "Brye needs someone to help erase that line, and we all believe you're that person."

"Don't you think I should have a say so in the matter?" Her voice, as serene as the gentle breeze whispering through the trees, navigated through the oscillating night. A split second later, her inexhaustible presence came with it. Brye rested her right foot on the first step leading to the deck landing. She rested her elbow on the pine banister. There was no trace of anger or irritation. In fact, in the blanched evening light, because she had eavesdropped, she presented to them a glowing smile of atonement.

"Once I got the little ones off to sleep, I checked on the older kids—they're in the day room, threatening to blow the walls down with their blaring music." The day room, equipped with pool and ping-pong table, big screen plasma TV and stereo sound system, was built adjacent to the sun deck. To drive Brye's point across, the sudden wail of rap music ripped a hole in the wall and rumbled through the serene territory like a herd of stampeding buffalo; creatures large and small scurried for cover. Low-pitched base notes agitated the deck floor, crept along bare legs, and burrowed deep in the gut like severe indigestion. Ignoring the ruckus, Brye reached up and pushed a strand of hair off her forehead. "I thought everyone else had gone into town, so I started to take a walk, heard voices, and took the pathway leading to you all."

She took the six steps up to the landing and began clearing away discarded wine cooler bottles and empty pop cans. "Why don't I get you guys something more to drink?"

Both Chad and Sam jumped to their feet. They both began in unison, "Why don't we help—"

"I can handle it." Brye waved them back into their seats, empty wine bottles flashing brightly against an inky background. With gathered bottles, she halted at the deck entrance. "Besides, it'll give you time to finish talking about me behind my back." She turned to go. On second thought, she twirled to face the sedate group. "Oh… by the way…while you're planning my future, you should ask Chad about his. It's reported he's getting engaged soon…and it's not to me." She disappeared into the dayroom. An earsplitting burst of consonance escaped the partially opened door.

George was the first to react following Brye's retreat. A burst of laughter dispersed into the night, fraternizing with the bellowing music. "Don't you just love her? Caught in the act and she didn't even blink an eye."

Mary Ann nodded. "She's so secure in who she is it doesn't matter what anyone says about her."

"I think it's true that she doesn't let other people's opinion bother her. What I don't believe is that she's secure with herself," Lisa said. "Because if she were all that secure, she wouldn't be so…lonely."

"Maybe if she found herself a good man—"

Lisa, an active feminist, immediately cut Mary Ann off. "What makes you think bringing a man into Brye's life would help solve her problems?" she snapped. "Hell, 95 percent of the time, the man *is* the root of the problem."

The incredulous scowl Mary Ann hurled at Lisa struck her dead between the eyes and threatened to knock her off her seat. "Correct me if I'm wrong, but aren't you the one who offered Chad your full support." Falling silent to take a quick breath, her words poured forth in a burst of anger, "And another thing, with that attitude of yours, I'm surprised Sam's stayed with you as long as he has."

Sam rolled his eyes toward the blinking stars. "I'll thank you to keep me out of this."

"Look," Merissa broke in, hoping to diffuse the situation before it turned ugly. "I mean this in the nicest possible way, but I think you all need to butt out of matters that don't concern you." She swiped at a brown moth fluttering around her head. The flying bug floated down the stairs and disappeared into a row of spruce trees. "Brye's a grown woman. She's a beautiful woman. And I think we all can agree that if she wants a man, she won't have any problems finding one."

"Merissa's right," Jack agreed. His demeanor apologetic, he gaped at Chad. "Although we believe you and Brye would make a good couple, we're wrong for interfering."

"Wait a minute," Lisa said, unprepared to give in so easily. "Is it true…about your engagement?"

Curiosity alone had urged Chad to listen without interruption. He had hoped to gain greater insight on Brye from the people she closely worked with. But he'd been wrong. They retained less data than he possessed. And what information he did obtain only led to more questions. In fact, one of Lisa's statements had struck a raw chord. Was there a man at the root of Brye's problems? Was he that man?

No. He couldn't be. Brye had been plagued by an unknown entity long before he'd entered the picture those many years ago, yet he'd been no closer to an answer then, than he was now.

It was his turn to establish an apologetic smile. "I'm sorry," Chad said. "Caught up in your conversation, I should have stopped it long before Brye walked in on it." His eyes dropped to Lisa. "There's been several published reports on an upcoming engagement…*my* engagement. But just because it's written in the tabloids, or plastered on social media, doesn't necessarily make it true." Inside the day room, rap music was replaced by a song just as loud, but was more conducive to the adults' eardrums.

"Secondly," Chad continued, wanting them to believe his and Brye's relationship was nothing more than friendship, "Brye and I go back a ways. We went to NYU together." It was a long stretch; nevertheless, it was the truth. "Whatever you see…whatever you *think* you see between Brye and I…we are nothing more than friends."

A smokescreen. The layers, laid on thickly, did not limit Lisa's vision. More was going on than either Brye nor Chad was willing to admit. In a voice mollifying her disbelief, she asked, "Have you ever considered going into politics?"

"Is it safe to come out?" The door opened wide enough for Brye to slip her head through. Her glowing smile threatened to brighten the entire outdoors.

The sudden appearance saved Chad from responding. His look of relief converged with Brye's amused stare. "Come on out, Brye. I can assure you the wolves have pulled in their fangs—at least for the moment."

She shoved the door with her left shoulder. Heaping four wine coolers and two diet Cokes in the crook of one arm, she held a third Coke can out to Chad. She then dished out the other drinks. Hitching her right hip along the deck railing, she asked, "Why didn't any of you go into town with the others?"

"You're kidding…right?" Sam asked. "The only place I'm going is to bed."

"You got that right." George yawned, his mouth shaped into an elongated O. "What'll you bet the others'll be dragging themselves back in here shortly?"

Brye laughed. "I'd be better off hanging out with the younger crowd. You guys are old and tired!"

"That's right, we are," Jack replied. "And damn proud of it at the moment."

At the end of his haughty declaration, the door flew open once again. Out trudged Kirk with Shansey, his girlfriend of nine months, glued to his side. "We're going for a walk on the beach," he announced.

In the dusky twilight, Brye peered at her Apple Watch. "Make sure you're back by twelve."

Kirk halted in his tracks. "That's whack, Brye. I'm eighteen years old, we're on vacation, and I should be allowed to come and go as I please."

As usual, Brye took on his defiance with calmed ease. Mildly, she retorted, "What's whack, dear heart, is that you fail to understand that *I* care little whether you come back tonight at twelve, tomorrow night at twelve, or midnight New Year's eve.

"What *is* my concern, however, is one seventeen-year-old Shansey. Her parents agreed to allow her to vacation with us *only* on the stipulation that I personally keep a vigilant watch over her. You, of all people, know I take my responsibilities seriously."

Brye captured his chin between thumb and forefinger. Maintaining an unflinching eye, she stared down his nose. "You are perfectly welcome to stay out as long as you like. Shansey will be back here at twelve. Do we understand each other?"

"Yes," Kirk muttered, his enthusiasm fizzled into the buzzing night.

"Shansey?" Brye asked, keeping a vigilant watch on Kirk.

From the first day Shansey had met Brye, she'd been enamored with the supermodel's beauty, fame, and fortune. If it pleased Brye, Shansey would agree to have her hair dyed, fried, and plastered to the sides. "Yes, ma'am," she timidly answered.

Brye released Kirk's chin. Her hand dropped to her side. Still, eyes adhered to his, she requested, "Now I'd like you to repeat back to me what time she's to be back."

"Brye!" Kirk grumbled, jaws twitching, eyes blazing with indignation.

"Now...please!" she softly demanded. "So I'll know, when you walk in here one hour after twelve—or even one second afterward—your defiance was calculated and done with aforethought malice."

A light switch clicked on in the back of Kirk's mind as a plan of action formulated. Before Brye's eyes, his irritation waned. "Shansey will be back here at twelve," he eagerly promised.

The reply came much too quickly to satisfy Brye. "I don't mean for you to come in the front door at twelve, make an appearance, then sneak out the back way at twelve-oh-five, Kirk. I want her back here, in the lodge, until rise and shine tomorrow morning."

A slow grin transformed Kirk's insolent appearance into that of a man who couldn't win for losing. Sometimes he forgot Brye was only seven years older than he. Being young herself, she had to have tested and perfected all the angles as a teen. In actuality, he'd be surprised to learn that Brye had never, not once, attempted to deceive her parents—of course, given their open marriage and sordid lifestyle, they had never had reason to give her any rules to follow.

Kirk raised his hands in irrefutable surrender. "Okay, okay. I give. Twelve o'clock...here...for good. I got it."

"Good." Brye breathed easier. Another disaster thwarted. "Now go and have a good time. Oh…one more thing." As the two young teen's clamored hand-in-hand down the stairs, Brye caught Kirk's full attention. "I hope you have some protection with you."

A few muffled snickers erupted from the adult population. Kirk was not amused. Surrounding by nothing but blackness, his face beamed as bright and red as Rudolph's shining red nose in a gusty, winter snowstorm.

"Damn, Brye! Why you wanna front me like this?"

"*Excuse* me, Kirk!" Innocent facial features contorted into feigned maidenly confusion. "Repellent. I'm talking about mosquito repellent. I hear the mosquitoes can be murder up here."

As Shansey broke into absorbed laughter, Kirk dragged her off into the cover of darkness. Not once did he look back.

Hard as she tried, Merissa could not embody the suppressed chortle begging for a much-needed release. It started out as a sniffle, transformed into a cough, then exploded into full-fledged, foot-stomping, side-stabbing, belly-jiggling snorting.

The inextricable fanfare started an undulated avalanche. Four couples broke down at the hilarity of the situation. An upsurge of wind lifted the laughter by its wings and sent it flurrying over the moonlit lake. Minutes passed before the laughter filtered out and died.

Impressed by the manner Brye handled not only Kirk, but the other kids as well, Jack praised as if toasting her for an award. "You were unbelievable." An avid game player, he compared the verbal match to a chess tournament. "Watching you and Kirk was the equivalent of watching a chess game. Two generals squaring off for battle. Kirk executed his first move, you countered with exemplary patience and skill. As the game progressed, you stripped him of all pieces. In the end, *wham!* Checkmate." He chuckled. "Are you sure you've never had kids?"

Monthly, fifteen to twenty-five children thrived underneath the care of her guardianship. But no, Brye had no children of her own. Only a twin brother whom she practically raised from the moment of conception until his death. Still…no…there had never been any children of her own. Only a set of twins who'd never had the chance to see the light of day, but with Bethany and Anthony appearing to be their exact reincarnates. And no, Brye had no children.

Deep-seated pain raced across Brye's habitually controlled facade before she had time to slam down the brakes. She did not want to talk, or think, about the children she never had. Instead, she wanted to...what?

Contemplating the answer, her sadness entangled with Chad's. An irrefutable bond difficult to ignore and next to impossible to run away from, joined the hapless lovers together; a bond strengthened by the love they shared for each other as well as the babies they had long lost. Caught up in his astute alertness, Brye became aware of several revelations: Chad also suffered from the loss of their children, and Brye wanted to move into his arms to be comforted...to comfort.

"She probably learned how to handle kids from personal experiences," George broke into Brye's disturbing preoccupation. "All grown up, she's Ms. Innocent Incarnate. As a child, I bet she was a holy terror."

Eyes solidly fastened on Chad, Brye solemnly answered, "It's a bet you'd lose. I was a good kid. The kind of daughter most"—she almost choked on the words—"most parents would have been proud of." Squeezing her eyelids shut, Brye swallowed down pain that dusted the back of her throat.

Heedless to her torment, George teased, "Most kids grow up believing they're perfect little angels. Why would you say anything less?"

Sadly, Brye shrugged her shoulders. Opening her eyes, she turned her sights toward the lake to hide her trembling lips. "I could never put anything past you, could I, George?"

The conversation trudged forward. Brye, aware Chad maintained a reticent eye upon her, walked out of the conversation altogether. She wanted so badly to step out of her body. An invigorating breeze brushed lightly across her face. She released her hair from its restraints. Inhaling deeply the refreshingly clean mountainous air, her resilient lungs overextended from the conscious effort. Heart and respirations slowed, her mind took flight and soared freely...high above the lodge...into the sparse, scattered clouds. From a distance, she could hear voices talking, joking, laughing, but she did not concern herself with their liveliness. Far removed, she was where she wanted to be. Nothing, no one, could touch her in her flight of fancy.

Studying Brye, with the moonlit glaze cloaking her vision, the dark downy hair caressing soft features, a half-smile playing across sensuous lips, and a serene lake as a picturesque backdrop, Chad knew he'd never seen a more deceptive sight.

Chad had witnessed Brye's mental departure to...where? What had provoked her to turn inside herself? Had it been the short discussion pertaining to her own adolescent behavior?

Thinking back, Chad realized he knew nothing of Brye's childhood—she'd never, not once, discussed that aspect of her life. While they had been seeing each other—somehow the words "seeing each other" seemed inadequate in comparison to what he and Brye had felt for each other, or at least what he *believed* they'd felt for each other—when they had been...romantically involved?...Chad had met Brye's parents once. Only once. And at his insistence.

Dinner. At her parents' Manhattan apartment. The evening had turned out to be a huge success. Brye's parents had been cultured, enchanting, and in every sense of the word completely devoted to their daughter and her happiness—they'd welcomed him with open arms. Brye, on the other hand, had appeared apprehensive, on edge, anxious for the evening to end.

At the time, he'd chalked it up to nervousness on Brye's part. Nervousness induced by his first meeting with her parents. Now, looking back, he knew something...what...sinister?...had befallen Brye and her parents. Something he hadn't noticed then and couldn't lay his finger on now.

The dinner they shared was the last time he'd seen her parents. Ashamed to say, but he hadn't as of yet asked Brye about their well-being. He made a promise to do just that as soon as the two of them were alone.

"How 'bout taking in eighteen holes of golf with me in the morning?" George asked, dragging Chad back into the conversation.

Chad drew a steady finger around the top of his condensation-soaked Coke can. "Sunday morning would be better. I promised I'd go fishing with the twins first thing in the morning."

"It's a date. But that still leaves me without a playing partner for tomorrow."

"Can't you forget golf for one day?" Merissa huffed. "You can golf at home. But we've never been to Lake George, and there's so much to do…like shopping, for instance," she hastily added.

"I can tee off at 0600, play eighteen holes, and be back here long before your stores open. How about you, Brye?" An itch begging to be scratched, George was prepared to take on anyone willing to accept the challenge. "Would you care to join me for eighteen holes?"

No answer.

"Brye?"

Mentally floating over the small group, Brye experienced a slight pull of gravity.

"Brye?"

Slowly at first, then more expeditiously, the ground rose to meet her.

"Brye?"

Whoosh. Slam dunked back to earth.

Somewhat woozy, Brye blinked at George.

"Are you okay?" he asked.

Regaining her footing, Brye smiled. "I'm fine…really. What was it you asked?"

"You wanna get out on the golf greens with me in the morning?"

"Sorry, I have a fishing date. Besides, I don't golf."

"You don't know what you're missing."

"Once, years ago, I attempted to teach her, but—" Chad stalled, giving Brye the opportunity to complete the sentence.

Amazed, Brye didn't know what surprised her more: Chad telling everyone they had known each other years prior, or Chad broaching the subject of her short-spanned golf career. "But I wasn't"—Brye rummaged through a long list of words before she came up with the best suited—"focused. Well…" Unable to uncover feelings of shame for the direction in which her golf lessons had developed, Brye stifled a giggle before completing. "I *was* focused, but it wasn't on golf." Eyes playful, with devilish smile, she exchanged an intimate moment with Chad. She, just like he, remembered.

"Chad?"

On the immaculately swept golf course, at the onset of their third tee—a par 4 at 395 yards—Brye still remained unacquainted to the basics of the game. The morning sun, beginning its junket toward the western horizon, had just taken its first bite out of the chilled early-morning air.

Ignorant to Brye's plight—her sharpened senses had taken on a life of their own and was now threatening mutiny—Chad intimately aided Brye in her golf stance. Like two spoons fitting snugly together, Brye and Chad's body posed in perfect alignment.

Front grazing back, thighs rubbing against thighs, arms squeezed tightly together, fingers locked as one…how was Brye expected to centralize her thoughts on Vardon grips, proper posture, and full swings when the heat radiating off his body, the swaying aroma of his aftershave cologne, the bolstering effect his efficient grip engendered within her, assaulted every sense of her normal state of being?

"Chad?" she attempted again, breaking her stance and his concentration.

"Sweetheart, you need to pay closer attention to my instructions." His warm breath fondled her right temple, transforming her body into one huge, quivering block of Jell-O.

Yes, her hormones were definitely riding roughshod over her sanity.

Brye loosened her grip on the driver. Twisting her body within his arms, she faced her teacher. An impudent grin flittered across her overheated face. One tantalizing finger dallied along the edges of his open collar. "Don't get upset, Chad," she cooed, "but I'm not in the least bit interested in chasing a ball—a little ball whose actions prove to be a lot smarter than mine—across this land.

"But I can get interested in chasing around *your* ball," she stated lasciviously. Drawing her hand around the back of his neck, Brye urged his head downward. Slowly, surely, she captured his mouth with her own.

Before allowing the kiss to take hold, gently, firmly, Chad pried Brye loose. "Brye…honey…we've only played two holes. How do you know you're not interested if you don't give yourself time to catch on?"

"I've given it all the time I need." At the base of his neck, Brye wound strands of raven-colored hair around insistent fingers. "And I know there's *other* things I'm *more* interested in."

Chad gingerly peeled Brye from his body. Pushing her to arm's length, he beseeched, "Just try. Okay? Give this a chance?"

Brye stepped out of his reach. Frustrated, she swiped a strand of hair away from her forehead. Her eyes darted left to right as she inhaled the scenic environment. To the right, a bank of trees skirted the rich horizon. An idea began to take root.

"Fine," she said, pilfering the driver from Chad's fingers. "For you, I'll try."

Feet planted shoulder length apart, knees flexed, fingers firmly gripping the club, wrist locked—Arnold Palmer himself could not have been more impressed. Without the benefit of a practice run, Brye drew back into a full swing.

Chad examined her stance and instantly noticed that her aim was completely off kilter. "Hold it Brye, you're—"

Whomp! Too late. The club struck home. The golf ball sliced through the air, cracked against the bark of a tree, then rustled through the leaves as gravity reached upward and seized the ball by the tail.

"Your form was better. Your aim leaves a lot to be desired," Chad informed candidly. He pulled a second ball from his golf bag. "Why don't you swing again."

"No. I'm going after that one."

"Brye!" He'd wanted so much to teach her the game, but from the moment they had begun lessons, she hadn't been able to keep her mind on the sport. And now he wasn't having any luck holding his exasperation in check. "You'll never retrieve that ball."

Brye's intent was not geared toward retrieval. "Ye of little faith!" Interweaving their fingers, she attempted to pilot Chad toward the dense area.

Rooted on the spot, Chad stood his ground. "It's a waste of time, Brye," he wearily recognized.

Studying him, Brye wondered what it was with this game that turned him into a total stick in the mud. Head tilted to one side, she said, "Please."

Looking down into a face pleading for mercy, Chad's resolve weakened. God, how he loved her, he thought to himself. Stretching his arms outward, he glided his knuckles along the side of her face. "If you asked me to chase a ball halfway around the world, despite how futile the task might be, I'd be powerless to say no, because I'm powerless to deny you anything."

"Oh, Chad." A flood of warmth channeled throughout her body. "That is the sweetest thing you've ever said to me." Lifting on her tiptoes, she pecked the underside of his chin. "Now," pushing sentimentality aside, she abruptly pulled away and barked, "Let's get going! That ball isn't going to wait forever." Dragging Chad in with her, she dove under the concealment of cedars, cypresses, and elm trees.

Camouflaged by willowy splendor, Brye dropped her driver and attacked Chad. Tugging the bottom of his shirt out of his white cotton pants, she glided her hands underneath and ran teasing fingers along solid muscle mass.

"Brye?" His skin shuddered uncontrollably underneath her sensual assault. "What're you doing?"

"If you have to ask"—she nibbled at his earlobe—"I must be doing something wrong." Hooking the bottom of his shirt between thumb and forefinger, she raised the loose material and exposed a flat stomach and hairy chest. Leisurely, she drew heated circles around his nipple with eager tongue.

"Brye?" He sucked in a sharp, faltering breath, his senses flooded by passion.

"Hm?" Working her way past his neck, she addressed all her attention to his right ear.

"Do you realize where we are?" he moaned, finding it difficult to dive for cover underneath her passionate onslaught. Shutting his eyes, his head rolled on his shoulders as Brye quickened the urge to make love to him.

"Of course I realize where we are." Brye applied herself to the opposite ear.

"We can't do this here." Belying his words, he wrapped his arms securely around her impassioned body. Molded together, two bodies swayed in time with a gentle breeze.

"I've never known you to be a party pooper, Chad," Brye whispered close to his ear. She lifted his shirt over his head and dropped it at her feet.

"Dammit, Brye." Roughly, Chad pulled at her clothing. Popping the button of her walking shorts, he pulled down her zipper.

Clutching at one another, they fell onto a pillowy mound of red-clay dirt.

Twenty minutes later, Brye and Chad reemerged and stumbled into the direct pathway of a rumbling golf cart.

Two long shadows fell across the driver's line of sight. Surprised, he slammed his foot on the breaks. The gas-powered mobile came to a jerking halt.

"Are you okay?" he shouted. Startled to see two haggard individuals darting out of the bushes, the thought of almost hitting them sent his heart slamming against his chest. But as he took a closer look, he realized that the man and woman weren't haggard at all. In fact, they looked as if they'd been… He blinked back his shock.

Brye struggled to keep her grin from exploding onto the scene. Hands clasped behind her back, balancing on the balls of her feet, she stared with open-eyed innocence at the driver.

Despite the long hair and wide sideburns, the man clearly looked to be well over retirement age. Folded in his seat, a rotund belly dangled over a broad cowhide belt and hung precariously over his lap. Wearing a skintight yellow-canary pullover shirt and brightly colored polyester pants, he resembled an Elvis Presley throwback.

Feeling extremely generous, Brye extended the driver a smile guaranteed to raise a dying man from his sick bed. "We're fine," she answered.

The concern masking the man's face eased into indulgent wonder. Taking in Brye's disheveled appearance—hair helter-skelter, white shirt and shorts wrinkled and adorned with grass and dirt stains—he still thought this young lady to be one of the most refreshing creatures he'd ever set his tired eyes upon. His gaze then flickered to Chad. "What were you two doing in there?" he suspiciously asked.

"We were searching for my ball," Brye rushed to answer. Following the man's line of vision, she reached over and lifted a strand of grass from Chad's hair.

"Mm-hmm!" he stated with obvious cynicism. "And did you find it?"

Mischievousness danced around Brye's satiated expression. Unabashed with not having a ball in hand, she answered. "Yes, we did." Dangerously, she grinned at Chad. "In fact, I found several." The implication struck home.

Chad cringed with embarrassment. His hands covered his mouth as he choked on a cough. The older man broke into rich, deep laughter.

"Since everything's okay, I guess I'll leave you two to…whatever." He started the golf cart. With a final jerk, he pulled off.

"Have a good day!" Brye cheerfully waved after him.

Not looking back, the man flicked his hand in acknowledgment. Chuckling to himself, he good-heartedly thought, *To be young again.* He then wondered if he and his wife were too old to come out here and play with his balls.

Alone, Chad visibly relaxed. Blowing out an insipid puff of air, he squinted at Brye and hissed, "I can't believe you did that! I can't believe you *said* that!" Plunging back into the trees, he pulled out the forgotten driver. "Let's get out of here."

"Chad?" Brye hung back. Her taunting tone tickled his sanity.

Back rigid, perturbed, Chad pivoted on his toes. The gleam in her eyes brought him up short. Not understanding why he was upset, he readily understood that what had just transpired between the two of them had been beautiful, exhilarating, spontaneous. Brye excited him. Their making love in a secluded yet public place had enticed him. The possibility of being caught had also been a powerful source of stimulus for him. So what was the problem? Was it that Brye had introduced a side to him he hadn't been aware of?

He didn't know. At the moment, he was only aware of two things: he loved Brye, and he loved making love to her. Where they made love was of no consequence to him.

Bringing his mouth crashing down on hers, he issued her a deep, longing, tongue-lashing kiss. By the time they tore apart, both were left breathless, heaving for more.

Grabbing her hand, Chad muttered, "Let's get out of here."

"Does this mean my golf session is over?"

"For now."

The golf paraphernalia was packed in a hurry. They made it as far as Chad's red corvette before falling into each other's arms again. Within the tight confines of the sport's car, they made love again before pulling off.

Twice afterward, Chad returned with Brye to the golf course. Both times, they never made it past the third hole, leaving him to accept the fact that Brye would never embrace the game of golf.

The conversation continued to progress without Brye or Chad. And fifteen minutes later, the couples dispersed. It was time to rest some weary bones.

Under the boisterous singsong of the impromptu night concert, as the couples dragged themselves off to bed, rhythmic reggae filled the moody ambiance. Fireflies straggled the air like dancing Christmas lights. Brye silently followed the flight plan of one as it crossed over her line of vision. And for one instant, as the teens replaced one CD with another, all fell quiet; the dusk before dawn.

Then it whispered to Chad on a warm summer's breeze. His words, his sentiments, his heart, molded into a powerful, intrinsic love song: Boyz II Men's "On Bended Knee."

Heartfelt lyrics blended into Chad's exposed soul as he finally accepted what he had assiduously fought against the many years he'd been without Brye. He wanted her back…for the duration of his life…for always… He allowed the song to express what he could not bring himself to say.

Darlin', I can't explain…where did we lose our way…girl, it's drivin' me insane… And I know I just need one more chance to prove my love to you…if you come back to me, I'll guarantee, that I'll never let you go…

Drawing himself out of his chair, Chad moved to stand directly in front of Brye. He slid purposeful fingers underneath her flying hair and began kneading strained neck muscles. And together, they took heed…

Can we go back to the days our love was strong? Can you tell me how a perfect love goes wrong? Can somebody tell me how you get things back the way they use to be? Oh God give me the reason… I'm down on bended knee.

Gentle yet firm fingers, tender music, caressed their way into Brye's mind…her heart…her soul. Leaning into his body, she rested her forehead against his chest. His heart racing against her ear mimicked her own. A wistful sigh spilled into the warm night as the passionate words flushed through her.

Gonna swallow my pride, say I'm sorry… Stop pointing fingers, the blame is on me… I want a new life, and I want it with you… If you feel the same, don't ever let it go…

The atmosphere sizzled with passion. Wild animals crooned to their mates. Tree limbs swayed to the beat of the impassioned plea. In its show of support, a full moon sheathed the troubled lovers in a lustrous ray of hope. An assemblage of stars appeared to separate, then reunite in the shape of a heart. And for several inspiring moments, Chad and Brye believed in the power of love.

Wanna build a new life…just you and me… Gonna make you my wife…raise a family…

The animated world converted back to its original state as the love song ended. But the moving encounter left Chad and Brye emotionally fried.

Despite what they desired, in spite of the tender sensations warming their hearts, how could they prepare for a future when the past had not been overcome? Chad wished with heavy heart and soul he could be man enough to let the past go. He wished it would soundlessly slip away like some nonentity with no substance or meaning. He wanted to start over with Brye right here, right now. But he couldn't. Her hidden past had held a direct bearing on his life…his happiness. He could not let it go. It was imperative she help him understand.

For Brye, as she watched his rising chest, as the flow of life passed through their bodies, she felt complete. His entity blended into hers. They were of one. Earlier, they had shared a golf memory. Seconds ago, they had shared a song. At the moment, they were sharing one soul. And when Chad stifled a yawn, Brye shared that as well.

"Maybe you should turn in now," she spoke softly, reluctantly, the past few moments slipping out of her reach. "It's been a long day."

Chad's fingers rested along the base of her neck. He quietly demanded, "We need to talk…really talk. It's time, Brye. It's time for answers."

Her response came in a cautious shake of her head. Brye wasn't certain she could give him answers because there were few she had to give. Something—an incident from her distant past—truly frightened her. Something so horrific, she religiously struggled to hide it from even herself. She could not allow Chad to penetrate those veiled memories. She had to stall, at least until she was ready to face her own tormented history.

Sliding out from under his heady grip, Brye reared back. She stared up into his steamy expression. "I don't mean we can't talk or you can't ask your questions. I only mean that I don't want to discuss it tonight." She shrugged. "I'm feeling exceptionally vulnerable right now. I'm also feeling a bit nostalgic. Both sensations usually carry with it a lot of baggage—generally in the form of pain." Again she shrugged. "I'm not certain my conscious awareness can handle the overload."

Brye slid away from the deck railing. She pulled herself upright. Her body posted so close to Chad's, the tips of her breast flattened against his expansive chest. Ignoring the insidious ache rising in the pit of her stomach and ferrying toward the nature of her womanhood, she captured his face between the palms of her hands. Floating her thumb around moon-filled eyes that clearly reflected strains from a long-winded day, she voiced, "Why don't you go to bed?"

His questioning stare prompted her to implore, "Please!"

Chad searched her face with restless eyes. A hint of sadness took precedence over her beauty. There was a time, during the many months they'd been a couple, when the unhappiness had no longer been evident. At the time, he believed he had been the exorcist expelling her demons. Could he do it again? Did he even want to tackle the job?

The answer was yes. But this time he wanted to do it right. Before, he hadn't really expelled her demons. He'd merely shoved them aside, leaving them to emerge on another day.

For now, he decided, he would not push. Instead, he'd wait until she was ready.

His head dipped. His mouth brushed lightly over hers. Drawing back, he asked, "Are you coming?"

"Not right now." Brye dropped her hands to her side. Doing an about-face, she wrapped her arms around her chest while skimming the glistening water with her eyes. "I'd like to be by myself for a while."

Chad stepped up behind Brye. He dropped his hands to her shoulders. Lowering his face into her hair, he inhaled a hint of Mystique. Eyes squeezed shut, he silently agonized over whether to remain or withdraw. Finally, without uttering a good night, he backed away and entered the lodge.

Secluded in his room, Chad's fatigue dropped on him like a man hitting the ground without a parachute. Crossing over the braided, area rug, his weary body collapsed onto the Native American motif blanket veiling the bed. The soft cotton embraced his exhaustion, devoured it, and sent him floating on a layer of swaying clouds.

Drifting on the border of lethargy, Chad forced himself into semi-awareness. Not one stitch of clothing had been removed from his person. Struggling to pull himself upright, he undressed in a hurry then dragged himself into the shower.

Nude, twenty minutes later, Chad tumbled into bed. But now sleep eluded him. After several minutes of staring at the pine beams stretched across the ceiling, he tossed his feet overboard and guided his legs into a pair of faded jeans. Shirtless, barefoot, he traipsed through the dimly lit hallway. Western-style hurricane lamps palely lit each end of the lengthy corridor.

On deck, he sailed over the darkened area with drifting eyes. Vague shadows jumped from behind trees, bushes, and winding bends. And out of the corner of his eye, he caught a scant movement.

There she sat, Indian style, back against a cedar tree, staring out into nowhere. It reminded him of the first time he'd met her. His angel. Now, just like then, he sensed that if he approached her, she would take flight and run…for good. Today, they had made progress. He wasn't prepared to step backward.

He remained where he stood. If she was aware of his presence, she didn't let on. When sleep overcame him, he steered back to his room. Exhausted, he slid his body under cool, crisp sheets. He fell asleep with the perpetual image of Brye floating amidst his weakening convictions.

"You got one! You got one!" If any of God's creations were, perchance, snoozing in the mid-morning sun, Anthony's piercing outcry exploding onto the scene and reverberating off the forest trees, startled them out of their well-hidden burrows and nests. "Reel him in, Brye. Hurry up and reel him in."

This was not a moment Brye had enthusiastically looked forward to. When she'd agreed to accompany Bethany, Anthony, and Chad, the thought of actually catching a fish appealed to her almost as much as having her hair dyed purple, shaved around the edges, and spiked clear to the ends.

But here she stood. Five minutes into casting her line, and a fish just happened to mosey along and take a bite out of her perfectly arranged morning. How did she ever get so lucky?

She stared at Chad in a hopeless daze. The bedeviled grin riding sensual lips irritated her to no end. She wanted to reach over and smack that complacent look right off his face.

You just don't know how lucky you are, Chad Collier, her mind speared at him. *If the twins weren't here, I'd—*

"You're losing him, Brye." Bethany's enthusiasm bubbled over like the flowing stream they fished in. "Reel him in!"

Ripples of water augmented to monumental proportions as the medium-sized fish flounced back and forth. Right now, it fought for its life. Frankly, Brye hoped it would win.

For the benefit of Anthony and Bethany, Brye put on her most spirited face and began drawing in the line.

Much to her chagrin, the fish finally broke surface. Its scaly body performed amazing acrobatic feats as its tail whipped to and fro in the wind. Ecstatic, the twins jumped up and down with glee. Clapping their hands together, their excessively boisterous encouragement cut into the sanctity of the unruffled forest. Preoccupied with the distasteful image of handling the slimy, scaly, smelly, nauseous, water creature, the twins barely penetrated Brye's chaotic thoughts.

Fortitude. It took every ounce of tenacity for Brye to grip the casting line inches above the hooked fish. Every few seconds, it would rouse and fly into a series of spasms. Whether the movements were voluntary or involuntary—she didn't know nor did she care—Brye refused to lay her hands on the flopping creature until it came to a dead halt.

At long last, the slowly dying fish dangled freely in front of her nose, swaying along the tide of a lofty breeze. *Ugh!* she thought to herself, watching the mouth and gills struggle for oxygen. *Fishing definitely sits up there, one notch above golf on my list of activities I need to set aside for another day. A day I'll hopefully never see in this lifetime.*

"What do you think, guys?" she asked, hoping to prolong the moment she'd actually have to touch the squirming thing.

"You actually caught your first fish," Anthony praised. He studied the sleek build, the overlapping scales, the speckled body with reddish-pink stripe running down the length of his torso.

Anthony was in awe.

"Are you gonna clean and gut it for supper tonight?" Bethany asked. She, as well as Anthony, were thrilled at the prospect of eating fish caught by their own hands. Brye, on the other hand, did not share the same enthusiasm. Her stomach staggered at the thought of feeding on the loathsome creature.

"Maybe I'll take it back with us." Brye spoke slowly, inventing words as she trudged along. "I mean…this is my first catch of the day…of the century. Maybe I'll have it stuffed, then mounted." She grinned at Chad, pleased with herself for coming up with a plausible excuse for not dining on it for dinner.

"Do you know what kind of fish it is?" Anthony interrogated. "Can you really have it stuffed?"

Chad smiled to himself as he watched Brye keep her repulsion down to a tolerable level. Despite her obvious distress, she handled the fish like a trooper. He decided to take pity on her overwrought soul.

"It's a rainbow trout," he answered. Gripping fish and hook, he easily separated the two. "And yes, it could be mounted. But in this day and age—in *any* day and age—catching an eight inch rainbow trout is not a feat many sportsmen—or sportswomen—brag about."

"Now," he said, dropping the fish in a net gaming bag and lowering the bag into the cool stream, "you two better go check your lines. Make sure nothing's nibbled at your bait."

The twins needed no further urging.

"Thank you." Forgetting the earlier exasperation she'd aimed at Chad, she recalled the patience he implemented while instructing the twins on the art of fishing. He would make a wonderful father. With a tinge of regret, she pushed the sacred thoughts aside. "The idea of touching that thing was not sitting well on my stomach." She punctuated her words with a weak smile.

Chad found himself drowning inside her childlike demeanor; several years had been erased from her controlled facade. Along with her youthful appearance, no longer was there a sign of the lost, vulnerable, little girl he'd observed the night before. A completely different person stood in front of him today. This person was relaxed, amusing, confident—only not so confident she wanted to cavort with the fishes—and extremely energetic. Even the sadness had been pushed aside—to be resurrected at a later time no doubt.

Early morning he'd stumbled, half asleep, half dead, into the brightly lit dining room. Bethany and Anthony, already there and waiting, were eating breakfast. Chad had guzzled two cups of very strong, very hot, coffee before telling the twins that Brye might not be up to their fishing expedition. Much to his surprise, she bounced into the dining room wearing a sports bra, a pair of running shorts, and a sweatshirt tied around her waist. Acting as spry as a hummingbird contentedly buzzing from flower to flower, Brye had informed him that she'd be ready as soon as she jumped into the shower—she'd just completed a four mile jog along a panoramic trail. As she sprinted off, thoroughly astonished, Chad had shaken his head at her backside. When had she had time to sleep? Did she sleep? If she slept, how much time did she allot for that minor necessity of life? It was another mystery Chad found imperative to solve.

"I guess fishing isn't your forte," he said, taking control of her fishing pole.

"Next year, remind me to take the kids someplace where fishing is prohibited by law," she mumbled under her breath, not wanting the twins to overhear.

His entire face shifted into a gear she held no awareness of—as if she'd said something profound and he was dying to call her attention to it.

"If that's an invitation to join you," Chad said with a roguish grin. "I graciously accept."

"Why don't you worry about getting through the next several days? Then…we'll see."

Baiting her line with a live minnow, Chad deliberately pushed the wiggling creature at her face. "Why don't you worry about getting through the next hour?"

Repulsed, Brye puckered her lips. She shoved the pole back at him. "I believe I'm going to get through this next hour fine, thank you very much! Over there." She pointed toward a large, shady, Sycamore tree. "Wa-a-a-y over there. You three carry on without me."

A small smile played along Chad's lips as he stared after Brye. It was good seeing her in this fashion. Happy, spirited, unencumbered from all worries.

Unrolling a blanket she'd brought with her, she meticulously stretched it out under the tree. Next, she dug into her backpack and pulled out a paperback. Book in hand, Brye made a niche in the soft grass as she settled down to read. Smiling, waving, she dropped her face into her book.

"She's not really into this, is she?" Anthony asked. Head slanted to the side, he studiously eyed Brye.

Reluctant to turn his back on the picture of pure innocence Brye portrayed, Chad took a stance beside Anthony. Golden rays of sun streaked the young boy's hair with multicolored hues. Chad ruffled his fingers through strands so much resembling Brye's.

"You are such a remarkably astute young man," he praised, his mind muddled with the large amount of pride he felt toward Anthony.

"What does *astute* mean?" Bethany asked.

"It means"—he sought for an interpretation easily understood by six-year-olds—"observant, perceptive, aware."

"Astute." Bethany rolled the word around her tongue. Since coming to Brylinn, between Brye and Mama Linn, her vocabulary steadily heightened. And last night, while watching a popular sitcom, Jordan had declared how much she "idolized" the teenaged star.

Idolized. Bethany had liked the word the moment Jordan had defined it. The tangible definition had identified the feelings she retained for Chad; she idolized him more than any other man in the world. And that said a lot considering she had never "idolized" anyone before—not even television stars. After taking a few seconds to mull over her two new words, Bethany stored them away for later referral.

Chad planted himself on top of a large bolder jutting from the moist ground. Situated between Anthony and Bethany, as he cast his line, he noted Bethany's red and white bobber twist and turn for several seconds then dive under the water. "I think you've got a bite, hon." He pointed to her line.

Tingling with excitement, following Chad's explicit directions, she reeled in her first catch of the day.

Two hours later, having caught five fish—two bass, one crappie, two trout—and partaking in the most stimulating of conversations he had ever held with two six-year-olds, Chad exhaustively crawled onto Brye's blanket.

"Don't stray too far," he shouted at the twins as they took off on an exploration expedition of their own. "And be extremely careful."

"We will," Anthony and Bethany cried in unison. In a matter of seconds, they had moved beyond the trees and out of the line of sight.

"Those two are amazing." Lying flat on his back, he laced his fingers behind his head.

Brye lowered her book. Brightly shining eyes smiled down at Chad. "Yes, they are. And you… You're wonderful with them."

Chad released his fingers. Reaching upward, he brushed a strand of hair away from Brye's forehead. "They make it easy for me. Sometimes it's a strain keeping it in my head that they're only six years old."

Brye tossed her book aside. Stretching her body beside Chad's, she rolled onto her stomach and propped her chin onto her balled fist. "They like you, you know," she said, staring down into his placid features.

"And you, Brye Grayson? How do you feel about me?"

Brye's heart had opened up tremendously as she, under the cover of her book, kept a vigilant eye on the three. Chad was good to them, he was good *for* them, and never had she seen the twins as happy as they were, catching fish, with Chad by their side, entertaining them with every breath he took. It was dangerous, she knew, but her heart swelled with so much love for Chad and for the twins. This once she decided to allow herself the luxury of believing they were a real family. "I like you too." She couldn't believe she had said it. Yet she was glad to have spoken the heartfelt words.

Afraid to see his reaction, she flipped to her back. A diaphanous cloud gingerly floated above her head. Studying it intently, she debated on whether it looked like a donkey's or a mule's head. Was there a difference? Of course there was. Could she point out those differences? No, not at the moment. But then did she really care about the physical aspects of donkeys and mules.

"How much?"

Brye snapped out of her senseless deliberations. "How much what?" she asked.

"How much do you like me?"

"I plead the fifth." Brye kept her eyes on the roaming donkey/mule. *Isn't a mule the offspring of a male donkey and a female horse? Yes, but what does that have to do with anything?*

"Do you like me enough to go dancing with me tonight?"

Brye rolled to her side. The sight of his handsome, Herculean profile took her breath away. "Excuse me?" she managed with some difficulty.

"This morning, I promised Mary Ann we'd go dancing with them tonight."

"Okay." She flopped onto her back. A downy woodpecker pecked fiercely at a Sycamore branch. She studied the bird for several seconds. "I'll go," she said, surprising Chad.

It was Chad's turn to roll to his side. Facing Brye, eyelids crimped into a curious glare, he repeated, "Okay? Just like that? No screaming, no fighting, no punching or kicking? Just 'I'll go.'"

She switched her gaze from the bird to Chad, grinned, and asked, "What did you expect me to say?"

"I expected you to say no. More specifically, I expected you to say, 'Hell no!' I expected you to scream at the top of your lungs, 'I wouldn't go dancing with you if you were the last man on earth, Mr. Collier.' And, in saying all that, I'm saying I expected you to put up more of a fight."

Her eyes rolled over his broad shoulders, massive chest, flat stomach, and stopped short at the bulge straining in a pair of carpenter shorts. A long, lean sex machine. The thought carried a flush to Brye's cheeks. Returning her eyes to the cloud, she said, "I'm not impossible to get along with, Chad. You of all people should know that."

A long time ago, Chad had thought he'd known all there was to know of Brye. In reality, he'd only skimmed the surface. He'd only seen what she had allowed him to see. There was so much more, so much depth. If he started digging now, maybe he'd see the light of day by the turn of the century.

"What?" Brye said, observing the familiar reflection cropping up on his face. "What were you thinking about…just now?"

"I was thinking that I thought I did know you." His voice became teasing, inviting. "Look at us." He did a roundabout with his eyes to take in the bountiful countryside, the blue sky, the perfect weather, the solitude. "Look at where we are. At one time, you would have been screaming to jump my bones."

"Jump your bones?" Her laughter sounded so vibrant, so alive. Shivers of gratification warmed Chad's entire body. He felt a sense of pride knowing he had invoked that scintillating sound from her.

Back on her side, face-to-face, she made merry with her dancing eyes. "Mr. Collier! You are the adult here. You're supposed to set the standards. You've known my kids for what? One week now? And instead of encouraging them to rise to your level of maturity, you've followed them down into the den of inequities."

Chad appeared contrite—for a fraction of a second. The grin he'd tried so hard to conceal burst through like a ray of sunshine. "Hey…would you have rather I said knockin' boots, bump and grind, rock my world?"

Brye's eyes widened in fictitious shock. "Oh my god! You have been talking to my kids?"

"What can I say?" Chad admitted with a grin spread from Lake George to clear across the state of New Jersey. "I'm doing my part in bridging the generation gap."

"It is such a wide gap to close, isn't it, old man?"

Chad and Brye shared laughter. An opulent, potent, cleansing chortle. Yet something other than shared laughter occurred. Once again, they felt the mingling of souls. The sensation left them both lightheaded and breathless.

Flopping down on his back, Chad lifted his arms and cradled the back of his head inside his hands. Beyond the scope of the grand tree, the sun beat a ferocious path along the forest greens. Yet where he and Brye lay, a cool breeze stroked their unsettled bodies. Chad felt far removed from the world stretched beyond the boundaries of his vision.

There was so much bad blood between him and Brye; so much bitterness; so many words said, as well as unsaid. But here, today, under the protection of the shady Sycamore tree, they'd found a safe haven—they were able to put the cruelties of life's injustices far behind them. And here, today, they exonerated the other of their respective sins. It was a day to be reckoned with. A day to be embraced, cherished, then stored for safe-keeping—much like one would safe keep precious jewels, delicate crystals, treasured heirlooms.

Tomorrow, the balance might falter in the midst of their wake. Today, nothing could upset their perfectly scaled domain.

"Chad?"

Chad's eyes were closed. The soft lilt of her voice did wicked things to his mind and body. "Hm?"

"If the twins weren't here…with us?" She licked her lips before nervously trudging forward. "You…me… here…now? Would you… Would we have?"

His eyes kicked open. Beneath the glare of dark lashes, he said, "I think you and I both can agree that there's an underlying sexual current commanding our every movement when we're together." He shrugged, unashamed to admit, "Even when we're apart. It's inevitable, Brye. It's gonna happen." He drew his right hand from behind his head. Stalwart fingers slid around her throat and settled at the back of her neck. "I want you, Brye. I've not denied that fact since you've reentered my life. I want to make love to you. And, yes, if Anthony and Bethany hadn't been here helping to maintain a respectable distance between us, we would be making love now. At this very moment."

Chad had said he wanted to make love to her. He hadn't said he loved her. He hadn't offered to commit himself solely to her. He hadn't mentioned going to Jennifer and telling her to take a flying leap off a soaring airplane...without the aid of a parachute, she guiltily mused.

At the age of sixteen, an age supposedly depicted of innocence and sweetness, Brye had stopped counting the number of men she'd fended off; men who'd wanted to sleep with her. Advantageously, Brye demanded more from herself; she wanted more for herself. She also desired more from Chad. And being invited into Chad's bed was synonymous to being invited into Jennifer's domain. Chad and Jennifer were sleeping together. A fact. Chad and Jennifer were expected to announce their engagement sometime in the near future. Another fact. Where was Brye expected to fit in that sordid scenario? She didn't know. She did, however, know that she had no desires in becoming a fundamental component within a three-way math problem. And although she wanted Chad just as much as he wanted her, she refused to give in to a few minutes of indiscriminate passion—particularly when love wasn't a part of that equation.

Incorporating the attributes of a femme fatale—her mother would have loved this—Brye set out to prove to Chad that he could not have her.

She lowered her voice by several octaves, sounding husky, tempting, sensual. "You are a very virile man, Chad Collier."

Lifting his kneading fingers from around her neck, she settled his hand on the ground between their heated bodies. "And sexy." She trailed a shapely, medium-length, unadorned fingernail down the middle of his breastbone. "Extremely sexy." Her finger continued a downward path, fluttering along a taut stomach, down the front of his shorts, halting directly on top of the intensifying inflation manifesting between his legs. Beneath her finger, he became one solid, shivering, hunk of mass. Pleased with the reaction she induced, she continued her mental attack. "I know how much you enjoy sex, Chad. I know how much you want me." Head dropped, her tongue flickered amazingly close to his ear. "But I never knew you were into threesomes." Abruptly, she pulled away. Her hand fell innocently onto the blanket.

Not put off by her sudden retreat or her verbal jab, Chad recaptured her hand and positioned it back on target. Pressing her palm firmly against his hardened member, sucking in his chest as desire detonated millions of tiny pleasure points along his throbbing torso, he rasped, "Yes…you're right. I do enjoy making love to a woman. *One* woman. Particular when that woman retains all the qualities necessary to satisfy my needs and desires."

"And does Jennifer do that for you?" She exerted a small amount of pressure through her fingers.

Chad closed his eyes as her deliberate onslaught played havoc with his firing brain cells. "In her case, I can honestly say she's lacking in some qualities."

"All of which are human." Brye squeezed a little tighter before releasing her grip and dropping on her back.

Propping himself up on one elbow, Chad peered down into a face void of any emotion. In the corner of his eye, he spotted a woodchuck lazily rambling past. "Do I detect a note of jealousy?"

"What you detect is a note of genuine interest. Tell me, Chad, why does someone like you—someone who can be so kind, caring, and sensitive—pick someone like her, who's as dehumanized and as cold as the fish I caught today, for a lifetime friend, companion, and mate?

"I can't imagine she'd ever give birth to children. The thought of tainting that perfectly manufactured body of hers would be way to traumatizing. Prolonged consideration alone would probably lead to a multitude of emotional scars." Somewhere in the distance, a motorboat revved to life.

"But if by some chance the queen of perfection did decide to go through with a pregnancy, I have no doubt she'd give birth to a flawless baby who, prior to entering this world, would have already attended and graduated with honors at the University of Etiquette, Style, and Supremacy. Not to mention the fact that the baby would no doubt make his trip though the birthing canal already bathed, powdered, diapered, and smelling like a rose."

Chad shot into a sitting position. "You *are* jealous."

The surprise he generated sounded genuine to Brye's ear. "No… yes…no. Not in the way you think?"

"In what way?"

"I'm not jealous of her, I'm jealous of how you relate to her. I'm jealous at what she represents to you." Brye pulled herself up to Chad's eye level. Stuffing her knees under her chin, she wrapped her arms around her legs. She looked away. Her eyes darted after a dragon fly skimming the surface of the rippling stream.

"You look at her and see the prefect wife…the perfect life. You look at her and know she's the perfect showpiece clinging to your arm…the perfect mouthpiece…the perfect hostess. You know she'll always say the right thing. You know she'll always do the right thing. You know she'll always be the woman you want her to be—at least as long as she is in the public eye." Brye grimaced at the reality of her own societal standing within Chad's life. And then you look at me." Brye swallowed. She turned away to hide the pain echoing off her heart. "When your eyes fall on me, you see a conniving bitch…a money-hungry charlatan…an embezzler. You look at me and see someone you would like to take to bed but would never invite home to be introduced to your mother."

Whatever the origin of her anguish, the pain was authenticated by the quiver in her voice, the tremble of her chin, the constrained look in her eyes. Her grief was real. And Chad's every instinct said she needed reassurances. She needed love.

"Brye?" She didn't respond, so he leaned closer. "Look at me, Brye."

Her eyes remained in front of her.

"Brye?" He clipped her under the chin with thumb and forefinger. Brute strength alone forced her to confront his piercing stare. "You're wrong on all accounts, Brye.

"If I truly believed Jennifer was the right woman for me, we would've been married long before now. As it stands, we're not even engaged."

He cradled her face between the palms of his hands. "And you…I look at you and see a woman, a beautiful woman, a wonderfully fascinating woman, who might have gotten into some trouble years ago but, for some inexplicable reason, was afraid to take me into her confidence. I see a woman who took money from my family, not because she wanted to but because she didn't feel she had any other recourse."

As he spoke, life returned to Brye's eyes. She pulled out of his reach. A half smile teased enticing lips. Silently, she studied him. "Are you serious?" she finally asked in astonishment. "Is that what you really see when you look at me?"

"Yes," he somberly informed.

A bear crashing through the forest would have been less surprising than the spirited laugh Brye flung in his face. This was Chad speaking. Her Chad. The same Chad she'd met and fallen in love with years ago. There was no bitterness, no rancor, no need to seek revenge. Instead, here was a man ready and willing to give her the benefit of the doubt. They had come a long way over the past few weeks.

"We've made tremendous progress, Chad," her comment blazed with fascination. "A couple of weeks ago, you wouldn't have granted me the time of day." Bending forward, she puckered up and plopped a huge, sloppy, lip-smacking kiss on top of his stunned mouth. "There's hope for you yet. And at the rate you're going, I'll have you believing I never took your lousy money."

Chad wasn't certain how to respond. It was one thing to forgive her of her sins. But he could not disregard her betrayal as if it had never come to pass, particularly when he possessed hardcore evidence of her deception.

Given no time to reflect further, Bethany volleyed onto the scene.

Chest heaving, words choppy—more from exhaustion than worry—Bethany blurted, "I can't find Anthony. I turned away to watch this pretty red bird pecking at a tree limb. And before I realized it, Anthony was gone." As she caught her breath, her sentences were delivered more evenly. "I called out, but he never answered."

Heart pumping wildly, endless possibilities of Anthony's whereabouts forayed Chad's mind—none of which proved very favorable. On his feet long before Bethany finished her sentence, Brye was a mere fraction of a second behind him. "Take me to where you last saw him."

Brye couldn't block the alarm speeding through her. "Chad?"

He turned. Their eyes met. The fear Chad detected reflected a mirror image of his own. He wanted to pull Brye into his arm—to assure as well as be reassured—but he needed to maintain a level head for them all.

Awarding her with a lucid smile, he said, "We'll find him. Don't worry."

Brye wasn't convinced until she dropped on one knee in front of Bethany. Grabbing her lightly by the shoulders, Brye asked, "Bethany?"

Just that, in the form of a question. It was all Brye needed to say. It was a private conversation between two people not linked by blood, but bound by something intrinsic, more profound…something enduring.

In silent wonder, Chad beheld Bethany as she closed her eyes and opened her mind. Head cocked to one side, she listened, felt, sensed. Chad did not comprehend what was taking place inside her pigtailed head.

Bethany reopened her eyes. "He's fine."

With a sigh of relief, Brye nodded, accepting Bethany's word as gospel. She stood. Slipping her fingers into Bethany's tiny yet secure grip, she said, "Then let's go find him."

Thirty minutes later, and still no sign of Anthony, Chad decided it would be best to split up. Within minutes of parting from Brye and Bethany, trailing the bank of a second stream hidden deep within the forest walls, he finally ran across Anthony. His heart lurched into his lungs and threatened to arrest his normal breathing pattern.

A mixture of rocks, boulders, and stones created a jagged and unsafe trek across the rapidly flowing stream. Highly imaginative and extremely energetic, Anthony spotted the protruding stones for what they resembled—a ticket to the other side. Surefooted as a chimpanzee frolicking in the trees, Anthony had effortlessly slipped across. After exploring a world full of exciting discoveries, he had finally decided to rejoin the others and was now crossing back.

"Stay where you are, Anthony!" Chad yelled. "I'm coming to get you."

Face beaming with delight, Anthony waved with so much vigor Chad feared he'd lose his footing and tumble into the water. In horror, he watched as Anthony continued to scramble toward him.

"Dammit, Anthony!" Alarmed, his voice pitched with fright. "I said wait right there!" Chad had already begun to hop the projecting boulders. As he crossed over, he silently prayed Anthony wouldn't slip and break his neck.

He didn't have to worry. The harshness in his voice froze Anthony on the spot. Terror shrouded his eyes. Panic embraced his small frame.

Gathering him up, Chad barely noticed the stiffness embodying Anthony. Once they hit solid ground, he lowered Anthony to his feet and decided to give him a bear hug first, chastise later. He dropped to his knees and reached toward the paralyzed body.

"Don't hurt me! Please don't hit me!" Anthony broke from his paralysis. "I'll be good! I swear I'll be good!" Protecting his head with folded arms, Anthony cowered in front of Chad.

The anguished pleas, the face contorted in fright, brought tears to Chad's eyes. Shaken at the pitiful sight, he silently swore to himself. How does one physically and emotionally scar a six-year-old so severely that the slightest sign of affection directed toward him is interpreted as a threat to his own personal safety?

Never having lived with that kind of pain, Chad could not grasp the full extent of Anthony's fears. Nevertheless, he did digest—a repulsive taste which left him gagging on his presumptions—the lengths to which intimidation had been applied to influence this subservient behavior. And he did empathize, as well as sympathize, with Anthony's tragic dilemma. Then and there, he vowed to do everything in his power to help ease, if not erase, the pain and bad memories the twins had endured, and retained, within their short life spans.

Hands shaking from his own fright, Chad took hold of Anthony's wiry wrist. Gently prying the tiny hands away from a face wrecked with anguish, he only succeeded in inciting another bout of earth shattering wails.

With his own aggrieved emotions unraveling into thin shreds, Chad dragged the struggling body tighter into his chest. His arms wrapped securely around Anthony. "I would never hurt you, Anthony. I could never hurt you." Patiently, Chad rocked as he continued in a soft monotone. "I know you don't know me well enough to trust me, but you have to believe me when I say I would never do anything to cause harm to you. And I swear"—his voice cracked as he closed his eyelids to stay the impending tears—"I'll never let anyone hurt you or your sister again."

The words were born out of sheer desperation, yet Chad spoke with such passion and conviction, he knew he would take any steps necessary in order to keep his promise. "All I ask is you have a little faith in me," Chad added, providing Anthony with the much-needed warmth and strength the little boy had been denied most of his life.

A hushed stillness blanketed the forest clearing. The sun disappeared behind a straying cloud. The air stood stagnant. Leaves on trees ceased their restless fidgeting. Birds terminated their singsong chirping. Even the stream seemed to have come to a radical standstill. And unbeknownst to the two aggrieved figures, Brye and Bethany stood motionless, waiting in the wings, desperately clutching each other's hands. For one urgent moment, the world had ceased to function. It was as if all walks of life waited anxiously to see how this dramatic scene would play out.

Gradually, Anthony's tears subsided as Chad's effectual declarations took hold. With the exception of Bethany, Brye, and Mama Linn, Anthony had not received much love in his life, and certainly never from a member of the same sex. Any male figure playing a significant part in his life had only treated him with resentment and persecution. And now, with Chad's calming nature, his capable, reassuring grip, and the promises made to take care of him, Anthony wanted nothing more than to believe Chad. He wanted to believe in this man who showed nothing but patience and kindness toward him. He desired a male authoritarian figure in his life he could trust as well as confide in.

Pushing away from Chad, tears drying, Anthony sniffled loudly, "Are…Are you mad at me?"

"Of course I'm not mad at you." Chad smiled and swiped at Anthony's tears with a gentle thumb. "I am upset at your actions, though. You could've been hurt disappearing the way you did. While crossing the stream, you could have fallen off one of those rocks… hit your head…been swept away in the stream. You could have gotten lost. You could have been attacked by a wild animal." Chad met Anthony's wavering eye. "Are you getting the picture here? Or do I have to go on and on with a list of endless possibilities of the trouble you could have gotten yourself into?"

Chin quivering, eyes brightly lit with more unshed tears, Anthony shook his head back and forth.

Chad pulled him back into his arms. "Do you realize how worried we were?"

"I'm sorry," Anthony sobbed against Chad's shoulders.

"All is forgiven if you promise to never run off again by yourself."

"I pro…pro…promise."

"Good. I'm going to hold you to that. Chad parked himself on the bank of the stream. Pulling Anthony down beside him, he draped an arm around the boy's shoulder. Closing his eyes for a quick second, Chad pondered what to do next. He blew out an anxiety-filled puff of air. Knowing more needed to be said, not certain what it was or how to go about saying it, Chad counted to three and prayed the right words would come. "Now we need to talk about anger and when one person gets mad at another. Okay?"

Hesitancy leaped into Anthony's boyish grace, yet bravely, he nodded like a man.

"I need you to understand, Anthony, that it's okay to show your anger—even if you're very close to that person and you love them very much. As long as the anger is channeled in a constructive, not destructive, manner, it's all right to acknowledge your frustrations." To gain more time and organize his thoughts, Chad picked up a small stone and skipped it across the water. The stone issued little plopping sounds as it struck the water four times. Turning back to Anthony, Chad squeezed his shoulder. "Do you know what a destructive pattern would be?"

A crocodile tear dropped from the corner of Anthony's eyes. Sliding listlessly along his cheek, the huge water droplet trickled to the ground beside him. He knew the answer to that question well, having been treated like a punching bag his entire life. "It's when someone hurts another person. Maybe by hitting or screaming or calling him bad names."

"That's right," Chad agreed. "But that's the wrong way to express one's anger. Do you know what the right way is?"

Anthony shook his head no. Abuse was the only expression he'd ever endured—he could not relate to anything else.

"The right way is by sitting and talking, like we're doing now. Calmly… Showing respect for one another's feelings…always taking the other person's opinion into consideration." Bowing his head toward Anthony, they tapped foreheads. "Do you think you could do that?"

Anthony extended his first smile. The sun trotted high above two lowered heads. But Anthony's simple gesture of happiness warmed Chad's skin more than any sizzling rays could.

"Oh, by the way"—Chad gently tapped Anthony on the bridge of his nose—"this anger thing works both ways. We both have every right to express our feelings to the other. Which means it's perfectly acceptable for you to get mad at me. Just remember to come to me so we can discuss it and straighten the bad stuff out."

"I could never get mad at you," Anthony notified, staring at Chad with huge, forgiving eyes.

"Of course you could…and you will at one time or another." The blank look on Anthony's face hurdled Chad into seeking a sufficient example. One Anthony could fully understand. *How would Brye handle this?* he thought to himself. *What would she say?* "Let's say I fed you spinach for dinner," Chad cautiously trudged forward.

"Ugh!" Anthony stuck his tongue out in loathing. "I hate spinach."

"You see"—Chad bent and kissed the top of Anthony's head—"you will probably get mad at me when I force you to eat it."

Anthony nodded to himself, deep in thought. A nuance of understanding burnished a bright hole in the back of his awareness.

"The destructive way to handle that anger is to go stomping off, lip out to here"—Chad grabbed Anthony's bottom lip and playfully stretched it well beyond his top lip—"while mumbling to yourself during the entire meal."

Giggling, Anthony jerked away from Chad's light pinch.

"The constructive way to handle your anger would be to come to me and say—" Chad waited for Anthony to finish the sentence.

Anthony grinned, falling in line with the game. "I'd say, why are you making me eat this nasty green stuff when you know how much I hate it?"

"Then I'd say, 'Because it's good for you. It has lots of much needed nutrients.'"

"I could take *Flintstones* vitamins and get more than my daily allowance."

"It'll make you grow up big and strong like Popeye."

"Popeye's a cartoon character. All the spinach in the world won't make me look like him."

"Okay. Then how about wrestlers? Spinach can help you grow to look like one of those sizable men."

"Nope. I think steroids do that." Anthony dipped his hand in the stream and swished it back and forth.

Incredulously, Chad gawked at Anthony. *This kid is unbelievable.* "Are you sure you're not a sixteen-year-old hiding out in the body of a six-year-old?"

The tears were long gone. Anthony beamed up at Chad. "I'm sure." Reestablishing their game, he asked, "Does this mean I don't have to eat my spinach?" His hand came out of the water. Huge droplets flew everywhere as he shook the excess moisture off his skin.

"No, it doesn't. Because now I'm the one who's mad," Chad lightly teased. "In fact, I've grown tired of being nice, and I'm sick of your smart-aleck remarks, young man. So eat your spinach or you won't get any dessert."

Retreating within himself, Anthony took time to consider the gravity of the situation. His left cheek blew up like a hot-air balloon as he dragged his tongue along the polished skin aligning the inside of his mouth. A decision teetering in the balance, he asked, "What's for dessert?"

Not expecting the question, Chad blindly stumbled inside his head as he pursued an answer to the unforeseen question. What was the going dessert for boys Anthony's age? Had chocolate remained the universal favorite since his childhood? He took a wild shot in the dark and skipped another stone in the water.

"Chocolate cake with a double dip of chocolate ice cream, smothered in chocolate syrup, and topped with chocolate sprinkles."

Anthony's mouth watered as a vivid image of the cake emerged. "Okay. I'll eat my spinach."

"Good." A wave of relief washed over Chad. Moments later, the sense of relief faltered, sapping him of all energy.

"So"—fine lines etched along Chad's brow intensified his apprehension—"are we straight with this?"

"I think so."

"We're buddies?"

"Yes."

Chad pointed a balled fist at Anthony. "Good. Give me some dap."

At the same moment, Anthony tapped Chad's fist with his own. Brye's silent support came in the form of a touch along his shoulder blades. Nimble fingers, lightly grazing his back, gifted him with the strength he'd misplaced. Pushing himself off the ground, he pulled Anthony to his feet as well. Briefly, his eyes connected with Brye's. Based on the smile of encouragement she awarded him, he had no doubt she'd witnessed the entire emotional episode.

Are you all right? Her silent question reached out to him.

I need a hug. His half smile returned.

A slight nod of the head, and Brye turned on Anthony. "And you, young man, do you know how much of a scare you gave us?" Brye grasped his chin between thumb and forefinger. Shaking his head gently, she asked, "Do I have to go through the entire spiel of why you shouldn't run off by yourself?"

"No, you don't," Anthony replied, grinning at Chad. "Mr. Collier's already given me a taste of that spiel, thank you very much!"

"Did you learn anything?"

"Yes." His baby blue eyes fell onto his sister. A Cheshire cat grin altered his serious appearance as he passed a silent, and elusive message to his twin, *Wouldn't it be neat if we had a father like Mr. Collier?*

"Good. Then I imagine we should be getting back. It's way past lunchtime, and we have a long hike in front of us."

Growing serious again, eyes murky with sincerity, voice sinking, he apologized, "I am sorry, really, for running off and scaring you."

Bending at the waist, Brye accepted his apology with a quick brush of her lips along his cheek. "I know you are." She straightened her body. "Why don't you two run ahead and start collecting our supplies? Chad and I will be right behind you."

The two look-a-likes dashed ahead.

Not thinking twice about her actions, Brye readily slipped into Chad's arms. As she enwrapped her arms around him, as he clung tenaciously to her, she sensed his desperation, his doubts, his fears. And as Chad gathered strength from her nurturing embrace, he grew alarmed as the familiar contours of her cloying body teased his pensive emotions.

"You handled the situation very well," Brye applauded, and strove to ignore the galvanizing oscillation his nearness created within her own body.

"I kept wondering what you would do or say. I prayed I wouldn't make the situation any worse by saying something inappropriate or doing something that was way out of line." He sounded strained, depleted to the bone. As usual, his need to make love to her ran high, but the desire to brave this conversation reigned even higher. "But most of all, I felt angry for what he's had to go through his entire life. I swear, Brye, if I could get my hands on the people who've abused those two…" Chad trailed off, anger seeping, leaving Brye to fill in the blanks.

"Your feelings are only natural," Brye informed. "I experience the same feelings each and every time an abused child comes to Brylinn." She peered into his enraged face. "You have to remember, Chad, that although these kids had a rough beginning, they're doing all they can to put the past behind them. I'm doing all I can to help them. And although their past will always be with them, they're learning how to cope. So it's extremely ineffectual for you and I to waste time dwelling on the parents' inhuman conduct. Our place is to focus on the abused child."

"You're right, I know. But it's difficult to be objective. Particularly when a child, a child seemingly as happy and bright and wonderful as Anthony, cowers at your feet because he's deathly afraid of being struck." Chad closed his eyes. The image, now a permanent fixture ingrained within his mind, twisted inside his gut. "God, Brye, you don't know how I felt when he begged me not to hurt him." His eyes slowly opened. Brye glimpsed a hint of tears begging to be released.

"It's okay, Chad." Brye pulled him back into her arms. Together, they stood, drawing from each other's strength. And when Brye felt Chad had regained himself, she deposited a light kiss on the side of his neck; on the very spot his heart pulsated; on the very spot life surged through him. Wanting to give more, needing to receive more, begrudgingly, she slipped out of the restorative clench.

Slipping her left hand solidly into Chad's, she smoothed her right palm across Chad's cheek. "You have made a friend for life with Anthony, as well as Bethany. You realize that, don't you?"

Chad turned endeavoring lips into Brye's warm touch. Kissing her open palm, he said, "Next to you, I'd love nothing better than to have those two remarkable kids become part of my life." His emotional aspirations came straight from the heart.

As they trailed after the twins, Brye noticed she'd become more in tune with the bountiful land surrounding her. Mother Nature had rebalanced itself. The sun forged an exhilarating trail of radiance along her sensitized skin. The stream flowed with an effervescence visible to all who were pure in heart as well as spirit. The bracing aroma of cedar and pine skimmed the forest walls. A band of lively forest animals joined in sprightly chorus. The whistling wind served as back-up accompaniment.

Yes. Mother Nature had returned to its natural, resplendent state. Life surged through Brye as never before.

A significant omen. Whether good or bad, Brye knew not which. Was this the quiet before the storm? Or had her pretentious display of an existence ultimately taken a turn for the better?

17

THE STAR-CROSSED LOVERS CARVED their own blazing path in the clandestine moonlit night. Arm in arm, Brye—barefooted, two-inch black sandals slung in hand—and Chad, strolled along a private beach grazing a modest share of terrain riding along the perimeter of Lake George. Miles and miles of shimmering lake stretched before them. An iridescent half-moon, stars bursting with animated vivacity, virtuously adorned an indigo sky. Frenzied evening ambiance mellowed into a lazy, obliging night. The air remained inert, with the exception of an occasional draft levitating the provocative scent of Mystique through the circumspect darkness.

The palpable aroma of Brye's designer's perfume forged its own intrusive route inside Chad's brain. It drew a parched streak directly to his loins, leaving in its wake an unrelenting thirst begging to be quenched. Chad feared he would be unable to deny his self-imposed famine much longer.

The tranquil seclusion, the private walk along the beach, the dazzling half-moon beaming down at them—this was clearly a night foreordained for lovers. And although Chad and Brye had not made love in years, today, they'd shared intimate thoughts, intimate caresses, and intimate laughter. Chad desired to inscribe a memorable signature at the end of a remarkable day; he wanted to make love to Brye until the break of dawn.

"I'm sorry about tonight." Brye's voice, soft, apologetic, pitched Chad's hormones into intermission—at least for the moment, if not for the duration of the night.

Several hours earlier, Brye and Chad had met members of Brye's staff and their significant others at a local dance spot. One dance later, and instant recognition ripped into Brye and Chad's intimate evening. For one hour, earnest fans besieged Brye. Untiring, graciously, she accommodated each devotee accordingly—signing autographs, dishing out beauty tips, answering semi-personal questions, lightly joking. In the face of the tenacious crowd, Brye remained controlled and unwavering. Submitting undivided attention, capturing hearts in the process, she imparted upon each individual a sense of warmth and mutual regard.

Shortly after receiving a slight reprieve, she suggested they quietly slip out the back way. She and Chad had jumped into the Jeep Wrangler he'd rented and had instantly found themselves on the secluded beach.

"No apology necessary." Chad lightly squeezed Brye's fingers. "This is the first time we've been alone since our arrival," he noted.

"That can't be helped." The slight edge in her voice startled Chad. "The kids take up a great deal of my time. You are aware of that fact. I can't drop what I'm doing with them merely to spend time with you." Slipping her fingers out of his grip, she pulled ahead by several feet. Tiny grains of sand pressed warmly against the soles of her bare feet.

"Whoa, Brye!" Chad clenched her securely around the wrist and spun her around to face him. In a whirl of skirts, a swell of perfume, and a swirl of long, soft, curls, she met him with a biased eye. Her sudden flare-up ambushed him. His present train of thought scattered in the aftermath. Several painful heartbeats later, he recaptured the fleeing appreciation of the brief time they'd spent together. "Don't get defensive on me. I was fully aware of the circumstances when I signed on for this little excursion. And for the record"—he leaned over her, jacket pushed back, one hand planted firmly on his hip, the other clenching her wrist—"I wasn't asking you to renounce your responsibilities. I haven't asked you to run off with me, and I didn't intend for you to ignore all else because of me. I merely wanted you to know that it feels good, being here like this, with you."

In the quick instant Brye turned on Chad, something strange, something enigmatic, something—wonderful?—clutched at her plagued being. She faced him with an unsteady eye. Confused, she inhaled his overpowering presence, his familiar manly scent, the intensity in those swaying baby blues. The pleasant sensations his fingers transmitted to her as they rode along her willowy wrist.

Embracing his princely features with an avid stare, Brye attempted, unsuccessfully, to divert her mind beyond his pressing caress. She also attempted, unsuccessfully, to quell her racing heart. It was time to return to their highly charged discussion. But she, unlike Chad, wasn't able to salvage their existing conversation. Mind completely voided, she couldn't begin to recollect what they'd been discussing. Had she been agitated with him a few seconds earlier? If so, what had been the cause?

She didn't know.

She did recognize, however, that if she didn't turn tail and run—not walk—as fast as she could, she'd be lost to Chad forever.

Legs laden with heaviness, Brye stumbled out of his grip and away from his overly consuming presence. Flinging her back to him, she desperately wanted to get away. But her overwhelming desire, her need to make love to him, superseded her common sense. She stood rooted on the spot. Her sandals listlessly slid out of her loosening grip.

Chad, not unconscious to Brye's treasonable state of mind, found himself struggling with his own obligatory passions.

"Brye?" He reached out to her. His fingers grazed along her back.

"No...don't!" She flung a distressing look at him, belting him between the eyes. "I can't breathe," she choked, chest heaving. "I can't..." In unladylike fashion, Brye plopped her pulsating body down on the grainy soil. Bare legs stretched out before her, flowing skirt fanned out against pale sand, Brye dropped her clasped hands into her lap and stared out over the lake. Mentally, she began gathering up her wayward emotions.

Concerned, Chad hunkered down beside her. "Don't shut me out, Brye. Please."

She raised hopeless eyes to him. "I can't breathe when you're so close, Chad." She fanned herself with the palm of her hands. "I can't function properly. I can't...think." Pushing on his arm, she wailed in desperation. "Move away from me...please."

Sliding his legs out from under him, unmindful of his thousand-dollar ivory-colored suit, Chad parked himself in the sand.

"No…no…that will never do." Brye fanned him further away. "Over there. Go sit over there."

Somewhere along the way, the situation had ceased to be grave. In fact, Chad was finding it rather comical. Skidding his bottom over sand, he moved a few feet away. "Is this okay?" he asked, incapable of maintaining an honorable expression. Perfected pearly white teeth grinned endlessly against the blackened night.

Above, the taunting moon grinned mercilessly against tantalizing stars. Below, Brye found her body avidly reacting. "And stop looking at me like that!" she barked, irritated.

Chad's smile instantly dried up. Head tilted, he asked, "Is there anything else I can do for you?"

Fighting a losing battle, Brye murmured in an undertone, "Yes…" The rest of her sentence was indecipherable.

"What?" Chad cupped his fingers over his right ear and pointed it in her direction. "I didn't quite make that out."

"I said…yes." A resigned sigh mingled with the gentle wisp of a cool breeze. Brye groaned in unconditional surrender. "I'd like for you to kiss me." Where had that come from? She hadn't meant to say the words. Yet she had said them. And she had meant them. Holding her breath, she waited for his response.

It didn't take long, but to her, the delay seemed enduringly drawn out.

Removing his suit jacket, Chad stretched it across the sand behind Brye. Slowly, supporting her back with his arm, he lowered her to the ground.

Fascinated, Chad's face hovered directly above Brye.

"You are the most remarkable, bewitching, unpredictable creature I've ever met in my life. And I've missed you, Brye. God, how I've missed you!"

Brye walked her fingers along his shoulders, halting at the base of his neck. Twisting thick strands of hair around her fingers, she pulled his lips down to greet hers. A hair's breadth away, she mumbled, "And you, Chad, talk too much."

Their lips touched, mingled, frolicked tenderly together. The kiss lingered, swelled with passion, grew frantic with the need to sample and then devour.

Bodies in frenzied motion took on minds of their own as the urgency to luxuriate in one another took control.

Brye desired Chad. She needed him. Mind and body begged for instant gratification. Whimpering against lips teasing her into total capitulation, Brye's aching body arched urgently toward his.

Impassioned with his own crazed hunger, Chad sunk further down her inflamed body. Releasing her breasts from the gathered restraints of her halter-style dress, Chad cupped one quivering nipple while rolling a tongue over the other.

Eagerly accepting his shameless offerings, Brye pushed her chest deeper into his mouth. She lost herself in the raging influx of sensation storming her frenzied awareness; concentrated pleasure embraced every nerve fiber of her being.

Chad dipped his nose in the silky cleft lying between her breasts. Running a zealous tongue along her breastbone, he implored, "I want to make love to you, Brye."

"Yes" she moaned, head buried in shampoo-scented hair. "Yes, please,"

But what about Jennifer? The words flew at her on the tail end of a balmy breeze.

She doesn't have to know. No one ever has to know.

But you'll know.

And I will know. Her mother's voice, coming out of nowhere, knocked the inclement wind right out of Brye's sails. Behind closed eyelids, she envisioned her mother's maddening smile. A knowing smile. An intrusive smile slapping Brye back into soberness. Her body congealed underneath Chad's uninhibited touch.

Her abrupt recoil instantly seized Chad. Hoisting himself off of Brye, he towed his trembling body upward. Eyes overshadowed by fevered desire challenged Brye.

"What is it?" he rasped, holding his impatience in check. "Is something wrong?"

"I can't do this, Chad." Anguished lines surfaced around her eyes and mouth. "I'm sorry, but I can't do this just yet."

Chad's heart pumped erratically in his head, his chest, his loins. His ears heard the words, yet his body could not readily accept them. "You want me just as much as I want you, Brye. You can't deny it. You can't deny *us*. You can't deny the desire we harbor for one another."

Incapable of answering, ashamed to confront him, she turned away from his empowering stare.

The heat generated from Chad's closeness permeated Brye's skin, her mind, her soul. The heat of her desire ignited once again. Inhaling slowly, deeply, she fought to gain control. Her heart, her body, did not want to deny Chad. But to him, it was all about sex. It was all about desire. It had nothing to do with love. Despite how much she wanted him, she could not allow herself to be used. She could never live with herself if she did.

In the end, Brye did not have to answer Chad. Her intractable expression was all he needed by way of a reply. Rolling into a sitting position, liberating a tenuous breath, he rummaged shaky fingers through tousled hair. Then, standing on wobbly legs, he scuffled away—far away—from Brye's mind-jolting proximity.

With Chad's sullen withdrawal, the cool air seemed to swoop down and entangle Brye within its frosty clutches. She quickly repositioned her clothing. Shaking off granules of sand from Chad's evening jacket, she shrugged her arms into the lengthy sleeves.

"Chad?" she inquiringly called out to him. In the shadows, she observed him carry out his own shaky ritual as he gathered himself.

He shoved his shirttail inside his pants…and did not respond.

Brye pushed herself off the ground. Bare feet shuffled in the cool sand. The sound of the lake mildly lapping against the secluded beach muffled her approach. When she lightly laid her palm against Chad's forearm, they both jumped from the unanticipated jolt.

"Please don't be angry, Chad. I don't want you to be angry," Brye pleaded. Stuffing her sandals inside his jacket pocket, she wrapped her arms around his chest. "I just need you to understand."

The childlike simplicity reverberating in her tone thawed Chad's somber mood. "I'm not angry!" he declared, rougher than intended.

Spinning on her, a fleeting glance took in her mournful, exposed, appearance. Loose hair flapped tamely in the mild wind like a baby bird experimenting with its wings. Nervously, she chewed on her bottom lip. The dismal slope of her shoulders underneath the weight of his jacket touched his heart, relaxed his mind. Any minute, he expected the oversized coat to swallow her whole. His heart, his tone, softened dramatically. "I'm not angry. It's just"—he paused, imparting a lame smile—"it's taking me a little longer to cool down." He spread his arms wide. "As you can see, a cold shower is not an option I have readily available to me at the moment."

A glint of amusement colored Brye's smile. "You can always use the lake as a substitute. I'm sure it'll douse your…less than honorable intentions, amongst other things."

"Under the circumstances, I don't think it'd be a good idea if I strip to my bare essentials."

Brye's face drooped. The night had not gone as planned. Wishing she could make it better for him, unable to, saddened features spilled into the tender night. Afraid to move closer, wanting to, she stood in place. Shaking the strands of fluttering hair out of her line of vision, she finally managed, "I'm sorry, Chad."

"So am I," he quietly responded. In the obscure light offered by the moon, Chad stole a quick look at his watch. "It's close to one, Brye. We should be getting back."

Brye turned her head into the black of night. The diversionary tactic proved unnecessary. She could not hide tears she could not produce.

The canter back to the lodge was tedious and took on the mien of a distasteful task neither party wanted to partake in. The mood, compared to the lighthearted stroll at the beach, deteriorated drastically. The ambiance had grown heavy, the conversation strained. Both Brye and Chad walked a conservative distance apart. Careful not to brush against the other, both were painfully aware of the unmanageable love struggling to breach the solid walls suspended between them.

In Brye's eye, the day had been too perfect, too full of memorable pleasures to have it end on such a sour note. At all costs, she could not let that happen. Closing the distance between the two of them, she linked arms with Chad and formed a human shackle. Much to her delight, his tension slowly dissipated into the surrounding blackness.

"Did you know that you're the first man ever placed on a pedestal in Bethany's eyes?" Brye asked, hoping to bring the conversation back to a light note.

Chad chuckled. "How did that happen?"

"Besides the obvious of your being extremely handsome and next to impossible to resist, the way you handled Anthony today turned out to be the defined element launching you straight to the top of her 'the-one-person-I-most-admire' list."

Face grave, Chad peered down at Brye. "If I'm so impossible to resist, then why aren't we making love…right now?" He halted. Swinging Brye around to face him, he captured her upper arms with a commanding grip. "We are two grown adults with strong healthy sexual urges. We're not bound to anyone by marriage, Brye, so why are you resisting this? Why are you denying what we both desperately want?"

Brye visibly paled. Turning away from his compelling plea, her voice reached far into the darkness. "I'm not certain I could resist you, Chad. I'm not even certain I *did* resist you. In fact, I have this sinking feeling that I've only postponed the inevitable."

Chad dropped his hands to his side. He stuffed them inside his pants pocket. "Why do you make it sound like a fate worse than death?"

"Because for me, it would be." She moved around him and picked up her pace.

Not understanding the meaning of her statement, sensing her reluctance to discuss it, Chad decided to let the matter drop—for now. Mercifully changing the subject, he ambled behind her and said, "I've been meaning to ask you about something that happened this afternoon."

"What is it?" she asked, grateful for the switch in subjects.

Two steps behind, Chad could almost discern the sigh of relief silently escaping Brye's lips. "Before we began looking for Anthony, you and Bethany were so sure he was fine. How was that?"

"Twins endure a special connection," Brye stated, simply, matter-of-factly, "There's a unique bond constructed between them… physically, emotionally, mentally, as well as spiritually. Bethany reached out to him with her mind. In return, she didn't sense him to be in danger…at least she didn't sense that he perceived himself to be in danger. It was enough to keep us from worrying."

Sounding slightly skeptical, Chad asked, "You honestly believe twins exhibit some form of extrasensory perception with each other?"

"It's not a matter of what I believe, it's a matter of what I *know*. And yes, to a certain extent, twins have the psychic ability to sense each other's pain. One twin can even experience the very same trauma, at the precise moment, the other twin is subjected to it."

The intensity of her recitation, the certainty resounding in the stirring night, it was as if she associated this particular subject matter with her own personal experiences.

Chad stepped in time with Brye. He altered his pace to accommodate hers. As far as Brye's beliefs went, he decided to accept her at face value. Individuals—lovers, friends, husbands, and wives—from all walks of life mentally connect with their soulmates. Why wouldn't twins be at the head of the game? Moreover, he and Brye connected on an intimate level. So much so, he sensed her need to be comforted at this very moment.

The palm of his right hand descended along a slender arm. Lacing their fingers, he gently squeezed. The unassuming contact was all that was necessary.

Brye smiled in gratitude. Joined together, she carried his fingers to her mouth and planted a kiss on the back of his hand. Their arms lowered, they strolled along in companionable silence.

When the cypress trees surrounding the lodge came into view, Chad remembered the question he'd been longing to ask. "How're your parents?" he lightly queried, certain the air had completely cleared between them.

"My parents?" She stiffened.

So much for clearing the air, Chad thought, instantly recognizing her withdrawal. Bracing himself for her response, no amount of preparation or anticipation readied him for her answer.

"My parents are dead." It was a fact, and stated as such. No emotion was exhibited visibly or verbally.

In comparison, Chad's immediate reaction made up for Brye's lack of reaction. Literally, he nearly tripped over his own two feet. "But how? When? Why didn't you call me? Why didn't you tell me sooner?" He fired the questions in shocked disbelief.

Methodically, as cool as a red rose floating on top of an ice-laden crystal bowl, Brye handled each question as they struck her.

"They died in a fire…at their Manhattan apartment. It happened right after you and I broke up. I didn't call you because we weren't exactly on speaking terms at the time. I didn't tell you before now because it's been years, and I've put it all behind me."

The dullness in her voice, the scarcity of emotion, alarmed Chad. Unbelievable as it may seem, she had disassociated herself with the reality of the circumstances. He recognized this as a defense mechanism. It was her way of coping. From what? He had no idea.

"Have you, Brye? Have you really been able to put it behind you?" God forbid, if his parents parted from this world, he'd find it difficult to speak of them without the bereaved tear in his eye or the emotional crack in his voice—not after one year, not after ten, not after one hundred years.

One of Brye's greatest assets was that she did not lie. If asked a question she could not readily answer, she responded to the best of her abilities. If confronted with an inquiry she found too taxing to approach, she effortlessly sidestepped it. In response to Chad's disturbing question, she simply chose not to answer.

The steps to the deck loomed before them. Right foot falling on the bottom step, right hand grasping the railing, Brye heavily pulled herself upward.

Her intentions made perfectly clear to Chad—she wanted to flee and escape his probing questions—he locked fingers around her wrist. In mid-climb, Brye halted.

"Please, Brye. Don't shut me out. Please…tell me what happened," he pleaded. "I want to know."

Brye dropped her face in her open palms. God, but she didn't want to do this. She hated dragging the past into her present. She hated that remembering reminded her of the empty shell of a life she had led before her parents' death. It reminded her of all she'd lost… all she'd never really had… It reminded her of all she'd be willing to give up in order to gain the kind of life she'd always dreamed of…a life she longed for. And most importantly, dragging her past into the present buoyed innermost emotions—intricate emotions she was not prepared to face—dangerously close to the surface.

Heavily, she dropped onto the third step. She would tell him what he desired to know. But barely skimming the surface, omitting crucial details, she related only the basics.

"One week after you and I—" She squeezed her eyes shut, regrouping her train of thought. Inhaling deeply, expelling it slowly, she started over. "Not quite two months pregnant, I began hemorrhaging." Brye neglected to add that the bleeding had been induced by a one way trip down a flight of stairs; the end results of a headlong struggle with her drunken father. "I didn't lose the babies right away. In the hospital, I hemorrhaged off and on for several days. The third night of my stay, I began to bleed heavily. Three hours later, the babies spontaneously aborted. Ironically—" She trailed off, fists wound into sealed knots. She squeezed so tightly, her fingernails forged deep craters within her sensitive skin. "At the same time I lost my babies, a fire broke out in my parents' apartment. The official report maintained that it started when someone fell asleep with a lit cigarette in their hand and a spilled bottle of liquor dripping off the side of the bed." Brye failed to say that neither of her parents had ever smoked. She also failed to mention the third individual—the one who had actually started the fire. There was a high probability that her drunk parents had been engaging in a *ménage à trois* at the time of the fire. Her voice shook with trepidation. "I lost my parents, along with my babies, all within the same time frame."

Brye fell silent. She wrapped her arms protectively around her chest as if stilling herself from some unknown entity. And from the deepest, darkest, innermost recesses of her brain, it came at her. Aimed toward the forefront of her awareness, it steadily took form, growing larger by the second.

Fighting against its existence, Brye pushed it back...back...way back. She shoved it deep down into the abyss in where it struggled to break free from. Whatever she hid from herself, she would eventually have to confront it. But for now, she couldn't—wouldn't—face the truth dangling just outside her grasp.

"Jesus!" Chad finally managed to exclaim. The irony of it all had not gone unheeded. The loss of the unborn babies—their babies—had actually resulted in saving Brye's life. If she had been in that apartment, on that particular night, she would most likely have died along with her parents. The mind-boggling revelation sent chills running up and down his spine.

Chad plopped his hulking body beside Brye. His arm lowered over her shoulders. Pulling her into his body, he asked, "Are you okay?"

Eyes met. Her face looked drawn, spent. "I try not to talk about it much." The tips of her mouth angled upward, sadly. "I try not to talk about it at all."

He understood now why she retained misgivings in reliving the past. It was all so painful. Tilting his head, with foreheads tapped together, he whispered, "Thank you for telling me."

Brye held both sides of Chad's face between the palms of her hands. His skin felt slightly roughened from a hairy shadow probing the lower half of his face. Yet touching him felt so good. Being with him felt too good. Amazingly, she felt safe whenever she was with him. She felt as if nothing could touch her...no one could do harm to her. She also knew it was dangerous to be harboring such emotions. A high sense of security lowered her guard. And Brye couldn't afford to let her defenses down.

Her thumb played around the perimeter of his lips. Underneath the stirring touch, she felt him tremble. "I wish—" she began, trailing off.

Under the dim shade of night, Chad brightened with anticipation. "You wish what, Brye?" he urged.

Shaking her head, she dropped her hands away from his face. She stood. "It's late. We should be turning in."

Disappointed, pushing it out the way, he climbed to his feet. "Let me walk you to your room." Chad deposited her at her door. "I'll see you in the morning," he said. Releasing her arm, he started down the long hallway.

"Chad?" Brye called after him.

Chad walked back. Face-to-face, he was caught off balance when Brye threw her arms around his neck. Winding her fingers in his hair, she pulled him downward while she raised her lips to meet his.

The kiss began slow, tender. Gingerly, she moved her mouth, her body, against his. Then aggressively, she pressed deeper into him. His mind went into a tailspin as her tongue fiercely probed his mouth, as she clutched demandingly at his shirt, pulling, lifting, sliding her fingers underneath. Open palms smoothly glided along the peaks and valleys forming his rib cage. The potent touch carried a moan to his lips and shivers along his heated skin.

And her mouth. God! Her mouth began to lower, traipsing along his chin, his neck, drowning in the V of his open collar. She appeared to be searching, seeking, looking for…what? Chad didn't know. As soon as his mind began to rocket into parts unknown, a sudden chill invaded him.

Opening his eyes, Brye appeared to have dropped through a hidden portal. The closed door looming before him was tantamount to the massive barrier Brye had constructed around herself. The barrier, both barriers, mocked him cruelly. One was bent on keeping him out of her room, the other meant to keep him from getting too close to her heart…her life. If he had a say, neither would be standing much longer.

"Dammit, Brye! What are you trying to do to me?" he mumbled under his breath. Unsteady on his feet, he began a long, laborious walk to his room, his primary goal geared on gaining access, as quickly as possible, to a cold shower.

En route, he spotted Anthony, wearing Spider Man pajamas, precariously sliding out of his bedroom door. Preoccupied with whatever had taken control of his mind, he did not see Chad coming up from behind. Furtively, Anthony crept along the semi-lighted hallway. His bare feet padded soundlessly against the hall runner.

"Hey, Champ!" Chad softly called out, bent on finding out the circumstances behind this stealthy night run. "What's up?"

Visibly, Chad watched Anthony's small body stiffen. He jerked around, almost toppling over in the process. Frightened, bulging eyes stared up at him.

"I…I…" Nervously, Anthony shuffled back and forth.

"Hey!" Chad dropped to his knees in front of the unsettled little boy. The altered appearance startled him. Anthony's skin was pasty gray, blending naturally inside the gloomy hallway. His tiny limbs trembled violently. Chad could actually feel the ground beneath him shudder. Blue eyes were as large and dark as the indigo sky. They also reflected terror. "I thought we were buddies." He assured in soothing tones. "Don't you know that buddies can tell each other anything?"

Undecided, Anthony stared blankly at the hurricane light hanging over Chad's shoulder. Whenever he had nightmares, he went to Bethany or Brye. But Chad was different. Chad, Anthony believed, was a man with no fears. He'd probably never been scared of anything or anyone in his entire life. Anthony respected Chad, just as much as he respected Brye. But Brye had seen him frightened before. Chad had not. And Anthony didn't want Chad to look at him with disgust in his eyes. He didn't want Chad to think him a wuss.

"We *are* buddies, aren't we?" Chad urged, knowing something terrible had frightened him.

"I had another nightmare," Anthony blurted, unable to look at Chad.

"A nightmare?" Chad lifted Anthony into the air. Enfolding him within his arms, he took in the fresh scent of soap, along with all the other wonderful smells associated with a little boy. The two lone figures ambled toward the outside deck. "Do you have them often?"

"Not as often as I used to." Anthony hesitated a fraction of a second before wrapping his willowy arms around Chad's neck. "When I have them, I go to Bethany, and then Brye…well…it's as if she senses when I need her because she comes around every time I have one."

Chad pushed the sliding door open and stepped out into the cool night air. Sitting in the exact spot he'd shared with Brye less than a half hour ago, he encircled Anthony within his arms and hugged him securely to his chest.

The night had settled into hushed splendor. A sea of darkness generously opened its arms, drawing the two bodies into a world inclusive of peace and solace. A soothing breeze washed warmly over Anthony's shivering body. And the trees...the cypress trees...

One year earlier, Anthony and Bethany had contemplated running away under the cover of twilight. But the dark frightened Anthony. Danger lurked...too many burrows where evil could spring forth...too many unknowns. The Bogeymen mingled with the dark abyss, prepared to pounce on an unsuspecting boy and his twin sister, anxious to drag them into parts unknown...never to be heard from again. And the trees...the trees were the worst. With their scabrous bark and their scraggly limbs, Anthony believed trees were demons from hell, specifically created to attack when least expected.

But as Anthony lay cradled inside Chad's manly strength, as the overlapping Cypress leaves waved sprightly against an unruffled setting, as the man on the moon—with a wink and a nod—smiled down at him, he sensed no hidden agendas in the isolated darkness; there were no phantoms lying in wait. And from this moment forward, Anthony ceased to be afraid.

"Does Bethany have these nightmares as well?" Chad asked as Anthony's quivering torso gradually abated.

"She doesn't have them anymore...or at least she hasn't had one in over five months." Burrowing himself deeper inside Chad's lap, Anthony felt safe, secure, warm.

"Do you feel like talking about your nightmare?

From day one, Brye had impressed upon him the importance of confronting his fears. Facing them meant walking the road to recovery. And although he'd only discussed his fears with Brye or his twin sister, tonight, he didn't hesitate to open up to Chad.

Thirty minutes later, his words ceased to flow. For a short time afterward neither spoke. Anthony's trembling was fewer and further in-between, and now only came in short, swift, bursts. Chad secured a firmer grip, pulling Anthony closer. The small comfort he offered wouldn't be sufficient enough to ease the suffering Anthony had lived through, but he prayed to God it would help. He only wished he could do more.

"You know your nightmares can't hurt you. They're just bad dreams." Chad found himself saying. "And your mother"—it angered him to speak of Anthony's mother, so he decided not to go there—"you're safe now, you'll remain safe…and that's all that matters."

"When we first came to Brylinn, Brye would say that to us a lot." Anthony managed a small smile. "We didn't believe her, but she said it didn't matter. She said to give it time. We would eventually see for ourselves how safe we were. Eventually, we did believe, and we learned to believe in Brye. And you know what?" He pulled far enough away from Chad to point trusting eyes at him. "Not only do we believe in Brye, but we also believe in you."

"I'm glad you do, Sport. And I promise I won't let you down." Unshed tears, resembling the twinkling stars above, speckled Chad's unwavering stare. An influx of love grappled with his heart. How could he have become so emotionally involved with this boy in such a short period of time? Was it because Anthony's image resembled what Chad believed his son would have looked like had he been born? Was Chad looking at Anthony and Bethany as surrogate children; as replacements for the ones he never knew? He didn't know. He didn't care. At the moment it just felt good having someone depend on him by blind faith alone. "There's something I want you to do for me," Chad said, resting his chin on the top of Anthony's head. "Brye's going away on tour soon. Has she told you about that?"

Silently, Anthony shook his head up and down.

"Well, I'm going to give you my office, cell, and home phone number. While she's away, or even when she's in town, if you need me, if you need *anything* at all, I want you to call me. Do you think you can do that for me?"

Again, he felt the nod of Anthony's diminutive head.

"I don't care what time it is. I don't care how insignificant. If you feel the need to talk, call."

"I promise," the meek voice came back at him.

"I'm going to hold you to that promise."

In answer, Anthony's arms snaked around his waist. The joy Chad felt could not be described in words.

High above, a shooting star streaked across the expansive universe. The luminous speck splintered the midnight sky with a blazing trail of brilliance. Traveling light-years through time, the heavenly body went in search of a better life, much like a child chasing after a dream.

Head shot off Chad's chest, chin pointed to the heavens, Anthony's voice quivered with excitement. "Did you see that?"

"Hmm," Chad answered, amazed at how an inconsequential incident could bring about so much pleasure. "You should make a wish. But don't tell me what it is, otherwise it won't come true."

Anthony didn't have to think long or hard. Easily he thought of the one thing he yearned for more than anything else in the world. Smiling to himself, he settled back into Chad's soothing hold. Of course, he would keep his wish to himself. He wouldn't even tell Bethany. That in itself would positively guarantee it would come true.

Twenty minutes later, Chad laid Anthony's sleeping head upon his awaiting pillow. The bed covers snuggled around a face free of worry, anguish, and sadness, Chad tousled the dark hairs peeking out from underneath. He silently backed out so as not to disturb Anthony's roommate. Closing the door softly, he strolled back toward the direction of Brye's room. If awake, he would inform her of the last hour's events. Of course, he could have easily waited until the following morning, but in all reality, he would use this excuse in order to see her again before settling in for the night.

18

After leaving Chad stranded in the isolated hallway, laboring for air, Brye stood in the middle of her room wondering what had taken possession of her. For no apparent reason she'd lost all self-control and had literally, sexually, attacked Chad.

Flinging off his jacket, along with the rest of her clothing, she dove headfirst into the shower. "It's time to get a grip on yourself, Brye," she mumbled as the cool water juiced down her body; a body aching to be touched by no one other than Chad; a body begging to be released from its painful suffering and self-imposed celibacy.

Determined to push the sinful thoughts out of her mind, Brye turned her attention toward Anthony and Bethany as she rushed through her shower. They had taken to Chad like three puzzle pieces fitting together: perfectly, snugly, merging three units into one. All three appeared to belong together. Brye didn't know whether to be jealous or grateful; the twins were finally opening up to a diversity of individuals.

Brye had worked with the twins for ages before finally getting them to confide in her. Yet enters Chad, and in a matter of minutes, he bowls them over with that irresistible, impossible-to-resist charm.

After some contemplation, instead of being annoyed, tossing an oversized pink nightshirt over her head, she fell into bed with a smile on her face.

Normally it took time before she surrendered to sleep. This night was different. Maybe it was due to the pleasant thoughts she carried to bed…perhaps it was because she'd been subjected to one of the most enjoyable days of her life. Whatever the reason, it all proved to have a culminating effect; Brye was lulled into a false sense of security. She effortlessly succumbed to a desecrated world far beyond her reality.

Because as usual, she dreamed.

Perfectly rounded glittering spheres dangled above the crowded dance floor and spun on its silver pivot like planet earth rotating on its axis. Shimmering bursts of light darted back and forth, creating agile walls as animated as the couples dancing within them.

Lost in the depths of the packed couples, absorbed in each other's presence, Brye and Chad remained oblivious to everything around them. Chad's lips felt like velvet rose petals as he drew a delicate trail along Brye's left ear.

"Do you know how good you smell?" he asked, taking in the engaging scent of Mystique. "And do you know how wonderful you look?" Slightly pulling back, desirous eyes praised her dazzling looks. Light makeup, hair pinned in a French roll, large, spiraling curls cascaded down the right side of her face. Black, ankle-length halter-dress exposing a delicately tanned back; a wide patent leather belt accentuated a slim waist; matching two-inch sandals adorned her feet; diamond stud earrings graced delicate lobes; a pulsar black and gold watch garnished her narrow wrist.

Smoothing her fingers along Chad's wide, muscular shoulders, she said, "Do you know how good you feel to me?" To prove her point, she shimmied her body closer. Instantaneously, she experienced the crux of his desire. The sharp intake of breath brushing close to her ear carried a smile to her face. She pressed closer. So close, a toothpick couldn't have slipped through the two clinging bodies.

Luxuriating in the irresistible feel of his hard torso, swaying in the breeze of soft mellow music, Brye closed her eyes and rested her head on his inviting shoulder.

The evening, topped off by a wonderful day, couldn't have ended more perfectly. Early-morning fishing with Anthony and Bethany, the afternoon had been spent jet skiing with many of the older kids. Renting a Jeep Wrangler, late afternoon had been spent, once again, with Anthony and Bethany—Chad had taken them into town to buy a monumental amount of swimming apparatus, with the intent of providing swimming lessons the following Sunday afternoon. And now she danced in the arms of the man she loved, a man she knew she would love for the rest of her life. And even if Chad didn't, or couldn't, return those same sentiments, it wasn't a deterrent for the impassioned emotions building inside her.

"Brye?"

A soft, harmonious, voice called out from the depths of the club's surround sound.

"Did you hear that?" Perplexed, Brye looked questioningly at Chad.

"Hear what?" he asked, smiling into her flushed face.

Doubts surfaced. Brye shook her head. "Nothing," she replied, dropping her head back to his shoulder, shutting her eyes.

"Brye?"

Although the voice sounded faint against her ears, it wiped out all sound blasting from the loudspeakers. Brye peeked over Chad's shoulder.

Somehow—maybe when her eyes had been shut—the dance floor had cleared out. Only two couples remained: Brye and Chad, along with one other pair. The man—middle-aged, distinguishably handsome—Brye held no knowledge of his identity. But the woman, although Brye only glimpsed her backside, appeared remarkably familiar. Thick, luxurious hair pranced down a long, graceful back and stopped just above a paper-thin, exposed, waistline. Skin-hugging, red sequined dress outlined an eye-popping, mouth-drooling, tongue-hanging, curvaceous body. She possessed the kind of body all women spend their entire lives striving to obtain, but never acquire, and all men would willingly give an eyetooth to possess.

As Brye looked on, the faceless woman channeled her hands seductively over her partner's body. Her lithe fingers roamed and performed lewd acts everywhere she touched. She performed sinful acts that could have gotten her arrested for indecent exposure—excluding the fact that there probably wasn't one man in the place who would turn her in, not to mention that one had to find a policeman ready, willing, and able to arrest her.

She kissed him. A penetrating, lip-smacking, tongue-lashing, suck-his-tonsils-right-out-of-the-back-of-his-throat kiss.

The inflamed woman's partner kneaded her taut buttocks with left hand. His right hand exposed one fleshy, quivering breast. His tongue snaked downward, drawing a pink voluptuous rosebud into his mouth. Abruptly, the woman pushed away. Everybody, everything, faded into the background. Only two women were left standing.

The unidentified woman did a slow pirouette as she turned and locked eyes with Brye. Ruby red lips glided into the most congenial of smiles.

Her mother. Her heart-stopping, free-spirited, take-them-for-everything-they've-got, sumptuous mother. Brye had created an exceptionally good living for herself on her looks alone, but she could never hold a candle to the throngs of magnificence bequeathed to her mother on the day she had been born.

What a waste, Brye thought to herself. And her second irrational thought: How like my mother to be roaming the face of the earth with someone other than my father.

Brye could not have hid her irritation if she had been paid to do that very thing. "What do you want, Mother? And why do you insist on tormenting me?"

Her mother appeared contrite. "Why, Bryson? I thought you'd be happy to see me."

"You're nonexistent, Mother. You're no more. Dead as a doorknob, flat as a board, cold as an icicle." Stopping short, Brye cocked her head to one side. She studied her mother astutely before adding, "Scratch that last remark. How can you be cold as an icicle when you burnt to a crisp on the day of your death?"

To Brye's right, a small round table materialized out of nowhere. Two crystal fluted glasses filled with a white Chardonnay waited patiently to be consumed. Brye handled them both, courteously offering one glass to her mother.

"I think a poem is in order here, Mother, don't you?" Tilting the rim of her glass to the voluptuous woman, Brye recited:

Ashes to ashes.

Dust to dust.
Why don't you lay down for good, Mother?
And stop creating all this fuss.

The glasses released a soft "ting" as the rims tapped together. Both drank greedily.

"How apropos." Intensely proud of her daughter's brilliance, she presented Brye with a conciliatory smile. "And what a touching poet you've become."

"Drop dead, Mother!" Brye's lips curled into a satisfied sneer. "Oops. I forgot. You already are."

"You know, sweetheart, I may be dead, but at least I went to my grave knowing who and what I am. You, on the other hand, haven't got a clue."

"Maybe I don't know who I am, Mother. But I do know that I go to bed at night, every night, with my self-respect intact. Could you say the same?"

"Such facetiousness, my dear child." She shook her head heedfully. "I didn't teach you to be so facetious."

"If my memory serves me correctly, you didn't teach me one damn thing! Everything I learned, everything I am, is not because of you, Mother dearest! At least I can stand with my head held high and honestly say I'm nothing like you."

"You're facetious," Ashley continued as if Brye hadn't interrupted, "and you're a tease." Primly, she touched her glass to her lips. Downing a small amount, she added with a hint of malice, "You slither that delectable body of yours against your friend there, offering him what he so badly wants. You incite him, entice him, turn his body into molten wax, drive his senses wild with need and desire, then you turn and walk away, shutting him down cold."

Slamming her empty glass down against the octagon-shaped table top, the glass shattered into injurious slivers but registered no harmful influence upon Ashley. Eyes fiery with contempt, she hissed, "No, you aren't like me, my darling child, you're nothing like me! And in your quest to be so different, you've become worse than me!

"You flaunt yourself. You flirt. You walk around batting those sorrowful eyes of yours, and then you look at men as if to say, 'I know you want me, I know you would do anything to have me. But you can't, and you won't. So look and enjoy because that's all you're getting from me!'" Brye's mother smiled, the most enchanting of smiles. "But you know what, dear heart? That little game of yours is going to backfire one day."

Unperturbed, Brye stared at her mother indifferently. "It really amazes me on just how little you really do know me—or should I say knew me? Because if you had known me at all, you'd know that what you spew out of the side of your dead mouth is a bunch of crap. Ying-yang, Mother. You speak with forked tongue." Chin tilted upward, she added, "I've always tried to carry myself in a dignified manner. I don't flaunt myself, I've never chased after any man, and I've never led another man on just to drop him outside, cold, at my doorstep. So think what you will, Mother. Say whatever makes you feel good. But know that I don't give a damn about what you or anyone else, for that matter, thinks of me. Because I, and only I, can validate who I am."

To Brye's chagrin, her mother did an about face and changed tactics. "And who you are is a direct extension of myself. You may not see it now, but you are heading down the same path I walked along."

"How can you say that?" Brye grunted, genuinely mortified. "I would never, ever follow in your footsteps."

"You say that now, but look at you. Look at your relationship with Chad."

Hesitant at first, when Brye spoke, she did it with very little conviction. "Chad cares for me...very much."

"Of course he cares, honey. They all care in their own little way. Chad cares enough to invite you into his bed. The question is, does he care enough to invite you into his life...permanently?"

Something flickered deep within Brye. Was it anger? Pain? Fear? Whatever? Ashley had struck a nerve. Pressing the point further, she said, "I give you one week to fall into his bed...to give yourself completely to him. And when it happens, let's see what kind of a commitment he offers."

Backing away from her mother, the frigid stare she hurled matched the stiffness of her tone. "This conversation is dead, Mother. And so are you." Turning her back, she reached out to Chad, who waited patiently on the sideline. She moved gracefully into his welcoming arms while chancing one last glance in her mother's direction. Infuriated at witnessing her mother smile insidiously at her, Brye waved her hand in the air as if brushing off a pesky fly. "Go away!" she barked.

As ordered, her mother faded into concealed obscurity. "One week, my darling daughter." Her words drifted from the central core of a swirling mist. "You'll see. In one week, you'll be no better than I." In a puff of smoke, and gales of charmed laughter, her mother dissipated into the surrounding brilliance.

Brye slammed the lid securely on her mounting rage as Chad's comforting grip embraced her. Contented once again, she pushed the events of the last several minutes into her throwaway pile of nefarious memories.

Eyes closed, head relaxed against Chad's shoulder, she found herself drifting back into the same liberated serenity she'd established before her mother's rude interruption.

A sigh of well-being tickled the softness of her lips. Her hands began a free roam along Chad's solid frame. But as her mind registered the subtle changes her fingertips detected along his stalwart backside, her eyes flew open in distressed confusion.

"Tyson!" she exclaimed, staring into her twin brother's expressionless face. "I should have known. Why are you following her *around?"*

"You and I have a lot to discuss, darling sister."

"We have nothing to discuss." Brye's feet stopped moving. She struggled inside his constricting grip. "Now let me go."

"Why did you let me down, Bryson?" He held her fast to his body. "You promised to always be there for me. You promised to always take care of me. But you let me down. I wouldn't be where I am today if it weren't for you."

"And where is that, Tyson? Are you in hell? Is your soul burning in hell?"

His eyes grew hard, cold, incensed, as he stared into Brye's impassive features. Disregarding her question, he growled, "It's all your fault. Why, Bryson? Why did you let me down?"

"You let yourself down," she snapped. "You chose your own destination. I had nothing to do with it." Hands sprayed against his chest, she attempted to push away. "Now let go of me."

"What's the matter, Bryson? You think you're too good to dance with me." His teeth flashed menacingly. His voice turned vicious. "Dad always said you were an uppity bitch. He said you always rode that righteous ass of yours higher than the rest of us." Determined hands along her backside slid lower…lower…cupping her buttocks and squeezing.

Brye cringed with revulsion. "Take your vile hands off me, now, Tyson!" Hands balled into a closed fist, she flailed at his chest."

"Ahhh, Bryson?" Exhibiting little strain, he shrugged off her blows. "Don't you love me any longer?"

To Brye's horror, with each blow she rained upon him, he pulled her closer into his body. "Damn you, Tyson! Let me go!"

"Say it, Bryson," he sneered at her. "Tell me you love me."

The more she battled, the tighter he held on to her. Unable to break away, she swung her one free hand backwards. Concentrating all her strength into her right arm, she propelled a powerful blow, aiming directly at the side of his head. Direct contact sent a thousand jolts of pain zigzagging along her arm. And if the pain in her hand was a true indication of the measure of force delivered behind the blow, she could well imagine the damage she'd done to her brother.

Howling like a wounded banshee, he instantly dropped his hold. Backing far away, Brye kept a wary eye on him.

As she stared into his face, sheer terror overcast her anger.

Tyson had mutated into a demented monster. His hands covered one side of his ravaged features but did not hide the damage done by her very own hand.

Blood. Dark red droplets. Thick pools of fluid gushed between his spread fingers. And the bone. Brye could see crushed bone. And brain matter. Large chunks of brain matter oozed from his open skull.

Shaking violently, Brye turned her right palm upward. "Oh God!" she moaned. She wore the badge of blood stained hands; bloody hands flashing at her like neon lights. And skin. Dead skin peeled from his face and clung loosely to her fingers. "Oh God!" she screamed again, losing all sense of reality.

"Bryson?" His voice sounded deeper, thicker, more sinister.

Appalled, Brye gaped at him. The transmutation attacking his face took several horrific seconds to register.

His right eye—the left eye was just an empty, ragged socket—grew wild, deranged. His lips were drawn back into a snarl—only, God help her, he didn't have lips. Only disintegrating flesh. Dead flesh dangling from blistering gums surrounding rotten teeth. One side of his skull was caved in. His hair was matted with fresh blood.

"Tell me you love me, Bryson." Arms stretched outward, the Frankenstein she'd created lunged toward her.

"No!" Immersed in fear, alarm ripping her apart, Brye found her legs too rubbery to move. "Stay away from me!"

"Don't you want to give your baby brother a hug, Bryson?" He slid closer, one leg dragging behind the other. "Maybe even a kiss?"

"Don't touch me! Don't touch me! Don't touch me!" she chanted in a mournful wail. Her sanity was inescapably coming into question. If she could not free her heavy foot, if he touched her with those long, decrepit talons, she would be lost to madness forever.

In slow motion, unable to do little else, she watched in chilling horror as her brother—or what used to be her brother—crept closer and closer and closer…

"Brye, wake up!" An anxiety ridden Chad attempted to shake Brye out of her turbulent slumber. Seconds earlier, pausing outside her door, he'd been struck by the sounds of tormented cries. He burst through the unlocked door. Not knowing what to expect, he spotted Brye wildly thrashing in bed.

Head whipping back and forth, palms shoved in front of her face, she flailed at whatever horrific creature her mind had invented. Chad raced to her bedside.

"Wake up, Brye!" He shook her shoulders more forcibly. In return, her eyelids shot open.

Terror. Real terror. Intense terror penetrated the very depths of her core. Facial muscles drawn, skin pale, she stared unseeingly at Chad.

"Don't touch me!" she cried out. Caught completely unaware, Brye blindly shoved against Chad's chest. "Keep away from me!"

Chad found himself propelled off the edge of the bed. He hit the floor with a booming thud.

By the time he'd peeled himself off the ground, Brye had scurried backward. Trapped against the headboard, knees drawn up, arms tightly wound around her legs, eyes remained wild, panicky, clouded, as she fixed them on Chad.

"It's me, sweetheart. It's Chad." Edging along the bed, he spoke low, consoling.

He reached out to touch her, and she frantically swung at his arm.

"Don't!" Exposed body and mind pressed insistently against the headboard, as if commanding it to swallow her alive.

Making no further effort to approach her, Chad continued to talk calmly, caressing her raw senses. Tender words began to seep into her tormented world. Her terror began to subside.

Projectile eyes did a futile one-hundred-yard dash around a dimly lit room lurking with shadows…and unknown factors. Certain no signs of menace prowled within the confines of the murky space, her eyes then settled on Chad. From one end of the emotional spectrum to the other, her expression transposed from fright, to bewilderment, to suspicion, recognition, and then relief.

"It's me, baby. It's Chad," he acknowledged, helping her set a firm footing on reality.

"Chad?" she repeated uncertainly.

Before he could respond, she flew into his arms. Crushing herself against him, she clung to him with the desperation of a woman striving to adhere to every ounce of sanity remaining within her.

God, but the dream seemed so real; she could still see it all so vividly. Pressing her cheek into Chad's shoulder, she willed herself to gain control of her jagged breathing. She forced herself to flush the nightmare out of her poisoned system.

"You had a bad dream?" Chad tenderly stroked her backside; compassionate fingers wound in and out of her disheveled hair.

"Yes." Her words sounded muffled against his chest.

"Do you have them often?"

"More often than not," she admitted vaguely. "Although this one was a bit more morbid than its predecessors."

"Do you want to talk about it?"

"I want to forget it."

Chad did not push the matter. Falling silent, he continued to hold her…comfort her…offer her strength and support.

Amazingly, Brye found herself thinking less and less of the atrocity she had awakened from. Instead, Chad's gallant presence ignited already heightened senses; the faint scent of his efficacious aftershave, along with his transitory touch, also initiated a calming effect. Against his staunch chest, her heart drummed an acoustical incantation to the beat of an Indian love elegy—passionate, bittersweet, malevolent. Brye heaved a sigh of regret. So close yet so far away, in love, in life, in understanding.

"Why are you here?" she asked, scooting away from his analgesic touch.

Chad remained perched on the side of the bed. He kept a vigilant watch on Brye. "Earlier, after I left you, I spotted Anthony sneaking out of his room. He told me he had a nightmare. He was seeking out Bethany."

"And you came to tell me?"

"Only if you had been awake. I paused at your door and heard you cry out."

Brye flung the tousled bed linens aside. She started to climb off the bed. "I should go to him."

Chad gently pushed her down by the shoulders. "Anthony's tucked safely away in his bed. I held him until he fell asleep."

He stood. Piece by piece, he abandoned his clothing. Clad in jockey briefs alone, he announced, "Now I'm going to do the same for you."

About to protest, deciding it would be better—much, much better—to sleep with him rather than with the night terrors, Brye teased with a bravado he'd grown to know and love. "Who was it that said chivalry is dead?"

Cuddled snugly together like two stacked teaspoons, Brye nestled deeper into the niche burrowed by Chad's semi folded lap. Chad slid one arm under Brye's neck. He tossed the left arm loosely around her narrow waist. The heat radiating off his person wrapped itself around Brye, embracing her, devouring her in its entirety, warming her to the bone. Chad lying beside her, arms protectively securing her, was the only weapon she needed to safeguard herself against the night demons—a megadose of sedatives could not have been as effective.

In short order, Brye found herself drifting back into a world filled with darkness and uncertainty. Only this time, she felt safe and secure.

Long after Brye had fallen asleep, Chad remained awake, alert, watchful. The events of the past hour replayed itself inside his agile mind. If he had not been given privy to Anthony's reoccurring nightmares, as well as learned the significance behind them, he would have missed the gravity of the circumstances rousing Brye's night apparitions. The evidence mounted.

The deep seated sadness, the wall she had constructed around herself, the lack of trust, the overpowering need to provide for abused children—there was no doubt she had been abused. In what form, he could not guess. His first inclination, and the most likely, was that she'd been sexually abused. But he tossed the notion aside as he recalled how she had come to him those many years ago as a virgin.

Then again, he scurried to rectify, a person could be sexually abused without the tangible act of penetration coming into play.

Equally as well, she could have been physically or mentally abused. With the thought, however, more questions surfaced. Questions with no answers.

How badly had the abuse affected her?

Badly enough to modify her sleeping habits? Badly enough to alter her entire life? Their lives? Somehow, it was all interconnected.

One thing was for certain: Brye's pain tunneled deeper than the twins, or the other kids at Brylinn. The kids generously spoke of their grief like outsiders looking in. The abuse had occurred; although it wasn't the end of the story, it also wasn't the end of their lives. Ready to put their anguish aside, they were prepared to do whatever it took to rebuild their shattered subsistence.

Brye, on the other hand, was not striving to cure whatever ailed her. She had never been able to talk about her past, let alone accept it. She could not follow her own advice to the kids; she had not yet begun the healing process.

It angered Chad. It also frightened him. If Brye could not embrace whatever haunted her, what chance did they have for a future?

As if he could safeguard her well-being, he pressed her now at peace body securely into his chest. Sighing heavily, he closed his eyes and waited for sleep to overtake him.

Six hours later, Chad found himself waking to the warm sun streaking merrily across his body and the enticing sight of long dark eyelashes flashing in his face. A chorus of sparrows sang tunelessly outside their lace curtained window.

"Good morning." Her smile was serene, heartwarming. All traces of the night's misadventures clearly banished from her thoughts. She'd awakened several minutes earlier to the comforting feel of his stalwart leg thrown over her thigh, his fingers lightly grazing a full breast. Immediate arousal engulfed her. Trying not to wake him, she cautiously flipped over to face him. Preying on the few minutes allotted to her, she'd used the time to study his strong, admirable features.

"Good morning yourself." He yawned and stretched. His muscular, tanned body coasted seductively against Brye's stirring senses. The percale sheet slid dangerously low. Brye kept a concentrated eye on the wavy muscles in his chest, the six-pack abdomen, and powerful biceps. She felt her face flush as his brawny flesh contracted, then released.

A goner. Brye languished in the thought of their making love; if Chad moved to consummate the act, she would be powerless to prevent it from happening.

"What time is it?" he asked, turning her away from her wayward—or were they wistful?—images.

"It's late. A little after eight."

He met her with a whimsical eye. "For most people on vacation, eight's considered early."

"I'm usually up by four. This is the longest I've slept in years."

"And here I was under the impression that you didn't sleep at all," he lightly teased.

Outside her room, a herd of individuals nosily slipped past. Brye and Chad were oblivious to all but themselves. She traced his shadowed chin with a light touch of her finger. "It's all your doing, you know?"

"What's all my doing?"

Brye's breath caught in her throat as her finger slipped inside's Chad's mouth. Her entire body tingled as he suckled. "My sleeping in this morning. You are extremely efficient at chasing the bad dreams away."

Something, some form of emotion, intermingled with Brye's childlike expression. Was that love Chad witnessed in Brye's eyes?

Maybe it was a trick of the early-morning lighting. Or maybe it wasn't. Whichever, they could not hide from the past much longer; they could not disregard the emotional ties driving the two bodies together.

Voices permeated Brye's terracotta walls: one teen asked another to join him out at the pool. The male voices slowly faded as they moved further past Brye's room.

"Do you want to talk about last night?" Chad asked, releasing her finger from in between his lips.

"I would rather I didn't." Her collapsed tone said she wanted to forget the entire episode but wouldn't deny him answers if he pushed the issue.

Yes, Chad wanted to confront her about the nightmares. He needed answers pertaining to the suspected abuse. He desired to know of her prior relationship with her parents. Instead, for the moment, he dropped the inquisition. Not wanting to force her into opening up to him, he'd rather she supplied answers of her own free will.

With his mind emptying, Chad became intricately aware of the woman lying beside him. Flecks of sunlight shimmied across her face. Despite the rumpled nightshirt, the disorderly hair, and the lack of morning grooming, he noted how peaceful she looked. Unable to control himself, he inclined his head and kissed her. One touch, and they were lost. Clutching, groping, pulling, kissing, squeezing, feeling, before either realized it, they lay naked, Chad stretched atop Brye.

Voice thick with passion, Chad nuzzled her ear, "If you don't want this, tell me now, Brye."

In response, she cupped her hands over rock solid buttocks and pressed him into her eager body. Insurmountable pleasure ripped through his groin and invaded the inner depths of his mind. Moaning, Chad moved to guide himself inside her. At the onset of penetration, however, a steady rapping on the closed door interrupted the two would-be lovers. It couldn't have come at a more ill-timed moment.

Chad tossed Brye the most mournful, pathetic, frustrating look she'd ever seen in a man. Confronting the sudden impulse to laugh at him—he looked so adorable with those big baby-blue puppy dog eyes pouting at her—she thrust the whim aside.

Providing him with the most apologetic of smiles, sympathetically, she spoke with her eyes, *I have to answer it.*

Disgruntled, discouraged, and very much deflated, Chad arduously rolled away from Brye. On the far side of the bed, lying on his back, he covered his eyes with his forearm. Tediously, his chest rose and fell. It took great effort to calm his racing heart, cool his heated breath, and quell his roaring hormones.

"Who is it?" Brye called out, hoping to gain command of her own thunderous emotions.

"It's Bethany. Can I come in?"

In a panicked state and a flurry of bed linens, Brye jumped off the bed. Prior to her feet hitting the floor, she shoved Chad with a powerful thrust.

"What the hell?" Arms flailing, legs beating against empty air, limbs entangled in the top sheet, Chad's strapping body hit the hardwood floor like a large boulder spilling off a high cliff: the surrounding area shuddered on the moment of impact." Groping the edge of the bed, he laboriously fought to free himself from the binding linen tangled around his legs. Once he was free and clear, he pulled himself into a standing position.

"Dammit it, Brye!" he angrily barked. "What do you—"

"Shhh! Don't talk so loud," Brye interrupted in an overwrought whisper. A virtual tornado, she whirled around the room scooping up discarded clothing and tangled sheets. "Just a minute, sweetheart," she called out to Bethany.

"In the bathroom," Brye demanded, shoving Chad's balled clothing at him.

"What?" He stared incredulously. "You don't expect me to—"

"It's either the bathroom or under the bed," Brye spat at him. "You choose."

"I'm a grown man, for heaven's sake!" Chad snatched his clothing out of Brye's grasp. He started for the bathroom. "I can't even remember the last time I got caught with my pants down or was forced to hide until the coast was clear." He ducked into the bathroom. No sooner had the door shut, it swung back open. "This is unbelievable," Chad bellowed. "*You* are unbelievable! And you owe me, Brye. I expect us to finish what we started. Do you understand?"

In the process of sliding her nightshirt over her nude body, Brye flipped her head back to toss the heavily fallen hair out of her face. She had desired to consummate their reunion as much as he had, and now her body suffered from a longing gone unfulfilled. She could barely shove her disappointment aside. With fallen face and dispirited heart, dolefully, she apologized. "I really am sorry, Chad."

He softened at the dismal picture she presented. His tone grew gentler. "It's not your fault." He shrugged, extended an accepting smile, and admitted, "I'm just blowing off steam."

"I'll be right there, Bethany," Brye cried out for the child's benefit alone. Sprinting up to Chad, she kissed him on the lips. "I promise to make it up to you."

Chad cupped her on her left buttock and pinched her closer into his groin. "I'm going to hold you to that," he growled.

"And I'm going to look forward to you holding me to it." Then, repentantly, Brye abruptly grabbed Chad by the arm and swung him around. Pressing her palms against his back, she shoved him out of sight. "Now get in there and don't come out until I call you." Brye closed the door on his answer.

"Bethany," Brye greeted with a welcoming smile as she pulled open her bedroom door. "What are you doing here?"

"I missed you at breakfast," she said, looking over Brye's sleeping attire. Her youthful features transformed into grown-up concern. "Are you feeling okay?"

"I'm fine…perfect even." Brye stepped aside, allowing Bethany space to slip into her room. "I overslept."

Bethany's eyes grew wide with understanding. "That's right." She plopped down beside Brye. The bed springs creaked as she excitedly jumped up and down. "You had a date with Mr. Collier. Did you have a good time? How much do you like him? Are you two—"

"First of all, it was not a *date* date—we went out dancing with a few of the others to…socialize. And yes"—Brye halted the bunny hopping by pressing the palms of her hands firmly into Bethany's shoulders—"I had a good time."

"Do you like Mr. Collier?"

"Bethany!" Brye cried in mock horror. She shot off the bed and padded around the room collecting items for her morning ritual. Uncertain if she was dodging the question, the answer, or herself, Brye asked, "Just why are you here?"

Bethany reminded Brye of their planned cruise around Lake George.

Brye promised to meet her in the day room after she'd dressed. But to her mortification, Bethany made herself at home.

"I can wait." She hopped off the bed and spread the lace curtains open. The western designed room flooded with undiluted sunshine.

"Oh, honey, you don't have to." Brye inwardly groaned. "I have to jump into the shower…it may take me a little while."

"I don't mind waiting…really," she added, turning away from the window.

The bleak smile Brye shoved at Bethany hardly made a dent in the otherwise magnificent rays. She drifted toward the closed bathroom door. "I'll be out shortly."

"Brye?"

Brye turned and smiled.

With the wisdom of someone keenly aware of the intricate patterns of love, life, and the pursuit of happiness, Bethany acknowledged, "I like Mr. Collier too."

Brye's grin vacillated to a lesser degree. She inched the door open and slipped through the narrow crack.

The tile—of earth tone color and scheme—tickled Brye's bare feet as soon as she stomped onto the cold flooring. Richly painted walls, pedestal sink, oak finish medicine cabinet, shower stall peeking behind a shower liner colored in shades of indigo, topaz, dove gray, and cranberry; the interior design intended to draw away from the scant size of the private chamber.

At the moment, the grand scheme was extremely ineffectual in diverting Brye's attention. Colliding into the massive, living, breathing, barricade of a human being absorbing three-quarters of the confining space, Brye concurrently established the room to be too small to retain the both of them. Signing praises to God that Chad had gained enough sense to cloth that tantalizing physique of his, she peeled herself off of his hairy chest.

"Are you okay?" Chad asked, grabbing her by the elbows. He spoke low, not wanting to alert Bethany to his presence.

The simplest of contact, as Chad touched her now, jarred the most sluggish of senses. Even now, her craving for him shifted into full blown hunger pains. "I need to take a shower," she breathed. Slinking past his strangling nearness, his searing gaze cut through her every movement. Her fingers shook slightly as she pulled the shower curtain back and turned on the ceramic hot and cold tap. Water spilled from the shower head. A warm moist mist immediately invaded the confines of the tiny room.

A whimsical grin caught Brye's eye as she flipped around to face Chad. Afraid to ask what flashed behind those baby blues, afraid she already knew, Brye snapped, "Do you mind?" The severity of her words were cushioned by the amused smirk darting across her lips.

"Watching you?" Chad planted his hands on his hips. "No, I don't mind at all."

An exasperated sigh echoed off the walls. Brye whipped her nightshirt off, draped it over Chad's head, and dove under the steaming water pellets.

"Would you like company?" Chad called out. He could still smell the sweet scent of her skin as he towed the nightshirt over his face. "I could be of great assistance."

"Don't you dare come near this curtain, Chad!" Brye yelled over the running water. But no sooner than the demand was issued, in dazed stupefaction, she watched as Chad, fully clothed, shoes and all, dove recklessly into the shower.

"What are you—" Taken aback, she balked as Chad clamped his hand over her mouth.

A split second later, she heard the bathroom door open. Bethany called out, "Did you say something to me, Brye?"

Chad removed his binding hold. Brye was quick to answer, "No, hon…no. I was just…singing to myself."

Alone once again, Brye fell, headlong, into Chad's mesmerizing eyes. *What are you doing here, Brye Grayson? You should get out…now. Before it's too late.* "You're all wet." She ignored her own warnings, pushing her fingers through his soaked hair strands.

Nodding, he ran his fingers along a glistening cheek. Water droplets, sparkling like flawless diamonds, drew Chad closer to skin bedecked by the shimmering jewels. Running a tongue along her silken skin, he desired to draw nourishment from every inch of her moistened body.

"Chad?" Brye moaned. Throwing her head back, warm water sluiced down her face, shoulders, and breasts. Greedily Chad drank from her, driving Brye into a mindless frenzy.

"Chad?" Brye repeated, wanting so much to get lost inside his caressing touches. "We shouldn't be doing this," she spoke unconvincingly.

Chad's soaked shirt clung seductively to his chest. Brye ran her hands under the now translucent fabric, separating human skin from inanimate material. Kneading taut pectoral muscles, she found great pleasure in knowing it was she who induced the uncontrollable quiver underneath the touch of her tenacious fingers.

Legs shaking with desire, she found partial relief as Chad lifted her by the waist. Wrapping her legs tightly around his grinding hips, she clung to him in shameless rapture.

The prelude to their lovemaking balanced between wild, wonderful, and wet. The uninterrupted pulsation of deluge streaming along Chad's body did not extinguish the blaze raging deep from within; and it was Brye, and Brye alone, who could proficiently drown the fire burning intensely within his soul.

As if Brye understood his thoughts, his every need, she ripped open his shirt, popping several buttons in her frenzy to strip him of his clothing. She craved Chad. She desired his body. Every nuance of her touch translated this need. But it was only when Chad moved to join the two bodies in union, when he released himself from his pants, did Brye tear away from the flaming planet Chad propelled her toward; her mind was involuntary transported back to reality.

"No, Chad." She groped at him, begging to be released. "We can't do this. Bethany's in the adjoining room."

It took several seconds for her earnest pleas to register within Chad's frenzied state of being. But as it did, he promptly lowered her to her feet. His lips stretched in disgusted disapproval at his thoughtless actions. "You're right. I shouldn't have—"

"It's not your fault," Brye rushed to exonerate him of all guilt. "It's me. At the very most, I shouldn't lead you on the way I do. At the very least, I shouldn't encourage you at every inopportune moment." She glanced up at him with sorrowful eyes. "I'm the one who's sorry. But I promise, I'll make it up to you…and it'll be worth the wait."

"I'm going to hold you to that. But in the meantime"—he gave his sodden clothing a quick once over with a problematic eye—"what are we going to do about my appearance?"

Drenched down to the puddles in his Gucci dress shoes, Brye hid her smile as she did her best Robert DeNiro impersonation. "You talkin' t' me?"

"Brye-e-e?" her name came out in a mournful wail. "Don't do this to me…please."

Brye ducked out of the shower. Drying herself off, she grabbed toothpaste and toothbrush. Meticulously scrubbing her teeth, she ignored Chad's urgent appeals to obtain dry clothing. She ignored the growing puddle of water snuggling at his feet. She ignored the irrational—or was it rational?—impulse to jump back into the shower with him and make mad, passionate love. Instead, she hurriedly dressed in olive-green walking shorts and beige crop top, forked her fingers through wet hair, threw him a flying kiss, and teased him with the most enchanting of smiles. "You're on your own, *bud*!"

Chad was left drowning in a puddle of water as well as his own sorrows.

The corridor was void of all human occupancy when he struck out for his own room. Dripping wet garments hung heavily against his body. Ruined shoes flopped loosely in his hands. Bare feet slapped pitifully against the hardwood floor. And like Hansel and Gretel leaving a trail of bread crumbs behind, puddles of water droplets mocked Chad as he sloshed down the long corridors.

Every sodden step carried him closer to his room. It also brought with it a sense of relief; if his luck continued, he would not be accosted. One more corner, and he'd be home free.

Stopping short, he maneuvered the sharp bend only to spot George knocking on his room door.

Too late. Before he could duck out of view, George caught sight of him. His gaze shifted downward, then slowly upward, absorbing every inch of Chad's bedraggled appearance.

Voice neutral, face straight as an arrow, George said, "You didn't make breakfast. Since we planned a nine o'clock tee off, I thought I'd check to see if we were still on for the day."

"I'll be ready in twenty minutes," Chad assured, unable to meet George's questioning eye.

George stepped aside to give Chad access to the door. "Do you mind my asking," he said, incapable of letting the outlandish moment pass, no matter how hard he tried to ignore it, "did you fall in the lake on your way to breakfast?"

Knowing the dining room was inside the lodge, Chad wrapped his fingers around the doorknob.

George broke out into a beguiling grin. "You know Brye missed breakfast as well. Do you know anything about that?"

"Why would you assume I keep up with Brye's eating habits." He jerked open the door. George made no effort to depart. "Is there something else you needed?" he growled, stepping across the threshold.

"No…no…nothing at all." George continued to grin maniacally, although he tried his damnedest to contain his mounting laughter. After several seconds of fighting with himself, his shoulders jerked uncontrollably as his laughter burst forward and traipsed down the sunlit hallway.

"I'll be ready shortly." Chad slammed the door in the face of George's unnerving chortle.

Sloughing out of his wet clothing, Chad cursed the moment the sun had risen. Then again, the insurmountable resurrection had found him resting his weary head upon Brye's silken brow. In resigned frustration, he reluctantly admitted that he would willingly walk fifty miles in sodden clothing if given a second chance to awaken in Brye's bed, his limbs entangled within hers. Sighing heavily, he indulged in a cold shower.

Tenisha woke to the aromatic odor of freshly brewed French Vanilla coffee. Bacon, eggs, and pancakes also stormed her jaded system. Squinting at the brightly illuminated numbers covering the face of her bedside clock/radio/telephone, blinking against the blinding brightness, she pinpointed the time to be either nine o'clock, or nine-oh-eight, or nine-eight-eight, fuzzy eyesight contributed to her inability to discern zeros from eights.

Sinking further into a cloud of downy softness, her polyester fiberfill pillow cradled her weary head, neck, and shoulders. Eyelids dipped in closure, Tenisha mulled over the past evening's events.

Entering her home after a long day of photo shoots, she found the brownstone spotless. Dinner—grilled shrimp and vegetable kabobs, corn-on-the-cob, tomato and lettuce salad, cherry cheesecake—had been prepared, was warming, and waiting for immediate consumption. A floral bath had been drawn by an even-tempered, amiable, attentive, dressed-to-kill husband.

Appreciative of the effort—grateful she hadn't been forced to don boxing gloves when entering her home—his unanticipated attentiveness had not moved her enough to want to ignore all the bad treatment she'd endured, by his hands, over the last several months.

Surprisingly, though, the night had been a huge success. After her bath, she'd slipped into a black silk tank dress—forgoing the ultra-short, ultra-sexy, ultra-guaranteed-to-make-your-husband-forget-all-the-other-women-in-his-life ensemble TyJuan had laid out on the bed.

After dinner, he'd played a medley of Luther Vandross love sonnets—ultra-guaranteed-to-get-a-rise-out-of-a-philandering-husband-so-he-could-make-it-with-his-estranged-wife—and they'd danced long into the night.

For the first time since God knows when, there had been no flinging of founded or unfounded accusations. There had been no blaming the world for their steadily escalating problems. And despite the fact that she was horny as hell, when they finally called an end to the evening, she went to bed alone.

Under the wineberry print comforter, Tenisha lifted her right foot. She flexed it, then twirled her ankle. Round and around and around. She sighed and continued her ruminating.

To be fair to TyJuan, he had made an honest effort to burst the jarring dissension ballooning between the two of them. But even that hadn't been enough for her to fall into his eager arms. To be honest, she wasn't certain she wanted to make love to her husband...ever again. Because if she did make love to him, that would mean she had exonerated him of all his sins—past, present, and future. And if she made love to her husband, it would mean that she validated the drinking, the physical abuse, the verbal attacks, and the extramarital affairs.

Of course the drinking, as well as the abuse, she experienced firsthand. The extramarital affairs she had no visible proof and could only guess at. Yet in Tenisha's mind, the probability of his cheating ran extremely high.

Despite the lack of physical confirmation, her assumptions were shaped by proof nevertheless. Subtle proof. The first being TyJuan's recent lack of interest in slamming "the Man." Generally his favorite subject, obviously he'd discovered other diversionary tactics to peak his highly opinionated interests.

The constant phone calls—or should she say hang-ups when she picked up his phone—added to her suspicions. More times than not, he took his phone calls in a different room. There was also a slight decline in his drinking. Of course, the drinking alone didn't mean much in itself and, technically, she should have been grateful, but he was spending more and more time out of their flat, and if he wasn't job searching or out drinking with his "dawgs," then what was he doing and who the hell was he doing it with?

Lastly, and the most significant clue of all, was the direction in which their sex life had taken. In a word, *zip*, *zilch*, *nada*. They had none; sex was null and void. And the kicker: TyJuan hadn't batted an eye after informing him of her decision to sleep alone the preceding night. He'd just proffered a conciliatory smile, saw her to the door of their bedroom, spotted her cheek with a chaste kiss, then left her to ponder the meaning of life. It also left her wondering: if he wasn't getting it at home, if he wasn't complaining about not getting it at home, then where the hell, and with whom, was he getting it from.

Tenisha lowered her foot. Her eye raised to the sixteen inch color television built into her white oak canopy bed, a wedding present from her parents. She'd spotted the bed in a magazine weeks before her marriage had taken place. Unbeknownst to her, her father had purchased the expensive item. By the time she and TyJuan had returned from their Hawaiian honeymoon, the bed had been ready and waiting for the happy newlyweds.

Although her daddy hadn't approved of TyJuan or the marriage, he'd accepted him because of her—his only daughter. Tenisha wondered if she'd be as accommodating with her offspring as soon as they opted to date someone she couldn't stand the sight of. She doubted she would be as generous as her own father.

Her father. Her first true love…until Marcus.

No. Not Marcus.

Yes. Marcus.

TyJuan blew into the bedroom, sending Tenisha's reckless thoughts scurrying into the early-morning blaze. Wearing a poignant essence of eau de coffee, he literally and uncharacteristically bounced up to the bed.

"Hey, baby?" he buoyantly greeted. "Did you sleep well?"

"Yes…thank you." Her legs, followed by the rest of her body, inched out of bed. As he leaned against the dressing drawer, she silently studied her husband. *Why are you so damned chipper this morning?*

"Good." He parked himself on the edge of the bed. "Breakfast is served whenever you're ready."

Tenisha raised a questioning brow. *And so energetic. What's gotten into you, TyJuan?* "Actually, I am kinda hungry." Her long, brown legs swung to the floor. Deciding to take advantage of this windfall, guessing it would not last past the dinner hour, she said, "Give me a few minutes to freshen up."

"I'll give you as much time as you like. And Tee"—he stilled her with fingers pressing gently into her forearm—"I know things haven't been all that great for us in a while. But I'm gonna do my damnedest to make it up to you." He applied a little pressure. "Despite what I've done, despite the stupid things I've said, I really do love you."

For a quick second, their eyes fastened. *Yeah, right. And I'm gonna win the twenty-million-dollar lottery.* Tenisha was the first to break eye contact. Oddly enough, she didn't believe him and she really didn't care. She also wasn't feeling magnanimous enough to forgive him. But then again, maybe she didn't want to.

Why the sudden change of heart, Tenisha. Is it because of Marcus?

Don't talk to me about Marcus, she silently admonished herself.

Slipping away from a touch that did not inspire or stimulate, she murmured something inaudible as she wandered toward the adjacent bathroom.

TyJuan seared Tenisha's backside with an indulgent leer. He then began smoothing silk sheets, plumping pillows, and tucking in corners. He felt good. He felt great. He felt like he could tackle the world…plus his inflated wife. After she'd gone to bed last night, he'd slipped out of the apartment to smoke a little crack-cocaine. He'd done some more this morning. Later on in the day, one of his newly found female friends would be introducing him to heroin. No doubt, he would fuck her afterward. Right now, the world was a damn good place to live in. And he, TyJuan Davidson, could afford to be generous to his wife. After all, she was springing for his drugs.

Running a flat hand over the taut covers, he resisted the urge to pull a quarter out of his pocket and bounce it on top of the bed.

19

BRIGHT AND EARLY TUESDAY morning—actually, it couldn't be considered bright since it was much too early yet for the sun to consider rousing—instead of taking up residence in the dining room, Brye and Chad relaxed in the antiseptically clean kitchen. Vague shadows and images danced around the industrial-sized, silvery polished appliances, sinks, and countertops. Somehow, the kitchen seemed to be the most ideal place to hang out in on the last morning of their stay.

Peace and serenity had befallen the lodge. The quiet before the storm. Soon the natives would be stirring. But for now, Brye and Chad basked in blessed tranquility. Indulging in a morning cup of coffee, they quietly reminisced over the past four days.

"Have you forgiven me for leaving you to fend for yourself the other day?" The smile she granted him was neither innocent nor apologetic.

Chad's jawline tightened in merciless contemplation. "Not only have I *not* forgiven you," he growled in mock bitterness, "but I'm in no frame of mind to discuss it."

"What if I told you I'm willing to do anything to gain your forgiveness." She ran a suggestive finger along the inside of Chad's sleeveless arm, assuring him of her sincerity.

Her less-than-honorable intentions could not be shelved. As usual, thoughts of making love to Brye sent his raging hormones spiraling into another dimension. Every day spent with her, he found it increasingly difficult to hold back the desire threatening to incinerate him in its entirety.

Brye validated the libidinous glare Chad displayed; she identified well with it. For every day she spent with him, she found herself powerless to abstain from the intimacy she'd denied herself for so many years.

"We could go back to my room." The words were weighted down with a yearning to great to ignore. Brye tickled the inside of Chad's wrist with a taunting finger.

The offer sounded too good to refuse. Yet Chad did, with considerable reluctance. "You know I'd love nothing better than to take you up on your offer, but I have no desire for a repeat performance of the other morning." Shuddering underneath Brye's sizzling touch, he added, "Besides, when we make love, I don't want it to feel like we're making love in Grand Central Station. I want it to be in a quiet, romantic setting. And I want to be able to concentrate on us."

Disappointed, yet understanding perfectly, Brye said, "Sometime after we get back, I'll fix us a deserving, intimate, dinner. Afterward—" A sudden bout of shyness attacked her. She allowed him to draw his own conclusions.

"Just don't keep me waiting too long," he growled.

"The sooner the better," Brye wholeheartedly agreed. Her fingers lightly rested atop the back of his hand. Quietly they sat, relishing in fun memories as well as embellishing in the anticipation of memories soon to be created.

To Chad's reverence, despite his growing desire to make love to Brye, he was not overwrought with disappointment. What he felt, whatever he was feeling, he owed to his coalition with the kids at Brylinn. He felt a sense of parenthood. No doubt about it, kids were time-consuming, strength-draining, highly demanding, impetuous-performing creatures. Having kids meant losing a part of oneself. Time was no longer yours. Sanity was forever being called into question. From moment to moment, one's patience balanced on a weakened tightrope, and more times than not, the frail lines would snap.

Yet despite the great loss of solitude, and the huge deprivation of one's energy, there was so much more to be gained. And although Chad hadn't fully grasped the sense of what all he had attained, he recognized that being held responsible for children meant a whole new world of emotions had opened up to him; a warm rush of paternal instincts flowed throughout his humming system. This was a new game he had entered. A game structured around rapidly changing rules and ingeniously thought out strategies—on the part of both adult and child. Through it all, he also recognized that it had become a tremendous challenge—a test of wills perhaps—in snatching time alone with Brye. But—and he reveled in this wisdom—the time he did manage to spend with her alone was that much more welcomed and cherished.

"Can I have a cup of coffee?"

Engrossed in their own quiet reflections, neither Brye nor Chad had taken note to Bethany's soft footing padding along the kitchen floor.

"Why are you up so early?" Brye asked, her voice as mollifying as the first morning rays infiltrating the boundaries of their secluded little world and warming them with its welcoming embrace.

Dressed in light blue cotton pajamas and large fuzzy cat slippers, Bethany stepped closer to Brye and Chad. She was shy in her answer. "I've really enjoyed the trip—it's the first time Anthony and I have ever been anywhere—and we've had an awful lot of fun, but—" She trailed off, those beautiful innocent eyes dropping at her feet.

"But you're glad to be going home," Chad concluded for her, pulling her close to his side. She nodded hesitantly.

"You miss Fred and Wilma?" More statement than question. Before their stay at Brylinn, Bethany's and Anthony's days gravely hovered over them like a tyrannical cloud bursting forth in a wrath of destruction, ravaging beyond repair, with no concern for the damage left behind; each day of their young lives had been met with consternation, terror and pain. Now, a real future stretched out before them—a future they could reach out to. There were people who loved them just as much as they were capable of loving. Life had taken on an entirely new meaning for Bethany and Anthony.

A huge smile spread along the early-morning light, enticing the sun to glow that much more brighter. "You think they've driven Mama Linn bananas?"

"No," Chad replied with a jaunty grin, "I think Mama Linn's driving them bananas."

Bethany giggled. She threw her arms around Chad's neck, hugging him tightly. For Chad, it was a meaningful moment meant to be put away and cherished along with the many other memorable moments he had collected over the long, fulfilled weekend.

"Can I have a cup of coffee?" Bethany asked again. Pulling away from Chad, she grabbed the ladder-back chair planted beside him.

About to deny her the inappropriate request, Brye's response stunned Chad into cryptic silence.

"Of course you can, sweetheart." Peeling herself out of her seat, Brye quickly jumped to complete Bethany's request. "Whenever I'm away from Brylinn for a few days," she explained to Chad, "the first morning I've returned, Bethany and I usually sit around the kitchen sharing coffee and recent escapades." Steadily she pulled down two cups, two saucers, two teaspoons from the sandblasted cabinets. "It's become sort of a ritual for us."

With newfound interest, Chad watched as Brye mixed Bethany's "coffee." A slight smile teetered on the edge of laughter as he recalled the age-old saying, when someone poured a handful of sugar in a cup filled with about three inches of coffee, "have a little coffee with your sugar." In Bethany's case, it was "have a little coffee with your milk."

Three parts whole milk, one part coffee, a pinch of vanilla and sugar; in all actuality, Brye mixed the smallest amount of coffee to give Bethany's milk a rich piquant shade of winter-white.

The timer on the microwave sounded. Brye removed its contents and placed the warmed mixture in front of Bethany. She then went about mixing a cup of hot chocolate. After warming it, she placed the cup and saucer by the empty place setting beside her chair. Like clockwork, Anthony entered.

"So this is where everybody is." He pulled out the chair in front of the hot chocolate.

Entranced, Chad looked into the creamy dark swirls of hot chocolate, then at Anthony, and finally at Brye. It was as if she had expected him; it was as if this intimate assemblage had been prearranged. An intricate bond far beyond their similarities in appearance connected Brye and the twins. Their ties reached higher than the tallest mountain, ran deeper than the road to China, traveled well beyond the end of time. They were linked by horrific tragedies of the past, nightmares forged into the present, and, hopefully, promises of better days to come inside the near future.

Brye, Bethany, and Anthony related extremely well with each other; they related as a fraction of one whole. Chad wondered if he would ever achieve that same solidarity; he wondered if he really wanted to. Suddenly he felt overwhelmed. Maybe he was taking on more responsibility than he wanted or needed. Maybe he was getting in way over his head.

But as he joined in jovial conversation, as they laughed over hilarious predicaments having occurred on the Fourth of July, Chad realized that he welcomed the long-term responsibilities the twins represented. After all, the two delightful creatures were the closest individuals to the son and daughter Chad had never met.

The sun was finally peeking its fiery head above the rugged horizon. But thick, bleary clouds formed around the edges of the mountain tops, deliberately taunting the sun, giving it a run for its money, as if to say, "You've lived on borrowed time long enough. Now it's our turn."

"It's getting late," Brye announced. "I think you two better scoot along and get dressed. The kitchen staff will be along to boot us out of here any minute now."

Anxious to begin the long trip home, the twins quickly adhered to Brye's request.

"The kids have really enjoyed your being here." Fingers laced around her coffee cup, the dark liquid resembled a tumultuous whirlpool as Brye swirled the remainder of her coffee around in circles. Her eye trained in the center, she felt a similar stirring rumbling in the pit of an unsettled belly.

Chad smiled, knowing he'd enjoyed the trip just as much. Wanting to offer financial help, now was as good a time as any to announce his good intentions. "I'd like to help compensate you for this trip. I'd also like to provide financial backing for Brylinn."

Stunned by his request, Brye fell silent. She lowered her coffee cup. Trembling hands slid under the table and fell heavily in her lap. She didn't want his money. She never had, and she refused to take it now.

When she spoke, she articulated with deliberate caution. "Your offer is greatly appreciated, Chad, but it really is not necessary."

The tone she used was one he recognized so well: she was detaching herself from him, from the moment, from the situation in hand. "I want to do this, Brye."

"No!" The answer was thrown at him genially, yet firmly. "We don't need your money, Chad."

Ever so slightly, a spark of anger tinted Chad's better judgment. No sooner had it appeared, however, just as quickly, it disappeared.

It lasted long enough for Brye to decipher it.

"So say it," she ordered through her controlled impulses.

The tension had suddenly grown thick with furor. It was a mistake broaching the raw subject without the benefit of a dispassionate eye. Nevertheless, Chad recklessly rushed forward. "*You* don't need the money or the kids don't need it?" Chad asked between clenched teeth.

She understood perfectly yet asked nevertheless, "What're you implying?"

"It means that you didn't have any problems *needing* my money years ago, so why the hell would you deny it now?"

Voice steady, Brye struggled to bury her rising irritation. "I never *needed* your money, I never *wanted* your money, I never *took* your money! I didn't want it then, and I don't want it now." She pulled her hands out from underneath the table. Propping her elbows on the tabletop, she dropped her chin on steepled fingers. Wide, innocent, violet-tinted eyes stared openly at Chad. "Tell me something, Chad, if I were in such dire straits for money back then, why didn't I just marry you?" Long, inquisitive eyelashes batted maidenly at Chad. "I think it's safe to say that if I had, I would have secured more than enough capital to last me a lifetime."

Yes, it was a major flaw in Chad's veiled reasoning. He had asked himself that very question on numerous occasions. But he refused to acknowledge his doubts—particularly since it infuriated him in seeing her appear so innocent, so smug, and so damned gorgeous at the same time.

Instead, he asked, "Tell me something, Brye, the day we went fishing, you stated that in another week, you would probably have me believing you hadn't extorted a million dollars from my family—is that because you hoped to use your feminine charms to convince me otherwise?"

Any other set of words would not have affected Brye so violently. It was only when her integrity came into question that she chose to attack in full force and with rash vehemence.

"I would never, *ever*, use charm or any other inappropriate behavior in an attempt to convince you of something that we both know to be totally false!" she hissed at him. "The other day, I merely meant that I hoped you would use the good sense you were born with to see that I wasn't the devious person you perceived me to be."

The slight tick beating furiously against his temple alerted Brye to his wrath. "Why wait for my good sense to kick in." He ran a deceptively benevolent finger down the side of her strained features. "Why not enlighten me instead? Why don't you tell me what really happened prior to our splitting up?"

Brye jerked away from a touch threatening to obliterate every ounce of pride and self-respect she painstakingly safeguarded. But then, what use was there in sheltering herself if she was destined to spend the rest of her life alone because of it. Sighing loudly, for one brief second, she found herself faltering.

No, she ultimately screamed out in her mind, she would not compromise her self-taught ethics and values to seek acceptance from him. The chair's legs produced an ear-splitting screech as she shoved it from underneath the table. Brye shot upward. To calm herself, she kept busy by removing soiled cups and saucers from the tabletop.

"If I told you what *really* happened," she informed, bustling around the kitchen, "if you can't see for yourself what is clearly before your very eyes, then that would mean what we shared so long ago had only been a lie." She presented a stiff and unyielding back as she stacked dishes in the huge, glistening double sink.

If Chad considered himself a master at playing corporate games, Brye was the champion at retaining secrets; she was an expert at locking feelings away so the rest of the world could not catch a glimpse.

Slipping up from behind, he clutched her wrist with a persistent grip. Turning her around, he forced her to face him. Stoic eyes confronted, converged, challenged. His love for her was shoved aside, completely ignored…forgotten. "And wasn't it a lie?" he quietly asked.

Her tone took on a hard edge. "Was this a lie?" She flicked her head around to include the kitchen they stood in, the lodge they'd spent the last several days in. "Was this entire trip a deception…a falsehood of the heart…your heart?"

He clamped his free hand over her other wrist. Roughly, he tugged her against his body; despite their many conflicts, he craved to possess her. His breath was hot against her flushed cheek as he growled into her darkened eyes. "Why don't you tell me, Brye. Was this entire trip orchestrated for my benefit?"

Intoxicated by his nearness, she prayed she would not succumb to his unrestrained sexuality. Brye called on all her strength to break away. Palms outward, fingers flattened across his chest, she pushed Chad away. The attack was so sudden, so unexpected, he stumbled over his own cumbersome feet.

Brye stormed out of the kitchen. She spoke in a calm and gentle tone that belied the inner turmoil. "Go to hell, Chad Collier! And don't bother coming back…ever!"

Close to three in the afternoon, Chad entered his affluent midtown Manhattan apartment. His luggage slipped out his harried fingers and hit the tiled flooring with a loud thud. There was time to hit the shower, then spend a few hours catching up on a backlog of paperwork at Romanique Cosmetics. His mood, which had steadily slipped from bad to worse since his fight with Brye, matched the downpour of rain which had finally broken loose just as the bus hit the edge of town. Massive rain pellets beat relentlessly at his Gothic arched windows and strummed a destructive rhythm against his pulsating temple. Although the heavy drapes were pulled open, the atmosphere of his living room was as lifeless and gray as cement. His dark, undesirable disposition coordinated well with his present surroundings and necessitated the urge to remain isolated from the general public.

Feeling as if he'd been flung into the Hudson River with a cement block attached to his leg, oppressively, Chad sunk into the center of the jacquard-leaf, eight-foot long sofa. Eyes clamped shut, his head fell backward.

The bus ride home had been excruciatingly long. The entire duration, Brye had maintained an insufferable distance between them. When she spoke to him, *if* she was forced to speak to him, she treated him with respective distinction and politeness befitting the king. It irritated Chad to no end. Brye irritated him to no end.

With all he knew of her—which was little of nothing but more than he'd known before the trip—was it finally time to just let go? Should he cut his losses? Firsthand, he bore witness to her deep-rooted pain. Catching a glimpse of her soul enabled him to expose a part—albeit a small portion—of the secrets she struggled to keep hidden. Did he really want to walk away from all that? Did he really want to involve himself with a woman who concealed more secrets than all the involved players inside the Watergate scandal?

Was a decision really necessary on his part? Because after today, he had a sinking feeling that he'd exhausted all avenues of reconciliation where he and Brye were concerned. Hell, at the very least, he wasn't even certain he wanted to reconcile their differences. If she couldn't admit to her problems, if she wasn't prepared to open up to him, who was he to concern himself in her business.

"Mm-hm." The sound came at him over the low rumble of thunder.

Chad opened his eyes and lifted his head. Dressed in nothing other than black, lace panties and bra, Jennifer's tall lean body struck a seductive stance in the middle of the open double doors leading to his bedroom.

"I've come to give my man a proper welcome." Confident and proud, she slithered toward him like a snake eager to poison its victim. Much to his surprise, mind nor body reacted to her corporeal advances. At least not until his head dropped heavily onto the back of the sofa and his mind scurried back to a different place and time. A time merely a few days old. The place: Lake George.

Chad found himself back on the private beach, Brye's body slithering with passion underneath his. Her unrestrained fingers shuffled along every inch of his ignited body, bringing it closer to its zenith.

"Let's go to bed," Brye seductively whispered. But as he opened his eyes, as he realized who guided him toward his bedroom, he felt like the proverbial lamb being led to slaughter. And somewhere in the distance, the roar of thunder disturbingly mocked him.

Close to two in the morning, scheduled for an eight o'clock curtain call, Brye finally stumbled her fatigued body into bed. Sleep did not readily come. With aching heart, she mulled over Chad's unpredictable—or maybe it was predictable—conduct: one moment he treated her as if he couldn't succeed in living without her, the next minute he acted as if he hated her guts.

Just what did it all mean? What did he really want from her?

A self-pitying groan broke the stifling silence ensnared within her painted walls. A sinking feeling ambushed her weary brain, informing her that she had let her guard down much too soon with Chad. Unfortunately for her, she found it implausible to believe that she wouldn't lower her defenses once again. But she could hope, and she could pray, and she could maintain a far enough distance away from him to just maybe, possibly, hopefully, guarantee not to make a complete fool of herself by throwing a body in extreme heat down at his feet, begging his forgiveness, imploring for a second chance, beseeching to be made love to.

She flipped to her right side. Her eyes opened but stared unseeingly at the painting of the old-fashioned village ensconced within an antique-white frame.

In the short months Brye and Chad had made their reacquaintance, he had rekindled a flame she believed to have long dwindled out; the ashes scattered desperately in the wind, scurrying nowhere, scurrying everywhere, lost to her forever. In those same short months, Chad had also extinguished the burning fire. But not as a lover would, caressing, stroking, propelling her body into a burning inferno until the fiery blaze consumed her body alive. In all actuality, he had dumped an ice cold bucket of water over her unsuspecting head, mercilessly dousing what little faith she'd had in him, leaving her body and mind exposed and susceptible to the deadly internal forces threatening to destroy her.

Brye flipped onto her belly. Her cheek pressed firmly into her thick, fiber-filled pillow. She rotated to her back, lying spread eagle. After completing a succession of tosses and turns for several unendurable minutes—she flipped to her left, then back to her right. She laid on top of the comforter, then burrowed underneath. Finally pulling herself in a fetal position, sheets tucked securely under her chin, she fitfully dozed off. And when Brye fell into an unsettled sleep, as usual, her mother's patronizing aura taunted her.

20

Countdown: three days till take off. Committed to a whirlwind, six-week tour—twenty-four cities, forty-five personal appearances, a talk show interview, three commercials and numerous layout shoots—most of Brye's journey would be trafficked via the Romanique Cosmetics' luxury liner. Her complete entourage consisting of a bus driver, personal assistant, hair and makeup artist, personal dress designer, professional photographer, and gofer. Romanique Cosmetics spared no expense.

Aside from missing her kids, Brye was anxious to embark upon her grueling schedule. Bent on keeping as much distance as she could between her and Chad, this tour, a befitting diversion, would guarantee their complete dissolution.

With each step bringing Brye closer to Chad's office, dread beat her over the head like a hailstorm pounding the streets of New York.

Thank God his office door is shut, Brye noted with exaggerated relief as she approached Rhonda's secretarial desk. She gravely thought, *With any luck, after meeting with Brian, maybe I can slip out without confronting him,*

"Brye!" Rhonda greeted, genuinely pleased. "At last, a sane person flying in the midst of all this insanity."

One side of her hair piled haphazardly atop Rhonda's head; the other side, released from its restraints, fell down the side of her face and over her eyes. Pen and pencil resembling rabbit ears poked out the top of her head. Lipstick had mellowed to a dull gleam, olive-colored eyes, desperate and wild. As she conversed, her fingers danced to a tune opposite her mind as she struggled to complete her latest assignment. Documents, various packages, unfinished projects, spilled over the edges of her desktop.

Frazzled. No other word suited Rhonda's fragmented appearance. Extremely proficient at her job, during the most highly charged situations, when everyone else ran around like a chicken with its head chopped off, Rhonda remained undaunted. If temperaments ran high, she diffused the situation. If there was a problem, her voice was that of an arbitrator. Her duties ran above and beyond the call of an executive secretary. And, respectively so, she was paid well for her accomplished services.

Witnessing her discombobulated state both amazed and amused Brye. But before she could comment, Rhonda's interoffice intercom beeped.

"Rhonda!" Brian's booming voice overtook the office. "I need the stats on those overseas sales."

Rhonda rolled her eyes toward the ceiling. "They're on your desk. Next to your right hand."

Silence. Then, "What about the pro—"

"Underneath the stats."

"There's a conflicting timetable with Brye's schedule. Did you—"

"Changes have been implemented, confirmed by the appropriate parties, and approved with your initials three hours ago. Kierra has a revised scheduled and is going over the travel plans with the driver as we speak."

More silence. "Is there anything else I should be kept apprised of?" Brian scrupulously asked.

"God, I hope not," Rhonda mumbled under her tongue.

"Excuse me?"

"I said," she spoke distinctively, "it's getting hot."

"Maybe you should have the air conditioner checked," Brian petitioned.

"Maybe you should check yourself," Rhonda snarled at her intercom seconds after Brian disconnected.

Brye laughed, knowing Rhonda's irritation was borne more out of frustration, rather than disrespect toward her boss. "I take it he's driving you crazy."

"*That* is an understatement," Rhonda torridly confirmed. "Don't get me wrong, Brye"—she suddenly showed signs of a woman with a guilty conscience—"I enjoy working with Brian. And I enjoy my job. But in his desire to kick this tour off without a hitch, he's checked, and double-checked, and triple-checked the most infinitesimal of details. And in his overzealousness to make things perfect, he's limiting me in my own job." Her eyes flowed over her overflowing desk. But as the elevator chimed, her gaze bounced upward, outward. The doors slid open. Its passenger—Darryl Dempsey, department head of Romanique Publications—emptied out and strolled past. He smiled, greeting them in passing.

"I've been unable to get anything done," Rhonda completed once the area was clear. With wide, pleading, eyes, she swung her gaze back to Brye. "Help me...please! Get him out of here...for an hour or two...long enough for me to get something done," she wailed profusely.

Rhonda reminded Brye of the kids at Brylinn whenever one came to her requesting a toy they desired, or a trinket, or even the freedom to go out on a much desired junket with one of their friends. Then there were times when they would ask for her alliance, particularly when acknowledging that their insensible actions would send Linn off in a tyrannical rage. Brye could no more deny Rhonda, than she could her own kids. Promising to do all that was within her power, she stood outside Brian's door ten minutes earlier than her scheduled appointment.

"Am I too early?" Brye pointed to the empty hall behind her. "Or should I turn tail and abide my time until you're ready for me."

"Don't you dare!" Brian bustled to the door and escorted Brye into his office. "You are like a breath of fresh air in this otherwise stale office of mine."

A delighted burst of laughter coddled Brian like a lover's embrace. The audacious sensations unsettled him. Drawn to Brye in a capacity other than an employer/employee relationship, Brian resolved himself to gain, and maintain, a dispassionate eye. Besides, realistically, he had to concede to the fact that every man setting eyes on Brye wanted her in some form or fashion—and Chad was no exception.

Unaware of Rhonda's desperate plea to marshal him out of her life for a few hours, Brian would soon discover that his desire for her, which had been deposited on a back burner, would not sit idly in the caustic heat.

"I have entered the den of metaphor-spewing maniacs—eloquent though they may seem," Brye lightly teased, grabbing the chair slathered against the side of Brian's desk.

"What do you mean?" Brian asked. He waited until Brye was properly seated before occupying his own chair.

"Rhonda said something similar to me when I approached her earlier. I can only guess that the tour is running everyone ragged—excluding me, of course." Brye put on the air of an uppity socialite secure in her conviction that wasting brain cells on such mundane tasks ranked one notch higher than scooping dog poop. "I've been given the honors of having such a fine planning staff available to me, I've not had the need to worry my pretty little head over such trivial matters."

"And we wouldn't want to overwhelm that pretty little head of yours, now would we?" Brian added in good-natured humor. For a short period afterward, Brye and Brian amused each other with light banter. And when Brian advance toward their business affairs, Brye initiated her own plan of action.

"I asked you here because I wanted to advise you of some of the changes in your agenda." The leather in Brian's chair squeaked profusely as he buried himself more comfortably within its cozy confines. His fingers stretched toward her updated schedule, but Brye reached the gold-trimmed, leather-bound day planner first. She splayed her fingers across the top.

"Kierra can update me on the changes, Brian." Scooting toward the edge of her chair, she challenged him with an offer she hoped he wouldn't refuse. "What I'd like to do is invite you to lunch. Maybe a short walk in the park afterward—to work off our meal."

The invitation, eminently unexpected, caught Brian completely off guard. Recovery was not swift. Nor was it pretty. His jaw was halfway to the floor before he caught himself. Noiselessly, he slammed it shut. But when he reopened it, lost his train of thought, shut it again, he resembled a ventriloquist's dummy speaking without the aid of the ventriloquist.

"Brye," he finally managed to sputter.

The denial was evident in coming. Brye would not accept his refusal. If need be, she would prey on his guilt.

Brye arrested Brian with an aggrieved pout. "You've asked me out for a bite to eat on several occasions. I've denied you each and every time. But I have to tell you, Brian, I'm not as gracious at handling rejection as you are—particularly when the first man I've ever asked out declines my offer."

"Are you telling me you've never asked?"

"Not ever," Brye admitted, a slight tinge of embarrassment soiling her cheeks. "If you turn me down, I could be traumatized for life. I mean, how does one recover from a bruised ego?"

The solemnity in which she stated her case intimated to Brian that she might have turned serious on him, though he didn't believe it for one second.

He picked up a pencil and tapped the eraser on the desktop. "Brye, in another year, you will have obtained a PhD in social psychology. If anyone can learn to get over rejection, you can." Word for word, he matched her somberness.

Brye looked injured. "You're turning my lunch invitation down, *plus* you're patronizing me." Feigning indignation, she shot out of her chair. "If that's the way you're going to be, fine. Forget lunch. Forget you ever knew me." Amidst an obstinate huff, she stormed out of the office.

What the hell happened here? Brian's heart clutched at his chest at the thought of upsetting Brye. But as his eyes remained trained on the door Brye had mere seconds ago tore out of, he felt a receding in his heartbeat as she stuck her grinning face back around the threshold.

"You're just going to let me walk out of here?" She now presented her entire million-dollar body to him. "I didn't make you feel guilty in any way?" She rolled her eyes to the ceiling in manufactured disbelief. "I must be losing my touch."

Laughing in relief, Brian thought about her offer. In an attempt to be honest with himself, he wanted to go out to lunch with her, yet he didn't want to go. He was afraid of where their lunch might end. Then again, he was afraid of where the lunch might not end. He was confused with the entire ordeal, yet maybe he was actually thinking clearly. Or maybe he wasn't thinking at all. And as he gazed into those twinkling eyes of hers, he thought about the drug commercial: the frying pan and the egg.

Except in his case, he visualized beef and potatoes. He thought, *This is my brain. This is what Brye does to my brain. Pure hash.*

He blurted out his decision before he could change his mind. "Okay. I'll go to lunch with you."

"What's that?" Brye moved deeper into the room. Her fingers slid behind her ear, pushing one delicate lobe forward. "I didn't quite hear you."

"Don't make me repeat myself, Brye," he growled good-naturedly. "Let me finish—"

"No!" Brye dropped her hands on top of his. Forcing him out of his chair, she pushed him toward the door. "Your work can wait until you get back. I, on the other hand, am starving." Hands splayed across his back, she shoved him along the way.

"You are unbelievable," Brian noted, smiling down into her face, grateful for the chance to spend time with her outside the limitations created by the office.

The posh elevator embraced its convivial passengers. As the steel jaws gracefully sealed them from the rest of the world, Brye reached up and straightened Brian's paisley tie. Then she rested open palms against his suit jacket lapels. "That's why you can't resist me," she noted, grinning up at him.

Seconds prior to Brye and Brian waltzing onto the elevator, Chad strayed from his office. "I couldn't get Brian on his intercom. Can you locate him for me?"

Without breaking stride or lifting her eyes, Rhonda aimed her office-supplied Bic toward the closing elevator. "He just left for lunch with Brye."

Rage, unbridled jealousy, tapped into the core of Chad's inner sanctum. His fist clenched into a tight fist as he watched the intimate manner in which Brye groped at Brian.

Close to three in the afternoon, the weather prevailed windy and warm yet not uncomfortably so. A Canadian storm front exerted minor pressures over the state of New York. Although rain did not look imminent in coming, like a child engaging in a game of hide-and-seek, the sun intermittently peeked its resplendent head from around darting, distended, clouds.

After indulging in a relaxing lunch at a sidewalk cafe in Greenwich Village, Brye and Brian struck out at Washington Square Park for an unhurried stroll. The tempo in the village moved to its own variable beat. Like native New Yorkers, Brye and Brian slipped into the vacillating pulse with relative ease.

Arm-in-arm, wandering south on MacDougal Street, Brian remained oblivious to the various shops and the mingling odors of prepared food flanking his senses—his attention remained transfixed on the intriguing woman accompanying him.

Peasant blouse exposing smooth, tanned shoulders; ankle-flowing gauze skirt; flat sandals with long ties crisscrossing around the calves of her legs; bangle bracelets and large hoop earrings; hair absent of constraints; cheeks heightened in color by an unruffled expression; perfected skin tinted by a touch of sun—her exotic appearance was deceptively unveiling. She resembled an untamed gypsy; an individual whose mind and spirit soared with the wind; someone who drifted with the tide.

Brian believed otherwise. She was definitely no free spirit. In fact, he believed her to be existing in an altered state of being. Her mind was trapped in a locale far removed from the present, a place she did not want to be, yet could not tear herself away from.

For two hours, Brye had effectively managed to extort his life story from him. He laughed at his first boyhood crush directed at his sixth-grade teacher. With profound melancholy, he recalled the childhood pranks he and his best friend survived during his teenaged years. He grimly recalled the first and only time he had experimented with marijuana—he'd come home stoned to the hilt at the age of fifteen. His father had beat the holy crap out of him, threatening to break every finger in both hands if he ever lifted a joint to his lips again. Years later, he would admit to his father that he hated the feeling that crashed down on him from the consummation of that one single joint. For him, it had been a sinking feeling of not being able to maintain control. It was the identical sensation he had experienced when undergoing a root canal.

The hygienist had offered him nitrous oxide, and he agreeably accepted. During the entire procedure, he floated somewhere between the stratospheres and never-never land. Completely removed from reality at large, if the world had crashed down on his head, he would have been powerless to save himself. Once his mind settled to near normal, he swore he'd never inhale the stuff again.

And, finally, dispirited, he spoke of his marriage that had never come to be. For four years—his college days—he dated and fell in love with a woman harboring her own self-serving ambitions, her own desires, and her own agenda. It wasn't until after they had gotten engaged that realization struck: it would never work. She searched for something he could never give her, and she would not give him the family he so desired. To this day, they continued to exchange Christmas cards, but not their personal reflections.

Now that Brye knew all there was to know of one Brian Paxton, he longed to gain an equitable amount of insight into her.

"I've bored you with my entire life story, Brye. It's time to reciprocate." A series of left and right turns found them standing on the intersection of Greenwich and Sixth Avenue. Halting at an outdoor produce market, Brian bought Brye a bouquet of flowers. Irises. "The same color as your eyes," Brian noted, snapping one off at the stem and gliding it behind her ear." Fingers cupped under her elbow, they continued west on Eighth Street. "Tell me about yourself, Brye?" he requested, weaving through window shoppers wistfully peering into storefront windows.

"There's nothing to tell." Brye buried her nose in the sweet fragrance exuding from the flowers.

"There's always something to tell," Brian insisted.

"Not in my case."

Exasperated, Brian asked, "You're going to make this difficult for me, aren't you?"

"I don't mean to."

The untainted look she cuffed him with told Brian she meant every word. "Then how about if I ask you some questions?"

"Brian!" Wearily, Brye protested, "Are you turning this outing into a question and answer period?"

"It's only fair. After all, I did—willingly, I might add—answer every question you aimed at me."

Still, her reluctance lingered.

"How about if I only ask twenty questions?" Brian compromised. Intersecting with the industrious traffic, they crossed over to MacDougal Street.

"Ten personal questions," Brye countered with little enthusiasm. "Anything more has to be under the category of general topics."

"Who determines whether it's personal, or general?"

"I do."

"Not fair, but agreed," Brian acknowledged, knowing it would be in his best interest not to quibble over the terms. He began on what he thought was a harmless inquest. "Why did you go into social psychology?"

Brye shrugged. "There's a rumor going around implying that most practitioners go into the field in the hopes of fixing themselves?"

"Excuse me?" He guided Brye past numerous women's and men's apparel shops.

"That's number two," Brye counted.

"Uh-uh!" Brian roughly disputed. "That question goes under the heading of general topics."

Again, Brye shrugged. She would grant him that one. "Can you define social psychology?" she asked with indifference.

This time it was Brian's turn to shrug. It was a question he had no clear answer to. "The study of social patterns and how it affects one's behavior?" It was a stab in the dark. Apologetically, he added, "I'm sure it's more involved than that, but it's the best I could come up with on such short notice."

The horn of a red Isuzu Trooper blasted maddeningly at a bicyclist riding a Schwinn. The unrelenting shrill endeavored to blow the rider right off his seat.

"Actually, your definition is as good as any other. Even the professionals have problems defining the study of social psychology. Psychologists define it one way, sociologists define it another. As a field of study, it is not now nor has it ever been clearly defined. But for our intent and purpose, and to simplify a concept that goes far beyond the simplicity stage, I will define it as this: social psychology is the systemic study of social and economic advantages—or disadvantages as the case may be—as well as personal factors which influence individual social behavior. Which is to say," she basically summarized, "it's the study of learned social behavior influenced by the behavior of others."

Brye paused. "So...I guess what I'm trying to say is that maybe I went into the field to gain a better insight of who I am and why my family was the way they were. Maybe I longed to understand the controlling forces molding me into the person I am today. Maybe I hoped to fix myself."

Baffled by her lack of emotions, wherever her problem lay, Brian wondered if instead of confronting her issues straight up, she had distanced herself as far away as possible. "Have you made any progress in fixing yourself?" he asked.

"Not at all," she easily admitted.

They sideswiped a group of young teens taking up the entire sidewalk. Brian asked, "Why is that?" The smile on her face, a cross between sadness and recognition, pulled at Brian's gut.

Brye ruefully answered, "Have you heard the one about the attorney who represents himself has a fool for a client?"

"You're saying that you decided not to treat yourself?"

"Bingo!"

"Brye." In the middle of West Ninth street, Brian swung Brye around to face him. Disquietude poured from his eyes. "If there's a problem, why don't you talk to someone about it…seek out a therapist?"

"That's two questions in one, which brings the count to six." Hugging her flowers to her chest, she answered his question with vague incisiveness. "A therapist is only as good as his patient allows him to be."

"Which means?

"Which means a therapist can't help someone who doesn't want to be helped."

"And you don't want to be?" His mouth funneled into benevolent puzzlement.

"Not at the moment…no…I don't."

Brian felt like a dog chasing around after his own tail. He understood no more of Brye now than when he first began this Q&A session. His feet began to move, his questions traveled an alternate route. "What is it you want out of life, Brye? What'll make you happy?"

The very essence of Brye took on a dreamlike aura of a young woman anticipating attending her senior prom with the first true love of her life. "I want a big family. A real family equipped with marriage to a husband who adores me, a bunch of clinging, time-consuming children, and wonderful in-laws who double as doting grandmother and smothering grandfather."

Her answer both stunned and fascinated Brian. "Many career women of today push thoughts of marriage and family toward the back of their mind until much later in life."

Slightly embarrassed, Brye smiled. "I know I stand the chance of setting the feminist movement back fifty years, Brian, but I mean it when I say I want a family—plus all the trimmings that come with it. I don't think I'll ever be complete otherwise."

"You know," Brian said, grabbing Brye's hand and tugging her along, "I have wonderful parents who're dying to become grandparents."

Brye halted. Her feet plastered firmly to the pavement. She felt the slight tug of her shoulder socket as Brian attempted to tow her along.

Her resistance urged him to stop. He turned and was met with a teasing grin. "Why, Brian," she giggled, "was that a proposal?"

"Hey…I'm willing to go for it if you are." Brian grinned back.

Daintily waving her hands in front of her face as if genuinely flustered, batting those lovely, dark eyelashes, Brye took on the air of a maidenly southern belle. "My, my, my, Mr. Paxton. Aren't we being a little too presumptuous here? And to think, as of yet, our lips have not had the pleasure of savoring one another."

It was then Brian acted on a staggering urge he'd been suppressing the last several hours…hell, since the first moment he had met her.

"A minor problem which can promptly be rectified," he assured. Eyes locked on Brye, Brian leaned closer. Temples pounding, heart fluttering with anticipation, gradually, their lips made contact. But before the kiss had time to unfold, a sledgehammer of guilt rammed into Brian's chest, knocking him backward. His head whirled with haziness, yet it remained clear enough to know he could have possibly opened himself up to sexual harassment charges. He pleaded for forgiveness. "Brye, I'm sorry. I don't know what came over—"

The remainder of his sentence was lost as Brian's mouth collided into Brye's. Surprising them both, Brye's fingers snaked around Brian's hair, pulling him downward to greet her. Lips joined, theirs was not a demanding kiss, nor was there an urgency to feed upon one another. Instead, there was tenderness as gentle as spring rain. Their bodies barely grazed each other as his hands rested lightly upon her shoulders. And when his tongue flickered over Brye's closed mouth, he did not attempt to force himself and pry her lips apart—he gave her the right-of-passage to choose in which direction their unhurried kiss would travel.

With only the slightest of pauses, willingly, Brye opened her mouth and invited Brian inside. Her fingers explored the strength of his back as she pulled him into her body.

A busy thoroughfare, during prime time hours, as the kissing couple lost touch with reality, a steady flow of individuals trudged past. Some onlookers glanced with dull interest, most ignored them altogether. This was New York City in the summertime. In this town, stranger things had happened.

When Brye and Brian finally broke free, the shocked couple blinked back their surprise. The pleasures derived from Brian's kiss had been enjoyable—not once had she felt a sickening pull in the pit of her belly—but she instantly took note of the lack of passion overwhelming her system. Fireworks had not ignited. Her heart did not drum erratically against her chest. Her insides weren't threatening to implode. Nor did Brye feel as if she would melt by the slightest touch of Brian's hands or by his searing glance.

In effect, being with Chad, kissing Chad, making love to Chad, ranked right up there with the tumultuous sensations one experienced when ambushed by an earth-shattering quake, registering 9.0 on the Richter scale. Brian, in essence, was merely an aftershock.

"The kiss was nice, Brian..." Brye turned her troubled gaze away. She silently eyed a mother wheeling a baby stroller.

"Why do I feel a *but* coming on here?" he cautiously asked.

Without knowing what was in store, sensing something, Brian issued a smile so full of understanding and forgiveness, Brye found herself wishing she could give herself completely to him. But she tragically recognized, in her heart, compared to Chad, he'd always come in second—and he deserved so much more than that.

"It's my turn to apologize." Brye lightly stroked his clean-shaven face with her open palm. "My reasons for kissing you were purely self-serving. There was no consideration for your feelings, or with the concern that I might be giving you false hope." Dropping her hands to her side, she pulled away. "I've denied myself this for so long." Her arms spread open to include Brian, their leisurely walk, the flowers she clutched within her grasp, the kiss, the enjoyable afternoon she'd spent with him. "I guess I just wanted—" Her sentenced trailed off. How was she supposed to tell him that she only kissed him to prove a point? There were no other comparisons in Brye's life; she had endured with memories, alone, for so many years, she had written off every available male seeking a relationship with her because she didn't believe any of them could ever compare to Chad; she kissed Brian on the off chance he could wipe out blessed memories of her former lover. She now understood that no one would ever be able to sweep his memory, or his place, out of her shattered heart.

Confiding in Brian only enough for him to gain some insight, she said, "I've been hurt by some people who should have always been there for me...people I should have been able to trust. In the aftermath, I've found it extremely difficult to trust others, and almost impossible to begin a relationship with a man."

Arms linked, they weaved their way back to Washington Square Park. "Anyway," Brye continued, "it was true when I told you earlier that I'd never asked a man out on a date. It tells me that I've come a long way over the past few years. But I still remain unprepared to get involved in an intimate relationship."

It was important to see the expression on his face when she approached him with the best proposal she had to offer. Again, she stopped her pacing. Meeting him face-to-face, looking him directly into his eyes, she meekly acknowledged, "I know most men hate to hear my next line because they feel it's really a brush-off, but Brian, please don't get angry when I say I'd really like for us to be friends."

The condensed version Brye submitted helped Brian to read between the lines: somewhere, somehow, by someone, she'd been severely hurt. The emotional scars she sustained hindered her from charging back into the dating game; the fear of being mortally wounded kept her stranded on the sideline. There was no room for life, love, or happiness in the shell of an existence she created for herself. A vibrant woman with so much to give; it was all so terribly tragic.

"Friends would be nice." Brian granted her with an inspiring smile. "At least this way, we've established the boundaries of our relationship. And I can stop mooning over you like some lovesick teenager."

"You never mooned," Brye established, delighted he had accepted her terms so genially.

"Maybe not," Brian righteously admitted, "but it doesn't mean I didn't want to." He offered his hand for a handshake. "You want to seal our newfound friendship?"

Brye opted for a hug instead. Tossing her arms around his neck, she kissed him on the cheek. "Thank you...for everything."

In companionable comfort, they walked the several hundred yards back to Brian's emerald-green Infiniti. Questions continued to plague Brian. One particular question had to do with Chad. He could not hold his tongue.

"Tell me about you and Chad?"

Beside him, he felt her stiffen. "You've used up your ten questions," Brye cautiously reminded.

"Let's just say I'm taking advantage of my newfound friendship."

Laughter ensued, the tension ebbed, and Brye said, "You are incorrigible."

"It's my middle name."

In answer to his question, Brye considered feigning ignorance; she considered pretending as if there was no merit to his inquiry. But she decided not to insult his intelligence or make herself look like a complete idiot denying what he obviously had gained some insight into. Therefore, she simply stated, "Chad and I have a past together."

"Your past has intercepted with the present," he stated contemplatively.

Uncertain if he spoke to her or to himself, vague to whether he asked a question or merely issued a statement, Brye mumbled, "Yes." Then she asked, "Did he have anything to do with my becoming spokesperson of the company?"

"Everything. He said whatever it took, he wanted you aboard." Their eyes mingled. "You two were lovers?" Brian boldly asked.

"Yes. Over six years ago."

"What happened?"

She floundered over her response before answering truthfully. "He thinks I've wronged him."

"Did you?"

"No." Brye foresaw the next question. She saved him the breath. "His father played head games with us." Brye shrugged in apathy. "I guess we didn't trust each other, or our love, to question the validity of his father's allegations."

"What was Daniel Collier's reasoning for tearing you two apart?"

"I didn't live up to Daddy dearest's standards. I wasn't good enough for his precious baby boy. Chad asked me to marry him, I accepted. But in his father's eyes, he saw me, the marriage, as a misalliance."

Brian had been a relatively bright boy during his early school years. In college, he had maintained a 3.5 grade point average. He was a quick study and had found it imperative to make something out of his life. His ability, enthusiasm, and willingness to appropriate information was like a sponge soaking up water; he excelled in his chosen vocation. From stock boy to Chad Collier's right-hand man, his creativity and keen intelligence was what carried him rapidly through the ranks of Romanique Cosmetics. Through it all, he maintained a judicious cliché in the back of his mind, often repeated by his fourth-grade teacher; Mr. Carruthers. Although he couldn't recall the specific words, it was something to the effect of "The only stupid question was the one gone unasked."

And right now, he had no qualms in asking Brye. "What the hell is a misalliance?"

The sun ducked behind a volatile rain cloud. An eerie glow cast around the stalled couple. A shadow of pain eclipsed Brye's tanned features. Turning away from Brian, she focused on a band of artists displaying their sublime creativity. Her voice cracked with grief. "A marriage to a social inferior."

Brian almost fell flat on his face. "Shit!" he muttered, witnessing the calamity of emotions badgering Brye's composed dignity. Without thinking, instinct impelled him to pull Brye into his chest and cradle her within his arms. As he comforted her, his mind raced ceaselessly.

All the pieces fit: Daniel Collier's initial reaction when he learned of Brye's signed contract; the unpredictable behavior—manifesting itself in the past few month—afflicting Chad's solid-as-a-rock composure; the years of pain and suffering Brye had incarcerated into her own quintessence like a prisoner being held in solitary confinement.

Ironically, he recalled the conversation he held with Chad days before Brye signed with the company: Brian had wanted to take Brye into his arms, ease her pain while telling her he would take care of her. He understood now that it wasn't in the cards, nor was it his place. Those privileges had been reserved for Chad. But would Chad accept the honors?

"Why did he hire me, Brian?" Brye's words tumbled against his chest. "I still don't understand what he wants from me?"

"You don't know?" Brian continued to stroke her tensed backside as she pulled far enough away to catch his eye. Brian had assumed she'd been crying, but her eyes were dry as the pavement they walked on.

She shook her head vigorously, gypsy hair flying wildly in her eyes.

"He wants you, Brye. When you shuffle through all the anger and resentment, anyone with half a brain can see that he wants you." Brian confronted her with a steadfast guarantee. "He still loves you."

Brye digested the poignant words. If—and it was a very big if—Chad still loved her, he had forgotten how to show it. No, she didn't know what to believe any longer. Nor did she want to linger on the subject. Thoughts of Chad remained confusing as well as painful. Yet she was very much grateful for the amount of understanding Brian had presented toward her.

A thin smile touched grim lips. "You are proving to be a very invaluable friend, Brian. Thank you."

"Any time, lovely lady." He pulled away. Interlocking fingers, he pulled her along the final few steps remaining to reach his car. "I hate to do this, Brye, but it's time I got back to the office."

"Do you have to?" Brye moaned. Thoughts of Chad were immediately shoved aside. In its place, inspirations of keeping Brian out of the office the remainder of the day took precedence.

"Yes, I have to. I have a lot of work to do." Brian marveled at how fast she bounced back. He imagined it was all a front for his sake.

"I have a much better idea." The sun had miraculously popped out again, sharpening the glitter of mischievousness dancing in her eyes.

"Dare I ask?"

"Only if you agree to go along with it." She smiled. A glowing smile tinted her eyes a deeper shade of purple.

"When you look at me like that, how could I possible resist?" He opened the front passenger door. "Where're we going?"

"Trust me." Brye's body conformed to the soft leather seat. She said little else.

Brian maneuvered around the front of the car. Climbing into the driver's seat, he wondered, with a smile on his face, what he'd gotten himself into.

21

Jealousy polluted Chad's reasonably sane state of mind much like a malignant tumor running rampant amongst normal tissue cells. Spreading, devouring, consuming him alive, the destructive pathway left behind an embittered shell of a man.

Holed up in his office since eight, after a long, unsettled night, Chad stewed, growing more antagonistic with each passing minute. Ears cocked toward the open office door, his mind labored more on the sounds befalling the reception office rather than the drudgery staring at him from the top of his desk.

After spying Brye and Brian step onto the elevator yesterday afternoon, with growing agitation, he had obsessively waited for their return.

Up until six o'clock the prior evening, certain neither Brian nor Brye would be returning, he'd given up his vigilant watch, left the office, and seethed in the midst of a brewing storm.

Bitterness, comingled with rage, fermented most of his evening. His thoughts loitered on two cheating individuals. Where had they gone? Why hadn't Brian returned to the office? Were they still together?

After much deliberation, he had picked up the phone and called Brian at home. No answer. He dialed Brye's number. He got Brylinn. More specifically, Kirk. His words continued to lash out at Chad.

"She's in Atlantic City...won't be back until tomorrow...staying at Trump Plaza Hotel and Casino...do you want the number?"

Chad had instantly dialed the hotel and casino.

"No...Brye Grayson is not a registered guest," he'd been promptly, yet politely, notified. "Yes...Brian Paxton is registered, would you like me to connect you to his suite?" Minutes passed. The rings were long and drawn out. "I'm sorry, sir, there's no answer. Do you wish to leave a message?"

Chad did not wish.

By ten, and still no appearance of Brian, Chad summoned Rhonda.

"He'll be in early afternoon."

Several hours later, low voices invaded his office walls. Chad sat up straighter, ear tuned toward the outer office.

Brian had finally straggled into the office a little after one.

For the next two hours, Chad contemplated confronting him. But what could he say? And how could he say it without sounding like a jilted, insanely jealous lover—which is exactly what he was acting like?

Anger ripped at him like a knife gutting out his intestines. *How stupid can you be?* he raged. One fight, and she had immediately searched for bigger game. Played for a fool once too often, it was time to sever his ties…for good.

Deep down, however—and he could no more admit this to himself than he could admit that he'd lost all touch with reality—Chad feared that cutting Brye loose would be equivalent to cutting out his own heart.

The soft tinkle of her voice pierced the inner depths of his soul. The melancholy hum halted him in his rampant tracks.

Brye had finally arrived.

"How did you do it?" Seated in her swivel oak chair, Rhonda grinned conspiratorially at Brye. Gone was the frazzled confusion of the day before. Her circular desk was cleared of all but a few minor projects. Hair and makeup held up well under the normal wear and tear of an eight-hour workday. The atmosphere surrounding the reception area presented a more relaxed, welcoming ambiance. The inner office intercom played light, mellow tunes. Even the leaves of her potted spider plant, which had drooped under the heaviness of the office fanfare the day before, stretched taller, emerged greener, appeared contented. This was a huge difference from the prior afternoon.

"Not only were you able to get him away from the office"—Rhonda rolled her hand into a ball and tucked it under her chin—"but since he's been back, I haven't heard a peep out of him."

"I can be very persuasive when need be." Brye leaned closer into Rhonda's desk. Her fingertips rested lightly upon a manila folder.

"Persuasive, my ass," Rhonda jocularly quipped. "It's those remarkable...*assets* of yours. Any man would willingly follow you into the depths of hell for a chance to be close to those worldly goods."

Brye threw back her head and laughed. "Are you suggesting I purposely used my feminine wiles to lure Brian into my evil clutches?"

"Not purposely." Rhonda wore a wicked smile. "Unlike the Pied Piper—who used a flute to lure his unsuspecting subjects—all you have to do is strut your stuff, and the mindless creatures come scurrying out of the woodwork."

A shadow passed to the right of Brye. Rhonda's gaze chased after the slight distraction, Brye followed suit.

Chad. He stood, obstructing his office door, hands plunged deep into the pants' pocket of his teal-green, double-breasted suit. Other than his squared jawbone, his facial cast supplied no clue of his enraged state. The ventilation around them—which had shifted from pleasingly temperate to unmercifully stifling within the few seconds of Chad's appearance—said all to the chatting women.

"May I see you for a moment, Brye?"

It was not a request. Simply put, it was a demand.

Good luck, Rhonda mouthed.

In Chad's current frame of mind, I'm going to need it, Brye thought. Back straight, chin forward, head held high, the epitome of dignified splendor, Brye strolled into Chad's office.

"Hold my calls," Chad ordered. He shoved aside to admit Brye. The door firmly cut Brye off from any outside support.

This was Brye's first visit to Chad's office. Twice the size of Brian's, lavishly designed in an ultra-modern, ultra-sterile, and ultra-pretentious motif, it wasn't quite Chad's style, but it possessed all the necessities of life and then some. Up until now, she had been led to believe that Chad had never been one to flaunt his wealth.

"I inherited it from the last occupant," Chad confessed. Despite his anger, he could still read her thoughts. "At the time I took it over, I didn't think my stay here would be lengthy enough to bother with redecorating." He ordered her to take a seat, then wandered toward his bar. "Would you like something to drink?"

Brye did not respond. All evidence indicated that this would be no social call. It suited her to remain on guard. She continued standing, eyes remained fixed on him.

Her lack of reply compelled Chad to abandon the bar. Turning back toward the center of the room, he hitched his right hip on the arm of a chair. Undaunted by her silence, he coolly asked, "How was your evening?"

So he planned on toying with her. A full report from Kirk verified Chad's knowledge of her whereabouts the night before.

"Did you call me in here for a business meeting? Or is this a witch hunt?" she jabbed, arming herself for the fight.

Chad did not throw a sucker punch of his own. His was a direct blow to her heart.

"Are you fucking Brian now? Does he know he's dealing with a conniving, cold-hearted, money-grubbing bitch?"

The bitterness and anger Chad displayed toward Brye drove her back several steps. It also knocked the fight right out of her. Underneath the unfounded animosity, she unearthed pain. Pain indirectly caused by her, but principally engendered by his own father. For that reason alone, she would never tell him the truth behind their collapsed relationship. She had never known what it felt like to be raised by a loving family. And in Daniel Collier's unorthodox way, he loved and wanted what was best for Chad. She would not be the one to shatter the illusions of the man who had given him life.

Her cool, calm manner infuriated Chad even more. As long as he'd known Brye, she seemed to be able to effortlessly maintain a tight rein on her emotions. From the first moment he had laid eyes on her, she'd been the one in control of their destination; she had yanked the plug from underneath his happiness. Through jealous eyes, he saw it all as an elaborate scheme; an ongoing plot he had somehow ventured into once again. Well, it was time to leap off this rocky roller-coaster ride. It was time he took the reins back into his own hands and gain control of this three-ring circus. And in the process, he planned on possessing Brye—if not for a lifetime, then only for a few minutes.

"What I don't understand is why you targeted Brian." Chad interlocked his fingers, resting them on his upper thigh. His mannerism was that of a friend establishing the boundaries of a genial discussion. "Brian is a remarkable person, employee, and friend. I don't deny he's invaluable to the company. But for you, Brye, financially, he's not your usual mark." Chad smiled pleasantly. "Correct me if I'm wrong, but don't you go after men who can afford to give a million bucks away for one quick fuck? Brian, although he makes a damn good living, does not have that kind of money to toss aside."

Anger flashed from deep within and desperately desired to spill over into the golden office. Somehow, she managed to hold onto her wrath. "Can I go now?" she asked.

"You'll go when I say you can!" His expression had taken on a hard-edge glare.

Brye closed her eyes and ears against the vehemence resounding in his voice. Maybe had she fought back, she could have talked him through his anger. Had she forced him to recognize his preposterous allegations, they might have been able to put the past behind and begin afresh. If she had told him she loved him, he may have said he loved her back and then begged for her forgiveness. In the end, Brye remained quiet; she allowed his anger to run its course.

"Maybe you don't care about Brian at all," Chad sneered. "Is it possible you're using him to get to *me*...to make me jealous? Maybe, over the years, you have realized you could get more from me than a million dollars. Before, you went after the bronze. Now you're going for the gold." Chad intended to push her; he wanted to push. He wanted to witness her loss of control, just as he felt himself slipping further into despair. And what he was about to do, what he was going to say, would probably leave him with no passage to turn back on; Brye might never be able to get beyond his heartless performance.

Chad removed himself from the chair. He planted himself in Brye's face. They stood so close, Brye could feel his breath stroking her brow as he bent over her. "Your youth and beauty won't last forever, Brye. You're going to need a steady cash flow to keep Brylinn going." He leered down at her. "I'm willing to give you all you need. But you know what you have to do in return."

The gold and glitter of the room dimmed to a greenish-gray. The air grew deathly still, ominously quiet. They had landed inside the eye of the hurricane. Could the two catastrophic lovers ride out the duration of the storm with no permanent damage inflicted upon their shattered souls?

Brye reeled from Chad's callous proposal. Validating his pain, as well as knowing the root of its existence, did not make her any less impervious to his verbal beatings. And to suggest she would ever use him as a means to an ends was not only eminently disturbing, but it was something she might never be able to forgive Chad for.

The room caved in around her. It was time to throw in the towel. Brye twirled away from his reach, determined to get out of the room and put as much distance as she could between them. But before she accomplished that feat, Chad imprisoned her wrist within his wrenching grip. Roughly, he swung her around to face him.

"I said you can go when *I* say so!" Chad had not had one drink, nor had he ingested any drugs, yet he was brazenly drunk on his anger. He was flying defiantly high because of his jealousy; his deranged behavior was that of a man dangerously out of control.

Fronting each other, Brye and Chad openly glared. One was all inclusive of animosity, jealousy, and distrust; the other was an indiscriminate miscellany of emotions incorporating understanding, sadness, pain, and love.

Brye was the first to break the oppressive silence. Voice quivering, she asked, "Why are you doing this to me, Chad? What is it you want from me?"

"I want you, Brye!" Chad growled, authenticating Brian's words of the day before. His mouth came crashing down on hers. Pain and anger transmitted to Brye via his gluttonous kisses and the possessive manner in which his fingers roamed her body. His frontal attack was neither gentle, unhurried, nor full of loving caresses. This was an intentional, disarming approach. His mind ravaged with suspicion, Chad sought revenge as well as sole gratification. No concern for Brye's needs factored into this moment.

The crazed manner in which he stormed Brye both exhilarated and excited her. She was tired of fighting the urge to resist him. She was tired of denying herself his love. More than anything, she wanted this. She needed his strength. And if making love sealed their unity for life, the pain she endured her entire life would have been worth it.

Chad grew hard underneath his blinding assault. His body sought relief. From Brye.

Only she could release the yearning thirst he had harbored for her since the first day she'd come back into his life.

He was like a ticking time bomb threatening to explode; if Brye did not defuse him, he would erupt into thousands of unrecognizable pieces. Deliberately, persistently, pressingly, he urged Brye to her knees.

Anxious to reacquaint herself with his body, eager to reestablish an intimate relationship, lacking shyness or intimidation, Brye knelt before him. Fingers gifted and accommodating, she released Chad's hardened member from its inflicting constraints.

Stomach muscles dramatically constricted. The audible intake of breath dislodging from the back of Chad's throat encouraged Brye onward. Initially, her decisive fingers embraced him, stroked, teased, drove him toward a near frenzied state. When Brye felt the jolts of involuntary shudders ravage Chad's mind and body, she used her tongue to finish the job her fingers had started. Tasting him, nursing him as an infant suckled his mother's breast, Brye tormented him with pleasurable pain. Her tongue, hot, wet, anxious to satisfy, drove him further into her demanding mouth.

Unrestrained advances, each deliberate stroke, sped Chad's mind to a near-frenzied state of being. He found himself floating on a wave of undulated pleasure. Abruptly, the wave matured, developed into a turbulent surf, swelled, crested, and then hurled Chad into uncharted waters. A sea of exquisite ecstasy washed over him, submerged him, filled him with such intense satisfaction he wasn't certain he would survive the unparalleled experience. Several efficacious seconds later, Chad found himself rising to the surface, gasping for air.

Despite what had just transpired, before his vision returned to near normal, a hazy image of Brye pleasing Brian in the same fashion lit another fire underneath his smoldering wrath. Chad could not let that impassioned reflection go.

He had entangled her hair around his knotted fingers. Pulling away, his voice cold and mechanical, he numbly stated, "You have fulfilled your obligation. You may go now."

The abrupt manner in which he brushed her aside startled Brye. His intonation was stiff, remote, amazingly clear. Pushing herself to her feet, face heating to a beet-red, she glared incredulously at him.

His facial muscles reflected that of his frosty tone. It was then Brye understood. She had just been used in the worst possible way. Astounded with the dire revelation, she fell two steps backward. All the while, her eyes burned into his. *How could he do this to me?* she cried out in her head. *Not this! Anything but this! Does he hate me so badly he's willing to destroy me emotionally?*

"Don't look at me like that!" he snapped. There was no shame as he slid himself back into his pants. "Whatever happened between us in the past, whatever has happened in the last few weeks, it's over. We're even." He zipped up his pants. "As far as your contract is concerned, as long as your work remains satisfactory, it'll remain unchallenged."

Pain jabbed viciously at Brye's soul. She forced back a sob as she attempted to channel the hurt in accordance with her usual manner; she strove to shove it aside. Only she found it impossible to do.

Finding no other recourse, maliciously, she struck out at him.

"You mean it'll remain untouchable as long as I fuck the boss on the sidelines," she angrily hissed at him.

"Don't flatter yourself, Brye." Chad straightened his shirt as well as his tie. "Although you are definitely the best when it comes to giving head—"

A streak of lightning, Brye's hand whipped through the air seeking skin contact. She wasn't fast enough. Before the palm of her hand cracked against the side of his face, Chad's fingers snaked out and clamped over her wrist.

"Make no mistake, Brye. I don't give a shit about your contract or what you do with it! If you want to continue working for Romanique, fine. If you don't, I'll release you. Either way, I'm through with you." He roughly shoved her aside. "Now get the hell out of my office!"

Brye stumbled backward and almost tripped over a brass trash can. Righting herself, shying away from the indignities suffered by Chad's own hands, knees threatening to give out on her, she hurried toward the door. Halfway there, the ringing of an outer office phone infiltrated her fight or flight response. Her mind raced at four times its normal tempo. Suddenly, running away did not appeal to her as the appropriate answer. Her mind set, she chose to fight. She would not go out defeated—despite how much she wanted to run. He had just treated her like a two-bit hooker. If he wanted her out of his life, so be it. But it would end on her terms. Not his.

Her newly found aspirations lifted her sloped shoulders. Seconds later, a sudden sense of defilement nearly sent them drooping again. Determined to carry this to the bitter end, Brye took a steadying breath. She could do this, she told herself. After all—and for the first time in her life she found herself admitting—she was her mother's daughter.

"Chad?" Brye pivoted to face him, her rigid body framed by the marigold walls.

He met her with a steely gaze.

Brye wore a silk, body-slimming tank dress. The hem rode provocatively high above supple knees. As she kicked off her high-heeled pumps, her arms twisted behind her back. Reaching high, she unzipped her dress...slowly.

"When was the last time you made love to a real woman, Chad?" Seductively, she lowered the strap on one side of her dress. "When was the last time you touched real breasts?" She lowered the other strap and pushed her dress down toward her waist. Her upper half exposed a lacy, peach-colored bra.

It's working, she thought to herself. Chad stood mesmerized in anticipation of her every movement. Pure, unadulterated lust betrayed his underlining hostility.

"I'm talking about breasts that haven't been pumped up with silicon or saline or soybean or whatever the hell they're using these days." Unsnapping the front hooks, firm, perfectly symmetrical breast bounced out of their retainers. The satin bra slipped through her fingers and dropped in one soft pile at her feet. In response to the chilled air-conditioned room, pink protruding nipples pointed invitingly at Chad. Pleased to see him ogling her with the look of a man barely able to control himself, Brye shimmed her dress over her hip and tossed it across the arm of the leather sofa. Standing tall, she wore nothing but matching thongs barely covering the soft curls of her womanhood.

Chad's glands began to salivate like a doomed man in anticipation of his last supper. Perfect in every way that counted, she appeared before him, so delicate…so feminine…so artistic…all woman.

"When was the last time your hands ran over a woman's body that wasn't pinched, or tucked, or reshaped, or tainted, by another human's hands?"

She kicked her shoes out of the way and shimmied toward him. Eyes sealed with his, she unbuckled his belt and unzipped his pants. Slowly, seductively, she smoothed her hands along his backside, dragging his slacks down as she went. On her knees, she removed him of shoes, socks, slacks, and underwear.

Tantalized by her unexpected seduction, Chad could do nothing but follow where led. Dressed in nothing other than shirt and tie, he found himself being pulled down to the carpeted floor. Brye maneuvered his body to her own satisfaction; half supine, half sitting, Chad lay propped on his elbows.

Brye stood. She stepped far enough away for him to view her as she clipped her thumbs over her thongs and removed them. As planned, with the exception of pulling off his pants, she had not touched him to bring his arousal to its peak. And in its heightened state, it resembled a stalwart oak tree: tall, solid, majestic.

"Do you want me?" Brye questioned, lasciviousness dripping from her every word.

"Yes," he audibly croaked. Brye tossed her panties onto the beveled-glass table. Straddling his chest, she lowered to her knees. Brye's breasts, leaning inches into his face, drew his immediate attention. His tongue snaked out to capture one jutting nipple.

Anticipating his actions, Brye pulled away. "Do you want me more than what's her name?" From this moment forth, she refused to utter that woman's name across her lips.

Forgetting his jealousy, unable to call to mind why he'd been so angry, not remembering or caring about "what's her name," Chad truthfully answered, "I have never wanted anyone as much as I've desired you…ever."

Satisfied he spoke the truth, Brye stationed herself above Chad's groin. Knees bent and pressing into the soft carpet, she lowered herself over Chad's throbbing crux of desire. Head lowered, her eyes followed their joining as one. With deliberate slowness, she pushed herself downward. Spellbound, Brye and Chad watched as he disappeared inside the folds of her womanhood. He trembled as her warm moistness, the binding muscles, the sweet remembrance of her body enfolded him. And as he filled her with his masculine virility, Brye was barely able to control her desirous need to have him…totally. It had been so long, much too long, since she'd been with Chad in this way. She wanted him so very much. It took every ounce of will power to slow her racing actions. The way the relationship stood between the two of them, this may be her one and only chance to make love to him. Not only did she want to savor the moment, but she wanted Chad to commemorate on this day for the rest of his life. She wanted him to remember what he was turning his back on. Lost in the thought, Brye moved feverishly against him.

"Oh God, baby!" Chad moaned. His body melted into liquid fire. The high intensity of heat inflamed mind and soul. This is what he desired for far too many years. This is what he missed. Brye. His Brye. And the staggering influx of sensations she incited within him as she molded herself around him. The muscles in his buttocks constricted as his lower body rose from the floor. Pushing the length of himself deeper inside her eager body, he strained for everything she had to offer.

"Don't move," Brye immediately demanded. "Just lie still. Let me make love to you."

All movement instantaneously came to a halt. Anxiously, Chad waited. Utilizing her pelvic muscles, firing a steady barrage of contracting and releasing motions, Brye massaged him with her palpitating insides. But as she did so, she found herself climbing toward a higher plain. Her mind and body faltered under her premeditated actions. She could not fight the incredible flow of titillation seizing control of her total being. Wheels in motion, no matter how hard she tried, she could not slow her thundering heartbeat or the desperate urgency to end her self-ordained abstinence. Not able to maintain her tight rein, she rocked recklessly against Chad.

Underneath her frantic undulations, she could feel Chad straining against her. She knew then he was also fighting to gain some resemblance of control. Brye refused to allow him to achieve command of his own faculties.

She reached behind her body and dragged purposeful fingers along his inner thighs. Deliberately stroking him with a tender touch, she whispered honeyed attestation guaranteed to drive a man insane with desire.

And it did.

Where Brye was concerned, when it came to their lovemaking, all constraints were usually forfeited. And just like then, he could not hold on to one ounce of self-control.

Chad homed in on the thin layer of sweat beads teasing Brye's upper lip. He watched as the tip of her tongue peeked out at him, then grazed her lip, licking away the moisture. The provocative sight propelled his desire to greater heights. His eyes then dropped to firm, taunting breasts. Breasts which danced in tune to the oscillations of her body. The captivating vision sent his senses soaring through the ceiling. But it was only when her fingers played along the interior of his upper thighs—when she whispered how much she welcomed making love to him, how good she felt with him inside her—that the powerful explosion ripped body and mind apart. Five minutes before, Chad had believed he had experienced the orgasm of a lifetime. But nothing had prepared him for the high-voltage shock wave rippling through his system, followed by the series of potent aftershocks rendering him mindless.

As Chad bucked tenaciously against Brye, the boisterous shockwave passed through Chad and jarred Brye's awareness of all else except her mind spiraling outward. The times she and Chad had made love those many years ago had been countless. Yet nothing could compare to the overwhelming, fulfilling influx of emotions seeping into her every pore. As the tremors overcame her body, she bit her lip to keep from screaming. This was a bittersweet moment for her.

Several spellbound seconds later, Brye steadied herself. Inhaling a rich, recovering breath, she was up and dressed before Chad secured an inkling of her veiled movements.

Fully dressed—with the exception of her panties—steadfast and cocksure, Brye strolled over to Chad. She bent at the knee, her shoulder grazing the edge of his desk. She looked down into his flushed face. Undisciplined guilt savagely bit into her mind for the avenue she had been forced to take. She had just broken her own Cardinal rule: she'd slept with another woman's man; a man who had not pledged his undying love to her.

But he had bequeathed his love to her. He'd asked her to marry him…six years prior. In spite of everything that had taken place between them, Brye could not let go of his promised affirmations.

She waited for Chad's breathing to subside and his eyes to open.

When his baby blues finally came into focus, they did so with so much love, so much compassion, it threw Brye off balance. And after the phenomenal moment they had just shared, Chad was ready to forgive her anything.

"Brye, we need to talk." Pulling himself into a sitting position, he reached out to her.

She shot to her feet and backed out of his range, afraid of the influence his touch would generate. Today he had hurt her terribly. She could forgive but not easily forget. The lines in her face hardened as she glared at Chad.

"Earlier," she reported, "you told me to get out because you were through with me…for good." She smiled the most angelic of smiles. "Well, Chad, I *am* through with you." Her smile turned upside down. "I will carry through with the tour as planned. During that time, I'll consider my options in quitting Romanique Cosmetics. As soon as I'm back, I'll inform Brian of my decision."

Brye stepped closer. "Since you have chosen to treat me like a prostitute, let's make it perfectly clear; I have just given you a freebie." She dropped her panties onto his lap. His member, once firm and unbending, lay flaccid against a solid thigh. Evidence of their lovemaking, glistening against the afternoon light, left a mocking trail of dankness along his tanned skin.

"Keep the change." Brye swirled on her heels, then floundered out.

In front of his office door, Brye faltered. Her heart pounded recklessly against inflexible ribs. Chad had been deliberately cruel to her. In turn, she viciously retaliated. For the first time in her life, she used her body to prove a point. But it was nothing to be proud of. A heaviness settled over her heart. Never had she felt more sickened with herself than at this very moment.

Grateful Rhonda was not at her desk, Brye stumbled into the elevator and out to her car. The drive home proved to be excruciatingly painful.

In the spirit of doing what she did best, Brye attempted to thrust the last half-hour back into that remotest part of her brain; that part of her brain she used to store and lock all events threatening to cause irreparable damage to her mental harmony.

Most likely, and highly probable, she would not be able to push those crucial last moments out of her consciousness because she didn't want to. Despite the outcome, their lovemaking had been nothing less than extraordinary. Even now, her body continued to bask in the aftermath. And although she left Chad fuming in his office, in truth, he remained with her on her ride home. For Brye could still taste Chad, she could smell him all over her body, she felt him moving urgently inside her. And the evidence of their lovemaking, his thick seepage trickling down her legs, was testament to the joining of souls with a man she loved more than life itself.

Within her mind, Brye began to feel the presence of another entity.

You're a fool, darling daughter. Even now. After the way he treated you, after the way he spoke to you, you're ready to forgive him. He's ripping your soul into shreds, and you haven't got the guts to stop him.

Don't even start with me, Mother! Whatever you say, whatever you might believe, Chad made love to me out of anger and jealousy. Yet despite it all, he still wanted me. And regardless of what he said, he still cares for me. I allowed it because I love him. I'll always love him. And he loves me. Brye sighed in certainty.

Of course he loves you, dearest daughter of mine, her mother assured. They all do when in the midst of fucking.

The low hum buzzed around Brye's head like a lonely mosquito swarming around a campfire. Leave me alone, Mother.

Gradually, as Brye struggled for control, the murky presence of her mother receded into the background.

The remainder of the drive home went undistributed, with Brye replaying her and Chad's explosive copulation.

There was something deeply profound in the volatile manner in which their bodies had communicated; their destinies had been interwoven into one. If Chad could get beyond the wall of anger and pain, he *would* recognize the sealing of their destiny. If he couldn't rise above the anger, she promised herself to uphold their affirmation to stay away from each other.

In the meantime, she continued to cling to hope.

Emotionally and visibly shaken, despite the cool interior of his surroundings, sweat poured from Chad's tunneled brow. Ego bruised, speechless, his anger sizzled as Brye stalked from his private office. His emotions were scorched with what? Fear? Anger? Frustration? Love? Less than a few seconds prior to her exit, he had contemplated forgiveness.

Dressing in a flurry of bitterness and madness, Chad's mind reached outward, searching for some form of punishment for Brye.

Amply clothed, he swung around and faced his desk. His eyes dropped to the floor. A vivid image of their love making spread before him like an eagle taking flight. A contemptuous voice crucified him for his senseless actions.

Now look what you've done. You drove her away. And she walked out with your heart in her hands.

"Shut up! You don't know what the hell you're talking about!"

You're lost without her. You were a goner before she reentered your life, and you're a goner without her now. Go after her, man, or you'll never recover.

"I don't need her in my life."

Oh well. It may be for the best anyway. She'll probably never speak to you again. I mean…whatever abuse she suffered as a child, it had to have been a walk in the park compared to what you just did to her.

"How do you know she was ever abused? Her act was no doubt contrived. She's a con artist. It was all part of a master scheme to gain my sympathies…and my money."

Some things can't be faked, Chad. Her terror, her pain, her sadness—it's not bogus.

"She's a good actress."

Did she fake the torment she suffered on the night you woke her from her nightmare? Was the alacrity of her heartbeat pounding erratically against your chest a sham?

"How do you know that was her heartbeat? It could have been mine beating tumultuously against her breasts."

Exactly! You love her.

"Shut up!"

She holds your life in her hands and you're too stupid, too blind, too stubborn to admit it.

"I said shut the fuck up!"

In a burst of rage, Chad whisked his arms over the top of his desk. An array of paperwork—folders, contracts, and other mindless drudgery—spilled to the floor, sweeping away the graphic vision of him and Brye making love. The deafening outburst erupted into the peaceful quintessence of the outer office.

In the reception area, Brian apprised Rhonda on the proposed date and time of the upcoming mid-month department head's meeting. Proficiently, she pledged to have the interoffice memo typed and distributed by the end of business hours. As she made a notation on her scratch pad, a deafening cacophony, coming from Chad's office, shattered the working pair's organizational deliberations.

Both Brian and Rhonda burst into Chad's private office. Both were stunned at the chaos staring back at them.

Earlier, while chatting with Brye, Rhonda had gained a sense of Chad's cloudy mood. Until now, she had no inkling that a storm had actually been brewing. But looking down at the mess covering his office floor, she realized that the storm had ruptured into a full-fledged microburst—and she and Brian could easily drown from the tumultuous tsunami Chad rained down upon them.

Not uttering a vowel, giving Chad a wide berth, Rhonda moved to the fallen mess. She stooped and began picking up the clutter.

"Leave it!" Chad barked.

"It's okay. I don't—"

"Dammit, Rhonda, I said leave it!" He jammed his fingers through his hair. His hands then rested on the back of his neck. "I created this mess. I can clean it up." His eyes passed fleetingly over Brian. "If you two will excuse me..."

Turning a questioning eye toward Chad, Brian asked, "Is everything all right?"

"Everything's fine." Chad blew over to the door and opened it.

Baffled, yet unable to find the words, Rhonda was the first to step out.

Brian, unable to step away without showing concern, paused before exiting. "If you feel like talking, you can come to me... anytime."

"I'll take it under advisement." Chad had to halt himself from slamming the door in Brian's face. Inhaling deeply, he quietly closed it to their prying stares.

"What's going on?" Rhonda whispered as if Chad's ear was glued to the other side of his office door.

Brian shrugged. "I don't have the foggiest."

"I could tell he wasn't himself when he asked to speak to Brye."

Brian's eyes widened in understanding. "Brye was in today? When was that?"

"About forty minutes ago. You didn't see her?" Rhonda asked in surprise. "She came in to see you."

"No…no, I didn't see her." That disclosure grounded Brian to an alarming halt. Understanding that Brye was the catalyst behind Chad's thunderous behavior, he headed to his office. Bent on contacting her, he needed to know how well she faired in the damaging aftermath.

Behind closed door, Chad sat slumped in his executive chair. The phone lay at his fingertips. Unconscious of his actions, his fingers tapped a steady beat on top of the headset. Coming to an instant decision, he punched a number into the base. It was time to eradicate Brye from his mind, his life, forever.

Later that evening, after a quiet, romantic dinner at Le Bernardin, an elegant seafood establishment, Chad proposed marriage to Jennifer. Her exuberance could not be contained had she bottled it and stuck a cork in the top. Anyone hoping to catch a glance at the enthralled socialite had to stare upward. She was flying so high her head threatened to collide with the checkered ceilings. After her acceptance, they lingered over a bottle of Dom Perignon while planning their future. As the evening dragged forward, and Jennifer chattered endlessly, Chad tilted his champagne glass and stared inside; the chalice was off-kilter and empty, much the same as his life.

News of the impending marriage between one of the most eligible bachelors and the beautiful socialite ran rampant the following morning. Sources were dug out from underneath rocks, favors were called on the carpet, all for the privilege of uncovering exclusive information on the prominent couple. All major news stations, radio stations, tabloid news shows, and talk shows scrambled for personal interviews—all for the sake of higher ratings.

Through it all, Brye readied herself for the promotional tour: there was so much to arrange with little time to arrange it. And later, her kids were giving her a good luck/going away party. Much too busy, she neither watched television or listened to the radio, nor was she tied to social media or Instagram. All through the day, she managed to remain oblivious to the most talked about current affair—at least until her front doorbell interrupted her frenzied state of affairs.

"Brian!" Brye leaned into him. She pecked him on the curve of his mouth. "What a nice surprise. I wasn't expecting you." Grabbing him by the arm, she pulled him past the foyer and into the living room. Waving him into a chair, she asked, "Did you come to wish me well? Or is there some last many changes—" Brye trailed off. She took note of Brian's tense stance and his forlorn appearance. Her smile froze. Something was wrong. "What is it?" she managed to stutter.

"You haven't heard?"

Her legs grew weak. In nervous anticipation, a tingling began at the tips of her finger. "What is it?" she repeated more forcibly.

"I'm sorry to be the one to tell you this." He took a step closer.

The unfavorable prickle migrated along Brye's arm, traveled inward, and raced toward her heart. The walls spun crazily around her. "Just tell me…please!" The last word ended on an agonized whisper.

"Chad announced his engagement to Jennifer." He took another step closer. "It's been all over the news media." Another step. "I thought you might have heard by now, so I came to see how you were holding up." He reached Brye just in time to catch her before she hit the floor.

The last thing Brye remembered before passing out was the acrimonious sound of her mother's inflated laughter.

22

TWO WEEKS. ON THE road for fourteen days, and Brye trudged in and out of cities, in and out of department stores, in and out of photo shoots, makeup, designer's clothing, and the bus. The keynote speaker in several women's groups, functions, high school assembles, and abuse centers, the supermodel never asked; she merely followed where led.

She, along with her entourage, practically lived on the luxury liner.

Some days were more hectic than others. Early morning, they would roll into a city just in time for her to speak at an important breakfast function. Afterward, she would make personal appearances at major department stores. Afternoons, she would reload the bus, steering toward another department store, in another city, in time for an evening appearance. Nights were usually spent on the road, and Brye had become extremely efficient in taking five-minute showers or quick sponge baths. There was no time for herself. There was no time to think. Yet it was all a blessing in disguise. She had no time to dwell on the impending marriage of Chad. Tonight would be different, however. It was her first evening off since embarking upon the promotional tour.

A one day layover in Kansas City, Missouri, registered at the InterContinental on the County Club Plaza, her suite was luxuriously equipped with two bathrooms, a large bedroom separated from the main sitting room by French doors, two televisions, phones throughout the suit, a well-stocked refrigerator, and an astounding view of the plaza.

Brye would celebrate her night off by taking a long, soothing, hot bubble bath. Afterward, she would call the twins, then Marcus; the only downside of the tour being she missed them all terribly.

Drawing her bath, she poured a capful of Mystique bath gel under the force of the running tap. The unique fragrance promptly filled her senses as well as permeated throughout the spacious bathroom.

Barefooted, she padded back into the main room. With remote control in hand, she flicked through channels until she stumbled across her latest commercial.

A smile took flight as she sat down to watch—

A department store shopper—male, tall, handsome—indecisively mulled over purchasing either a double-breasted blue stripe suit or a single-breasted gray stripe.

"Definitely the blue stripe."

A voice—soft, sexy, confident—sailed delicately over his shoulder. He turned to see a captivating woman looking over his choices.

"Are you sure?" he asked, pulling the double-breasted suit closer into his chest.

"Positive." The breathtaking woman rendered him a heart-stopping smile. "With this shirt and tie"—she presented him with a light blue French-cuffed shirt, and a silk Jacquard weave tie—"you will be the best dressed man at your dinner party."

He looked surprised. "How did you know I was invited to a dinner party?"

She merely graced him with an elusive smile. "How about this gold tie chain? Every man should own at least one."

He laughed. "Anything else?"

After she rung up his purchases, he turned and walked away. Abruptly altering his direction, he walked back to the register. She hadn't been wearing an identification badge, and he wanted to get her name, maybe ask her out for a cappuccino.

Nowhere in sight, confused, he walked around in a circle.

"Excuse me?" He stopped a wandering salesman. "I'm looking for the woman who sold me these purchases. Could you get her for me?"

The clerk's brow crinkled in bewilderment. "I'm the only sales associate in this department, sir. I have no idea who you're talking about."

"There was a woman…a beautiful woman…she rang up my purchases."

"She couldn't have, sir. I'm the only one authorized to use the register."

The baffled man began digging around in his shopping bag. "I have the receipt here."

Along with the sale's receipt, he pulled out an engraved card smelling richly of a fascinating fragrance. It read:

> MYSTIQUE: ALL MEN CRAVE A LITTLE INTRIGUE IN THEIR LIFE. ALL WOMEN DESIRE TO BESTOW IT UPON THEM…

Pleased with the final outcome of the commercial, Brye dashed into the bathroom grinning from ear to ear. She shut down the water faucet.

Two other commercials ensued. One was scheduled to be shot the following morning on the terrace of a plaza cafe.

The unknown woman would be eating lunch. The male customer from the department store enters with a party of three. He spots the intriguing woman watching him, but by the time he can break away from his small gathering, she's disappeared. Again, a fragrant card will be left by her place setting: "MYSTIQUE: ALL WOMEN DESERVE A FEW WELL-KEPT SECRETS OF HER OWN."

The third commercial had not been written yet. But it would fall in line with its predecessors.

The telephone rang just as Brye began to strip down to nothing.

"Hello?"

"Brye. It's Kierra. I'm calling to see if you'd like to go out with the gang. We're going to get some barbeque…maybe take in a few sights…listen to some jazz."

Kierra, Brye's personal assistant, was instrumental in sustaining a trouble-free tour. She handled all arrangements, upheld the hectic schedule, thwarted all crisis, and remained the unflagging link between Brian and herself. Day in and day out, she worked tirelessly by Brye's side. If anyone warranted a few hours off for some much-needed rest and relaxation, it was Kierra.

"Thanks for inviting me, Kierra. But I already have a date—with a hot tub, a telephone, and a king-size bed. Maybe next time."

Kierra bid her a quiet, restful night. "I'll see you at five," she pledged. The line went dead.

Brye eased her weary body into the bubbly, fragrant bathwater. A loofah sponge accommodating a generous portion of Mystique body gel worked wonders for her tension. Within minutes, her skin felt revitalized; it tingled with newly found effervescence. Her muscles lost their strained tightness. The pressures of the past two weeks evaporated into the steamy atmosphere. The constant churning in her mind eased and became one with the gentle ripples in her bathwater. Her eyelids grew heavy. Soon her level of consciousness dropped to a semiconscious state. As it did, she felt herself floating on a downy layer of protective clouds. All her problems dallied behind.

Funny, she pondered, as she transported toward a transcendental phase, *I'm drifting backward. Why am I drifting backward?*

Seconds later, her consciousness existed no more; her subconscious remained the prevailing force, drawing her back into time. Mercifully, she did not think ugly thoughts. Instead, she remembered a time met with sweet gratification.

Hands tightly clamped over her ears, Brye attempted to block out the exaggerated moans of pleasure coming from the next room—her mother's and father's bedroom. But it was her mother entertaining some "client" twice her age who commandeered Brye's attention.

Disgusted, Brye slid her stereo headphones over her ears. She tuned into a radio station playing music from the '80s and '90s and set the volume to blaring.

Ritually, her mother, or father, or both, invited "guests" home. For hard, cold cash, they performed whatever sexual acts fit their fancy. Her mother and father were beautiful, charismatic people. They were skillful at their "chosen" profession, they were rich because of it, and they only catered to an elite clientele.

Brye figured they were "loud" with their screwing—Brye could never call what they did lovemaking since it was merely sex for hire—because they hoped to draw her into the "family business." Her mother maintained that Brye was bred from the same seed, which meant she had the same commanding sex drive; which meant she should be following in their footsteps; which meant the ungodly noise they created should stir something within her; something that would beguile Brye into joining them. It was all so conspicuously contrived…all so transparently convoluted.

Strangely enough, tonight, the erotic sounds procured a dynamic effect on Brye. Usually, as soon as their coupling began, Brye would either leave the room and go into another part of the large apartment, get out of the apartment altogether, or she would immediately throw her headset on. Tonight, she'd been slow in her response time. Ashamed at the slowness of her reaction, she continued to listen and grew flushed—overheated would probably be a better description. By the time she turned away from the indecent display of infidelity, Brye's own sexual desires had augmented to unbearable dimensions.

A five-by-seven-inch oak-framed picture of Chad smiling that alluring smile of his was stationed on Brye's bedside table. She caressed his glossy photo with a tender eye. A stirring of love and desire warmed her chilled soul.

Her mother was right about one thing: Brye did have a gluttonous appetite for sex. But it was nothing genetically acquired. Her overzealous libido was a direct cause of her relationship with Chad.

No other man now or in the future would ever instill the all-inclusive devotion she fostered for the love of her life. Before Chad, Brye didn't believe she would ever be able to trust a man—let alone make love to one. But here she was, unable to keep her hands off the object of her true desire.

But it was more than just a sex thing. Brye was insanely, unequivocally in love with Chad. And as far as she was concerned, the "ultimate" act was meant to be shared between two people who loved each other dearly; sex was not, particularly in this day and age, meant to be a casual sport.

Sadly enough, her parents obviously held no awareness of the true meaning of love. Because if they had, they wouldn't have embarked upon the life they now led.

Brye picked Chad's picture off her night stand. She hugged it close to her chest. He'd been in Europe, assisting his father with a business deal for the past week. She missed him terribly. She had not met his parents as of yet, and Chad had invited her along for that very reason. But out of respect for his parents, she had declined—since the trip was strictly business, Brye didn't want to distract him, nor did she want to obstruct his creative juices in any way.

Brye stared at the red illuminated numbers on her bedside clock. Midnight. Chad's plane should have gotten in at nine. He should be back in his own bed by now. They had made arrangements to meet the following day for lunch. Brye decided she couldn't wait any longer.

Not giving herself time to change her mind, she threw on her clothing, left the apartment, and twenty minutes later found herself standing at the door of Chad's Manhattan loft.

Several months earlier, Chad had given her a key. This was the first time she actually used it.

Brye opened the door to a room sweeping with obscure shadows. Despite the remote atmosphere, Chad was here. His inspiring presence warmed the very skin on her body and touched the very core of her soul.

Stealthily, she moved across the darkened room. Piece by piece, she removed her clothing, leaving a trail of soft piles behind.

By the time she hit the bedroom door, her fervid body called out to her lover.

Sound asleep, Chad was oblivious to her night visit. Silently, Brye stole toward the bed. Slowly, she slid the cotton sheet down his naked body. Her eyes immediately drifted down to the rigid member encompassed in a feathery bed of dark locks. If Brye hadn't known better, she would have believed he'd been waiting for her.

Moist with anticipation, her heart pounded enthusiastically as she guided him into her pulsating entrance. Bodies joined, elbows locked, hands flattened on each side of Chad's head, Brye's breasts hovered just above his tranquil features. Eyes trained on Chad, she moved fervently against him. Inebriated with the feel of him swelling deep inside her, she could not restrain herself any longer. Her movements grew frenzied.

Chad's eyelids flew open as Brye began her ascent into the heavens.

"Jesus, Brye!" His voice caught in the back of his throat. "I thought…" A rush of pleasure bulldozed his aroused body.

"I can't…" He stiffened, attempting to slow his tempestuous transit.

"Don't," Brye moaned, her unbridled actions dictated by mindless desire. "Don't…stop…please…"

"I'm…losin' it…"

"Chaaaad?"

"I'm…sorry. I can't…control…" Grabbing her buttocks, Chad stabbed deeper inside her wet tightness. A strangled cry rose from the depths of his throat as he spilled his juices inside her. His body bucked uncontrollably.

It was good. It was sooooo good.

"Oh…Chad!" Grabbing a section of the fitted sheet on each side of Chad's enraptured facial appearance, Brye's hands spasmodically clenched into tight fists. Her body writhed recklessly against his. God, but it was oh so good.

Several unconstrained moments later, Brye collapsed onto Chad's heaving chest. With the exception of strained breathing, the room fell silent.

This should have been the happiest time of Chad's life. With marriage plans in the works, he should have been the epitome of joy and happiness. His parents praised his decision, Jennifer walked on air, yet Chad looked at his upcoming walk down the aisle with as much excitement as a man sitting on death row.

Weddings plans were the last thing on Chad's mind. When his bride-to-be asked for his advice, he conveniently bestowed upon Jennifer and her parents, free rein to proceed in any way they saw fit.

In all actuality, not contemplating the wedding freed Chad's mind. Since his last bittersweet exchange with Brye, all he seemed to do, all he was capable of doing, was meditate over their hazardous situation. Getting engaged to Jennifer, so he thought, meant Brye would become inaccessible to him. It had not worked out as expected.

Forbidden fruit.

He looked at Brye as someone he could not acquire. But *that* troubling reality elevated his urgency to claim her for himself once again. For two weeks, all he had done was live and breathe Brye Grayson. He still wanted her. He was willing to go to any lengths to have her…even if only for a few hours.

The flight attendant's voice, booming through the cabin of the 747, sliced into his snarled reverie. "Ladies and gentlemen, the captain will soon be making his approach to MCI Airport. A flight attendant will soon be around to collect all discarded items. Please make certain all tray table and seat backs are in their upright and locked position."

Chad peered out the window of his first class seat. In the waning light, miles of emerald green pastures garnished with distant farmhouses reached upward and snatched the plane right out of the pale sky. As the jet approached its landing, Chad's mind continued to dwell on the woman he could no longer pretend he hated. Bits and pieces of the flight attendant's parlance bit into his driven thought patterns.

"We welcome you to Kansas City… On behalf of the captain, crew, and myself, we'd like to thank you for choosing our carrier… If we could be of further assistance, please… We hope your stay is a safe and…"

Soon, Brye. Chad unbuckled his seat belt as the plane eased down the stretched tarmac. *I'll be there soon.*

This was a spur of the moment trip, a clandestine rendezvous. It had not been planned. Nor had he informed anyone of his New York departure—including Brye. In no way did he expect her to be receptive to his sudden appearance, particularly after the harsh way they ended their relationship. But Chad had encountered this overwhelming need to see her, be with her, make love to her. And he planned to do just that before his chartered 5:00 a.m. flight back to La Guardia.

Brye awakened with a start. The bathwater had grown cool to the touch. Mind hazy, eyes blinked in rapid succession as they rolled over the quiet room. Something had awakened her. Her mind attempted to digest what that something had been.

The sound, more distinct, came at her again, a not-so-lightly rapping on her suite door. Brye scrambled out of the tub. Body dripping wet, she wrapped herself in a white posh robe the hotel furnished for its guest. She flew out the bathroom, wet feet leaving a scent of water behind.

"Just a minute," she called to the persistent tapping. At the door, she stopped to peer through the small security peephole. Distorted yet very much recognizable, Chad occupied the wide-angle image. Astounded at the unexpected sight, her heart fluttered. Her hand flew to her chest in an attempt to stay the uncontrollable quiver. Bracing herself, she disengaged locks and swung the door open.

No words were spoken. Their eyes engaged and sealed. Chad took in her clean, fresh appearance, the surprised look pouring from her eyes, and the caution in her dazed expression. A trace of Mystique exuded from her wet skin. He'd pulled her out of her bath. And she looked too damned desirable to ignore.

Brye deciphered the carnality rising in Chad's mannerism and instantly knew why he'd come. She should have minded. She should have turned tail and ran. She should have told him to get the hell out of her suite and never come back. But she didn't. She couldn't. The sad truth was that she wanted him just as much as he wanted her. Prepared to do anything to accommodate his visit, all that mattered was that he had come to her. Tomorrow would come soon enough for self-recriminations. Now she had tonight.

Brye backed deeper into the room. Her eyes remained fixed on Chad. The only lighting in the room came from the television set. Audience laughter spilled from the color tube as a whimsical sitcom rolled across the screen.

Chad followed Brye into the small foyer. But not before exhibiting the "Do Not Disturb" sign on the outside of the door. He reengaged locks. A bathroom lay to Chad's left. His eyes ducked inside the darkened chamber for a split second before finally fronting Brye. Silently, she loosened her belt. The material felt cottony soft as it slid down her moist body. The robe surrounded her feet in a fluffy pile of luxurious splendor—his angel stood in layers of velveteen clouds.

His body ached with a burning urgency. His overnight bag slipped from his fingers. Without prelude, he rushed into her waiting arms.

The first kiss, and the subsequent others, intoxicated Chad's senses. "Oh God!" he groaned into her neck as her fingers danced along his chest, shoulders and backside. Inhaling her damp skin, the feel of her body responding to his, incited his groveling hormones. Anxious to remove his clothing, he urgently pulled at his tie.

"No." Brye covered his frenzied fingers with her own. "Let me undress you." Tenacious fingers slowly guided over the front of his pants as she unbuttoned and tugged on his zipper. Brye floated to her knees, hauling his pants along with her. Removed of shoes, socks, and trousers, she deliberately tormented his flesh by guiding her tongue along his inner thigh. Drawing him into her mouth, she lingered a few minutes longer before rising to her feet. Inch by inch, she undid the buttons on his tailored shirt. Eagerly, she planted debilitating kisses along his exposed skin. And as she lowered the material over his brawny shoulders, Brye captured his mouth. In an abandoned entanglement of desire, her tongue dove in and out as his garments shared company with Brye's fallen robe.

Unable to deny himself any longer, Chad lifted Brye into his arms. With little effort, he found his way to the bedroom. Together they tumbled onto the bed.

Sweet remembrance.

Too well, Brye and Chad honored the other with methodical precision; they played each other like a cherished musical instrument. In lyrical fashion, two bodies communicated in sweet melody. As Chad plunged into Brye, they moved to a rhythm, pleasing to the senses as well as the soul.

Their lovemaking emulated a tender rhapsody, a sonata—a composition of music performed by one or two instruments performed in three or four separate sections.

In quick succession, the overture advanced lazily, caressingly, erotically stirring all thought and reasoning. It soon rose to a crescendo, toward a higher intensity, as drums pounded in an untamed inflection of pleasure. Climaxing to a consuming fanfare of brass horns, the symphonic arpeggio concluded into a cadence of harmonic pulsations.

A command performance. Shakily, they held each other. Moments later, the music began again as insatiable bodies requested an encore.

The intemperate night progressed quickly. In his desire to make love to Brye in every conceivable way possible, sleep was not sought nor was it required.

Nonstop, they made passionate love for hours. Bodies bathed in sweat, bed linens soaked with the fruits of their labor, the scent of lovemaking moistened the air.

Lying prone, legs spread apart, Brye shoved her head into her pillow to stifle screams of blessed fulfillment. Above her, Chad's fingers, his tongue, played magically over her languid body. He probed, stroked, taunted, searched for, exposed, and then penetrated her most sensitive body areas. He was like a dogged man on a treasure hunt. Upon completion, every inch of Brye's body endured total exploration, all treasures thoroughly uncovered.

An onslaught of blinding lights stormed the inside of Brye's head. Unbridled spasms torpedoed her body, turning her flesh into galvanized tissue.

Spent, Brye had lost count of the many orgasms Chad had incited within her. Yet she knew she had reached her limit; she was too weak to go any further.

As Chad slid his tongue along her backside, Brye moaned in protest. "I can't, Chad. Please…no more."

Ignoring her quivering pleas, with stalwart knees, Chad prodded her shaky legs apart. Stretching outward, he lowered himself on top of her debilitated torso.

His strained breathing fondled the interior of her ear. The rise and fall of his chest tickled her backside. His fingers reached above Brye's head, interlocking with her fingers. His groin, slick with the fluid of their lovemaking, slid smoothly into Brye. A perfect fit, their bodies melded into one.

The decision to take her from behind stemmed from a possessive need to own her body, mind, and soul. Maybe that was the very reason he had agreed to marry Jennifer: with little effort on his part, his current fiancé would willfully walk through fire to reach their marriage alter.

A diehard urgency propelled Chad to obtain the same devotion from Brye. And because he could not procure what he so badly coveted, he spent a great deal of his time imagining he hated the woman centered atop the axis of his own inadequacies.

But when he entered Brye, every time he filled her with his love, she possessed him. She had a way of encircling him with her strength and spirit. She grabbed hold and pulled him deeper inside, swallowing him whole, taking everything he had, then giving it back tenfold. And once it was all said and done, it still wasn't enough. For Chad could not get enough. In the end, greedily, he sought more.

This time, as Chad made love to her, there was no tenderness in his touch. Fast and furiously, he hammered into her backside. Mere seconds earlier, Brye believed she had nothing left to give. Yet Chad was quick to induce an avid response. She hitched her hips higher, offering more of herself.

"Sweet Jesus!" Chad groaned in her ear as undulated ecstasy charged through him. "Come with me, baby. Don't let me take this trip alone."

"Chad?" Brye whimpered into her pillow. Her mind began an intense spiraling outward. Seconds afterward, her body followed.

Chad plunged deeper as her insides collapsed around him. Swept away on a magic carpet with Brye navigating at the helm, the carpet rose, ascending higher…and higher…and higher… Together they soared over the universe, steering in the direct pathway of a turbulent blast of wind. Vacillating dangerously for several intense seconds, climatically, they reached their zenith.

At long last, the carpet tipped. Plummeting back to earth, Brye and Chad became lost within the sounds of silken gratification.

"Don't move," Brye pleaded as Chad labored to roll away.

"I'm too heavy to remain on your back for long, Brye," he whispered throatily.

"Please?" Brye felt the bulk of his weight settle over her. Content, she squeezed his fingers. Chad kissed her earlobe in answer.

Beyond their exhausted bodies, the room settled into restored silence. The television from the main room displayed an early-morning news show. Heavy drapes drawn back, bright streetlights soared through the window and washed over the sweaty lovers.

The weight of Chad, converging into Brye, reassured. She felt safe, secure, and very much anchored. She longed for this moment to go on forever but knew it could not. It did not matter. This night would remain a part of her for the duration of her life.

Languidly, her mind teetered on the edge of reality and obscurity. But as her thoughts drifted off, Chad's heat also slipped away. She was jolted back to awareness.

Brye flipped over. Her upper body shot upward as she pulled her legs close into her chest. Her body violently reacted to the loss of warmth and shelter his intimacy had provided. Her heart already agonized over the void he created.

"I have to go," Chad announced, heading for the bathroom.

"Yes," Brye solemnly answered.

Chad did not look back. He disappeared through the bathroom door.

Seconds later, Brye heard the shower running. Without hesitation, she went in and joined him.

***

Stiff, sore, and very much satiated, Chad settled into the commodious seat of his chartered jet. The entire night, he and Brye had not spoken a total of thirty words. Yet they had communicated in ways most husbands and wives did not achieve in marriages lasting a lifetime. And he could live a lifetime and never appropriate these same palatable feelings with Jennifer. The sensations Brye provoked within him were too glorious to relinquish. Yes. It was time to rethink the temperamental choices he'd created for himself.

Images of Brye rose to the surface of his wavering consciousness. Chad smiled to himself as fatigue encompassed him. His head lulled against his spent shoulders. Before the plane's engines roared to life, he was fast asleep.

23

JENNIFER USED HER KEY to enter Chad's unruffled apartment. Stepping inside, she practically tripped over her fiancé's leather overnight bag. Staying her curiosity, she softly called out his name. Not receiving a response, she crept toward his bedroom. Spread-eagle, fully clothed, minus his shoes, Chad slept.

Backing into the main room, Jennifer stooped to the floor. She unzipped the bag, intent on examining the hidden contents.

Noon, the day before, had been the last contact Jennifer had held with Chad. Despite her many attempts, she had not been able to locate him. Something was going on inside her fiancé's head. Midnight, she had let herself into his empty apartment. She waited until 4:00 a.m. By eight, she started ringing his office.

"He'll be in late," she had been notified. Her second attempt found him attending a business meeting. "Chad will be unavailable for the next several hours." Her next move had been to show up at the office unannounced. She had missed Chad by two minutes; he'd called an early halt to his day—something Chad rarely did.

Three o'clock in the afternoon, and here he was, sleeping off… what? What had transpired in the past twenty-four hours? Hopefully, his bag would provide her with much needed answers.

Digging through the contents, she noted how everything seemed to have been hastily stuffed inside. A wrinkled suit, shaving kit, an airline boarding pass—destination: Kansas City, and a box of…

Anger flashed across Jennifer's perfectly painted features. It all began to sort itself out. Fuming, she grabbed the box of condoms—an unopened box—and shook it in midair.

He has the audacity to chase after that bitch! she raved to herself. *And he couldn't even wear protection!*

Maybe it wasn't what it seemed at all, she strove to convince herself. Maybe prewedding jitters impelled her to question Chad's every move.

Prewedding jitters, my ass! she thought to herself. If anyone was having those, it clearly was not her.

What state had Brye been in last night? One way to find out. She reached into her purse and pulled out her cell phone. Stepping into the foyer bathroom, she closed the door and lowered her voice so it would not filter into his bedroom.

"Will you hold, please?" Rhonda's greeting came at her.

Impatiently, unconscientiously, Jennifer walked out of the bathroom and glided into the kitchen. She took in the room with a circular sweep of her head. Nothing fancy, the kitchen was designed in masculine colors. Crown moldings, oak cabinetry amid stainless steel appliances, Jennifer yawned at the simplicity of it all. For a man with Chad's wealth, he retained rudimentary taste. Of course, all that would change once they were married. Faster than Chad would know what hit him, she planned on throwing him out of this place and moving him into a mansion equipped with nothing but the best money could buy.

"May I help you?"

Any other time, Jennifer would have lit into Rhonda for keeping her on the line for so long. Given the circumstances, however, she mustered the most convivial attitude she could manage. "Has Chad come into the office again?" she required, knowing full well he hadn't. Rolling her eyes at the answer, she politely responded, "Thank you. If you do hear from him, please have him call me. Oh, by the way," she added, as if on an afterthought, "how's the promotional tour going?"

She half listened to the reply. "And which city is Brye touring in now?" Her speculation confirmed, Jennifer muttered something discernible, then severed the connection.

Stuffing the condoms back into Chad's bag, instantaneously she came to a decision. Jennifer blew out the door in a vaporous puff.

Hands formed into a steeple, elbows planted on top of the massive rosewood desk, Daniel stared out the elegant arched windows adorning the east wall in his New Jersey estate study. A panoramic view of the posh grounds extended well beyond the boundaries of the window.

Careful not to make a sound, Jennifer observed him with a prudent eye. There was no need for her to worry any longer. She had dumped the entire load in Daniel's lap. The concentrated look drawn across his stern features meant his mind had dissected the situation and was now searching for the most effective means in eradicating the problem.

There were no delusions of who and what this man personified. He possessed a brilliant business sense, yet he was equally as devious. He played hardball when necessary, and he played for keeps. If need be, he would become Brye's worst enemy. A smile struggled to stay buried. *The bitch won't know what hit her.* Jennifer had done right by confiding to Daniel.

"Your parents are planning a formal engagement party." It had not meant to be a question. It was a stated fact.

"Yes." Jennifer's smile brightened in confident expectation.

"I strongly suggest you plan the party for one week from this Friday."

"That would be pushing it." Her pessimistic approach stretched Daniel's facial muscles into an irritated frown. Jennifer had made a grave mistake in challenging his request. She rushed to rectify her error. "I will handle the arrangements myself," she stated with unblemished certainty.

"Good." He pushed himself out of his chair. Coming around to stand in front of her, he offered her his unconditional support. His touch was warm and inviting as he pulled her to a standing position. Arms linked, he escorted her toward the study's sliding doors. "Why don't you concentrate on your engagement party and your upcoming wedding? I'll take care of the rest."

His smile beamed bright and deadly. *Just like his wrath*, Jennifer mused. It felt good to be on the home team.

"Home," Marcus mumbled to himself as he steered down his barren street. The heat was so intense he actually visualized steamy vapors floating above the sizzling asphalt. Later, as the sun settled lower in the western zone, the genteel neighborhood would fill with walkers, joggers, and children riding bicycles, skateboards, or roller-blades. But now there wasn't a brave soul daring to venture outside the perimeters of air-conditioned domiciles.

"God, it's good to be home." After a taxing day at the office, Marcus was looking forward to making himself a light dinner, putting his feet up with tray in lap, and transforming into a couch potato for the duration of the evening. Four houses away from his brick dwelling, he slowed his Lincoln SUV to a crawl. Stomach muscles clenched into a tight knot, his knuckles gripped the wheel tightly. A Ford Explorer was parked in his drive. He hadn't seen Tenisha since the day before the twins' birthday party. Why was she here? What had made her come?

It didn't matter. For whatever reason, he was glad to see her. Up until this moment, he hadn't realized how much he missed her.

The Navigator inched beside the Explorer, then came to a braking halt. He stepped down onto the hot pavement.

A large elm shaded his front stoop. Tenisha sat underneath the protection of the tree in a sleeveless sundress and a pair of wedged-sole thongs. As Marcus drew closer, she stood but almost faltered behind his ample good looks and his eye-catching physique.

"What're you doing here?" Marcus asked, stepping up to his porch.

"It's nice to see you too," Tenisha countered, squinting at the glare of the sun.

Thrown aback, Marcus apologized. "I'm sorry. I didn't mean to sound put off with your company. It's just that—"

"You became discombobulated at the unexpected sight of my dazzling beauty," she teased.

Yeah…something like that. Keys in hand, Marcus plowed past her. He spoke over his left shoulder. "I meant, why are you sitting out here in the heat?"

"Because I don't have my own set of keys."

Marcus turned to face her. Beads of sweat licked the underside of her chin. Several rounded pellets trickled down a long, delicate neck and settled in the deep fissure separating well-formed breasts. Marcus found himself wishing he could follow with his tongue. He averted his yearning stare, not wanting her to witness the animal carnality smearing his vision. To reorganize his hazardous thoughts, he concentrated on unlocking the front door. Once opened, he pushed it ajar and waited for Tenisha to precede.

Inside, the central air reached out and snatched at Tenisha, encompassing her sticky body with a welcoming embrace. She shivered at the dramatic drop in the temperature. "That feels good." She pulled the top of her dress out several inches to allow the cool air to storm the pores composing her naked skin.

Marcus tried not to ogle. "Why don't I get you something to drink?"

"Water will be fine." Tenisha followed him into the kitchen. She explained the reason behind her visit. "TyJuan is busy tonight. I wasn't in the mood to sit home alone, so I've come in search of a dinner partner."

"Am I your last resort?" Although he thoughtfully asked the question, he cared little of her answer. She was here. It was all that mattered.

You are my only choice. Noncommittal, Tenisha shrugged. "Everybody seems to be busy these days," she vaguely responded.

Since the Fourth of July weekend, her relationship with TyJuan had progressively traveled downward. He spent a great deal of his time away from home. His drinking had recommenced, and Tenisha believed he was experimenting with drugs. She retained no concrete evidence. Only a strong suspicion. Until today. Today she'd come home to a pigsty of an apartment and a monthly bank statement.

In the midst of the pigsty, she uncovered drug paraphernalia, and her opened bank statement reported large withdrawals tallying up to several thousand dollars. Incapable of dealing with either incident, Tenisha had fled the "happy" home. She knew she would eventually have to make a decision surrounding her failing marriage, but at the moment, the resolution was nowhere within reaching distance.

Marcus handed Tenisha her ice water. Their eyes converged as she seized the glass. As she drank, with troubled mind, he pondered over her sudden appearance. The strain she endured was evident. Her smile had been grim. Worry lines enveloped a gloomy brow. The color in her eyes had dulled to a unpolished shine. Words gone unspoken were easily picked up by Marcus's ears: Tenisha was having major problems at home. Now, more than ever, he wanted to gather her within his arms.

"Tell you what"—he removed the empty glass from her hand—"why don't I fix us some dinner? There's a movie coming on later I don't want to miss."

"I accept as long as I get to assist with dinner."

"Uh-uh." Marcus dropped the glass into his dishwasher. He loosened his tie, then removed his suit jacket. "Tonight, you get to sit back and relax."

"But—"

"But nothing," he injected. "No arguments. Next time, I'll let you buy me dinner. Deal?"

Tenisha smiled. This giant of a man was good for her. "Deal."

"Good. Just give me a few minutes to get out of this suit and rescue Rainbow from his cage." With jacket hooked over his index finger, he walked up the back stairs. Yelling over his shoulder, he announced, "Mi casa is su casa. Make yourself at home."

Twenty minutes later, he came down wearing jeans and a T-shirt, with Rainbow roosting on his shoulder. They were a grand sight to see.

"Hello!" Rainbow spoke, head cocked to the side, beady eyes watching Tenisha.

"Hello yourself," Tenisha responded. When she first met Rainbow, she'd felt a little self-conscious—or maybe just plain silly—striking up a conversation with a bird. Over the past few years, she learned quite a bit observing Brye's interaction with Rainbow. Eventually, it had become second nature to treat the exotic bird like another person. After all, most of the time, he talked like one.

Graceful in his descent, Rainbow soared to the floor.

"Are you sure I can't be of some assistance?" Tenisha asked.

"There's no need," Marcus assured. "Yesterday I baked vegetable lasagna. With Brye not here to raid my refrigerator, I have plenty of leftovers. A few minutes in the microwave, along with a fresh Caesar salad and some garlic bread, and we have our meal. It won't take long at all."

Seated at the kitchen table, Tenisha viewed the detailed manner in which Marcus moved around the kitchen.

After he washed and dried his hands, the discarded paper towel went directly into a trash bin underneath the sink—not on the counter or dropped on the floor where TyJuan would have tossed it.

Utensils were used and promptly stored in the dishwasher—not thrown about to clutter counter space.

Crumbs and spills were timely wiped away—not left to attract summer ants. Spices were returned to their original holding position—not tossed negligently aside, never to be seen from again.

By the time dinner was served, the kitchen looked as clean and as organized as when he initially began preparations for their meal. Every moment Tenisha spent in this man's company, her admiration for him heightened in major leaps and bounds.

"Would you like to eat in here or in the formal dining room?"

"Here will be fine." Eating in the formal dining room meant an intimate touch would be added to the evening. It was difficult enough being in the presence of Marcus without Brye as a buffer. If she didn't keep their interaction at a companionable distance, the relationship could get heated…quickly.

"Fine."

Tenisha insisted on setting the table. The perfect gentleman, Marcus held out her chair. Stretching her linen napkin over her lap, Tenisha dug in.

"It's very good," Tenisha praised, savoring her first bite. "But then I'm not surprised." She took another bite. "You cook as well or maybe even better than I. You certainly keep a better home. You're an extremely good dancer, you're well organized, intelligent, sensitive when need be, protective of your friends, and an all-around good guy. Is there anything you don't do?"

"As a matter of fact, there is."

"Well?" Tenisha waited, fork perched in midair.

"You'll laugh."

"I won't." The skeptical look he tossed her, prompted Tenisha to add, "I promise."

Marcus appeared to be weighing his decision. After a voiceless debate on whether to take her at her word, he lowered his fork to his plate. He leaned against the back of his chair. "I don't do dentists."

"Excuse me?" she queried, unsure of his meaning.

"I have this aversion to dentists. I hate them. I hate going…I have since I was a kid."

Tenisha couldn't help it. She began to giggle. But the scowl on his face turned her giggles into a feigned coughing spell. "Excuse me," she said, beating herself on the chest. She picked up her glass of lemonade and drank. "Something caught in my throat."

"You were laughing," Marcus accused.

"I was…not," she choked on the lie. "Okay, okay. I *was* laughing. But I wasn't laughing *at* you. I was laughing *with* you."

His eyelids drooped. "I don't recall laughing."

Tenisha lowered her drink. She leaned forward, her breast pressing indiscriminately against the table edge. "Tell me why you're afraid of the dentist?"

Marcus shoved his plate aside. He propped his elbows on the table. "I remember the first time I went in—I was three years old. A family checkup. My sisters went before me. I think, by mutual consent, they decided to scare me. Each one of them came out moaning and groaning. Complaining on how much it hurt. Add that to all the drilling I heard, and by the time I sat in the dentist's chair, I was scared shitless.

"The hygienist wanted to take X-rays—a 'few pictures' was how she put it—but of course, I didn't understand what was going on. So when she came at me with this huge monster of a machine, I ran. With film in my mouth and lead apron around my neck, I shot out of there and ran right out the front door. Five adults, including my mother, chased after me. I was clear out the building and practically a mile away before anyone caught up to me." Marcus stopped talking, partly because he was out of breath, partly because he didn't believe Tenisha could hear him over her riotous laughter.

"You promised not to laugh," he calmly reminded.

"I know. I'm sorry." Her fork dropped to her plate. Her hands covered her mouth. The giggles spilled from in-between her fingers. "It's just that the visualization in my head looks so pitiful." She made an honest effort to quell her incessant chortle. Dropping her hands to her lap, she looked contrite. "I'm sorry. Go on."

His left brow lifted in question. "Go on?"

"Please."

"From that moment on, not only did they have to strap me into the chair, but my mother stayed with me to hold my hand."

"How long did that go on?"

"Until I was twenty-one."

Tenisha almost spat a mouthful of food into Marcus's face. "Twenty-one…huh? And what do you do now?"

"I brush my teeth often, I floss after every meal, and I only visit the dentist when necessary."

She tilted her head. "And when do you deem it necessary?"

"When my mother schedules an appointment without my knowledge. She then calls Brye and tells her what time the appointment is scheduled. And without forewarning, I'm ambushed and hauled off to the dentist."

The kitchen filled with more of Tenisha's uproarious laughter. "But you're so…so…" She ended in a fit of laughter.

"Big," Marcus finished for her. "Don't even go there, Tenisha. Since when did size set the stage for inner doubts and fears? I'm afraid of dentists. Plain and simple."

"You're right." Tenisha snickered. "It's just that your story sounds so absurd, it's hard to be—" She halted and stared at him with wide-eyed skepticism. "You were making it all up, weren't you?"

"I was not." Marcus looked as if she hurt his feelings. "But if I *had* made it up, at least I can say it put the gleam back in your eyes." When they had first met, Tenisha had always appeared so strong, so self-confident. Lately, in spite of her tough woman's exterior, a little lost girl had been hiding underneath. Sometime during dinner, she had found herself again. Marcus took great pride in knowing it was he who had helped in recapturing her splendid nature.

Unable to fight temptation, he reached across the table and tenderly stroked the side of her face. "You are beautiful. But even more so when your entire face lights up with laughter."

His voice was just as warm and soothing as the touch of his fingers caressing her face, stirring her insides. And although his hands were large and bulky, they were as equally soft and gentle.

Tenisha wanted to close her eyes and bask in the reverence of his solid touch. She wanted to rest her weary brain and yield to Marcus's fostering care. She wanted to fall into his arms and succumb to his restrained advances.

Not wanting him to read all that reflected in her eyes, she lowered her gaze to her plate.

Afraid he'd gone too far, Marcus dropped his hand. His half-eaten dinner plate scraped against the tile top as he slid it back in front of him. They continued to eat in strained silence. The sexual tension mounted.

Several drawn-out seconds later, Tenisha attempted to douse the heated moment. She guided the conversation back on safe ground. "Earlier you mentioned something about a movie you wanted to watch?"

Marcus nodded. "*North By Northwest.*"

"With Cary Grant! I love that movie. I can't even count the times I've seen it."

The room cleared of all tension. "Probably not as many as I have."

"I doubt that. I'm an avid fan of all those old Turner classics: *To Kill A Mockingbird, Maltese Falcon, Casablanca, Raisin in the Sun, Psycho*...to name a few. I love 'em all." A faint smile flickered across Tenisha's valued memories as she recalled her childhood days. "I loved spring breaks, summers, and Christmas vacations, not because it was a much-needed respite from the daily routine of mundane classwork, but because my father used to let me sit up with him at night and watch the late shows.

"We'd sit in front of the television with popcorn, or potato chips, or Oreo cookies, or ice cream, or whatever dessert my mother fixed for dinner, and we watched our favorite movies. It was our time together. And I soaked up every minute of it." Tenisha sighed. The sunny childhood memory encircled her skin with a warm glow. "I still sit down to watch an old black-and-white, or a musical like *Seven Brides for Seven Brothers* or *Calamity Jane.*" Reluctantly, she admitted, "Because of my busy lifestyle, I don't get to sit down and watch them as often as I'd like it to."

Marcus couldn't fathom TyJuan not jumping at the chance to spend late nights in bed, arms encompassing Tenisha, watching old classics. It was certainly an opportunity Marcus would never pass up. He asked with great caution, "Does your husband enjoy oldies as well?"

A half grin, half smirk intersected with Tenisha's pleasant regard. "TyJuan's idea of an oldie is waiting six months to a year for a feature film to come out on cable TV."

"Well...he doesn't know what he's missing." Marcus's tone remained neutral. "I, myself, could watch classics all day and all night. And I consider myself to be extremely knowledgeable on the subject."

Tenisha grinned. To her, his cocky attitude was an invitation to be challenged. She decided to put him to the test.

"What was the title film Clark Gable made his musical debut in? And what was the name of the song he sang and danced to?"

"*Idiot's Delight* and 'Puttin' on the Ritz,'" Marcus smugly answered. "Your turn. In the 1951 version of *The Thing*, who played the Thing?"

"James Arness. But I liked the remake better. I'm an avid fan of Kurt Russell." Enjoying the game, she proceeded to ask, "In the 1958 movie *The Viking*, who were the three leading male characters and how were they linked to one another?"

Marcus hurled a look that said, "Is this the best you got?" He answered, "Kirk Douglas, Tony Curtis, and Ernest Borgnine. Kirk and Tony were half brothers. Both were fathered by Ernest." Grinning wickedly, he came up with a question that was certain to stump her. "What was the name of Mickey Rooney's first movie?"

"*Broadway to Hollywood.* He was ten years old. What was his age when he first worked with Judy Garland?"

"Seventeen." He also recited the name of the movie and the subsequent others the two shining actors had costarred in.

On and on it went. Both hoping to trip the other. Neither succeeding. And two minutes prior to the start of the movie, Tenisha and Marcus sat in front of his television, a carton of pineapple sherbet shared by both.

Spoon in mouth, Tenisha pondered over the past few hours. Not once had Marcus asked her about her marriage, yet she sensed she could discuss her personal life with him if the need arose.

Her life with TyJuan seemed far removed from where she sat at the moment. She also understood that sitting here with Marcus perpetuated the growing problems in her marriage. Soon she would have to make some major decisions. But it would not be now. Because now, she wanted to enjoy the time she had left with Marcus.

"Marcus?"

"Uhmm," he mumbled, a spoonful of sherbet melting in his mouth.

"Earlier you made a statement about being my last resort for dinner. Well"—she reached across the sofa and grabbed the sherbet carton—"you were the only person I wanted to come to tonight." She dug out an enormous lump of sherbet. Leaning toward Marcus, she slowly guided the spoon toward his mouth.

For fear he would say the wrong thing, for fear he would do the wrong thing, he silently accepted the humble offering.

Spellbound, Tenisha glimpsed a sliver of his tongue as it made contact with the spoon. Sensual lips sealed shut. She witnessed the bob of his Adam's apple as the chilled substance took route and traveled downward.

Tenisha's insides simmered as the atmosphere sizzled around her. Her lungs struggled to suck in the cumbersome ventilation. Her fingertips itched with an irrepressible urge to reach out and touch him. Her mind shut down to all else except to the idea of making love to him. And all the while, she wondered if this is what it felt like to be swallowed whole by a man.

He could barely tolerate the look she affronted him with, as if she wanted to toss aside the sherbet and take him on as dessert. Quite frankly, he loved nothing better than to be served up to her on a silver platter. But, battling his own emotional conflicts, fortunately for him, his conscience was winning. Wrapping his fingers around Tenisha's hand as she continued to clutch the spoon handle, he pulled it out of his mouth.

"I think we've had enough of this stuff," he gruffly stated, removing the silver utensil and the carton of sherbet from her hands.

"Not yet I haven't." A thin layer of sherbet coddled his lower lip. Tenisha leaned toward him, giving way to the urge to lick the smooth substance.

Have you gone crazy? she berated herself. *What the hell are you doing?* Common sense getting the best of her, she tugged backward. "Maybe you're right. Maybe we have had enough."

Marcus breathed a sigh of relief. He went to put the ice cream away. With head tucked deep inside the freezer, he grabbed a couple of ice cubes and ran them over his heated face and neck. With Tenisha sitting by his side, in his house, watching television, it promised to be a long night. It also promised to be an enjoyable one.

In spite of it all, Marcus smiled to himself as he knowingly thought, *There's no place like home!*

Jamie and Jordan Farrow had spent the past four hours with their mother and her boyfriend. Prior visits had been supervised, but once Debbie Farrow complied with a court order and attended parenting classes, she'd been granted unsupervised visitation. Jordan wasn't certain how her mother had gained the privilege while her boyfriend—Gary Dowding—remained in the picture. Unless she had put one over on those social worker people, which was easy to do.

Excluding Gary and his loathsome presence, the two girls had spent the entire time at Coney Island, laughing, teasing, reminiscing. The day had been near perfect. Until now.

Now her mother wanted to leave them alone with Gary while she ran to the corner grocery store to pick up a can of biscuits—Gary refused to eat a meal, any meal, with the absence of bread. Jordan and her mother stood on the stoop of a Brooklyn brownstone. The tip of the sun still peeked above ground, seasoning the horizon with an orange-yellow glow. Although the heat had not slacked off, the streets swarmed with individuals suffering from cabin fever. Sounds of laughter, music, chanting, and basketball fraternized with the warm current flowing though the awakening neighborhood.

"Please don't leave us with *him*, Mom! Please!" Jordan pleaded.

At the age of twenty-seven, Debbie Farrow's once maidenly features were now worn out, tired, aged by the harsh realities of life. Pregnant at the age of fifteen, she left her family to begin a new and exciting life with the twenty-year-old father of her unborn baby. Six years later, pregnant for the second time, she dejectedly admitted that the worst kind of loneliness was the one endured while living with one's intended life partner.

With one child and another on the way, once again, she began anew. For years she struggled to keep her head afloat and her kids fed. She also scrambled to keep sunshine in their little hearts. And then, two and a half years ago, she met, fell in love with, and moved in with Gary. And in the process, insurmountable tension had become a fact of life for the wannabe family.

Debbie sighed. Exhaustively, she glided her palm over the crown of her daughter's head. "It's gonna be all right, honey." She loved her daughters dearly, but she was so tired of being the cushion between Jordan, Jamie, and her live-in lover. "I won't be gone long." Thankfully, in Gary's infinite wisdom, he understood her girls' disdain; after being the sole recipient of their mother's love for years, they resented his presence and the time she now devoted to him. He did not fault them for the stand they had taken. And every day Debbie stayed with this kind man, she thanked her lucky stars she'd found someone as understanding and patient as Gary.

Tears of desperation swelled. "Then take us with you…please," Jordan begged.

Debbie pulled Jordan into an indulgent hug. "Just give Gary a chance? For me?" Met with no answer and an unyielding body, her voice raised in faint irritation. "Why can't you accept the fact that I love Gary? He's a big part of my life…just as you and Jamie are."

Jordan pulled out of her mother's grasp. Why could her mother not see through that awful man? Why didn't she accept their word when they told her he hit them? Malice nourished her next set of words. "If the social workers knew you lied about Gary, if they found out he'd been with us on this visit, they wouldn't allow you another unsupervised visit."

"Are you threatening me?" Anger flashed, then instantly hopped aboard the crest of a surfing breeze; the mild current carried her irritation away from the crumbling stoop. Debbie didn't want to do this. Not now. There were only a few hours left before she delivered her daughters back to Brylinn; she intended for them to be memorable ones.

Determined to grant Gary time with the girls, she kissed Jordan on the tip of her head. "I promise I won't be long." She marched down the stairs, leaving an anxiety-filled Jordan staring after her.

A girl of Jordan's age rode past on rollerblades. "Can you come out and play?" she yelled.

Jordan had been away from Jamie much too long. She had to get back into the house. "Maybe later," she yelled, ducking inside the screen door.

The living room was drab—shabby curtains, lumpy couch, scarred furnishings, and crumbling wall plaster—but Debbie maintained a clean home. With no sign of Jamie or Gary in the living room, fine hairs prickled her arm as she stared at a jelly glass—utilized as a drinking utensil—turned on its side. Liquid seeped through the couch, turning the burnt orange material into an ominous shade of brown.

Danger lurked in the air. She could feel it, smell it, touch it. Panic-stricken, Jordan dashed toward the kitchen. In vain, she tried to convince herself of a virtual impossibility. *Maybe he'll behave himself. Maybe as long as he knows the authorities are watching him, he'll leave us alone. Maybe he realizes his mistakes and is trying to change.*

Yeah…right. And maybe there're such things as the Great Pumpkin, the Easter Bunny, and the tooth fairy. Maybe—

A piercing scream shattered the currently agitated atmosphere. Jordan burst through the shuttered kitchen doors.

"Let her go!" she screamed at Gary.

Clasped between his powerful grip, Jamie hovered above a sink filled with dish water. Her face dripping with liquid, the front of her blouse soaked, Gary was forcing her head under, depriving her of much needed oxygen. In horror, Jordan stared. His thin, lengthy face was bloated with rage. Long greasy hair fell into crazed eyes. He looked deranged. He looked impaired. He looked larger than life and too much for Jordan to tackle.

"I said let her go!" Jordan frantically searched the kitchen for a weapon. Something. Anything she could use against him.

Ignoring her, Gary pushed Jamie's head back into the water. All day he had to play Mr. Nice Guy to these insufferable brats. Minute by minute, his patience had steadily worn thin. But when he asked Jamie to bring him another glass of wine, and she tripped and spilled it all over his shirt, it had been the final straw.

"Maybe next time you'll be more careful!" he snarled, pushing her head further into the water. Several agonizing seconds past before he lifted a sputtering Jamie out of the water. Crying, screaming, pleading, Jamie begged to be released. "I'll teach you, you goddamn brat, if it's the last fuckin' thing I do!" Her head went back under.

"Get away from her!" Jordan yelled. She lifted an empty frying pan sitting on top of the stove. Her swing was wide and frantic. Gary ducked. The pan barely grazed him and only resulted in fueling his biting anger. Still holding Jamie down, he grabbed hold of Jordan with his left hand. Roughly shoving her aside, he yelled, "You interfere with me again, and I'll give you more of the same!"

Flying backward, Jordan hit the kitchen wall. Pain fired along her back as she slid to the floor. In a stupor, her eyes glazed over from the piercing discomfort.

Gary turned his attention back on Jamie. By now, she'd gone limp. As he pulled her head out of the water, a burst of lightning streaked across his vision as fierce pain split open the back of his head. A millisecond later, blood dripping from his wound, unconscious, he fell to the floor with Jamie in tow.

Chest heaving, confused and shocked, Debbie stood over the man she had loved for over two years. A few seconds after leaving for the store, she realized she'd forgotten her purse and had returned to confront this horrific scene. The folding wood chair she'd cracked over his head slipped out of her hands. She dropped to her knees and pulled Jamie into her arms.

"She's not breathing," Debbie quickly assessed. "Oh God! What do I do!" she moaned. Paralyzed with fear, her mind sent out nothing but scrambled jargon. Unable to gather her erratic thoughts into some semblance of order, she rocked back and forth while cradling her daughter's motionless body within her arms. Unconsciously, she swiped at the excess water running down Jamie's face.

This was her fault. She could blame no one but herself for this. She should have known her babies would not lie. She should have trusted them.

"Mom!" Jordan had broken out of her daze. She knelt beside her mother and baby sister. Her face, her voice, quivered in fear. "She's not breathing, Mom. You have to do something!"

"Yes. Yes. I have to do something," Debbie rushed to agree. In her present state of mind, she was grateful to be given a task. *But what? What should I do? CPR! My daughter needs CPR!* Pulling herself together, hands shaking, Debbie lowered Jamie to the floor and positioned her inert body. On her knees, applying a head tilt/chin lift maneuver, having been taught CPR several years ago, she inched her ear toward Jamie's mouth.

Nothing.

Debbie's heart dropped to her knees. But now that she had direction, she carried out her duty with painstaking precision. She initiated rescue breathing. After two sufficient puffs, she felt for a pulse.

Thank God Jamie's heart continued to beat. "Call 911!" she shouted at Jordan. "Now!" Jordan hopped over Gary's stationary body as she dashed to make the call.

Debbie continued with her rescue breathing. "Breathe for me, baby! Please breathe for Mommy!" she chanted in between breaths. "Come on, Jamie! Do this for me! Please!"

Debbie continued for what seemed like hours—but in reality was only thirty seconds—when Jamie gasped for air. Coughing, sputtering, huge gulps of water purged from her lungs as terrified eyes flew open. Debbie quickly shoved her daughter's head to the side to prevent her from choking on her on fluid.

"Mama?" Jamie sounded weak, her voice was strained, hoarse, grainy. The sound was like music to Debbie's ears.

Collapsing with relief, Debbie sank to the ground. She pulled Jamie into her arms and hugged her tightly, afraid her daughter would backslide if she released her. Tears of joy, and sadness, spilled down her face. "I'm here, baby. And I swear, no one will ever, ever hurt you again."

As Jordan took her place beside her mother, Debbie pulled her eleven-year-old into her shaky embrace. "I'm sorry. I'm so, so sorry. I should have listened. I should never have doubted you two. Please forgive me. Please."

And as police and ambulance sirens drew nearer, Debbie vowed to make a better life for her girls.

TyJuan was embarking upon a stimulating trip. A much-welcomed, sought-after junket. Excited as a little boy going off to the circus, he hopped aboard his scheduled flight; a skyrocket transporting him to a land of unmitigated rapture.

Where he was flying, there would be no racial inequalities; he did not have to cross any color barriers. Nor did he have to concern himself with climbing a social ladder or plowing through a status boundary.

Where he would land, no one questioned his joblessness; there was little concern for his monetary depravation, nor did anyone feel the need to front him with the lack of choices he made in life. In effect, he was about to visit the perfect world. A place where prevalent issues and endless problems lingered no more.

Grinning to himself, several seconds after shooting up, TyJuan's eyes rolled to the back of his head. As his chin slumped to his chest, he mellowed out, strapped himself in, and prepared to enjoy his ascent into the heavens. Life had never felt so good.

24

St. Petersburg, Florida. Late night. Much too late for Brye to be out walking alone. But she could not sleep. *The engagement party is tonight,* she ruminated. *It's taking place at this very moment.* Impossible to sort out her blistering thoughts, Brye had not been able to remain and brood in her hotel suite.

A clear night. Overlooking Tampa Bay, a full moon bounced off the shimmering surface. Thousands of blinking eyes peered down at her. Moist, cool sea air filled her lungs and clung tenaciously to her skin; she hoped her invigorating surroundings would clear her mind.

Barefoot, pants rolled several inches above her ankles, oversized sweater hanging on a sluggish body, Brye listlessly strolled along the hotel's private white sandy beach. She shivered. Not from the glacial breeze sailing off the bay's surface, but from her own benumbed thoughts.

Why was she so out of control? Why couldn't she resist Chad? Why did she dissolve inside his arms every time he tossed her a bone? God, but it was so sickening. Her impetuousness disgusted her. How could she throw away lifetime pledges for a few minutes of reckless abandonment? Reckless abandonment that meant nothing to Chad.

Actions spoke louder than words. But in this instance, Chad had never said he loved her, nor had he acted like he wanted her for anything other than a quick and easy lay.

He just enters my life and takes what he wants, then exits again as if nothing's ever occurred between us. No one the wiser. Not his mother, not his father, nor even Jennifer.

Why did she tolerate his insensitive behavior? What made her put up with him?

Because you need him.

Despite her running doubts, she recognized and accepted how much she loved him. But she could not decipher the enigmatic feelings Chad fostered for her. Since their last night together, over and over, Brye had replayed his final departure.

At her suite door, he had looked down at her with such concentrated tenderness. "Are you still having nightmares?" Spoken softly, quietly, his words barely rose above a whisper.

Brye nodded yes, weary eyes remained trained on his.

He leaned forward, lightly brushing her forehead with firm lips. "No more nightmares," he softly commanded. Just that simple, as if he had waved a magic wand over her head. Since then, her night terrors had not reached out and subdued her by its crushing clutches.

How he had accomplished that feat, she did not know. Power of suggestion, maybe? Or maybe she was just getting tired. Maybe this grueling tour was finally catching up to her. Lately, she found herself crashing at night and forcing herself awake in the morning.

The upside of it all was that she slept without nightmarish interference.

Guided by the blanched light of the moon, Brye continued her lone walk on the isolated beach. She took note of nothing or no one as her feet shuffled in the soft sand. She only concentrated on Chad's engagement party. His wife-to-be had reserved the audacity to overnight Brye a personalized invitation. A calculated move on Jennifer's part. She gloated while displaying her awarded trophy. Brye could not fault her for that.

Brye moved farther away from her hotel and deeper into the fists of darkness. Her mind went even further; she was oblivious to the hushed footsteps slithering from behind. She didn't sense danger until the malevolent presence emerged behind her. By then, it was too late. The assailant whipped out a dagger and slathered it across her pulsating throat. The cold, sharpened edge rode dangerously close to her carotid artery. She stiffened from the sudden attack yet fear did not yet run roughshod over her mental state; this felt like an out-of-body experience.

"What's a pretty young thang like you doing out all by yourself?"

His voice grated against her depressed nerve fibers. The rancid stench of whiskey rushed past her ear, drowning her senses. Rough, prickly hair growing from the lower half of his face scratched the side of her cheek. A wave of revulsion washed over Brye.

"You and me are gonna have a lotta fun, baby."

His voice grew raspier in Brye's ears. It finally struck home. His intentions were clear. She began to shake. "Please...don't," her voice trembled.

"Oh yeah, Bryson. Beg for me. I love it when you beg. It turns me on even more."

He pressed a hardened groin into her backside. His fingers slid under her sweater. Brye recoiled. Offensive fingers crept along repelled skin. Sickened as he roughly squeezed the tip of her breast, she shut her eyes to the bright lights of the city. There was a great big world out there filled with thousands upon thousands of individuals—none of whom could help her. She could only help herself. She opted to not degrade herself by begging. It would do no good. Brye chose to fight. She had done it many times before. She could do it again. She would stop him from violating her. Or he would rape her dead body.

The hand gripping the knife moved an inch higher. His left hand continued to fondle her breast. He moaned something incoherent. Brye wanted to throw up. Instead, she dropped her chin. The knife passed to the left of her mouth. She sunk her teeth into solid flesh, applying as much pressure as she could into that one bite. He howled in pain. His left hand furiously slammed into her backside. Her teeth buried deeper. The knife dropped silently to the sand. The assailant finally tore his arm away from her inflicting grip.

"Bitch!" he screamed. Grabbing her by the wrist he flung her around to face him. He punched her in the mouth with a balled right hook. Brye's head whipped backward. She ignored the pain and wasn't certain if the blood she tasted was his or her own. Swinging her arm upward, she dug in and dragged her fingernails down the side of his face. Digging in firmly, his skin gave way to strong nail beds. He backhanded her. Again and again. She pulled her nails free, believing her head would rip from her shoulders as a burst of colorful lights lit up the surrounding darkness yet crippled her eyesight. Blindly, she flung out at him. Prepared for the counterattack, he grabbed both her flailing wrist.

"You fuckin' bitch," he fiercely swore. "When I get done with you, you're gonna—"

His breath expelled in one long anguished hiss. Brye had just executed her most debilitating move: a knee lift to the groin. Lucky for her, she hit dead center. He bowled over in pain. Private parts howled in protest as the assailant dropped to his knees. Pressing her advantage, Brye interlocked all ten fingers. Strength and determination went behind one final blow. As if holding a golf club in hand, she swung at his bent head.

Fore! She insanely thought as the direct hit rolled him on his side.

Not waiting to see if he clutched enough power to come after her, Brye turned. She sprinted down the beach and ran toward the security the lights offered. Urgently, she ran toward safety.

Bone weary, yet Brye continued to vigorously scrub the deranged attacker's scent off her bruised body and out of her system. At full force, she ran the water as hot as she could tolerate and scoured the filth of his grubby paws off her skin.

For the past six hours, she'd been questioned by the police, examined by a doctor, poked, prodded, and photographed to procure evidence—the most important being the skin scraped from underneath her fingernails—questioned some more, and, finally, she supplied a description to a police artist who sketched a composite drawing of the perpetrator.

A very good likeness, Brye had been satisfied with the final results.

The offer to provide a reasonable facsimile of the assailant after she'd undergone a good night's sleep went unheeded. It had been dark. It all happened so fast. Brye wanted to give them all the information she could while it remained fresh in her mind.

Despite her earnestness to cooperate, there still remained something about the night that continued to elude her. Something the attacker had said to her. For whatever reason, her mind intentionally chose to block a frame of information away from her memory bank. No matter how hard she tried, she could not penetrate the strategically positioned impediment. Yet Brye understood that the expunged information was vital, if not to anyone else, it mattered to her own well-being. Soon she would have to sit down and challenge herself. It was imperative she uncover what her mind assiduously guarded.

Certain she finally cleansed the crushing stench out of her system, her skin as crimson as a broiled lobster, at 5:27 a.m., she stumbled out the shower. Hurriedly drying herself off, her thoughts continued to oscillate.

I've called and informed Brian of the assault. I've alerted Linn to the possible news' frenzy. I've called the front desk and left a seven o'clock wake-up call for Kierra, along with ensuing instructions. I've asked the desk to hold all calls. Is there anything I'm forgetting?

With no time to consider the question, she was dead to the world as her fatigued body connected with a firm mattress.

Two hours later, twenty-nine-year-old African American Kierra Martin supported a service tray—topped with a carafe of coffee, china, silverware, and staples—between her body and the peach and blue patterned wall. Short and petite, Kierra possessed what many a photographer appraised as solid bone structure and admirable facial features: dominate, proud, ancestral. Eminently photogenic. A section of her long fashionable braids fell in her line of vision as she dipped her head toward the door's lock. The security key slid smoothly into Brye's slot. Maneuvering key, door lever, and the coffee service, somehow, she managed to enter without spraying the carpeted hallway with coffee or the little server packets of creamer and sugar.

Upon entering, she instantly gained a sense of discord. The same clothing Brye had worn the night before haphazardly trailed away from the suite entrance and headed toward the open bedroom door. Brye was too much of an organizer to have just deposited her clothing onto the floor. But that reason alone was not what set off alarm bells. Every morning, prior to their early-morning parley, Brye would have either already completed a four-mile jog, or she would have worked out in the hotel's private health spa.

Every morning, Kierra walked into a suite blaring with upbeat music. And Brye would usually be stepping out off an invigorating shower. This morning, the hotel suite spread before her exposed and destitute. A sense of dread bowled over Kierra. She slid the coffee tray onto the sideboard. Pouring a cup, she waltzed over to the open bedroom door.

In bed, bareback facing her, Kierra stared at Brye with growing apprehension.

"What the hell?" she mumbled to herself. *Why is she still sleeping?* She placed the coffee cup on the bedside table. Strolling over to the closet, she ripped Brye's robe off a padded hanger.

Standing over the stilled body, Kierra called out several times before Brye stirred.

25

ONE SPRING DAY, AFTER an early school dismissal, Bryson elected to dash home, grab a pair of walking shoes, and head to the Museum of Modern Art.

Although she expected no one to be home, she quietly slipped into the apartment.

Much to her disgust, a sight too horrifying to comprehend accosted her in her parent's living room. It was the first time Bryson realized that the mind could do strange things to protect its owner's mental stability. Until it was certain she could survive the revolting scene, her brain refused to process what her eyesight engulfed.

Gradually, Bryson recovered her senses. A sour taste rose from the depths of her stomach. Clamping her hands over her quivering mouth, she strove to quell her lurching stomach. However, it was apparent after a few seconds of struggling with herself that she could not hold down the bile. Bryson stumbled into the bathroom.

The floor broke her fall as she dropped to her knees. In one forceful surge, her afternoon lunch exploded outward. She hovered over the toilet bowl in wait for her quivering stomach to cease its acerbic hemorrhage. Beads of sweat exploded across her forehead and the back of her neck. Her mouth tasted of acidic waste. Moaning, she protectively wrapped her arms around her now tender belly.

After she jettisoned her entire lunch in one loud swoosh, the liquefied contents overflowed into the city's sewage system.

Squeezing her eyelids shut, she tried to block out the vision permanently embedded within her memory banks. Shakily she climbed to her feet. Knees wobbly, feet unable to support her taxing weight, she eased her body back down onto the plush, bathroom carpet. Her pounding head dropped into waiting palms. Eyes tightly sealed, yet the repulsive vision could not be suppressed, it remained as clear as if she had never left the living room.

Her mother and twin brother completely nude, engaged in lewd and lascivious acts. And why wasn't it surprising to Bryson that her father stood on the sideline, cell phone camera in hand, taking pornographic photos.

Bryson attempted to remove the nauseating spectacle out of her head. But she could not shake it nor the feeling of uncleanness out of her surging mind. Struggling to gain her footing, she frantically tore at her clothing.

She needed to undergo a very hot shower. Filth and vile incinerated Bryson's skin much like an army of red ants devouring a depleted body staked to the hard ground. She desperately needed to rid herself of the site of her family's damaging violation.

The bathroom grew hot and humid as Bryson set the water as hot as she could tolerate. The mirrors streaked heavily with steam. She laboriously scrubbed at herself. And when she'd scoured her skin raw, only then did she climb out of her self-ordained baptism.

Body towel wrapped around her stinging torso, she aimed for the toothbrush. In midair, her hand hovered over the soft-bristled brush. Her nostrils flared at the abrupt intrusion overpowering her sixth sense.

A nefarious stench clawed at the air, threatening to suck Bryson's oxygen dry. Icy clutches of fear wrapped itself around her lungs, depleting her of the vital provisions of life, much like a parasitically leech attaching itself to her body, draining her of all blood.

Fear. Anger. The two indomitable emotions were interchangeable as Bryson wrestled to take control. Several cleansing breaths later, anger conquered all.

Bryson spun on her heels. Eyes dilated with resentment, she angrily faced her twin brother. Hard, piercing eyes took in his partially clad body. He wore no shirt, no shoes, and no ready apology. Unzipped jeans bared red bikini briefs. "Get the hell out of my bathroom!" she fiercely demanded.

The stalwart force behind her leveled verbal attack flung Tyson backward. The illustrious smile he wore on his face vacillated between shock and amazement. As long as he could remember, Bryson had never uttered a harsh word to him. The obtrusive loathing reddening her cheekbones sent him teetering off balance. When he regained his composure, he smiled, yet it didn't accommodate the same brilliance as before.

"You don't mean that." He took a tentative step forward.

"I do mean that, you filthy piece of slime!" Bryson took one step backward. "How could you do it? How could you let her talk you into it? She's our mother, for god's sake!"

"You don't know anything about it." In two strides, Tyson was upon Bryson. Securing her by the shoulders with a vise grip, he barked, "She loves me. Just like Dad loves me. And—"

"Are you fucking him too?" Bryson sweetly batted her eyelids at him.

The anger flared. His eyes clouded, as he viciously backhanded her.

Bryson's teeth shattered from the blinding impact, yet she continued to stand defiantly before her twin.

"I hate you. And I hate the people that spawned you. You're nothing but scum…all of you. The lowest of low. The sickest of the sick. Dregs of society." Her head reared back as he struck her again.

"You mean nothing to me!" Bryson continued, barely skipping a beat. "You are nothing to me!" Emotionally, Bryson was severing her ties. There was no turning back. "I hate you and I hate myself because you're a part of me."

Tyson suddenly reeled backward. This time, although she hadn't lifted a finger, Bryson had done the slapping. Confusion, hurt, pain shattered his bleeding heart. He couldn't bear the thought of Bryson hating him. She was a part of him…the biggest part. If he lost her, he'd die.

"You don't mean that." His voice was low, childlike. "You can't hate me. You love me. You'll always love me. I'm a part of who you are."

Bryson cruelly pushed past him. "If I have to, I'll take a knife to myself and rip out the part that contains you."

"Bryson… No!" It was an anguished cry.

"I hope you fry in hell, Ty!" Standing in the middle of the bathroom door, Bryson swung around to face him. Face ablaze with contempt, eyes narrowed into dangerous slits, she announced, "Twice in the past several minutes you've struck me—not to mention the other times in the past few

years you've raised your hand to me. If you ever hit me again, in any way, shape, or form, I'll kill you! I swear I will."

"You couldn't," Tyson whimpered. "You wouldn't."

"I can. I will." There was no forgiveness, nor was there remorse. Her shoulders lifted in a resigned shrug. "As far as I'm concerned, you're already dead to me."

"Bryson?" Tyson yelled after her. She kept going.

"Brrryyyy?"

"Brye?"

"Brye…it's time to get up," Kierra repeated more forcefully.

Groggily, Brye's mind grew alert to her present surroundings. She was also made aware of the stiffness in her body. "Oh God!" she moaned to herself, every nerve-ending screamed out in spiked agony. It felt like a two-ton Mack truck had just run over her, shifted gears, then backed over her again.

"Kierra?" she groaned, forcing her eyes open.

"I'm here."

"Coffee…please." Brye slid her bare legs out from underneath the sheets. Sitting upward, she offered Kierra a full view of her bruised back. The wide-spread discoloration was highly discernible even in the dim morning light.

"Oh my god, Brye! What happened to your back?" Fear, as well as shock, flooded Kierra.

Brye seized the moment to face Kierra. Again she cried out in amazed alarm, "Jesus, Brye, your face! What the hell happened? Are you okay?"

"I was attacked last night." Brye slid her arms into the proffered robe. She then took the coffee Kierra handed her. "Then I spent the biggest chunk of my night being questioned." Warming her fingers around the heat the coffee cup offered, Brye took several small sips before reciting the events of the past night.

"Why didn't you call someone?" Kierra questioned; the realization that she and the others had been out partying while Brye had undergone her attack was more guilt than she could withstand. "Why did you go through all that questioning alone? We should have been there with you."

Brye blinked back the fuzziness. "You couldn't have done anything to have stopped the attack. And once it was over, I decided that none of you should lose sleep because of me."

"Dammit, Brye! We should never have gone out and left you. We should have—"

"You weren't hired to be my babysitter," Brye reminded with emollient sensitivity. "I don't want you feeling guilty about this because I'm the one who screwed up." Brye sampled more of her coffee. The strong concoction did little to warm her insides or revive her weary brain. "I told you I'd be staying in for the night. But I couldn't sleep, so I decided to go out. On that decision alone, I should have left a message of my whereabouts. But barring all that, I should never have gone out alone to begin with."

Brye laughed. But there was no humor. Only a hollow emptiness echoing in her ears. "Born and raised in New York City, you think I'd have been more attuned with my surroundings." She squinted at the bedside clock: 7:37 a.m. She needed to get the day going.

"It's going to be an extremely hectic day. We better get started. I need you to start making some phone calls." Brye shakily climbed to her feet. She stumbled into the bathroom.

Kierra stared in unabashed disbelief. "You aren't thinking about working today! You can't." She barked, "Look at you!"

In the bathroom, Brye shoved fallen hair out of her bruised face. She squinted in the mirror. The damage wasn't as bad as it had appeared the night before. Puffiness resembling a bloated balloon floated beneath a red-rimmed left eye. A purplish bruise the size of a silver dollar burned brightly against chalky features. Her tongue glided along the tender skin inside her mouth where she'd bitten herself. All-in-all, she considered her face to be salvageable.

"Actually," she attempted to tease, "I feel a whole lot worse than I look."

"How can you joke about this?" Kierra exploded, coming to stand at the door, guilt, fear, anger, interchangeable, all three emotions mingled inside her bloodstream, threatening to pollute her entire system. "What happened to you is every woman's nightmare. But you don't appear to be upset. You don't appear angry. In fact, you act as if you just survived a trip to the amusement park. How can you be so indifferent over such a contemptible act?"

Brye pushed away from the mirror. Her eyes fell on Kierra. A heavy sigh breezed past her bruised lips. She took a seat on the edge of the bathtub. Swallowing arduously, she began, "When he first put that knife to my throat, I didn't feel much of anything. There was no fear…or anger. And then, just that fast"—Brye snapped her fingers in midair—"I disassociated myself from the entire situation. And when he"—Brye shut her eyes against the repugnant memory—"touched me, all I cared about was getting away—or die trying. It wasn't until I was sequestered in the security office of this hotel, waiting for the police, when I had time to contemplate what happened. That's when I lost control." Brye's hands began to shake as she relived the moment yet again.

"That's when I grew frightened. My insides turned to ice. Nothing I could do, nothing anyone could say, could warm me… still. Even the continued assurances of my safety didn't help. And when the police finally came, I not only lost control of my emotions, but I lost control of my life. I *had* to be questioned. I *had* to seek the assistance of a doctor. I *had* to have photos taken…had evidence removed from my person." Brye shook her head. She wrapped her arms around her heaving chest. "Suddenly, so many people had full control over my life. And I couldn't do a thing about it."

As she spoke, Kierra lowered the toilet lid. Sitting down, she listened intently.

Brye stared at Kierra with a prudent eye. "To lose control is one of the most frightening, degrading things that can happen to a person. The man who assaulted me attempted to demoralize me. In fact, he dictated every move I made last night. But now, today, we're talking about my job…*my* livelihood. I will not let him take control by forcing me to drop out of sight."

"It's not a question of whether he still has control, Brye. You took back control when you elected to fight. And you were in complete control as soon as you reported the incident," Kierra wisely pointed out. "But right now, it's about being able to cope with the aftermath. Your mind and body have been abused. Mentally and physically. This is a matter of taking time to recuperate."

Kierra continued to push. "So what if you take a few days off? A week even. It wouldn't be considered a rash reaction on your part. In fact, everyone would expect you to cancel the tour—we've only two weeks left on the circuit anyway—and no one would reproach you for doing just that."

Brye stood. She turned on the shower. Hot steam inundated the bathroom. "It's not a matter of what I *want* to do, it's a matter of what I *have* to do. Please understand, I need to maintain my sanity."

Kierra nodded. Although she didn't agree, she understood perfectly. Brye felt the need to keep busy. She wanted to keep her mind occupied. Kierra respected her decision. She would, in the meantime, maintain a vigilant watch over her. If the supermodel showed any signs of strain, she would report it directly to Brian.

Experiencing momentary dizziness, Brye grabbed the edges of the sink to stabilize herself. She swayed for several seconds before recovering.

Kierra sprang to Brye's aid. She grabbed hold of her elbow. "Are you okay?"

The room came back into focus, her vertigo slowly subsided. Brye smiled a most opulent grin in spite of her current circumstances. "Of course I am." She moved away from Kierra's concerned grip. This was a new day, a new time. Last night's events would be shoved aside; it was how she managed all critical ordeals. Strangely, it was a wonder her radical approach hadn't induced a nervous breakdown before now. Surprisingly, she did not suffer schizophrenic or psychotic tendencies. Gratefully, she had not been impelled to designate sections of her mind to multiple personalities, demented or otherwise.

Pushing the dreary thoughts aside, Brye said, "We need to get busy."

It was Kierra's cue to gather pad and pencil.

As Brye showered, she doled out orders. "Things are going to get frenzied today. I need you to call Marcus and Tenisha for me… first thing…before they hear the news elsewhere. Explain to them what happened. Tell them I apologize for not calling but will contact them as soon as I can. Tell them—" Brye hesitated. She thought about the generalized message. Both Marcus and Tenisha would be furious she hadn't taken the time to make the call herself. She needed to personalize the notation, turn it into something more intimate. She needed to say something that would take the edge off their anger. "Tell them I love them." Brye's heart skipped a beat. It was the first time she ever verbalized the words out loud about her dearest friends. But she knew she meant it. And the realization of knowing she had room in her heart to love others carried with it a sense of security. Maybe she was finally learning how to get on with her life.

"You also need to call Romanique…after you've spoken with Detective Baumbard. I spoke to Brian earlier and promised we would keep him updated.

"As soon as I get dressed, you need to get Cory up here. ASAP. It's going to take a miracle to fix my face. I want these bruises completely covered by the time I get in front of the public eye."

On and on Brye went, covering all bases and last-minute details. Although she felt like crawling back into bed and pulling the sheets over her head, never would she ever admit it to anyone. The tour would continue without interruption.

It had been two days since Chad had stepped foot in the office. He rode up the elevator, bent on collecting his briefcase. Important contracts needed his attention before Monday morning.

At Jennifer's request, he'd taken two days off in preparation for their engagement party. Why Jennifer wanted him to remain accessible to her for the past several days had remained a mystery to him. Particularly since he had not contributed to the planning in any way. And especially since Chad didn't know why he allowed this farce of an engagement to continue as long as it had.

The engagement party had gone off without a hitch. His parents, as well as Jennifer's, had considered it a huge success. Chad had looked upon, as well as attended, the party as a spectator; he had held no interest in it whatsoever. The entire evening, his thoughts catered to Brye: What was she doing? Did she hate him for this? Was she thinking about him? Did she think of him or their last night together?

On and on it went, deep into the troubling night. Even after going home with Jennifer. Particularly before, during, and after they had engaged in sexual intercourse.

Scornfully, Chad laughed. With Jennifer, he couldn't even bring himself to say lovemaking any longer. Chad "made love'" to Brye. In every sense of the word. With Jennifer, he merely participated in the sexual act—and even that wasn't very satisfying.

The elevator doors parted. Chad stepped into the reception area. The office, at least on this floor, was generally empty on weekends. The sight of Rhonda sitting at her desk, talking animatedly into her phone headset, sent electrical shocks scurrying along Chad's spine. He walked deeper into the spacious room and was even more surprised to see Brian's door open. Altering directions, he headed toward his right-hand man's office.

Chad picked up on the yelling long before he hit the door.

"Dammit, Kierra! I don't give a shit what she wants!" Brian belted into the receiver. "You tell her it's either the bodyguard or we abort…right now. It's her choice. And it's nonnegotiable!"

A shadow fell across his desk. Brian's head flew up. Chad lounged just inside his office door. Frantically, Brian waved him in. "Fine," he said. "If anything else comes up—and I don't care what it is—call…regardless of the time."

The beginnings of a tension headache badgered Brian relentlessly. Brows pleated into a tight grimace, he massaged the bridge of his nose. "Brye was attacked last night by knife point," he warned Chad.

Stunned into silence, Chad's heart quit beating, then sluggishly jump-started, and leaped into his throat. For weeks now, he'd been walking on shaky ground. But now, with the discerning news Brian ambushed him with, his world ceased to exist as he had known it. If anything happened to Brye…

"Attempted rape," Brian continued.

"Brye?" Chad managed to utter. Knees knocking with fear, he collapsed into a chair. "Is she—"

"She fought him off and was able to get away." The steady pulsation radiating from the base of his nose strangled the blood vessels riding along his skull. Wearily, awake since her call at three in the morning, he was hoping to do all he could to make things right on this end. "She's sustained some ugly bruises. Kierra says she's pretty shaken up, but she refuses to take a few days off to recuperate. And she is defiantly determined to continue with the tour."

"How did it happen?" Chad queried. "When did it happen?" His facial muscles constricted in fear. For Brye. For him at the thought of losing the only woman he loved.

"Late last night. Everyone went out to a club to listen to live reggae. Brye remained behind. She couldn't sleep, so she went out for a walk."

It's my fault, Chad silently condemned. His hand balled into a tight fist. *She couldn't sleep because of me. She had her mind on the engagement party*. He knew it as well as he knew his own name.

"Since the attack, everyone's running on a short fuse. Tempers are flaring. Everyone's barking at the other. They're all blaming themselves for not being there when Brye needed someone. And Kierra says, through it all, Brye's been working double-time striving to convince everyone that she's the one at fault."

Half listening, Chad's insides shook. For the first time since Brye had forged a tumultuous passageway back into his life, he was able to see with deliberate clarity. What he now realized, all he could see, is that he loved Brye, and his entire behavior over the past few months sickened him. Vowing to himself, if Brye could forgive his behavior, he would do whatever it took to make their relationship right.

Able to pull his mind together, for the first time in weeks, Chad functioned at top capacity. He fired off a barrage of questions. "Did she report the incident to the police? Have they gotten involved?"

"They've begun an extensive investigation," Brian enlightened. His knuckles beat against the top of his desk. "During the ensuing struggle, the assailant dropped a double-edged dagger. For whatever reason, he forgot to retrieve it. They've already obtained fingerprints. They've also retrieved skin samples from under Brye's nails where she scratched him across the face."

"Are you sure Brye's okay? You said she has some bruises. Where are they? Was she badly hurt?" Chad pulled himself straighter and freed his mind, intent on soaking up every ounce of information Brian delivered.

"Kierra says he slapped her around a bit, punched her in the back." Brian's eyes dropped to his bouncing fist. He stared as if its actions were brought on by its own accord. The involuntary action halted in midair.

Trepidation quickly shifted into anger. If given the chance, Chad would not hesitate to kill the bastard who'd done this to Brye. If needed, he would search the world's four corners until he found the assailant. "Why didn't anyone call me?" The question was moot since Chad had spent the night with Jennifer. If they had attempted to call, they wouldn't have connected with him.

Brian accosted Chad with an undeviating eye. He knew Chad had been with Jennifer, hosting an engagement party. He could have called his cell phone but had refused to interrupt the festivities. "Rhonda was instructed to phone your apartment every half hour until she reached you. I don't know if she's been able to stick to that schedule, however, because the phone's been ringing off the hook all morning long. News reporters looking for a story, fans wanting to offer words of comfort, employees calling in to see if they can be of any assistance."

"You said Brye refuses to cut the tour short. What steps have we taken to protect her?"

"I've hired a bodyguard." He failed to report that he, himself, had wanted to jump on the plane and go after her himself. "He was on a plane to Florida one hour after I spoke with Brye this morning." A faint smile popped across Brian's worn features. "In no uncertain terms, she made known her disapproval. But whether she likes it or not, I put my foot down on this one."

Face drawn and set, Chad prepared to take command once again. "Right now, Kierra's our eyes and ears. She's the closest to Brye. She's seen her, spoken to her. Does she have any concerns with Brye continuing the tour?"

"Brye says she can finish…she *wants* to finish." Brian swirled in his chair. He rotated toward his window. A splash of sunlight drizzled across his forearm. "Kierra believes she will. But she also says Brye is the one holding the entourage together, trying to deflect their guilt. She's also handling the press as well as satisfying fans and curiosity-seekers. Kierra's afraid all the added pressure will eventually take its toll." Brian frowned. His head lowered. His fingers stroked throbbing temples.

"Within the past twenty-four hours, Kierra says Brye has only had about two hours of sleep. This morning, she nearly fainted in the bathroom."

Chad stared at Brian without speaking, yet his mind reeled from the piquant news. His brain flew through some quick calculations. Five weeks ago, he had made love with Brye for the first time in years—without protection. It was highly plausible Brye suffered from the added strain and pressures of her crushing night. It was also conceivable that her grueling schedule over the past four and a half weeks had been taxing to her already overloaded system. But he could not overlook the feasibility that she could be pregnant…with his child. One way or another, he needed to find out.

Just then, Rhonda stuck her head in the door. "Chad, you have a phone call."

"Take a message," he barked. "Then hold any other calls I might—"

"He's been calling all morning," Rhonda cut in. "He wouldn't talk to Brian…said it had to be you."

Sighing in frustrated acquiescence, Chad asked, "Who is it?"

"A young boy. Says his name's Anthony."

Chad's hand whipped across Brian's desk to reach his phone. He stabbed at the blinking light. "Anthony? Is everything all right?"

Anxiety-ridden, in finally reaching Chad, the relief rushing through Anthony's tiny voice traveled miles across the line and touched Chad. "Mama Linn said that a bad man hurt Brye last night," he managed to say. "Have you talked to her? Is she doing okay?"

Chad expelled a silent whiff of air. He should have guessed Anthony would be having a tough time digesting the news. He rushed to reassure. "No, Anthony, I haven't spoken with her. But yes, from what I understand, she's doing fine."

"But you don't know that for sure because you haven't talked to her yourself." Anthony hesitated. He redirected the subject. "When I lived with my mother, whenever she hurt me, Bethany's always been there to comfort me. We've been there for each other. And now, whenever I have a bad dream, or whenever I feel sad, Brye's there for me...for Bethany. She's never let us down." Again Anthony paused. When he continued, his tone cracked with emotion. "There's no one there for Brye, Mr. Collier. She doesn't have anyone to hold her or comfort her or tell her everything's gonna be all right. She's going through this alone and she shouldn't be by herself."

Anthony, Bethany, and Brye were linked by a spiritual and emotional bond. From the first day in seeing the three together, Chad had recognized their close ties. In Anthony's need to comfort Brye, the sensitive young boy also possessed the need to be comforted. He was afraid for Brye. He was afraid for himself, for his sister. Anthony was as afraid to lose Brye—the only person he'd learned to put his trust in other than his twin sister—just as he, himself, was afraid. At all costs, Chad needed to dispel the clinging fears—for himself as well as for the twins. In his heart, he knew Brye would expect nothing less of him.

Decision struck, he praised, "It never ceases to amaze me on how wise you are for a six-year-old kid. But you're right, Anthony. Brye does need someone. She needs us. Put Linn on the phone, I'm going to have her pack you and Bethany a bag. We're going on a trip."

After issuing orders to Linn, he disconnected. Under normal conditions, Brian and Rhonda would have afforded Chad his privacy. Today, with all hell breaking loose, they had listened to his one-sided conversation. Both wondered about the composition of the call. Both pondered over the identity of Anthony and Bethany. Both were wise enough not to ask.

Forthwith, Chad barked out his plan of action. Down to the minuscule of details, with Brian and Rhonda filling in the spaces he overlooked, Chad meticulously planned the next few days of Brye's life. Upon leaving to pick up the twins, he was assured all would be in place once his plane settled down at St. Petersburg-Clearwater International Airport.

"So," Rhonda remarked, her tone one of prying concern. "What do you make of all that?"

Brian shrugged. It was not something he usually did, imbibe in office rumor. But in this one instance, he could barely suppress his answer. "I think Jennifer is going to be short one fiancé when Chad gets back."

"Oh well," Rhonda shrugged, not the least bit overthrown or displeased, "it's something we all have to learn some time during our short life span."

"What's that?" Brian wearily asked.

"We can't always have everything our daddies promise to buy us!"

Her desk phone began blaring off the hook. Rhonda raced after the rowdy sound.

"Our client is extremely dissatisfied with the services rendered," the displeased baritone spoke over the telephone.

"I ran into some unexpected problems," the gruff voice on the receiving end noted.

"You were paid well to anticipate unexpected problems."

"Things got out of hand."

"I'm not interested in your problems. I'm only interested in solutions. You are a hot item at the moment. I need to devise a solution that will cool things down at bit."

The line fell silent. The disgruntled baritone then said, "You will continue to lay low until I can obtain some identity papers for you. We need to get you out of the area as soon as possible."

"How soon will that be?"

"Within the next few days...no longer than a week. Just hang tight. If you're caught before we get to you, you're on your own."

"I won't get caught."

The line went dead.

"That stupid fuck!" The baritone slammed the burner phone down hard on the table. His eyes bored relentlessly into a large, unsavory character standing at attention. "Our client is not happy. He hurried to point out that he didn't pay us so he could take risks. And with the cops obtaining that fool's fingerprints, hair, and skin samples, it's only a matter of time before he's caught. And once that happens, it won't be long before he turns state's evidence."

An unmerciful frown emulated his intractable mood. "He will have to be eliminated. Immediately." He nodded, satisfied he approached the most suitable solution for everyone involved. "I'll get back to you with details."

The standing man nodded in acknowledgment. He turned and left the room.

Still lying in bed, Jennifer had been basking in the night's glorious events when the news of Brye's attack flickered across the television screen. In morbid fascination, she listened as the story unfolded before her pleased eyes.

Although she would never accuse Daniel, nor would she ever speak of this matter to him, without a shadow of a doubt, she recognized his handiwork.

This should do it. Jennifer's laughter exploded with unconfined giddiness. This should make the bitch turn tail and run...maybe she'll even rip up her contract with Romanique Cosmetics.

She jumped out of bed and danced around the room. This was cause for a celebration. But first she would call Chad and see if he had heard the news. She might even be woman enough to offer Brye her condolences…and good riddance.

Jennifer halted in front of a full-sized mirror. She grinned wickedly to herself. Yes, this was turning out to be a splendid day all the way around.

26

IN THE FRAGRANCE SECTION of Nordstrom's, Brye surreptitiously peered at the time while signing what she believed to be her millionth autograph. Scheduled to begin the shoot for her third Mystique commercial in one hour, she should have been back in her hotel room by now. Yet she found it extremely difficult to extract herself from the monopolizing crowd.

As suspected, the entire day spilled with disorderly order. First she had to contend with her own entourage. Cory had remained beside himself the entire time, diligently working at repairing her face. Brye found herself continually reassuring him it wasn't his fault; she had to reassure the others as well.

Next, she had to battle the news media. After issuing a short statement for the press, she was carted off to the Pinellas Square Mall.

There, between the makeovers Cory provided, the endorsement of Mystique body products, the well-wishers, curiosity-seekers, and autograph hounds, the morning slipped by quickly yet much too frenzied.

A thirty-minute lunch break was spent with a carton of yogurt mixed with a Q&A session with the St. Petersburg's police. Afternoon turned out to be an instant replay of the morning. Through it all, record sales for Romanique products climbed to an all-time high.

And, finally, there was Tank—her appointed bodyguard.

Tank?

His mother knew what she was doing when she named that one. With a body to match his title, he stood six feet six inches tall and extended outward as wide as a brick wall. An ardent bodybuilder.

When notified that she was the proud recipient of her own personal bodyguard, Brye had imagined him to be stern, impersonal, impenetrable, and very much unapproachable. She had expected someone wearing a penetrating glare, a sour expression, and a dry sense of humor. She figured him for a stuffed shirt, wearing government-issued shades, dark business suit, and hair trimmed to perfection.

The moment she met him, she instantly absorbed his appearance, and he immediately dispelled all preconceived notions.

On his first day on the job, Tank wore a pair of loose-fitting jeans, chambray shirt—which did little to hide his powerful physique—and a pair of Reebok leather cross-trainers. Light brown hair was drawn back into a long ponytail, diamond stud earring pierced his left ear. His amiable demeanor was one of someone not having to prove himself…to anyone. But then with a body like his, why did he have to? And when he laughed—a deep, lazy, unpretentious chuckle—Brye decided she liked it, and she liked him. Having a bodyguard wouldn't be as bad as she had imagined. If nothing else, he blended well with the rest of her party.

A cue from Kierra engendered Tank to step up to Brye's side. He led her away from the buzzing crowd and beyond the lingering aroma of merging perfume. With Tank on one side, Kierra on the other, they strolled past women's apparel, rode down the department store's escalator, and trekked toward a private office.

"There's some people here to see you." Kierra paused just outside the closed door.

Brye groaned. Her eyes rolled toward the ceiling. "Please…no more detectives," she whined.

"They're not detectives."

"Then who?"

"Why don't you find out?" Hand on the brass doorknob, Kierra swung it open.

Inside, Anthony and Bethany occupied themselves with a box of crayons and a *Grimm's Fairy Tale* coloring book. Chad hovered over them singing praises to their artistic creativity.

Brye's sudden appearance drove the twins out of their chairs. They tore across the room to get to her. Astonished, yet exhilarated at the unexpected sight, Brye dropped to her knees and gathered the scrambling twins into her welcoming embrace, into her heart, into her senses. She inhaled deeply the sweet scent of their childhood aromas. She basked in the devoted alliance the three of them shared.

"I missed you two soooo much." Brye planted a kiss on their foreheads. "But what are you doing here?"

Brye was met with a double dose of tolerant smiles.

"Mama Linn told us what happened," Anthony started.

"And we wanted to make sure you were all right," Bethany finished.

"Are you really all right?" they cried in unison.

"Much more so now since the two of you are here." Brye needed this, and she needed them, but she hadn't realized how much until this very moment.

"We thought, after what happened to you, you might need a hug?" Bethany offered.

"So you flew all this way to give me one?" Brye smiled at the twins with amused disbelief. She pulled them back into her arms. God, but they felt so good. "Well, you're right. I do need a hug. And I thank you, my loves. You two are just what the doctor ordered."

On the sidelines, overseeing the emotional exchange, Chad finally recognized his childish behavior for what it was. He'd done nothing but hurt Brye these past few months. And when she looked up into his face, when he witnessed the reflection of love and gratitude bouncing off her exhilarated expression, he knew now that he wanted Brye for not just as a bed partner, but as his lifetime mate, lover, and wife. It was time to let go of the anger and pain. It was time to accept and trust the love he sustained for this sensitive and loving creature. But Chad also understood that he could not pledge his undying love, nor petition for her hand in marriage until he dissolved his rash engagement with Jennifer.

"Thank you for bringing the twins to me." Brye pushed herself off the floor. She reached outward to rest her fingers lightly within Chad's palms. To anyone looking, it was a friendly gesture of gratitude.

"Even if the kids hadn't called, I wouldn't have been able to stay away." Unsatisfied with a mere touch of her hand, unable to hide his feelings any longer, not caring who watched, Chad dragged Brye against his chest. In front of the twins, Kierra and Tank, his mouth sought and found hers.

Unable to restrain himself, this was not a chaste kiss. His kiss matured, grew passionate, and was definitely all-consuming. Every tangled emotion overloaded his system—his love, his need, his desire, his remorse—went into that one efficacious kiss.

Responding to the changes Brye sensed within Chad, she matched his ardor with her own and allowed herself to get lost in a miscellany of delicious sensations…all which drove her to a point teetering just above the edge of ecstasy.

And as the small group absorbed the arcane scene, the heated contact was greeted with varying degrees of interest and concerns.

The twins shared conspiratorial grins. Their plan was working perfectly. Since hearing of Chad's impending marriage to another woman, they had set out to sabotage the wedding. In their attentive eyes, there left little doubt that Brye and Chad remained two halves of one whole. The two headstrong individuals would never be completely functional unless they accepted what fate held in store for them. And in assisting their destiny along, when first learning of Brye's attack, Bethany and Anthony decided to take advantage of the situation. First and foremost, for their own peace of mind, it really had been imperative they see Brye for themselves—they needed absolute proof of her safety. But if it meant hurling Chad and Brye together in the process…well, it was something that couldn't be helped.

Tank greeted the scene playing out in front of him with a blind eye. The kissing couple was none of his business. His job was to protect Brye. Anything else lodged out of his jurisdiction. And right now, she appeared to be doing fine without any assistance from him.

Kierra, on the other hand, strove to divert her probing eyes as well as her rising curiosity elsewhere. She was unsuccessful in both endeavors. The preceding evening, Chad had been the guest of honor at his own engagement party. Yet at this very moment, he laid a kiss on Brye that was so heated with passion, it threatened to overload the entire department store's central air-conditioning.

That is not a kiss of friendship or of gratitude, Kierra thought to herself. Totally mind-boggling, it couldn't help but rile her curiosity.

Kierra finally broke her attention away from the intriguing sight. Converging her focus on the twins, she stared into eyes so intense, so serious, she wondered what happened to the little kids inside. Raised in a one-parent home, she understood what it meant to become hardened by circumstances journeyed beyond one's control. She recognized the look all too well; the twins' pensive expressions were of kids who'd literally passed over their carefree days; she stared into faces of little people living with the weight of the world anchored on their shoulders. Her heart reached out to them. She rushed to offer, "There's a place to get ice cream in the mall. Why don't we give Brye and Mr. Collier a chance to"—she stumbled, searching for the most appropriate passage—"talk."

"Yeahhhh!" Anthony's and Bethany's smile lit up their eyes with anticipated delight. Kierra couldn't help but grin at their beaming faces. *This is the way they're supposed to look: exhilarated, lighthearted, and free of all worries.*

"Can we go, Mr. Collier? Please?" Their bodies jumped up and down in unison with their spirited chant.

"Of course you can." Chad released Brye. Her lipstick silhouetted his swollen lips. "Brye and I need to talk. Tank, I'd appreciate if you keep an eye on the twins for me."

Tank nodded. Although he'd been hired by Brian, Kierra had installed within him that Chad was top dog. Tank got paid to go wherever he was told.

Kierra had picked Chad up from the airport in the Camaro Convertible she'd rented for their four-day stay. The striking similarities between Brye and the twins had astounded her. Another mystery: how were the four of them interconnected? She cared enough about her job not to ask. She did, however, call attention to the parallelism.

"Let's go, little Brye. You too, little man." She caught them both by the hand.

Strolling out the door, Bethany asked, "Why did you call me 'little Brye'?"

"Because you look so much like her."

"You think so?"

"I know so."

"But she's so pretty," Bethany wistfully noted.

"Maybe so. But she doesn't hold a candle to you."

Listening to their parting repartee, a lump developed in Brye's throat. She could have kissed Kierra. With little or no effort on her part, she had drawn Bethany and Anthony out of their reserved shells.

"Are you sure you're all right," Chad asked as the room emptied out.

"A little sore," Brye answered in truth. "And Cory worked on my face longer than usual to cover the bruises. But all-in-all, I'm feeling pretty lucky." With facial tissue in hand, Brye delicately patted at the artificial color playing along Chad's lips.

"I should have been there for you."

Brye dropped her hand from his mouth. She bowed her head to keep from looking into his eyes. "You were…otherwise engaged." It was not an accusatory statement. It was merely a reflective thought she chose to verbalize.

"I'm sorry, Brye." He spoke softly, unusually repentant.

She nodded but did not raise her eyes to encounter his.

Chad clipped her under the chin with thumb and forefinger. Gently, he raised her face to meet his. "I'm *really* sorry, Brye," he repeated, his loving emotions intensified with the piercing look he honored her with.

His apology stretched farther than his inability to have been her support system in the past sixteen hours. It delved further into their lives, encompassing all aspects of their connecting world, reaching back into their blazing past.

Brye began to drown in his mesmerizing baby blues. Persuasive eyes were bathed in so much love, that for the first time in years, Brye attained a sense of hope for her future; a future embarked with Chad at the helm.

"Soon we're going to have a long talk about our future." It was if Chad had read her mind. He lifted her fingers to his lips. Nuzzling each exquisite digit with his mouth, he pleaded, "All I ask is that you give me a little time to rectify the mess I've created over the past months. If you can see your way clear of doing that, if you can forgive me for what I've put you through, then I promise I'll be able to freely discuss our relationship and where we want to go with it."

"I have forgiven you." Brye didn't have any idea what had triggered the newfound changes within Chad, but her beacon of hope began to illuminate bigger and much brighter. She would give him as much time as he needed.

Chad reluctantly pulled away. A tapestry duffel bag took up space in the corner of the large office. Lifting it in the air, he prompted, "Why don't you change into these? We're leaving as soon as you get dressed."

"Leaving?" Startled, Brye stood in a fog of confusion. "But where? I have a commercial shoot in thirty minutes."

"Your schedule has been cleared." Chad unzipped the bag. He removed a pair of belted cotton denim shorts, a button front sleeveless shirt, and a cotton denim baseball cap.

Brye came out of her stunned lethargy long enough to protest. "But—"

"No buts, Brye!" Chad firmly apprised. "You've been working nonstop for four weeks, some days putting in anywhere from sixteen to eighteen hours. It's time for a break, and it won't kill you to take three days off for a bit of rest and relaxation. I've canceled the commercial shoot. We'll refit it into your schedule as soon as I feel you're up to it." Along with a smile to soften his words, he handed over her shorts. "This is a direct order coming down from your boss. And I will not tolerate insubordination, Brye. Besides, I promised we'd take the twins to Disney World, and I don't think you want to disappoint them."

"Disney World, huh?" Brye grinned. Chad's abrupt transformation threw her way off-kilter, but she was ready, willing, and able to take full advantage and follow his lead. She gathered her clothing. "You planned it so I couldn't refuse, didn't you?"

Chad returned her smile with a lopsided grin of his own. "I decided not to depend on my own exceptional good looks and persuasive charm to convince you into taking a few days off."

"It's a good thing too. Just because you're used to having your way with women every time you flash those gorgeous baby blues doesn't mean your unsavory methods would have worked on me."

"No?" With dangerous intent, Chad stepped closer. "What *do* I have to do to get back into your good graces?"

Brye took one step backward. "There's nothing you can do."

"Are you sure about that?" Two wide steps forward, and he stood over Brye. Fevered bodies stood so close, two hearts pounded as one. "Not even if I did this?" His head dipped. His tongue ran a moistened trail along the delicate chords protruding from her piquant neck.

"Not even that." As Brye spoke, her heart danced at double time.

"How about this?" Chad's dropped his face lower. Playful lips shuffled along the swell of her breast.

"No," Brye whimpered. Her actions belied the word. Grabbing a fistful of his hair, she pressed him into her fluttering chest.

"God, sweetheart!" Chad stepped out of the game and stepped back into real life. "Why can't I get enough of you?"

Brye also lost sight of the game as she regained her sense of their close surroundings. "We can't do this, Chad. Not here." Pulling together her frazzled emotions, she put some much-needed distance between them. Smiling mischievously, she added, "If you maintain your distance and be a good little boy, I'll concede to the fact that you know how to tweak a woman's button in all the right places."

"Your buttons are the only ones I want to tweak, Brye. For now and forever."

The significance of his words hung heavy in the air. From across the room, body frozen in place, Brye blinked demurely at Chad. Not knowing how to respond, uncertain she wanted to, she turned her back on Chad and began to undress.

"Could you watch the door while I throw my clothes on?" she tossed over her shoulder.

A sharp intake of breath, a string of curse words reverberated off the four walls.

Alarmed, Brye swung around to confront Chad. "What's wrong?" she demanded.

"Your back," Chad swore to himself. The anger swelled, built to a crescendo, and then threatened to blow like a volcano on the verge of eruption. Several long strides, and he stood at Brye's side. Twisting her around, he scrutinized the bruises on her back. "Did he do this? I could kill him for laying a hand on you!" Inflamed irises emitted glowing balls of fire. The sparks flying around Brye generated enough fuel to set the entire mall ablaze. Brye set out to extinguish the fury fueling the embers.

In soothing circular motions, she ran her thumbs along the incensed lines buckling his handsome features. "I'm really looking forward to spending this time with you and the twins. Please don't ruin this for me by dwelling on the attack. Let the police handle it." Her caressing touch lowered and lingered on his broad chest. "I'm fine. I really am," she rushed to emphasize. "The fact that I have this uncontrollable need to make love to you tells me he did not traumatize me as badly as he could have. Can we decide, here and now, that for the next three days, all talk about my assault is off limits?"

Chad's burning rage lowered to an insignificant spark. His expression visibly mellowed. Right now, he wanted to tell her how much he loved her but knew the words weren't appropriate—at least not until he settled matters with Jennifer. So he abided himself by saying, "Do you know how proud I am of you?"

Eyes shining as bright as prized gems, Brye shook her head from side to side.

"I'd like to show you. But if I do, you'll probably never get your clothes on and we'll never get on our way. So how 'bout a rain check?"

"I'm going to hold you to that."

"Good." Chad moved back to the door. Brye rushed to finish dressing. Chad found it difficult maintaining his distance and composure as Brye taunted him with her partially clad body. When she stood before him, completely dressed, only then was he able to breathe a huge sigh of relief.

Pulling her hair back into a ponytail, Brye put the baseball cap on her head. "I'm ready when you are."

Chad pulled a pair of mauve-colored shades from the tapestry bag. Sliding them over her eyes, he said, "Now we're ready."

At the door, he hesitated. "Oh, I forgot something." Chad pulled his cell phone out of its holder clipped to the waist of his jeans. "Something for you from everyone at Brylinn. They all wanted to give you a message, and the quickest way possible was to record it. We have a ninety-minute ride from here to Orlando. You can listen to it in the car if you like."

A warm glow of affection gushed from Brye's smile. Appreciative of the support everyone offered, she had to swallow past the lump in her throat before answering. "I'd like that very much," she finally managed.

"Then let's go."

This time it was Brye's turn to hold back. "Chad?"

He turned and stared silently into her soft expression.

"Thank you." It was all that needed to be said. Yet the depth of her utterance went far beyond those two simple words. It went way beyond thanking him for bringing her the messages, the twins, and himself. Underneath it all, Chad sensed Brye was also thanking him for finally letting go of the past. And he had let go. So much so he looked forward to the future. Their future. Again, Chad wanted to tell her how much he loved her. He also wanted to demonstrate that love.

Smothering his desire, Chad inclined his head. Their foreheads lightly touched. For several seconds afterward, in the hushed atmosphere, they stood united. Finally pulling away, he commanded in gruff voice, "Let's go find the twins."

27

Joe Zimmerman, an average male, living an average life, working at an average job, considered himself to be a run-of-the-mill individual; an ordinary guy, a regular Joe Blow trying to make a living the best way he knew how. He figured himself to be an honest man. Well…as honest as they come anyway. If solicited on the street to buy stolen merchandise, he saw nothing wrong in purchasing the hot items. Hell, after all, he hadn't had a hand in the actual burglarizing. And if Joe came across a lost billfold loaded with cash and credit cards, he'd gladly return it to its owner—minus a service fee of course, which would rack up to be the exact amount of money stuffed inside the wallet. And then there was the time Joe walked out of a grocery store with a sack of groceries, along with money in hand he intended to use for his purchases. But right before doling out his dollars, a highly disruptive exhibition occurred several aisles down.

The explosive commotion interrupted the normal everyday flow of production. Attention turned elsewhere, the cashier neglected to collect all monies due, and Joe managed to slip out the store's automatic doors without being accosted for money owed. All the while, not once did it occur to Joe that the cashier would suffer any mishap over the unfortunate incident, nor did it cross his mind that she could lose her job. To Joe's cynical eye, everyone had problems. In fact, he held enough of his own and refused to waste time worrying about others.

In his entire forty-three years of living, Joe Zimmerman had never considered himself to be a lucky man—nor was he unlucky. He didn't hold illusions of who or what he could make of himself or his life; just a middling man trudging through life. He didn't claim to be an opportunity seeker, but if opportunity knocked on his door, well…let's just say he would not fail to invite it in.

And the day he spotted Brye Grayson at Disney World was the day that a goldmine fell into his unsuspecting lap.

For months, his girlfriend had been riding him about spending the day at the highly innovative and popular tourist attraction. Too old for such nonsense, nonetheless, he finally complied. Loaded with one of those disposable cardboard box cameras, Joe set out for his once-in-a-lifetime experience.

One hour into the swing of things, he spotted the illustrious supermodel. Disguised in hat and dark shades, he could pick her out anywhere. A devout fan, in his eyes, she was the most beautiful woman he ever set eyes on—not that he would ever admit that to his current girlfriend.

Joe figured he knew all there was to know about Brye Grayson—at least he knew everything the press could dig up to write about her. What he didn't know and what he figured no one else knew, were the people she was gallivanting around the theme park with: two kids and a man. They looked and acted like a family; a real family. And the kids possessed the same distinguishing features as Brye.

Instantly, his mind worked overtime. He could get exclusive pictures and sale them for thousands of dollars to one of those tabloid magazines. Hell, maybe he would contact several magazines and wait it out for the highest bidder. He could make a fortune.

At a reasonable distance, with girlfriend in tow, he followed them around, snapping picture after picture. At times when Brye and her male companion became so engrossed with each other, he bravely inched closer.

Once he finished the entire roll, he sought out a Kodak stand to buy another camera. By the time he obtained the equipment he needed, however, Joe had lost sight of his ticket to fame. No matter. He had taken enough pictures to set him up big time.

That same evening, he deposited his film in a one-hour photo mat. Too late to pick up his processed film the same night, he stood now, in the check-out lane, waiting behind two other customers.

Nervously, he tapped his foot. What if the film's overexposed? What if the lighting had been all wrong? What if the lens hadn't focused properly? What if the photo mat lost his films? What if they ruin his pictures? What if?

Joe couldn't turn his mind off. So many things could have gone wrong, and he wouldn't be able to breathe easier until he held the celebrated pictures in hand.

One down, one to go. The woman with the baby stroller stuffed her package into her purse. Stepping aside, she wheeled her baby out of line and out of Joe's memory banks for the remainder of his life.

Fidgeting even more, Joe started humming and beating the palm of his hand along his jean-clad thigh in time to a rhythm conducted only inside his mind. Calling undue attention to himself, he only became aware of the boisterous spectacle he was making, only when the lanky man standing in front of him turned to blind him with a scorching look.

The perturbed man squelched Joe's nervous flutter with a smoldering dart of an eye. Mumbling an incoherent apology, Joe blessed him with a feeble smile. The abrasive man turned away, paid for his purchases, and then stomped out the door.

Joe stepped up to the counter. Giving up his claim check, he waited with bated breath until the clerk returned with his items. In a hurry to look over his purchase, Joe thrust a fifty-dollar bill at the cashier, then dove toward the clearing.

"Don't you want your change?" the startled man called after him.

Joe returned, snatched up his money, and almost fell out the door.

On the outside, it wasn't until his lungs screamed for much-needed air that he realized he had hold of his breath. Gulping an ample amount of the stifling Florida heat, head hung low, pictures pressed protectively against his side, he stumbled toward his 1983 Chevy Impala.

The interior of his car felt like the inside of a baked oven. Profuse sweat streamed down his forehead. Damp and sticky, his shirt readily adhered to his soggy back. Joe reached across the seat and rolled down the passenger window. A hot, humid breeze sifted inward. It only added to the stifling heat.

At the moment, Joe didn't care. If things went as planned, he'd be able to buy himself a new car. A truck, actually. Dodge Ram. Midnight blue. Fully loaded.

He forced himself to come out of his fantasizing long enough to look over his handiwork. Fumbling with the closed envelope, he pulled out the much desired photos. His breath discharged in one, long, satisfying hiss.

Her image smiled up at him bigger than life itself. Initially, Joe hurriedly shuffled through the stack, making sure each photo was picture perfect. Then he took his sweet time in examining each one. There was Brye hugging the little girl; laughing down at the boy; staring mesmerized into her male companion's face. Joe wondered if the man knew how lucky he was to be with the supermodel.

But by the way the unidentified male gazed at Brye, the way he touched her, the way he kissed her, Joe figured he damn well knew how lucky he was.

In one shot, they all sat on a park bench, eating ice cream. All except Brye. Joe had snapped the picture as she sampled her male companion's cone. He took another picture of the man pressing the cone against Brye's nose. And another of Brye laughing as the man licked the ice cream off.

Unbelievable!

In another picture, the man had actually snatched Brye's cap off her head, lifted her sunglasses, and gave her a kiss smack dab on the lips. He held a clear shot of Brye Grayson. Proof positive. No one could dispute the authenticity of her identity.

Joe found himself daydreaming as he continued to maul through the photos. He saw himself sitting next to Brye, licking her, kissing her, doing all kinds of shameful things to her million-dollar body. And as he fantasized, he found himself growing hard.

"Get a grip, man!" Joe shook himself out of his absorbed world. "It will never happen. The pretty lady would never give you the time of day." *Maybe not*, he thought to himself, *but I have her pictures.*

Joe climbed out of his car. Before selling to the highest bidder, he decided to treat himself to a second set. His own personal collection. His girlfriend would never have to know. More at ease than when he first entered the photo establishment, Joe walked through the door happily humming to himself.

In the living area of the three-bedroom, three-bath, commodious condominium, Brye and Chad laid on a sofa which doubled as a queen-sized sleeper. Part of a vacation rental, the condo was large enough to accommodate eight people with minimal strain. Stretched out along the couch, legs intertwined, naked bodies partially clad by a thin percale sheet, Brye's head lay in the crook of Chad's arm. The atmosphere sizzled with their lovemaking.

Right knee bent, resting along the channeled back of the sofa, elbow propped on the rolled side arm, Chad stared down into Brye's tranquil facial cast.

"You look content." He nuzzled teasing lips along the side of her forehead.

"I *am* content," Brye purred. Soft, radiant eyes embraced Chad, encompassed his sanguine features with their glowing exuberance. The last three days had been heaven-sent. Gifts from above. And like an ill-fated person who knew happiness did not last forever, Brye cherished every second. As the room fell silent, she relived the past several days.

The first evening, the entire drive from St. Petersburg to Orlando had been spent dozing in the car. Before settling into their condo, Chad had awakened her; Brye, the twins, and Chad had enjoyed a relaxing meal in the sheltered atmosphere of a quaint seafood restaurant.

Afterward, late night, the small intimate group prepared for bed. An extremely long day for Bethany and Anthony, jet lag soon crashed down on the two animated souls.

Baths were quickly executed, and the twins' minds shut down seconds before their tiny bodies hit their pillows.

A kidney-shaped Jacuzzi—already bubbling and awaiting its occupants—built directly into the floor of the master bedroom instantly caught Brye's attention. Taking a quick shower to scour off the day's makeup and grime, she wrapped a body towel around a torso beaten down with exhaustion. Barefoot, padding toward the Jacuzzi, silk strands of plush carpet embraced her toes, fondled the tired digits, and eased her over-fatigued feet. The luxurious sensation charged along the calf of her legs, darted along her thighs, invaded her body and caressed the core of her brain.

Her towel slipped to her feet. As her big toe dipped into the foaming water, the bedroom door opened. Towel slung low around a lean waist, Chad stood in the doorway.

The door soundlessly closed behind him as he stared into Brye's brutally stamped face. The discoloration around her eye and mouth fueled his quelled anger once again. He struggled for several seconds to get his fury under control.

Strolling over to Brye, as if he could heal with a heartfelt touch, he tenderly kissed the bruises on her face and backside. Then, silently, they climbed into the bubbling pool.

The concentrated heat seeped through every inch of Brye's pores, soothed her weary soul, and infused her convulsive mind. Before she knew it, her eyelids grew heavy, and her limbs were laden with lead. The pampering flow of water drew her downward.

"Brye?"

Brye woke with a start. She stared at Chad through weighted lids.

"Let's get you to bed."

Chad lifted her out of the Jacuzzi. Propped on her feet, through hazy eyes, she watched Chad kneel before her. Temperate hands roamed over her unresponsive body as he toweled her dry.

God, but I'm so tired. Brye swayed. *Why do I feel so drained?*

Back in Chad's arms, he hauled her off to bed. The mattress shifted under the pressing weight of two bodies, then shifted again as Chad rolled off. Tucking the sheets under her chin, he strolled toward the bedroom door.

"Don't go," Brye managed to stay awake long enough to plead, voice heavy with sleep.

Chad hesitated at the door.

"Please."

Chad backtracked. He slid under the cool sheets. Burrowed against the rock solid length of his body, Brye promptly fell asleep.

Sometime during the night, she awakened. They made incredible love, then drifted back off into contented slumber.

The next time she became aware of her sheltered surroundings, Chad's side of the bed had grown cold. Early morning sunlight pranced around the perimeter of the peach-and-green-colored room. Seconds after blinking the sleep away from her eyes, the twins, along with a smiling Chad taking up the rear, burst into her room, carting a loaded breakfast tray. Chocolate-filled croissants, Belgian waffles, eggs, bacon, fruit, orange juice, coffee—enough to feed an army. Veiling her naked body behind the bedsheets, Chad aided in sliding her arms in the silk robe he had carried into the room. Once presentable, the twins, dressed in their night clothing, climbed into bed beside her. Carving out his own niche, Chad joined them. The morning meal was shared and picked clean by all.

And thus set the pace for the duration of the trip: Brye being waited on hand and foot by Chad and the twins.

Between Disney World, Universal Studios, Sea World, and beach combing, their days had been fun-filled and exhilarating. For Brye, she partook in family gatherings she had never experienced and had always longed to be part of.

Through it all, whether in the car, or back at the condo for a short intermission, or even bumming on the beach, whenever Brye remained still for longer than a few minutes, she'd fall fast asleep.

Never had she slept so much in her life. The sudden alteration did not disturb Brye, however. The small amount of concern that did interfere with her mellow mood was shoved toward the back of her mind. If anything, she contributed her tiresome spirit to Chad's diligence in watching over her; it freed her mind from dwelling on her anguished soul and aided her in concentrating more on Chad and the twins. And much to her surprise, even her dead mother seemed to be cooperating with her happy-go-lucky mood; she hadn't made a contagious showing in weeks. Right now, Brye felt like the luckiest person alive.

Leaning over Brye, Chad took note of her sparkling eyes and the serene smile teasing full lips. Even her bruises appeared to be gradually fading. Despite having just made love, he continued to ache for her. From the very first day they had met, there remained this deep longing to have her. Over the years, the longing had only increased in intensity.

Maybe it was because he possessed the power to own her body but had never been able to grasp her mind. And to top it all off, he now faced the possibility that she carried his baby.

Not once, within the five week span of making love to her, had he worn any protection. Nor had he discussed birth control with Brye. As far as he could tell, she didn't use any. Next, he had to consider the large amount of sleep she seized at the drop of a hat; positively not the act of the woman who, until a few weeks ago, eliminated the word *sleep* from her vocabulary as well as from her daily activity roster.

With a sudden twinge of regret, his mind flew back to the past and the twins they lost; twins that would have been the same age as Bethany and Anthony. Twins that could have possibly been Bethany and Anthony. For a fleeting moment, Chad wondered if their failed history was trying to rectify itself.

Brow converging in dazed wonder, Chad's eye roved over Brye's quiescent form. Their last night together, Brye would be climbing aboard the tour bus in less than six hours. Hours earlier, the bus had driven to Orlando in preparation for the trip to Savannah, Georgia. Kierra had called and offered to take the twins to the movies, giving Chad and Brye a few intimate hours on their own. As soon as the condo had emptied and the front door had closed on the world beyond, as if they had shipped their kids off for a weekend at the grandparents, Brye and Chad took advantage of their newly acquired freedom. The stolen moments were utilized making love.

Gazing at her now, already, he felt an immediate stirring in his loins. Conceivably, this assiduous need to hold her, make passionate love to her, take care of her, stemmed from the long drawn-out years they had been separated from each other. Now he was trying to make up for lost time.

"What are you thinking about?" Brye had finally come out of her absorbed world long enough to find Chad soaking up his own ambiguous thoughts.

Chad met Brye with a profound eye. His fingers gently glided along her flat belly. He loved the notion that she might be carrying his baby. He hated not being able to discuss it with her until he dissolved his relationship with Jennifer. "I was thinking about you… how you were really feeling?"

Brye glided a pedicured toe along the interior of Chad's athletic thigh. Eyes twinkling devilishly, she hummed, "I feel fat and lazy and…hungry."

Chad chuckled. "Hungry for me?"

Looking sheepish, she answered, "Would you get mad if I said I craved a large pizza?"

Thoughtfully, Chad asked, "With Italian sausage?"

"I wouldn't have it any other way."

"And pepperoni?"

"Of course."

"Onion?"

"I've some breath freshener in my purse."

"Extra sauce and extra cheese?"

"You're a man after my own heart."

Stark naked, Chad extricated himself from Brye's limbs and jumped off the couch. "Let's do it." A man completely at ease with himself and his body, he strutted through the condo with no shame. A brochure boasting local eateries equipped to deliver lay hidden in a kitchen drawer. With pamphlet in hand, Chad circled the butcher-block bar separating the two rooms. He drew up a barstool while skimming through the ten-page advertisement. Reaching for the phone, he made the call.

Brye listened to his strong, confident voice, and a surge of pride swelled within her. She loved this man so much. How she had managed without him for so many years went way beyond her comprehension. But then, if she had to admit to herself, what she had been doing could not be placed on the same even keel as living. Not really. She had walked on the edge of limbo for far too long. Not knowing how to feel, not wanting to open her mind and heart had become second nature. But Chad had come back into her life. He had breathed life into her stalled lungs. He had stimulated senses anesthetized for longer than she cared to admit. And God help her soul, she had become dependent upon him.

Brye climbed off the couch. She wrapped the sheet around her naked body, tucking an end just beneath her armpit. "Don't forget the—"

"Mushrooms," Chad finished into the phone. Leaving name, address, and telephone number, he hung up.

"Great minds think alike," Brye stated. Moving up behind him, she threw her arms around his neck.

Velvety strands of hair sailed along Chad's trembling chest, sharpening his senses, arresting his breath. He loved her. And he loved the way her provocative fingers liquefied his torrid skin as she trailed a pathway of flames down the length of his upper torso. Her inflamed touch singed the ends of the fine sprays of hair dusting the area between his legs. She engulfed his stimulated member with a need too powerful to ignore.

A slight turn of his head, and he found his nose buried into the bracing aroma of Mystique scented hair. "Great minds think alike, huh?" he breathed into her neck. He shut his eyes against the sensuous flux of pleasure titillating throughout his body. "Tell me, Brye, what am I thinking right now?"

"What you're thinking," Brye teased, her migratory fingers steadily taunting him, "is not repeatable to the general public."

"Ah…but it's not the general public I'm interested in repeating it to." Grabbing her arm, he wheeled her around to face him. His sinewy thighs anchored her yielding hips. Drawing his mouth along her ear, he whispered something so deliciously arousing, Brye found herself blushing like a virginal bride. But her actions were less than chaste when she loosened the sheet and allowed it to spill down her solicitous body. She was far from wholesome as she dropped to the carpeted floor, spread her knees, and invited him to enter her private domain.

Time seemed to have come to a standstill as Brye waited for Chad to join her. At his own pace, he cruised toward the floor. Eager for their bodies to coagulate into one gratifying mass of passion, Brye grabbed him around the waist and yanked him downward.

"Impatient, are we?" Chad asked. His teasing smile displayed profuse amusement. Appreciative of the woman lying underneath him, ready to give herself to him completely, like a consummate epicurean, Chad luxuriated in the feel of her inviting body, the smell of her tantalizing scent, the passion behind her fiery demands. The need to savor this moment ran high. Despite Brye's urgent cries to douse the wildfire raging within, Chad continued to build on those flames. With deliberate and calculating movements, he fueled her passion, intensified the heat, and inflamed her ignited flesh into a raging inferno.

Finally, when Brye could stand it no longer, Chad pushed himself inside her throbbing vortex, filling her with his own desire. Yet much to her antagonistic disbelief, he continued to taunt. Leisurely sliding in and out of her, the distended yearning to have her thirst quenched was mocked by Chad's unhurried performance. And although she brazenly arched against him, dug her fingers along his steely backside, greedily pushed him deeper inside her, Chad obstinately held onto the handler's reins; he refused to be thrown from the driver's seat. Coaxing Brye into reckless abandonment, Chad commandeered her mind and body. He pushed and continued to push, until she moved beyond all rhyme and reason. He drove her forward until all that erupted from his impassioned lover was engendering pleas to be released from the restrictive bonds of tormented pleasure. And when he finally emancipated her from his binding constraints, when she cried out his name in sweet surrender, then and only then did he let go of the reins.

Barefoot, wearing a pair of lace-trimmed shorts and crop top, Brye ducked into Chad's bathroom. Over the running water, in deep resounding voice, he sang a medley of Chicago's greatest hits. Singing until he couldn't recall a stanza, he then switch to another of their more popular melodies.

Brye smiled to herself. If they had taken a shower together, she'd still be in there with him now, and they would have missed their dinner. As it happened, she had demanded they go into their separate corners. Finished with her shower first, she met the delivery man at her door.

"I hate to interrupt your impromptu concert," Brye yelled over the running water, "but the pizza's here and I have no money."

"My billfold's sitting on the dresser," he promptly offered. "Take whatever you need. I'll be out in a sec."

Perched in the middle of his room, Brye's eyes roamed and settled on the black leather wallet. She pulled out a twenty and a ten-dollar bill. Noting a slightly thick piece of paper folded in quarters, as it slipped out and dropped to the floor, Brye hurriedly swooped down to retrieve it. She then dashed out to pay the pizza man. Trading the pie for the $30, she told him to "keep the change" and shut and locked the door behind him.

The heat radiating from the bottom of the box warmed Brye's open palm. She slid the large cardboard box onto the coffee table. About to enter the kitchen to pour several glasses of lemonade, she suddenly realized she still clutched the fallen paper.

Absentmindedly, she unfolded the documents—two stapled sheets—to its original eight and a half by eleven size. While walking back to Chad's bedroom, her eyes rapidly skimmed over the document. When she realized what taunted her, her footsteps slowed, then halted altogether. All color drained from her face.

Towel slung low around his waist, body glistening with a fine mist, Chad strutted out the bathroom. "Did you find—" Brye's ashen face, the hurt preempting the violet hue of her eyes, struck him mid-sentence. The room had grown deathly quiet. So quiet, Chad could hear the nervous ticking of his heart. "What's wrong?" he demanded, taking one step forward.

Brye held the paper out in front of her as if it could shield her body from his seductive touch. She attempted a smile, but it faded into the now oppressive air. "I wasn't snooping…it dropped… fell out of your wallet… I didn't mean…" Giving up all attempts to explain, her voice faded into a low moan.

Knowing what Brye held in her possession, cursing himself for not getting rid of it years ago, as if it were poison, Chad held back from grabbing the venomous proof. Warily, he could only stare at Brye.

"Why?" Brye rasped. "Why did you keep this?"

"Brye." It was all he could say. Anything else would have been tactless. For how could he explain how distressed he had been when they first broke up? How could he explain how it had affected his life? How could he admit that he wanted to destroy her as he had believed she had destroyed him?

But in the end, he didn't have to explain; Brye knew exactly why he had held on to the toxic reminder.

"How could you? Why would you?" Her voice cracked, then came back stronger. It was one thing to strike out at her in a fit of rage. But Chad had, with malicious intent, sought her out to render some form of mental harm, exact his own means of justice. "All this time, all these years, you've wanted to seek revenge. And somehow"—her arms spread in front of her, taking in the entire room—"this all ties into it, doesn't it? How could you?" she repeated in anguish.

The distrust, her flagrant accusations, ripped Chad's chest apart. Blood pounding in his veins, beat relentlessly against his brow. He forced himself to remove the acrid records from Brye's shaking fingers. He stared down at it, although word for word, he knew by heart what was written there.

It was the contract. That damned contract Brye had signed years ago, relinquishing Chad of all rights and responsibilities of their baby in exchange for a million dollars. The second page held a copy of the actual check drawn on his father's personal checking account.

Funny, but he had always looked at this document as poison. Years ago, it had excreted its lethal toxin on his unsuspecting life, yielding nothing but pain and suffering. It had destroyed everything he believed in, taken away everything he sought to secure his future with. And now, resurrected again, with no antitoxin to counteract its cursed effects, just as infallible as before, it had risen like a powerful phoenix, stronger than ever, ready to destroy all he had worked hard to reestablish.

Not wanting to lie, afraid she would see through him if he did, Chad reluctantly admitted, "At first, yes. I wanted to extract my pound of revenge. I wanted you to pay for using me the way you had. But somewhere along the way, all the hurt, all the bitterness, didn't seem to matter anymore. Nothing mattered but the love I felt for you. I love you, Brye." He spoke with such intensity, Brye found herself wanting to believe. "I've always loved you. And my love is what I can't get past."

Brye's features crumbled into an anguished grimace. She wanted to accept him at face value. But the fact that he carried that cancerous document verified that his bitterness had run as deep as a bottomless well. So deep he'd kept the papers near and dear to his heart to imprison the detest he harbored for her. It aided in keeping his wounds open; it encouraged his severed heart to fester.

"What was the turning point for you, Chad? When did you decide to give me clemency?" With pained expression, she pushed. "Was it when you thought someone else could take me away from you for good? Was it when you thought I slept with Brian?"

"I've put that behind me, Brye." He longed to reach out to her, enfold her within his arms. Instead, he could only stand there, plead his case, and pray she understood. "I've already forgiven you for that."

Brye laughed, a bitter, insane cackle. "How sanctimonious of you, Chad! And extremely patronizing." Her eyes flared in brilliance, then died in intensity—as if life had suddenly siphoned out of her.

"Like a ping-pong ball, you've been bouncing back and forth between my bed and Jennifer's. Tell me, Chad, which one of us should forgive you for *that*?" At least he had the decency to look embarrassed, Brye thought to herself as his face turned an unrecognizable color inconsistent with the progressive shades of tint supporting the color spectrum.

"Brian and I are friends, Chad," she abruptly alerted him. Despite it all, she could not stand the thought of intentionally hurting him. "Nothing more. There's a story behind why we flew to Atlantic City. But we didn't go there to fall into bed together."

Chad nodded, accepting her declaration as truth. Sluicing through all the misery and madness, he believed her. "I love you, Brye," he vehemently announced, hoping that if anything got through to her, his love would. "I've made so many mistakes where we are concerned...where Jennifer is concerned. But if you give me time, we can work all this out." With an anguished cry, Chad tore the contract into tiny shreds. Each time he ripped away a strip, he emphasized with zeal, "We can get beyond this, Brye. I *have* gone beyond this. It's in the past. All that matters is the future...*our* future. I love you. And through it all, despite how angry I was with you, despite all the bitterness I felt toward you, my love for you has always been the predominating factor. Despite how much I willed myself to hate you, it just wasn't feasible." The tattered pieces fluttered harmlessly to the floor, to be swept away and discarded. For Chad, it symbolized their problems—as if this unpleasantness could be whisked away and tossed in the trash. For Brye, it wasn't that simple.

The uncertainty, the vulnerability, flaunted Brye's prudent features. This all witnessed by Chad, he knew he would do whatever it took, say whatever necessary to convince her of his love; he could not lose her, not again. He rushed to attack the obstacles legislating her ambiguous thoughts. Crushing her to his chest, he wound his arms tightly around her. Met with a stiff, unyielding body, arms dangled listlessly by her side, Chad refused to let that deter him. Soothingly, hypnotically, his breath was a mere whisper transgressing into the subterfuge of her weakening senses.

"When I heard you had been attacked, I thought my entire world had fallen apart. It was then I realized that I couldn't live without you." As his appeasing phrases soothed her swelling fears, temperate fingers molded her inflexible body. Stroking and caressing, gradually, Brye buckled under his discriminate onslaught.

Chad pushed his advantage, hating himself for doing so. He needed Brye's forgiveness, but was it worth it to prey upon her vulnerabilities? "This trip has been good to us, Brye. It's been good for us. It's made me rethink my mistakes. It's forced me to realize what I really want out of life." Brye's arms lifted. Ever so lightly, she placed them around his waist. In response, Chad brushed his lips against her temple. He continued to push. "Don't you feel it too? We've been like a family, haven't we, Brye? With Anthony and Bethany here with us, it's as if we've recreated the family we were meant to have."

"Chad?" Brye had never been able to resist this charismatic, forceful, yet receptively sensitive man. More so now that he was swearing his undying love to her. Add that to him referring to the four of them as a family, and he had secured her love and support for life. She loved him. With all her heart and soul, he meant the world to her. If he was willing to let go of the past, then why should she deny him that right? Brye's body melted against his. Her fingers slowly flowed over his bare back. Kneading his steely muscles, she throatily declared, "Our pizza is going to get cold if you don't let me go."

Chad tightly clamped his eyes shut. He said a silent prayer. Somehow he'd broken through. Insurmountable elation engulfed him.

It was also very short-lived.

"That's what microwaves are for." Chad roughly grabbed a handful of her hair. Pulling her head to where she was almost bending over backward, he dragged impatient lips across the delicate skin of her neck. "Right now, I want to make love to you."

Brye trembled with desire. Her chest heaved for air as Chad buried his head in between two jutting breasts. A demanding throb, originating between her thighs and broadening to conquer her mind, seized her immediate attention. Brye shut her eyes to the influx of honeyed sensations.

"*Brye?*" The voice came out of nowhere; singsong, high-pitched, and very much feminine. Unquestionably her mother's.

Startled, Brye's eyes flew open. Her head turned in the direction the imposing sound had surfaced. Then she saw her. In the brass-framed beveled mirror. A clear image of Brye's mother grinned back at her. Brye blinked several times. A fragment of her imagination, Brye conjectured, yet her mother refused to fade back into the shimmering background.

To Brye's growing alarm she realized that her mother was no longer restricting her destructive activities to midnight raids. She was now transgressing into reality. Shaking in undeniable fright, Chad mistook her actions for unrestrained passion. He emitted a low cry of pleasure. Snatching Brye's blouse over her head, he addressed his attention to her delectable breast.

Wearing her trademark ruby-red lipstick, a white, super-short, skin-tight, flesh-exposing, slinky dress, Brye's mother smiled knowingly.

Look at him. Her eyes roamed over Chad's towel-clad body. *He thinks sex heals all wounds. All men do. You throw them a bone, and they're happy. They think all is right with the world.*

One shapely hip cocked to the side, hand poised on top, her mother was pleased to elaborate. *It's the wrapping, my daughter dearest. All men want a woman with beautiful packaging. I've been trying to teach you that lesson for years. Men don't care about the total package. It's the body they go after. Take Chad, for instance. He doesn't trust you. He doesn't have faith in you. He doesn't believe you when you tell him you didn't take his father's precious million dollars. He doesn't even care about the money—men are used to paying for exquisite playthings—all he cares about is owning you, making love to you.* Her mother smiled ever so dearly—ever so apologetically. *I'm surprised at you, my sweets. You, who've always held yourself above the rest of us. You, who've lived by a higher standard set by no one other than yourself. I can't believe you'd allow him to think he paid a million dollars for services rendered.*

He loves me, Mother, Brye spoke inside her head. *He loves me, and he believes in me. If I tell him I didn't take the money, he'll believe me because now, he also trusts me.*

To give credit where credit was do, her mother didn't even attempt to hide her disbelief. She snorted in beguiling cynicism. *If you believe that loaded pail of horse shit you're shoveling out the side of your mouth*—she nodded toward Chad—*ask him. Prove it to me... prove it to yourself. Ask him if he still believes you took the money. And when you get your answer, ask him if he cares that you took it.* In a swirling puff of dense fog, her mother gradually dissipated.

By the time the mirror cleared, Brye's fluid movements had come to a complete standstill.

She stiffened under Chad's guiding tutelage. He instantly sensed her retreat. Into where, he did not know. But when she mentally came back to him, her body had grown cold, her eyes looked haunted. Fear crept along his spine. Afraid he had lost her again, Chad secured her chin and forced her to meet his solicitous eye.

"What's wrong?" He could not cloak his uneasiness.

"I need to know one thing." Brye pulled out of his reach. Staring at him with open-eyed expectations, she asked, "Do you believe me when I tell you I didn't take your family's money?"

Chad's world came crashing down. It was an extremely important question to Brye. If he answered to her satisfaction, they could go on with their lives...plan their future together. But God help him, he could not lie. He could not say what she badly wanted to hear.

"Brye... I..." The damage done, Brye shut down right before his very eyes. The look she thrust at him created the same effect as deadly fingers clamping over his heart and closing down on his arteries. Chad rushed to explain. "The money means nothing to me, Brye. Not a damn thing."

"But you believe I took it?" she persisted.

Frustrated, Chad walked over to the king-size bed. His legs buckled under him, he dropped onto the mattress. Systematically, he tried to explain why he'd come to the only conclusion left to him. "I had the original signed contract. A contract with your signature. A contract issuing you a million dollars in return for your relinquishing me of all parental rights. Then there was the copy of the check my father wrote to you." Chad halted. He forked his fingers rigorously through his hair. He gawked at her with pained expression. "It's in the past, Brye. It doesn't matter anymore. It certainly doesn't matter to me."

"But it *does* matter, Chad." Brye's tongue caught in the back of her throat. Her voice sounded ineffectual, completely used up. "To *me,* it matters." She hid her face in her hands, then dropped her arms to her side. Her shattered heart exposed through the anguished expression she wore. "Blind faith," she whispered. It's what the children at Brylinn bestowed upon her. Was it too much to ask the same from Chad? "Do you see, Chad? I don't want you to forgive me for something you think I did. I want you to believe…to *know*…to trust that I didn't take your father's money. Even if you can't possible explain how it happened, you should believe me because I say I didn't take it." She pointed a quivering chin at Chad. "How can you love me when you can't even trust me?" Defeated, Brye turned to go.

Chad chased after her. At the bedroom door, he caught her by the arm. "Then tell me what to believe," he pleaded in sheer desperation. "Please help me understand."

"I can't, Chad. You have to figure it out on your own." There were two reasons why Brye would never admit the truth to Chad. The first, she wouldn't be the one to destroy the superficial image his father had built in Chad's shaded eye. Second, she was afraid he wouldn't believe her. She feared Chad would denounce her as a liar and a cheat.

Just like he's doing now, she sardonically thought to herself. Shrugging in hopelessness, Brye broke away from him and dashed to her room.

Chest heaving, she cringed against the closed bedroom door. Scared she lost Chad forever, her legs slid out from under her. Her distressed body crumbled to the floor. To add to her infinite problems, her dead mother had made an appearance today. Brye understood perfectly that the visceral sighting had been a direct result of an overloaded, overwrought, overactive imagination. But up until now, she had been able to control those toxic images—at least on a conscious level. Her mother, father, and brother had always remained locked away on a subconscious level. Never had they appeared in her conscious state—never had she allowed it. But somehow her mother had found a way to break through the barrier separating subconscious from consciousness. Her mind reeled from the implication. It meant emotionally and mentally, she was too drained to continue hiding from herself and holding her buried past at a distance. It meant that soon she was going to have to stop running. Soon she would have to confront and do battle with her complex emotions.

Weighted down with the notion that her world was steadily falling apart, Brye pushed herself off the ground.

"Brye?"

A knock on the door spun Brye around like a spinning top. Eyes burned a hole in the wood as she stood glued to the spot. Making no effort to move toward the door, she also made no effort to speak.

"We need to talk, Brye."

Brye slid over to the walk-in closet. She pulled out her suitcase and began to pack. To shut out the low drumming of Chad's continuous appeals, she switched on the bedside radio. After a moment's thought, she flipped the sound up to a thunderous pitch.

"Dammit, Brye! I got a phone call from your personal assistant one day after the fact. After the news media inundated the world with minimal details. Do you know how worried I was? Are you so busy you couldn't see your way clear of taking a few minutes to call me yourself? Tell me you were okay."

Marcus was pissed. So much so that thousands of miles away, steam produced by blind fury poured from Brye's EarPods inserted in her ears. After packing her bag, she decided to call and apologize for not having spoken to him sooner. Perched on the cherry-finished settee fronting the end of the bed, Brye stretched her feet out before her and settled in for the long haul. The thing to do now, she decided, was to sit back and wait until he ran out of gas.

"Marcus?" Brye attempted to cut in.

"And now you have the nerve to bless me with a phone call four days later. Four *fuckin'* days later. Why bother at all? Why not just mail a letter? Hell, it probably would have reached me faster than this phone call had."

Sitting down on the bed, Brye covered her face with a shaky hand. Seconds later, in slow circular motions, she rubbed at her drumming temple. God, she'd give anything if she could just let loose and cry. She so much wanted to cry.

Marcus's flurry of allegations continued to pound at the perpetually growing fissure she used to call a brain.

"Marcus?" she tried again.

"I thought we meant more than that to each other, Brye. And Tenisha? What about Tenisha? She's been worried sick about you. If not me, you couldn't at least see your way clear of calling her."

"Marcus…please," Brye broke in as soon as he'd come up for air. Her eyes trailed the length of the room. They stopped at the Jacuzzi. Maybe she should jump in, headfirst, she tediously considered.

Marcus came out of his tyrannical rampage long enough to hear the desperation resounding in Brye's voice. Silently, he cursed himself. "Brye, I'm sorry. I'm just frustrated. Pay no attention, okay?"

"I'm the one who's sorry, Marcus. I really am. It's just that… afterward, things got kind of hectic. And I wanted to call…I knew you'd be mad because I hadn't called, but—"

Marcus thought about kicking himself. After surviving her traumatic episode, he should have known she would be fragile. And the sound of her voice told him she was almost at the breaking point.

"Listen, sweetheart," he dropped his tone by several octaves, "I shouldn't have put you in the position where you had to go on the defensive."

"Marcus… I…" Brye's voice cracked.

"Talk to me, Brye," he quietly urged. "Tell me what's wrong?"

"It's nothing…really."

"Don't give me that bullshit!" Despite the cursed words, he spoke gently to offset his harsh dialect. "Remember, I know you better than anyone. And I know you're hurting right now. So tell me what's going on."

Brye continued to rub vigorously at her forehead, thinking that if the burdensome pulsation did not cease soon, she would more than likely rub a hole in the side of her head. "I guess," she slowly began, not really knowing what she was about to say, "in a world of insanity, I needed to hear a voice of reason."

The line went dead for an attenuated moment. Marcus was the first to break the strained silence.

"Look, Brye, why don't I take a few days off from work? I can come out there. We don't have to talk about the attack if you don't want to…we can do or talk about whatever you want."

Brye forced herself to sound light and cheery. "I love you for offering, but it really isn't necessary. Besides, it's not the attack that's weighing on my mind. It's Chad. He brought Anthony and Bethany out here to see me. They're here now."

"Ahhh…the Great One," Marcus answered in masked awe.

Brye was taken aback by her friend's calm response. "Why don't you sound shocked?"

"Did you know he's been spending time at Brylinn?"

Brye drew back in surprise. "No. He didn't tell me…neither did you," she added in an accusatory tone.

"He's a natural with the kids." Marcus paused. "One day, I was showing the twins how to clip Fred and Wilma's wings. As soon as they heard Chad come in, they took off. Needless to say, I was left holding the clippers."

Inwardly, Brye smiled. She'd done the right thing in calling Marcus. He could always cheer her up. "Ohhhhh," she teased. "Is my poor baby feeling neglected? Maybe a little bit jealous?"

"Well"—feigning hurt, he sniffed like a whiny brat—"how am I supposed to feel? For years, I've been the only man in your life. And then *he* walks in, takes you away from me, and then goes after the kids."

Brye snorted in response. "How could he take me away from you when you've never had me? You've never even wanted me. And if I recall, on numerous occasions, you've said that we aren't—how should I put it?—color coordinated."

Marcus laughed. "I know what I told you. But that was a smokescreen to hide the real truth."

"Which is?" Smiling to herself, Brye began twirling a strand of hair around her index finger.

"Which is; I wanted to go down in the Guinness Book of Records as the only man on earth who turned down Brye Grayson—the most desirable woman in the world—*after* she'd thrown herself at my feet."

Brye clamped her hands over her mouth to hold in the laughter. "That's a bald-faced lie!" she retorted in mock indignation. "I never threw myself at your feet."

"Maybe you did, maybe you didn't. It's my word against yours. And in this day and age, when people thrive on gossip and innuendoes, who do you think they're going to believe?"

"You are totally, categorically, unequivocally, insanely wasted out of your mind."

"I might be," Marcus coolly agreed. "But you know what you are?"

"What's that?"

"You, my darlin', are smiling…at this very moment. Despite how bad you were feeling a few minutes ago, I actually got you to laugh."

Brye instantly sobered. "You did not," she adamantly denied.

"I did to. So admit it, you feel much better now."

"Okay, okay," Brye acquiesced. "You're right. I do feel better."

"Admit it, I'm just like taking a dose of medicine."

"More like a dose of castor oil."

A low rumble erupted over the telephone lines. When Marcus's laughter subsided, his tone was full of serious intent. "Now that we've decided unanimously that you're feeling better, tell me what's going on. What happened between you and Chad?"

Brye remained silent for a full thirty seconds before answering. Marcus patiently waited.

Finally, she said, "Chad told me he loved me tonight."

"Oh…that explains it then." But it didn't. By rights, Brye should be floating on cloud nine. She should have been the happiest person on the face of the earth. Instead, she responded to Chad's declaration of love as if it were a death sentence.

For the next thirty minutes, being the best friend he could be, Marcus leant his ear, he offered his sympathy, and he gave his full support. Not once did he offer advice. Brye was one of the most intelligent women he knew. When it was time, when she was ready, she would do what needed to be done.

He did ask, "Has Chad spoken to you about Jamie and Jordan?"

Alarm yanked at Brye's troubled heart. "No, has something happened to them?" Brye asked, fearing the worst. And when Marcus relayed the events putting Jamie in the hospital overnight, Brye thanked the Lord the girls would be all right.

"Her ex is in jail. He did spend a few days in the hospital after Debbie busted the back of his head open," Marcus continued. "Child abuse and attempted man slaughter charges have been filed against him. No charges have been filed on Debbie."

"Is Debbie okay?" Brye asked.

"Yeah. She's staying at Brylinn for the time being," Marcus informed. "At least until she can regain full custody of her kids. When she does, she says she's going to go back home to her mother—to live in Iowa. Chad's promised to pay for their flight."

"Chad?" Stunned, her eyes whipped around the room as she continued to question him. "How did he get involved in this?"

"Before he and the twins flew out to you, he spoke with Debbie, promising to do all he could to help her get back on her feet—and he visited Jamie at the hospital."

Brye could hardly believe her ears. She needed time to think. Blowing a long, controlled breath out of her lungs, she decided to end their phone conversation.

"Have I told you that I love you?" Surprisingly, the words rolled smoothly off her tongue.

"You have via a messenger. But it's nice hearing it firsthand. And I love you too."

Brye hung up. A small smile clung to her lips. It slowly faded as she looked at her suitcase waiting in front of the closed bedroom door. Chad had gotten the candid message that she didn't want to talk to him. Reluctantly, he finally left her alone.

Soon she would have to face him. The news of what he had done for the Farrow family softened her heart. But she wished it hadn't.

Kierra and the twins would be coming back any minute. Grabbing her bag in hand, Brye opened her bedroom door. Now was as good a time as any to confront him.

"We need to talk, Brye." Facial lines drawn, fully dressed, Chad sat on the living room sofa. Cold and uneaten, the pizza topped the coffee table.

Shaking her head, Brye strained to make her feet move. She headed straight for the door. "We've already talked. And it hasn't gotten us anywhere."

Chad stared hopelessly at her suitcase. "So you're going to just walk out of here…walk out on us?"

"No, Chad." At the front entrance, she turned and met him with an impenetrable stare. "You're the one who walked out on us… you walked out on *me*! And I'm not talking about tonight. I'm talking about years ago…when you didn't—" Brye arrested the sudden rise in anger. Already she had said too much.

Chad picked up on her slipped tongue. Quick as a cat, he flew off the couch and landed directly in front of her. Determined fingers, pressed into Brye's shoulder, sent electrical shocks zigzagging down her body.

"When I didn't what, Brye? What were you going to say?" His eyes blazed fierce and arduously into Brye's stoic expression.

Pulling out from under his demanding touch, turning away from his swaying eyes, Brye dropped her suitcase. It landed on the carpet with a soft thud.

"Dammit it, Brye! What are you not telling me? What are you hiding from me?"

Spared from answering, Tank, Kierra, Anthony, and Bethany came rollicking through the entrance.

Despite the pleas, in spite of the twins verbally voicing their disappointment with her earlier than scheduled departure, Brye left the apartment with Tank and Kierra flanking her sides.

Behind the closed door, three bodies stood inert while indistinct thoughts rummaged through them. For a long while, all remained oppressively quiet. It was a frightening moment for them all—as if Brye had been their lifeline; as if her spirit alone was the glue that held them together. And once she walked out the door, emptiness settled over their barren lives in less seconds than it took a professional car thief to empty a busy thoroughfare of a Mercedes Benz or a Jaguar.

"She's mad at you, isn't she?" Perceptive as usual, Bethany was the first to call attention to Brye's immediate exit.

"Yes, she is," Chad admitted. Dropping his arm around Bethany's shoulder, he pulled her against him.

"Don't worry, Mr. Collier," Anthony said. "Everything's gonna work out okay." And he honestly believed it. After all, he had wished upon a shooting star. One day, Chad and Brye would be his and Bethany's parents.

Chad nodded. He knelt on bent knee to get, more than give, a reassuring hug. As he held on tightly, he prayed to God Anthony was right.

28

MIND IN A TAILSPIN, spinning wildly out of control, for the past seven days Brye remained in center stage of Chad's distraught emotions.

How was she doing? How was she feeling? Was she pregnant? Would she tell him if she were? God, how he loved her.

Stranded in his office, television on, sound low, remote control parked close by, every few minutes he would flip through the channels in search of a news station or talk show that might offer the latest updated information on Brye or her attacker. Not accepting his phone calls, any information directed to him came directly from Kierra or Brian.

Torture. The thought of losing Brye for good felt nothing short of hell. The first time he believed he'd lost her, he had buried himself in a bottle of booze with a two year refill provision. He allowed the fast lane to swallow him alive. For years, he had been too far gone to feel any pain. But now, attempting to maintain some decorum of normalcy, he felt nothing but emptiness. To be put out of his misery had to be better than the slow death he now suffered.

Knuckles pressed into his desk, he pushed himself out of his chair. Lumbering into his inner office bathroom, he splashed cold water over his face. As he toweled himself dry, he gaped at the accursed image staring back at him in the mirror. Face drawn, lips tight, eyes cloudy, Chad hadn't slept nor eaten much in the past week. His face disclosed every bit of that strain.

The intercom buzzed, drawing his attention back to the inner office.

"Chad…Mr. Zangerfields's on line four. He wants to discuss revisions on that contract we sent over to him."

"Have Brian take the call, Rhonda, please."

"Right away."

The past week, Chad had been delegating more and more work to Brian. It left Chad time to go over the last few minutes he'd spent with Brye. It left him time to ponder over where he'd gone wrong. He diligently searched for what he'd missed.

Once again, her shadowed accusations ran roughshod over his muddy thought patterns.

You're the one who walked out on us…you walked out on me. And I'm not talking about tonight. I'm talking about years ago…when you didn't—

"When I didn't do what, Brye?" Chad mumbled to himself. The passionate manner in which she'd spoken the words, the quiet determined zeal flaming her eyes. Those tell-tale eyes. Violet-colored eyes reflecting pain, sadness, and…truth. Windows to her soul.

More and more, he believed the breakup to be his fault. He believed he had overlooked something; something so markedly obvious he couldn't decipher it because it dangled so close to his nose it distorted his impassioned vision.

But it was there. All he had to do was focus.

Chad dropped heavily into his swivel chair. Leaning backward, head dropped back, an image of Jennifer flashed behind closed lids. On top of all else, he still hadn't confronted her. By the time he'd returned from Orlando, she and her mother had flown off to Paris in search of a wedding dress. It would have been highly improper for him to hit her over the head with news, damaging to her ego, directly over the phone. He promised himself he would confront her as soon as she returned, which was any minute now. Ironically, no matter how much he desired to see Brye, he promised himself he would not beg for an audience until he straightened out the mess he had created with Jennifer.

Thinking about Paris induced him to recall a time, years ago, when he'd flown overseas for a week. It had been during the time he had been seeing Brye. Having asked her to accompany him, she had graciously declined. It had been a drawn-out, burdensome week without her.

Missing her more than humanly possible, Chad returned home in earnest anticipation of being with her the following day.

Late that night, he fell asleep with her on his mind. He dreamed. A vivacious, stimulating fantasy of Brye making love to him. The image presenting itself was so genuine, felt so real, his mind surrendered to the potent impulses. Their bodies, joined as one, moved together in synchronized uniformity. But somewhere along the way, the hazy image revolved into a four-dimensional seduction. Not only was her presence vivid, but he could feel, smell, and touch her. Eagerly, his body responded to the mental and physical stimuli.

And just as his mind exploded into a cacophony of blinding stars, his eyes embraced her. She hovered above him, locked in a passionate love dance, draining him of everything he had within. Their lovemaking had been phenomenal. Chad had fallen in love all over again.

Shuddering in the aftereffects, Chad tightly wrapped his arms around Brye. "That was unbelievable!"

Brye lifted her head from his chest. Face glowing from satiated pleasure, she beamed down at Chad. "I take it you were pleased with my welcome home present?"

"*Pleased* is such an ineffectual word for what I'm feeling right now." His satisfied grin matched his lover's. "In fact, right now, I'm feeling so generous I want to give you a gift." Lightly, he slapped her naked bottom. "Now get off me, woman, so I can get it."

"Nooooo!" Brye groaned. Dropping her head down, she wailed into his chest, "Don't make me get up. It feels sooooo good lying on top of you."

"I promise I'll save your position." Chad rolled to his side, throwing Brye off.

"Yeah…well…" Her voice caught in her throat. Stretched on her side, head propped upon her balled fist, greedy eyes soaked up

Chad's magnificent body as he strutted across the room. Her lips stuck out in an obvious pout. "What if I don't want to reclaim my position?"

"You'll want to." He carried over a medium-sized elegantly wrapped gift box. Plopping down beside Brye, he said, "Particularly after you see what I've brought you."

Hidden shadows darted around the dim room. Chad flipped on the bedside lamp. Soft light splashed across Brye's exulted features and continued to stretch outward, daintily encompassing the brass bed. Much to Chad's surprise, she stared at the gift-wrapped box as though it would bite.

With strained smile, Brye stated, "You didn't have to."

Her sudden change in demeanor alarmed Chad. Whatever the problem, it had risen unexpectedly. "I wanted to. Now open it," he prodded.

Brye pulled herself into a sitting position. Repelled at touching the gift, reluctantly, she took custody.

In the glowing light, Chad witnessed Brye's shaking fingers as she carefully removed the colorful wrapping. Watching her, Chad wondered if she stalled to keep from seeing what lay inside.

The hinges on the velvet box creaked open. Brye's eyes were cloaked as she peered inside. A small gasp escaped her lungs. Artistically presented to her on a bed of soft, black velvet lay a necklace and matching earrings.

The necklace: an elegant prong-set pear-shaped amethyst encircled by sixteen precision-cut diamonds and suspended from a one-half inch wide fourteen carat gold chain. The amethyst and diamond pierced drop earrings were just as ethereal and just as refined.

"I saw them in a jewelry store window. They reminded me of you," Chad explained. "When your smile touches your eyes, whenever you laugh, every time we make love, those violet-colored eyes of yours change into a deeper shade of purple. A shade matching the amethyst."

"Chad?" Unable to go forward, shutting her eyes, Brye's fingers covered her mouth.

"You don't like them?"

Eyes tightly shut, Brye nodded up and down. "I do like them. They're beautiful." She greeted Chad with a glistening stare. "But I can't accept them."

Her teary eyes resembled sparkling teardrops dripping from an amethyst pool. The priceless reflection resembled his gift of love. "I bought them for you, Brye. I wanted to show you how much I love you."

"No, Chad." Leaning forward, she ran a loving touch across the jagged growth of his early-morning shadow. "I don't need you to buy me expensive gifts. I don't *want* you to give me extravagantly impressive presents." Her voice broke, a single tear dropped from the corner of her eye. "It's not what I need at all."

"Then what do you need?" he spoke in gentle undertone.

"You." Brye moved into his waiting arms. "I only need you. Nothing or no one else matters but you."

Rocking back and forth, Chad soothed, "You have me." And when he pulled her at arm's length, when he stared deep into somber eyes, there was no doubt in his mind that she meant every word.

Chad shot up straighter in his chair. His heart raced. He blinked in understanding. In some way, he had betrayed Brye. He didn't know how, couldn't figure it out, but he understood now that he let her down.

Brye had spoken the truth. She had not taken the million dollars. And she had told him so, not just verbally but in her eyes as well. Just like the night she had refused to take the gift purchased in Paris. It had been there all along, but he had refused to see it.

Yet and still, he remained no closer to the answers he needed. He still had no proof of what really took place those many years ago. And how could he confront Brye without proof. If he simply went to her and asked for forgiveness, she'd look at him with suspicion. She would probably believe he hadn't changed at all but had only hoped to appease her. It was imperative he find out fast. Before he lost Brye for good.

Minutes later, he received the much sought-after answers. It came in the form of Jennifer blowing into his office like an unexpected hurricane. She flailed a magazine wildly over her head. Her less than ladylike behavior reminded Chad of an overzealous cowboy striving to rope cattle.

"Damn you, Chad Collier!" She flung the magazine at his chest. "How dare you make a fool out of me!"

Startled at the frontal attack, Chad caught the magazine as it flew across his desk.

"Not only could you not wait until after we were married before you started humping around, but you weren't even smart enough to be discreet! How dare you!"

Speechless, dodging bullets fired from her smoking irises, Chad deflected his attention to the magazine thrown at him.

He stared at a copy of *Private Affairs*, a popular tabloid magazine. Although the caption—"The makings of a family?"—drew Chad's attention, the photo on the cover is what captured and held his fascination. With King Stefan's Banquet Hall poised as their backdrop, Brye and Chad were kissing on a park bench. The twins looked on with pleased expressions.

More interested than he cared to admit, he thumbed through the five-page article. More pictures followed a story that proved to be vague, utilized a lot of innuendoes, yet could not be construed as libelous. It made note of his mad dash—with two small children holding a remarkable resemblance to himself as well as Brye—to be by the supermodel's side. It also laid out a short summary of his life, his wealth, and his recently announced engagement to Jennifer. Shamelessly, it hinted that there might be trouble in paradise.

"Is this the new Mrs. Chad Collier and family? Only time will tell," the article ended.

"Do you know how embarrassed I was to step off the plane and be slapped in the face with this thing? This piece of *shit*!" Jennifer hovered over Chad like a pouncing wildcat. "And my mother…what do you suppose my mother thought of this crap?"

"Jennifer," Chad climbed to his full six feet three height. He remained calm. "I don't know anything about this, and I certainly didn't mean to hurt you, but I should tell you that Brye is the reason I asked you to marry me. I was furious with her, and I guess, in a way, I thought I would be getting back at her if I married you."

Behind the permanent makeup, Jennifer visibly paled. She couldn't believe the words falling from his lips. And she positively would not accept them. Her fury corrupted all rational thinking.

"Just what are you trying to say to me, Chad?" She stood, hands bearing down on her hips.

Chad moved around his desk. "I'm saying I love Brye. I'm saying—"

"No!" With murder in her heart, lips drawn back in attack, she barked, "I won't let you do this. And you're a fool if you think your father—" Her eyes enlarged at the blunder brought on by her maniacal rage. Clamping her mouth shut, she turned away from Chad.

The implication of what Jennifer had almost said slammed into Chad like a football tackler plowing into the quarterback. Although knocked senseless for a few short seconds, he had been allowed open passage into the game. "What about my father?" He circled Jennifer as she attempted to avoid his stare.

Jennifer rushed to retract the words she misspoke. "Your father is not going to sit around and let this magazine malign your character…*my* character!" As she ad-libbed, her eyes darted nervously from one wall to another.

Her twitching was enough to verify the truth.

In a last ditch effort to put a halt to Chad's unwelcomed declarations, Jennifer said in a most placating tone, "I know you're upset about this. I also know you're very busy. Why don't we give ourselves a chance to cool down?" Before he called off the wedding, she backed out the open door. "We'll talk later." She parted, throwing him a goodbye kiss.

Stunned, deliberating over the inference of Jennifer's botched disclosure, Chad never even considered going after her and informing her of their canceled engagement.

Instead, he pondered over his adoring father. Could he have been behind their breakup? Could he, for some inexplicable reason, hate Brye so much he deliberately sabotaged the relationship?

All of sudden, the pieces began to drop into place. And although small gaps remained unfilled, the puzzle was clearer than depicted minutes before.

"Dammit!" Chad cursed. He suddenly realized that he had proof. For all these years, he'd carried that proof in his wallet. Yet not once did he ever consider checking out his father's story. "How could I have been so stupid?" he chastised, mentally beating himself against his skull.

Chad leaned over the top of his desk and grabbed his phone. He jabbed at the numbers, finally making that long awaited call. Years ago, he'd been given a copy of the front of the check. But he'd never seen the back; he'd never actually witnessed Brye's signature endorsing her betrayal.

When his father's CPA answered, Chad barked into the phone. "I need some information, Cliff. And I needed it yesterday."

Sounding bored, in his high nasal lilt, Cliff answered, "I'll see what I can do."

"Almost seven years ago, my father wrote out a check for one million dollars. It was made out to Brye Grayson. Could you find out if that check was ever endorsed and presented for payment?"

"I'll need some time to—"

"Now, Cliff!" Although Chad had shredded the copy, he had stared at it often enough. From memory alone, he recited the check number.

Cliff fell silent. "I'll have to approve this with your father—"

"Check with him afterward. I need to know now!"

"Give me a few minutes to look it up. I'll call you back."

Prepared to hold the phone for as long it took for the CPA to check his notes, his microfiche, his computer, or whatever the hell he utilized to store his father's important documents, Chad snapped, "I'll wait." Holding the phone to his ear, he shook his head incredulously. To look back now, his father's story hadn't even washed. Chad should have verified it himself. He should have confronted Brye afterward. He should have had enough faith in what he felt for her, what they felt for each other, to never have accepted a half-baked story. Instead, he crawled away like the jilted lover, his pride tucked tightly between his legs.

Okay. Now that he had figured out what had happened on his end, he needed to figure out why Brye had signed the damn thing.

Because my father went to her and said I wanted no part of her or the baby.

The appalling thought struck him with as much impact as a cold shower rushing over his body.

But his father hadn't been the one to confront Brye. Just as abruptly, Chad recalled the press conference set up to announce Brye as their spokesperson. Brye had to be introduced to his father; she had never met him before, hadn't known him from Adam.

Chad groaned. How the hell had he let that slip? Years ago, his father had told him that Brye had come to him asking for money. But she hadn't. So…who approached her?

More puzzle pieces slipped into place.

One of Dad's flunkies. Someone had been ordered to go to Brye. Chad would bet his last dollar she'd been told that he would pay to free himself of her and the baby. Hurt and disillusioned, she had signed the contract because she believed it was what he had wanted. Afterward, she had either refused the check or tore it into shreds. Chad could see it all so clearly. And now he waited for conformation.

"Chad?" Cliff burst into his reeling insight. "In answer to your question: No. The check was never presented for remittance."

"Bingo!" Fist balled, Chad struck himself on his thigh.

"Excuse me?"

"Nothing. Thanks, Cliff. I owe you one." Chad didn't know whether to be elated or if he should kick himself for figuring it out six years too late.

"But why, Dad?" Chad muttered to himself. "Why did you do it?" Not ready to confront his father, he decided to go to Brye first. Maybe she could shed some light on the why part, if he could convince her to forgive him. That in itself would be the biggest obstacle to conquer.

"You got a few minutes?"

Chad looked up to see Brian lingering in his doorway. "Come on in." Chad slid over to the wet bar. He pulled two bottles of green tea out the pint-sized refrigerator. Handing one to Brian, he twisted his top and tilted the bottle to his lips.

"I just saw Jennifer," Brian notified. Keeping a vigilant eye on Chad, he searched for a clue to his present state of mind. Since his return from Orlando, his boss had been extremely efficient in running the office yet had remained withdrawn to the people he worked with. As a friend, Brian was genuinely concerned. Cautiously, he trekked. "She practically bowled me over while hopping onto the elevator."

Peering at Brian over the rim of his bottle, Chad nodded. He reached across his desk and grabbed *Private Affairs*. "She gifted me with a present."

Chad gave him time to canvass the magazine. The entire duration, Brian displayed no visible hint of his private thoughts until his eyes washed over the cover story. And then Chad was only met with a curious lift of one brow.

"So what do you think?"

The pages produced an insignificant breeze as Brian flipped through the magazine one last time. "I think I'm smart enough not to answer until I know how you feel about this."

Chad moved away from his desk. He fell onto the leather couch. "I know that what I should be feeling is a far cry from what I actually feel."

Brian dropped beside Chad. "Okay. Let's take it one step at a time. First…tell me what you *should* be feeling?"

"I should be furious that someone's invaded my privacy… Brye's privacy. I should be upset at the idea that, that same someone trekked around Disney World, taking pictures, all for the sake of money. I should be dialing up that magazine, screaming bloody murder, threatening to sue." Chad slipped the magazine out of Brian's grip. He stared down at the cover page. "But I feel neither angry nor threatened by this."

"Okay. Now that we've established that we won't be suing the pants off these guys, tell me how you really feel."

"I'm not sure if I can explain this or that you'll even understand."

"So try me."

In a matter of minutes, Chad's world had been turned upside down. The one person he trusted the most—his father—proved to be the one he knew the least. The need to talk to someone ran great. Sitting forward, Chad studied his plastic bottle as if it sprouted tea leaves right before his very eyes. Wearing a tight smile, he said, "I feel like I've been breathing stale air all my life, and all of a sudden, fresh ventilation is available, but my lungs are having difficulties coping with the shock." His head barely moved as he turned an inherent eye toward Brian. "I feel as if I've been unwittingly letting others pull my strings, I've finally broken free, but I'm not certain which way I should turn with my newfound freedom."

Chad drank down half his tea, wishing he had something stronger. "I've been dating Jennifer for three years now—not because she suited me, but because she suited my father. Not once have I looked at Jennifer as a woman I could, or would, or want to love. She was just someone who satisfied my immediate needs. Whether a showpiece on my arm or whether to warm my bed at night, she served my purpose well. It could have been anyone." Accepting the truth for what is was, Chad shrugged in indifference. "It just happened to be her."

Staring at his empty bottle, wondering how it got that way, Chad continued, "My parents liked her. Her parents liked me. Hell… why not get married? She was doing for me what any other woman could have done." He shook his head in self-reproach. "In going over it now, it all sounds so cold and calculated. So convoluted. But it all stemmed from thinking that I wasn't capable of loving anyone else again."

"But then Brye reentered the picture," Brian mindfully interjected.

"'Reentered?'" Chad gaped at Brian, surprised at his choice of words.

Brian nodded. "Brye told me you two were lovers years back.

Chad's brow spiked in undiluted surprise. "What else did she tell you?"

Brian met Chad's fixed stare head-on. Certain he was breaking Brye's confidence in repeating part of their past conversation, he was almost as certain Chad had reached a crossroad. He was now seeking guidance on which course to follow. A slight pause delayed his answer. "She told me your father played mind games with the both of you."

Chad turned away, but not before Brian witnessed the aggrieved expression closing over his countenance. The muscles in Chad's jaw clenched, released, and clenched again.

"She was right." His voice sounded distant, uncommonly alien. "Unfortunately, I didn't gain any insight into *that* critical piece of information until"—Chad glanced at his watch—"twenty-minutes ago. Ironically, as I reacquainted myself with Brye, what happened in the past—or at least what I *thought* happened in the past—didn't matter anymore. I discovered that I was too young to be straddled down for the rest of my life with a woman I did not love, not when I knew I was still capable of loving. And particularly *not* when I knew it was possible to have a life with the woman I loved…have always loved…have never ceased loving."

"But before that, something happened to push you over the edge," Brian prompted. "Something that drove you into asking Jennifer to marry you in the first place."

A sardonic smile bit into the lower half of Chad's face. "I found out you and Brye flew off to Atlantic City."

Brian nearly misted himself, the sofa, and Chad with the tea he had just tipped over his lips. Choking the mouthful down, he blurted, "I don't deny that we went. I certainly can't dispute our having a good time. But it was all very innocent, and we went as friends. Nothing more."

"I'm aware of that," Chad admitted, no trace of animosity tolling his voice.

"Tell me about the trip to Orlando?" Brian asked, anxious to change the subject. "Something happened down there." His gaze swept over the magazine. "Something other than having your *family portrait* taken?"

"To summarize it all, it blew up in my face."

"Brian," Rhonda's voice hurled at them through the office intercom, "your three o'clock appointment is here."

"I'll be there shortly." Brian stood. He dropped his empty bottle in the trash standing next to the door. "How about dinner tonight? My treat."

A little life sparked in the midst of Chad's melancholic expression. "Are you asking me out on a date?"

"It doesn't look to me like you'll be getting any other offers anytime soon."

Chad let loose a hearty laugh. It was his first since returning from Orlando. "You might be right about that. Brye's not returning my calls. And Jennifer...well...you saw the way she departed."

"So you two are officially un-engaged?"

"She never gave me a chance to call it off." Chad stood. He tossed Brian a whimsical eye. "Why? Are you interested for personal reasons of your own? Maybe considering dating her?"

Brian easily picked up on the not-so-subtle insinuation. "No way, Chad. She's not my type. Come to think of it," he considered, "she's not *your* type either."

"How do you know what my type is?" Unaware of his actions, Chad unconsciously wound the tabloid magazine into a tight roll.

Brian snatched the publication out of Chad's fingers. The pliable material sprang back to its original shape. He pushed the cover into Chad's face. "Your type of woman is the kind who would opt to spend one day at Disney World rather than spend an entire month on the French Riviera." Brian leaned into the doorjamb, the magazine now tucked under his arm. A sly grin reached out and grabbed Chad. "Actually, the reason I asked about your breakup with Jennifer is because there's a money pool circulating around the office. Everyone came up with an actual date on when it would happen. I bet on tomorrow. So if you could see your way clear..." He left Chad to draw his own conclusions.

"You're joking, aren't you?"

"Afraid not. Someone wanted us to bet on who—Jennifer or Brye—would actually get you in the end. But no one was stupid enough to lay their odds on Jennifer."

Unmitigated laughter invaded Chad's office once again. Brian shoved himself away from the doorjamb. Tossing Chad the magazine, he said, "We'll confirm time and place later." Then he was gone.

Smiling to himself, Chad concluded that he could actually accomplish some work. *Things must be looking up.*

Two major natural regions of the eastern United States composed the unconstrained state of North Carolina. The Appalachian highlands and the Coastal Plain. The Appalachian highlands embodied two sectors: the Blue Ridge, engulfing the mountainous section, and the Piedmont plateau, which enfolded tame rolling hills, dense pine forests, and man-made lakes. Whereas the majority of the natural lakes spread throughout the Coastal Plain, most of the lakes dotting the highlands were man-made. It did not take away from the states natural beauty but, in fact, added to it.

For thirty-six hours, the Piedmont slopes would be Brye's home away from home. She shared a two-bedroom suite with Tank in a posh hotel architecturally designed in the image of an illustrious nineteenth-century Southern plantation. Exterior and interior columns, vaulted ceilings, stately fireplaces, cozy balconies overlooking artistic landscaping, and if Brye stepped onto her balcony and peered to the south, she viewed a trellis-walled gazebo with clinging rose vines overlooking a man-made lake.

With cell phone clamped securely between shoulder and cheek, Brye only half listened to Kierra as she worked her way across her bedroom. Feeling a bit claustrophobic, she drew the heavy curtains open. Late afternoon light greeted the bedroom with a wave of its attenuated fingers.

"Chad called again," Kierra stated. "He'd like for you to call. He says it's extremely urgent."

"All his phone calls have been urgent—so he says," Brye patiently reminded. Deciding she was not encountering panic attacks but was suffering acid indigestion instead, she unlatched the window's lock and opened the large sliding window. Her room was immediately assaulted with the cleansing scent of pine and azaleas.

"Would you please, please, please just call?" Kierra whined.

"I fail to see why it's necessary," Brye stubbornly replied. "After all, I'm in constant contact with Brian." The fresh air was not helping. Shutting her eyes against the colorful azalea bushes fronting her room, Brye willed the queasiness to go away.

"Dammit, Brye," Kierra cursed, more from irritation than anger. "You may be able to write your own ticket, but the rest of us peons have to work hard for a living."

"Are you saying I don't work hard?" Feeling slightly overheated, despite the roaring air conditioner, Brye picked up the script for the Dante jeans commercial shoot and began fanning herself. Puffs of hair danced around her head as the mild breeze foraged her face.

"What I'm saying *is,* Chad is my boss. I just want to do my job. But you're putting me in the middle of whatever is going on between you two." She paused. "Just call him… Pleeeeezee!"

Brye laughed, although she did not feel joyous. "I'll think about it."

"Bryeeee!" Kierra screamed into the phone.

"It's the best I can do for right now." *Why do I feel so warm?* Brye asked herself.

Kierra sighed. If she proved to be lucky, she would make it through this tour without an ulcer, without her blood pressure skyrocketing through the ceiling, or without any other job related health hazards—like her sanity gone awry. Frustrations mounting, she elected to change the subject, although she knew Brye would refuse before she popped the question. "Why don't you come out with us tonight? See some of the city. We'll have fun."

"Thanks, Kierra, but I can't. Four more days of this grueling schedule, then I'll be off to California to shoot my last two commercials. I need to study my lines before then."

"Promise me you'll call me if you need anything."

"I'll be fine. I have Tank, remember?"

"Call me anyway."

"Yes, ma'am!" Brye ended the call. She unbuttoned the top three buttons of her short-sleeved silk blouse and aimed her makeshift fan toward her sweltering breast. The fresh air was a godsend, so she left the window open. But bending forward, she allowed the cold air coming from the air conditioner to blast her dead in the face.

"Why do I feel like I'm having hot flashes," Brye uttered over the chilled breeze. "I'm much too young to be going through menopa—"

Oh my god! Brye screamed out in her mind. In a panicked state, she launched herself across the bed and grabbed her excessively large black leather purse. In her hurry to reach the opposite side, the weight of her body slammed the bed's headboard into the wall. The jolting collision caused the Claude Monet replica of *The Artist's Garden at Giverny* to crash against the dresser drawer and plunge to the floor. Disregarding the deafening disturbance she had created, Brye swept the bag into her clutches. But before she had time to scatter the contents on top of the bed, Tank burst through the bedroom door.

"Are you okay?" he demanded, taking in the room in one quick yet efficient sweep.

Distracted with the task at hand, she could not carry a normal conversation. "I…uh… Yes…I'm fine."

"Are you sure?" Tank inched further into the room. He picked up the painting and placed it so that once again, it stood sentry over Brye.

Brye dug out her personal day planner from the mess she'd dumped on top of the bed. Staring blankly at Tank, as if he had just materialized, Brye smiled apologetically. "I wasn't being very careful. Thank you for retrieving the painting."

Loud knocking prevented Tank from answering. He aimed his hulking body toward the suite door. "Your schedule was pretty merciless today, you haven't had dinner yet, so I took the liberty of ordering something for you."

The thought of food sickened her churning stomach even more. Swigging back the acrid taste covering the inside of her mouth, she smiled faintly. "A bodyguard and nursemaid too. How did I ever get so lucky?"

Alone, Brye opened her day planner. Her mind futilely searched for possible answers as she fingered through the dates.

I'm never late, she fumed to herself. *My cycle is regular. Just like clockwork. In fact, the last time I was ever late was when I was expecting…*

She stumbled unsteadily over the recollected image. "When I was expecting Chad's babies," she uttered softly to herself.

Anesthetized with the sobering thought, Brye's fingers automatically drifted across a flat abdomen.

Pregnant. The signs were irrefutable. The inescapable fatigue dropping on her head at any odd time of day; the endothermic hot flashes; the crippling nausea and weighted down breasts; she'd endured the early warning signs of pregnancy before. It seemed she was destined to weather them once again. Her mind paced over possible methods in which to confirm her explosive condition. She needed to know. And she needed to know fast. But walking into a drugstore and buying a home pregnancy test was strictly out of the question. She could not afford to have someone recognize her.

"I wanted to surprise Brye. If I had called to tell her I was coming, it wouldn't have been a surprise. Duh!"

The jutting voice, furious and condescending, barged into the suite, taking the beeline expressway to Brye's bedroom. It crashed through her undulated thoughts.

"Tenisha!" Brye squealed in jubilation. For the moment, her present predicament ceased to exist. "It's all right, Tank!" Brye okayed as she threw herself into her friend's arms. "What are you doing here?"

"I wanted to surprise you." She threw Tank a withering look. "What's up with Kevin Costner here?" The piercing look turned appreciative as her solicitous eye did a slow intake along his eye-popping physique. "Oops, my bad. He's more like Arnold Schwarzenegger—without the accent," she glorified, her misappropriated annoyance momentarily forgotten.

"I was trying to explain that no one enters without clearance." Inwardly, Tank's patience steadily deteriorated, yet outwardly, he remained solidly intact.

"And I was explaining that since I didn't know anything about obtaining a clearance, it's obviously too late to get one now because I'm already here."

"And I'm so glad you have," Brye said, deflecting the precarious moment. "But what are you doing here?"

"I'm on vacation. I decided to sponge off you for several days, then I was going home to visit my parents."

"You're more than welcome to sponge as long as you like." Rendering a repentant smile to Tank, she grabbed Tenisha's twenty-six-inch pullman. "As long as you don't mind bunking with me."

"I'll take those," Tank promptly offered. He secured the suite door, then peeled the pullman from Brye's fingers. Lifting her garment and overnight bag, he carted them off to Brye's room.

"What's going on between you and TyJuan?" Brye turned on Tenisha. She assumed this to be a spur of the moment trip, with Tenisha desperately needing to put some distance between herself and her husband.

"Do we have to get into this now?" Tenisha asked with an exasperated sigh.

"Yes. We do. Then we can forget about him and enjoy the rest of your visit."

Resigning herself to adhere to Brye's request, Tenisha dropped onto the cream-colored sofa. "I'm tired. And I needed to shut my mind down for a little while."

Of all people, Brye related well with Tenisha's sentiment. Sitting beside her friend, she offered comfort, and a shoulder to cry on if need be. "TyJuan hasn't gotten any better?"

Tenisha rolled her eyes in disgust. "If you only knew the half of it."

"Tell me."

"He's not only drinking, but he's sleeping around as well. Unexplained large amounts of money have been withdrawn from our joint account." Her eyes tapered into narrow slits. "He's graduated to drugs."

Horror-stricken, Brye's mouth worked but nothing came out. She grabbed Tenisha by the hand and said, "You have to get out of there. Now, Tenisha. Before he does something to you."

"It's not that easy." Tenisha slipped her hands out from under Brye's pressing fingers. Knees together, she sandwiched her palms between her thighs. "I can't just walk away without trying to help him."

Brye mashed her lips together, determined not to begin a fight. When the impulse became too intolerable to bear, she said, "You can't help him. Only he can help himself. And he doesn't want to do that. So you need to cut him loose…cut his finances loose. Otherwise, it's going to get worse."

"It's not that easy," Tenisha mournfully repeated.

"Of course it's not. The first step is always the hardest. But if you want, I'll be there with you every step of the way."

Deep in thought, as if really contemplating the idea, Tenisha uttered, "What would my parents say?"

Enlightenment sank in. Brye frowned. "Don't tell me you're holding back because you're afraid of what your father will say."

Tenisha turned away from Brye. "He warned me not to marry him in the first place."

"So you made a mistake. You fix it, then go on with your life."

"I don't expect you to understand, but my father was always there for me. He supported me. In everything…everything except my marriage to TyJuan. How can I just walk away? How can I say to my father that he was right all along and I was wrong?"

Brye stared at Tenisha in total disbelief. For as strong a person Brye knew Tenisha to be, it was difficult to sit here and accept this self-pitying attitude her friend was drowning in. Shaking her head from side to side, Brye established, "But I do understand. I understand perfectly. The only thing keeping you in a marriage turned bad is your pride. And…misplaced self-respect." Brye stood. She walked around to face Tenisha, then dropped to her knees in front of her. Sliding her friend's fingers within her own, she said, "What's that saying? 'Pride goeth before a fall.' Get out, Tee. Get out now before it's too late."

Tenisha's chin trembled. The more she tried to force the tears down, the more her chin quivered. Fortunately, Tank walked in, deflating her morose mood. Her smile overrode the pain. Tenisha proclaimed, "I've done enough talking about my sad state of affairs. I've come to have a good time…so let's have a good time."

"Agreed." Brye stood up. "But you are aware that I am on tour? So wherever I go, you go with me. And that means long bus rides."

Looking chagrined, Tenisha teased, "You mean I can't fly first-class to your next destination and meet you there?"

"You're sponging off me, remember? The rule is: if the spongee expects to sponge off the sponger, then the spongee's presence is an absolute requisite."

"If you want to get technical about it," Tenisha rectified, "I think I'm the sponger. You're the spongee."

"Whatever!" Brye brushed aside the correction with a wave of her hand.

"Then I demand to be fed. All I've had this evening was a package of stale nuts—and they weren't even roasted," Tenisha complained.

Again, a soft tap came at the door. As Tank angled across the room to answer, Brye smiled sweetly and remarked, "Guess who's coming to dinner."

Faced against one another, Tenisha and Brye sat Indian-style atop Brye's king-size bed. A deck of cards sandwiched between them, they indulged in the middle of a tie-breaker game of gin rummy. Both wore bedtime attire; Brye in a purple pajama set offsetting her eyes, Tenisha wearing a large plaid nightshirt with matching panties.

Tenisha's play, she pulled the top card from the face-down pile. Studying it intently, surreptitiously, she said, "Marcus sends his love."

Brye lowered a card hand that seemed to be mocking her. Covertly, she stared at Tenisha underneath the protection of long eyelashes. Her tone remained light, not accusatory. "You've been seeing Marcus?"

"We have a mutual adoration for seasoned movies—particularly black-and-whites." Tenisha discarded a four of hearts.

Brye was aware of Marcus's veiled affinity toward Tenisha, and now she picked up on the dreamlike quality resounding within Tenisha's tone. She didn't want to see either of her friends hurt, nor did she want to sound preachy. Stepping lightly, she questioned, "What does a 'mutual adoration for seasoned movies' mean? Does it mean you've seen each other, you're seeing each other, or you've seen each other while stepping out to the movies?" Brye drew a ten of spades. With a hopeless shrug, she discarded that same card.

"We've spent some evenings together…enjoying old flicks." Tenisha lifted an ace of hearts. She melded the ace of hearts with the ace of clubs and the ace of spades. Spreading the cards out on the cottony comforter, she threw away the jack of diamonds—her final card—and announced, "Rummy. You owe me a root beer float."

Brye tossed her cards down. "You two been getting along okay?"

"We've been getting along fine. You of all people know what an evening spent with Marcus is like. He's strong, yet gentle. He's sensitive, honest, and fun to be around. He's a good cook, a good housekeeper, and to top everything off, he's all that plus a box of chocolate-covered nuts."

"I don't want his resume, Tee. I want to know what's going on between you two." Brye pooled the deck into one pile.

"Nothing's going on. And that's a major feat in itself, considering how horny I've been lately. Oh, by the way"—she blinked at Brye through a libidinous glaze—"the way I feel, you should tell Tank to lock his bedroom door tonight. Otherwise, he might be getting a night visitor." She giggled. "Wet dreams could take on an entirely new meaning for him."

"Tenisha!" Brye exclaimed. Accustomed to her friend's risqué assertions, she joined Tenisha in inane laughter. Cards gathered, she climbed off the bed.

Overdramatizing her frustrations, Tenisha flopped backward onto the bed. "I need a man!" she moaned, squinting at Brye.

"So why are you looking at me like that?"

"Like what?"

"Like the big bad wolf about to devour Little Red Riding Hood."

"Don't even go there, girlfriend! Excluding the fact that you're missing all the major vital body parts, you aren't even my type."

"Excluding the fact that I'm missing all the major vital body parts, I seem to be the only person you've been able to lure into bed lately."

Tenisha groaned. "Please don't remind me." She stretched upward and turned off the bedside lamp.

Brye dropped the deck of cards on top of the dresser. Turning off the main light, she slid under the cool sheets. "Just make certain you remain on your side of the bed."

"Go to hell!" Tenisha quipped. Sinking into her semisoft pillow, a half-moon lit up the bottom half of her worn features. It had been a long day. After arguing with TyJuan over the money he'd been spending, after he'd come reasonably close to striking her, she had decided to put some much-needed distance between them. Without thinking twice, she'd jumped on a plane and flew to North Carolina. Her last conscious thought before slipping into blackness: she was glad to be here.

Five o'clock the following morning, Brye left Tenisha slumbering while she and Tank went out for her daily jog. Above, the eastern horizon transformed from a midnight shade to a purplish haze in preparation for the rising sun. Below, a slight breeze sighed through magnolia and dogwood trees. An aromatic diversity of sweet ambrosia filled the air. Bright red cardinals speckled the trees, sparrows sweetly crooned from deep within azalea bushes.

This was the only time of day the world seemed at peace with itself. All things, everyone, mingled in perfect harmony.

Everyone except Brye. Not only was she not in tune with the world, but her body refused to harmonize with her psyche. With every step she initialized, her stomach muscles contracted, then lurched into the forefront of her awareness.

Pure torture. Step upon agonizing step, Brye wondered if she could make the second half of her run. Deciding she couldn't, she barely breathed Tank's name as he tracked, unaware of her agony, beside her.

Maybe I can finish, Brye foolishly decided. She gulped down the fresh morning air, not because she couldn't catch her breath—she'd been running much too long to be out of wind after the completion of two miles—but because she hoped the steady influx would still, or at least, hinder, her rolling gut and allow her to finish her early run. No such luck.

"Tank?" she called again, her voice straining against the morning breeze as her feet came to a complete standstill. Tank abruptly halted and turned a concerned eye to Brye.

Not expecting to see a bloodless face with wide frightened eyes and puffing cheeks, the bodyguard immediately moved to her side. He supported her with one hand pressing into her stomach, the other resting against her shoulder. "Are you all—"

Before he could finish the sentence, Brye bowled over. Hands balanced against quivering thighs to support her upper body, face distorted in wretched agony, in one unnerving heave, she torpedoed her entire stomach's contents on top of Tank's recently purchased Nike's.

29

The Woman's League luncheon and fashion show was scheduled to begin in a little under two hours. Buried in a cramped dressing room, Brye stared sightlessly into the brightly lit wall mirror. As Cory's expert fingers navigated over her face and hair, Brye vividly remembered her early-morning fiasco. After showering Tank's shoes with her liquefied innards, surprisingly, relief immediately flushed through her. However, convincing Tank of her sudden improvement was another story in itself.

He wanted to call a doctor. Brye refused, He suggested they call Brian. Again she refused. He advised her to take the day off and rest. Brye insisted her health was fine.

His mission, should he chose to accept it, was to furtively visit a drugstore and buy her a pregnancy kit. Not giving a reason for wanting that particular item, she left him to draw his own conclusions. She did, however, extract a promise from him: he would not mention the pregnancy test to anyone. To her absorbed relief, he complied without question.

Presently, Tank was holding sentry on the other side of her dressing room door. But earlier, he'd disappeared long enough to adhere to her bidding. Once he'd returned from his mission, his head had popped inside. Issuing a subtle nod in confirmation, he ducked out, wondering if he'd done the right thing in contacting Brian. He promised he wouldn't discuss the pregnancy test to anyone. He did not, however, promise to keep her vomiting a secret. Out of concern for Brye, he thought it best to inform Brian of her present state of health.

On pins and needles, Brye was eager for the afternoon to end. For her own peace of mind, it was imperative she return to her hotel room and administer the confirming test. One way or another, she would learn with certainty whether she carried Chad's baby or not.

"What's another word for *lively*?" Tenisha asked. Sitting comfortably in a director's chair, legs stretched outward, feet propped on the dressing table, her head dipped deep inside a crossword puzzle. Collectively, Brye and Cory added their educated input.

"Spirited," Cory was quick to answer. Much like the caress of an artist intimately stroking his canvas, Cory brushed a light shade of melon-colored blush along Brye's cheekbones.

"Three letters," Tenisha established.

"Fun," Brye responded, slipping out of her own absorbed world.

"Last letter begins with a 'y.'"

The dressing door suddenly exploded inward. In an irrepressible swirl of colors, cologne, and cockiness, Frederico Flandeno—the renowned fashion designer whose creations Brye would be modeling—presented himself with a boisterous flourish to the three unprepared occupants.

"Brye…dah-ling," he purred.

Strutting up to Brye with more sway in his hip than she and Tenisha had in their entire body, she stared in wide-eyed fascination. Concentrated eyebrows, a pouting mouth in direct opposition to his authoritarian stare, Frederico Flandeno was someone used to getting his way, be it by praising, sulking, or demanding. Wiry, emphatically excitable, he was impeccably dressed in a lime-green double-breasted suit. Buzz cut hairstyle, gold cross earring dangling from his right lobe, several gold necklaces, and an extravagantly ostentatious gold pinkie ring, Tenisha looked at a man who was very comfortable with himself; a man who cared little of what others thought of himself. But then, with the millions he made each year, along with his lustrous reputation acquired by his sensational creations, why shouldn't he be comfortable with his own identity.

"I'm sorry I wasn't here to personally greet you, but…" He shrugged, and smiled, and presented his arms in an obliging gesture that said, "Que sera, sera?"

He smacked two kisses in close proximity to her ears. "You are absolutely glowing, my dear. How do you do it?" he praised.

"Thank you, Frederico." Brye blushed, wondering if her pregnancy had anything to do with that absolute glow. She waved a hand toward Tenisha. "Have you met my friend?" She did not wait for an answer. "Tenisha Davidson…Frederico Flandeno."

"Is this *the* Tenisha Davidson," Frederico squealed with the jubilation of a crazed supporter greeting his longstanding idol. "You do just mah-velous work, dah-ling, particularly when you're working with models wearing *my* creations. You have a way with lighting and angles and colors and…ohhhh…it makes me shiver all over."

Brye met Cory's amused image inside the mirror. Both found it difficult to choke back their laughter. Both wondered if Frederico had just experienced a self-induced orgasm.

As an artist, Tenisha knew and respected Frederico's creativity and artistic mind. Until today, she had never met nor did she know him personally. Although her initial impression had proved to be somewhat unsteady, she found herself beaming in the light of the unsolicited praise.

"Thank you so much for your greatly appreciated approval, but credit should go where credit is due, which is back on your lap. After all, I don't bring anything into your creations…your creations carry it all into my photographs."

In the mirror, Brye hid her laughter as Cory rolled his eyes to the ceiling. And as she continued to regard the engaging adulation passed back and forth between Tenisha and Frederico, she decided they were caressing egos much like lovers embarking upon a journey of passionate love making. *Totally sickening*. But as Brye studied their ecstatic expressions, she realized it wasn't a game with either of them. They actually retained mutual respect for the other.

"I would love to sit here and chat some more, but I do have a show to put on." As he spoke, he continued to lay a light hand on Tenisha's arm. In less than five minutes, they had become besties. "Let's do a late lunch afterward, I'd love to hear how you got started in your career."

"I'd like that." Tenisha beamed with pleasure.

"Good." He flashed an unsettled smile at Brye. "One of my models called in sick. I've got my people on the phone trying to replace her. I hope to call in some markers, but if everything falls through, I hoped—strictly on your approval, of course—you might consider modeling more of my fashions than you were originally fitted for."

"That won't be necessary," Brye assured with cast iron confidence. Eyes sparkling impishly, she announced, "You already have a replacement."

Reading her mind, Tenisha exclaimed, "Oh no you don't!"

"Look at her, Frederico." Brye opened her arms, palms waving in the air as if presenting Tenisha to the world. "She's gorgeous. Even at her worst," Brye teased, her eyes darting over the tousled hair, light pink cotton blouse and shorts, with pink canvas shoes to finish off her casual ensemble.

"Don't go there, Brye," Tenisha warned, her eyes shooting spitfire.

Brye ignored Tenisha's battle cry. "What do you think, Frederico?"

Frederico's left hip jutted outward. He plopped one balled fist upon the distended hip bone, the other stroked his hairless chin in thoughtful contemplation. Everyone in the cluttered dressing room could hear his mind ticking. Time slowly marched forward. Several pensive minutes later, his voice tingled with excitement. Yes…yes…" His head bobbed up and down. "I can work with this."

"Of course you can," Brye speedily agreed. Her smile flowed as wide as the Hudson River.

"Can she strike a pose?"

"Of course she can," Brye assured. "She taught me everything I know."

"Don't I get a say so in this matter?" Tenisha barked. They were talking like she wasn't in the room.

"Come on, Tee. I've always wondered why you worked behind the camera instead of in front of it. Haven't you ever thought of becoming a model, even the tiniest bit?" Brye held her hand out in front of her face, thumb and forefinger spaced an inch apart.

"No…well…maybe," Tenisha answered, her voice quivered with uncertainty.

"You can do this."

Tenisha didn't doubt that she could. At one time, she had retained notions of becoming a model, had actually modeled some in her early teens. But her heart had always been set on photography. On her sixth birthday, her father had given her a camera. As time went on, it became her third eye. She'd driven her parents crazy. At the most inopportune moments, she snapped pictures of mother, or father, or anyone else who had the misfortune of crossing her artistic path. And one of the proudest moments of her life was when she snatched the job of photographer for her high school year book—four years in a row.

But maybe she could do this…just once. It would be fun.

The idea unfurled its wings and took flight. Frederico recognized the slight spark highlighting Tenisha's caramel coloring. He pounced. "It's settled then. I'll get my seamstress, Cory will do your makeup and hair." He raised his hands to the ceiling. "God bless America. We're in business once again."

Smacking two kisses next to Tenisha's ear, he remarked, "You have made a friend for life, dah-ling." In the same gust of colors, cologne, and cockiness he had entered on, he hopped aboard the returning flight and took off. With the absence of his effervescent grandeur, the dressing room appeared much drearier than it had been a moment earlier.

"He's so…so…" Tenisha searched, unable to arrive at an adequate synonym apropos to his demonstrative mannerism.

"Colorful?" Cory offered. Running nimble fingers through Brye's hair, he began pulling it into an upsweep.

"Flamboyant?" Brye proposed on the end of Tenisha's shaking head.

"Excitable?" Cory submitted, pinning Brye's hair.

"Gay?" Brye said, a slight smile teasing her lips.

Tenisha looked down at the crossword puzzle she had not as of yet set aside. Mouth molded into a surprised O, she excitedly blurted out, "That's it!" She began penciling in the letters: G…A…Y. "That's my three letter word for lively!" she exclaimed.

Cory and Brye stared at each other inside the lighted mirror. This time, the laughter could not be repressed. Several confused seconds later, Tenisha joined in.

The toilet lid closed with an explosive bang as Brye pushed it shut. A weighty sigh pushed through her partially closed teeth as she dropped onto the cold seat. Arms pressed tightly into her chest, she waited for the results of her home pregnancy test to materialize.

On the conclusion of the fashion show, for two hours afterward, Brye had lingered to discuss Romanique products, current fashions, and women's issues in general. Tenisha and Frederico had slipped away to croon courses of "What a mah-ve-lous job you did, dah-ling!" at each other.

Finally breaking away, Brye had rushed back to the hotel in her urgency to test her urine before Tenisha caught wind of her surreptitious activities.

Sitting forward, Brye propped her elbows on top of her thighs and settled her chin on top of her linked fingers.

She didn't have a clue of what she would do if this test proved positive. Would she go to Chad? Of course she would, Brye thought with a definitive nod of her chin. This was his child too, and he had a say so—albeit, a small say—in what the baby's future entailed.

In Florida, Chad had declared his love for her. Aside from him believing she embezzled money from his family, he had forgiven her; he actually said he had put the past behind him. Unconditional love was what he was offering her. Should it matter that although he didn't trust her, he was willing to accept her?

The bathroom door flew open, interrupting Brye's perplexed quandary.

"Here you are," Tenisha breathlessly exclaimed. "Frederico and I had a long talk over expresso, and…" She halted. Head tilted inquiringly to one side, she stared openly at Brye. "What're you doing in here?" Her eyes slowly rolled over to the intrusive kit spread atop the marble vanity. "A pregnancy test?" she blurted in confused wonder. "You're taking a pregnancy test?"

"I... You... I..." Hopelessly tongue-tied, Brye shrugged in apparent distress.

Tenisha slid further into the room. She looked down at the strip stretched atop the marble vanity. "It's pink." She turned back to Brye. Dumbfounded, she asked, "What does that mean? Pink it's a girl, boy if it's blue? What the hell does pink mean?" On the edge of hysteria, her voice steadily climbed.

"I...I don't know," Brye admitted, her face squinted into a puzzling state of complexity. Again she shrugged. "I didn't read the instructions all the way through."

Tenisha scooped up the empty box. Reading the written instructions, she mouthed the words as her eyes moved along the printed lines.

"White if it's negative, pink means you're pregnant." The box slowly lowered to her side, her back slumped against the wall. As if her friend had challenged the most phenomenal of miracles since the Virgin Mary, she mumbled, "You're pregnant? But how can that be?"

Although Brye had suspected as much, had all but prepared herself of its high probability. Hearing it out loud added an entirely new dimension to her precarious circumstance. In more of a state of shock than Tenisha, her listless body slid off the porcelain throne and crumbled to the floor. "How could this have happened?" she uttered in nonsensical despair. "How *did* this happen?"

"Forget *how* it happened." Tenisha sank down beside Brye. "I'm sure if you go back to sex education 101, you'll figure that out. The real question here is, *who* did it happen with?"

The answer was soon in coming.

"Brye?" Tank's voice stretched into the bathroom from across her bedroom.

"I'm in here, Tank."

His huge frame filled the bathroom door. His eyes swooped over the motley scene confronting him. They settled on Brye. "Is everything okay?"

"Everything is fine," Brye assured, eyes clearing. "Thank you, Tank."

Tank proffered his hand. "You have a visitor."

Brye accepted his offer. Under the power of brute strength, she found herself hoisted off the floor. "Who is it?" she asked.

His response almost sent her tumbling back to the floor. After she had righted her footing, she hurried through the door.

The stunned look on Tenisha's face mimicked Brye's to perfection. Scrambling to her feet, she followed, not wanting to miss this for anything in the world.

In the main room, face-to-face, there was no proper greeting.

"I want some privacy so we can talk." Jennifer had not asked nicely. In fact, she hadn't asked at all. She had taken on the air of a woman expecting the servants to jump at her every whim.

The arrogance infuriated Brye, yet she presented a warm and unassuming smile. "Whatever you have to say can be said in front of Tenisha. And Tank was hired to look after my own personal safety." Her smile grew wider. "He stays as well. After all, we can never predict when a crazed fan might start brandishing a knife or gun."

"Then I guess you don't have to worry about me…since I'm not now nor have I ever been a fan of yours, crazed or otherwise." Jennifer's faith in Daniel's abilities had steadily declined; his well-made plans had backfired in their faces. After the badly handled confrontation with Chad, Jennifer had decided to hop a plane and approach the source directly. If necessary, she would personally take Brye out of the equation on her own.

"Is that so?" Brye took a step closer to Jennifer. Hands crossed under her breast, her stance emerged tall and defiant, her tone remained gracious and confidential. "And I guess it's also safe to assume that you didn't fly all the way down here, tapping on my door, to sell me Girl Scout cookies?"

Not as adept at confining her detest as well as Brye, Jennifer's lips sneered in unencumbered contempt. "What a brilliant assumption." Her eyes rolled disdainfully over the length of Brye's relaxed body. "And this coming from a woman who has no use for a brain.

Particularly when the only part of you men are interested in is your body."

A cat fight. Claws brandished, both woman were out to draw blood. Captivated, Tenisha's eyes bounced back and forth from one woman to the other. Not once had she seen Brye enraged or out of control. Even now, Brye met Jennifer with an imperturbable manner—yet she had every right to rip the eyes out of the egotistical bitch's socket. But Brye's unruffled nature only added insult to injury; her calm demeanor carried a greater amount of vehemence to her biting deliveries. Giving ten to one odds in Brye's favor, Tenisha had no doubt Brye would be the one delivering the mortal blow.

"You can rest assured," Brye was saying, "that your visit has become the highlight of my day. But if you don't mind, why don't you get on with what you've come to say so we can board you back on your broomstick and send you flying back to Manhattan."

Jennifer turned a vexed eye toward Tenisha, then at Tank. The superior stance she personified was one of Imperial Queen subduing her lowly subjects. Neither budged, however, and she was forced to confront Brye. "This is a private matter."

With a casual lift of her shoulders, Brye responded, "If the accommodations are not suitable to your liking, I suggest you kindly leave." Brye walked over to the sofa. She sat without offering Jennifer the same.

Jennifer flung a look of disapproval at Brye. She found Brye's etiquette—or lack there-of—atrocious. Unable to hide her contempt, she finally barked, "I want you to stay away from Chad!" Glaring down at Brye, she continued to stand, intent on proving her superiority.

Brye smiled knowingly into Jennifer's raging features. She refused to be intimidated. Dropping her hands into her lap, she said, "I hate to burst your bubble, Jennifer, but I'm not the one you should be talking to." Settling more comfortably into the sofa, Brye continued, "I think you better take a seat. It's time I brushed you up on current events."

Jennifer glowered. Seconds later, she dropped into a spider-back chair opposite Brye. Sitting stiffly, back rigid, she waited.

"Tenisha can testify to the fact that I never wanted the spokesperson's job at Romanique. I didn't even know Chad was part of the company. But I found out later—after I signed the contract—that Chad had personally handpicked me for the job. There were no other contenders, and he ordered Brian to do whatever it took to get me on board. And Fourth of July"—Brye paused to secure Jennifer's wavering eye—"I never invited Chad to spend the holiday with me. I was practically standing with one foot on the bus when he showed up, packed and ready to go."

Tenisha's head bounced back and forth from Brye to Jennifer. In wide-eyed fascination, she couldn't believe her ears. Chad had been secretly seeing Brye. He'd vacationed with Brye…sleeping with Brye…more than likely the father of Brye's baby.

Tenisha could barely conceal her jubilation. "Wait a minute. You and Chad? He actually went to Lake George with you?"

"Yes, he did," Brye openly admitted.

"And you didn't tell me," she pouted.

"You didn't ask."

"That's kind of a moot point, don't you think, since I didn't know you were *seeing* him?" Childlike pout replaced gleeful indignation.

Brye tossed Tenisha a look of exasperation. "Wake up, Tee. *That's* the point I'm trying to make. I wasn't *seeing* Chad, he was *seeing* me."

"Well, excuse me, Ms. Thang, but that's the same as saying six of one, half dozen of the other." The sofa absorbed Tenisha's weight as she collapsed beside Brye. "The meaning is the same, no matter how you phrase it."

"Excuse me!" Jennifer interrupted, caustic lines cutting into her exquisitely carved features. "But could you two put a cork in it and continue this Laurel and Hardy act some other time? I would like to get out of here, and the sooner Brye finishes her fantasizing, the sooner I can speak my piece."

"'Fantasizing?'" Brye repeated, raising her chin in heated defiance. "'Fantasizing?'" she urgently stated again. "I guess I was *fantasizing* when Chad showed up at my hotel, unannounced and certainly not expected—much the same as you've done today—in

Kansas City, Missouri, and spent the night with me. And I imagine I was merely *fantasizing* when Chad flew down after my attack and carted me off to Florida, spending the following three days afterward with me." Much to Brye's surprise and pleasure, Jennifer had gone a sickeningly shade of green underneath her salon-induced tan as her eyelids lowered.

Brye was pleasantly surprised. Evidently, the arrogant woman had some prior insight into Chad's recent sexual forays. Again, she felt pleased with herself. "Well, I declare," Brye egged sweetly, "I do believe we might be eating a little crow for dinner tonight...you think?"

"I've come to make you a deal," Jennifer spoke, her tone less confident.

Brye's brow crinkled in mild curiosity. "I'm listening."

"I want to marry Chad. I *plan* on marrying Chad. But I need you to help steer him in the direction of our wedding altar."

Tenisha coughed. She strangled on the irony of the situation. Right out from under Jennifer's nose, unwittingly, Brye had seduced Chad from the arms of a woman who had everything delivered to her on a silver platter. Chad would never marry Jennifer—at least not when he discovered that Brye carried his child. Of this Tenisha was certain. She smiled to herself. This alone had been worth the trip. Seeing this woman—and Tenisha used the term loosely—come into her own, had topped off an already extraordinary day in grand fashion. "Is she saying there's trouble in paradise?"

"I'm saying that Chad is...misdirected...because of you, Brye," Jennifer candidly acknowledged, ignoring Tenisha. "I'm saying I want you to help guide him back to where he belongs."

"Why should I?" Brye leaned forward, her face lit up in a blaze of confusion. "What's in it for me if I agree?"

For the first time since entering, Jennifer smiled. An afflicted smile. Lips drawn back over perfect white teeth, she resembled a condemned dog ravaged with rabies. "Because whatever happens between Chad and I, Daniel Collier will never allow you to have him. You aren't good enough to wed his son...you never will be. And, if you help me, after we're married, I promise to turn a blind eye to you and Chad's illicit affair. I'll allow you two to carry on as you wish—as long as it's done in a discreet manner."

Brye stiffened. Her eyes sank into the back of her head. After each of Chad's covert trysts, she had browbeat herself for accepting the backseat position Chad had placed her in. But hearing the truth cross someone else's lips was equivalent to having ice water tossed in her face. It forced her to wake up to the reality.

"A mistress?" She could not control the pain, or rage, any longer. "Are you saying you'd allow me to become your husband's kept woman?"

"I'm saying this alliance can be beneficial to the both of us."

A virtual cannonball, Brye shot off the sofa. Smoke trailing behind, she flung the door open. The exterior hallway stood free and clear. Had it been packed with hundreds of individuals, it would not have stopped Brye from launching her blind fury.

"Get the hell out of here!" she forcefully ordered. "Or I'll have Tank bodily throw you out!"

Once a venomous snake, Jennifer now pulled back her fangs. She shed her skin and donned an identity more conducive to her personified image. She was now the ideal guest, the perfect woman. With the grace and poise befitting a queen, Jennifer levitated to her feet. An alluring one-piece pantsuit hugged her hour-glass body like an ardent lover. She smoothly floated across the room. Her feet halted in front of Brye. "You are a smart woman, Brye. I know you can't delude yourself into thinking you have a future with Chad. This is your only chance." She stepped closer. Harsh words laced with saccharin, she sweetly acknowledged, "You started from nothing. You were born into nothing. And with credentials such as those, Daniel Collier will never allow you to become a member of his family."

Brye's anger shot past Jennifer's shoulder and slammed into the door directly across the hall from her room. Her fury dissipated into the solid wood.

She managed to keep the emotion out of her speech.

"My coming from nothing meant that the only place I could go was up. I've had plenty of room to advance in life. I've had plenty of space to grow. And I *have* moved up in the world, Jennifer. Because of my background, I've struggled to make a better person of myself. And I've done that.

"As I get older, I continue to improve myself. There are no limitations to what I can do, learn, or become. But you—" Brye hesitated. Face set in stone, eyes bright with vehemence, she completed, "As for you: once a bitch, always a bitch."

"Say what you will, Brye," Jennifer easily responded, "but this *bitch* will be marrying Chad." Calmly, Jennifer passed through the door. "Think about what I said."

"Why don't you think about this?" Gathering her strength, Brye effectively slammed the door in Jennifer's face. The walls siding her floor, plus the ones several levels below, roared behind the tremulous blast.

Chinese-filled take-out cartons topped Brian's ivory-finish dining room table. Chopsticks in hand, Chad piled a generous amount of shrimp fried rice onto his stoneware dinner platter. Dumping empress chicken on top of the rice, he then added lo mien noodles, one spring roll, and two crab Rangoon to his plate.

He and Brian had worked late at the office. By the time they'd walked out, Brye's interview loomed before them. For the second night in a row, they opted to eat dinner together. Choosing Chinese takeout, the food was then hauled to Brian's spacious loft to be eaten in front of the television.

"Leonard Shaw's doing his monologue now." Brian's footsteps tapped rhythmically against the white-and-black-checkered ceramic tile. "We probably have about ten minutes before Brye's guest appearance." Brian picked up a plate and delved into the overflowing cartons.

Carting his plate over to the refrigerator, Chad stuck his head in. The side door crawled with soft drinks, flavored teas, carbonated water, beer, and wine coolers. Chad reached for the carbonated water. He wanted to keep his mind clear.

Just as Chad and Brian settled in front of the entertainment center, Brye was announced as Lionel's first guest. Blood congregated inside Chad's head. Dizzy from a wave of desire, he gawked with wide-eyed intensity as Brye's statuesque frame emerged before him.

A black slim-fitting column dress enhanced an admirable torso. The long slit fleeting up the side of her dress blessed Chad with a glimpse of lengthy thighs sheltered by jet black sheer silk stockings. Hair pulled back and secured by a large bow, black teardrop earrings danced below dainty earlobes.

"She looks great," Brian admitted, eyeing her progress across the length of the television screen.

Eyes bolted to the sixty-five inch LCD color screen, Chad nodded in consummated agreement. A twinge of jealousy surfaced when Brye hugged her host in welcome. She then favored him with a gift pack of their top selling men's cologne and body products. He displayed his gratitude by way of another hug and a fleeting kiss on the cheek.

As far as talk show ratings went, Leonard Shaw was at the top of his game. He wasn't necessarily an extremely attractive man. It was his charismatic nature and voluble brown eyes that hauled in the most hesitant of interviewees into a bracing, most-often-talked-about-long-after-the-show confrontation. Tonight would be no different.

With the exchange of the initial pleasantries dismissed, Leonard settled in for the interview. The first question sent Brian shooting out of his seat.

"Shit!" He slid his plate onto the cocktail table. "I knew this would happen. I tried to contact Brye earlier to inform her of the photos in *Private Affairs* but couldn't get through to her. Kierra has family in North Carolina, so Brye gave her most of the day off to visit. I've left messages at the front desk, but I can only assume Brye hadn't picked them up." Along with his jabbering, he nervously paced in front of the television.

"Sit down, Brian!" Chad commanded, a bit harsher than intended. He watched as Brye admitted, with casual indifference, that she knew nothing of the photographs. "Brye can handle this."

As he studied her, the woman sitting in front of him exuded a sense of someone relaxed, at ease, apathetic to the jarring situation thrust upon her.

"Can you tell us why multimillionaire, entrepreneur, and recently engaged Chad Collier rushed to be by your side after your attack?" Leonard Shaw interrogated Brye as she thumbed through the pages with a detached eye.

Chad noticed the emphasis he laid on the words "recently engaged." It was enough to make his teeth grit.

On the edge of his seat, he observed as Brye looked up from the magazine. She hit Leonard with the most amusing of smiles. "From what I can tell of these photographs, I'd say he was consoling me." She held up the front cover for an audience point of view. As the camera zoomed in, she purred, "*Effectively* consoling me, wouldn't you agree, ladies?"

"Yes!" a boisterous chorus sang out under the euphony of laughter.

Chad couldn't help but smile himself. *That's good, Brye,* he thought to himself, *you're not openly admitting to anything.*

"Can you give us some insight on Chad and his three-year love interest and fiancé's current engagement status? Has the wedding plans been delayed, canceled? Or are they continuing as planned?"

"Again—and I'm only referring by what I see in front of me—from what I can tell from these pictures, it doesn't look as if we took the time to discuss his impending marriage. That's something you'll have to discuss with Chad and his fiancé."

Leonard smiled, somewhat ineffectually. "Are you trying to tell us that there is no basis to these photographs?"

"What's that saying? A picture's worth a thousand words." Indifferently, she shrugged. "Then again, in this day and age, with programs like photoshop at everyone's disposal, anything's possible."

"So you're saying the photos have been faked?"

Unflappable, Brye retained her million-dollar smile. "I'm saying that I could spend the rest of my life refuting the validity of this story. And the truth of the matter is Chad Collier's personal life is just that—his personal life. I would never dare to speculate on it.

And as for these pictures...well...I did not authorize them nor had I been made aware of their existence until this very moment." Again, unconcerned, she shrugged. "Therefore, I'm going to allow the general public to draw their own conclusions."

"Attagirl, Brye," Brian openly praised, impressed. Several minutes ago, his appetite had diminished. Now it had returned in full force. He dove into his platter with zeal.

The duration of Brye's interview proved to be entertaining, as well as enlightening. As usual, she handled herself well as she discussed fall fashions, makeup, the latest in Romanique products, and finally, the assault. With each subject, she relayed real-life anecdotes she had undergone during the last five weeks of her tour. Anecdotes which kept her audience spilling over the arms of their seat in the throes of laughter. And at her closing, she thanked everyone for their bolstering support, kind words, and the many cards and letters she had received after her traumatic experience.

Brian held the remote in hand. "Do you want to see the rest of the show?" he asked on the tail of Brye's appearance.

"I've seen enough."

The TV screen went blank.

"Can I get you something else?" Brian asked. Scrambling to his feet, he grabbed Chad's empty platter.

Chad peered offensively at his half empty bottle of carbonated water. "I think I need something stronger to drink."

"Scotch and water?"

"That will do."

"Be back in a minute."

Seconds later, Brian passed Chad his drink. "Brye's performance tonight has bought you some time. But come morning, there's going to be an influx of calls regarding your engagement. Jennifer's phone is probably already ringing off the hook." Brian sat down with beer in hand. "Soon you've got to come up with an official statement to go hand in hand with that magazine."

"I'm aware of that," Chad assured. "But until I speak with Jennifer, all statements are on hold."

Brian nodded in acceptance. Only his nod continued longer than necessary. Catching the subtle alteration in moods, Chad noted, "You're holding something back."

Brian threw back a swig of his drink. The volatile spirits chilled the back of his throat, yet warmed the pit of his stomach as it hit rock bottom. Uncertain he wanted to alarm Chad with so little facts, he hesitated.

"Despite Brye's strenuous hours, she looked good tonight," Brian hedged.

Chad made no comment. Patiently, he waited for Brian to get to the point.

"I received a call from Tank today." Brian assiduously studied the pale shade of his drink. "He's concerned about her health."

Chad's ears perked. He found himself perched on the edge of the sofa.

"They were out jogging when Brye suddenly vomited."

Chad looked away. His eyes became fixed on the lithograph painting hanging over a brass plant stand. The four-foot planter confined a Boston fern with attenuated healthy green limbs stretching down to the parquet floor.

"What I'm about to confide has to remain between the two of us." Chad wet his dry lips with his drink. The potent liquid loosened his tongue. "Nothing's been confirmed, and I'm not sure if Brye's aware of it, but there's a good chance she's pregnant."

Startled, like a semiautomatic assault weapon, Brian fired questions at Chad in short, rapid bursts. "Pregnant! But how? You mean Brye? You! Are you sure? When did you— What the hell?"

"No, I'm not sure," Chad readily admitted. "But her vomiting could easily be attributed to morning sickness. And while we were in Florida, she slept every chance she got, which means her fatigue could also be associated with the early signs of pregnancy."

"Do you have any idea what this could do to her career?" Brian abruptly barked, his loyalty for the company, and the sudden need to shelter Brye, kicked into protective mode and rose above all else. "She's Romanique Cosmetic's spokesperson, for god's sake! Not to mention a role model for millions of susceptible young minds. How the hell do you think it's going to look when it's announced that she's pregnant *and* unwed?" Brian slammed his bottle against the rolled arm of the sofa. "Dammit, Chad, didn't you even think about using protection? If not for your safety, then for hers?"

"Spare me the dissertation on safe sex, Brian. I'm already aware of the repercussions."

"I find that hard to believe," Brian snorted.

"I don't give a shit what you believe!" Chad furiously retorted. "And I certainly don't give a damn about how this is going to look to the public. All I care about is Brye."

"The way you've been acting the past few months," Brian vengefully recalled, "I find that hard to believe as well."

Nostrils flaring, chests heaving, both men glared angrily at the other.

"Dammit, Chad," Brian rushed to add. "You of all people know that emotionally, Brye is under a lot of pressure. Did you even consider what this might do to her?"

Chad's face fell. Suddenly he felt as if Brian had stuck a fork in him, allowing the hot air to escape. Deflated, he dropped his face into the palm of his hands. After several minutes of drowning in his own sorrow, he exposed his hidden thoughts to Brian.

"Maybe, subconsciously, I wanted her to get pregnant." He hung his head in shame. "God, Brian! I would never have slept with Jennifer without protection. With Brye, I never bothered…not once.

"Maybe, subconsciously, I believed that if I got her pregnant, she'd come back to me…for good." Unexpectedly, Chad laughed. "In thinking about it," he pathetically admitted, "it sounds crazy to me now. In fact, since Brye's resurfaced, my entire life's been turned upside down. Hell, I haven't even been able to recognize myself lately."

"That's okay." Brian grinned, his anger dissipating into thin air. "We haven't been able to recognize you either."

"It's been that bad, huh?"

"Worse."

Their laughter trailed off. The room settled into a stoical silence. Chad was the first to cut through the depressive stillness.

"I love her. I want to spend the rest of my life with her." He sighed, the irony of the situation stabbing viciously at his heart. "She's probably carrying my child and she won't even return my calls."

Before Brian could respond, the telephone rang. He dashed into the kitchen and grabbed the cordless phone mounted on the wall.

"Brye!" he exclaimed, instantly recognizing the caller. Dumping his empty beer bottle into the sink, he moved back into the living room.

"You handled yourself beautifully tonight," Brian reassured. He tossed Chad a knowing look before dropping into his oversized recliner chair. Pushing backward, the footrest flew upward to grab hold of his spent legs. "I'm sorry you had to go into the situation blind."

Chad lent his ear to the lopsided conversation. His heart thumped recklessly against his chest; Brye was close yet so far away. He wanted to snatch the phone away from Brian and beg her to talk to him. He wanted so much to speak with her, tell her how much he loved her, beg for her forgiveness. In the end, he merely sat there and listened.

"Yeah," Brian was saying, "he showed me the article."

She must have asked if I've seen the magazine, Chad thought to himself.

"He's sitting right here. Why don't you ask him yourself?" Brian petitioned.

Chad stiffened. He waited in agony for Brye to inform Brian that she did not want to speak to him. However, dazed, he reached over and took the phone Brian held out to him.

"Hello." He sounded slightly hesitant, breathless, uncertain.

"Hi." At any other time, on any other day, Brye might have refused to talk to Chad. Since her pregnancy was confirmed, however, she felt nothing but leniency toward the father of her unborn child. "How are you?"

Her harmonious voice brought music to Chad's bleary soul. "I'm fine." Chad looked on as Brian struggled out of his comfortable chair. His friend pointed toward the kitchen; Brian was leaving Chad to his own demise. Chad imparted a beholden smile. If he was lucky,

Brye would send him to his death quickly, mercifully, and in the absence of witnesses.

"And you…how are you?" he asked, keeping an eye on Brian's backside until it disappeared.

"I'm okay. I'm doing fine." Jennifer's impromptu visit had forced Brye to make some definite decisions. She was prepared to inform Chad of those choices.

"Brye?"

"Chad?"

They spoke simultaneously. Nervous laughter ensued.

"You first."

"You first."

Again in Dolby stereo. An expansive pause followed.

"I had a visitor today," Brye was the first to push forward. "Jennifer." She did not mistake his sharp intake of breath.

"Brye, I'm sorry. Did she—"

"It's okay…really, she was unable to extract her pound of flesh."

Another pause. Chad waited for the bad news.

"She asked me not to interfere with your exchanging of wedding vows. In return, she would turn a blind eye and allow me to become your mistress."

The sharp knife that had been jabbing at his heart earlier now worked its way down his chest, had slipped into his belly, and was now ripping his gut apart. "Brye, I'm sorry."

"I don't know whether to respect her for wanting you so badly that she's willing to share you, or to just call her the biggest fool on this side of planet earth."

"Brye—"

"Please," she quietly interrupted again. "Please let me finish."

Afraid to allow her free rein to complete her thoughts, Chad feared she would call a halt to their perilous relationship. He did not want to risk losing her. In the end, he nodded as if she visualized his every movement. He then began his slow descent into a bottomless pit of despair.

"The thing is, Chad, this time around, we were wrong in allowing our relationship to go as far as it did. It shouldn't have happened—not as long as Jennifer was a major factor in your life. What we did went against every moral fiber of my being, Chad. I'm not very proud of myself right now. You forced me to alter my—" Brye rethought her position. "No. That's not quite right. You didn't force me into anything. It takes two. I wanted you just as much as you wanted me. But I'm not as magnanimous as Jennifer, Chad. I don't want nor do I need to share a man…any man. It was wrong. And it'll never happen again."

Chad sunk further into the ominous pit. Brye's foot, crashing down on his head, forced him under.

"The next time I go into a relationship with a man—*if* I go into a relationship with a man—it will be for keeps. All or nothing, Chad. I won't settle for anything less. I will not be some man's plaything…a weekend excursion…a time out from the main event. Do you understand?"

In that one moment of revelation, a light-heartedness surged throughout Chad's entire system. The weighty burden driving Chad downward miraculously lifted. Instead of drowning in a pool of emptiness, he floated on a willowy blanket of promises for the future.

Although Brye hadn't outright given him a second chance, she hadn't slammed the door in his face either. She was telling him to get his life in order, cut loose the excess baggage. Afterward, they would talk. For now, it was enough; it was an endowment to the future he sought to secure with the woman he loved.

"I understand." His placating tone caressed the inner sanctum of her soul. "All or nothing, Brye. It's the way it should be, my love."

30

The nature park had closed one hour after sunset. A quarter moon beat a murky path along the foliage-lined bicycle trail. Under the safe haven of balmy trees, sprouting shrubbery and tropical vegetation, a solitary figure merged amongst the shadowy overcast.

Stealthily, he made his way to the prearranged meeting spot. Acute cries produced by earnest night creatures shifted through the temperate air and stifled the sound of the lone man's shuffling feet. Wearing sneakers, faded jeans, and a white T-shirt, his only distinguishable feature was the partially healed jagged scars sprouting from the corner of his left eye. It traveled downward, settling into the bed of a recently grown beard.

He reached a clearing but remained sheltered in the wake of an immense palm tree. A twig snapped harshly at a distance behind him. His heart shot straight through the roof of his mouth. Body tense, prepared to fight, he spun to confront the unknown danger.

"Jumpy, are we?"

A low, resonant voice shot at him from inside the darkness. The face was obscured by shadowy light, yet the imposing torso was clearly recognizable.

"Wouldn't you be," the scarred man answered, visibly blowing out a shaky breath, "if you'd spent the last two weeks in hiding?"

"You got me there," the second man answered, shouldering past him. Entering the clearing, he turned. A circumspect glance down the length of the shorter man's fading scars influenced him to say, "She did that to you?"

Dark brown eyes flared in consolidated fury. "The bitch! If I ever get—"

"Save it, man," the resonant voice commanded. He had no intentions of spending the next several minutes listening to a bunch of should've, could've, would'ves. "You had your chance and blew it." Anxious to complete the transaction, he slid a thick manila envelope from out of his inside breast pocket. He tossed it, underhanded.

The scarred man caught the flying package in midair. In search of more lighting, he moved further into the clearing.

Right where the bigger man wanted him.

Head down, the scarred man shuffled through the hundred dollar bills and the fake ID. "What a minute." Growing anxious, his fingers ruffled through the crammed contents again. "Where's my plane ticket? I thought I was leaving town tonight?"

"You are. But where you're going, you won't need the aid of a plane."

As soon as the scarred man looked up, the spinning bullet slammed deep into his hard skull. The silencer stifled the roar of the explosion; the blast erupted like a dampened firecracker. The scarred man never knew what hit him. But before he hit solid ground, the manila envelope was back in the hands of the executioner. Guiding the envelope into his inside pocket, he pulled out a plastic baggy bountiful with a fine, powdery substance.

Opening the bag, a hefty amount of white powder salted the inert body. The rest of the cocaine flittered away into the midnight breeze. Tossing the half empty bag next to the dead man, the tall man turned and walked away, never looking back.

The following morning, on the edge of the break of dawn, two dead bodies were discovered. One in St. Petersburg, Florida, the other hundreds of miles away in the Bronx. One male, one female. For one, the cause of death was instantly recognized: execution-style gunshot wound to the head. The cause of death for the other was just as easily recognizable but unconfirmed for several hours. The medical examiner's official report: respiratory failure secondary to an overdose of heroin. Although the two tragedies weren't directly connected to the other, both would alter the course of Brye Grayson's haunted life.

Cold...smelly...unaesthetically appealing...deathly inert... idyllic words synonymous to the drab morgue Brye had just set foot into. Swept back into Florida, she had flown in from California to positively ID the body of the man the police suspected to have attacked her. Blessedly, she had finished both commercial shoots two days ahead of schedule. After identifying the body—if she could identify the body—she had nowhere else to go but home.

Sandwiched between Tank and Detective Baumbard, Brye wandered down the cheerless corridor. Their combined footsteps echoed through the bare hallway. The sight of Chad chatting casually with another detective assigned to the case floored Brye. Her feet grew heavy with lead as the distance shortened between them. Although heart and mind reached out to him, physically, she was afraid to touch him. Not having spoken since the night of her interview, his current status with Jennifer remained a mystery. Brye refused to award herself with false hope.

Confronting him, she found herself floating in the pools of his responsive baby blues. "What are you doing here?"

"I've come to take you home."

Although his eyes washed over her with such illustrative warmth and sensitivity, Brye did not attain a sense of what ticked behind them. She redirected her focus to the detective standing at Chad's side.

Latino, mid-thirties, lean-built, well-dressed, malleable features which had the ability to alter in accordance with any given situation. Be it cold as ice, hard as steel, or soft as a baby's bottom, when necessitated, he was the more compassionate of the two detectives.

"Detective Gurerra." Brye smiled, proffering her hand. "Even under these circumstances, it's nice to see you again."

"Granted"—he slid warm fingers into hers—"this isn't the best of circumstances to be meeting under, but this is a situation that'll take you one step closer into getting your life back in order."

For a brief moment, something unidentifiable flickered beyond his dark features. However short-lived, his poker face had slipped before skidding firmly back into place. Be it reluctantly, unintentionally, or willingly, he was holding back information critical to Brye's well-being. Brye opted to sidestep the issue for the time being.

"Well, then, if all preliminaries are completed, let's get this show on the road and my life back on track."

Chad slid his fingers into Brye's. To reassure, he applied light pressure. Grateful for his supportive attendance, Brye squeezed back. A united front, they walked through the swinging double doors.

Inside, the body lay on a cold, steel cart with a white sheet tossed over it.

It's as if he's being presented to me on a silver platter, Brye mused in gruesome fascination. During her college years, a course in anatomy physiology had been required. For an entire semester, she had worked with a cadaver. Also, she had been offered the opportunity of viewing an autopsy. Dead bodies were not new to her. But when Detective Baumbard stepped up to the cart and slipped the sheet down, Brye was morbidly drawn to the ghastly pallor, the ragged scars, and the small gunshot wound decorating his forehead and staring back at her like a third eye.

Pulling out of Chad's comforting reach, she stepped closer. But as she did so, the memory of that night came flooding back to her. She found herself hurdled back into time, transported back on the white sandy beach of St. Petersburg. She could feel him rubbing his hard-on against her tensed body. She smelled his stale cologne and the sour stench of liquor on his breath. But worst of all, she could hear him.

"Oh yeah, Bryson. Beg for me. I love it when you beg."

The sentence slammed into Brye much like the bullet finding its way home in the dead man's skull.

Bryson... Bryson... Bryson... Bryson...

Her name ticked inside her head like a time bomb on its final count down before detonation.

He knew my given name! How could I have blanked that out? she screamed inside her head. *How did he know my name?*

Because it wasn't a random attack.

"Oh God!" Brye faltered. Her body shuddered uncontrollably. Her mind spun wildly. *But why?* she asked herself. *And who?*

"Is this the same guy?" Detective Gurerra asked, witnessing Brye's apparent distress.

Brye did not hear the Detective. She was only conscious of the unanswered questions ripping her brain apart. Her fingertips pressed into the side of her temples. She shook her head wildly in an attempt to throw off the frightening reality.

"It's okay, Brye." Her distraught reaction roused Chad. He reached out to pull her into his arms. "I'm here. I'm not going to let anything happen to you."

Panic-stricken eyes drilled into Chad. But it wasn't Chad she saw. It was his father. And suddenly she understood. Her soul trembled with fright, and the dread she was feeling swiftly surged into full-blown terror.

In a crazed frenzy, Brye tore away from Chad's constraining clutches. "Don't touch me! Don't you ever touch me again!" She backed into the frigid tile. Wild eyes, chest heaving strenuously, Brye was clearly lost in a world invented by her own cognizance.

"Brye…" Cautiously, Chad inched toward the frightened body cringed against the wall.

Completely out of control, she screeched at him, "Stay away from me!"

"Brye!" This time, Detective Gurerra attempted to approach her. "It's okay. It's going to be okay." He continued to speak lightly, unpretentiously, as if attempting to talk a jumper off a high-rise. Eventually, his soft tone penetrated Brye's ensnaring panic attack.

The overwhelming terror gradually seeped into the dreary atmosphere. The pounding of her heart caustically drumming inside her ears began to subside. The fear remained but gradually became manageable. "I'm okay." Frail from the emotional eye-opening disclosure, her pulse beat weak and thready, her voice simulated the same. "I'm sorry. I just..." Inhaling deeply, she raised her hands to her face. Sliding open palms up and over her temples, she pushed her fingers through tussled hair. "I guess... I don't know..." she struggled to explain. "My mind...I think it went back to that night... the attack..." She feebly smiled, trying to pull herself together. "I'm okay." She looked around. "I want to get out of here."

The relieved detectives promptly ushered Brye out of the oppressive room.

Minutes later, Brye found herself seated in a colorless office not much more appealing than the morgue itself. Coffee in hand, she stared unseeingly out the window as the detectives relayed everything they knew of the dead body lying on the cold slab. Only half listening, she wondered why Daniel Collier hated her so much. Why had he hired someone to physically attack her?

Like a hypnotist with gold pendulum in hand, the answer swung back and forth in front of her blurred vision: *Daniel wanted to scare you off into quitting the tour, which would give him the ammunition needed to have Chad fire you for breaching the contract.*

And now the question was, what was she going to do about it?

I'm going to break it off with Chad...for good.

All her hopes, her dreams, the desires Chad had mustered within herself the past few months now seemed as dead as the body she had just identified. Her happiness was no longer a possibility. She could never tell Chad what his father had tried to do. And it was blatantly clear that Jennifer was right: Daniel Collier would never allow her and Chad to be together...he would never allow them to be happy.

Of course, she could always try and tell Chad about his father's deceit, but there was no guarantee he would believe her. Daniel Collier had corrupted his son's mind against her before, and he could most certainly do it again.

But what if I'm wrong? she tried to convince herself, knowing for certain Daniel Collier's hand was all over this.

In thinking about the man who had attacked her, Detective Baumbard had said that they had not uncovered a name as of yet.

This man did not have a record, had never been in the service, nor had he ever had his fingerprints taken.

Gathering together all her professional knowledge, Brye understood that a man didn't just wake up one morning and decide to become a sex offender. It was a psychotic affliction ailing a perpetrator every second of every minute of every day. At certain times, he could possibly suppress his runaway inclinations, but the majority of the time, when gone untreated, his destructive behavior generally exerted itself upon the world with disastrous results.

The dead man's estimated age balanced somewhere between the years twenty-eight and thirty-five. If he were a true sex offender, Brye didn't believe he could have gotten away with sexually assailing women for many years while managing to sidestep the law.

And if he had been killed in a drug bust gone awry, if he were a mere drug dealer, it still continued to mark her with unanswered questions. If he'd traveled down the road of crime and drugs his entire life, why didn't he own a rap sheet? Was he so quick-witted that he'd eluded the police department all these years? And if he were that smart, why did he decide to one day deviate from the norm and attack her?

No, in every way she tried to rationalize it, the outcome was the same: He had spoken her name…her *former* name. A name no one held any awareness of except Chad…and his father.

Worried sick over Brye, Chad continued to keep a vigilant eye. He did not fully comprehend what had taken place inside the morgue, but he would never forget the look of terror, mixed with hate, dimming Brye's short-lived recognition. It was the same identical look he'd seen after having awakened her from her horror-stricken nightmare at Lake George.

Chad also couldn't ignore how Brye shied away from him after her stormy episode. He couldn't disregard how she continued to withdraw from him, even to the point where she refused to look at him. Something profound was troubling her. Something not only the dead man triggered, but his own presence had set off as well. Even now, face pinched and ashen, lips taut, her wayward mind was clearly not attached to the physical body seated before him.

As he studied Brye, she seemed to awaken from the self-induced trance. Facial muscles loosened, cloudy eyes cleared and fell on Detective Gurerra. She opened her mouth and remarked with emphatic certitude, "You're keeping something from me."

Detective Gurerra frowned. Detective Baumbard coughed into his balled paw. Shaggy hair, large nose, droopy ear lobes, he reminded Brye of an affectionate Saint Bernard. Short, stocky, less meticulous in dress and temperament, Brye became aware that it had been his singular decision to shroud the truth from her.

"Please tell me?" It was a desperate plea.

"Tell her," Detective Gurerra ordered.

Detective Baumbard coughed again. His heavy bottom pressed into the metal desk. He stretched his legs outward and crossed his arms over his chunky chest. "We called in all our markers. We hit up all our informants. As far as we can tell, if he *were* dealing drugs, no one inside nor outside our district knew of him, nor bought from him."

In slow understanding, Chad's face crumbled and fell. Although he understood the implication, he asked nevertheless. "Just what the hell are you trying to say?"

"We're saying that it could have been a drug deal gone bad. Or it could have been an execution style killing made to look like a drug deal gone bad…to throw us off track."

"We just don't know," Detective Baumbard added.

"We may never know."

Brye inhaled the reality of the situation with quiet acceptance. All her suspicions had been confirmed. She nodded. "Thank you for telling me."

The duration of her time spent with the two detectives left no clear mark on her mind. She remembered nothing up and until she was whisked off to the airport and settled into the private jet taking her due north.

The unvarying buzz of the jet's engines droned like an incessant bee against Chad's pulsating eardrums. Beside him, chair back in a resting position, Brye dozed. Even in sleep, her body shifted away from him. Since leaving the morgue, she had very little to say. She was systematically shutting down to him. He refused to allow that to happen.

For the umpteenth time, his mind replayed the distressing news the detectives had finally seen fit to release: "The killing may or may not have been drug-related." Either way, what did it have to do with Brye?

Chad turned a wary eye to the woman dozing beside him. In sleep, all pressures and worries etched into her face earlier had softened in virtuous splendor. She looked young, innocent, and intensely vulnerable. Chad resisted the sudden urge to reach over and push away the loose strands of hair hiding her left cheek. Instead, he dropped his eyes and watched the steady rise and fall of her swollen chest. The equanimity her body depicted at this moment was a big difference from the headlong panic he'd witnessed a few short hours ago.

He still couldn't release from his thoughts how her eyes had ripped into him—as if she'd suddenly remembered something. Something so horrifying, her mind couldn't accept the bitter truth.

God...he recalled the terror overshadowing her eyes—as if she'd been staring at a ghost. Or maybe not a ghost. Something or someone his presence had reminded her of. Someone connected to him in some way. Someone like...his father!

No! Chad released a low, agonizing moan. His father would never intentionally—

Chad found it discerningly impossible to finish the defiled statement. His father *would* intentionally hurt Brye. He had done it before and would do it again, without qualms, and at the expense of his own son's happiness.

But would his father go as far as to hire someone to physically harm Brye. Chad didn't believe so. But what he believed didn't matter. It's what Brye believed that counted. And Chad held no doubts that Brye believed his father was the mastermind behind the entire sordid plot.

"Dammit, Brye!" Chad spoke softly, his words lost in the insistent hum storming the cabin. "When are you going to learn to trust me? Talk to me? Let me in on what you are going through?"

But as he vehemently spoke the words, he knew he had never given her reason to trust. Trust was something he would have to earn. Chad vowed to do whatever it took to gain it.

As his eyes remained locked on her tranquil features, he witnessed a steady transformation. Agitated, her eyes severely vacillated behind quivering lids. Deep creases tunneled a crooked route along her delicate brow. Her head began to whip back and forth violently. Soft, frightened whimpers erupted as unseen manifestations threatened to destroy the private sanctuary she'd built around herself.

"It's okay, sweetheart," Chad soothed close to her ear. "It's all right. Don't worry. I promise I'll never let anyone harm you again."

"Chad?" Eyes closed, half asleep, dreamily Brye called out his name.

"It's me, baby. I'm here." Chad trailed soft kisses along Brye's temple.

Brye's turbulent actions ceased. She drifted into buoyant calmness, floating somewhere between a light trance and partial awareness. Chad continued to mark her face with tender kisses long after she'd settled down.

Brye was dreaming…a dream of a different caliber. In this one, although mother, father, and twin brother relentlessly taunted her, there was no malicious intent. Instead, they seemed to be warning her—in their usual contemptuous mocking fashion, of course. All three spoke of her continuous battle to run away and hide from everything that proved significant to her. First she ran away from the feelings she harbored for her own endearing family, and now she ran away from the life she could have with Chad. Her family found it quite amusing actually. Her mother went as far as to sound extremely pleased with herself when she informed Brye that the four of them would be spending the rest of eternity together. Inasmuch as

Brye chose to run, her loving family would be goading her the entire way. Hell, it was the least they could do, her brother warned with a lascivious wink and a nod. And he would personally make sure he remained close—extremely close—behind.

It was a sickening, frightening thought. With each passing moment, Brye grew weaker in her ability to fight off her personal demons. She couldn't continue to hold back the truth for much longer. Soon she would have to face what she'd hidden away for so long.

As her family's sneers augmented in intensity and duration, a gentle kiss, as light and delicate as the first winter snow, brushed against Brye's troubled soul. She then felt another land on her weary brow, and another mark her pale cheek.

Puff!

Methodically, the first kiss snuffed out her father.

Pop!

The second kiss wiped out her twin brother.

Whoosh!

The third kiss banished her mother to a state of total nonexistence. It was then Brye recognized that Chad could not only chase her personal demons away, but he could also aid in banishing them out of her life forever if she allowed him entrance into her private domain.

Chaste kisses lifted Brye out of one sheltered haven and settled her safely down into another. Since birth, Brye had been a fighter. She was a survivor. With or without Chad, she would continue to survive. But her life would be so much brighter, fuller, happier with Chad by her side. And life with Chad was worth battling for.

No. She would not let Daniel win. Not this time. Not ever again. From here on out, she would battle with the same underhanded tactics Chad's father utilized.

A strong sense of well-being washed over her as she became more attuned to her present surroundings. Her eyes remained shut, yet she sensed Chad's closeness. She basked in the pampering warmth his nearness offered. She flourished in the efficacy of his sweet kisses. Her body ached for more. As Chad's complaisant lips barely grazed the corner of her mouth, she reached up and grasped a thicket of hair skimming the base of his neck.

Caught off guard, Chad did not resist when the slight downward tug brought his mouth into direct contact with Brye's. Surprised by the intensity and demanding nature behind her impassioned kiss, he was even more startled with the staggering influx of emotions siphoning through his arteries and spilling into the pumping chambers of his heart as her lips played along his. God, but he loved her! How had he managed to endure those many years without the very woman who breathed life into his collapsed lungs? She pumped life-sustaining sustenance into his undernourished system. But how could he expect Brye to forgive him for doubting her all these years when he wasn't certain he could forgive himself?

These collective thoughts were momentarily eclipsed by Brye's darting, demanding tongue.

Breathless, their lips finally parted, but their foreheads continued to touch.

"Hi," Brye greeted, her sweet breath intermingled with Chad's.

"Hi yourself." He smiled. "How are you?"

"Fine." Brye smiled seductively into his eyes. "Don't I look fine?"

He pulled back slightly and gave her a quick once over. "You look wonderful," he admitted. And she did. Before she'd fallen asleep, her features had been pale and lifeless, her violet-colored eyes equally dulled in comparison. Now her lips were red and swollen from the impassioned kiss, her cheeks were treated with a natural glow, and her luminescent eyes twinkled with recently found vivacity. Indeed, she looked great.

Seconds earlier, the flight attendant had swept past to check on Brye's and Chad's momentary needs. The ardent exchange awaiting her congenial eye validated her visual inspection: their needs were being met just fine. An avid romantic, she smiled to herself as she wavered down the aisle. Minutes later, she was back again, asking if Brye or Chad cared for a drink.

Reluctantly pulling away from Brye, Chad declined but asked for a glass of water. "You need to drink a little something," he informed Brye. "You may even want something a little stronger before we finish our talk."

The burnished shine in Brye's eyes flickered. "I'm not quite ready to talk about us, Chad. I need time to work some things out in my mind first."

Chad nodded in understanding. Gripping the water the flight attendant passed to him, he turned his full attention to Brye. "We have all the time in the world to decide where we want to go with this relationship. I promise not to push the issue."

An abbreviated frown marked Chad's handsome features. "What I wanted to discuss—" He hesitated, finding it difficult to continue. Apprehensively, Brye stared at his Adam's apple as it bobbed up and down. "I needed to discuss the twins. Yesterday morning, the police found their mother. She died from an overdose of heroin."

Horror-stricken, Brye clutched at her throat for much-needed air. Her mouth worked, but she could get nothing out over the massive lump threatening to cut off her breathe. Before realizing what she was doing, she grabbed the glass of water Chad gripped in his hand.

And as the jet continued northeast bound, as Brye continued along her tortured journey, inside the next twenty-four hours, she would soon be exposed to a series of related and unrelated incidents that could potentially send her emotional stability over the edge permanently.

31

"I don't care if she's dead! I'm glad! I hated her!" It was an expected outburst by a six-year-old boy who had been hurt too many times by a woman who had never grasped the concept of motherhood. Yet the impulsive declaration triggered an intrinsic reaction within Brye. All of a sudden, her mind spiraled toward another dimension. Chad, the twins, Central Park, slipped beyond her reach.

Brye found herself stumbling around unfamiliar territory. An intricate maze. Extremely dark, the air she inhaled prevailed dense, damp, and musty. And the distressing sounds—mother, father, twin brother—mercilessly taunted her with madcap laughter.

Like a special effects movie, as her feet moved in front of her, the walls sped past at an extremely high velocity. Whenever she gained ground and turned a corner or slanted bend, she found herself at a dead end, with the closed-in space spinning wildly about her, and her family's derisive chortles inundating her overwrought senses. Anxiety level high, she attempted to backtrack but found it an impossible task. With everything weaving out of control, she could not tell where she had been or in what direction she headed.

Chest heaving, breath labored, she picked up speed. Fear clung to her like darkness clinging to midnight. She had to find her way out. If she couldn't, she knew she'd be lost forever. She ran until her lungs threatened to explode. Tripping over a dirt mound appearing out of nowhere, Brye found herself spiraling forward. Her body rolled over and over. She finally came to a halt, lying flat on her back, head dizzy with hopelessness. Fatigued, despondent, she possessed very little strength to go on. Only sheer desperation forced her back to her feet. In one last-ditch effort, she urged herself forward. And then she saw it: an infinitesimal pinpoint of light. It was enough to give her hope.

Faster and faster, she ran toward eternal salvation. The tiny speck of light increasingly grew larger. Never breaking stride, exhilarated, she finally broke into the luminous clearing. On this side, Chad awaited. His warm, encouraging smile reassured her.

Oblivious to the role Anthony had played, at length, he unwittingly forced her to face her own demons. She was finally able to release herself from the self-imposed prison she had banished herself to. And although snatches of her anguished past remained a distant blur, total recall was imminent. In time, the memories would freely flow.

Within Brye's mind, the prognostic manifestation seemed to have taken place over an extended period of time. In all actuality, it had transpired in only a few seconds. Taking heed to Anthony's heated assertion, Brye pulled him onto her lap.

"It's okay to have those feelings." Unhindered, Brye stamped her seal of approval. To her astonishment and relief, she actually accepted her words to be true—for Anthony as well as herself. "As long as we talk about it, and you learn how to work through your feelings, it's good to get it out."

Seated in front of the children's carousel, laughter rose and touched Brye's heart. As she took in the untainted scene of spinning kids, Brye gathered Bethany alongside her twin brother. "What about you?" Snuggling the two small bodies close, she asked, "Do you want to talk about how you feel?"

Bethany felt guilty for the lack of emotions she retained for her mother. Did it make her a bad person because she couldn't muster any deep feelings for the woman who gave birth to her and her brother?

She tentatively broached her true sentiments. "I'm not sure I hate her. And I'm sorry to hear she's dead. But I'm glad she can't come back to hurt us any longer."

Submerged in intrinsic affection, Chad stood sentinel over the three huddled heads as they lost themselves in their hushed conversation.

In many ways, they were so much alike: the vulnerability; the battling of private wars; the deep-seated desire to be loved, held, protected; an unchallengeable bond connected the three together…for life.

Throughout Brye's promotional tour, Chad had spent many hours with the twins because it had given him a sense of closeness to Brye. Somewhere along the way, he learned to love them as if they were his own. It was a startling yet comforting revelation.

"Do I have to go to the funeral?" Chad broke out of his embracing thoughts in time to hear Anthony ask.

"Not if you don't want to," Brye proclaimed, giving him a firm yet gentle squeeze. "But I've been thinking about this and I want *both* your opinions on it."

The twins looked up at her with bright, trusting eyes. In subdued anticipation, they waited.

"Before I tell you my idea, I want you to know that this is strictly *your* decision." She captured Chad's show of support before continuing. "And that means if you don't like my idea or if you have a better one, then I want you to speak freely what's on your mind. Do you understand?"

Several joggers darted past as Brye attained the twins' comprehensive nod. She proceeded, "Because you're the only surviving relatives the police are aware of, your mother's body will be released in my custody. There's no law that says we have to have a funeral. So if you don't want one, we don't have to arrange it."

Dropping her lips between the two heads, Brye planted a kiss on each temple. "But what you two need to do, what we *all* need to do, is gain a sense of closure."

"Closure?" Bethany repeated. Her childlike face squinted in fierce concentration in her attempt to fully grasp the indistinct word.

"It's where we call an end to the past. We lay it to rest. Set our bitterness aside so we can get on with our lives."

"And how do we go about doing that?" Bethany inquired. She wanted so to forget the past and begin anew with Chad and Brye as her parents. And she was willing to do whatever it took to achieve that dream.

"I thought we might have your mother cremated."

"Do you know what that means?" Chad asked, stepping into the conversation for the moment.

"No," the twins spoke concurrently.

Sitting next to Brye, Chad swung his left arm around and let it dangle along the back of the park bench. As he clarified the meaning, with the twins perched in her lap, Brye rested her weary head on Chad's supportive chest. She compiled energy from his strength as the sun wrapped the four bodies within its eager grasp.

"With your mother's remains—her ashes—we can do whatever you want," Chad concluded.

"You can spread them over a rose garden," Brye volunteered. "You can throw them out in the ocean. You can toss them into the air and let the wind carry her away. Or you can even keep her if you want. It's entirely up to you."

"Do we have to say anything to her?" Anthony asked, not certain if he'd speak to her, even if she were alive, looking well, and standing in front of him at this very moment.

"Not if you don't want to. But it's perfectly all right to tell her you hate her. It's all right to show her your anger. It's important for you to get your feelings out, Anthony. It's important you release the hurt and bitterness in a constructive way so it doesn't fester inside...so it won't destroy all that you are." Her eyes sought and found Chad's. Unspoken communication flowed between them. If the same advice had been adhered to years ago, they would never have had to endure life without the other's love.

"I don't want you to spend the rest of your life running away from your nightmares," Brye concluded. She dropped a light kiss on Anthony's cheek. "Do you think you can do this? If not for me, for yourself?"

Tears collected in the corner of Anthony's eyes. If Brye wanted him to do this, it could be done. He nodded in agreement.

"How about you, Bethany?" Brye's lips barely grazed her forehead. "Does this sound like an idea you might agree to?"

"I *want* to say goodbye to her," Bethany ardently admitted. "I want to tell her that despite everything she's done to hurt us, she did not destroy us. I want to tell her that despite it all, I forgive her."

Brye closed her eyes to the potent words Bethany had just expressed. Words no six-year-old should ever have had to recite, let alone be familiar with. When her emotions were back in check, she reopened her eyelids and was confronted with Chad's stirred expression. "It's settled then. It's time to lay the demons to rest. This is a time for healing…for all of us."

Driven by blind rage alone, Tenisha careened into Brye's drive and skidded to a screeching halt before realizing Brye wasn't scheduled to return until the following evening.

After spending four brainless fun-filled days with Brye and three soul-searching nights at her parents' home, Tenisha had finally come to a much-labored decision: she resolved to grant her marriage one last chance. Midmorning, she'd returned to her Manhattan apartment with the sole intention of convincing TyJuan to check himself into a drug and rehabilitation center. Afterward, she was prepared to go through counseling. If their marriage did not survive, it would not be for lack of trying on her part.

All her well-laid plans soared out the window and squashed onto the concrete sidewalk the moment she stepped into her messy apartment. Lacy bra and panties, a micro-mini dress—none of which belonged to her—led her into the occupied bedroom. The owner of the racy clothing laid brazenly exposed in her bed, next to her insolent husband. Unaware company had arrived, they both lay dead to the world. Pangs of anger blinded her vision. Red—in the form of fresh blood—was the only color clouding her eyesight.

The first impulse gripping her enraged emotions was to grab a kitchen knife and render bodily damage to the two dormant bodies. But she had no desire to spend the next twenty-years of her life locked up for a double homicide, even if it was justifiable. Taking another route, she gathered up the woman's clothing, grabbed a butcher knife, and pretended TyJuan lay underneath the garments she brutally shredded into tiny pieces. She then dumped the contents of the woman's purse into the garbage disposal. Salvaging the copper-colored lipstick, she wrote an eminently expletive message in big, bold letters across the bedroom mirror. Finally, she grabbed a pitcher of ice water and unloaded the entire load on top of the unsuspecting bodies. As two sputtering, swearing heads came to life, Tenisha high-tailed it out of the apartment.

"Damn you to hell, TyJuan!" Tenisha shut down the engine of the Explorer. "You want it to be over? Fine, it's over!" She hopped down from the vehicle and drew a straight pathway to Marcus's front door.

"Can I come in?" she asked as Marcus poked his head out.

Her unexpected appearance shook the very ground he traipsed upon. Stepping aside, he swallowed his elation. "Of course you can." Inside the hall entrance, he turned and judiciously studied her. The joy in seeing her was instinctively veiled. The nervous manner in which she portrayed herself caught his full attention.

Hands linked behind her back, chest jutted outward, sullen eyes that refused to look him in the face, a nervous twitch of her right foot, and Marcus sought to put her at ease.

"When did you get back?"

"This morning," Tenisha unclasped her hands and pointed shaking fingers in the direction of Brye's home. "I pulled into Brye's drive before I remembered she wouldn't be back until tomorrow night." She attempted a smile. It failed miserably. "I thought I'd come see you instead…that is, if I'm not interrupting anything. Did you have any plans for today?"

None that couldn't be altered. "Nothing definite. I thought I'd pick up a few of Brye's kids and bring them back over to help me get her house back into good living condition. Nothing's been dusted or polished since she's been away."

Several loud squawks rose from the living room as Rainbow searched for his owner.

Taking heed to the ear-shattering ruckus, Marcus spoke over it, "Would you like to grab a seat while I feed Rainbow?"

"Can I use your bathroom?" Tenisha requested on impulse.

"You know where it's at." Marcus inhaled the floral scent of her perfume as she slipped past. The front of his jeans tightened as the bulge in his pants grew more pronounced.

Leaning over the porcelain sink and into the bathroom mirror, Tenisha stared dubiously at her wavering expression. Guilt shuffled along the perimeter of her conscious thoughts. The notion of playing with Marcus's heart did not sit well in her stomach. He deserved better. She understood that. But the somber thought did not alter her intentions. If anything, despite her nervousness, she also shook in great anticipation at the thought of seducing the unsuspecting man.

Tenisha splashed cold water over her face. She removed all traces of makeup before exiting the guest bathroom.

Rinsing his morning dishes in one side of the double sink, Marcus became aware of her closeness seconds before she spoke, but he was not prepared for the sizzling sensations bolting along his backside as she wrapped her yielding arms around his solid waist. He stiffened at the feel of her supple body melding into his.

Tenisha nestled comfortably against his massive frame. "I thought about you a lot while I was away," she spoke softly, sensually. She whispered the truth. Over the past several months all she thought about was Marcus. She probably sabotaged her marriage because of him. For that reason alone, it had become the deciding factor in giving TyJuan another chance.

He stiffened. "Tenisha, I—"

"Don't say anything." Nimble fingers pranced along Marcus's expanded chest. Her exquisite touch forged an undiluted path of pleasure directly to his heart. "Just listen…and feel." Her fingers glided lower, spreading over the very essence of his desire. "I have no promises for tomorrow, Marcus. I don't even know what's going to happen in my life several hours from now. But I do have now… this moment. And I'm offering it to you. I'm offering myself to you. I want to make love with you."

Marcus wanted to do nothing more than push her away. He wanted to will his legs to turn tail and run. But for the past few months, she'd become the axis his existence revolved around. Her dark and lovely features were what he envisioned when looking at other women. Her high-spirited, extremely contagious laughter filled his head at all times of the day. He thought of her upon waking in the morning. She invaded his thoughts until he fell asleep at night. She shaped the substance his dreams were carved out of.

But this was no dream. Tenisha's industrious fingers vicariously chipping away at his rooted willpower happened to be real. And he could not summon the strength to turn away from reality.

A mercurial pulsation stormed the length of his yearning body and ravaged all reasonable thought. A low moan rose from the back of his throat. His lower body moved to the rhythm of her skillful touches. His head fell backward as mind-altering passion ripped apart his quintessence. Volatile senses gone amuck, he grasped for some conformity of control as Tenisha began to lower his zipper.

Marcus topped her long delicate fingers with his massive hand. Gliding a tender touch along her forearm, he grabbed on tightly and flipped her around. Positions switched, now her backside glazed his front. Closing his eyes against the glorious feel of sensuous curves rubbing against his hardened desire, he lowered his lips close to her ear.

"Please don't be mad at me later because I'm too weak to resist you now."

"You're one of the strongest men I know," Tenisha sighed. Wearing a taut-fitting, beige, linen vest—no bra—the swell of her breast spilled over the top two undone buttons. Marcus cupped one breast while working loose the rest of her buttons. God, but she felt good. How many times had he dreamed of this moment?

He sprinkled tiny kisses along her brow. "I understand you're not promising me a bunch of tomorrows. But it doesn't matter. I'm going into this with eyes wide open, and I accept whatever you have to offer. If this moment is all we'll ever have, I swear I'll make it last a lifetime."

As he spoke, he played with her breasts, squeezing, molding, massaging, inciting audible gasps of pleasure from Tenisha.

Never having kissed Marcus, Tenisha longed to feel his lips upon hers. Twisting her head to one side, she hooked her fingers around the base of his neck. Applying firm pressure, she tugged his head downward.

Without preamble, their lips locked. Knowing this might be the one and only chance he had with Tenisha, Marcus set out to arrest her senses. Not wanting to play fair, he longed to create a situation she would find impossible to walk away from.

Tenisha's knees grew wobbly at the potent assault he rained upon her. Like a power-generated vacuum, full lips and wandering tongue sucked in every bit of her mouth. From the tip of her head to the bottom of her feet, her insides were swept away on a sizzling current. And as his wet tongue roamed freely over her lips and face, his fingers dragged down her quivering body. Downward...downward...sending a flurry of butterflies scurrying heedlessly underneath her skin. His galvanizing touch ignited every inch of her body. Each tiny pore had turned into a launching pad, activated to blast off at any second.

And then his roving fingers invaded the interior of her linen pants, seeking out the most delicate, most sensitive, the most heated site of her entire being. Probing, stroking, the hot juices of her desire saturated his penetrating finger.

Maybe it was the fact that she hadn't been with a man for several months. More than likely, it was the dexterous fashion in which Marcus manipulated her body, whichever, Tenisha found her ravenous flesh responding eagerly.

Slightly bending at the knees, spreading her legs apart, she willfully opened herself up to him, giving herself freely. An admixture of moist, delicious, fiery heat originated in the heart of her soul, diffused outward, and encompassed her mind and body. In a matter of seconds, her molten insides went into automatic meltdown as the explosive heat bombarded her sweltering system. Crying out in gratifying release, unsteady fingers clung to the edge of the sink as her liquefied legs gave way.

"Marcus?" she breathed his name in one soft, satisfied sigh.

As her body began to solidify, Tenisha collapsed against him. Laborious panting subsided, then increased in intensity as his hardness pressed urgently into her backside.

"Did you enjoy that?" Marcus whispered close to her ear.

"Yes," she managed to utter in between gasps.

"Would you like more?"

Tenisha turned to face him. She linked unsteady fingers around his neck. Burning desire deepened her caramel-colored eyes. "Only if you join me."

"It'll be my pleasure."

In one effortless swoop, Tenisha found herself folded inside Marcus's powerful arms. He carried her up the stairs and to his bedroom, exerting very little effort. Treating her delicately as an antique china doll, he removed her clothing and gently deposited her onto his bed. He stepped back. In her direct line of vision, blazing eyes fixed upon her as he proudly stripped to his bare necessities.

Spellbound by his magnificent build, Tenisha's desirous eye drank in every inch of his powerful physique. She hated comparing him to TyJuan, but in all reality, there was no comparison. Her husband had nothing on this man. Strong, expansive shoulders, bulging biceps, a massive chest powdered with coarse dark spirals of hair, Herculean thighs. And protruding between his massive thighs, presented erect and surrounded by a mass of tightly wound hairs, proudly stood the focal point of his manhood.

Satisfied with the attention she flourished upon him, Marcus moved to the side of the bed. He pulled out a square cellophane wrapper from the bedside stand.

"Let me," Tenisha offered. Scooting over to his side, she took the wrapper and removed its content.

As Marcus stood before her, he gasped as Tenisha ran a finger along the length of his hard shaft. Encompassing him in her entire hand, he felt thick, hot, and heavy. The feel of him prompted her juices to flow once again. Anxious to consummate their union, she utilized her tongue in sliding the condom on. The cries of pleasure bursting from Marcus enticed her to linger…to stroke…to please.

When the taunting pleasure propelled him toward a crazed frenzy, Marcus grabbed her by the shoulders and pushed her down on the bed. Before he could begin a slow descent down her body with his yearning tongue, Tenisha urged, "Foreplay can come later. Right now, I want to feel you inside me."

"Are you sure you want to do this?" To ask was the most gentlemanly thing to do, but a gentleman was the last thing he wanted to be right now.

"Don't make me wait any longer, Marcus," Tenisha demanded, her body pressing demandingly into his.

Marcus was quick to oblige.

And when he filled her with his masculine strength and vitality, as he pushed her toward her limits, when she soared to heights she'd never attained before, Marcus ceased to exist as a conquest—he had now become a necessity of life.

Blessed silence greeted Brye and Chad as they stepped through the portal of her private domain. Pleased to be home, she rambled through the lower level while embracing her cherished possessions with a tender eye. Except for the layer of dust hugging her well-suited furniture like ivy clinging to Princeton's walls, everything stood in its proper place. In the kitchen, fondly, she picked up the African violet perched on the plant shelf above the double sink. *Marcus did a good job keeping you alive,* she thought, smiling warmly at the almost-next-to-impossible-to-grow exotic plant.

"Tenisha must be over at Marcus's," Brye assumed. Pulling into her drive, Chad's limo had eased behind her best friend's Explorer. Since she was nowhere in sight, it was safe to infer where she was spending her time. "I think I'll jump in the shower and head over that way."

"If you ask nicely, I'll wash your back for you." Elbows crossed over his chest, Chad leaned against the refrigerator door.

"I know what you're trying to do, Chad Collier, and it won't work." She deposited the potted plant back in its original position. Feet spread apart, hands on hips, she stared defiantly into Chad's innocent expression. After eating lunch with the twins and dropping them back off at Brylinn's, Chad had insisted Brye spend the night at his place. "To rest," he submitted. "Nothing more."

Brye's day had begun long before she walked into the morgue at 6:00 a.m. It was now three in the afternoon. The last eight hours had been profusely emotional. On the exterior, Brye donned her stress and strain with skill. Inwardly, Chad believed her to be a waking volcano on the verge of erupting.

"What am I trying to do?" Chad mildly asked.

Brye needed time alone to sort out her thoughts, to work out her problems, to handle her business. She could do none of those things with Chad hovering over her like a mother hen. Adamantly, she refused his offer. "You think that if you can't get me to stay with you, you're going to hang out here and babysit me. But I'm not going to let you." Taking his hand, she tugged him toward the front entrance.

"Can't I at least stay until Tank gets back?" he good-naturedly whined. Despite his attempt at keeping things on a frivolous level, his concern for Brye peeked out from behind his calm exterior.

"No, you can't." At the front door, Brye swung around to face him. Face set, determined, she reassured, "I'll be fine, Chad. Really. And Tank will be here shortly, so stop worrying."

"Won't you at least tell me where you sent him after our plane landed?"

"No…I won't. But to make you feel better, as soon as I'm through with my shower, I'll head over to Marcus's. He'll protect me until Tank gets back."

"But I want to protect you." He'd taken on the tone of an over-imaginative little boy brandishing a plastic sword, devising to do battle with the make-believe dragon.

Brye grinned. "Do I detect a note of jealousy?"

Chad grinned back. "Should I be jealous?"

"A little jealousy is a healthy emotion." Skepticism crept into her cheerful features. "But this isn't about that. This is about your trying to stall."

Chad dropped the happy-go-lucky pretense. He allowed his apprehension to escape. Pulling Brye protectively into his arms, he proclaimed, "I love you. I can't help but worry."

Afraid she would never feel as safe nor as protected as she felt at this moment, Brye clung to Chad in sheer desperation. On the plane home, she'd come up with an idea that would either make or break their relationship. The thought of losing the man she loved for good, once again, ate savagely at her heart. She forced herself to look into his concerned features. The smile she produced did not encompass her eyes. "Please don't worry. And please try to understand. I need some time to myself for a while. I need to get my head straightened out."

In agonizing reluctance, Chad succumbed to her reasonable appeal. He longed for her to reach out to him, confide in him, yet for whatever reason, she was not prepared to entrust her faith in him. He unwillingly bowed to her wishes.

Chad graced her with two kisses. One on each eyelid. "Will you at least let me take you out to dinner tonight? So we can talk."

Unable to hold his penetrating gaze, Brye dropped her eyes to midpoint along his chest. "I'm not sure I'll be ready to talk about us, but I'd love to have dinner with you…here. I don't think I'll feel up to getting dressed and going out."

Chad did not let his disappointment mar his concerned features. He clipped her under the chin. His touch was as gentle as the look he showered her with as he lifted her eyes to meet his. "Fine… whatever you want to talk about is okay with me. I'll bring dinner."

His kiss was feather light. "I love you," he declared before walking out the door. He hopped into the limo while pondering over his father. He had evaded his parents since officially calling off the engagement to Jennifer five days earlier. He initially wanted to confront certain issues with Brye before making contact with the man who raised him. Since unanswered questions of Brye's assailant hung precariously over his head, Chad decided to alter his plans. He would challenge his father first. Maybe then he could get the answers Brye desperately searched for.

As his driver pulled out Brye's driveway, Chad called his father but was disappointed when he was informed that he could not acquire an audience with him until the following day. With a change in plans, he decided to go home, shower, then return later in the evening.

32

THIRTY MINUTES AFTER CHAD's limo floated out of Brye's drive, as Brye crossed over into Marcus's recently mowed backyard, Marcus and Tenisha polished off a late lunch of grilled chicken salad, marinated tomatoes and cucumbers, and an ice-cold pitcher of sun tea.

For two solid hours, Tenisha's world had ceased to exist as she'd known it. For the first time in her life, she'd made love to a man who, in total disregard to his own hormonal surges, sustained a predilection to fulfill her every sexual need and fantasy. A mindless puppet on a string, a quivering clump of Jell-O, Tenisha had granted Marcus carte blanche over her entire body. Charitably, abundantly, he had embraced her with an empowering touch, intoxicated her with his potent prowess. He sent her mind spiraling to euphoric proportions. Total gratification. It had been the most exciting, exhilarating, enchanting lovemaking she'd ever experienced. One hour afterward, mind and body continued to tingle from the aftereffects.

Marcus could not keep his eyes off Tenisha as she stacked dirty dishes in the partially loaded dishwasher. One of his tailored shirts swallowed her upper body. Firm, perfectly rounded buttocks forged a symmetrical outline against the tail end of the cotton material. Long, smooth, exquisitely shaped thighs and legs taunted him as she moved from sink to dishwasher.

As she pranced around his kitchen, guilt did not riddle his brain. He felt no remorse for having made love to a married woman. Not yet. That would come later. For now, the only emotion feeding his system was love. Pure and unadulterated. He loved her; a love so conclusive, so crucial to his very subsistence he could not deny her importance any more than he could deny himself food, drink, or sleep. And knowing his heartfelt sentiments would never reach her ear—at least not as long as she remained married—he was thoroughly prepared to show her.

"Come here." His voice came out low, husky.

"A girl lets you have your way with her, and now you think you can order her around?" Tenisha genially quipped. Bending over the dishwasher, she swung the door shut, secured it, and then spun around to face Marcus. The ardent gleam he fired at her, piercing the center of her heart, had as much efficacy as if he struck her with a dart saturated with an aphrodisiac.

"Please…come here," Marcus lightly amended.

Unable to resist, eager to comply, Tenisha's transit across the room deemed slow and sensual, with the intent to arouse.

The bottom of Marcus's chair slid noisily across the dappled tile as he slid out from underneath the table. Firm fingers glided around Tenisha's trim waist. With a specific purpose in mind, he guided her hips between his sturdy thighs.

One by one, Marcus undid the buttons on the shirt clothing her body. Exposing firm, projecting breasts, his thumbs drew jolting circles around delectable nipples; nipples looking as tantalizing as plump, juicy raisins. The appealing sight warranted all Marcus's attention. Leaning forward, a zealous tongue flickered toward Tenisha's eager breast. Hungrily, he drew the trembling point into his mouth. Ambrosial pleasure. Marcus diligently sapped her of all strength.

Head flung back, mouth formed in an O-shape, Tenisha moaned with pleasure. She straddled Marcus's hips and dropped onto his lap. Her chest pressed impatiently into his face as she caught his head between her hands and pulled him closer. It was then the back door swung open.

For several distressing seconds after Brye stepped into the occupied kitchen, her mind transported back into time. Back to a time when she stumbled across another scene too indigestible to swallow. It wasn't until her feet were planted firmly back into the present that she realized the two pertinent episodes were, in fact, completely different.

Snared by a flurry of movement, Brye uncomfortably looked on as two indecent bodies struggled for decency. The room pulsated with nervous tension. Shirt tugged taut against bare breast, extremely jittery, Tenisha cleared her throat.

"Brye! You're back. I wasn't"—she widened her proclamation to include Marcus—"Marcus and I weren't expecting you back until tomorrow."

Astounded eyes took in Tenisha's harried appearance. They then accusingly searched out Marcus. Ultimately, unable to maintain any form of composure, Brye dropped her pained gaze to the floor. "I'm...sorry," she urgently mumbled. "I...I didn't mean to interrupt." Spilling out the back door, she tore across the yard and stumbled into the sanctity of her own home. Not once did she respond to Marcus's pleas for her to return.

Bursting through the sliding patio doors, Brye took the stairs two at a time. She dove into the upstairs hall closest, shuffling through liquid hand soap, toothpaste, cotton balls, needles, thread, and cleaning fluid. She searched until she uncovered furniture oil, a feather duster, and a dusting cloth. It was time to get her house back in living condition.

But unable to muster the strength to tackle the job, in her study, she dropped into a cane-back chair. In quick succession, her head dipped forward as her eyes sought a few minutes of uninterrupted respite. But as Brye drifted along the sea of obscurity, turbulent waves crashed down on her head.

A rapid tapping traipsed upon what little security Bryson's sealed bedroom offered. In bed, wearing a long-sleeved nightshirt draped over bare thighs, Bryson stuffed her head under her pillow. The knock on her door persisted. She forcibly clamped her eyelids against the unwanted intrusion.

"Bryson?"

No answer.

"Bryson…please?"

Agitated, Bryson pulled herself up in bed. She slammed her fist into her pillow. "Go away, Tyson."

"Please…I only want to talk," he called through the door.

"No!" It had been a week since she walked in on the incestuous behavior perpetrated by her brother and mother. She'd endured one nightmare after another because of it. Repulsed with the persistent vision, Bryson couldn't stand the sight of her twin, let alone having to tolerate speaking to him.

"Two minutes, Bry. Please. Can you at least give me that?" Bryson ignored him. Tyson continued to passionately plead for an audience with her.

Bryson felt a small tear at her heart. Despite it all, he was still her brother. And as she listened to him beg for charity, he did come off sounding repentant.

Minutes passed before Bryson climbed out of bed. Bare feet padded soundlessly toward the door. Several months ago, she'd installed a dead bolt and safety chain as added protection to the original lock. She unfastened all three, all the while praying for the day she'd never have to live in dire fear of her safety ever again.

Opening the door a crack, she peeked out at her brother.

"I'm sorry, Bryson." She could hear the affliction of pain. "I can't stand this rift between us."

Foolish as she might be, Bryson allowed his desolate countenance to enclose her heart. She felt the vital organ melt somewhat. She opened the door and invited her brother in.

"I know you don't agree with what I've done, but does that have to interfere with our relationship?" Tyson touched Bryson on her left cheek. "I love you, sis. That'll never change. Isn't there anything I can do to gain your forgiveness?"

His soft caress, the urgency in his voice, spilled into Bryson's drained soul. It had been so long since she'd experienced any form of affection. A driving desire to feel loved motivated her forgiving response.

Her heart melted some more. She opened her arms and invited her brother in.

"Oh, Bry!" Bodies pressed together, Tyson's fingers rode up and down Bryson's backside. He groaned into her neck. "I love you so much."

A touch of lust marred the close, intimate declaration. It riled Bryson's nerves like an agitated python. One minute, she was basking in the love her brother offered. The next minute, as the initial stirring of his desire poked at her lower abdomen, hate consumed every ounce of love she had ever sustained for him.

Tyson's tongue grazed her earlobe. "You feel so good to me, Bry." He drove his hard-on against her pelvis. Simultaneously, his fingers gripped her buttocks and tugged her against him.

Horror-struck, a sharp, tingling sensation ate at Bryson's skin as the small hairs on her arms and legs rebelled against Tyson's offensive actions.

Bryson struggled against his chest. He kissed her on the corner of her mouth. Her stomach contents fidgeted nervously. About to lose her dinner over his illicit seduction, she snapped. "Take your filthy hands off me, Tyson!"

Holding her tight, Tyson fondled her lush bottom. "Let me make love to you, Bry. Let me show you how good it can be." So much alcohol maligned his breath, Bryson was growing lightheaded from the smell alone.

She choked on her own bile as she pounded him with balled fist. This was too loathsome for her to handle. Tyson was not a slimy snake. He wasn't a wolf disguised in grandma's clothing. Nor was he a stinking, disgusting pig. This was her brother. Her own flesh and blood. Her twin. And the reality of it all drove Bryson toward the brink of insanity.

"No!" she howled, determined to break away. Scorn ripped at her youth and beauty. A guise created by the demons of hell remained. She bopped him against his ears with open palms. The exploding pain urged him to release her. Leaving her heart behind, Bryson dove for the 9mm semiautomatic weapon she'd purchased off the streets a few short weeks ago. At the time, little had she known she'd have to use it on her own brother! Grabbing it from the drawer of her bedside stand, Bryson aimed it directly at Tyson's stunned face.

"Damn you to hell, Tyson!" Gone over the edge, yet her voice, her stance, her hands did not waver. "So help me, God, I'll blow your fuckin'

head off!" Chest heaving, eyes crazed, Bryson swore to herself that she would never, ever be taken in by him again. Brother or not.

"Put the gun down, Bry!" Tyson ordered, witnessing the intent burning inside her deranged stare. Hands out, palms open, he stepped toward his sister.

"Don't come any closer, Tyson," she snarled at him.

He took another step. "Bryson?"

"I swear I'll shoot." She gripped the gun's trigger.

"Put it down, Bry." He inched nearer.

Bryson's index finger moved purposefully.

"Bry?"

"Brye?"

Brye's head shot forward. Slightly disoriented, she stared down at her hands. The dust rag remained clenched inside a tight grip.

"Brye?" Tenisha sounded more insistent.

Glassy-eyed, Brye stared at her.

"Where the hell were you? I've been calling your name for several seconds."

Brye stood and shook the cobwebs out of her head. She sidled up to the fireplace. Lifting a brass candlestick, she polished it to a brilliant shine. The image staring up at her looked blanched, drawn. Despite the cool, controlled air circulating her body, beads of sweat dotted her pinched forehead. Her hands suddenly began to shake. Careful not to drop the candlestick, Brye replaced it on the mantel.

Concerned, Tenisha stepped closer. "Brye?"

"I'm sorry," Brye finally answered. "I didn't hear you come in." She picked up her supplies and sauntered out the room.

"Well?" Tenisha asked, trailing after Brye. She was surprised with Brye's lackluster attitude.

"Well what?"

"Well…let's hear what you have to say about Marcus and myself."

Brye halted. She turned a vacant eye to Tenisha. Shrugging, she proceeded toward the downstairs bedroom. "What's there to say? You two are grown adults."

"But?" Tenisha egged.

"But what?"

Spoiling for a fight, Tenisha glared angrily at Brye. Maybe it was because she knew Brye would be right, although the censured words had not yet crossed her disciplined lips. Maybe it was because she was frustrated with her home situation and just didn't give a damn at the moment. Or maybe it was because, secretly, she was mad at Brye for walking in and ruining her intimate moment with Marcus. Whatever the reason, Tenisha was eager to bring it on.

"Come out with it, Brye. I know there's a bunch of disapproving thoughts circulating through that virtuous head of yours."

"What you do is your business." Brye reached overhead with the feather duster and waved it back and forth across the ceiling fan.

Tenisha scowled. Pushing further, she incited, "So you're not going to shove TyJuan in my face?"

Forfeiting the detached stance she had been determined to take, Brye lowered her arms. The feather duster dropped futilely to her side. "He's *your* husband, which means he's already in your face." Brye swung around to face her. "Why, Tenisha? Why did you do it?" She shook her head in sheer bewilderment. "I know TyJuan hasn't been a good husband lately, but is that sufficient enough reason to go out and take a lover?"

"Why not," Tenisha croaked. "He did it. In fact, my welcome home present was walking in on him in bed with another woman."

"So you decided to use Marcus to get back at TyJuan?" Brye turned her back on Tenisha. Her eyes shot out the bow window and across the trimmed hedges to Marcus's ornate brick home. Despite the combined walls separating them, she knew he was close at hand. "Why did you draw Marcus into this? Why couldn't you wait until you ended it with TyJuan?"

"Maybe I'm not ready to end my marriage with TyJuan." Silly as it might seem, Brye's cool, calm exterior infuriated her even more.

For ulterior motives unknown to Tenisha, she wanted Brye to give rise to her inexhaustibly controlled temper.

"So you're going to demean what Marcus feels for you by making him participate in a seedy affair? You're going to allow him to hang out in the shadows and wait for you to visit whenever you can juggle him into your hectic life? You're going to aid him in losing his own self-respect?"

Agitated beyond reason, Tenisha vindictively noted, "Why not, Brye? After all, *you* did it." Arsenic poisoned her tainted declaration. "You need to check yourself, girlfriend! You're the last person to be throwing stones. You not only had an affair with another woman's fiancé, but you weren't even smart enough to use protection."

The reaction Tenisha received was nothing she anticipated. She had expected Brye to explode with uncontrolled anger. She imagined Brye rushing to her side, kicking and screaming, prepared to scratch her eyes out. She figured Brye would verbally attack, declaring her unbridled hatred toward Tenisha. But she did not expect to see the hurt now obscuring Brye's ashen features; she had not anticipated Brye to turn sad, dejected eyes on her.

"Did you ever consider *that's* the very reason I know what I'm talking about?" She looked down at the floor, then turned back to face Tenisha. Pain-filled eyes shimmered with unshed tears. "I love you. And I love Marcus. I'd hate to see you two go through all I've suffered."

Tenisha did not have the foggiest idea why her human battery refused to wind down and die, but despite the pain routing through Brye, she continued her attack.

"Maybe you're upset because I ruined your plans. Maybe you hoped to have Marcus for yourself if your affair with Chad didn't work out." Her smile turned lecherous. "After all, you *are* the other woman in his life."

Unresponsive, Brye's lips twitched as she stared at Tenisha. For the first time in a long time, she wished with all her heart she could cry. She begged for the sweet release of tears. But no matter how hard she tried, they would not come.

Razor-sharp knifes sliced through Tenisha's heart. She had said enough…too much. She'd done more damage than intended. She was not pleased with herself or the heart-wrenching pain she caused Brye. Unable to confront the injury inflicted by her own hands, too distressed to hang around and apologize, she backed away. Seconds later, she tore out the front door, climbed into her waiting vehicle, and sped out the driveway.

As soon as the Explorer careened down the drive, Brye crossed to the kitchen. Back facing the patio doors, she eased into a kitchen chair. She did not have to wait long for Marcus's appearance. The sliding doors barely sounded as they rolled softly on their gliders.

Their confrontation was short but not sweet.

"She was vulnerable, Marcus. You knew that! Why did you let it go as far as it did?"

Marcus skirted around the table to catch Brye's eye. She looked frazzled, worn down to paper thin. Just like Tenisha, a murderous mood overrode all else. Unable to cater to her emotional instability, he reported, "Not all of us are as dehumanized as you, Brye. We can't turn our feelings off and on at a whim or a mere snap of a finger." The thick hairs above his upper lip twitched in marked irritation. "If I've failed to live up to your high standards, I'm sorry."

Deathly silence blanketed the sullen room. Hands balled into tight fists, Brye stared at her blanched knuckles. She sneaked a peek at her gold wrist watch. Bone-weary, and it was only four o'clock.

Brye did not want a battle with Marcus. Too exhausted to continue, she needed to conserve what little energy she had left. In anticipation for her long overdue confrontation with Chad's father, she opted not to get into a knock-down, drag-out fight. Throwing in the towel, she hefted her fatigued body out of her chair. "Please make sure the patio door is closed when you see yourself out." She left the room.

Baffled, Marcus stared at her retreating backside. For some unexplainable reason—or maybe it could be explained away—Brye was hurting more than usual. But at the moment, he was of no use to her. He was of no use to anyone. He only wanted to sit in a corner and lick his own demanding wounds. Soundlessly, Marcus walked out the kitchen.

Brye's footsteps treaded heavily on the carpeted stairs as she climbed toward her bedroom. Midway up, harmonious chimes boomeranged off the enclosed walls. Turning around, she retraced fatigued steps and headed toward the front entrance.

"Were you able to get everything you needed?" Brye questioned the caller as soon as the door swung inward.

"Are you sure you want to go through with this?" Tank asked, sidestepping Brye and entering the sedate home.

"This isn't a matter of what I *want* to do." Brye's eye dropped to the metal briefcase Tank carried in his powerful grip. "It's a matter of what I *have* to do."

Sure-footed, instinct alone propelled Tank toward the living room. He dropped the case on Brye's sofa. "When do you want to do this?"

His reply came in the form of a telephone ring. Excusing herself, Brye went to silence the insistent blare.

Back in less than two minutes, Brye said, "In answer to your question, would one hour be soon enough?"

Tank frowned. He angled the opened suitcase so Brye could peek at its elaborate contents. "Well, I guess we should go over how all this works."

33

At Tank's request, Brye dressed for her impromptu meeting in a denim mini skirt, sleeveless baby blue midriff top, and two-inch matching sandals. Nothing concealed her firm tanned arms, nothing hid her long lavish legs. The only accessory adorning her partially clad body was a two-inch wide belt, with intricately designed belt buckle slung low beneath her waistline.

Bare all, tell all. Her flagrant display of the licentious attire was expressly worn for the sole intentions of drawing Daniel Collier's immediate focus on her body and off the minute camcorder entangled in her belt buckle.

Used to wolfish jeers and canine growls, Brye ignored the carnivorous stares and lecherous grins Daniel's driver and flunky tossed at her as she entered the stretch limo. She did, however, take heed to Daniel's appreciative arched brow.

The driver settled in behind the wheel. A second man, Daniel's lackey—tall, dark, and delusive—sat beside his boss and across from Brye.

Brye had met them in a remote woodsy area along Palisades International Parkway inside New Jersey; continuing northward bound, the parkway sped toward the entrance of New York State.

The engine idled quietly. The air conditioner effectively hummed in the foreground, yet the stretch limo remained rooted to the spot. Tank loitered behind the limo in his black Nissan Marano.

Patiently, Brye waited for Daniel Collier to initiate the conversation.

"How nice of you to dress for the occasion," he sarcastically remarked. Although he wore an absorbed grin, intrinsic anger hovered directly behind the brink of cold, steel-blue eyes.

Brye followed his lead. Just as pleasantly, she responded, "I'm so glad you approve."

"I do." His face darkened, then recovered its amiable facade. "But it does make me wonder"—he paused for effect—"you look very sleazy, my dear." Again he paused, as if his observations would hurt him more than it would her. "You dress as if you are—how should I put this?—a desperate lady of the night in search of a much-needed fix."

Just as Tenisha and Marcus had done earlier, Daniel Collier baited Brye. Only with her friends, she refused to rise to the occasion. This very moment, confronting Chad's father, is what she had prepared for. The ensuing minutes were crucial, and would prove to be her moment of glory, or her greatest defeat.

Brye tossed back her head and liberated a soft, sensual laugh. From the start, she meant to establish to Daniel that he could neither intimidate nor rile her. Casually crossing her legs and slightly twisting in her seat, she intentionally presented the two men a wide-angled view of flawless thigh, smooth skin, and exquisite legs—legs that seemed to fill the entire length of the limo. "Why Mr. Collier," Brye exclaimed, "I'm surprised and somewhat disappointed in you. Given your worldly knowledge, your exceptionally high IQ, and the vast number of connections accessible to you"—tell-all eyes swept over the menacing yet well-dressed man sitting next to Daniel—"you of all people should know that one's dress does not make the person. Take him, for instance." Again, Brye incorporated Daniel's unscrupulous companion into her animated discussion. "Although he's sporting a five-hundred-dollar business suit, you and I both know that underneath the regal attire lies a common street thug."

A slow heat crept along the back of his sidekick's neck. His jaw tensed, his hands balled into hard fists. Impressed with the measure of self-control he sustained, Brye decided to give him points for not flying out of his seat and wrapping long beefy fingers around her pulsating neck. On reconsideration, however, she elected to take back her points for his inability to conceal what little reaction he had shown.

Daniel's reaction was not as self-contained. An enthralled, boisterous laugh erupted into the cool exterior of the limo. "Bold, brassy, and beautiful! Qualifications I like in a woman."

Brye's smile faded. "But they're not qualifications you'd have for the woman destined to be your son's wife?"

Time to get down to business, Daniel's facial muscles hardened. "It's time we speak frankly to one another."

"Silly me." Flustered, Brye batted silky lashes at him. "And here I thought we were already doing that."

Daniel's lips lengthened into a tight grin. A covert message passed from boss to lackey. Before Brye realized it, the ungainly man sitting by Daniel's side pulled a large manila folder out of a leather briefcase lying next to his burly body. As if it held the names of current Oscar winners, with a grand flourish, he delicately handed the prized possession to Daniel. Daniel, in turn, passed it over to Brye.

"Look at it!" he harshly commanded.

Brye stifled the urge to salute him and repeat, "Aye, aye, Captain!"

Within her hand, she treated the envelope as if it would blister her skin. Her fingers treaded lightly as she uncovered what lay hidden beneath the flaps of the unknown.

Photos. Glossy prints. Pornographic pictures of her mother and twin brother. *So this is what happened to the photos my father took*, Brye repulsively surmised. With the death of her parents, Brye had assumed the revealing pictures had fried in the apartment along with the rest of their belongings.

Six in all. Her heart pumped frozen icicles through her veins. Her toes curled in her sandals as veiled eyes barely skimmed the first two nauseous photos. Having seen enough, she slid the pictures back into their hiding place.

Eyes and tone balmy, she inquired with inflexible coolness, "What do you want?"

"I want you to get out of my son's life…for good. I want you to resign your position at Romanique Cosmetics. Make up some excuse." He shrugged, unconcernedly, and waved his hand in the air. "I don't care what. I just want you to get the hell out."

"How much time do I have?"

"Forty-eight hours." He glanced at his Rolex. "The clock starts now. Once your time is up, these pictures will be splattered in every tabloid magazine in the country. And as an added bonus"—his aristocratic features brightened, as if a brainstorm had just washed over him—"I might even have your face superimposed on some of your mother's pictures. Wasn't it you who said 'with today's technology, pictures can be altered'?" His laugh was harsh, terrifyingly chilly. "I can see the headlines now. 'Supermodel and twin brother…caught in an incestuous love affair.'"

Brye refused to flinch. "I can be sued for breach of contract."

"You call it off, I'll handle my son. I can guarantee you won't be sued."

Brye's fingers tapped absentmindedly on top of the manila envelope as her mind twirled in a senseless whirlwind. Halfheartedly listening to Daniel, she knew she could care less about the photos or who viewed them. She cared even less with what people thought of her. In the past few hours, she'd been able to confront most of the hidden secrets as well as the hatred she harbored toward her family. And now that she was finally coming to grips with the errant skeletons heedlessly spilling from her closet, she could give a damn if others couldn't or wouldn't accept her. All she wanted, all she needed, was secured time to confide her past to Chad. She needed to entrust her fears to him as well as her desires. She welcomed informing him of their upcoming blessed event. But most of all, she endeavored to entrust her faith in him.

"Where did the pictures come from?" she asked, suddenly curious as to how he'd gained access.

"I commissioned your father to take them. I told him that a client was willing to pay thousands of dollars for pictures of his wife and son…together."

Brye winced. She noted the emphasis he imposed on the word *together*. The rest of his statement, however, sank heavily into her mind like a rock settling in a swamp.

"You knew my parents?" Surprise, combined with genuine interest, registered in the midst of her doleful expression.

"Quite well," Daniel admitted. Feeling generous, he decided to admit to the extent of his relationship with her parents. "I personally recommended both your father and mother to many of my business associates. In return, on occasion, your mother and I spent time together. Imagine my surprise when my son approached me with testaments of love for the daughter of associates who made a living by selling sexual favors."

Concurrently, Brye experienced cold chills and hot flashes. She did not want to believe Daniel, but the smug look aligning his brow told her otherwise. "But why?" she asked, struggling to understand. "Why did you sleep with my mother? Wasn't your marriage satisfying enough?"

Daniel glowered at her puerile naiveté. "My marriage is a separate entity from my business affairs. Sleeping with your mother had nothing to do with my love for my wife—it was purely a physical act."

"You hated me and broke up my relationship with Chad because of who my parents were?" Brye asked, struggling to understand.

Blatant shamelessness stripped Daniel of his brittle iciness. Brye shivered as he covered her from head to toe with a lecherous leer. Feeling violated, he had just stripped her naked with his deliberate eye.

"I don't hate you. In fact, I'm proud Chad has such impeccable taste in women." He sneered knowingly, "I bet you are as good a fuck as your mother! And if my son wanted to sleep with you on the side once he married, I would have no objections with that. But whether my son loves you or lusts after you, it is my duty as his father to make sure he obtains the best in life. And you, my dear, are unequivocally not it—at least not where a marriage is concerned."

"But I can make him happy." It was a desperate plea spoken against unheeded ears.

"Your mother was charming, witty, intelligent, beautiful, and sensual. Yet in spite of all her outstanding qualities, she was still nothing but a high-class whore." Facial lines etched in granite, he callously added, "It doesn't matter whether you could make my son happy or not. You come from inferior stock. And I will not allow inferior lineage gain access to my bloodline. "

Brye's eyelids narrowed into incensed slits. Much to her surprise, she would make her stance, even if it meant defending her own mother. "My mother may have been a whore, but she was proud of who she was and what she did for a living. From day one, she never hid her occupation from me or my brother. I've always known her for who she was." Brye dropped her hands on the doorknob. "I feel sorry for Chad." She shook her head in transparent disgust. "Your son doesn't have a clue who his father really is."

Brye swung the door open. "Oh, one more thing." Brye turned and flattened Daniel with a rock-hard stare. "If I agree to do this, will you call off your dogs?"

"My dogs?" Daniel repeated. He sat there, personifying the innocence of a chaste altar boy.

Brye nodded, her eyes remained leveled. "You allowed one of them out of his kennel in Florida."

His features altered into a show of benevolent sympathy. "You're talking about that unfortunate incident in St. Petersburg. That must have been a harrying experience. Anyone else would have went into seclusion for months—sometimes years afterward…"

Brye completed the entirety of his unspoken sentence: "And if I'd laid down and yelled uncle, we wouldn't be here now, having this conversation." Again, she shook her head in disgust. "For some of us, it takes a while longer for no win situations to sink in. Nevertheless, I need confirmation that there will not be a reoccurrence of the incident that took place in St. Petersburg."

"If you step out of the limelight and stay away from my son for good, I'm sure that psychos like the guy who confronted you in Florida would cease to bother you."

It was the most he'd commit to. It was enough for Brye. She stepped out of the limo.

"Oh, Brye?" The electric smoke-tinted glass lowered. "Don't forget your photos." Daniel handed them over through the open window. He flashed her the blazing Collier smile—the one guaranteed to turn women's heads, whatever their age. "Let's just call this incentive. For all intents and purposes, it should encourage you to do the right thing."

Brye did not waver. She tenaciously clung to her self-respect. With photos in hand, she moved with slow, dignified steps. The walk toward Tank's waiting Nissan, however, proved torturous. Her eyes barely grazed over the hanging cliffs, nor did she note the Hudson River's calm waters. But as she stepped one foot into the SUV, her gaze reached across the wide river and settled on the George Washington Bridge. As traffic sped across, it truly amazed her that despite how tightly the noose surrounded her neck, life continued, unencumbered, around her.

Once she settled safely inside the black leather interior, her courage dissolved. "Tank?" Her voice matched her lagging heartbeat, weak and thready.

"Just hang tight, kid. We're almost home free." Dropping the gearshift in drive, Tank steered to the left of the white stretch limo. Executing a series of sharp twist and turns, when the distinguished front end of the Lincoln disappeared from his rear-view mirror, he notified, "Okay, we're in the clear."

Apprehension seized her by the throat, impeding normal speech pattern. "Did…Did we get it?"

He lifted the DVD out of the recording device. Flashing it at Brye, he smiled encouragingly. "You did well, Brye."

Then and only then did she collapse into the black leather seat.

Tenisha felt far removed as she strolled through the apartment she called home for the last three years of her marriage.

An immense sense of loss played heavily over her heart. Sadness encompassed her. Beneath it all, relief flooded through her. She'd come to a decision. The marriage had been over months ago, yet she had been too stubborn to admit failure to her father.

Brye had been right. She couldn't help TyJuan. He had to do it himself. But he was a long way from admitting he had a problem.

No matter. Tenisha promised she'd do all she could to help him, if he wanted help. But she would do it from afar. It was time to call an end to her farce of a marriage. For fear of losing herself entirely, she had to get out from under. If she didn't, she would lose what little self-respect she held on to. Hell! Her pride had already dropped by the wayside. If it hadn't, she wouldn't have gone after Marcus like a bitch in heat. She cared for Marcus a great deal. And their lovemaking had been an unforgettable experience. But Brye had been right about him as well. He deserved more than a fly-by-night affair with a married woman. She wanted Marcus. She needed him for more than one afternoon. But she would never be with him again. At least, not until she was able to put some semblance of a normal life back together.

Tenisha's bags had gone untouched since her earlier arrival. She hefted them to her side and steered them toward the door.

"You're back."

Bloodshot eyes glared at her. A bottle of Jim Beam remained glued to his fingers. Unsteady on his feet, he leaned against the bedroom doorjamb for support. TyJuan gaped unflinchingly at Tenisha. Then, moving deeper into the living room, he clumsily staggered. "I'm sorry about what happened earlier." Despite the amount of alcohol he obviously ingested—by the looks of the near-empty bottle he held in hand—his speech was not incoherently slurred. "I wanna explain—"

"Save your breath, TyJuan." She stared at him with sad, regrettable eyes. "You'd only lie anyway, so why not save us both the misery?"

"But—"

"Just so you know, I'm leaving." Tenisha dropped her bags on the floor. She stepped closer to TyJuan. It proved to be a fatal mistake. "I'm getting a divorce. It's over."

Anger distorted his drunken state. "What da ya mean ya wanna divorce? I made a mistake. Ya wanna cut me loose 'cause of a simple mistake?"

"A mistake!" Tenisha croaked, her voice rising in irritation. "Is that what you call sleeping with another woman in my bed? A mistake?" Her emotions converged into a potpourri of outrage. "I guess next you're going to tell me that your drinking is a mistake…your doing drugs is a mistake…your refusal to look for a job is a mistake? Well, let me tell you about *my* little mistake!" Fury pressed Tenisha into confessing her culpable sin. "After I left here today, I found me a man ready and willing to make love to me…someone who knows how to satisfy a woman."

The thought of her looking at another man made his blood ferment. But the implanted vision of her sleeping with someone else drove him into a blind rage. His face crippled into an ugly mass. Tenisha never saw it coming. For a man whose heart pumped 100 percent proof alcohol by volume, his hand was lightning fast as it streaked forward and shot around her head. Viciously, he grabbed a handful of her hair. Her burning scalp seared from the callous mistreatment. Any attempt made at twisting out of his torturous range intensified the acrimonious pressure attacking her firing nerve fibers. Her mind collapsed in agonized pain.

"You bitch," his hissed. "You wanna be with anatha' man…then he's gonna hafta wait 'til I'm through with ya." He raised the liquor bottle to his lips with his free hand. Siphoning the remaining contents, he forced Tenisha's head up while simultaneously launching the glass bottle across the room. It hit the wall with a reverberating crash. The bottle shattered. Different sizes and shapes of glass scattered everywhere.

TyJuan's mouth invaded Tenisha's. He jammed his slobbering tongue, the acrid liquor, down her constricted throat. Struggling against him, Tenisha drowned from the sour stench of his breath, the thick, invading tongue and the biting taste of hard liquor. Determined to fight, hands squeezed into balled fist, she hammered him on both sides of his scruffy face. Increased pressure squalling against his eardrums induced a sensation of vertigo. Equilibrium thrown off balance, TyJuan stumbled backward. It gave Tenisha time to scramble toward the door. As her fingers grazed the brass knob, TyJuan threw his drunken weight into her back. Spiked pain scaled her spine and darted along her shoulder blades. She dropped to her knees. TyJuan trapped her neck between rigid fingers, pressing incessantly into her windpipe. Weightlessness bathed Tenisha. Refusing to give in, she reached behind her and made contact with solid flesh; she manhandled his spongy balls. Not in a position to do major damage, Tenisha still managed to cripple him with a shattering squeeze. He loosened his crushing grip long enough for her to feign to the left and ram her elbow into his midsection.

Moaning, TyJuan crumbled over in pain, Tenisha rolled out from under him. She pushed herself to her feet and made a mad dash toward the bedroom. In flight, she hurriedly pulled the extension cord of a crystal-base table lamp out of the wall socket. She thrust it at TyJuan. Already on his feet, he ducked, but the lamp caught him square on the shoulder. Howling in pain, gripping his wound, he tore after his wife. As if entering a football game, TyJuan flew after Tenisha, tackling her from behind. Bodies entangled, they fell and skidded across the carpet.

Tenisha went under kicking and screaming. Yet it wasn't enough to hold TyJuan at bay. Landing on top, he straddled her chest and pinned her arms and shoulders under his knees. Excruciating pain screamed inside her head, yet it was nothing compared to the anguish she endured when he rammed his fist into her mouth. Nor did it equal the heedless torment of destruction he pummeled about her head and face.

Hot searing pain stabbed ferociously at her outraged senses. Shock rippled through the remotest part of her brain. The bitter taste of blood inundated her mouth and the back of her throat, threatening to block her already pinched air passages. Unable to fight any longer, Tenisha gave herself in to the senseless beating. The last thing she envisioned as the jaws of darkness mercifully reached upward and pulled her down into its soothing embrace, was TyJuan's wolfish incisors baring down on her.

Close to six, the ringing phone reverberated within the confines of Brye's uninhabited home. Brye cursed her blunder for not remembering her cell. Sliding the front key into the lock, she threw open the door and chased after the relentless sound.

She scooped the cordless phone off the sofa. "Hello?" Breathless, she addressed the unknown caller. A weak, raspy discord nettled her unprepared ears. Eyes trained on Tank, she nodded as he mouthed the word *coffee*. A rigid point of her finger navigated him toward the kitchen. She turned her full attention to the phone. "You have to speak up. I can't hear you."

"Brye?"

Terror encroached upon Brye's already frazzled nerves. Her legs grew wobbly under the weighty strain of unadulterated fear. The markedly frail and debilitated voice was undeniably and frighteningly recognizable. And she knew. As if Brye secured a direct pipeline into Tenisha's home, she knew TyJuan had abused her friend in a way that was too reprehensible to envision.

"Tee?" Brye quivered. Her knees rocked. "Are you hurt badly?"

"Brye…he…he…"

The steadily crumbling sound urged Brye onward, "It's okay, Tee. It's going to be okay. Are you at home?"

"Yeees."

The word blew across the wire in one attenuated agonizing moan. Like a fragile egg, Brye felt her composure cracking. "Just hold on, Tee. I'll be there soon." Dropping the headset, Brye sprinted up the stairs taking two at a time. "Forget the coffee, Tank!" she yelled over her shoulders. "We don't have time!"

The moment she hit her bedroom door, she stripped herself of the racy attire. In one minute flat, she dressed more conservatively: a pair of stonewash jeans and a long, sleeveless silk shirt. Racing down the stairs in less than two minutes, she was grateful to see Tank waiting by the front door with keys in hand.

Spurred by the urgency in her voice, he watched as Brye sprinted toward him. "Where to?" he asked.

"Tenisha's. I'll give you the address when we're in the car." Her voice took on a shrill note. "Drive like your life depends on it." The door banged shut behind them. A premonition. It reminded Brye of an explosive gunshot shattering the tranquil neighborhood setting. A foreboding of events to come.

Three tortuous hours later, Brye grimaced with reflective pain as she witnessed Tenisha maneuver her battered body from the stretcher over to her waiting hospital bed. She moved with excruciating slowness. Although she remained at Tenisha's bedside, Brye's mind's eye revisited the ugly scene confronting her and Tank when they had burst into Tenisha's demolished apartment. Phone spilled on top of her, Tenisha lay passed out on the living room floor. Her once unmarred face now congealed into a bloody, bruised pulp of her former self. One eye completely swollen shut, the other narrowed into a scanty, bloody slit. Nose swollen, possibly broken, lips distended and discolored to an unsightly purplish hue. A tremendous amount of blood garnished her crushed features.

As gentle as allowed, Brye cleared away as much blood as she could manage without causing Tenisha any more undue harm. To her astounded relief, there seemed to be no permanent damage—the massive dose of blood seemed to be the direct cause of an unrelenting nose bleed. Her relief was augmented when the ED doctor at Mount Sinai Medical Center confirmed Brye's unprofessional opinion. Still, it was advised for Tenisha to remain overnight for observation purposes only.

After the tests, at Tenisha's insistence—Brye had wanted her to rest prior to her interview with the police—she issued her statement as well as had photos taken of her bruised condition. Swearing out a complaint, she wanted TyJuan prosecuted to the full extent of the law. If he wouldn't help himself, Tenisha no longer lodged aspirations in saving him. If nothing else, maybe time in jail would help him see the error of his ways.

"Brye?" One crushed lid hopelessly sealed tight, Tenisha searched Brye out with her remaining good eye. But when the supermodel's face inched into sight, Tenisha claimed a distorted view through a swollen opening.

The last few hours futilely slipped through Brye's fingers. She focused her attention on Tenisha and pulled up a straight-backed chair alongside the hospital bed. Sliding her fingers into Tenisha's, she gently squeezed. "The nurse just gave you a sedative. You should relax and let it take effect.

"I just wanted to say—"

"Shhhh...shhhh," Brye hushed with a soothing touch across Tenisha's bruised forehead. "You need to rest."

Tenisha's tongue and eyelids drooped under the heaviness of the needless beating. The sedative given her was also taking its toll. Her face felt as if it were on fire—as if a lighted match maliciously danced underneath each individual nerve ending. She longed to give in to the beckoning blackness, darkness which offered to hold her hostage for many hours to come. Refusing to yield to the welcoming proposal, she longed to settle matters with Brye. "I want to say I'm sorry...for this afternoon."

"It's not necessary, Tee." Brye's smile was filled with warmth, understanding, and forgiveness. "We're friends...practically family." Brye laughed. She continued to lovingly stroke Tenisha's forehead. "If you want to disregard the fact that we grew up in different cities, with different families, and have different skin color, I'd say we were as close as any two sisters can be."

Tenisha found herself smothering a chuckle. "Don't make me laugh, Brye. It hurts when I laugh." She attempted to sound gloomy, yet a little bit of sunshine broke through her murky features.

"May God strike me down with a cream-filled eclair if I make you laugh," Brye teased, bending forward at the waist. She replaced her caressing fingers with a light touch of her lips. "Rest now. When you're up to par, if you like, we'll discuss this then."

"Brye?" Tenisha's voice sounded distant, allowing the painkiller to carry her away in its intimate clutches.

"Yes?"

Avoiding any contact with mirrors that would expose ghastly reflections of herself, Tenisha finally gave in to the gnawing question. "Does my face look bad?"

Brye quickly surveyed her swollen, bruised, features. Every time she looked at her friend, it took every ounce of control to maintain the anger…the pain…swarming just beneath the surface. She did not hesitate in her answer. "Of course it doesn't."

Tenisha attempted a smile. It resembled a sneer as only one side of her distended lip floated upward. "Now you're lying to me."

Again Brye did not hesitate. "Of course I am. But it doesn't matter. The doctor says in a couple of weeks, you'll be as good as new. Now go to sleep. I promise I'll be here when you wake up."

Since entering the emergency room, Tenisha had begged Brye to remain by her side. Brye had. And she would continue to do so. But now that she was resting comfortably, it was time to make some important phone calls. Four hours past her date with Chad, she knew he was worrying senselessly. Brye also wanted to contact Tenisha's parents. At this aggrieved time in her life, her friend needed all the love and support she could get.

As promised, Brye remained by Tenisha's side, holding her hand, long after she'd fallen asleep. Then, as carefully and quietly as possible, she slipped out of the room.

"What do you mean you're HIV positive?" On the brink of spontaneous combustion once again, TyJuan's wild, demented eyes bored a large crater in one of the many lovers he had taken over the past few months. "Why the hell didn't you tell me you suspected something before I fucked you?"

Thin, lanky, sunken cheekbones, Erin Frazier depicted the waif-look to proficiency. Bubbly dark-colored eyes resembling the cartoon character Betty Boop, she stared offensively at TyJuan. "I didn't suspect anything. I get tested every six months, and this time, the test came back positive."

"How can you sit here and be so goddamned nonchalant about this? You have *AIDS* for god's sake! I could have *AIDS*!" Before laying the destructive news on him, Erin had offered TyJuan a glass of cheap wine. Forgoing the glass, he tipped the bottle to his lips. Drowning himself in the entire bottle before coming up for air, he wished like hell he would pass out, wake up in his own bed, this morbid nightmare just a distant memory.

"I don't have AIDS," Erin detailed the facts to him as placidly as if she were explaining the ABCs to a classroom filled with kindergartners. "I'm HIV positive. There is a difference."

TyJuan's stomach muscles clenched into a tensed knot. "Not for long there isn't." Images of dying a horrid, painful death beat a brutal path along his alcohol-hazed mind. "How could you do this?" he roared. "How could you do this to *me*?"

Erin learned a long time ago to not cry over what could not be changed. Much too late to do anything about her condition now, she needed to concentrate on maintaining a positive attitude and getting the most out of the remainder of her life. "It works two ways, TyJuan. You could have easily used protection when you took me to bed. It was just as much your choice as it was mine."

"You bitch!" Bile rose up from the bowels of his stomach and bubbled over like a pan of water boiling over a hot stove. Out of control, he backhanded her across the mouth. "I could kill you for what you've done to me!"

The sharp blow practically sent Erin's head spinning off her shoulders. Eyes bulging with fury, hand pressed against her stinging lip, she dodged into her bedroom. About to chase after her, TyJuan stopped in his tracks and cautiously eyed her as she stepped out of the bedroom waving a Smith and Wesson.38 Special revolver.

"You ever lay a finger on me again, you son of a bitch, and I'll personally blow a hole in your sorry ass!"

"Put the gun down." The sight of the cocked gun instantly sobered TyJuan.

"Go straight to fuckin' hell!"

"I have a feeling we'll both be going down under," TyJuan sneered. Not caring if he missed—hell, as far as he was concerned, he was already a walking dead man—his movements were swift as he threw the wine bottle. Hitting Erin dead center in the face, the gun went off as it fell to the hardwood floor. The lethal bullet plowed harmlessly into the wall. The rubber heel of TyJuan's Rockport's came up and plowed into Erin's midsection. An agonizing breath expelled from her lungs as she bent forward. Spiked pain churned liberally through her folded body. TyJuan dove for the gun.

Unfortunately, Erin did not get off as easily as Tenisha. As she was bound over with pain, TyJuan raised the butt end of the gun and rammed with full force against the bridge of her nose. On contact, he felt, more than heard, the crushing of delicate bones shattering into ragged pieces. Blood spewed down the front of her top as she cried out in tormented anguish. Ignoring her distress, his comely features were no longer recognizable. Vengeful, demented eyes glowered at Erin. "You got off easy, bitch," he ruthlessly snarled. Pointing the gun to her head, he finished, "I could kill you right now and they would never do a thing to me." His maniacal laugh would remain with Erin for the duration of her days on earth. "Justifiable homicide is what they would call it." Forcing the gun downward, the stainless steel collided with her skull. A brilliant display of sparks discharged inside her head seconds before Erin fell into a unconscious heap.

His rage abated for the moment, TyJuan calmly stepped over her body. Gun in tow, he left the flat, not giving two hoots about the debilitated body sprawled across the floor.

Chad woke with an uneasy start. The unfamiliar room bathed in swarthy shades of color, he blinked back the dim fuzziness. Back muscles stiff from the uncomfortable position he'd fallen asleep in, he began driving the kinks out of his coiled spine. As his muscles sighed in sweet release, it suddenly hit him: he was at Brye's and had fallen asleep upright in her winged chair. Arriving just after seven to a vacant home, Marcus had let him in with his key.

A faint tinkling entered from beyond the living room, alerting Chad to another presence.

Brye? Her features floated across his mind as he dashed into the well-lit kitchen. His relief was short-lived.

"It's you." Disappointed, Chad's face drooped as his hazy vision darted over Marcus.

Marcus flipped a beguiling smirk at Chad. "I take it you're not happy to see me."

Chad leaned back into the kitchen counter. Ankles crossed, legs stretched in front of him, he crossed his arms over his broad chest. "I thought you were Brye."

After allowing Chad entrance into Brye's home, Marcus had climbed out of his blue funk long enough to realize that Brye had come home earlier than expected. She had not called to inform him of her unanticipated arrival. Something—an uncontrolled tragedy perchance?—had altered her carefully laid plans. Marcus could read Brye like a book. This afternoon, despondency circled her head like preying vultures surrounding their afternoon meal. And her oppressive mood had nothing to do with finding Tenisha and himself in a compromising position. Not only was he guilt-ridden from not turning away from Tenisha this afternoon, but now he was bedded down with the weight of his harsh mistreatment of his close friend.

So as not to reveal his growing concern, Marcus turned his attention toward a glass bowl filled with a Caesar salad he had prepared at his home and carried over to Brye's. "So you haven't heard from her yet?"

"Not yet. And it's"—he sneaked a peek at his Rolex—"after eleven." Four hours. Four hours of waiting and not knowing where she had disappeared to. Unprecedented fear crept along his back, raising the hairs along his stiff neck. "You're worried about her too?' Chad had asked, hoping against hope Marcus would confirm his concerns to be unfounded. He halfheartedly expected the large man to declare Brye's absence as a misappropriation of time; she merely took off on a safe excursion, and the minutes had speedily escaped her. His delusions of grandeur were promptly crushed.

"I called Brylinn." Marcus pulled a couple of stoneware plates down from Brye's cabinet. "They haven't spoken to her since you and she dropped the twins off earlier this afternoon. She has not picked up her car yet. She did not forward her calls. Couple that with the unexplained sight of the coffee can placed on the counter with lid off and cell phone next to it, it leads me to believe she left here in a hurry." The lip under his mustache twitched in careful consideration. "Brye never goes anywhere without telling someone something." Filling both plates with the handmade salad, he then topped the romaine lettuce with strips of grilled chicken he'd grilled earlier. Adding a generous portion of parmesan cheese and homemade croutons, he studied his creation.

"Have you eaten?" he asked after the fact, hauling the plates over to the table.

Chad dropped his arms by his side. He walked over to the table. "I had planned on getting some dinner for Brye and myself. I guess I fell asleep before I got the chance to do that." The food did look appetizing. Despite his worries, Chad found himself ravenous.

"I fixed enough for Brye when she gets in." Although the word *if* had not been incorporated into Marcus's sentence, it hung over their heads like an ominous thunder cloud.

"I've made some iced tea," Marcus notified, "or would you rather have coffee?"

"Tea's fine. Can I help with anything?" Chad asked before settling in front of his plate.

"It's all taken care of." Marcus's moves were carried out with guided precision as he pulled tall frosted glasses out of a cabinet designated for all Brye's drinking utensils. A twinge of jealousy heated Chad's coagulating blood as he observed the ease in which the big man embraced Brye's home.

"Do you always do this sort of thing?" Chad asked, keeping the intonation controlled to cloak his boosted possessiveness of Brye.

"What sort of thing?"

"This." Chad spread his arms apart to encompass the impromptu dinner.

Marcus chuckled. He placed two filled glasses on the table. "More often than not." Not elaborating any further, he dropped his massive body into the kitchen chair and instantly diverted the subject. "Why did Brye come home early?"

"She didn't tell you?" Surprised, Chad stared at Marcus over his raised fork.

"We haven't really talked since she's been back." As he spoke, he thoughtfully examined a slice of chicken before taking a bite.

Chad observed an image of something—guilt maybe?—deepen the grooves in Marcus's restless features. "They found the man who attacked Brye." He creatively continued, "Some crazed enthusiast graduating from one of those fly-by-night medical correspondence schools performed a crude, yet highly effective lobotomy on Brye's assailant. They needed her to identify the body."

About to take another bite out of his salad, Marcus's fork poised in midair as he stared with open mouth. "Excuse me?"

"Although a bullet hole the size of a silver dollar altered the stone cold features of the dead man, Brye had no problems recognizing him."

"They found him dead?"

"Apparently so."

"So the case is closed?"

"Officially…yes."

Something in Chad's tone prompted Marcus to enhance, "Why do I get the feeling that a 'but' is missing at the end of that statement?"

Because Chad understood Marcus's unfailing concern for Brye's welfare, he held nothing back when recounting the entire day's events. From the unsupported suspicions the detectives dropped on Brye, to the death of the twin's mother, Chad confided it all.

Once everything was relayed, Marcus had no time to digest nor respond to the jarring news. All he could think of was how sorry he felt for not welcoming Brye home with open arms. At a time when she needed his full support, he callously shoved her aside.

The blasting peal of the wall phone relieved Marcus of his smothering guilt—at least momentarily. Shooting out of his seat, he ran toward the sound. Spilling into the living room, he spied the phone lying on the couch. Scooping up the receiver, he answered before the final ring had come to a complete halt.

"Brye Grayson's residence."

"No wonder I didn't get an answer at your place," Brye responded. "Would Chad be with you by any chance?"

"Brye?" Marcus almost collapsed from sheer relief. Reversing direction, he strolled back into the kitchen. Thankful eyes swung around to meet Chad's probing stare. "Where the hell are you and why haven't you called?"

"I'm calling now. Have you seen Chad?" she asked.

"You didn't call my cell?" he pouted.

Brye sighed and patiently explained. "I left my phone, Marcus, I have your home phone memorized, not your cell. Have you seen Chad?" she persisted.

"He's with me," Marcus admitted, feeling foolish as he looked over at Brye's forgotten phone. "He thought you two had a dinner date?"

Across the room, Chad guilty looked at his cell and realized it remained on airplane mode from their early-morning flight. He silently cursed himself while hovering over his chair. Poised, he was prepared to snatch the phone out of Marcus's hand but continued to listen to the one-sided conversation.

"Tell me what's goin' on," Marcus pleaded with unguarded impatience.

The line went oppressively still. Marcus felt the cool fingers of fear ruffle the fine hairs along his arms.

"Brye?" The chilled fingers steadily grew colder as the seconds ticked by without an answer.

With some consideration, Brye finally answered. "If I tell you, you have to promise you won't go off half-cocked and do something crazy."

Underneath the frigid fingers, Marcus's skin grew numb. "Just tell me, dammit!"

"Promise me, Marcus."

"Damn you, Brye!" he spat, more out of frustration than anger.

"Do it now, Marcus, or let me speak to Chad."

"Okay…all right…I swear…I won't do anything stupid." Marcus met Chad with a world-weary grimace.

Satisfied with Marcus's assurance, strained as it were, Brye went into graphic details—as told to her by Tenisha—the events up and through the time she found Tenisha's hammered and depleted body passed out on the floor.

Impatient to talk with Brye, Chad paced uniformly in front of Marcus. Not knowing nor comprehending what their conversation entailed, Chad perceived the news to be devastating. By the ashen gray tint blemishing Marcus's bronzed features and the death grip he subdued the phone receiver with, whatever bad tidings Brye issued, it hit too damned close to home. The suspense was like a jackhammer slamming in his gut. Half tempted to snatch the phone away from Marcus, he needed to alleviate his own sweltering uneasiness.

Rage threatened to erupt like a rumbling volcano. "I'll kill the bastard myself!" Marcus's unexpected outburst alarmed Chad further. He grilled Marcus with a querulous eye.

"No, you won't, and you can't," Brye quietly noted. "You promised, Marcus. Don't make me regret having told you. Tenisha trusted me not to, and I've violated that trust. She didn't want you to know."

In irritable defeat, Marcus covered his eyes with his hand. "What do you expect me to do?" he murmured with an intense urgency. "What the hell am I supposed to do?"

"You aren't supposed to do anything, Marcus. If you go after him, if you get yourself into trouble because of this, Tenisha will never forgive you, and she'll never forgive me for betraying her confidence." A few seconds of dead silence, then Brye continued, "Tenisha swore out a complaint against him. Let the law handle it from here."

Marcus squeezed his eyes shut against the insistent pounding galloping along the backside of his head. Of course he knew Brye was right. He understood she jeopardized her relationship with Tenisha in confiding in him. But it didn't depress the overwhelming urge to rip TyJuan's balls off and stuff them down a paper shredder. Again he sighed in defeat. Only this one sounded more resigned than the first. "Does she want to see me?"

"No," she answered, "but I wouldn't let that stop you. Although you can be a first-class jerk sometimes, you are, nevertheless, a kind and sensitive jerk. And"—she continued, with a teasing lilt—"you're *our* jerk! And she needs all the support you can offer her."

Marcus winced. The guilt of how badly he treated her earlier had not altogether withdrawn, but dozed lazily on the edges of his subconscious. The remorse, however, was driven to the forefront, after Brye's unsolicited description; it now beat him senseless on both sides of his head.

Anguished, Marcus turned his back on Chad as if the meager maneuver could grant him the privacy he desperately searched for. "Brye, about this afternoon… I'm—"

"I've already forgotten about it, Marcus. Why don't you do the same?"

"Brye?"

"One more thing," Brye concluded, "I'm going to tell you the same thing I told Tee's parents when I called them. Tenisha needs your full support. When you see her, she doesn't need everyone questioning her reasons for staying inside her failing marriage. She doesn't need to hear anyone going on about what a bad person TyJuan is. All she needs is your love, understanding, and support."

"Of which I have an overabundance of," Marcus said, turning to find himself staring into the face of an unstrung Chad. "Listen, I better hand the phone over to lover boy here. Right now, he looks like he's gonna jump down my throat."

Chad snatched the phone out of Marcus's tensed fingers. "Brye? Where are you? How are you?"

His voice, although frantic and somewhat tensed, gave Brye strength to carry her through the next several hours.

"I'm fine…really. Marcus will explain everything. I just wanted…I needed to hear your voice."

Chad's tone softened at her discernable weariness. "You sound tired."

"It's been a long day."

"I know, baby. I know. Why don't you let me come and pick you up? We'll drive up to the cabin. You can take a few days off to recuperate."

"I'd like that. But I can't leave Tenisha's side—at least not until her parents show up. They're driving in from Buffalo."

Although Chad did not, as of yet, know what was going on, it did not prevent him from pressing his advantage. "We'll talk about it when I get there."

Several more minutes passed before Brye called an end to their conversation. "I better go. I don't want Tee waking up to an empty room."

"I love you, Brye." Chad sensed a hint of a smile coming from Brye.

"It's just what I needed to hear," Brye stated before hanging up.

34

Tenisha's mind flew open long before her eyes were able to efficiently perform the simple task. Eyelids literally sealed shut, she acclimated herself to her present physical condition, as well as her existing surroundings. Aware she laid in a hospital bed, despite the pulling effects of the painkillers, in spite of the raw injuries draining her of much-needed strength, her intellect was up and running at full capacity; Tenisha was relieved to know she suffered no lingering brain damage. TyJuan had attacked her body with a vengeance but had been unable to scar her mind.

The puffiness mingling around the circumference of her eyes felt more pronounced than when she first fell asleep; she made no attempt to part her lids. Prior to sleep, her face had been devoured by a flaming inferno. The pain pill given her now doused those raging fires into smoldering embers. And her body, every inch of her pulsating torso screamed out for help; she felt like a much-used punching bag. All that notwithstanding, the unruffled darkness settled around her like soothing balm to her bleeding soul. Outside her closed hospital door, the muffled sounds of normalcy comforted her enhanced hearing. Inside the walls of her hospital room, Marcus relaxed her jittery nerves. And it *was* his familiarity she felt. Tenisha had no doubt about that. She felt his irrepressible presence, smelled the familiar masculine scent, sensed his distraught soul.

But why was he here?

Because Brye had called. Although Tenisha had begged her not to, her pleas had gone ignored, as Tenisha had known they would. No matter. After all, that's what friends are for.

"Marcus?" Her voice rang out stronger than expected, although her cheeks functioned as if stuffed with cotton balls.

"I'm here, baby." He slid his arm through the bed railing and intermingled his fingers with hers. Up until twenty minutes ago, he'd sat by her bedside along with Brye and Chad. All three had stood vigilant for several hours until he and Chad talked Brye into going home to rest. It had taken a lot of convincing, but she finally bought their hard sell and left with Chad unwaveringly in tow.

"How're you feeling?" he quietly asked.

"Alive." Tenisha attempted a smile. Her one good eye painfully opened. She bared witness to a wonderful sight. Marcus's brawny features hunkered above her in blurred and somber lighting. Worry registered in his eyes. She enthusiastically added, "And from this side of the bed, that feels pretty damn good!"

A hearty, relieved intonation erupted in the form of laughter. TyJuan may have wounded her pride, but he hadn't broken her spirit. Marcus was grateful for that. "Is there anything you need?"

Tenisha ran her fingers over the front of her face. She grimaced in pain. "Maybe a face transplant. This one has to look like one of Frankenstein's creations."

When Marcus first looked upon the mushy mass of flesh, he thought only a crazed animal could do such a thing. The hours he watched Tenisha sleep, his fury built in intensity, threatening to detonate and destroy everything within a square-mile radius. The destruction TyJuan had caused inflamed Marcus to want to pursue him just to put him down like the rabid dog he presented to be.

But now, staring into Tenisha's mutilated features, he begrudgingly swallowed his wrath. Not wanting to understate the damage done, neither did he want to overdramatize. Leaning closer, he ran soft lips across her beaten forehead.

"Hm? You look more like an overripe kiwi." His lips continued to play over her bruised and swollen face. "But so much juicer and a whole lot sweeter."

Tenisha laughed. It was short, meek, brittle. Nevertheless, it was a laugh. "That's the corniest thing I've ever heard you say." She squeezed his fingers. "It's also the sweetest. Thank you."

A comfortable silence embraced the new lovers. The subdued atmosphere deepened as Tenisha and Marcus buried themselves within a world of uncertainty.

For Marcus, he spent the time fashioning different forms of pain he could inflict upon Tenisha's husband's body.

Stretching TyJuan from here to eternity on one of those torture racks would be nice. Personally ripping his heart out of his chest would be even better. Maybe Marcus could take him bungee jumping; of course, he'd cut the rope as TyJuan plummeted toward the face of the earth.

On and on he went, with each punishment progressively more torturous than the last.

And for Tenisha, even in the dark, through closed, battered lids, she sensed Marcus's rage. She felt the suffocating heat filtering from his body. She deciphered the volatile images churning inside his brain, and she visualized the blazing glow of wrath spewing from the brutal slits swallowing the natural shape of his eyes.

Unwilling to give Marcus open passage to destroy himself in a welding pot of raw and undisciplined fury, Tenisha whispered. "Let it go, Marcus. Just let it go." Her fingers crept along his arm and found their way to his face. The roughness of his early-morning growth scratched her palm but invigorated her mind. She was going to be fine. Tenisha had no doubts of that. Bitterness did not play a part of her wounded spirit. She did not wish to seek revenge nor would she harbor any animosity.

Where TyJuan was concerned, a deep-seated sadness shaded the nucleus of her awareness. And sorrow. Sorrow for the destructive path their three-year marriage had taken…and ended. And relief. Relief because it was over. Her marriage was no more. The decision had been taken out of her hands once TyJuan had lifted his to do bodily damage to her. Regardless of the outcome, when she checked out of the hospital, she would never return to her husband. "Let it go, Marcus," she softly reiterated. "I swear to you that I have. And I promise you, I'm going to be just fine."

Her silent plea reached out of the darkness to touch him, caress his murderous thoughts, and soften his hardened heart. The afflictions discoloring her face had left no residual marks on her heart and soul. How she could be so generous toward TyJuan went way beyond his comprehension. He turned his face into her palm. "Is that what you want?"

His breath was warm and stimulating against her cool skin. Reopening her eyes to the extent in which her injuries would allow, she unflinchingly verified, "Yes. It's what I want. And it's what you have to do. For yourself. Not for me."

Her touch, gracing the side of his face, was as potent as truth serum; it would not let him enshroud the genuineness of his emotions. Marcus nodded back his tears but found it next to impossible to hold his tongue. "I love you, Tenisha." Cursing the neglectful slip, he backed out of her efficacious reach.

Tenisha's arm dropped heavily to the bed. "I love you"—the three most sought-after words in the universe. His impulsive attestation both thrilled and frightened her. Although she couldn't pinpoint the exact moment of conception, the seed had definitely been planted and had flourished to staggering proportions; Tenisha was irretrievably in love with Marcus as well. But after believing she'd fallen in love with TyJuan—she now understood that what she had felt for her husband had never harmonized with true love—coupled with the torment she sustained by his very own hands, she now doubted her own judgment.

Misinterpreting her hesitation, Marcus inched closer once again. Certain her nearness would be the death of him, he quickly pulled back. He stood and stepped away by several feet. His hands sought shelter inside his pants pocket. "It doesn't have to go any further than this, Tenisha. What happened today, what I said just now, does not have to go beyond this moment." Marcus's gaze fell on the window facing the east. Bright lights from outdoor security lamps poked through the slits of the closed mini-blinds.

"I'm putting the ball in your court, sweetheart. You can either pick it up and run with it, or you can let it roll off on its own. Either way, it's your choice. I'll abide by whatever you decide."

Whichever decision Tenisha came to, she knew she did not have to make it at this very moment. As she burrowed in her bed, sleep overtook her. "I'm tired, Marcus." She lifted her arm in the air. "Would you hold my hand until I fall asleep?"

Marcus rushed to her side and reoccupied his seat. Just as Brye had done earlier, he clutched Tenisha's fingers while lightly stroking her temples. And as the wheels of undisturbed repose charged through the night and kidnapped her battered soul, so did it steal away the brunt of his hostility. Never would he forgive TyJuan, nor would he forget, but for Tenisha's sake, because it was asked of him, he would let it go.

"I love you too, Marcus." Debilitated by sleep, dampened by darkness, yet the marvelous words were undeniably audible.

He could not regulate the strapping jolts of happiness firing through his charged synapses. He dropped his eyes and watched her stilled form. Lids shut tight, she uttered no other sound. Despite her slumbering appearance, whether intentionally or in sleep, she had declared her love. Marcus bent to kiss her forehead. Whatever harsh realities awaited him in the dawn's early light, in the tantalizing tresses of twilight, she had made him the happiest man alive.

Close to four in the morning, disturbingly sober, TyJuan's mind refused to shut down as he sat in his parked Lexus. Head tilted back, eyes closed, car situated in Brye's drive, he waited for his wife's friend, his friend, to appear. For several hours, he'd remained crammed into the driver's seat, his tempestuous mind replaying the grotesque scenes he'd written, directed, and starred in.

Drunk and delirious at the time of performing such monstrous acts upon Tenisha and Erin, stone cold sober now, every painful detail was as clear to him as the full moon hovering above the quiescent neighborhood.

Remorse gnawed away at him, threatening to consume him alive, leaving nothing behind except an empty shell of a man.

He'd fucked up. Big time. Nothing he could do or say would ever make up for the monumental pain and agony he rained down on his wife. Tenisha would never forgive him. Hell, she probably didn't want to ever see him again, let alone speak to him. But he didn't blame her. He couldn't. He had only himself to thank for the hellhole he just buried himself in.

A smile rich with irony covered the bottom half of his beaten face. What would Tenisha say if she knew he was about to pay for his sins? Would she forgive him then?

TyJuan sat up straighter in his cushioned seat. He rubbed his tired eyes, fingers shaking with uncertainty. God, but he wanted a drink…or maybe a long drag on a joint laced with PCP. But he would never be able to carry out his plan if he did not have his wits about him.

The HIV virus. For all he knew, he would soon be dying of AIDS. Sooner than that, he'd become a social outcast.

Out of a sense of obligation, when he was only six years old, his mother had forced him and his dad to visit his uncle in the hospital. He had been diagnosed as having full blown AIDS. TyJuan vividly recalled the repulsive, larger-than-life lesions covering his doomed mother's brother's face and body. He could not forget the deathly, emaciated appearance, or the hair that fell out in massive clumps. And lastly, TyJuan could not remove from his mind the insufferable manner in which his father had treated his brother-in-law.

A leper. His Uncle Jackson had been treated like the condemned man he had come to be. His father had refused to touch his uncle. He scorned every minute spent breathing the same air as Jackson. He had spooned out more false hope than Baskin Robbins dished out ice cream. And when they had walked away from the visit, TyJuan had never gone back. His Uncle Jackson had died several weeks later.

Condemned to walk the same down-trodden pathway, TyJuan would be granted firsthand knowledge of what Jackson experienced in the last agonizingly lonely days of his life.

TyJuan would not go out like that. He did not want to endure the sanctimonious condolences his so-called friends and family would extend toward him. He could not live through the suspicions revolving around his manhood. He could not control the repulsive looks people would greet him with, or the alienation he was certain he'd be forced to endure. No, TyJuan had no control over how others would respond toward him, but he did have control over one area of his life: death. In his hands alone, he held the power of his fate.

A low, scintillating beam dragged along the interior of his car. The bright light practically blinded him as it confronted him in his rearview mirror. His muscles tensed. Chilled blood felt thick and sluggish as it pumped through his contracting veins.

It was time. The wheels were spinning in motion. TyJuan was about to embark upon a journey he would never return from.

On the brink of limbo, Brye's head suddenly shot forward. Murky eyes scrutinized the dark-colored sedan settled in her double drive. The unexpected sight sent her drowsiness flying out the open window of Chad's Jeep and into the stilled night. "TyJuan's here." Her voice was amazingly calm in the face of obscure adversity.

Chad's knuckles tightened around the steering wheel. "Don't worry." Neck muscles bunched, voice tight, he proclaimed, "I'll take care of him." Navigating into Brye's drive, he maneuvered the Jeep around the parked Lexus.

"No. You won't." In the moon's overcast, Brye absorbed the angry lines dominating Chad's crimped features. "*I* will handle this."

"Dammit, Brye!" Chad blasted. Earlier, he and Marcus had seen the nonsensical destruction TyJuan had trounced upon Tenisha's delicate features. Both men had fought with some difficulty to swallow their surmounting rage, along with their overpowering need to seek revenge. No way in hell would he let that nutcase get close to Brye! "If you think for one minute I'd even let you go near him, let alone talk to him, then you're sadly mistaken."

Brye's heart picked up its pace as she stared at the hard set line of Chad's jaw. Unable to get upset with him, she understood his curtness was brought on by his love and concern for her safety.

She spoke gently, lovingly. "This isn't your choice to make, Chad. It's mine."

He swung a hard, piercing look her way. Even in the gloom of night, his stinging expression could send the mightiest of animals scurrying. It did not faze Brye. Stretching forward, she slid the back of her knuckles along the rugged hairs sprouting along his inflexible chin. Under the steady caress of her touch, she felt his tension slowly abate.

"I can handle him, Chad. I really can." With the exception of facing her own personal nightmares, Brye had spent her entire life confronting unwelcomed situations head-on. She endured a lifetime of distaste while clashing with omnipotent opponents—the most recent being Chad's own father. Jostling with TyJuan would be like swimming up to a harmless fish in the midst of a pool of hungry piranhas.

Brye drew a teasing thumb along the sexy curve of his lips. "I know I've never given you reason to trust me before, but I'm asking you to trust me now."

Cold hard guilt kicked Chad in the center of his chest. He blamed himself for the lack of trust plaguing their troubled relationship. If he had given her reason, maybe she would have confided in him in the earliest days of their blossoming relationship.

Unable to deny her anything—particularly when she stared at him with those saddened violet-colored eyes, especially when her face exposed her steadily declining endurance—he nodded in acceptance. Puckering his lips to plant a light kiss on her straying thumb, he then shut down the engine. "Just remember, I'll be right by your side the entire time."

Brye had handled more tragedy and pain in the past twenty-four hours than any human being should ever have had to endure in any concentrated period of time, let alone in a lifetime. And she'd come through it like a trooper. A normal individual would have crumbled under the heaping pressures long before now. And although he sensed Brye to be functioning at 40 to 50 percent of her total capacity, she still held strong. There was a toughness in her he could not deny. A toughness his father and he probably held a strong hand in erecting. His heart strings ached at the unsettling thought.

Chad jumped out the Jeep and skirted the front end. Opening Brye's door, he slipped strong, able fingers into hers and guided her out of the stalled vehicle.

For one heartfelt second, standing in the glowing rays of moonlight, nothing else existed for Brye and Chad, except each other. They stood so close, the combined heat of their bodies mingled into the night air and created a hot pocket in the cool midst of a light breeze. Eyes sealed on one another, Brye reached up and gently touched his bristly face with her open palm. Underneath her soft, extracting touch, a tingling sensation rippled Chad's sharpened skin. A metaphysical transference. Brye drew on his strength. An energizing glow radiated outward, originating at the tip of her fingers and drawing a burnished path along the side of his face. One moment, he was all aglow from her mystical touch. The next moment, it fizzled into the early-morning air. With a cognizant smile, Brye stepped away.

Strides long, determined, and purposeful, Brye marched toward TyJuan. Seconds after confirming their arrival, he'd climbed out of his car and clung anxiously to his door handle. Brye halted in midstride as her eyes drank in his haggard appearance. His clothing, wrinkled and frayed, appeared as if he'd worn them for days instead of hours. Facial lines strained, bloodshot eyes, at least a two-day growth dusted the bottom half of his aged face.

TyJuan stared back at Brye with eyes as dark and empty as an unfathomable sea. He got the impression that he was the last person she had expected to show up on her front doorstep.

"You look like hell," Brye greeted.

"I've been waiting for a while." TyJuan's eyes dropped to the ground, then lifted to meet her questioning eye. "I fell asleep in the car."

Uncomfortable, nervous, skittish, despondent—words Brye never thought she'd ever associate with TyJuan. The failing light of the steadily ebbing moon did not inhibit her from clearly viewing not only those four uncharacteristic traits, but some she could not easily identify.

"Why?" she asked, all wide-eyed and innocent.

For a moment, TyJuan appeared to have lost his train of thought. Thick brows thinned into a mass of garbled confusion. "Why what?"

Unclear to whether he was coming down off drugs, Brye sought a closer inspection. Afraid for her safety, Chad's fingers snaked around her forearm to restrain her from drawing nearer. Heeding to his subtle warning, Brye resigned herself to interrogate. "Why are you here? Why did you fall asleep in your car? Why do you look like that?" She shrugged, and frowned, and watched as the transient moon reshaped his face into something more dismal… Prophetic… Apocalyptic. A sense of uneasiness gathered in the marrow of her bone. "Feel free to answer one, or all if you'd like," she requested.

He chose not to answer any. "Have you seen Tenisha?"

Brye blinked at him with straight face. She sidestepped the question. "I wasn't scheduled to be back until this evening. Tenisha wasn't aware I was coming home earlier than planned," she hedged. "Why? Is something wrong?"

Behind Brye, Chad's stare was hard and unflinching. But when he looked down at Brye, when he touched her with the possessiveness of only a lover could, TyJuan perceived that Brye had found her soulmate for life. In the midst of his abysmal chaos, a ray of hope flickered. Brye had finally found love. It was something to cheer about.

For the first time since walking upon him, TyJuan acknowledged Chad. "Would you mind giving me a few minutes alone with Brye…please?" His tone was cordial, yet his desperation could not be dismissed.

"Actually"—Chad stepped up and around Brye, shielding her with an authoritative stance—"we're in a hurry." His smile, charming and disarming, sliced through the thinning night.

TyJuan sank further into himself. Chad was protecting his woman. He knew it just as well as he knew he would never again experience warmth from the morning's first emission of sunlight. TyJuan was not angered with the position Chad had taken. In fact, he wanted to urge the man to forever protect Brye…maintain her safety. He wanted to advise him to never let go and to forever cherish all that they shared. God help him, TyJuan wished now he had taken better care of Tenisha's love.

"I'll only take up a few seconds of her time." His left hip drooped as he endeavored to return Chad's smile. But his grin miserably fell, literally dropping off the face of the earth.

Brye could not ignore the despondency underlying his rushed words. She observed the torment drawing his bloodshot eyes into a vacuous cavity. For Tenisha, as well as herself, she owed it to TyJuan to hear him out. Gingerly, she peeled Chad's safeguarded fingers off her bare arm. "Why don't I meet you in the house, Chad?" She dug deep into her pocket and pulled out the silver key chain holding her house key. Dangling it in front of him, she smiled. "I won't be long."

Lips compressed together, Chad glowered at Brye. Ignoring the burning furor turning his eyes the same shade as the fading night, her stomach muscles rolled as she waited for the confrontation. To her dazed wonder and relief, he turned, walked away, and let himself into the house without causing a scene.

The dusky light of dawn wrapped its docile grip around the two lone bodies. All around them, birds, bees, flowers sluggishly awakened.

"What's going on?" Brye turned on TyJuan, hoping to extract some form of confession.

TyJuan turned away. He swallowed hard before swirling back to meet Brye's inquiring stare. "I'm sorry for the way I treated you the last time we saw each other." Dropping his head, he massaged the back of his neck with trembling fingers. "Lately, I haven't been much of a friend to you…to anyone. I've forgotten what it's like to be a good husband to my wife. I'm ashamed to call myself a man." His voice cracked. "I know I have no right, but I'm asking for your forgiveness."

Brye studied TyJuan's doleful expression. She searched for a hint of acrimonious mocking. There was none. Only intense sadness. "I forgive you," she stated with meaningful intent. Forgiveness for herself was easy; forgiveness for Tenisha was an entirely different matter. Her eyes remained trained on TyJuan as she waited for more.

He nodded, seemingly satisfied. "Can I ask a favor of you?" He patted himself down as if searching for…what? Remembering, he eyed his car. Yanking the driver's door open, his hands slipped inside, moved past the gun that remained oblivious to Brye's eye, and grabbed the sealed white envelope taking up space in the front passenger's seat. "If you could, I'd like you to give this to Tenisha for me."

Unable to grasp the scene unfolding before her, Brye's lungs constricted with foreboding. Throat collapsing around a swelled lump, she managed to utter, "It's done."

"Thank you." Their fingers touched as he handed the envelope to Brye. In a letter it had taken the better part of three hours to compose, TyJuan begged for forgiveness from his wife. He had also sworn his undying love. His only wish was that Tenisha wouldn't spend the duration of her life hating him for all the suffering he caused her.

A strangled sob rose from the hollow depths of TyJuan's lost soul. A sweaty palm clamped around Brye's wrist prior to her pulling the envelope away. Her eyes dropped to the tight clench he secured her with, then elevated to peer into the face of a condemned man. Quietly, she waited. For what? She did not know. Seconds later, she found herself cloaked inside a crestfallen embrace. She smelled, felt, and sensed…what?

"Tell Tenisha I'm sorry," he sobbed into the side of her head. "Tell her that I never stopped loving her. I just lost sight of that love."

TyJuan pulled away. He gave Brye one last grief-filled smile. "Take care of our girl." He clambered into the driver's seat. Brye turned and stumbled toward her front door. Her mind frantically searched for the truth, for that lost fragment hidden inside her hazy recollections. She needed to connect that final piece which would make sense of this bizarre scene playing out in her front yard.

She opened her front door and almost fell into Chad's awaiting arms.

"Are you okay?" he asked. But his voice struck her from a distance. Brye was lost in a fog of uncertainty and doubt. Her stumbling thoughts scrambled for an inkling of understanding.

What are your intentions, TyJuan? She gravely quizzed herself. *What are you trying to say?* Brye could still see the emptiness echoing inside his eyes. *What am I missing?*

Frantically, Brye replayed the entire scene over in her head. She visualized his anguish and heard the desperation. He had acted as if he sought penance for his sins…as if he desperately searched for a passageway to… She looked down at the envelope clutched in her trembling fingers.

Like a bolt of lightning slamming violently into her plagued visions, the final scrape of her imprisoned memory barreled through the recently unlatched portal. And at that terrifying moment, it struck her.

"Sweet Jesus…no!" Brye cried out in shameful fear. Heedless to Chad's startled expression, Brye tore out the front door. She flew toward TyJuan's sitting Lexus.

"No, TyJuan…don't!" she screamed at his obscure shadow. Reaching outward, the very same second she tore the car door wide open, an ear-splitting blast punctured her tender eardrums. Blood and brain matter splattered everywhere. Lost in unbridled hysteria, Brye flew backward. On her hands, buttocks, and feet, she scrambled away from the wounded scene. Screaming at the top of her lungs, fingers shaking in horror, she rubbed incoherently at her chest in a mad attempt to clear the splattered blood. To her dismay, the hideous stain grew in size and intensity.

"Brryyee?" Chad's booming voice echoed behind the gunshot, his heart thudded in time to his pounding footsteps as he dove after Brye. Fear as he'd never known before gripped tenaciously at his heart, constricting the four chambers from delivering precious blood throughout his veins and arteries.

Blood. So much blood. His terror strummed vigorously against his breast bone. Praying to God Brye had gone unscathed, he dropped to his knees. Determined and distressed, tremulous palms washed over her head and chest. To his staggering relief, she'd escaped harm—physically if not mentally. Encircling her within the folds of his protective embrace, he attempted to quell her anguished weeping. "It's okay, Brye. It's going to be okay."

"No! No! No!" Brye's head shook violently against his heaving chest. She struggled to bring the tears up. God, how she wanted to cry. Why couldn't she shed some much-needed tears? "You don't understand," she wailed into his shirt. "I killed him, Chad. Oh God! I killed him!"

Pushing her at arm's length, Chad captured Brye's oscillating head between restraining palms. "Listen to me," he spoke low, hypnotically, calmly. "You can't blame yourself for this. TyJuan killed himself. You had nothing to do with this."

Like frozen plumbing undergoing a lazy spring thaw, her tears began sluggishly, then burst forth in one violent whoosh. She soaked Chad's shirt as her weeping flowed unimpeded. "I had everything to do with it," she mournfully sobbed into Chad's chest. "I drove him to it."

"Don't do this to yourself, sweetheart." Chad gathered her into his comforting arms. "You are not to blame." Rocking her gently, protectively, Brye's tears began to show signs of abatement. She felt so safe, so secure, so loved. But she couldn't stay here. She had to go back. She had to face her past. She had to face the cold, numbing truth of her brother's death.

The tears spilled once again as she finally admitted what she had so inexhaustibly fled from her entire adult life. "My brother, Chad. I killed my brother!" One insufferable second later, Brye lost sight of reality as she passed out within Chad's arms.

35

"Bry?"

There was no fear as Tyson pushed his chest into the barrel of the loaded gun. "You can't shoot me. I'm a part of you. We think as one. And I know…" He paused. And smiled. But he did not display his usual charismatic charm and brilliance. Instead, his grin portrayed sadness, and remorse, and…love—there was so much love. "I know you won't shoot." He leaned toward her. His fingers wrapped around the cold, hard barrel. His palm slid down the long, steel length and blanketed her hand. "Give me the gun, Bryson."

Bryson's fingers, the gun, her body and mind, began to shake. Uncontrollably. In spite of his vile actions, despite her wanting to see him dead, Tyson was right. She could not shoot him. Defeated, an anguished cry rose from the pits of despair as she released her grip on reality.

"I hate you, Tyson," she whispered, the fight long fizzled out. "I'll hate you till my dying day. And just because I couldn't kill you under my own volition, I will always wish you dead." Bryson laughed…or was it merely a croak? Pain, anger, sadness, no longer commanded her beauty. What floated on the surface was unruffled acceptance.

She turned her back as well as her heart on her twin. For the moment. Forever. He ceased to exist.

Tyson's face spilled with sadness. A heavy heart fell uselessly to the floor. And Bryson understood that he understood she meant every word. All said and done, he walked out of her room with gun clenched in hand.

One week later, a sensation of despondency and doom haunted Bryson the moment she stepped inside her darkened bedroom. Disregarding the hollowness pulsating through her heart, she spoke unmercifully into the binding darkness. "Get out of my room, Tyson!"

Tyson slid from behind the concealing shadows. Like a pestilent disease anxious to destroy, depression flailed relentlessly at his person and obliterated all that he used to be. Bryson's implacable rejection had taken its toll. "I need to talk to you."

Bryson dropped her study materials on top of her bed. She reached under the shirred shade of her bedside lamp and flipped the light switch on. A small section of the room was instantly bathed in soft light. At the sight of Tyson's weathered features, she immediately wished she'd left the room in untroubled shadows. Cheeks sunken, skin ashen, lifeless eyes, Bryson stared into the beaten face of a man-child who'd fought with the devil and had lost. And when looking into those drowning violet-colored eyes, eyes identical to her own, eyes once filled with life and vitality, but now reflected condemnation and emptiness, she knew she stared into the dismal shadows of a floundering soul. She turned away from the miserable sight.

"We have nothing to talk about."

Tyson took a step closer. "In looking through your eyes, Bry, I've been able to take a good, long look at myself. I know what I did was wrong. I accept what I've done and I'm ready to take whatever measures necessary to get my life back in order. But I can't do it alone, Bryson. I can't confront Mom or Dad without you by my side." His face twisted with repugnance and shame. "I can't even face myself without your forgiveness…I can't face myself without your love."

"You know what?" Bryson's unmerciful stare ground into him like a heavy foot stamping out a smoldering cigarette butt. "I can't face you either. And as far as love and absolution is concerned, your soul will burn in hell long before I'd even consider giving you a four-ounce glass of cold water, let alone forgiveness." Storming over to the closed bedroom door, she grabbed the brass doorknob and hauled it open. "Get out of my room, Tyson! Get out of my life! I don't need you anymore. You are no longer a part of who I am. Mentally, emotionally, physically, I've severed our bond. Now get the hell away from me and stay away! I never want to see you again!"

A strangled cry liberated itself from the throes of Tyson's grief. Face crumbling, head bowed in defeat, he walked out of Bryson's room and out of her life forever.

Chest hoisting in undulated shudders, brow sweating, body shaking in undefined terror, Bryson lurched toward her antique, ivory-finish, framed mirror. She stared at her unwavering reflection. Haunted eyes stared back; the smoky image of her twin brother confronted her…condemned her soul.

Rooted to the spot by both fear and fascination, she sensed and could picture in her mind Tyson carry the 9mm semiautomatic to his temple. In morbid dismay, Bryson felt the icy barrel press firmly against her forehead. She felt the curved trigger as it methodically pulled backward. She heard the piercing explosion. And a millisecond before the shower of blood blinded her cursed eyesight, a penetrating, shattering convulsion ripped her world apart…

"Brye, are you okay?" The steady pounding on the bathroom door sent Brye's thoughts scurrying for cover.

"I'm fine." Standing under a pulsating stream of cascading water, Brye twisted the hot and cold ceramic handles to the off position. "I'll be out in a sec." It was time, she told herself. It was time to tell Chad the truth. Afterward, she'd let him decide which pathway their futures would embark upon.

Chad moved away from the bathroom door. At the cabin for one hour, and Brye had spent the entire interval inside the bathroom walls. Assured she was all right, bare feet slapped against the hardwood floor as he padded into the great room. Standing at the solid glass wall, he held a 180-degree angle of the surrounding woods, an isolated area guaranteed to protect from the roaming civilization at large. Early-afternoon sun beat upon the man-made lake, transforming the sparkling water into shimmering pools of burnished diamonds.

As his eyes slowly skimmed over the tranquil domain, his mind played over the tragedy that had unfolded before his very eyes. After calling 911, he and Brye had been detained and questioned for over two hours. Once they had been released and TyJuan's remains removed, Chad wasted several more minutes fighting the media circus. He'd then driven Brye to Mount Sinai to inform Tenisha of her husband's suicide. Afterward, Chad thought he'd have to throw Brye over his shoulder and haul her out of the hospital before the riotous news media stormed the place. But she had shown no resistance in leaving, and had actually seemed relieved to be walking away from the crazed frenzy that seemed to have grabbed her by the tail for the past thirty-odd hours and refused to let go.

Rotating his head on his stiff neck, Chad worked the kinks out of his bunched muscles. With the exception of the two catnaps he'd taken the night before, he hadn't had eight hours of sleep in over thirty-six hours. Neither had Brye. Their sleep was certain to be delayed a little while longer, however. It was time to discuss the rash statement Brye had uttered in the midst of their early-morning crises. They had not discussed her brother as of yet. A brother Chad had never held any awareness of. Then again, there were many things he'd been kept in the dark about. But if they expected to have a life together, it was time she learned to instill her trust within him.

"Hi."

Chad turned. Partially revived, Brye leaned against the bedroom doorway. The picture of perfect health, she wore one of his flannel shirts. Dark, damp hair fell in cascading tendrils down the side of her face and back. Her skin was scrubbed clean and produced a healthy shine. Glorious eyes reflected the energetic spirit that even thirty hours of living hell could not wrestle away.

A fiery heat flickered along his groin. Fighting against all odds, he crushed the urge to rush to her side, toss her on the floor, and get lost inside her luscious body. "You look…refreshed," Chad noted for the record. Hungry eyes greedily soaked in every inch of her semi-clad body.

"Yeah…well…believe it or not"—she tossed back a handful of moist hair—"I think I'm going to survive."

Despite the number of catastrophes hanging dangerously close over their heads, they were able to smile foolishly at one another for several seconds. But it was Brye who let the light moment slip. Her smile faded. She stared down at the large manila envelope she held in her hands. Slowly walking toward Chad, she held the damaging possession in front of her.

"There are some things I'd like you to see. There are many things I'd like you to know...about me...about my past, Chad. It's time you learn as to why your father doesn't want us together."

"Brye, I—"

Brye touched her fingers to his open lips. "Don't say anything... please. This is hard enough as it is. Just let me explain, then you can have your turn."

Chad nodded. Accepting her terms as well as the envelope she held, he slid his fingers between hers and walked them over to the sofa. They sat. He dumped the contents of the envelope onto the coffee table: one DVD and several eight-by-ten glossies of—

Chad blinked back his incertitude as his mind's eye refused to accept what his external vision clearly perceived. The young man copulating with Brye's mother was definitely not Brye's father. But the resemblance to Brye was so uncanny he found it impossible to fully grasp the context of the damaging photos. "This is your mother and...and..."

"My brother." Brye looked away before adding, "My *twin* brother."

For the next several hours, Brye spoke freely about her family; her parents' open marriage; the perversities and the prostitution. She relived the lonely existence she had led because of their sordid lifestyle. She confronted a life entailing no one but her brother. She spoke lovingly of the precocious twin she had loved, nurtured, and cared for.

She recounted it all. Holding back nothing. She spoke of the seduction of her brother by their mother; the incest; the willfulness to sell his soul to the devil. Finally, she apprised Chad of her rejection toward her brother and Tyson's inability to accept her emotional decision. And with tearstained eyes, once again, she relived her twin brother's suicide. And, in finally opening up, she emancipated herself from her sordid childhood existence.

Every word Brye spoke, every tear she shed, Chad shared with her. But now it was time to put the pain, the heartache, the past behind. "But he put the gun to his head, Brye, not you. He pulled the trigger."

"But I could have stopped him." Her fingers, wound into tight balls, dug sharply into the palms of her hand. "All I had to do was call out, tell him I loved him, tell him I forgave him. He would have heard me…he would have refrained from pulling the trigger." Brye shook her head in anguish. "I was tired, Chad. I couldn't hold us both up any longer, so I decided to cut him loose and save myself."

Brye dropped her head into her open palms. "This morning, TyJuan asked for my forgiveness. I didn't hesitate to give it to him. Why couldn't I do that for my own brother?" she wailed profusely.

"I'll tell you why." Prying Brye's fingers loose, Chad pulled her unyielding body into his arms. Leaning against the back of the sofa, he cushioned her with a soothing hug. "It was easy to forgive TyJuan his sins because emotionally, you weren't connected to him. But in your brother's case, there was an emotional, mental, and physical bond. When he hurt you, the pain ran much deeper."

Chad's able fingers worked through Brye's fast drying hair, stroking, caressing, sending electric jolts down the length of her body. "And for fear of sounding callous, your brother is the one who took the coward's way out. He's the one who ended it all by putting a bullet to his head. He's the one who walked away and left you to deal with this mess."

Brye stiffened in the face of his cold, heartless words. She attempted to pull away, but Chad clamped her firmly to his chest. "Eventually, you would have forgiven him, Brye. I have no doubt of that. But it was going to take time. And if your brother knew half as much as I know about you, he would have known you first needed to get over the betrayal. He could have hung around longer, fought a little harder to prove himself to you. But he didn't. And you have no reason to feel guilty." Chad brushed Brye's forehead with a tender kiss. His breath warmed her as he spoke quietly against her temple. "All that has happened with you and your brother is in the past, Brye. It's time to put it behind you. You need to tell Tyson that you forgive him. Then you ask for his forgiveness." Giving her another gentle kiss, he concluded, "It may not heal your wounds completely, but it'll be a beginning…your first step toward healing."

Of course he was right, Brye told herself, but she didn't have the strength to reflect. Chad's slumberous voice induced a sensation of weightlessness; she floated in the midst of a lazy cloud. She felt warm and protected. And she wanted to shut her intricate thoughts down—even if it was only for a short period of time. Long dark lashes tickled the tip of her cheeks as heavy eyes loosely shut. Chad's intimate caresses—the light kisses upon her temple, the tender strokes along her weary arm and backside—lulled Brye into a world void of all worries and concerns.

Then, recognizing where she headed, she forced her eyes open. She couldn't do this. She could not give in to the descending exhaustion until she exorcised all her malevolent demons.

"Chad?" Brye pulled out of his arms. She blinked back the crippling slumber, shoving the incoming drowsiness aside. "I love you. I love how you make me feel." She gifted Chad with an apologetic smile. "But I have to finish this. I have to tell you about myself… about my nightmares. You need to know why it's difficult for me to trust…to love. But I can't do this if you keep touching me…talking to me"—her heart melted as she stared into his smoldering baby-blues—"if you keep looking at me."

From the moment Brye had stated she loved him, all else was lost on Chad's ears. His beating heart called cadence upon his constricting chest. He grinned wickedly. "You said you loved me."

"Chad…please!" Brye hit him dead center with a look of reproof.

His smile instantly flattened. His eyes turned serious. This was important to Brye. Chad understood that. Yet he found it difficult to disregard her spontaneous declaration. "I'm sorry."

Brye scooted toward the edge of the sofa. She pushed herself off the sofa. As she strolled over to the glass window, she gulped down a stabilizing breath.

"I… We… My brother and I," she verbally stumbled, "were products of a sordid love affair, which turned into a sordid marriage, and escalated into a sordid lifestyle. Through it all, my parents pulled no punches with who they were or what they did for a living. Their profitable sex life was all we knew. In fact, many nights, we were left to take care of ourselves while they were out 'entertaining.'" Her reflection, shining in the clear glass, was borne out of pure scorn. "As soon as Tyson and I hit puberty, my parents began priming us for 'the business.'" Simultaneously, she used her fingers on both hands to produce quotation marks. "They easily seduced my brother. He willingly joined their immoral lifestyle. I refused to let them poison me. So they started leaving me alone with men. Men who wanted to take me to bed…take away my virginity. But I fought them off. Every single one of them." Brye moved away from the window. She pulled her bottom lip over her top as she carefully deliberated. "For a long time, I hated myself for not being like them…for not being one of them…for being the odd man out. And it took some time—many anguish-filled years later—but I finally recognized that there was nothing wrong with me. It was my adoring family"—the sarcasm flowed as wide as the Nile River—"who were the sick ones." Brye's shoulder's lifted into a resigned shrug.

"After a while, I stopped hating myself and started hating them. Only I ran away from that hate. I couldn't handle the reality of knowing I hated the people who should have been the closest to me. So I chose to shut down because it was much easier to arrest my feelings than to accept and cling to the loathing and bitterness I nourished for my parents and twin brother." Tears glistened as her poise melded into horror and shame. "Whenever I spoke of my brother to Marcus, every time I thought of Tyson, I convinced myself that I loved him. But I really didn't, Chad. I hated him. I hated them all. I was relieved they were dead. With their death came my sacred freedom." Brye's lips twisted into an ironic smirk. She turned and challenged Chad with an unwavering eye. "Only my family wouldn't release their stranglehold on me. Even in death, they chose to persecute me. They mocked what little happiness I had created for myself. Every night, in the form of embroiled nightmares, they tightened the noose they held around my neck."

The tears gushed. Chad shot off the sofa and rushed to her side. Brye patiently warded him off. Pushing renegade strands of hair out of her eyes, the free falling tears—cleansing tears—counterbalanced the blazing smile she presented to him. "I'm fine…really." She swiped away the tears and urged Chad back to his seat. Sitting across from him, the coffee table a barricade between them, she sniffled, loudly, several times before continuing. "Not until Anthony proclaimed his hatred for his mother did I realize what I'd been running away from for all these years. It was then that I finally faced the truth." Brye sniffled again. She shook her head incredulously. Her hair whipped loosely across her face. "God knows it would have made my life simpler had I accepted reality in the first place."

Red-stained eyes dropped to the long-forgotten pictures scattered on the tabletop. She gathered them up and began tearing them into shreds. Expelling a long, burdensome sigh, she progressed with her story.

"The first summer prior to my enrolling in NYU, I legally changed my name."

Somewhat changing directions, Brye ran down a different pathway. Chad quickly realized it all was intricately woven into one sinister tale of betrayal and deception. Drawn deeper into her life, he could not refrain from asking, "What did your parents say about your change in name?"

A stinging smile penetrated her desolate features.

"They didn't object. In fact, they thought it was quite amusing, actually. My mother even went as far as to tell me that I could change my name but I couldn't change the person inside. She said I could run but I would never be able to hide." Absentmindedly, Brye crumpled the now defunct photographs into shapeless, miniature pellets. "What they didn't understand is that I wasn't trying to change my identity. I was merely taking the first steps in distancing myself from them." Shoving the torn photos into one hefty pile, Brye grabbed Chad's attention with an unfettered eye. "And then I met you." Tenderness and love found its way to Chad's side of the room. "As long as I could remember, men came on to me like dogs in heat. But there you were, coming to see me day after day after day. Not once did you try to strike up a conversation, let alone say hi." In appreciative recollection, a small smile brightened her tormented memories. "You were afraid to approach me. You were the first man I'd ever known who was actually afraid to speak to me."

Chad reached across the way and touched Brye's cheek with the tip of his finger. His tone matched the ardor he witnessed in her demeanor. "I *was* afraid. There was so much sadness. I saw a vulnerability there that warned me away." His thumb grazed over her bottom lip, then reluctantly dropped away. "I was afraid you'd run and I'd never see you again."

"You were the first man, the *only* man, who ever made me happy…really happy." A sardonic smile now darkened Brye's brow. "My mother would always tell me that I was a slow starter, but the day I got my first taste of sex, I'd lose all self-control. She said, genetically, I'd inherited her and my father's strong sex drive, and one man wouldn't be able to keep me satisfied."

More from desire than embarrassment, crimson red stained Brye's bare cheeks. "I remember the first time you invited me up here…the first time we made love. I recalled the many times and the many different ways we touched each other." One particular memory deepened the color of her entire face. Spread eagle, Brye had bound Chad's sleeping and naked body to the four bed posts. She wakened him with a can of whip cream in one hand and a bowl of strawberries in the other. She feasted upon him for hours.

Dragging her mind back to the present, she released one long tedious breath. "The time we spent together had been phenomenal. But when I returned home, guilt took over. My mother's words continued to plague me." Her back suddenly rigid, Brye tightly gripped the edge of the couch. "I grew disgusted as well as ashamed for throwing myself at you the way I did. I kept telling myself that good girls didn't behave that way. And since I knew my mother wasn't a good girl, and she would have wholeheartedly approved of my torrid actions, I considered my wanton behavior highly improper."

"But it wasn't, Brye." When Chad had met Brye, he had considered himself to be an experienced lover. Brye, on the other hand, had clutched no experience in the art of lovemaking. But nothing could have prepared him for the reckless abandonment he released within her. Ready to please as much as receive pleasure, she had been all too eager to fulfill his every sexual fantasy. More times than not, she initiated, suggested, and ministered intemperate forms of intoxicating pleasure. Making love with her then, as well as now, was much like making love to a maverick: untamed, unrestrained, and prepared to ride beyond the limits. No one before or since Brye had ever come close to taking him to the heights she had driven him to.

"What goes on between two consenting adults is neither offensive nor shameful, Brye. Nor is there anything shameful in enjoying sex or taking it to the limits. Each and every time we made love was, and still is, the most memorable experiences of my life."

Brye confronted Chad with an earnest look. "Believe me, it didn't take long for me to realize that my way of thinking was totally screwed up." Her eyelids dropped. Afraid to meet his steady gaze, abashed at the intentional betrayal she perpetrated upon him, her voice lowered. "I never told you this, but right after we returned from the cabin, I went out with another man…another student. It was the worst, yet most enlightening night of my life." Brye visibly shivered at the unpleasant recollection. "Whenever he touched me—whether it was innocent or otherwise—my skin crawled. And when he attempted to kiss me good night, I wanted to throw up."

Brye was finally able to meet Chad's benevolent gaze. "The unpleasant experience helped me to realize that my love for you… our love…is what unlocked the door to my sexual desire. I loved making love to you, Chad. Only you. I loved seeing you shudder with desire by a slight touch of my hands…or whenever I executed an innocent kiss. But more importantly, I…loved…you!

"And when I found myself pregnant, when I told you I carried your child, you made me feel like the luckiest woman in the world." A gloomy shadow replaced the ecstatic hue tinting Brye's natural color. "And then one of your father's flunkies brought me a million-dollar check along with a message from you. He told me that you didn't want any part of me or the baby. He said the check was for services rendered. Services rendered," Brye scornfully repeated. She could not hold back the bitterness. "And it all came rushing back to me. The distrust, the insecurities, the anguish. All my life, my mother had grilled into me that the only thing a man wanted from a woman was sex. She bragged on how royally they would pay for that one thing—and I had a million-dollar check in hand endorsing every word she had preached to me."

Chad's gut twisted. He could spend the rest of his life striving to make up for the pain Brye had endured at the hands of his father. Maybe he would never succeed. But God help him, he would try. "Brye, you have to believe me when—"

"It's okay, Chad." Brye waved him into silence. Prepared to jump ahead of her story, she deemed it unnecessary to listen to apologies for something he had no control over. "Do you remember the first time you visited me in my home...months ago?" She did not wait for an answer. "You threw the name Bryson up in my face.

"At first, I thought your father had me investigated. But he hadn't, Chad. Your father knew of me long before you and I ever met...through my parents." The stoic expression Chad greeted her with sent Brye's mind tumbling inside a windmill. She needed Chad to believe her. Desperately. More than anything, she did not want to rely on the recorded DVD to extract his belief. Brye wanted him to believe because he held enough faith in her to believe. Jumping up, she moved around the table and plopped next to Chad. She gripped his arm tightly in sheer desperation. "Your father knew me as Bryson."

Brye watched the muscles in Chad's jaw twitch. Still unable to guess his thoughts, she struck him with the final knockout punch. "Someone else knew me as Bryson."

A sinking sensation struggled to stay afloat in the core of Chad's stomach. Every intuition told him that whatever Brye said to him now would change his life forever. Bracing himself, he asked, "What are you trying to tell me?"

"The man who attacked me, Chad. He called me Bryson. I completely blocked it out until I saw him lying on that slab in the morgue."

Her fingers dug sharply in his arm. His skin turned red, with half-moon indentations riding along the muscle. Chad was oblivious to the pain as he listened to Brye's tormented attestation. "Your father hired him...to scare me off...to scare me away...from you."

Chad's temple visibly pulsed. His rage quickly swam to the surface. Sad as it may seem, he couldn't decide on who he should be the angriest at. Himself or his father. Bent on exacting his own form of punishment upon Brye, he had neglected to pick up on his father's calculated plans.

No. That wasn't true. When Brye had attended the party his father hosted, he'd known then Daniel had been planning something. Chad had just chosen to ignore it. "If you believed this, why didn't you tell the police your suspicions?"

"Because he's *your* father."

Her impassioned statement knocked Chad backward. After all she'd been through, after all his father had done to her, she remained willing to protect him. Brye hadn't deserved what he and his father had done to her.

"Dammit, Brye! What took you so long to tell me?"

"Because he's your father," she quietly repeated. "I didn't want to destroy what you two have." Her eyelids lowered. "I was also afraid you wouldn't believe me."

So many emotions garbled Chad's agitated thoughts. Sadness, anger, disbelief, disappointment drove at him from every direction. Uncertain in which direction to vent his pent-up frustrations, he knew the best place to start was with his father. But for right now, he had to reassure Brye.

He gathered her into his arms. "I'm sorry, Brye. I'm sorry for everything you've been through…for everything *I've* put you through."

Mentally and physically, Brye was spent. She had exorcised Bryson Gray. And Chad was not running away. Nor did he look at her with scorn or disgust. And as the pounding of his heart intermingled with hers, she took in a breath that was lighter, purer, sweeter than the mountainous air. Blessed relief fluttered through her system like an exquisite butterfly floating on the breeze of a perfect spring day. For the first time in her life, Brye embraced hope for her future. A real future with Chad at her side. She pulled away from his tender clutches. In diametrical opposition to a body spent with lack of sleep, her voice registered spirited disbelief. "You *do* believe me?"

Chad hesitated before answering, "I have a confession to make." Reaching outward, he pushed aside a strand of Brye's falling hair. "After I returned from Florida, I was finally able to put two and two together. Only I didn't like the answers I came up with. I know now that you didn't take money from my family. I also know that it was I who threw away what we had." Chad shook his head in self-deprecation. How could he ask her to forgive him when he couldn't forgive himself? "God, baby. I should have trusted you. I should have trusted what we felt for each other. Instead, I got caught up in my own self-pity...my own pain and bruised ego. I did and said some unforgivable things to you because of my own inadequacies." He caught her hands between his. "I'm sorry. I'm so sorry. And if you'll let me, I'd like to spend the rest of my life making it up to you."

Chad lifted Brye's hand to his mouth. He spoke softly against her warmed fingertips. "And if you believe my father is behind your attack, then I don't doubt there's merit to your accusation. But please forgive me and try to understand when I say I don't *want* to believe. It's difficult to believe that my own flesh and blood, my own father, would go to such lengths to drive the woman I love away from me. I don't want to believe I've been so blind to his faults, I allowed him to play me like a puppet on a string."

His anger suddenly soared like an out of control brush fire. His face coagulated into a raging inferno. Releasing Brye, he flew off the couch and paced the length of the room. "Dammit, Brye! You could have been seriously hurt that night...you *were* hurt that night. And if my father had anything to do with it...anything at all, I swear I'll—"

Brye jumped up and threw herself into Chad's arms. "He's your father, Chad. Whatever he did, he did it out of love for you. He did it because he wanted the best for you."

Unable to believe his ears, Chad pulled away and directed his wrath toward Brye. "Do you hear yourself? With all that you believe, with all that you *know*, how the hell can you defend him like that?"

"I can because I respect his desire in wanting his son to have the finest in life." Arms hugging her chest, Brye spoke quietly, sadly. "Although I don't agree with his methods, I agree with his reasoning behind them."

Chad softened the raging storm as his vision washed over her swaying body. His heart swelled with the love he contained for her. Despite the horrors she endured at the hands of her own family, Chad fully grasped the extent of her belief in safeguarding family honor and values. She had not wanted to challenge the father/son bond, nor had she wanted to be the one to defile his relationship with his father.

So kind, so compassionate, so caring…so dead on her feet. She hung on by sheer willpower alone. For the past several hours, she had done nothing but bare her soul. For the past two days she'd slept very little. Emotionally expunged, Brye needed peace, she needed rest, and she needed to know how very much he loved her. He decided to offer his support on all accounts.

Startling her, he swung her in the air and cradled her in his arms. "What're you doing?" Brye yelped, although she was grateful to be off her feet.

"I'm putting you to bed." He carted her in the direction of the master bedroom.

"Oh." Brye draped her arms around his neck. "Will you join me?"

"Only if you ask me nicely." His voice low and seductive, he nuzzled her earlobe with a playful tongue.

"And how—"

The sound of car wheels rolling over gravel ceased Brye in mid-sentence and Chad in mid-route. Brye's legs swung toward the glass window as Chad turned to capture the identity of their caller.

"Tank?" Brye uttered in surprise. "Why is he here?"

"We needed supplies, so I called and gave him a list of things to bring up." Partially the truth, Chad had not been able to locate nor confront his father. Now that all the evidence had come in, wild horses could not keep him from seeking out the man who had terrorized Brye. Chad intended to drive back to Manhattan while Brye slept. Then he would pay Daniel Collier a long, overdue visit. Tank would remain behind to look after Brye.

In the bedroom, Chad flipped the intricately woven quilt back. Carefully, he placed Brye in the center of the immense handcrafted bed. Like a body weighted down with cement blocks, she sank deep into the mountain dew aromatic sheets. Eager to claim her for himself, the Sandman eagerly pranced behind drooping eyelids. Brye was all too willing to give herself to him.

Half asleep, rolling over in a fetal position, tongue laden with sleep, she murmured, "You'll come back to me, won't you? When you let Tank in?"

The love he felt for her transferred to the tip of his fingers as he lightly stroked her cheek with a gentle touch. "I will always come back to you, my love." But Brye was too far gone to hear his sacred promise. Tucking the sheets under her chin, Chad kissed her on the temple and left her to snatch the much-needed sleep her body craved.

And as soon as Tank familiarized himself with his new surroundings, Chad left for the city. On his way out, his eyes hooked on the forgotten DVD. Picking it up from the coffee table, he altered his route. Although he was anxious to find his father now, he was bent on looking at its contents before heading back into town.

As if competing in the Indy 500, Chad exceeded all speed limits as he drove to his father's New Jersey estate in record time. He burst through the closed double doors of Daniel's study. An ominous thundercloud traveling at close range eclipsed the sun streaming through the large window. Not in the mood nor the right frame of mind to placate, Chad barely took note of his ex-fiancé as he ordered, "Get out, Jennifer!"

Resentful of the tyrannical air of authority Chad had adopted toward her, stubbornly, she held her ground. "You can't come waltzing in here, making demands of me!"

"Now!" he hissed, eyes nothing more than viperous slits.

"Do as he says," Daniel ordered. Heaving himself out of his strapping chair, he stared into his son's enraged expression. One person floated behind the reflection of hatred Chad speared at him: Brye Grayson.

Daniel had made a grave mistake. He'd given her time to come to a decision. She'd used that time wisely.

Disapprovingly, Chad glared flagrantly at his father. "Is this another strategy session?" he quickly imparted once they were alone.

"Obviously, you barged into my office to tell me something." Daniel stared his son down with a inclement eye. "So why don't you come right out and say it?"

Chad refused to break eye contact, nor did he back down. "Did you orchestrate Brye's attack?"

Ambushed by the unforeseen question, Daniel determined that the best defense was a good offense. His chest puffed in indignation. "How dare you come in here hurtling unfounded accusations!"

Chad's anger flared. Closed fist slammed against the rosewood desk. "I want to know the truth…now, dammit! Or I swear I'll walk out that door and you'll never see or hear from me again!"

Regardless of all else, Daniel could not dispute his love for his son. Once before, Chad had walked away from him without thinking twice or looking back. At all costs, he had to prevent a repeat episode. A fog of defeat rose precariously over his head. Daniel fell heavily into his chair. "He was only supposed to scare her off."

The shock of having his father admit the truth crystallized Chad's heart. The love for his father was now frozen in time. And Chad didn't know what Daniel could do to engender the thawing of the icy chambers.

Whether "to scare her off" meant raping or maiming or just plain ridiculing, Chad knew it was pointless to ask how far the assailant would have carried it through to claim his promised compensation. "Did you have anything to do with his being gunned down in cold blood?"

At least he held the decency to turn a deathly white under his summer tan, Chad noted as he witnessed Daniel's pained expression.

"I had nothing to do with *that* unfortunate mishap." Daniel's voice, his eyes, his mannerism, did not waver. Nevertheless, Chad accepted his avowal as a lie. And Daniel witnessed that distrust. Heaving a sigh of defeat, he truthfully established, "After the debacle in Florida, his superiors considered him to be a liability—to *themselves*. I had nothing to do with the decision to eliminate him."

The fact that a contract had been carried out on the attacker did not trouble Chad in the least; as far as he was concerned, it had saved him the time and energy of tracking down Brye's assailant himself. What was reprehensible, however, was that not only had his father associated himself with the unsavory elements of the world, but he had also had the audacity to pollute Brye's unsullied environment. Despite the central air, the room had grown oppressively hot. No longer could Chad stand being in the same room as his father. He had to get out. The air was stale, oppressive, dirty. But before he put some much needed distance between himself and the man who'd given him life, he informed, "You better get used to Brye. I plan on asking her to marry me. She'll probably turn me down, but I'll keep after her until she finally accepts."

Daniel's brow deepened in anger. "Her mother was nothing but a common whore, Chad," he vehemently admitted. "We don't need that kind of publicity if her past ever gets out."

The back of Chad's teeth ground relentlessly as he glowered at his father. His voice remained amazingly calm. "Excluding the fact that *you* didn't mind her mother prostituting herself while you and your friends fucked her, Brye's mother has nothing to do with who Brye is."

So she had cursed Chad with the entire, sordid truth. Daniel blanched but regained his composure in the grand Collier style befitting his reputation. Shooting out of his chair, knuckles pressed into the rosewood desk, he leaned across the desktop and resorted to the last option available to him. "You marry her, and I'll write you out of my will."

An empty threat. They both knew Daniel could not intimidate Chad into complying. But Chad would take him up on his offer. His jeer turned merciless. "You don't get it, do you? I'm jumping ship now...cutting my strings...saying adios, Padre. So why wait until you're dead and buried? Draw up whatever papers you like, relinquish me of any and all your worldly goods. Being of sound mind and body, I'll eagerly sign them all."

The air seeped from Daniel's inflated ego. Taken completely by surprise, he turned a ghastly shade of pure terror. "You don't mean that!"

Chad's fingers rested on the solid brass door lever. "Brye remains spokesperson of Romanique Cosmetics. But as far as I'm concerned, you can consider this my resignation."

He turned to go. "Oh! One more thing." Peering at the long forgotten DVD, he tossed it on top of the desk. "You better hope Brye has a long and prosperous life," he growled. "Because if anyone so much as cuts her off on the highway, I'll see that Mom gets a copy of that."

A superficial bluff. Chad had just given Daniel the only copy in Brye's possession. It didn't matter. From here on out, he was dedicating the rest of his life in taking care of her. She need not worry about his father, or anyone else conspiring to do harm to her ever again.

Not taking the time to search out his mother, not even certain if she was here or at the South Hampton estate, Chad walked out. Much more needed to be accomplished before he could spend a few uninterrupted days with the woman he loved.

Less than two hours after Brye had fallen asleep, a slight tug in her lower abdomen drove her into a sitting position. Mind fuzzy, she waited for the discomfort to reoccur. It did. Minutes later. In the light of her previous miscarriage, mind suddenly alert, she carefully analyzed the trenchant sensations dragging along her pelvic region. Cramps. Although they weren't of the overwhelming or mind-crushing persuasion, they were coming at her regularly. Every couple of minutes. Fear prickled the tiny pores along her shivering arms as another spasm rocketed through her. Forcing herself to swallow the foreboding taste teasing the tip of her tongue, Brye shakily climbed to her feet. Gingerly sliding her legs into a pair of loose fitting jeans, she opened the bedroom door and stepped through.

The *New York Times* unfolded and spread around him. Tank turned his attention away from the paper and onto Brye. "You didn't sleep very—" In light of her pale skin and the alarm flaking her irisis, he charged to her side. "What's wrong?" he asked, grabbing her by the elbow and dragging her to the couch.

Brye allowed herself to be led. "Where's Chad?"

"He went back into New York to take care of some business." Hovering over her, Tank waited for her to sit.

She didn't. Brye squeezed his fingers as another cramp stretched across her belly and afflicted her wary brain. "I think you should get me to the hospital."

Tank had one question. "Should I call 911? Or can you make the drive?"

"If you take me to the nearest hospital, I can make it."

They switched directions and staggered out the cabin door.

For Brye, the next several hours were spent being poked, prodded, tested, and X-rayed. The pains continued to come, and she still had no answers. Sitting upright on a hospital stretcher, the sounds of busy activity reached her beyond the small cubbyhole the ER staff had confined her to. Wearing the fashionable hospital gown and foam slippers, Brye crossed her legs, lifted the end of the white sheet up and over her upper abdomen, then securely crossed her arms over her belly.

Fear continued to tower over her, and the not knowing only frazzled her mind more. If she lost this baby, she didn't know how she would survive. Blame had already settled in as thick as London fog.

"Are you comfortable, Brye?" Tank, standing beside the long cart, pulled her out of her dreary thoughts. "Can I get you a blanket? Another sheet?"

"I'm fine." Brye smiled weakly. "And thank you for being here with me."

"I can try to contact Chad if you'd like."

Brye shook her head from side to side. "Why don't we wait until we get some news."

They didn't have long to wait. A doctor Brye had not yet had the pleasure of being groped by sailed haughtily into the room.

Mid to late forties, stocky built, pointed nose and receding hairline, his only outstanding feature was the confident, yet not arrogant aura shrouding him much like the lab coat he wore.

"Ms. Grayson." Fingers outstretched, he took her right hand and shook with a firm, cocksure grip. "I'm Dr. Tarantino, a fertility specialist."

"Uh-oh! It must be bad news," Brye removed her hand from his stalwart clutch and braced herself to the incoming fireworks. "They've called in the big guns."

"I'm afraid so." Introducing himself to Tank, he wheeled a stainless steel stool up to her stretcher and sat down beside her. Bluish-gray eyes hit her with a no nonsense stare. "Let me inform you on what you've got here."

"Please do."

"Your pregnancy test indicated a positive reading." Keen eyes studied the clipboard—an impeccably summarized record of Brye's abrupt visit—as he continued. "But the ultrasound indicates that the embryo did not implant inside your uterine wall."

Brye stared past the good doctor and down at the off-white floors as she digested the news. How ironic. All this time, she'd been condemning herself for not taking better care of her body once she confirmed her pregnancy. In truth, she would never have carried this baby to full term.

"An ectopic pregnancy?" she asked with calm clarity.

Her voice barely touched Dr. Tarantino's ears. Telling a blissful expectant mother of her baby's impending demise had never been a highlight of his career. The compassion in his expression was authentic. "There's a high probability…yes. A mass was palpitated during your pelvic exam. And in the absence of pain as pressure was applied, if we are dealing with an ectopic pregnancy, it's safe to say that it hasn't ruptured yet." Dr. Tarantino pushed himself forward, rolling his stool closer. "Time is of the utmost. I need to go in, search for the embryo, and retrieve it before it causes major damage."

Brye nodded in acquiescence. Too tired to fight, she just wanted to get it over with. "Just do it." When the doctor didn't immediately leave her side, tediously, Brye caught Dr. Tarantino square in the eye. "There's more, isn't there?"

"In light of your previous miscarriage, it's likely something more is going on."

"Such as?"

"At this early stage, I don't want to speculate. The procedure I'm suggesting to you is called a laparoscopy. It'll not only help us locate the fetus, but it can also visualize the main source of the problem."

Again Brye nodded, noting her awareness of the diagnostic, and often therapeutic, procedure.

"Of course my main concern is eliminating the fetus before it ruptures." He frowned in contemplation. "If I do find the major cause behind your infertility, you're not under any obligation to agree to rectify the problem today. You can elect to have corrective surgery at a time conducive to your own schedule and with a doctor of your choosing." His frown flipped into a reassuring smile. "I'm just making you aware of your choices. And with laser surgery, if we can take care of the problem today, in the long haul, it may save you valuable time and another surgery later. If—"

"Fine." So many thoughts flew through Brye's oscillating mind—with images of ovarian cancer sucking up the brunt of her brain matter—so many emotions flushed through her overly taxed system. What if she could never have children? What if she was doomed to walk the face of this earth childless? Preoccupied with her grievous thoughts, the palms of her hand lightly glided up and down her flat stomach. *I never even got the chance to know you*, she speechlessly spoke to the baby she would never see. *I'm so sorry.* Her eyes swelled with tears. A lump sprouted in the back of her throat as she silently said her goodbyes.

"You have my permission to do whatever is necessary—barring a hysterectomy. If possible, I'd like to try for more children in the future."

Dr. Tarantino stood. Patting Brye's hand in understanding, he vowed, "You have my word. I will be conservative yet extremely thorough." With chart in hand, he strolled toward the door. "I'll have the nurse come in and have you sign the necessary forms."

Once he'd gone, Brye looked over at Tank who stood doggedly by her side. She mockingly thought to herself, *and the hits just keep on coming.* A single tear slid down her cheek. "I think you should try to find Chad now."

"I'm sorry, Brye."

Brye shrugged as if effortlessly brushing the matter aside. "Oh well." Her lips began to tremble. "It's the story of my life."

Sympathetic to her inner turmoil, Tank reached over and pulled her into his arms. "I'm not Chad, but will I do?"

Brye lifted her arms around his neck and sobbed into his shoulder.

36

Lost in a world created of her own accord, Brye drifted in a milieu of soothing darkness and calming peace. Every so often, vague images of Chad, Marcus, Kirk, Lynn, and the twins slipped into her unruffled continent. Not ready to share any part of the world she rejoiced in, Brye disapprovingly shoved the nebulous forms out of the realm of her self-contained universe. She would then sink contentedly back into a place where fears and torment remained ineffectual determinants.

Desiring to remain buried in the abstract, Brye only showed signs of recovery when mind and body joined forces to battle against her inherent stubborn streak. Metaphysical surroundings transposed into physical surroundings as she relinquished her hold on the commodious abyss she had created around herself. Begrudgingly, she dragged her disinclined awareness back into a world that only caused her pain.

Weighted down with lethargy, Brye's lids slowly fluttered open. Throat as parched as the desert air, the putrid taste in her mouth was strong enough to induce a gag reflex. An insistent throb extending along the lower half of her abdomen grabbed her immediate attention, but she chose to ignore it. A continuous IV, attached to a large gauge needle inserted into a prominent vein in the back of her hand, dripped a vital substance into her blood system. Unfamiliar with her surroundings, without exerting much movement, her eyes took in the private room doused in shades of blues, grays, and magentas. The fading light roughly indicated the time as early evening. In direct line of sight, a thirty-two-inch flat screen TV hung suspended in midair above her head. A bedside table, bedside nightstand, and two wide-ledge windowsills were loaded down with flowers, cards, boxes of candy and "Get well" helium balloons.

A slight turn of the head, and Brye's roving eye found Marcus. His massive body filled a multicolored upholstered club chair. His head was dipped inside a magazine with a title she could not discern from a distance.

"What time is it?" she asked. Her tongue felt thick and sluggish as if she'd spent several hours in a dentist chair instead of an operating room.

Surprised, relieved, Marcus's head shot upward. His smile was a small comfort to the pain inundating her body. "So…you've finally decided to join the land of the living."

Brye grimaced as she tried to pull herself into a sitting position. "If this is living," she groaned, "send me back to where I just came from."

Marcus flew out of his chair. With the bed's remote in hand, he drove the head to an upright position. "Is that better?"

"A little. What time is it?" she asked again.

"Close to seven."

Brye's mouth gapped in bewildered shock. "They were prepping me for surgery around six, how is it over so quickly?"

"No, sweetheart." Marcus slid a chair alongside Brye's bed. Sitting, he reached over the guard rails and took hold of her hand. "Your surgery was over two days ago. You've been in and out—mostly out—for the past forty-eight hours."

His affirmation brought it all crashing down on Brye's head. In the recovery room, prior to the move to her private room, she remembered Dr. Tarantino going over the perplexities of her surgery and the disease he diagnosed.

Endometriosis. Stage III. In both fallopian tubes, the chocolate-like cysts formed a sufficient enough blockage to prevent the fertilized egg from completing its predestined journey. Although endometriosis was not considered to be malignant, it still remained a long-term disease. Utilizing a laser, Dr. Tarantino had vaporized the visible adhesions. He believed to have arrested the disease, yet microscopic implants impossible to have seen may have been missed, thus promoting the growth of more adhesions.

On its own, the disease could reoccur at any given moment without warning. Add that to the reality that surgery in itself could cause a buildup of scar tissue—which could also impede a fertilized egg from making the jaunt down its intended pathway—and Brye was left holding a bag of ifs with no promises for the future.

With all the variables stacked against her, her chances of ever giving birth to a baby had steadily and rapidly declined. Although she had to live with those odds, and live with the possibility that she may never carry a baby, could she ask Chad to live with them as well?

"Do you want children, Marcus?"

The question was not expected. Unaware of where this conversation headed, he knew Brye well enough to grasp a general idea. Marcus stared into Brye's pale face for several intense seconds. He asked in a teasing manner, "Why, are you planning on giving me some?"

Brye slipped her fingers from Marcus's sheltering grip. Her gaze shot passed his right shoulder and settled on a large wicker basket containing a wide variety of colorful plants and flowers. She felt sick inside, as if the pain would never heal. And she was not in the right frame of mind or the best state of health to play games. "Please, Marcus."

The radiant twinkle in his brown eyes settled into a dull flicker. His huge chest heaved with a heavy sigh as he prepared himself for the hot seat. "Of course I want children."

"Why?" Her eyes remained trained on the floral arrangement.

He deliberated, or maybe hesitated, before answering, "Because not only do I think it's the greatest gift in the world to be able to create another human life out of the love two people share, but having children is a testament of that love which will be carried down through generations to come."

"But what if the person you love can't have children?" Her voice lowered, her eyes searched out the truth within his blank expression.

Marcus treaded lightly. The doctor had explained her situation to Chad. Chad had explained it to him. It had been distressing news, but it was nothing Brye could not battle and overcome. Particularly with Chad waging war at her side. "Brye, if two people love each other, it's not impossible to overcome the obstacles thrown in their pathway."

"But if you really wanted a child," Brye persisted.

"There are other ways in having a child besides the traditional means, Brye."

"Like adoption?"

"That along with other methods."

"But would you feel the same way about that child? Knowing that genetically, you didn't create him?"

Marcus was beginning to feel the rise of a slow heat intensifying against the rear of his jeans. He fidgeted in his seat. For one brief, guilty moment, he wished Brye had not fully awakened on his watch. But the thought quickly dispelled when he recognized how much Brye struggled to accept the hand dealt her. "To be honest, Brye, I've never thought about this, so I can't tell you how I'd feel." Once again, he reached for her hands and softly squeezed her fingers. "I can say that I'd like to think that I could treat someone else's child as my very own. I know that I have enough love within me to try."

It was the only answer Brye expected of Marcus. It was the same identical answer Chad would give her. But was it a good enough answer?

"Where's Chad?" she asked.

Marcus smiled, grateful for the change of subjects. "I relieved him of his duties thirty minutes before you woke up. He's been riding vigilant over you for two days. I made him go back to the cabin to rest for a little while. Unless I miss my guess, he'll be back soon."

Brye felt dirty, sticky, defeated. "I'd like to take a shower…wash my hair if I could."

Marcus automatically stood. He lowered a bed rail. "I'll go hunt down a nurse. Together, I think we can manage that."

Moving slowly, Brye was already inching her way out of bed. She wanted to be ready for Chad upon his return.

The relief of seeing Brye sitting in a chair, wearing her own gown and matching floral kimono, did not eclipse the inner withdrawal he sensed seeping from her very pores. Quietly, he lounged at the open door of her hospital room. Her flawless skin had regained some of its splendor. Her recently washed hair retained its luster. Her hushed voice sounded as if it grew stronger by the minute.

"So Linn was here with the twins," Brye was saying to Marcus. "I thought I was dreaming."

"Kirk drove them up in your car. The twins wanted to stay at the cabin with Chad, but Linn insisted on taking them back. They left you the huge stuffed bear sitting over there in the corner. Kirk left you the box of truffles. Linn left you her love. She said not to worry about the kids at Brylinn. She wants you to concentrate on getting your strength back."

Brye smiled to herself as her eyes flittered toward the four-foot bear wearing a plaid bow tie and matching knit cap. Drawing her attention back to Marcus, she asked, "And Tee, how's she holding up?"

The adoration Marcus harbored for Tenisha could not be concealed. His eyes lit up at the very thought of her. His voice softened as he spoke of the true love of his life. "She's holding up well under the circumstances. Her parents wanted to take her back to Buffalo with them for a few days, but in the light of TyJuan's suicide, they decided to stay here and take care of the funeral arrangements." Marcus grinned, his mustache quivering over his top lip. "She wanted to transfer into this hospital so you two could be roommates." He rolled his eyes to the ceiling. "I can imagine the wheelchair races you two would incite all through the hallways…the heart attacks you'd be inducing in all the horny old men trying to keep up with the two most beautiful women in this establishment."

Brye laughed, holding a thick pillow against her abdomen to quell the sharp stabs. As she looked upward, the laughter caught in her throat. Her smile slowly faded. "Chad!"

Chad entered. In three long strides, he stood at Brye's side. "It's good to see you up and about." He bent at the waist, offering her a kiss full on the lips. Brye abruptly turned her head. She presented her cheek instead.

Marcus could have taken a sickle and sliced through the tension spreading inside the room. "I think I'll get some coffee. Would you care for some, Chad?"

"Please."

Before leaving, Marcus cast Brye a look that pronounced, *He loves you. Don't do anything foolish.*

Eyes downcast, Brye ignored him and his insufferable expression.

Chad knew he and Brye were about to embark upon a fight. Over what? He could not imagine. Deciding it was best to get it over with, he filled the chair Marcus had just vacated. Sliding it on its legs, he only stopped when his and Brye's knees met.

"Why didn't you tell me you were pregnant?" he cautiously asked, leaning over and pulling her hands into his.

His nearness scrambled Brye's thoughts. Squinting in deep concentration, she said, "You don't sound too surprised."

"We weren't using any protection, Brye. I would have been more surprised had you not been pregnant."

"Did the doctor discuss the outcome of my surgery with you?"

Chad released her left hand. His index finger traced a loving pathway along the soft curves of her lower lip. "That it's going to be an uphill battle from here on out…yes, he informed me."

Brye swallowed hard. Her insides trembled. Whether it was from his intimate caress or from the pain she was about to inflict upon him, she did not know. In danger of falling apart, Brye resigned herself to get this over with as quickly and painlessly as possible.

"I may never be able to have a baby, Chad. Do you understand what that means?" Brye pulled away from his strength-depleting touch. Her face clouded with anguish. "I know your father hates me. But I had hoped"—she looked away from his profound stare—"I deluded myself into thinking he could love your child…*his* grandchild. But I can't even give him that. And I can't let you waste your valuable years with me, in the hopes that we might conceive a child. I have to let you go. You deserve a life with a woman who can give you everything you deserve in life."

Chad's jaw muscles worked as he stared at Brye. He considered the fixed glare of her eyes. It was senseless to argue with her. But his anger could not be brushed aside. An expert at constructing her own self-inflicted pain, at the moment, he felt no pity for her. He only felt sadness…for himself…for the love she was about to neglectfully toss aside. Unable to control himself, he unleashed his wrath. Grabbing her roughly by the shoulders, his fingers dug mercilessly into her arms as he dragged her body closer. There was nothing gentle in his touch or the kiss that came crashing down on Brye's surprised mouth.

His lips were cruel, demanding, exacting their own form of punishment. His hot, wet tongue delved deeper into her mouth, pleasing her, stroking her senseless, draining her of everything she had within.

An impetuous whimper crossed Brye's lips, spilling into Chad's fugitive thoughts. His head lowered, his fingers worked tenaciously at releasing the knot in her sash. He lowered the kimono off her trembling shoulders. His hands fell upon firm breasts, molding, shaping, turning her nipples into desirous mounds of quivering flesh. Easing the left spaghetti strap off her shoulder, Chad exposed her plump flesh. His mouth clamped down onto a hardened nipple, drawing her body closer.

Lost in a melody of pleasurable sensations humming up and down Brye's body, she threw her head back and thrust her throbbing chest into Chad's face. Unmindful of where they were, oblivious of the surgery she had undergone, forgetful of having just attempted to break off her relationship with Chad, she only concerned herself with dousing the heat setting her body aflame.

But as she captured Chad's head between the palms of her hands and dragged his face upward to meet her expectant lips, he abruptly thrust her wanton body away. With his aggressive withdrawal, a searing pain ripped through her. Unsure if the sudden ache resulted from his abrupt rejection of her, or from the recent surgical procedure, she could only look at Chad in dismayed shock.

"You want me?" he hissed, his eyes filled with unrestrained passion.

"Yes," Brye answered, her lips swollen from his ardent kisses.

"You love me?"

It was as if he poured an ice cold bucket of water over her head. Shuddering with disbelief in the midst of her unrestrained actions,

Brye could not lie. "Yes, I love you. But"—her words trailed off, her eyes dropped in regret.

"You can fuck me, but you don't won't to spend the rest of your life with me…is that it?" His lips were drawn back into a scathing sneer. "You are one fine piece of work, do you know that?" He stood up so abruptly, his chair went hurdling backward and fell with a loud bang against the linoleum floor.

He bent over and viciously slammed the chair back on its four legs. "For someone who is so exceptional at providing emotional strength and support to others, you are nothing but a coward when it comes to your own emotional stability."

His smoldering eyes were like hot ice, burning a fiery pathway to Brye's drained soul. The viciousness of his attack was a harsh blow to her already bruised body.

"What you're doing is no better than the violation your brother committed upon himself. Only with you, it's considered emotional suicide. You said it yourself: it's easier for you to shut down. It's simpler for you to step out of life than to confront the painful realities of everyday living—realities all of us face every time we challenge a new day."

Chad's expression mellowed. There was only tenderness when he dropped to one knee in front of Brye. "I love you, Brye. My love reaches down to the very depth of my existence. And I don't know how many times I have to say that to you or what I have to do to prove it, but I love you."

"I love you too, Chad. That's why I have to let you go." Her voice cracked with unrestrained passion. "I want your happiness. And I don't believe I can give that to you."

"Oh, baby." Chad dropped his face into Brye's lap. He inhaled the fresh clean smell of her body before lifting his head and meeting her woebegone expression. "Happiness isn't something that's handed to you on a silver platter. You have to reach out and grab it, fight for it, embrace it. Because once you find the one, that special person you want to live the rest of your life with, all those conquered hurdles makes it all so much more worthwhile." He raised her fingers to his lips. "I need you, Brye…only you. Yes, I admit, I do want children. But if we can't have them, at least I'll have you."

"How do I know that ten or twenty years from now, you won't resent me because I couldn't give you children?"

"Because you have to trust me when I say I could never resent you. You have got to believe me when I say you're all I'll ever need in life. Anything extra would be icing on the cake."

Brye wanted to trust him. She wanted to believe in him. But she couldn't. She wouldn't. All she ever wanted in life was a family. A *real* family. A close-knit family equipped with the strong, devoted husband and the time-consuming, adoring children. She wanted to be there for them with fresh baked cookies when they arrived home from school. She wanted to tuck them in at night, cradle them at their saddest moments, care for them at their sickest. So how could she ask him to settle for something less when she found it virtually impossible to do so herself?

Pulling her hands out of Chad's loving grasp, she whispered, "I'm sorry, Chad. But once before, I said to you that it was all or nothing for me. And since I can't have it all, I'll settle for nothing."

Something dangerously foreign flickered within Chad's eyes… something indiscernible to Brye's naked eye. Whatever lay beyond his fury truly frightened her.

Pulling himself up to his full height, Chad glowered down at Brye. After all they'd been through, after all the adversity they had overcome, how could she willingly throw away what they had so viciously fought for? "Fine. You want me out of here? Then I'm gone." He stomped furiously toward the door. Before heading out, he turned and flung at her. "But I'll be back, Brye. Like I said before, happiness isn't something that is handed to you on a silver platter. You have to earn happiness. *You* are my happiness! *You* are my life. And I have every intention of fighting to gain my life back. Mark my words, I'll do anything and everything within my means to have you. For good!"

He walked out of her room leaving a void so massive within Brye's aching heart, she wondered if she would ever heal from the mortal blow.

37

"Do you want to talk about it?"

Brye turned in response to the deep voice breezing past her ear. She smiled into the charming face of Brian. "Do you have the next several hours?"

"I have as much time as you need." His face became somber. He took her arm and threaded her in and out of the boisterous crowd. "It looks like you need a quiet place to rest your weary head…or maybe a sympathetic ear." He smiled warmly. "I'm renting you my office and my shoulder for as long as you like."

Brye bristled. "You can't very well walk out on your own party."

Paying homage to Brian, Brye had attended the office party which combined as both a congratulations and going away soiree. For Brian, it was to celebrate his recent appointment as CEO of Romanique Cosmetics. For Chad, it was his final farewell.

"Of course I can. Look around, everyone's filling up with champagne. They'll never know we've disappeared."

It was true. A lighted fountain spilling free flowing champagne stood in the center of the immense conference room. Ice sculptures, along with food and drink, proved abundant. Everyone merrily quenched their thirst as well as satisfied their taste buds.

Brye allowed herself to be led into the elevator and up to Brian's office.

"Okay. Tell me what the problem is?" Brian insisted, settling down beside Brye.

In a puff of exasperation, Brye blew her bangs out of her eyes. "Nothing." She sulked. "Everything. Since my hospital release, the last four weeks have been the most miserable days of my life." Brye folded her hands and dropped them in her lap. "I feel as if everyone's abandoning me."

Brian draped his arm over the back of the leather sofa. "I know you're feeling down now, but you have to trust that things will get better."

Brye's laughter erupted in the form of a bitter, sarcastic titter. "That's what the twins said to me before they walked out of my life."

Brian looked startled. "You mean those adorable little kids you were photographed with down in Florida? What do you mean they walked out of your life?"

"They found parents ready, willing, and able to adopt them."

"Are they happy?"

"By the way they sounded the last time I spoke with them, ecstatic would be more of an appropriate phrase."

Brian reached over, clipped Brye under the chin, and forced her to meet his stare. "Well, then, you should be happy for them."

Brye pulled away and stared down at her clasped hands. "I know I should…and I *am* happy for them. It's just"—she choked back a sob—"It's just that I miss them so much."

"Have you met the new parents?"

"I have not." She folded her arms across her lower chest. "Linn has. She says they're wonderful, deserving people, and the twins will have a good life with them."

"Is that the only thing that's bothering you?"

"Yes…no…yes." Brye fell over herself, trying to uncover the truth. She finally shrugged. And frowned. And stumbled over her embroiled feelings. "I don't know, Brian. I'm in my final year of college. I have a wonderful job. A wonderful boss"—she smiled fondly at the man baring a tender eye and a compassionate ear—"a house full of kids relying on me for their protection and happiness, but I still have this empty void in my life."

"And?" Brian urged.

"And…since TyJuan's funeral, Tenisha has been away at her parents', recuperating. Although I talk to her almost every night, I miss her physical presence. And Marcus—my next-door neighbor and best friend—has been busy doing God knows what with God knows who. And you've had your hands full taking control of this madhouse. So…I guess I've just been lonely."

"And?" Brian repeated.

Brye faltered. Her eyes roamed over Brian's office but nothing grabbed at her attention. The room was so incredibly quiet, it appeared to be mocking the last several weeks of Brye's life.

Unable to avoid the inevitable, but finding it difficult to admit to herself, she uttered, "And now I feel as if Chad has abandoned me as well. I thought…I hoped." She halted in mid-thought, knowing wistful thinking would get her nowhere. "He hasn't called. He virtually ignored me at TyJuan's memorial service. He didn't bother to show up when the twins and I scattered their mother's ashes. He hasn't approached me today, and I'm deathly afraid I'll never see him again." A lonely tear trickled down a quivering cheek. "He's also been spending time at Brylinn—on the days I'm not scheduled to be there."

Brian reached over with a caressing thumb. He wiped the tear away. "But isn't this what you wanted? Aren't you the one who called off the relationship?"

Delirium slapped her dead center. Her upturned nose wrinkled in crushed opposition. "So he's gonna hold *that* against me? I was days out of surgery and only hours away from gaining any sense of awareness. If anything, he should have given me the benefit of the doubt and wrote my reckless actions off as a delayed reaction from the anesthetic." Brye disapprovingly tossed her hands up in the air. "But noooo," she wailed, her tone sharpened by anger. "Instead, he goes about his life as if I never meant anything to him. He hasn't—" Brye ceased her barrage of nonsensical absurdity. Her eyes cleared, her mouth flew open in shock. "Jesus, Brian! I'm sounding like an irrational lunatic!"

Brian shook his head in wonderment. This was coming from a woman who had lived her entire life with her emotions under lock and key. Whether she was aware or not, the fact that she was able to express any emotion at all meant she journeyed along the road to recovery. In spite of the gravity of the situation, aside from the blanket of despondency encircling Brye, Brian found himself laughing.

"Irrational is good," he jokingly told her. "Irrational means you're at least feeling something. It means you're not drying up inside like a day old prune."

Unable to push her grief aside, Brye's anguish ended in a low moan. "Oh, Brian. What am I going to do? I love him. And I miss him. And I'm not sure I can live the rest of my life without him."

Brian sobered. He pushed his hand into Brye's. "Why don't you tell him what you just told me? Whatever the problem, you two can work it out."

"I can't do that." Now an emotional wreck, Brye combated the tears threatening to follow the first lone teardrop. The empty void that wrapped around her heart the moment Chad had walked out of her life was now threatening to devour her alive.

Feeling her pain, Brian pulled her into his arms. Coddling her close to his chest, he asked, "What can I do to help?"

"You're doing it?" Brye rested her head on his shoulder for a few calming seconds before pulling away. "Thank you for listening."

Brian beamed reassuringly into her now composed features. "Anytime you need a shoulder, I'm at your service."

Brye laughed. "Thank you. I'll remember that." She stood. "I think you've been away from your party long enough. It's time to get you back."

As they walked toward the elevator, Brye said, "Do you mind if I don't go back down with you? I think I'm gonna check out for the night."

"I don't mind at all, as long as you promise to call if you feel like talking. I don't care what time."

"Aye-aye, boss," Brye answered with a salute.

They rode the elevator down, the atmosphere more jovial then when first going up. And when the doors slid open on the floor accommodating the party, Brye hugged Brian before releasing him into the clutches of the monumental gathering.

"I really am happy for you," Brye noted.

"Prove it by continuing to make us money," Brian retorted. As he stepped across the steel threshold, Chad's indistinguishable voice called out.

"Hold that elevator!"

About to step in, he hesitated for a short second as his eyes fell on Brye.

"You leaving?" Brian asked, shoving the steel doors open.

"There are last-minute details I need to accomplish before my plane takes off."

Brian's eyes fell on Brye, but he addressed Chad, "Call me tomorrow. We'll say our goodbyes then." He shared a know-all look with Chad. Then the doors closed on top of his smiling face.

Chad's overpowering presence filled the confines of the elevator. Directly across from him, Brye could feel the heat radiating off his body, smell his familiar masculine scent. And the tension, the sexual tension, flowing between them could not be rerouted.

In order to still her flighty heart, Brye was the first to break the charged silence.

"You're leaving tomorrow?" she reaffirmed. Aching eyes swerved to confront him.

"Yes." He refused to look her directly in the eye.

Brye felt a sharp pain as a large chunk of her heart ripped away. "Where are you going?"

"Everywhere." He shrugged nonchalantly. "Nowhere."

Brye nodded her head as if she understood. But she didn't. Not really. There was so much needing to be resolved between the two of them. So much that hadn't been said. She wanted to scream to him that she hadn't meant a word she had spewed at him the last night they'd been together. She wanted to blame her moment of insanity on post-traumatic stress. She wanted to throw herself inside his arms and beg his forgiveness. She wanted to—

The elevator "dinged" the doors flew open. Not knowing what to do, unable to get her tongue to function, Brye stepped out into the underground garage.

"Brye?" Chad called after her.

She turned and painfully confronted him. The longing etched in his face sent shivers of passion along Brye's spine.

"Have lunch with me tomorrow…please?"

Brye couldn't deny him, even if she wanted to. She nodded.

"Would you mind coming to my apartment? My plane leaves at nine and—"

"You have last-minute details you need to tend to," she somberly finished. The astringent words wrapped tenaciously around her neck, slicing off her words. "I understand. If you like, I can bring lunch."

"It won't be necessary. It's already taken care of."

"Then I'll see you tomorrow?"

"I'm looking forward to it."

Eleven-thirty sharp the following morning, Brye nervously tapped her foot as she stood outside Chad's luxury apartment. With thoughts of arousing Chad, she had dressed for this occasion with care. Her hair was free of restraints because he loved running his fingers through the thick, dark strands. She wore the color periwinkle blue to deepen the violet in her eyes. And her dress…she had been extremely cautious with her clothing—not wanting him to think she hoped to seduce him, which is exactly what she was attempting to do. She ended up choosing an ankle-length spaghetti-strap dress. The silk material hugged her waist and hips but flared freely toward her feet. No bra, no panties, no stockings, making it easier for Chad to remove her of all clothing should he choose to make love to her.

Her heart, misfiring from ragged nerves, practically tore out of her chest as the massive door swung open. Unhinged by the astonishing sight waiting on the opposite side, Brye almost burst into tears as she dropped to her knees and tugged Bethany and Anthony into her pounding heart. Bethany looked absolutely beautiful in a floral design tea length dress with lace hem. Her hair was pulled back, tied in place with a matching floral bow. It fell in long shimmering strands against the length of her back. Anthony looked just as dapper in a double-breasted suit with floral tie identical to Bethany's dress.

Overpowering them with the love she fostered, Brye virtually squeezed the very breath from their lungs. Despite her delight, an undisciplined bout of rage colored this joyous moment.

These were *her* babies. The loves of her life. How could anyone enter the picture and scoop them up and out of her fostering care with no preamble? For one insane moment, she considered fighting for them.

"Let me look at you," she demanded, pulling out of their reach. Silently, she studied them. They wore bright and beautiful smiles. The sadness clinging to their eyes—once a tribute to their short, pitiful lives—had completely evaporated, leaving a burnished glow as clear and blue as sapphire diamonds. They stood before her with an uplift of head and chin—proud, wiser, older.

In the past several weeks, they had definitely grown up. But it wasn't the bad kind of growth; the kind one undertook in order to harden the skin for the necessity of their own primal survival. It was the good kind; a nurturing touch. Before, the twins had resembled tormented birds with clipped wings. But in the past few weeks, their primary feathers had been allowed to heal and grow. Discovering the capability held within their own reach, they opened their wings. Just a little. Until they overcame the fright of their newfound freedom. They then spread their wings wider, took flight, and soared to greater heights. In the process, they discovered what life could bring to them. They loved who they were. Their metamorphosis was truly phenomenal. Whatever resentment Brye felt toward the twins' newly adoptive parents, she would be forever indebted to them for eradicating their gloom and replacing it with blazing sunshine. "What are you two doing here?" she inquired, her face beamed with happiness.

"Since"—Bethany stumbled over Chad's name, but Brye was too exhilarated to notice—"Since Chad leaves tonight, he thought it might be good if we all got together."

Chad stood, pearly whites flashing, eyes twinkling at a distance behind the twins. He'd been studiously examining her from the moment she made her entrance. And if he had any doubts—which, of course, he didn't—about the major changes he had instilled within his life these past few weeks, they were instantly expelled upon witnessing the rapture the twins incited within Brye.

For the first time since entering the apartment, Brye was made aware of eyes burning into her soul. She looked up and spotted Chad. Afraid her tongue would give way, she thanked him with her eyes. He winked, then strolled over and offered his hand. Pulling her to her feet, his lips barely grazed her cheek.

"Thank you for coming," he greeted.

"Thank you for inviting the twins. I've missed them." *And I've missed you.* Desirous eyes soaked in every inch of his buffed physique. Wearing a short-sleeve jersey knit shirt and a pair of loose-fitting khaki-colored twill slacks, he looked completely at ease with himself and the decision he had made to rip Brye's world apart—not to mention the large chunks of her heart he dissected and dropped in the elevator the night before.

Guiding her out of the foyer, the twins at their heels, he entered the spacious living room and apologized, "Please excuse the mess. The moving men will be coming to collect my belongings tomorrow, and this stuff needed to be packed before I left."

His casual statement played havoc with Brye's bristling awareness. How could he be so nonchalant about this move? He was stepping out of her life. Possibly forever. The sight of loaded boxes and furniture sheathed with protective covering pained Brye's heart. Everywhere she looked, she was reminded of how easily Chad could pack up his life and move on to greener pastures.

Brye stifled her tears. "It looks as if you're all set to go."

Chad stared thoughtfully into Brye's tear-ridden eyes before answering, "I have a few important matters I need to wrap up…but, yes, I'm ready to go." His smile burned brighter. Despite the agony she felt, fire heated Brye's heart. "I hope you're hungry. The kids fixed your favorite meal."

"You did, did you?" Shoving down her grief, Brye grinned down at the two pleased faces. "Well, I'm delighted. And impressed."

Chad led Brye into the formal dining room. The exquisite Asian hardwood dining table was immaculately set with Chad's best china and sterling silver. Beautifully arranged freshly cut flowers enhanced the center of the table. Chad smiled at Brye's dazed expression as he pulled her chair out.

"You just sit right here and let us serve you," Anthony suggested, removing the floral arrangement and placing the crystal vase on the sideboard. He and Bethany then left the room.

Chad sat across from Brye. His eyes lit up with mischievousness. "This was all their doing, you know. The only thing I did was take them grocery shopping. So…" His grin grew wider.

"So if something's not to my liking," she finished for him, "I should blame them instead of you." Enriched laughter ensued. The charming sound sent an abundance of delicate butterflies rippling through Chad's abdomen.

"You should be ashamed of yourself," Brye noted at the end of her giggles.

"And you…" He missed Brye these past several weeks. God, how he missed her. Drawn to her as he never had before, Chad longed to reach across the table and take her within his ample arms. But since he couldn't, he satisfied himself by sitting before her and admiring her grace and beauty. He resigned himself into saying, "You are the most enchanting woman I have ever had the pleasure of knowing. With the exception of this pretty lady." He aimed his smile at Bethany as she entered the room carrying a large silver soup tureen. Behind her, Anthony carted a large covered tray.

Bethany visibly glowed from the warm praise. She pecked Chad on the cheeks before setting her handful down. She turned and left the room again. Anthony was not far off her tail.

Brye rested her jaw on top of her balled fist. Pointing her chin at Chad, she eyed him suspiciously. "So tell me how you managed to pull them away from their newly found family. I haven't been able to meet the adopted parents, let alone talk to them since they were introduced to the twins."

"I have some pull with their father."

Brye's eyelids popped open with wide-eyed astonishment. "You know their new parents."

"He knows them very well," Anthony answered. Walking around the table, he served Brye and Chad their soup.

Tomato.

Bethany dished out the sandwiches.

Grilled cheese.

Tears of pleasure prompted Brye's distant memory. "You two remembered."

"It was our first nightmare since moving to Brylinn," Bethany recalled. She took a large bite of her hot cheese sandwich. Long strings of melted cheese fell across her jutting chin.

"You came to our rescue, and we sat up the entire night eating tomato soup and grilled cheese sandwiches," Anthony added. "You said it was your favorite meal."

"And that it is," Brye admitted, taking a hefty bite of her sandwich. Dipping into her soup, she praised, "And you two did a wonderful job on the meal."

Their lunch flew by much too quickly for Brye. Their discussion ranged from the twins' new school, their classmates, and their newly found parents.

Brye experienced a bout of unjustifiable envy as she witnessed the adoration in their eyes as they spoke of their adoptive parents. These people were taking Bethany and Anthony away from her. She wanted to hang on to her resentment. But she could not. Because they never looked happier, or more content. So she decided to resign herself into being happy for them.

"Are you ready for dessert?" Anthony asked, shoving back his plate.

Brye grinned across the table at Chad. Stomach stretched from eating two sandwiches and one large bowl of soup, she sighed in gratification. "I don't know if I could put anything else in my stomach."

"But you have to," both Bethany and Anthony insisted. "You at least have to see what we have for you."

Incapable of saying no to their brightly lit faces, Brye easily capitulated. "Okay. But just a little."

The twins jumped up and ran toward the kitchen.

"Thank you," Brye pensively acknowledged, "for this." She encompassed the meal she had just eaten with a wavering smile. "I guess I needed to see them happy. I needed to know that they are happy before I could even think about letting them go."

Chad climbed out of his chair and filled the seat adjacent to Brye. His index finger trailed a sensuous path along the underside of her supple arm. His voice was low and throaty. "I know something else you can do if you really want to see them happy." Short bursts of electrical shockwaves darted along her weakening limbs. Even if the twins hadn't walked in and prevented Brye from answering, her tongue would have been sluggish in its response. Being this close to Chad, particularly after so many weeks of denying herself of his love and affection, did strange things to her mind and body. Forcing herself to pull away from his analgesic reach, Brye turned her focus to the twins. Between the two of them, Bethany and Anthony carried a large covered tray. Presenting it to Brye, they perfunctorily waited for her to remove the silver dome.

When she did, her eyes literally popped out of her head. A red velvet box.

She picked it up and gasped as the small container swung open on its hinges. A five-carat diamond ring, with five smaller accent diamonds skirting the larger stone, blazed brilliantly at Brye.

"Will you marry our daddy?" the twins asked in unison.

Brye almost fell on her face. "Your what?" Stunned, her eyes swiveled from one smiling face to another. As understanding set in, forgetting the pain and sadness she endured over the past month, a raging thunderstorm developed and washed away the joy she should have been encountering.

Springing out of her chair, she bulldozed the twins toward the door. "I need to talk to your *father* alone. Would you excuse us for a few minutes, please?" Gently pushing them out, she shoved the sliding doors together and thrust her full wrath upon Chad.

"How could you do that? How could you keep those kids—*my* kids—away from me? For weeks? Why would you use them as a pawn for your sordid little game?"

Chad's anger ignited, but quickly cooled down. "I'm not using them for anything." He climbed out of his chair and blocked Brye with his hulking frame. "I love them just as if they were my own. Hell"—Chad jammed his fingers through his hair—"they *are* my own. Do you know how many times I visited them while you were on tour?" He inched closer to Brye, their fronts almost touching. "I couldn't stay away from them no more than I could stay away from you." His fingers lightly stroked Brye's bare arm. "They're *our* family, Brye. They belong to us. Deep down, I knew it the first moment I laid eyes on them." His soothing tone mesmerized Brye. His blue eyes hypnotically pleased. "We've already created our family, Brye. We can raise them with a loving hand. Together. You and I. When they're old enough to have children of their own, *we'll* be the doting grandparents. And God willing, as the family continues to branch out, we'll be doting great-grandparents." His fingers slid higher and held Brye's face between his palms. "It has to start somewhere, Brye. Let it start here. Right now. With us. Marry me?"

Brye's heart began a slow meltdown. She loved him more than words could say. And she was now beginning to understand the extent of his love and the lengths he would go to prove it. The thought that she could spend the duration of her life without him went well beyond the realm of her reasonable intelligence.

Chad witnessed as a miscellany of emotions fused into one: love. She would agree to marry him. His mood turned jovial. He felt the urge to taunt her.

Amusement bordered along the perimeter of his validation. "My kids need a two-parent home, Brye. They need stability in their lives. If you don't agree to marry me, I may have to resort to asking Jennifer."

Brye's cheeks puffed with feigned indignation. "There is nothing stable about that artificial shell of a human being," she snorted. "And if she *did* agree to marry you, I swear to you, Chad Collier, Anthony and Bethany will be orphans seconds after you get the words 'I do' out of your mouth."

Chad could not contain his amusement. Rich baritone laughter burst upon the scene like a blazing sun shattering a stormy afternoon. Brye realized he'd been playfully toying with her. Rolling her eyes, she stuck her tongue out at him, turned away, and shoved her back at him.

A fatal mistake. With violet-colored eyes spewing spitfire, and that sliver of a tongue peeking out at him, she had looked too damned adorable for Chad to resist any longer. He fought to command the heat rising inside his pants. Damn, but his nights had been insufferably long without her in his bed. And his days had been pure torture knowing she was a mere phone call away, but he couldn't reach out and touch. But no longer. He would stake his claim on her here… now…forever.

Brye stiffened as his front rode sensually against her back. The mad pounding of his heart, the forcible pulsation invading his groin, drove Brye to a mad frenzy. Unaware of her own wanton actions, she pushed her backside deeper into his growing need and stifled an impassioned cry begging to be released.

"Marry me, Brye?" His sultry voice nuzzled her inner ear. His roving fingers gently sought her arms, her shoulders, her breasts. As tenacious lips heated cool spots along her pulsating neck, his hands roamed searchingly over her shivering body. Honeyed desire flowed freely through Brye's limbs, turning her knees to syrup. Another moan threatened to overthrow her. "I don't have a job, Brye, but I have two wonderful kids who need a mother. And I swear to you, I'll be a devoted husband and father." His tongue snaked out and ran circles around her ear lobe, his right hand lowered, lifted her skirt, and then floated up her bare thigh. Brazenly, he fondled her, caressed her with gently strokes. "Who knows? I might even become one of those modern-day house husbands. I'll take care of the kids while you go off to work." His mouth worked assiduously at the base of her neck.

Brye could not hold her tongue any longer. She whimpered. Her quivering body collapsed against him as it sought support. The atmosphere pulsated with an eagerness to see the two bodies reunite. Radiant threads of sunshine spun golden spools of passion around the two promised lovers. Straying from his intended role and transgressing into another, Chad lost himself in an influx of throbbing undulations.

"God, baby!" He moaned into her fragrant hair. "I missed you so much these past few weeks."

Mind twirling out of control, Brye could not verbally answer. She could, however, show him the extent of her desire. Rotating her head to one side, she eagerly sought his mouth.

Fervent tongues mated and copulated in tune to a passionate love song. Dancing, prancing, stimulating. The driving rhythm was only broken when the muffled sounds of adulated cries of pleasure erupted into the restless chamber.

"We…can't…do this…Chad." But even as Brye spoke, her fingers betrayed her by slipping between trembling bodies and encompassed the solidified protuberance begging to be removed from its constraints.

Brye's rummaging fingers spurred his body forward, but her heady words slammed his mind back to earth. Tortuously, delightedly, he returned to the task at hand. The ravishing of her body abruptly ceased. Chad whispered into her ear, "Don't worry, Brye. I don't intend to seduce you. Not with the twins outside the door. I was merely giving you a taste of promises guaranteed to be fulfilled after you promise to marry me."

In light of his conveyed affirmation, from this moment forward, Brye recognized that she would give him everything, deny him nothing.

"I promise to have your bath drawn and your meals prepared when you come home in the evening." Chad swung her around to face him. "Would you like that?" He kissed her on the forehead, the nose, the cheek. As uncompromising lips worked their way toward her mouth, Brye could not parry any longer.

"Yes," she answered, throwing her arms around him.

"Yes?" One eyebrow cocked, he touched her lightly on the mouth. "You're saying you'd like the hot baths, the home-cooked meals?"

"No…I mean, yes, I'd like that very much. But that's not what I'm saying yes to." Brye smiled into his bewildered expression. "Yes, I'll marry you."

"Yes?" he asked, afraid his ears might be playing tricks on him.

"Yes," she repeated, nodding her head in the affirmative.

Releasing a loud, boisterous whoop, he lifted Brye in his arms and spun her around the room. "I love you." He pulled her into his arms and hugged tightly. "And I will never, ever, let you go again."

"Promise me," Brye pleaded, seeking the reassurances, the security, the love she had never appropriated as a child.

"I promise." Holding her securely and safely against his heart, he vowed, "You will never have to worry about anyone hurting you again, Brye. I swear to you…I will do everything in my power to keep you unharmed and happy." His kiss reflected warmth, tenderness, protection. For Brye, it was if she had been forever sailing the ocean, battling raging waters plagued with torrential rains and squalling winds. But ultimately, gratefully, her hammered and debilitated ship washed into port. To shelter. To safety. Home.

When Chad finally forced himself to break free, the extent of his love converged into his supple features. He smiled into her flushed face. "Let's go tell Anthony and Bethany that they are the proud recipients of two bouncing, beaming, lovable parents."

"Do you think they'll accept us?" Brye teased, interlocking their fingers.

"Of course they will. Since we're much too immature to handle life on our own, they'll want to stick around and nurture us until we're old enough to strike out on our own."

Brye giggled. She rose on her tiptoes and pressed a lingering kiss along his close-shaven cheek. "I love you, Chad Collier. Thank you for not giving up on me."

As soon as Brye's acceptance had been reported to the twins, Chad whisked Brye away in a stretch limo. Traveling north on Interstate 95, Brye marveled as New York madness conceded to New England charm. But as they gained on their chosen destination and exited into Southport—a teeny tiny portion of Connecticut fronting an even tinier section of Long Island Sound, and boasting old-fashioned grace and majestic mansions—the limo turned due east on Center Street, then south on Pequot Avenue. As they glided along an extensive private road lined with stately homes sitting off the beaten path, Brye was then asked to seal her eyes. Begrudgingly, she did as told while the twins giggled in their seats opposite her and Chad.

The limo finally came to a rolling halt. Brye took note as Chad's tinted window whizzed downward. Although it was the end of September and the beginning of fall, the heat continued to cling tenaciously as if rebelling against the mighty change of seasons. With the window fully opened, humid air dove into the cool interior seeking refuge from the relentless sun.

"May I help you?"

Brye grew more curious as Tank's voice blasted from an intercom system.

"It's me, Tank," Chad answered. "Could you open the gates please?"

Electronic gates parted. Tank asked, "Is it safe to assume congratulations are in order?" Even with eyes closed, Brye visualized his beaming smile.

"Yes, it's safe to assume." Chad's arm draped over Brye's shoulder. "My bride-to-be is with us. You can open your eyes now."

As the long car rolled inside the wrought-iron gates, Brye's eyes popped open. Slowly traveling along a wide flagstone driveway, her gaze immediately inhaled the picturesque home looming ahead of them. A Victorian flaunting old-time charm. A white wicker porch swing hung graciously by its dangling chains. A long bed of colorful perennial flowers and plants encircled the old-fashioned porch.

"Do you like it?" The twins' exhilarated cries beat at Brye's eardrums.

"It's beautiful," Brye answered, sticking her head out the window for a clearer view. "Whose is it?"

The twins surreptitiously eyed each other. They giggled but did not answer.

"Why do I feel like I've missed the boat?" Brye asked Chad. "Is there something you're keeping from me?"

Before Chad answered, the limo came to a braking halt and Tenisha darted out the front door. She flung the door open before Brye or the driver had time to react.

"Tenisha!" Brye streaked out of the limo and gave her long-lost friend a huge bear hug. "What are you doing here?" Pushing her at arm's lengths, Brye took in her healed face and the stars twinkling in her eyes. She continued without waiting for a response. "You look great. No…you look more than great. You look wonderful. What're you doing here?" she asked again.

Tenisha wrapped her arms around Brye's waist. "I've come to take care of your needs for the day."

Brye's mouth flew open in confusion and lack of understanding. Tenisha laughed, hoping a fly, or a bee, or even the many butterflies darting around the colorful yard, would not take refuge in the wide opening.

"You'll see." She squeezed Brye's waist. "But first let me give you a quick—very quick—tour of the house. You're running late, so we haven't much time."

"Late for what? And what about Chad and the twins?" But as she sought them out, they had already disappeared. Frowning, she turned back and questioned. "What's goin' on?"

"You'll see," Tenisha obscurely replied. She herded Brye through the front door. A voluminous living room with two-story vaulted ceilings immediately took Brye's breath away. A cushioned, built-in window seat overlooked the front porch.

"It's sparsely furnished. It's just waiting for the owner to come in with her own decorative ideas.

"Who's the owner?" Brye asked.

Ignoring the question, Tenisha led her deeper into the impressive home. "We don't have much time, Brye. Save your interrogation for later. We have to get moving."

Although Brye was more than mildly curious, she did as Tenisha requested. But in the midst of her expeditious tour, she found it impossible to quell her rising oohs and aahs.

She appreciated a host of sensational architectural designs. Walls and walls of windows. A solarium and extravagant dining room flanked the state-of-the-art kitchen with vaulted ceiling and bay window breakfast nook. A family room opened to the outside deck by way of French doors. Double doors ushered into the library with built in shelves.

With six bedrooms and seven baths, Tenisha insisted they lacked the time to tour the more intimate chambers. But from everything Brye viewed, the home proved to be warm, not stuffy; voluminous but not overwhelmingly massive. This was a house ready to flourish under the gentle guidance of a loving family, not wither under the title of classical showpiece.

During the whirlwind tour, caterers, florist, and other unidentified workers approached Tenisha for advice on where to place this or how to arrange that. Quickly, proficiently, Tenisha solved problems as easily and effortlessly as if she lived here herself.

"I heard Tank when we pulled in," Brye mentioned as they climbed the split-level stairs to get to the master bedroom. "But I haven't seen him."

"This place has state-of-the-art security. Tank's overseeing it in the central office built over the five-car garage."

Brye halted at the top of the stairs. She hit Tenisha with a flabbergasted stance. "You sound as if you've been running this place."

"For the last two weeks, I have been." Not elaborating, she pushed Brye into the enormous master bedroom. The only room fully furnished in eighteenth-century tradition, Brye mooned over the mahogany king-sized bed with West Indies designed bedposts and the Southern-style chaise fronting a large brick fireplace. The sleeping area sported French doors leading to its own private deck. The master bath paraded a dressing area, double walk-in closets, shower room, double sinks, and two-person Jacuzzi tub.

"I love this place," Brye swooned. Gliding over to the bed, ever so gently, she ran a light finger over the multicolored comforter. "What's going on here, Tee? Why did Chad bring me here?"

The phone rang in response. Tenisha spoke into the headset, then thrust it at Brye. "It's for you."

"Hello, love."

Shivers of pleasure darted along her spinal column at the sound of his savory voice. "What's going on, Chad?"

"A wedding," Chad stated matter-of-factly. "*Your* wedding. It's a beautiful day for it, don't you think?"

Very much receptive of his honorable intentions, Brye gleamed with happiness. "What if I hadn't agreed to marry you…what would you have done then?"

"What's that saying? Absence makes the heart grow fonder? You missed me, Brye. And you were weakening. Long before the events of today. I had no doubt you'd say yes."

"So this was all a prearranged, elaborate plan to watch me sweat." Brye attempted to feign irritation, but her feet floated too far above the clouds for her spirits to be anywhere but elevated. "But how did you know for sure that I was ready to cave in."

"Brian told me."

"Brian!" Brye repeated in mild shock. "You mean he's in on this too?"

"You'd be surprised at the number of people I inaugurated in my campaign to assist me in convincing you to marry me."

A glow of happiness settled over Brye. Her voice dipped to a conspiratorial level. "You didn't have to whisk me away like this, Chad. I would have willingly cooperated."

"After everything that has happened between us over the years, I wasn't taking any chances." Chad chuckled. "Originally, I wasn't even going to let you out of my sight until after you said, 'I do,' but Tenisha assured me she would get you to the altar in time and in one piece."

With phone in hand, Brye strolled over to the French doors and peered out. Workmen steadily bustled around the impeccably manicured yard, transforming the area into a showplace the Queen of England would be proud to get hitched in. "I thought you had a plane to catch tonight?"

"I do. But you're coming with me."

Brye's heart sped into triple time before settling down to normal. "Where're we going?"

"It's a surprise."

"But I have to know what to pack."

"It's all taken care of."

"What about the twins?"

"I repeat, it's all taken care of. You, my darling, don't have to worry about anything but showing up at the altar."

Before Brye could respond, Tenisha tore the receiver out of her fingers. "Your time is up, Chad. If you expect me to get her to that altar, give me the time I requested." Her face crimped into an agitated frown. "One minute, Chad, or I'm slamming the phone down in your face."

Tenisha thrust the receiver in Brye's direction. Smiling sweetly, Brye put the phone to her ear and said, "You assigned me to this hard-nosed warden, so you have to live with it."

"Only for a few more hours, then you're all mine."

"I love you, Chad, but I better go. Tee's stomping her feet and giving me dirty looks."

"First, tell me what you think about your new home."

"Mine?" Brye could not support her weight any longer. Her legs folded onto the carpeted floor. She shouted in jubilation, "I love it! I adore it! I'm crazy about it! And you…and the twins."

"Speaking of which, the twins picked it out. But you can thank me the next time we're alone. But for now, you have a wedding to get ready for."

"Chad," Brye quickly sobered, "what about your family? Will they be here?"

The elongated pause bestowed Brye with her badly sought after answer. "You and the twins are the only family I need, Brye," he categorically confirmed. "I love you. Don't ever forget that." The line went dead.

"Are you okay?" Tenisha asked, peeling the receiver from Brye's fingers.

Brye's shoulders slumped in mortified sadness. "Chad's family isn't coming."

Tenisha shrugged. It was a matter she refused to concern herself with. Nor would she allow Brye to needlessly worry. "Daniel Collier is a jerk, Brye. And Mrs. Collier…well…she's married to a jerk. What more should I have to say? Except it doesn't warrant us spending any time worried about them."

Hesitantly, Brye grinned. "I guess that's all that needs to be said." Seconds passed, and her grin broke into a broad smile. Then she broke into a dismissive laugh. "You're right." Dragging herself off the carpet, standing once again on her own two feet, she stretched her arms outward. "Here I am, yours for the taking. Do as you see fit."

Tenisha giggled. "I'm glad you see it my way. Now let's get busy."

For the next two hours, caught in the midst of a flurry of charged activities—the fragrant baths, relaxing pedicures, soothing manicures, glamorous makeup and hairstyling—Brye and Tenisha caught up on the latest gossip. At times, their laughter soared completely out of control. On several occasions, their makeup had to be reapplied.

Finally, fully dressed, Brye and Tenisha stood admiring each other's magnificence in the closet's full-bodied mirror. Brye stood alarmingly beautiful in an ivory satin bridal gown. Queen Ann neckline and flattering bodice surfaced with resplendent pearls, shimmery sequins and lace appliques. A full skirt with layer upon layer of lace ruffles trailed the floor. A chapel-length train extended yards behind, and a delicate head wreath encompassed flowers, pearls, and Venise lace.

Tenisha looked just as splendid wearing a violet—a perfect match to Brye's eye color—satin and lace bridesmaids dress. Queen Anne neckline, keyhole back, slimming waistline and shirred sleeves, her floor-length dress emphasized but did not hug her eye-catching form.

"You look maaah-valous, daaah-ling!" Tenisha breathed, batting her eyelids at Brye.

"As do you, daaah-ling!" Blowing kisses past each other's ears, they broke out into gales of laughter.

"Oh…one more thing." Tenisha tore out of the bathroom. In only a few seconds, she was back twirling a blue garter belt around her index finger. "Here's your something borrowed and something blue." A sprinkle of memories long shoved aside powdered the forefront of Tenisha's mind. "I wore it at my wedding."

The sadness dimming Tenisha's caramel eyes induced Brye to asked, "Do you want to talk about it?"

"No," Tenisha somberly admitted. "For the first two weeks after TyJuan's death, that's all I talked about, it's all I questioned myself about. My marriage…how badly my life was going…why I hadn't left him long before he beat me…why he killed himself before waiting to see if he actually contracted the HIV virus?" Tenisha studied her perfectly painted face in the mirror. Despite her saying she didn't want to discuss the issue further, she wasn't quite ready to let go. "There was a chance—a good chance—he hadn't even acquired the disease. Statistics have shown that it's much more difficult for a man to acquire HIV from a woman than it is for a woman to contract it from a man. It would have taken weeks, possibly months, for the antibodies to show up in his bloodstream. And if it had… Well, there's medicine that could have helped halt the disease. In this day and age, HIV is no longer a death sentence." Tenisha paused. As if suddenly realizing what she was saying, her shoulders lifted in a gesture of hopelessness. "I can't think about it anymore. I don't want to talk about it any longer." She swung around to face Brye.

"When Chad called and asked if I'd help put together your wedding, I gratefully took on the entire project." Tenisha exhaustively rolled her eyes toward the skylights. "I was literally going crazy, actually pulling my hair out, trying to coordinate everything in the little time he gave me." Her gaze settled on Brye once again. Her expression was one of triumph. "But I did it. And I enjoyed every minute of it. And not once did I have time to think about my own problems. And—and this is the most important *and*—I'm not going to chide myself for not sitting at home mourning over a man who changed so drastically, that the person committing suicide a little over a month ago wasn't even the same individual I married. In fact, the man I married died months prior. I mourned over the death of TyJuan long before he pulled the trigger on himself."

Tenisha wrapped her right arm around Brye's waist. She steered her back into the master bathroom. Her face cleared, her smile beamed bright and promising. "I'll tell you what I *do* want to talk about."

For Tenisha, it had been touch and go the first few weeks of TyJuan's suicide. But with each passing day, the pain increasingly faded. TyJuan had left no permanent scars mentally, physically, or emotionally.

"What do you want to talk about?" Brye asked. Exposing one silk-clad thigh, she shimmied the garter along a long, shapely leg.

"I want to talk about what we're going to do about something old and something new."

Right on cue, a light tap sounded on the closed bedroom door.

Releasing Brye, Tenisha rushed over and threw open the door. "Marcus!" she exclaimed in feigned surprise. "What're you doing here?"

Marcus stepped into the room looking gallant and extremely handsome, wearing an off-white tuxedo and violet-colored cummerbund and tie.

"I've—" He stumbled over his lines. This was the first he'd seen of Tenisha since being released from the hospital. Her spirited loveliness stole his breath away. Shaking his head to clear his muddled thoughts, he began again. "I've come baring gifts." He finally tore his eyes away from Tenisha. Nonchalantly waving his hand in the air, he said, "You know…something old, something new."

An elaborate stage production, Brye thought to herself. Neither Marcus nor Tenisha would win an Oscar for their bad performances. Nor would they win anything for knowing how to treat the other with subtle discretion. Anyone looking into their shining faces could tell they were obviously two people very much in love.

"Please…don't let me interrupt anything," Brye moved her body between the two. "But I assume that package you're carrying is mine, and I'd like to have it."

"What?" Marcus spoke to Brye, but his concentration had already diverted back to Tenisha. Their center of focus was so heavily glued to each other, Brye wondered if she would need a bottle of acetone to peel them apart.

"Never mind," Brye good-naturedly quipped, snatching the package out of his hand. "You two carry on. Act like I'm not even here. Oops." She placed her hands over her lips and giggled. "I guess you already are."

Ignoring them both and the quiet conversation they held, Brye dropped to the bed and tore open the silver-wrapped package.

When she popped open the black velvet box, her mind spiraled backward. To another time and place when she'd last seen the exquisite gifts.

Her fingers shook as she tore open the card accompanying the box.

> My Dearest Love,
>
> I told you once that the amethyst and diamonds reminded me of you...of your sparkling beauty...and those angelic violet-colored eyes. Although you and I parted ways for a short duration of time, I kept these treasures—your belongings—as a constant reminder of the love we share. I knew if I held on to them long enough, somehow they'd find their way back to their true owner. Please accept my gift, Brye. And wear them as a symbol of my love for you. And I do love you. Now and forever.
>
> Welcome home.
>
> Your endearing husband-to-be.

"You like them?"

Brye looked up with tearstained eyes. Tenisha had slipped out, leaving her with Marcus.

"*Now* you notice me," Brye complained in mock irritation. "Two minutes ago, I couldn't even get you to give me the time of day."

Marcus's face fell. He stared as if it pained him to hurt her feelings. He dropped on the bed. "Brye, I..."

"Jesus, Marcus." Brye grabbed his hand and shook it. "Would you lighten up a bit? I was only kidding." Brye sought and captured his attention. "I never realized until today how bad you really had it for her."

Marcus's large chest appeared to have deflated several sizes smaller. "I've missed her. Although I've spoken to her over the phone about the details of your wedding, this is the first I've seen of her since she left the hospital."

"She looks wonderful, doesn't she?" Brye beamed proudly. "No residual marks left anywhere…be it mental or physical."

Despite how much Marcus wanted to discuss the woman he unwittingly fell in love with, this was Brye's day. It had been carefully, albeit expeditiously, planned. Planned with her happiness in mind. Her wedding day was meant to be the happiest day of her life. Switching his concentration from Tenisha, he turned his full attention and charm on her.

Lifting the amethyst and diamond necklace from the bed of satin clouds, he carefully examined the sparkling jewels before fastening the clasp behind Brye's exquisite neck. "These are beautiful, but they dim in comparison to the illustrious sparkles adorning your eyes."

The twinkle lighting Brye's ecstatic expression transcended the sound of her sharp tongue. "Spare me your false praise, Marcus. I know you only have eyes for Tenisha."

"Not today I don't." Marcus plucked one of the bedecked earrings from its resting place. He passed it to Brye. "In fact, today, there won't be a single man at your wedding who'll be able to keep his eyes off you. Every man in this place will look at Chad with resentment and envy." He waited until Brye pierced her right earlobe with the earring before handing her the match. "But underneath the jealousy, they're going to be saying to themselves, 'How did he get to be such a lucky bastard?'"

Brye captured Marcus's brawny features between the palms of her hands. "Do you know how much I love you?"

"I don't think your husband-to-be will take too kindly to you telling another man you love him, particularly on his wedding day."

"So sue me." She tossed her arms securely around his neck, careful not to smudge her makeup or smear the front of his tux.

They held each other for several seconds before Marcus grabbed her underneath the elbows and shoved her at arm's length. "Since

I'm giving the bride away, I guess it's my duty to give you that 'special' talk all fathers give their daughters prior to saying their wedding vows."

"You mean that much dreaded *sex* talk?" Brye asked, blinking innocently at Marcus.

During her stay in the hospital, Brye had finally confided in Marcus. Totally. Every area of her life had been exposed. Her troubled childhood, her twin brother's suicide, her parents sexual proclivities; Marcus had been given unlimited entrance to her innermost secrets and fears. He'd even been given privy to some of her most intimate moments she'd shared with Chad.

In the face of Brye's sprightly inquiry, Marcus chuckled. "The way you and Chad's been sneaking around the past couple of months, I think you could teach me a thing or two about sex." He tossed the empty jewelry box aside. "What I want to say will be short and sweet."

Marcus sheltered Brye's hands inside his own. "You have always been a beautiful woman, Brye. But you're even more radiant when you're consumed with inner happiness. "I've spoken with Chad to some length just to reassure myself that he's what you deserve. And you deserve to be happy. Chad says he'll do all that is in his power to maintain that thriving smile radiating from your soul. He plans on spoiling you rotten. And you better believe I'll be looking over his shoulder every step of the way." Tenderly, he squeezed her fingers. "I'll always be here for you, Brye. Don't ever forget that. We won't be living next door to each other any longer, but whenever you need me, you know where to find me, and you know I'll always be there."

"Oh, Marcus!" Not caring whether she marred her makeup or his jacket, she flew into his arms.

"I love you, sweetheart," Marcus pushed her away from him. "But if you ruin your makeup or if we're late for your wedding, both Tenisha and Chad will tar and feather my hide." He stood.

"Wait a minute," Brye balked. Grabbing his arm, she pulled him backward. He landed in a heavy pile on the bed. "Since we're having a tender moment and all, there's something I want to confess." Her eyes dipped to the carpeted floor. The color in her cheeks deepened to an embarrassing shade. "The day I walked in on you and Tenisha…well…I just want to say that when I saw you two together, deep down in my gut, I was a tad bit jealous, a little angry, and a lot more scared.

"With all the men crossing my path, with the exclusion of Chad, you are the first positive male figure who entered my life and gave rather than took. Not asking anything of me, you've never expected anything…except friendship. You've been good to me, Marcus. You're good *for* me. You are the closest, dearest friend I've ever had. And when I saw you and Tenisha together, I was afraid." The lines around her mouth deepened as she tried to hold back the tears. She looked away from his prying vigilance. "When I walked in on the two of you, I was afraid I was going to lose you."

Aside from the tough exterior Brye generally reserved for appearance sake only, there remained times when her insecurities poked through and slapped him dead center. At the moment, she appeared as vulnerable as a scared little girl who had just been told she couldn't play with her favorite toy any longer.

"Look at me, Brye." Forceful in his demand, he pinched Brye's chin and forced her misty eyes to meet his fuming gaze. "You will never lose me, okay? We will always be in this together…for the duration."

Appeased, a broad smile brightened Brye's shadowed features. Grabbing his wide lapels, she forced his nose down to converge into hers. "Just see that you don't forget that, *Daddy!*"

The bedroom door suddenly burst open. "What's taking you two so long?" Tenisha glowered. "Everyone's waiting."

Marcus jumped up. He offered Brye his hand. "Would you please do me the honors?"

Brye slid her fingers into his expectant ones. "It would be my pleasure."

Minutes later, arm and arm, Marcus and Brye filled the open portal leading to the gateway to her happiness.

Diana Ross's and Lionel Richie's "My Endless Love" filtered throughout the house speakers as Brian and Tenisha walked down the velvet-laid runway.

A small, intimate affair, approximately fifty folded chairs—twenty-five on each side—flanked the carpeted aisle. Brye and Chad's closest friends filled every chair.

Flowers, bows, ribbons, balloons, colorful streamers and flowing fountains graced the garnished courtyard. But Brye saw none of this. Her main interest, her only interest, reached way beyond the elaborate decorations and settled on the commanding figure dressed in tux and tails, heading the entire gala affair.

Tall, strong, defiantly handsome. Her soon-to-be husband. The warm reflection carried with it assurances of a wonderful life stretched beyond this glorious moment.

As soon as Brye and Marcus lit upon the doorway, Chad's quiescent heart somersaulted. As long as he lived, he would never look upon anything as heavenly as what evolved right before his very eyes: his angel, floating in a host of velvety clouds.

Across the way, their eyes fastened. Everything else, everyone else, disappeared by the wayside. For Chad and Brye, nothing else existed. Nothing but the two of them. This moment suspended in time. Forever.

Marcus shattered the spell Brye had fallen under as Bethany ended her short journey with her basket of rose petals in hand. His head leaned into Brye. "It's showtime, sweetheart," he whispered. "Are you ready for this?"

"I've been ready my entire life," Brye assured.

But as the "Wedding March" commenced, Brye caught a shadow falling in the corner of her eye. She turned and gasped. Chad's mother and father stood directly behind her.

Chad watched, the grin dropping from his face, as Brye executed a complete turnabout—long full skirts twisting around her legs—and disappeared into the house.

From his post, Chad was prepared to tear after her. From the doorway, Marcus signaled for him to stay.

"What the hell's going on?" Chad mumbled to Brian, his best man.

"I haven't got a clue," he answered. Directing his attention to the bewildered reverend, Brian assured, "I'm sure, whatever the delay, this will only take a few minutes."

The crowd had also watched the drama unfold. Suspicious murmurs filtered coarsely through the crowd.

Inside the cool interior of the home, Brye cautiously strolled toward Mr. and Mrs. Collier. Chad's mother was the first to react.

"I hope we're welcome at our son's wedding."

"Of course you are." Brye smiled warmly. "Chad will be honored by your appearance."

Mrs. Collier looked every bit the proud groom's mother. Hair pulled back into a tight chignon, tear-dropped pearl earrings and choker necklace adorned ageless skin. Elegantly dressed in floor-length, royal-blue, two-piece suit, V-neckline and pleated collar adorned the suit coat. The skirt featured a back slit riding just above her knees. The color offset the deeper shade of blue dancing in her observant eyes. Brye doubted if much got passed this sharp-witted woman. And was proved right by Mrs. Collier's next statement.

"I'm not certain what's going on between my son and my husband"—her eyes engaged her husband's stoic gaze—"since both choose to keep me in the dark. I am certain that whatever it is, it has something to do with you."

Just like Mr. Collier, Brye kept her facial expression neutral.

She reached out and lightly touched Brye's hand. "You are my son's choice as a wife. I honor that choice. I'd like to welcome you into the family." Once again, her eyes fell on her husband. "And as for Mr. Collier, whatever the problem, I'm sure he's prepared to put those differences aside for the day."

Witnessing Chad's mother up close and personal, whatever went on outside their stately mansion or in the midst of Mr. Collier's business affairs, Brye had no doubt that this woman ruled her own home with a firm hand.

A long way from being able to forgive Chad's father, an even longer way from being able to put her and Daniel's differences behind her, Brye decided, for Chad's sake, and at least for the day, she would put her reservations to rest—or at the very least allow them to take a long nap.

"I'd like that," Brye responded in kind. A resplendent smile settled on Mr. Collier. A truce—albeit a brief one—was offered by way of a handshake. "Thank you for coming, Mr. Collier. Chad will be pleased."

Daniel took her hand within his. Her grip was strong, warm, and indisputable. The smile he presented her was genuine. A worthy adversary, she had bested him. Of that, he could not dispute. And in his eyes, and for that reason alone, Brye had won his respect, if not his love. "Thank you, Brye."

Slipping out of Daniel's amicable graces, Brye said, "At the risk of seeming as if I'm rushing you—which in fact I am—we need to get you seated. The wedding had commenced the exact moment I noticed you two standing here."

Grabbing a server in a white jacket, Brye instructed him to find two more folding chairs.

Outside, Chad shuffled back and forth from one foot to the other. With each passing minute, he grew more and more tense. Finally, unable to stand the suspense any longer or terminate his mounting apprehension, he barked, "I'm going after her."

Brian dropped his hand on Chad's forearm. His face lit up with an amused smile. "There she is now."

Chad's eyes enlarged as he watched as a hired server hauled two chairs toward the front of the caravan of filled seats. But his mouth dropped open as Brye, long skirts gathered in right hand, dragged his mother by the left hand, his father trailing close behind, personally escorted them to their recently placed seats. Certain Chad's parents were situated comfortably, she dropped her skirts and floated toward the waiting Marcus.

With nothing less than adoration and love gleaming from within, Chad watched as his bride-to-be pause at almost every aisle to give someone a kiss, a hug, a stroke on the cheek, a pat on the hand.

Looks like the weddings vows are going to be postponed a few minutes longer, he reflected with approved amusement. Grinning profusely at Anthony and Bethany, patiently, he settled in for the duration. He could generously afford to grant her time. Because it was at his side she would eventually come to an allegiant halt. And it was by his side she would spend the duration of her life.

Epilogue

BRYE STEPPED ONTO THE sun-drenched deck. A gorgeous spring day. Warm, balmy, stimulating. A perfect day to give birth to a baby. Correction: two babies. Twins. Inhaling deeply through her nose, she exhaled profusely through pursed lips. Nimble fingers affectionately massaged the firm contours of her rotund belly. She'd been experiencing mild contractions in twenty-minute intervals, for the past two hours. Soon she'd have to inform Chad. For now, she was content in enjoying a few blissful moments of quietude.

The middling contraction subsided. Absently, Brye continued to caress Adrianne Renee and Andrew Chadwick Collier. Or as they were affectionately called, Adri and Andy. With the wonders of modern medicine, the babies were conceived six months after their wedding while on a family vacation on a private, secluded island in the Caribbean. The overconsuming love flowing through her heart for her unborn babies did not in the least dim the love she banked for Anthony and Bethany. She loved her children equally, completely, unconditionally.

Brye slid over to the deck railing. Her eyes skimmed over the glass-enclosed aviary Chad had built for the twins. Regardless of the weather outside, the temperature inside the massive domed birdhouse remained conducive to Bethany's and Anthony's feathered friends—Barney, Betty, Pebbles and Bam Bam had joined the ranks of the Collier family along with Fred and Wilma. Chad had spent a fortune landscaping the enclosed home. Dense with plants, trees, shrubbery and flowers, once inside, it gave the illusion of stepping into a tropical forest. Brye smiled and waved as Bethany crossed her line of vision. Three colorful macaws perched contentedly aloft her shoulders and arm. Waving happily to her mother, once again, she blended into the sheltering protection of lush foliage.

Brye's heart spilled with so much love and pride. This was her family. Never had she felt happier, nor freer…nor safer…nor warmer. It had taken time, courage, and understanding, but she had finally gone to Tyson's grave and expressed her love and forgiveness. She then begged for his forgiveness. And when a lightness billowed in her heart, and an awareness came to mind that her twin brother had forgiven her, she had finally been able to forgive herself. She had finally healed.

Afterward, the monumental amount of energy she had expended running away from herself for so many years kicked into high gear once again. But now she applied that same devotion and determination into raising her family first, overseeing Brylinn second, and maintaining her career third. And with Chad—her partner, lover, and lifetime soulmate—as the buttress of her strength and livelihood, all three areas flourished illustriously.

One surprising yet honored intrusion in the twins' life came in the form of Chad's mother. She had freely taken them under her protective wings and spoiled them rotten. So appreciative of the attention Mrs. Collier showered upon them, Brye did not have the heart to call a halt to her grandmotherly smothering. Even though deep down, Brye believed it was easier for Mrs. Collier to accept the twins—to proudly flaunt them around family and friends—because with their remarkable family resemblance and their trademark baby-blue eyes, she could effortlessly pass them off as having been genetically engineered by Chad.

In reality, although Mrs. Collier's generous actions may have come straight from the heart, she had not a clue to the definition of what a genuine family entailed.

A genuine family didn't necessarily have to be blood-borne or blood-linked. Nor did it have to be race-related. Family was born out of mind and spirit. It was born out of love, trust, and mutual respect.

Marcus held a family spot in Brye's heart. Tenisha, Lynn, the kids at Brylinn were all sum totals of Brye's extended family. Even Chad's mother had gouged her own special place. But with Daniel, there was a bridge both she and Chad found difficult to cross. And despite his many attempts to redeem the assuming position he had taken with Brye and Chad the day of their marriage, there remained a lack of trust. Maybe one day she would attain the level of confidence Daniel despairingly sought. It was a day she and Chad did not look forward to with great trepidation. They, in fact, looked toward that moment as the day a prodigious mountain had been reached, clambered up, and ultimately conquered.

"How are my babies doing?" Chad's temperate voice matched that of the pleasant day unfolding before Brye's very eyes. Wrapping his arms around her thickened waist, his nimble fingers worked magic along her distended belly.

Brye relaxed her swollen body against the muscular length of his supporting frame. The back of her head rested securely against his pounding chest. His inquiry was not only directed toward the twins she carried, but had incorporated his entire family.

"Anthony and Bethany are having the time of their lives playing with their little friends. Adri and Andy are anxious to come out and meet their new family. And I"—Brye turned within the circle of his efficacious hold—"I'm barefoot, pregnant, and incredibly happy." Pulling his head down, she greeted him with a taste of her yearning lips. Penetrating lips. Heated lips.

Shortly after returning home from their honeymoon, Chad had appropriated a faltering advertisement agency. Relentless, demanding, formidable, dedicated, recognized as being hard yet fair, he extracted loyalty and the same exacting drive from his employees as he practiced himself. In six short months, he managed to turn the company around—he was now pulling in a hefty profit, developing an entire innovative line of advertisement gimmicks for Romanique Cosmetics—featuring Mystique body and bath products. He managed to steal the account out from under the noses of a competitive advertisement company. Of course, knowing the CEO and being married to the spokesperson of Romanique did not hurt matters in the least. And shortly after procuring that major coup, it hadn't been difficult pulling in more and more accounts. His employees were, after all, remarkably talented. They had only needed someone at the helm to facilitate steering them in the right direction.

"Did your conference call go well?" Brye asked, breaking their passionate kiss to give some much needed air to her unborn children.

To get the advertisement agency up and running to its full potential, Chad imposed upon himself long and grueling weekdays. But regardless of his heavy workload, and because of Brye's hectic schedule, weekends were pledged to each other and their ready-made family. More times than not, Tenisha and Marcus joined in as well.

Recently, however, Chad had been approached by several businessmen in search of a partner and backer for a new business venture: construction of a medical building. Deciding it was time to diversify, this Saturday, he had spent his entire morning thoroughly researching the proposed project. On conference calls with planners, builders, and land developers, he procured cost and estimates as well as a projected target date for completion of construction. Soon he would make a decision on whether to back the proposed venture or not. But not today. The duration of this day was promised to his family.

Chad's thick brows lengthened into a repentant frown. He gently massaged her swollen abdomen with soothing circular motions. "I apologize for taking as long as I did, sweetheart. I got caught up in facts and figures."

Brye stared into a face livid with excitement. His eyes beamed with unconcealed enthusiasm. His voice trembled with the thrill of a new challenge. In many ways Chad possessed a number of qualities his father commandeered: ambition, adventurous, daring. Both continually strove to reach greater heights. But whereas Daniel measured success by power, prestige, and wealth, Chad measured it in terms of self-fulfillment. Also, unlike his father, Chad did not retain a ruthless bone in his body. Nor was he a vindictive person. But he loved to confront business challenges, and he was excellent at the game. And even though Chad had not yet agreed to support the venture, Brye knew it was only a matter of time.

Determined to give her full support, prepared to walk by his side whatever road he traversed, she acknowledged, "It's enough knowing we come first, my love. So it's okay if certain matters take you away from us over the weekend." An impish twinkle ornamented her eyes. "That is, as long as its business that's taking you away. Anything else will be wholly unacceptable—particularly when it's some artificially contrived blond bombshell hoping to get her claws into you."

Chad chuckled. He had never thought it possible, but his wife grew more and more carefree with each passing day. Marriage, pregnancy, motherhood—over the past eight and a half months, Brye had flourished dramatically. And inside the camera's scrutinizing lens, her distinguishable changes had not gone undetected.

There was no longer the perpetual sadness synonymous to Brye's career. Instead, the camera's eye detected and embraced a shining splendor…an internal bliss. And Chad prided himself in knowing he played a generous part in putting that devilish spark into his wife's very existence.

A light breeze blew strands of Brye's silky hair across her grinning face. Chad lovingly brushed the hair aside. "You are the only bombshell I want to spend the rest of my days with, Mrs. Collier."

"As long as you remember that, Mr. Collier, I think we'll get along just fine," Brye teased.

Voice heavy with desire, Chad said, "Just in case I do forget, why don't you refresh my memory now?"

"Don't you two ever give it a rest?"

Pulling apart, Brye and Chad turned toward the sound of Marcus's deep, playful voice. He slipped through the French doors with fingers linked through Tenisha's.

"The interior of your house was quiet, so we assumed you were out here," Tenisha established. Standing on her toes, she planted a kiss on Chad's cheek.

"Hey, big mama!" Marcus teasingly greeted Brye. His fingers automatically reached outward and sprayed Brye's huge belly. "I swear you're getting bigger and bigger every time I see you."

Like a musical accordion, Brye collapsed in feigned irritation. "How dare you say that to me," she admonished. "You know I'm sensitive about my weight."

"Yeah…right," Marcus chided. "You're about as sensitive as I am about the color of my skin."

Brye laughed in whimsical delight. Of course, he was right. In light of her first two miscarriages, as long as her unborn babies were healthy and steadily grew in size, she could have cared less if she resembled a beached whale. Fortunately, maintaining a nutritious diet for herself as well as the babies, as of her last check-up, she'd only gained twenty-eight pounds.

"If you've come here to insult me—"

"Not at all." Marcus looked chagrined. Dropping his fingers from Brye's extended belly, he moved over to Tenisha. He pulled her into his loving fold, his front flush against her back. "I've come baring good tidings. Tenisha has finally agreed to move in with me."

A chorus of congratulations filtered into the late morning breeze.

"Of course, I would much prefer if she married me, but—"

"I'm a little gun-shy right now," Tenisha sheepishly admitted. "I love this man. More than I ever thought capable of loving anyone. And my parents"—Tenisha's turned her head and smiled into Marcus' shining brown eyes—"particularly my father, adores him."

"What's not to adore?" Brye interjected with a teasing grin.

"He thinks I'm crazy for not taking Marcus up on his marriage proposal. But it's difficult for me right now."

Brye smiled in reflective understanding. She wrapped her arm securely around Chad's lean waist. But her eyes pinned down Marcus. "I remember once, this very good friend of mine suggested I take baby steps. If I hadn't listened, I wouldn't be as happy as I am today." Brye broke away from Chad and pulled Tenisha away from Marcus. Throwing her arms around her dearest friend's neck, she gifted her with stout encouragement. "I'm passing that same advice on to you. Take baby steps, Tee. Go at your own pace. Do what's best for you, and don't concern yourself with what others think, or say, or try to push you into. In the end, Marcus will be there offering support when you reach your chosen destination."

"You damn right I'll be there!" Marcus's intrepid eye showered Tenisha with a determination that would beguile the mightiest of queens in succumbing to his intractable will. "But in the meantime, I'm going to enjoy trying to convince you to bow to my irresistible charms."

With the certainty of her future intact, Tenisha was able to shove aside the dismal past few years of her life. "I think I like the sound of that." She moved easily into Marcus's arms. A steamy kiss followed. A kiss affluent with love, passion, and promises to come.

"What do you think?" Chad asked, smiling ardently into eyes outshining the glowing rays of sun. "Should we join them?"

"I think we'll only be setting a bad example for the twins if they walk up on two pairs of adults making out in broad daylight."

Chad's grin turned lecherous." Grabbing Brye by the waist, he hauled her to his chest. "I tend to disagree. I think it's good for them to see open and honest affection."

But before he could capture Brye with his eager lips, Marcus said, "Let's go celebrate. My treat. I'll even let the twins pick the place."

At the onset of Marcus's suggestion, a contraction poked insistently at Brye's lower abdomen. This one came at her stronger than the first couple. She took a deep, calming breath and leaned into Chad for support. Managing a smile, she said, "I don't care where we go as long as we take a detour to the hospital first."

A sharp jolt zigzagged across the center of Chad's chest. "It's time?" he asked. Concern as well as pride adhered to his unruffled diction.

"Yes. I think so. I've been having contractions regularly for the last several hours. But this one's a little more intense than the last."

"But it can't be time," Tenisha cried out in panic. "It's still early yet."

"It's okay, Tenisha. We were expecting this." Ever so gently, Chad lifted Brye into his supportive arms. "Brye was examined yesterday. The babies were in position, the sonogram estimated their weight to be around six pounds each, and Brye's doctor said twins normally arrive weeks before their actual due date."

"I can walk, Chad," Brye insisted. She lightly struggled against his broad chest.

"You need to conserve your strength, sweetheart," Chad ascertained. "And until you have to draw from it, let me take care of you." Carting her toward the French doors, he calmly barked out orders. "Marcus, you need to collect the twins. Have them clean up before you bring them to the hospital. Tenisha, I'd appreciate if you go up and get Brye's bags while I carry her to the car." He stepped into the house with Tenisha and Marcus at his heels. "Call Linn. Let her know what's going on. I'd appreciate if you would give my mother a call as well."

"Don't worry, Chad. I'll take care of everything." Tenisha leaned forward. She pressed her forehead against Brye's. "And you…relax, listen to your coach here, and everything will go as smooth as silk." She kissed Brye's temple. "I'm anxious to see my godchildren. Don't keep us waiting long."

She stepped back, and Marcus took her place. "Hang tough, kid, and you'll do just fine." He kissed her lightly on the lips. "I love you."

Chad swept Brye away on a crowning beacon of promises, a glorious future destined to be fulfilled existed just around the bend.

❧

"Sleep well, my darling. Sweet dreams." Chad brushed a good night kiss against Brye's stilled brow. It had been a long yet remarkably rewarding day. Drained to the bone, as soon as his wife's fatigued body crumbled into the hospital bed, her breathing had come at him slow and steady. Leaning over the bed rail, Chad gazed down at a vision bathed in harmonious tranquility.

And as he embraced Brye with a devout eye, his mind played back the birth of their son and daughter. The matrix of exalted emotions pumping through his heart and inflating his rising ego could not be put into words. First Brye, then Bethany and Anthony, and now Adrianne and Andrew. Chad had been granted the gift of a lifetime…his greatest achievement. His heart and soul. His lifeline. His family.

He was now complete.

Certain Brye slept soundly, Chad stole away from her bedside. Feet barely skimming the carpeted floor, he glided past the flowers, the gifts, the cards, and balloons. It was late. At home, Bethany and Anthony anxiously awaited his arrival. He had promised to tuck them in for the night.

Standing in front of the closed door, Chad turned and allowed himself the gift of gathering one more lingering, adoring sweep of his sleeping wife. His heart surged as he witnessed a tiny smile play along the edges of her closed lips. Satisfied nothing but pleasant images pranced behind her drifting eyelids, he quietly slipped out.

In calm surrender, Brye cruised on a billowy cloud of inner peace and lofty repose. No longer fearing what lay beyond the paradoxical boundaries of darkness, she embraced the healing retreat. And as she gravitated toward her rejuvenating haven, as usual, she dreamed…

Under the rigid tutelage of a nurturing sun, an oak sapling solidly rooted. Steadfast in its progression, its first limb pointed toward the heavens as if giving praise for its meager existence. Enduringly, one limb branched into two…two limbs divided into four. Unceasingly, the birthing process continued. From generation to generation, solid, stalwart branches expanded outward, upward. Spreading, reproducing, multiplying. Standing resolute against the blustery winds, inflexible against the beating rays of a fiery sun, uncompromising against biting wintery snowstorms, tall and proud, the magnificent oak proved to withstand the test of time.

About the Author

Michelle Denison has been a Kansas City resident for the majority of her life. She graduated from Washington High School, then continued her studies at the University of Kansas (Go, Jayhawks!), gaining a respiratory therapist degree. She has worked as a registered respiratory therapist as well as a certified hyperbaric technician for more than thirty-five years. She enjoys spending time with family and friends.

Printed in the USA
CPSIA information can be obtained
at www.ICGtesting.com
LVHW041044241124
797242LV00001B/6

* 9 7 9 8 8 9 3 0 8 3 2 1 7 *